Praise for

STEPHEN KING

and the #1 *New York Times* bestseller

THE BAZAAR OF BAD DREAMS

"If there are any lingering doubts about King's stylistic range, they should be put to rest by [this] collection . . . which features stories that seem to touch on every genre imaginable."

—*The New York Times*

"Impressive . . . meditations on mortality, destiny, and regret, all of which showcase King's talent for exploring the human condition . . . powerful."

—*Publishers Weekly* (starred review)

"Outstanding . . . ~~excellent~~ . . . s, his ability to grip . . . l with his prose mak . . .

. . . *Today*

"A gathering of short stories by an ascended master of the form . . . This collection speaks to King's considerable abilities as a writer of genre fiction who manages to expand and improve the genre as he works; certainly no one has invested ordinary reality and ordinary objects with as much creepiness as King. . . . A must for aspiring writers."

—*Kirkus Reviews*

STEPHEN KING

THE BAZAAR OF BAD DREAMS

STORIES

POCKET BOOKS

New York   London   Toronto   Sydney   New Delhi

Pocket Books
An Imprint of Simon & Schuster, Inc.
1230 Avenue of the Americas
New York, NY 10020

This book is a work of fiction. Any references to historical events, real people, or real places are used fictitiously. Other names, characters, places, and events are products of the author's imagination, and any resemblance to actual events or places or persons, living or dead, is entirely coincidental.

First Pocket Books paperback edition November 2016

POCKET and colophon are registered trademarks of Simon & Schuster, Inc.

For information about special discounts for bulk purchases, please contact Simon & Schuster Special Sales at 1-866-506-1949 or business@simonandschuster.com.

The Simon & Schuster Speakers Bureau can bring authors to your live event. For more information or to book an event, contact the Simon & Schuster Speakers Bureau at 1-866-248-3049 or visit our website at www.simonspeakers.com.

Interior design by Erich Hobbing

Manufactured in the United States of America

10   9   8   7   6   5   4   3   2

ISBN 978-1-5011-2787-8
ISBN 978-1-5011-1167-9 (hardcover)
ISBN 978-1-5011-1168-6 (ebook)

The following selections were first published in magazines: "Premium Harmony" in *The New Yorker*; "Batman and Robin have an Altercation" in *Harper's Magazine*; "The Dune" in *Granta*; "A Death" in *The New Yorker*; "The Bone Church" in *Playboy*; "Mortality" in *Esquire*; "Afterlife" in *Tin House*; "Herman Wouk Is Still Alive" in *The Atlantic*; "Tommy" in *Playboy*; "That Bus Is Another World" in *Esquire*; "Summer Thunder" in *Cemetery Dance*; and "Cookie Jar" in *Virginia Quarterly Review*.

Author's Note

Some of these stories have been previously published, but that doesn't mean they were done then, or even that they're done now. Until a writer either retires or dies, the work is not finished; it can always use another polish and a few more revisions. There's also a bunch of new ones. Something else I want you to know: how glad I am, Constant Reader, that we're both still here. Cool, isn't it?

—SK

I shoot from the hip and keep a stiff upper lip.
—AC/DC

Contents

THE BAZAAR OF BAD DREAMS

Introduction

I've made some things for you, Constant Reader; you see them laid out before you in the moonlight. But before you look at the little handcrafted treasures I have for sale, let's talk about them for a bit, shall we? It won't take long. Here, sit down beside me. And do come a little closer. I don't bite.

Except . . . we've known each other for a very long time, and I suspect you know that's not entirely true.

Is it?

I

You'd be surprised—at least, I think you would be— at how many people ask me why I still write short stories. The reason is pretty simple: writing them makes me happy, because I was built to entertain. I can't play the guitar very well, and I can't tap-dance at all, but I *can* do this. So I do.

I'm a novelist by nature, I will grant you that, and I have a particular liking for the long ones that create an immersive experience for writer and reader, where the fiction has a chance to become a world that's almost real. When a long book succeeds, the writer and reader are not just having an affair; they are married. When I get a letter from a reader who says he or she was sorry when *The Stand* or *11/22/63* came to an end, I feel that book has been a success.

But there's something to be said for a shorter, more intense experience. It can be invigorating, sometimes even shocking, like a waltz with a stranger you will never see again, or a kiss in the dark, or a beautiful curio for sale laid out on a cheap blanket at a street bazaar. And, yes, when my stories are collected, I always feel like a street vendor, one who sells only at midnight. I spread my assortment out, inviting the reader—that's you—to come and take your pick. But I always add the proper caveat: be careful, my dear, because some of these items are dangerous. They are the ones with bad dreams hidden inside, the ones you can't stop thinking about when sleep is slow to come and you wonder why the closet door is open, when you know perfectly well that you shut it.

II

If I said I always enjoyed the strict discipline shorter works of fiction impose, I'd be lying. Short stories require a kind of acrobatic skill that takes a lot of tiresome practice. *Easy reading is the product of hard writing*, some teachers say, and it's true. Miscues that can be overlooked in a novel become glaringly obvious in a short story. Strict discipline is necessary. The writer has to rein in his impulse to follow certain entrancing side paths and stick to the main route.

I never feel the limitations of my talent so keenly as I do when writing short fiction. I have struggled with feelings of inadequacy, a soul-deep fear that I will be unable to bridge the gap between a great idea and the realization of that idea's potential. What that comes down to, in plain English, is that the finished product never seems quite as good as the splendid idea that rose from the subconscious one day, along with the excited thought, *Ah man! I gotta write this right away!*

Sometimes the result is pretty good, though. And every once in awhile, the result is even better than the original concept. I love it when that happens. The real challenge is getting into the damned thing, and I believe that's why so many would-be writers with great ideas never actually pick up the pen or start tapping away at the keys. All too often, it's like trying to start a car on a cold day. At first the motor doesn't even crank, it only groans. But if you keep at it (and if the battery doesn't die), the engine starts . . . runs rough . . . and then smooths out.

There are stories here that came in a flash of inspiration ("Summer Thunder" was one of those), and had to be written at once, even if it meant interrupting work on a novel. There are others, like "Mile 81," that have waited their turn patiently for decades. Yet the strict focus needed to create a good short story is always the same. Writing novels is a little like playing baseball, where the game goes on for as long as it needs to, even if that means twenty innings. Writing short stories is more like playing basketball or football: you're competing against the clock as well as the other team.

When it comes to writing fiction, long *or* short, the learning curve never ends. I may be a Professional Writer to the IRS when I file my tax return, but in creative terms, I'm still an amateur, still learning my craft. We all are. Every day spent writing is a learning experience, and a battle to do something new. Phoning it in is not allowed. One cannot increase one's talent—that comes with the package—but it is possible to keep talent from shrinking. At least, I like to think so.

And hey! I still love it.

III

So here are the goods, my dear Constant Reader. Tonight I'm selling a bit of everything—a monster that looks like a car (shades of *Christine*), a man who can kill you by writing your obituary, an e-reader that accesses parallel worlds, and that all-time favorite, the end of the human race. I like to sell this stuff when the rest of the vendors have long since gone home, when the streets are deserted and a cold rind of moon floats over the canyons of the city. That's when I like to spread *my* blanket and lay out *my* goods.

That's enough talk. Perhaps you'd like to buy something, now, yes? Everything you see is handcrafted, and while I love each and every item, I'm happy to sell them, because I made them especially for you. Feel free to examine them, but please be careful.

The best of them have teeth.

August 6, 2014

When I was nineteen years old and attending the University of Maine, I'd drive from Orono to the little town of Durham, which is usually represented as Harlow in my books. I made this trip every three weekends or so, to see my girlfriend . . . and, coincidentally, my mother. I drove a '61 Ford station wagon: six in a row for more go and three on the tree (if you don't know, ask your dad). The car was a hand-me-down from my brother David.

I-95 was less traveled in those days, and nearly deserted for long stretches once Labor Day passed and the summer people went back to their workaday lives. No cell phones, either, of course. If you broke down, your choices were two: fix it yourself or wait for some good Samaritan to stop and give you a lift to the nearest garage.

During those 150-mile drives, I conceived a special horror of Mile 85, which was in the absolute nowhere between Gardiner and Lewiston. I became convinced that if my old wagon *did* shit the bed, it would do so there. I could visualize it hunkered in the breakdown lane, lonely and abandoned. Would someone stop to make sure the driver was okay? That he was not, perchance, stretched out on the front seat, dying of a heart attack? Of course they would. Good Samaritans are everywhere, especially in the boondocks. People who live in the boonies take care of their own.

But, I thought, suppose my old station wagon was an imposter? A monstrous trap for the unwary? I thought that would make a good story, and it did. I called it "Mile 85." It was never rewritten, let alone published, because I lost it. Back then I was dropping acid regularly, and I lost all sorts of stuff. Including, for short periods, my mind.

Fast-forward nearly forty years. Although Maine's long stretch of I-95 is more heavily traveled in the twenty-first century, traffic is still light after Labor Day and budget cuts have forced the state to close many of the rest areas. The combined gas station and Burger King (where I consumed many Whoppers) near the Lewiston exit was one of those shut down. It stood abandoned, growing sadder and seedier behind the DO NOT ENTER barriers marking its entrance and exit ramps. Hard winters had buckled the parking lot, and weeds had sprouted through the cracks.

One day as I passed it, I recalled my old lost story and decided to write it again. Because the abandoned rest area was a little farther south than the dreaded Mile 85, I had to change the title. Everything else is pretty much the same, I think. That turnpike oasis may be gone—as are the old Ford wagon, my old girl-friend, and many of my old bad habits—but the story remains. It's one of my favorites.

Mile 81

1. PETE SIMMONS ('07 Huffy)

"You can't come," his older brother said.

George spoke in a low voice, even though the rest of his friends—a neighborhood group of twelve- and thirteen-year-olds who styled themselves the Rip-Ass Raiders—were up at the end of the block, waiting for him. Not very patiently. "It's too dangerous."

Pete said, "I'm not afraid." He spoke stoutly enough, although he *was* afraid, a little. George and his friends were headed up to the sandpit behind the bowling alley. There they'd play a game Normie Therriault had invented. Normie was the leader of the Rip-Ass Raiders, and the game was called Paratroops from Hell. There was a rutted track leading up to the edge of the gravel pit, and the game was to ride your bike along it at full speed, yelling *"Raiders rule!"* at the top of your lungs and bailing from the seat of your bike as you went over. The usual drop was ten feet or so, and the approved landing area was soft, but sooner or later someone would land on gravel instead of sand and probably break an arm or an ankle. Even Pete knew that (although he sort of understood why it added to the attraction). Then the parents would find out and that would be the end of Paratroops from Hell. For now, however, the game—played without helmets, of course—continued.

George knew better than to allow his brother to play, however; he was supposed to be taking care of Pete while their parents were at work. If Pete wrecked his Huffy at the gravel pit, George would likely be grounded for a week. If his little brother broke an arm, it would be for a month. And if—God forbid!—it was his neck, George guessed he might be whiling away the hours in his bedroom until he went to college.

Besides, he loved the little cock-knocker.

"Just hang out here," George said. "We'll be back in a couple of hours."

"Hang out with *who*?" Pete asked. It was spring vacation, and all of *his* friends, the ones his mother would have called "age appropriate," seemed to be somewhere else. A couple of them had gone to Disney World in Orlando, and when Pete thought of this, his heart filled with envy and jealousy—a vile brew, but strangely tasty.

"Just hang out," George said. "Go to the store, or something." He scrounged in his pocket and came out with a pair of crumpled Washingtons. "Here's some dough."

Pete looked at them. "Jeez, I'll buy a Corvette. Maybe two."

"Hurry up, Simmons, or we'll go withoutcha!" Normie yelled.

"Coming!" George shouted back. Then, low, to Pete: "Take the money and don't be a boogersnot."

Pete took the money. "I even brought my magnifying glass," he said. "I was gonna show em—"

"They've all seen that baby trick a thousand times," George said, but when he saw the corners of Pete's mouth tuck down, he tried to soften the blow. "Besides, look at the sky, numbo. You can't start fires with a magnifying glass on a cloudy day. Hang out. We'll play computer Battleship or something when I come back."

"Okay, chickenshit!" Normie yelled. "Seeya later, masturbator!"

"I gotta go," George said. "Do me a favor and don't get in trouble. Stay in the neighborhood."

"You'll probably break your spine and be fuckin paralyzed for life," Pete said . . . then hastily spat between his forked fingers to take the curse off. *"Good luck!"* he shouted after his brother. *"Jump the farthest!"*

George waved one hand in acknowledgment, but didn't look back. He stood on the pedals of his own bike, a big old Schwinn that Pete admired but couldn't ride (he'd tried once and wiped out half-way down the driveway). Pete watched him put on speed as he raced up this block of suburban houses in Auburn, catching up with his homies.

Then Pete was alone.

He took his magnifying glass out of his saddlebag and held it over his forearm, but there was no spot of light and no heat. He looked glumly up at the low-hanging clouds and put the glass back. It was a good one, a Richforth. He'd gotten it last Christmas, to help with his ant farm science project.

"It'll wind up in the garage, gathering dust," his father had said, but although the ant farm project had concluded in February (Pete and his partner, Tammy Witham, had gotten an A), Pete hadn't tired of the magnifying glass yet. He particularly enjoyed charring holes in pieces of paper in the backyard.

But not today. Today, the afternoon stretched ahead like a desert. He could go home and watch TV, but his father had put a block on all the interesting channels when he discovered George had been DVR-ing *Boardwalk Empire*, which was full of old-time gangstas and bare titties. There was a similar block on Pete's computer, and he hadn't figured a workaround yet, although he would; it was only a matter of time.

So?

"So what," he said in a low voice, and began to pedal slowly toward the end of Murphy Street. "So . . . fuckin . . . what."

Too little to play Paratroops from Hell, because it was too dangerous. How sucky. He wished he could think of something that would show George and Normie and all of the Raiders that even little kids could face dan—

The idea came to him then, just like that. He could explore the abandoned rest area. Pete didn't think the big kids knew about it, because it was a kid Pete's own age, Craig Gagnon, who'd told him about it. He said he'd been up there with a couple of other kids, ten-year-olds, last fall. Of course the whole thing might have been a lie, but Pete didn't think so. Craig had given too many details, and he wasn't the kind of kid who was good at making things up. Sort of a dimbulb, actually.

With a destination in mind, Pete began to pedal faster. At the end of Murphy Street he banked left onto Hyacinth. There was no one on the sidewalk, and no cars. He heard the whine of a vacuum cleaner from the Rossignols', but otherwise everyone might have been sleeping or dead. Pete supposed they were actually at work, like his own parents.

He swept right onto Rosewood Terrace, passing the yellow sign reading DEAD END. There were only a dozen or so houses on Rosewood. At the end of the street was a chainlink fence. Beyond it was a thick tangle of shrubbery and scraggly second-growth trees. As Pete drew closer to the chainlink (and the totally unnecessary sign mounted on it reading NOT A THROUGH STREET), he stopped pedaling and coasted.

He understood—vaguely—that although he thought of George and his Raider pals as Big Kids (and certainly that was how the Raiders thought of themselves), they weren't *really* Big Kids. The true Big Kids were badass teenagers who had driver's licenses and girlfriends. True Big Kids went to high school. They liked to drink, smoke pot, listen to heavy metal or hip-hop, and suck major face with their girlfriends.

Hence, the abandoned rest area.

Pete got off his Huffy and looked around to see if he was being observed. There was nobody. Even the annoying Crosskill twins, who liked to jump rope (in tandem) all over the neighborhood when there was no school, were not in evidence. A miracle, in Pete's opinion.

Not too far away, Pete could hear the steady *whoosh-whoosh-whoosh* of cars on I-95, headed south to Portland or north to Augusta.

Even if Craig was telling the truth, they probably fixed the fence, Pete thought. *That's the way today's going.*

But when he bent close, he could see that although the fence *looked* whole, it really wasn't. Someone (probably a Big Kid who had long since joined the boring ranks of Young Adults) had clipped the links in a straight line from top to bottom. Pete took another look around, then laced his hands in the metal diamonds and pushed. He expected resistance, but there was none. The cut piece of chainlink swung open like a farmyard gate. The Really Big Kids had been using it, all right. Booya.

It stood to reason, when you thought about it. Maybe they had drivers' licenses, but the entrance and exit to the Mile 81 rest area were now blocked off by those big orange barrels the highway crews used. Grass was growing up through the crumbling pavement in the deserted parking lot. Pete had seen this for himself thousands of times, because the schoolbus used I-95 to go the three exits from Laurelwood, where he got picked up, to Sabattus Street, home to Auburn Elementary School No. 3, also known as Alcatraz.

He could remember when the rest area had still been open. There had been a gas station, a Burger King, a TCBY, and a Sbarro's. Then it got closed down. Pete's dad said there were too many of those rest areas on the turnpike, and the state couldn't afford to keep them all open.

Pete rolled his bike through the gap in the chainlink, then carefully pushed the makeshift gate back until the diamond shapes matched up and the fence looked whole again. He walked toward the wall of bushes, being careful not to run the Huffy's tires over any broken glass (there was a lot on this side of the fence). He began looking for what he knew must be here; the cut fence said it had to be.

And there it was, marked by stamped cigarette

butts and a few discarded beer and soda bottles: a path leading deeper into the undergrowth. Still pushing his bike, Pete followed it. The high bushes swallowed him up. Behind him, Rosewood Terrace dreamed through another overcast spring day.

It was as if Pete Simmons had never been there at all.

The path between the chainlink fence and the Mile 81 rest area was, by Pete's estimation, about half a mile long, and there were Big Kid signposts all along the way: half a dozen small brown bottles (two with snot-caked coke spoons still attached), empty snack bags, a pair of lace-trimmed panties hanging from a thornbush (it looked to Pete like they'd been there for awhile, like maybe fifty years), and—jackpot!—a half-full bottle of Popov vodka with the screw cap still on. After some interior debate, Pete put this into his saddlebag along with his magnifying glass, the latest issue of *Locke & Key*, and a few Double Stuf Oreos in a Baggie.

He pushed his bike across a sluggish little stream, and bingo-boingo, here he was at the back of the rest area. There was another chainlink fence, but this one was also cut, and Pete slipped right through. The path continued through high grass to the back parking lot. Where, he supposed, the delivery trucks used to pull up. Close to the building he could see darker rectangles on the pavement where the Dumpsters had been. Pete lowered the kickstand of his Huffy and parked it on one of these.

His heart was thumping as he thought about what came next. *Breaking and entering, sugarbear. You could go to jail for that.* But was it breaking and entering if he found an open door, or a loose board over one of the windows? He supposed it would still be entering, but was entering all by itself a crime?

In his heart he knew it was, but he guessed that without the breaking part, it wouldn't mean jail time. And after all, hadn't he come here to take a risk? Something he could brag about later to Normie and George and the other Rip-Ass Raiders?

And okay, he was scared, but at least he wasn't bored anymore.

He tried the door with the fading EMPLOYEES ONLY sign on it, and found it not only locked but *seriously* locked—no give at all. There were two windows beside it, but he could tell just by looking that they were boarded down tight. Then he remembered the chainlink fence that looked whole but wasn't, and tested the boards anyway. No good. In a way, it was a relief. He could be off the hook if he wanted to be.

Only . . . the Really Big Kids *did* go in there. He was sure of it. So how did they do it? From the front? In full view of the turnpike? Maybe so, if they came at night, but Pete had no intention of checking it out in broad daylight. Not when any passing motorist with a cell phone could dial 911 and say, "Just thought you might like to know that there's a little kid playing Freddy Fuckaround at the Mile 81 rest area. You know, where the Burger King used to be?"

I'd rather break my arm playing Paratroops from Hell than have to call my folks from the Gray State police barracks. In fact, I'd rather break both arms and get my dick caught in the zipper of my jeans.

Well, maybe not that.

He wandered toward the loading dock, and there, once again: jackpot. There were dozens of stamped-out cigarette butts at the foot of the concrete island, plus a few more of those tiny brown bottles surrounding their king: a dark green NyQuil bottle. The surface of the dock, where the big semis backed up to unload, was eye-high to Pete, but the cement was crumbling and there were plenty of footholds for an agile kid in Chuck Taylor High Tops. Pete raised his arms over his head, snagged fingerholds in the dock's pitted surface . . . and the rest, as they say, is history.

On the dock, in faded red, someone had sprayed EDWARD LITTLE ROCKS, RED EDDIES RULE. *Not true,* Pete thought. *Rip-Ass Raiders rule.* Then he looked around from his current high perch, grinned, and said, "Actually, *I* rule." And standing up here above the empty back lot of the rest area, he felt that he did. For the time being, anyway.

He climbed back down—just to make sure it was no problem—and then remembered the stuff in his saddlebag. Supplies, in case he decided to spend the afternoon here, exploring and shit. He debated what to bring, then decided to unstrap the saddlebag and take everything. Even the magnifying glass might come in handy. A vague fantasy began to form in his brain: boy detective discovers a murder victim in a deserted rest area, and solves the crime before the police even know a crime has been committed. He could see himself explaining to the drop-jawed Raiders that it had actually been pretty easy. Elementary, my dear fucksticks.

Bullshit, of course, but it would be fun to pretend.

He lifted his bag onto the loading dock (being especially careful on account of the half-full vodka bottle), then climbed back up. The corrugated metal door leading inside was at least twelve feet high and secured at the bottom with not one but two humungous padlocks, but there was a human-sized door set into it. Pete tried the knob. It wouldn't turn, nor would the human-sized door open when he pushed and pulled, but there was some give. Quite a lot, actually. He looked down and saw that a wooden wedge had been pushed under the bottom of the door; a totally dope precaution if he'd ever seen one. On the other hand, what more could you expect from kids who were stoned on coke and cough syrup?

Pete pulled the wedge, and this time when he tried the inset door, it creaked open.

The big front windows of what had been the Burger King were covered with chickenwire instead of boards, so Pete had no trouble seeing what there was to see. All the eating tables and booths were gone from the restaurant part, and the kitchen part was just a dim hole with some wires sticking out of the walls and some of the ceiling tiles hanging down, but the place was not exactly unfurnished.

In the center, surrounded by folding chairs, two old card tables had been pushed together. On this double-wide surface were half a dozen filthy tin ashtrays, several decks of greasy Bicycle cards, and a caddy of poker chips. The walls were decorated with twenty or thirty magazine gatefolds. Pete inspected these with great interest. He knew about pussies, had glimpsed more than a few on HBO and Cinema-Spank (before his folks got wise and blocked the premium cable channels), but these were *shaved* pussies. Pete wasn't sure what the big deal was—to him they looked sort of oogy—but he supposed he might get with the program when he was older. Besides, the bare titties made up for it. Bare titties were fuckin awesome.

In the corner three filthy mattresses had been pushed together like the card tables, but Pete was old enough to know it wasn't poker that was played here.

"Let me see your pussy!" he commanded one of the *Hustler* girls on the wall, and giggled. Then he said, "Let me see your *shaved* pussy!" and giggled harder. He sort of wished Craig Gagnon was here, even though Craig was a dweeb. They could have laughed about the shaved pussies together.

He began to wander around, still snorting small carbonated bubbles of laughter. It was dank in the rest area, but not actually cold. The smell was the worst part, a combination of cigarette smoke, pot smoke, old booze, and creeping rot in the walls. Pete thought he could also smell rotting meat. Probably from sandwiches purchased at Rosselli's or Subway.

Mounted on the wall beside the counter where people once ordered Whoppers and Whalers, Pete discovered another poster. This one was of Justin Bieber when the Beeb had been maybe sixteen. The Beeb's teeth had been blacked out, and someone had added a Notzi swat-sticker tattoo to one cheek. Red-ink devil horns sprouted from the Beeb's moptop. There were darts sticking out of his face. Magic Markered on the wall above the poster was MOUTH 15 PTS, NOSE 25 PTS, EYES 30 PTS ITCH.

Pete pulled out the darts and backed across the big empty room until he came to a black mark on the floor. Printed here was BEEBER LINE. Pete stood behind it and shot the six darts ten or twelve times. On his last try, he got a hundred and twenty-five points. He thought that was pretty good. He imagined George and Normie Therriault applauding.

He went over to one of the mesh-covered windows, staring out at the empty concrete islands where the gas pumps used to be, and at the traffic beyond. Light traffic. He supposed that when summer came it would once more be bumper-to-bumper with tourists and summer people, unless his dad was right and the price of gas went to seven bucks a gallon and everybody stayed home.

Now what? He'd played darts, he'd looked at enough shaved pussies to last him . . . well, maybe not a lifetime but at least a few months, there were no murders to solve, so now what?

Vodka, he decided. That was what came next. He'd try a few sips just to prove he could, and so future brags would have that vital ring of truth. Then, he supposed, he would pack up his shit and go back to Murphy Street. He would do his best to make his adventure sound interesting—thrilling, even—but in truth, this place wasn't such of a much. Just a place where the Really Big Kids could come to play cards and make out with girls and not get wet when it rained.

But booze . . . that was *something*.

He took his saddlebag over to the mattresses and sat down (being careful to avoid the stains, of which there were many). He took out the vodka bottle and studied it with a certain grim fascination. At ten-going-on-eleven, he had no particular longing to sample adult pleasures. The year before he had hawked one of his grandfather's cigarettes and smoked it behind the 7-Eleven. Smoked half of it, anyway. Then he had leaned over and spewed his lunch between his sneakers. He had obtained an interesting but not very valuable piece of information that day: beans and franks didn't look great when they went into your mouth, but at least they tasted good. When they came back out, they looked fucking horrible and tasted worse.

His body's instant and emphatic rejection of that American Spirit suggested to him that booze would be no better, and probably worse. But if he didn't drink at least some, any brag would be a lie. And his brother George had lie-radar, at least when it came to Pete.

I'll probably puke again, he thought, then said: "Good news is I won't be the first in *this* dump."

That made him laugh again. He was still smiling when he unscrewed the cap and held the mouth of the bottle to his nose. Some smell, but not much. Maybe it was water instead of vodka, and the smell was just a leftover. He raised the mouth of the bottle to his mouth, sort of hoping that was true and sort of hoping it wasn't. He didn't expect much, and he certainly didn't want to get drunk and maybe break his neck trying to climb back down from the loading dock, but he was curious. His parents *loved* this stuff.

"Dares go first," he said for no reason at all, and took a small sip.

It wasn't water, that was for sure. It tasted like hot, light oil. He swallowed mostly in surprise. The vodka trailed heat down his throat, then exploded in his stomach.

"Holy Jeezum!" Pete yelled.

Tears sprang into his eyes. He held the bottle out at arm's length, as if it had bitten him. But the heat in his stomach was already subsiding, and he felt pretty much okay. Not drunk, and not like he was going to puke, either. He tried another little sip, now that he knew what to expect. Heat in the mouth . . . heat in the throat . . . and then, boom in the stomach. Actually kind of cool.

Now he felt a tingling in his arms and hands. Maybe his neck, too. Not the pins-and-needles sensation you got when a limb went to sleep, but more like something was waking up.

Pete raised the bottle to his lips again, then lowered it. There was more to worry about than falling off the loading dock or crashing his bike on the way home (he wondered briefly if you could get arrested for drunk biking and guessed you could). Having a few swigs of vodka so you could brag on it was one thing, but if he drank enough to get loaded, his mother and father would know when they came home. It would only take one look. Trying to act sober wouldn't help. They drank, their friends drank, and sometimes they drank too much. They would know the signs.

Also, there was the dreaded HANGOVER to consider. Pete and George had seen their mom and dad dragging around the house with red eyes and pale faces on a good many Saturday and Sunday mornings. They took vitamin pills, they told you to turn the TV down, and music was absolutely *verboten*. The HANGOVER looked like the absolute opposite of fun.

Still, maybe one more sip might not hurt.

Pete took a slightly larger swallow and shouted, *"Zoom, we have liftoff!"* This made him laugh. He felt a little light-headed, but it was a totally pleasant feeling. Smoking he didn't get. Drinking, he did.

He got up, staggered a little, caught his balance, and laughed some more. "Jump into that fucking sandpit all you want, sugarbears," he told the empty restaurant. "I'm fuckin stinko, and fuckin stinko is better." This was *very* funny, and he laughed hard.

Am I really stinko? On just three sips?

He didn't think so, but he was definitely high. No more. Enough was enough. "Drink responsibly," he told the empty restaurant, and laughed.

He'd hang out here for awhile and wait for it to wear off. An hour should do it, maybe two. Until three o'clock, say. He didn't have a wristwatch, but he'd be able to tell three o'clock from the chimes of St. Joseph's, which was only a mile or so away. Then he'd leave, first hiding the vodka (for possible further research) and putting the wedge back under the door. His first stop when he got back to the neighborhood was going to be the 7-Eleven, where he'd buy some of that really strong Teaberry gum to take the smell of the booze off his breath. He'd heard kids say vodka was the thing to steal out of your parents' liquor cabinet because it *had* no smell, but Pete was now a wiser child than he'd been an hour ago.

"Besides," he told the hollowed-out restaurant in a lecturely tone, "I bet my eyes are red, just like Dad's when he has too marny mantinis." He paused. That wasn't quite right, but what the fuck.

He gathered up the darts, went back to the Beeber Line, and shot them. He missed Justin with all but one, and this struck Pete as the most hilarious thing of all. He wondered if the Beeb could have a hit with a song called "My Baby Shaves Her Pussy," and this struck him so funny that he laughed until he had to bend over with his hands on his knees.

When the laughter passed, he wiped double snot-hangers from his nose, flicked them onto the floor (*there goes your Good Restaurant rating,* he thought, *sorry, Burger King*), and then trudged back to the Bee-ber Line. He had even worse luck the second time. He wasn't seeing double or anything, he just couldn't nail the Beeb.

Also, he felt a little sick, after all. Not much, but he was glad he hadn't tried a fourth sip. "I would have popped my Popov," he said. He laughed, then uttered a ringing belch that burned coming up. Blick. He left the darts where they were and went back to the mat-tresses. He thought of using his magnifying glass to see if anything really small was crawling there, and decided he didn't want to know. He thought about eating some of his Oreos, but was afraid of what they might do to his stomach. It felt, let's face it, a little tender.

He lay down and laced his hands behind his head. He had heard that when you got really drunk, every-thing started spinning around. Nothing like that was happening to him, so he guessed he was only a little high, but he wouldn't mind a nap.

"But not too long."

No, not too long. Too long would be bad. If he wasn't home when his folks came home, and if they couldn't find him, he would be in trouble. Probably George would be, too, for going off without him. The question was, could he wake himself up when the St. Joseph's chimes struck?

Pete realized, in those last few seconds of con-sciousness, that he'd just have to hope so. Because he was going.

He closed his eyes.

And slept in the deserted restaurant.

Outside, in the southbound travel lane of I-95, a station wagon of indeterminate make and vintage appeared. It was traveling well below the posted minimum turnpike speed. A fast-moving semi came up behind it and veered into the passing lane, blatting its air horn.

The station wagon, almost coasting now, veered into the entrance lane of the rest area, ignoring the big sign reading CLOSED NO SERVICES NEXT GAS AND FOOD 27 MI. It struck four of the orange barrels blocking the lane, sent them rolling, and came to a stop about seventy yards from the abandoned restaurant building. The driver's-side door opened, but nobody got out. There were no hey-stupid-your-door's-open chimes, either. It just hung silently ajar.

If Pete Simmons had been watching instead of snoozing, he wouldn't have been able to see the driver. The station wagon was splattered with mud, and the windshield was smeared with it. Which was strange, because there had been no rain in northern New England for over a week, and the turnpike was perfectly dry.

The car sat there a little distance up the entrance ramp, under a cloudy April sky. The barrels it had knocked over came to a stop. The driver's door hung open.

2. DOUG CLAYTON ('09 Prius)

Doug Clayton was an insurance man from Bangor, bound for Portland, where he had a reservation at the Sheraton Hotel. He expected to be there by two o'clock at the latest. That would leave plenty of time for an afternoon nap (a luxury he could rarely afford) before searching out dinner on Congress Street.

Tomorrow he would present himself at the Portland
Conference Center bright and early, take a nametag,
and join four hundred other agents at a conference
called Fire, Storm, and Flood: Insuring for Disaster
in the Twenty-First Century. As he passed the Mile
82 marker, Doug was closing in on his own personal
disaster, but it was nothing the Portland conference
would cover.

His briefcase and suitcase were in the backseat.
Lying in the passenger bucket was a Bible (King
James version; Doug would have no other). Doug was
one of four lay preachers at the Church of the Holy
Redeemer, and when it was his turn to preach, he
liked to call his Bible "the ultimate insurance manual."

Doug had accepted Jesus Christ as his personal
savior after ten years of drinking that spanned his
late teens and most of his twenties. This decade-long
spree ended with a wrecked car and thirty days in
the Penobscot County Jail. He had gotten down on
his knees in that smelly, coffin-sized cell on his first
night there, and he'd gotten down on them every
night since.

"Help me get better," he had prayed that first time,
and every time since. It was a simple prayer that had
been answered first twofold, then tenfold, then a hun-
dredfold. He thought that in another few years, he
would be up to a thousandfold. And the best thing?
Heaven was waiting at the end of it all.

His Bible was well-thumbed, because he read it
every day. He loved all the stories in it, but the one
he loved the best—the one he meditated on most
often—was the parable of the Good Samaritan. He
had preached on that passage from the Gospel of

Luke several times, and the Redeemer congregation had always been generous with their praise afterward, God bless them.

Doug supposed it was because the story was so *personal* to him. A priest had passed by the robbed and beaten traveler lying at the side of the road; so had a Levite. Then who comes along? A nasty, Jew-hating Samaritan. But that's the one who helps, nasty Jew-hater or not. He cleanses the traveler's cuts and scrapes, then binds them up. He loads the traveler on his donkey, and fronts him a room at the nearest inn.

"So which of these three do you think was a neighbor to him who fell among thieves?" Jesus inquires of the hotshot young lawyer who asked him about the requirements for eternal life. And the hotshot, not stupid, replies: "The one who shewed mercy."

If Doug Clayton had a horror of anything, it was of being like the Levite in that story. Of refusing to help when help was needed and passing by on the other side. So when he saw the muddy station wagon parked a little way up the entrance ramp of the deserted rest area—the downed orange barrier-barrels in front of it, the driver's door hanging ajar—he hesitated only a moment before flicking on his turn signal and pulling in.

He parked behind the wagon, put on his four-ways, and started to get out. Then he noticed that there appeared to be no license plate on the back of the station wagon . . . although there was so much damn mud it was hard to tell for sure. Doug took his cell phone out of the Prius's center console and made sure it was on. Being a good Samaritan was one thing; approaching a plateless mongrel of a car without caution was just plain stupid.

He walked toward the wagon with the phone clasped loosely in his left hand. Nope, no plate, he was right about that. He tried to peer through the back window and could see nothing. Too much mud. He walked toward the driver's-side door, then paused, looking at the car as a whole, frowning. Was it a Ford or a Chevy? Darned if he could tell, and that was strange, because he had to've insured thousands of station wagons in his career.

Customized? he asked himself. Well, maybe . . . but who would bother to customize a station wagon into something so *anonymous?*

"Hi, hello? Everything okay?"

He walked toward the door, squeezing the phone a little tighter without being aware of it. He found himself thinking of some movie that had scared the heck out of him as a kid, some haunted house thing. A bunch of teenagers had approached the old deserted house, and when one of them saw the door standing ajar, he'd whispered "Look, it's open!" to his buddies. You wanted to tell them not to go in there, but of course they did.

That's stupid. If there's someone in that car, he could be hurt.

Of course the guy might have gone up to the restaurant, maybe looking for a pay phone, but if he was *really* hurt—

"Hello?"

Doug reached for the door handle, then thought better of it and stooped to peer through the opening. What he saw was dismaying. The bench seat was covered with mud; so was the dashboard and the steering wheel. Dark goo dripped from the old-fashioned knobs of the radio, and on the wheel were prints that didn't look exactly as if hands had made them. The palm prints were awfully big, for one thing, but the finger marks were as narrow as pencils.

"Is someone in there?" He shifted his cell phone to his right hand and took hold of the driver's door with his left, meaning to swing it wide so he could look into the backseat. "Is someone hur—"

There was a moment to register an ungodly stink, and then his left hand exploded into pain so great it seemed to leap through his entire body, trailing fire and filling all his hollow spaces with agony. Doug didn't, couldn't, scream. His throat locked shut with the sudden shock of it. He looked down and saw that the door handle appeared to have impaled the pad of his palm.

His fingers were barely there. He could only see the stubs, just below the last knuckles where the back of his hand started. The rest had somehow been swallowed by the door. As Doug watched, the third finger broke. His wedding ring fell off and clinked to the pavement.

He could feel something, oh dear God and dear Jesus, something like teeth. They were chewing. The car was eating his hand.

Doug tried to pull back. Blood flew, some against the muddy door, some splattering his slacks. The drops that hit the door disappeared immediately, with a faint sucking sound: *slorp*. For a moment he almost got away. He could see glistening finger bones from which the flesh had been sucked, and had a brief, nightmarish image of chewing on one of the Colonel's chicken wings. *Get it all before you put that down,* his mother used to say, *the meat's sweetest closest to the bone.*

Then he was yanked forward again. The driver's

door opened to welcome him: *Hello, Doug, been waiting for you, come on in.* His head connected with the top of the door, and he felt a line of cold across his brow that turned hot as the station wagon's roofline sliced through his skin.

He made one more effort to get away, dropping his cell phone and pushing at the rear window. The window yielded instead of supporting, then enveloped his hand. He rolled his eyes and saw what had looked like glass now rippling like a pond in a breeze. And why was it rippling? Because it was chewing. Because it was chowing down.

This is what I get for being a good Sam—

Then the top of the driver's door sawed through his skull and slipped smoothly into the brain behind it. Doug Clayton heard a large bright *SNAP*, like a pine knot exploding in a hot fire. Then darkness descended.

A southbound delivery driver glanced over and saw a little green car with its flashers on parked behind a mud-coated station wagon. A man—presumably he belonged to the little green car—appeared to be leaning in the station wagon's door, talking to the driver. *Breakdown,* the delivery driver thought, and returned his attention to the road. No good Samaritan he.

Doug Clayton was jerked inside as if hands—ones with big palms and pencil-thin fingers—had seized his shirt and pulled him. The station wagon lost its shape and puckered inward, like a mouth tasting something exceptionally sour . . . or exceptionally sweet. From within came a series of overlapping crunches—the sound of a man stamping through dead branches in heavy boots. The wagon stayed puckered for ten seconds or so, looking more like a lumpy clenched fist than a car. Then, with a *pouck* sound like a tennis ball being smartly struck by a racquet, it popped back into its station wagon shape.

The sun peeked briefly through the clouds, reflecting off the dropped cell phone and making a brief hot circle of light on Doug's wedding ring. Then it dived back into the cloud cover.

Behind the wagon, the Prius blinked its four-ways. They made a low clocklike sound: *Tick . . . tick . . . tick*.

A few cars went past, but not many. The two workweeks surrounding Easter are the slowest time of year on the nation's turnpikes, and afternoon is the second-slowest time of the day; only the hours between midnight and five a.m. are slower.

Tick . . . tick . . . tick.

In the abandoned restaurant, Pete Simmons slept on.

3. JULIANNE VERNON ('05 Dodge Ram)

Julie Vernon didn't need King James to teach her how to be a good Samaritan. She had grown up in the small town of Readfield, Maine (population 2,400), where neighboring was a way of life, and strangers were also neighbors. Nobody had told her this in so many words; she had learned from her mother, father, and big brothers. They had little to say about such issues, but teaching by example is always the most powerful teaching of all. If you saw a guy lying by the side of the road, it didn't matter if he was a Samaritan or a Martian. You stopped to help.

Nor had she ever worried much about being

robbed, raped, or murdered by someone who was only pretending to need help. When asked for her weight by the school nurse when she was in the fifth grade, Julie had replied proudly, "My dad says I'd dress out around one seventy. Little less if skinned." Now, at thirty-five, she would have dressed out closer to two eighty, and had no interest in making any man a good wife. She was as gay as old Dad's hatband, and proud of it. On the back of her Ram truck were two bumper stickers. One read SUPPORT GENDER EQUAL-ITY. The other, a bright pink, opined that GAY IS A **HAPPY** WORD!

The stickers didn't show now because she was hauling what she referred to as the "hoss-trailer." She had bought a two-year-old Spanish Jennet mare in the town of Clinton, and was now on her way back to Readfield, where she lived on a farm with her partner just two miles down the road from the house where she'd grown up.

She was thinking, as she often did, of her five years of touring with The Twinkles, a female mud-wrestling team. Those years had been both bad and good. Bad because The Twinkles were generally regarded as freakshow entertainment (which she supposed they sort of were), good because she had seen so much of the world. Mostly the American world, it was true, but The Twinkles had once spent three months in England, France, and Germany, where they had been treated with a kindness and respect that was almost eerie. Like young ladies, in fact.

She still had her passport, and had renewed it last year, although she guessed she might never go abroad again. Mostly that was all right. Mostly she was happy on the farm with Amelia and their motley

menagerie of dogs, cats, and livestock, but she sometimes missed those days of touring—the one-night
stands, the matches under the lights, the rough cama-
raderie of the other girls. Sometimes she even missed
the push-and-bump with the audience.

"Grab her by the cunt, she's a dyke, she likes that!"
some shitbrained yokel had yelled one night—in
Tulsa that had been, if she remembered right.

She and Melissa, the girl she'd been grappling with
in the Mudbowl, had looked at each other, nodded,
and stood up facing the section of the audience from
which the yell had come. They stood there wearing
nothing but their sopping bikini briefs, mud dripping from their hair and breasts, and had flipped the
bird at the heckler in unison. The audience had broken into spontaneous applause . . . which became a
standing O when first Julianne, then Melissa, turned,
bent, dropped trou, and shot the asshole a double
moon.

She had grown up knowing you cared for the one
who had fallen and couldn't get up. She had also
grown up knowing you ate no shit—not about your
hosses, your size, your line of work, or your sexual
preferences. Once you started eating shit, it had a way
of becoming your regular diet.

The CD she was listening to came to an end, and
she was just about to poke the Eject button when she
saw a car ahead, parked a little way up the ramp leading to the abandoned Mile 81 service stop. Its four-
way flashers were on. There was another car in front of
it, a muddy old beat-to-shit station wagon. Probably
a Ford or a Chevrolet, it was hard to tell which.

Julie didn't make a decision, because there was
no decision to be made. She flipped her blinker, saw

there would be no room for her on the ramp, not with the trailer in tow, and got as far over in the break-down lane as she could without hooking her wheels in the soft ground beyond. The last thing she wanted to do was overturn the hoss for which she had just paid eighteen hundred dollars.

This was probably nothing, but it didn't hurt to check. You could never tell when some woman had all at once decided to have herself a baby on the inter-state, or when some guy who stopped to help got excited and fainted. Julie put on her own four-ways, but they wouldn't show much, not with the hoss-trailer in the way.

She got out, looked toward the two cars, and saw not a soul. Maybe someone had picked the drivers up, but more likely they'd gone up to the restaurant. Julie doubted if they'd find much there; it had been closed down since the previous September. Julie her-self had often stopped at Mile 81 for a TCBY cone, but these days made her snack stop twenty miles north, at Damon's in Augusta.

She went around to the trailer, and her new hoss— DeeDee by name—poked her nose out. Julie stroked it. "Soo, baby, soo. This'll just take a minute."

She opened the doors so she could get at the locker built into the trailer's left side. DeeDee decided this would be a fine time to exit the vehicle, but Julie restrained her with one beefy shoulder, once again murmuring, "Soo, baby, soo."

She unlatched the locker. Inside, sitting on top of the tools, were a few road flares and two fluorescent-pink mini traffic cones. Julie hooked her fingers into the hollow tops of the cones (no need for flares on an afternoon that was slowly beginning to brighten). She closed the locker and latched it, not wanting DeeDee to step a hoof in and maybe hurt herself. Then she closed the back doors. DeeDee once more poked her head out. Julie didn't really believe a horse could look anxious, but DeeDee sort of did.

"Not long," she said, then placed the traffic cones behind the trailer and headed for the two cars.

The Prius was empty but unlocked. Julie didn't particularly care for that, given the fact that there was a suitcase and a fairly expensive-looking briefcase in the backseat. The driver's door of the old station wagon was hanging open. Julie started toward it, then stopped, frowning. Lying on the pavement beside the open door was a cell phone and what just about had to be a wedding ring. There was a big crack zigzagging up the phone's casing, as if it had been dropped. And on the little glass window where the numbers appeared—was that a drop of blood?

Probably not, probably just mud—the wagon was covered with it—but Julie liked this less and less. She had taken DeeDee for a good canter before loading her, and hadn't changed out of her no-nonsense split riding skirt for the trip home. Now she took her own cell phone out of the righthand pocket and debated punching in 911.

No, she decided, not yet. But if the mud-splattered wagon was as empty as the little green car, or if that dime-size spot on the dropped phone really was blood, she'd do it. And wait right here for the state police cruiser to come instead of walking up to that deserted building. She was brave, and she was kind-hearted, but she was not stupid.

She bent to examine the ring and the dropped phone. The slight flare of her riding skirt brushed against the muddy flank of the station wagon, and appeared to melt into it. Julie was jerked to the right, and hard. One hefty buttock slammed against the side of the wagon. The surface yielded, then enveloped two layers of cloth and the meat beneath. The pain was immediate and enormous. She screamed, dropped her phone, and tried to shove herself away, almost as if the car were one of her old mud-wrestling opponents. Her right hand and forearm disappeared through the yielding membrane that looked like a window. What appeared on the other side, vaguely visible through the scrim of mud, wasn't the hefty arm of a large and healthy horsewoman but a starving bone with flesh hanging from it in tatters.

The station wagon began to pucker.

A car passed southbound, then another. Thanks to the trailer, they didn't see the woman who was now half in and half out of the deformed station wagon, like Brer Rabbit stuck in the tar baby. Nor did they hear her screams. One driver was listening to Toby Keith, the other to Led Zeppelin. Both had his particular brand of pop music turned up loud. In the restaurant, Pete Simmons heard her, but only from a great distance, like a fading echo. His eyelids fluttered. Then the screams stopped.

Pete rolled over on the filthy mattress and went back to sleep.

The thing that looked like a car ate Julianne Vernon, clothes, boots, and all. The only thing it missed was her phone, which now lay beside Doug Clayton's. Then it popped back into its station wagon shape with that same racquet-hitting-ball sound.

In the hoss-trailer, DeeDee nickered and stamped an impatient foot. She was hungry.

4. THE LUSSIER FAMILY ('11 Expedition)

Six-year-old Rachel Lussier shouted, "Look, Mommy! Look, Daddy! It's the horse lady! See her trailer? See it?"

Carla wasn't surprised Rache was the first one to spot the trailer, even though she was sitting in the backseat. Rache had the sharpest eyes in the family; no one else even came close. X-ray vision, her father sometimes said. It was one of those jokes that isn't quite a joke.

Johnny, Carla, and four-year-old Blake all wore glasses; everyone on both sides of their family wore glasses; even Bingo, the family dog, probably needed them. Bingo was apt to run into the screen door when he wanted to go out. Only Rache had escaped the curse of myopia. The last time she'd been to the optometrist, she'd read the whole damn eye chart, bottom line and all. Dr. Stratton had been amazed. "She could qualify for jet fighter training," he told Johnny and Carla.

Johnny said, "Maybe someday she will. She's certainly got a killer instinct when it comes to her little brother."

Carla had thrown him an elbow for that, but it was true. She had heard there was less sibling rivalry when the sibs were of different sexes. If so, Rachel and Blake were the exception that proved the rule. Carla sometimes thought the most common two words she heard these days were *started it*. Only the gender of the pronoun opening the sentence varied.

The two of them had been pretty good for the first hundred miles of this trip, partially because visiting with Johnny's parents always put them in a good mood and mostly because Carla had been careful to fill up the no-man's-land between Rachel's booster seat and Blake's car seat with toys and coloring books. But after their snack-and-pee stop in Augusta, the squabbling had begun again. Probably because of the ice cream cones. Giving kids sugar on a long car trip was like squirting gasoline on a campfire, Carla knew this, but you couldn't refuse them *everything*.

In desperation, Carla had started a game of Plastic Fantastic, serving as judge and awarding points for lawn gnomes, wishing wells, statues of the Blessed Virgin, etc. The problem was that on the turnpike there were lots of trees but very few vulgar roadside displays. Her sharp-eyed six-year-old daughter and her sharp-tongued four-year-old boy were beginning to renew old grudges when Rachel saw the horse-trailer pulled over just a little shy of the old Mile 81 rest stop.

"Want to pet the horsie again!" Blake shouted. He began thrashing in his car seat, the world's smallest break-dancer. His legs were now just long enough to kick the back of the driver's seat, which Johnny found *très* annoying.

Somebody tell me again why I wanted to have kids, he thought. *Somebody remind me just what I was thinking. I know it made sense at the time.*

"Blakie, don't kick Daddy's seat," Johnny said.

"Want to pet the *horrrrsie*!" Blake yelled. And fetched the back of the driver's seat an especially good one.

"You are such a babykins," Rachel said, safe from brother-kicks on her side of the backseat DMZ. She spoke in her most indulgent big-girl tone, the one always guaranteed to infuriate Blakie.

"I AM AIN'T A BABYKINS!"

"Blakie," Johnny began, "if you don't stop kicking Daddy's seat, Daddy will have to take his trusty butcher knife and amputate Blakie's little feetsies at the ank—"

"She's broken down," Carla said. "See the traffic cones? Pull over."

"Hon, that'd mean the breakdown lane. Not such a good idea."

"You don't have to do that, just swing around and park beside those other two cars. On the ramp. There's room and you won't be blocking anything because the rest area's closed."

"If it's okay with you, I'd like to get back to Falmouth before d—"

"Pull over." Carla heard herself using the DEFCON-1 tone that brooked no refusal, even though she knew it was setting a bad example; how many times lately had she heard Rachel using that exact same tone on Blake? Using it until the little guy broke down in tears?

Switching off the she-who-must-be-obeyed voice and speaking more softly, Carla said, "That woman was nice to the kids."

They had pulled into Damon's next to the horse-trailer and stopped for ice cream. The horse lady (nearly as big as a horse herself) was leaning against the trailer, eating a cone of her own and feeding something to a very handsome beastie. To Carla the treat looked like a Kashi granola bar.

Johnny had one kid by each hand and tried to walk them past, but Blake was having none of that. "Can I pet your horse?" he asked.

"Cost you a quarter," the big lady in the brown

riding skirt had said, and then grinned at Blakie's crestfallen expression. "Nah, I'm just kiddin. Here, hold this." She thrust her drippy ice cream cone at Blake, who was too surprised to do anything but take it. Then she lifted him up to where he could pet the horse's nose. DeeDee regarded the wide-eyed child calmly, sniffed at the horse lady's dripping cone, decided it wasn't what she wanted, and allowed her nose to be stroked.

"Whoa, soft!" Blake said. Carla had never heard him speak with such simple awe. *Why haven't we ever taken these kids to a petting zoo?* she wondered, and immediately put it down on her mental to-do list.

"Me, me, me!" Rachel bugled, dancing around impatiently.

The big lady set Blake down. "Lick that ice cream while I lift your sister," she told him, "but don't get cooties on it, okay?"

Carla thought of telling Blake that eating after people, especially strange people, was not okay. Then she saw Johnny's bemused grin and thought what the hell. You sent your kids to schools that were basically germ factories. You drove them for hundreds of miles on the turnpike, where any drunk maniac or texting teenager could cross the median and wipe them out. Then you forbade them a lick on a partially used ice cream? That was taking the car-seat and bike-helmet mentality a little too far, maybe.

The horse lady lifted Rachel so Rachel could pet the horse's nose. "Wowie! Nice!" Rachel said. "What's her name?"

"DeeDee."

"Great name! I love you, DeeDee!"

"I love you, too, DeeDee," the horse lady said, and

put a big old smackeroo on DeeDee's nose. That made them all laugh.

"Mom, can we have a horse?"

"Yes!" Carla said warmly. "When you're twenty-six!"

This made Rachel put on her mad face (puckered brow, puffed cheeks, lips down to a stitch), but when the horse lady laughed, Rachel gave up and laughed too.

The big woman bent down to Blakie, her hands on knees covered by her riding skirt. "Can I have my ice cream cone back, young fella?"

Blake held it out. When she took it, he began to lick his fingers, which were covered with melting pistachio.

"Thank you," Carla told the horse lady. "That was very kind of you." Then, to Blake, "Let's get you inside and cleaned up. After that you can have ice cream."

"I want what she's having," Blake said, and that made the horse lady laugh some more.

Johnny insisted that they eat their cones in a booth, because he didn't want them decorating the Expedition with pistachio ice cream. When they finished and went out, the horse lady was gone.

Just one of those people you meet—occasionally nasty, more often nice, sometimes even terrific—along the road and never see again.

Only here she was, or at least her truck was, parked in the breakdown lane with traffic cones neatly placed behind her trailer. And Carla was right, the horse lady *had* been nice to the kids. So thinking, Johnny Lussier made the worst—and last—decision of his life.

He flipped his blinker and pulled onto the ramp

as Carla had suggested, parking ahead of Doug Clayton's Prius, which was still flashing its four-ways, and beside the muddy station wagon. He put the transmission in park but left the engine running.

"I want to pet the horsie," Blake said.

"I also want to pet the horsie," Rachel said in the haughty lady-of-the-manor tone of voice she had picked up God knew where. It drove Carla crazy, but she refused to say anything. If she did, Rache would use it all the more.

"Not without the lady's permission," Johnny said. "You kids sit right where you are for now. You too, Carla."

"Yes, master," Carla said in the zombie voice that always made the kids laugh.

"Very funny, Easter bunny."

"The cab of her truck's empty," Carla said. "They *all* look empty. Do you think there was an accident?"

"Don't know, but nothing looks dinged up. Hang on a minute."

Johnny Lussier got out, went around the back of the Expedition he would never finish paying for, and walked to the cab of the Dodge Ram. Carla hadn't seen the horse lady, but he wanted to make sure she wasn't lying on the seat, maybe trying to live through a heart attack. (A lifelong jogger, Johnny secretly believed a heart attack was waiting by age forty-five at the latest for anyone who weighed even five pounds over the target weight prescribed by Medicine.Net.)

She wasn't sprawled on the seat (*of course not, a woman that big Carla would have seen even lying down*), and she wasn't in the trailer, either. Only the horse, who poked her head out and sniffed Johnny's face.

"Hello there . . ." For a moment the name didn't come, then it did. ". . . DeeDee. How's the old feed-bag hanging?"

He patted her nose, then headed back up the ramp to investigate the other two vehicles. He saw there *had* been an accident of sorts, albeit a very tiny one. The station wagon had knocked over a few of the orange barrels blocking the ramp.

Carla rolled down her window, a thing neither of the kids in back could do because of the lockout feature. "Any sign of her?"

"Nope."

"Any sign of *anyone*?"

"Carl, give me a ch—" He saw the cell phones and the wedding ring lying beside the partially open door of the station wagon.

"What?" Carla craned to see.

"Just a sec." The thought of telling her to lock the doors crossed his mind, but he dismissed it. They were on I-95 in broad daylight, for God's sake. Cars passing every twenty or thirty seconds, sometimes two or three in a line.

He bent down and picked up the phones, one in each hand. He turned to Carla, and thus did not see the car door opening wider, like a mouth.

"Carla, I think there's blood on this one." He held up Doug Clayton's cracked phone.

"Mom?" Rachel asked. "Who's in that dirty car? The door's opening."

"Come back," Carla said. Her mouth was suddenly dust-dry. She wanted to yell it, but there seemed to be a stone on her chest. It was invisible but very large. "Someone's in that car!"

Instead of coming back, Johnny turned and bent

to look inside. When he did, the door swung shut on his head. There was a terrible thudding noise. The stone on Carla's chest was suddenly gone. She drew in breath and screamed out her husband's name.

"What's wrong with Daddy?" Rachel cried. Her voice was high and as thin as a reed. *"What's wrong with Daddy?"*

"Daddy!" Blake yelled. He had been inventorying his newest Transformers and now looked around wildly to see where the daddy in question might be.

Carla didn't think. Her husband's body was there, but his head was in the dirty station wagon. He was still alive, though; his arms and legs were flailing. She was out of the Expedition with no memory of opening the door. Her body seemed to be acting on its own, her stunned brain just along for the ride.

"Mommy, no!" Rachel screamed.

"Mommy, NO!" Blake had no idea of what was going on, but he knew it was bad. He began to cry and struggle in his car seat's webwork of straps.

Carla grabbed Johnny around the waist and pulled with the crazy super-strength of adrenaline. The door of the station wagon came partway open and blood ran over the footing in a little waterfall. For one awful moment she saw her husband's head, lying on the station wagon's muddy seat and cocked crazily to one side. Even though he was still trembling in her arms, she understood (in one of those lightning flashes of clarity that can come even during a perfect storm of panic) that it was how hanging victims looked when they were cut down. Because their necks were broken. In that brief, searing moment—that shutterflash glimpse—she thought he looked stupid and surprised and ugly, all the essential Johnny swatted out of him, and knew he was already dead, trembling or not. It was how a kid looked after hitting the rocks instead of the water when he dived. How a woman who had been impaled by her steering wheel looked after her car slammed into a bridge abutment. It was how you looked when disfiguring death strutted toward you out of nowhere with its arms wide in welcome.

The car door slammed viciously shut. Carla still had her arms wrapped around her husband's waist, and when she was yanked forward, she had another lightning flash of clarity.

It's the car, you have to stay away from the car!

She let go of Johnny's midsection a moment too late. A sheaf of her hair fell against the door and was sucked in. Her brow smacked against the car before she could tear free. Suddenly the top of her head was burning as the thing ate away her scalp.

Run! she tried to scream at her often troublesome but undeniably bright daughter. *Run and take Blakie with you!*

But before she could even begin to articulate the thought, her mouth was gone.

Only Rachel saw the station wagon slam shut on her daddy's head like a Venus flytrap on a bug, but both of them saw their mother somehow pulled through the muddy door as if it were a curtain. They saw one of her mocs come off, they got a flash of her pink toenails, and then she was gone. A moment later, the white car lost its shape and clenched itself like a fist. Through their mother's open window, they heard a crunching sound.

"Wha' that?" Blakie screamed. His eyes were

streaming tears and his lower lip was lathered with snot. *"Wha' that, Rachie, wha' that, wha' that?"*

Their bones, Rachel thought. She was only six years old, and not allowed to go to PG-13 movies or watch them on TV (let alone R; her mother said R stood for *Raunchy*), but she knew that was the sound of their bones breaking.

The car wasn't a car. It was some kind of monster.

"Where Mommy n Daddy?" Blakie asked, turning his large eyes—now made even larger by his tears— on her. "Where Mommy n Daddy, Rachie?"

He sounds like he's two again, Rachel thought, and for maybe the first time in her life, she felt something other than irritation (or, when extremely tried by his behavior, outright hate) for her baby brother. She didn't think this new feeling was love. She thought it was something even bigger. Her mom hadn't been able to say anything in the end, but if she'd had time, Rachel knew what it would have been: *Take care of Blakie.*

He was thrashing in his car seat. He knew how to undo the straps, but in his panic had forgotten how.

Rachel opened her seatbelt, slid out of her booster seat, and tried to do it for him. One of his flailing hands caught her cheek and administered a ringing slap. Under normal circumstances that would have earned him a hard punch on the shoulder (and Rachel a time-out in her room, where she would have sat staring at the wall in a boiling fugue of fury), but now she just grabbed his hand and held it down.

"Stop it! Let me help you! I can get you out, but not if you do that!"

He stopped thrashing, but kept on crying. "Where Daddy? Where Mommy? I want Mommy!"

I want her too, asshole, Rachel thought, and undid the car-seat straps. "We're going to get out now, and we're going to . . ."

What? They were going to what? Go up to the restaurant? It was closed, that was why there were orange barrels. That was why the pumps in front of the gas station part were gone and there were weeds poking out of the empty parking lot.

"We're going to get away from here," she finished.

She got out of the car and went around to Blakie's side. She opened his door but he just looked at her, eyes brimming. "I can't get out, Rachie, I'll fall."

Don't be such a scaredy-baby, she almost said, then didn't. This wasn't the time for that. He was upset enough. She opened her arms and said, "Slide. I'll catch you."

He looked at her doubtfully, then slid. Rachel did catch him, but he was heavier than he looked, and they both went sprawling. She got the worst of it because she was on the bottom, but Blakie bumped his head and scraped one hand and began to bawl loudly, this time in pain instead of fear.

"Stop it," she said, and wriggled out from under him. "Put on your man-pants, Blakie."

"H-huh?"

She didn't answer. She was looking at the two phones lying beside the terrible station wagon. One of them looked broken, but the other—

Rachel edged toward it on her hands and knees, never taking her eyes off the car into which their father and mother had disappeared with such terrifying suddenness. As she was reaching toward the good phone, Blakie walked past her toward the station wagon, holding out his scraped hand.

"Mom? Mommy? Come out! I hurted myself. You have to come out n kiss it bet—"

"Stop right where you are, Blake Lussier."

Carla would have been proud; it was her she-who-must-be-obeyed voice at its most forbidding. And it worked. Blake stopped four feet from the side of the station wagon.

"But I want *Mommy*! I want *Mommy*, Rachie!"

She grabbed his hand and pulled him away from the car. "Not now. Help me work this thing." She knew perfectly well how to work the phone, but she had to distract him.

"Gimme, I can do it! Gimme, Rache!"

She passed it over, and while he examined the buttons, she got up, grabbed his Wolverine tee-shirt, and pulled him back three steps. Blake hardly noticed. He found the power button on Julianne Vernon's cell phone and pushed it. The phone beeped. Rachel took it from him, and for once in his dopey little-kid life, Blakie didn't protest.

She had listened carefully when McGruff the Crime Dog came to talk to them at school (although she knew perfectly well it was a guy in a McGruff suit), and she did not hesitate now. She punched in 911 and put the phone to her ear. It rang once, then was picked up.

"Hello? My name is Rachel Ann Lussier, and—"

"This call is being recorded," a man's voice overrode her. "If you wish to report an emergency, push One. If you wish to report adverse road conditions, push Two. If you wish to report a stranded motorist—"

"Rache? Rachie? Where Mommy? Where Da—"

"Shhh!" Rachel said sternly, and pushed 1. It was

hard to do. Her hand was trembling and her eyes were all blurry. She realized she was crying. When had she started crying? She couldn't remember.

"Hello, this is nine-one-one," a woman said.

"Are you real or another recording?" Rachel asked.

"I'm real," the woman said, sounding a little amused. "Do you have an emergency?"

"Yes. A bad car ate up our mother and our daddy. It's at the—"

"Quit while you're ahead," the 911 woman advised. She sounded more amused than ever. "How old are you, kiddo?"

"I'm six, almost seven. My name is Rachel Ann Lussier, and a car, a bad car—"

"Listen, Rachel Ann or whoever you are, I can trace this call. Did you know that? I bet you didn't. Now just hang up and I won't have to send a policeman to your house to paddle your—"

"They're dead, you stupid phone person!" Rachel screamed into the phone, and at the d-word, Blakie began to cry again.

The 911 woman didn't say anything for a moment. Then, in a voice no longer amused: "Where are you, Rachel Ann?"

"At the empty restaurant! The one with the orange barrels!"

Blakie sat down and put his face between his knees and his arms over his head. That hurt Rachel in a way she had never been hurt before. It hurt her deep in her heart.

"That's not enough information," the 911 lady said. "Can you be a little more specific, Rachel Ann?"

Rachel didn't know what *specific* meant, but she knew what she was seeing: the back tire of the station wagon, the one closest to them, was melting a little. A tentacle of what looked like liquid rubber was moving slowly across the pavement toward Blakie.

"I have to go," Rachel said. "We have to get away from the bad car."

She got Blake to his feet and dragged him backward some more, staring at the melting tire. The tentacle of rubber started to go back where it had come from (*because it knows we're out of reach,* she thought), and the tire started to look like a tire again, but that wasn't good enough for Rachel. She kept dragging Blake down the ramp and toward the turnpike.

"Where we goin, Rachie?"

I don't know. "Away from that car."

"I want my Transformers!"

"Not now, later." She kept a tight hold on Blake and kept backing, down toward the turnpike where the occasional traffic was whizzing by at seventy and eighty miles an hour.

Nothing is as piercing as a child's scream; it's one of nature's more efficient survival mechanisms. Pete Simmons's sleep had already thinned to little more than a doze, and when Rachel screamed at the 911 lady, he heard it and finally woke up all the way.

He sat up, winced, and put a hand to his head. It ached, and he knew what that sort of ache was: the dreaded HANGOVER. His tongue tasted furry, and his stomach was blick. Not I'm-gonna-hurl blick, but blick, just the same.

Thank God I didn't drink any more, he thought, and got to his feet. He went to one of the mesh-covered windows to see who was yelling. He didn't like what he saw. Some of the orange barrels blocking the entrance ramp to the rest area had been knocked over, and there were *cars* down there. Quite a few of them.

Then he saw a couple of kids—a little girl in pink pants and a little boy wearing shorts and a tee-shirt. He caught just a glimpse of them, enough to tell that they were backing away—as if something had scared them—and then they disappeared behind what looked to Pete like a horse-trailer.

Something was wrong. There had been an accident or something, although nothing down there *looked* like an accident. His first impulse was to get away from here in a hurry, before he got caught up in whatever had happened. He grabbed his saddlebag and started toward the kitchen and the loading dock beyond. Then he stopped. There were kids out there. *Little* kids. Way too little to be close to a fast road like I-95 on their own, and he hadn't seen any adults.

Gotta be grown-ups, didn't you see all those cars?

Yes, he'd seen the cars, and a truck hooked up to a horse-trailer, but no grown-ups.

I have to go out there. Even if I get in trouble, I have to make sure those numbshit kids don't get smeared all over the turnpike.

Pete hurried to the Burger King's front door, found it locked, and asked himself what would have been Normie Therriault's question: *Hey afterbirth, did your mother have any kids that lived?*

Pete turned and pelted for the loading dock. Running made his headache worse, but he ignored it. He placed his saddlebag at the edge of the concrete platform, lowered himself, and dropped. He landed stupid, banged his tailbone, and ignored that, too. He got up, and flashed a longing look toward the woods. He *could* just disappear. Doing so might save him oh so much grief down the line. The idea was miserably tempting. This wasn't like the movies, where the good guy always made the right decision without thinking. If somebody smelled vodka on his breath—

"Jesus," he said. "Oh, Jesus-jumped-up-Rice-Krispies-*Christ*."

Why had he ever come here? Talk about numb-shit kids!

Holding Blakie firmly by the hand, Rachel walked him all the way to the end of the ramp. Just as they got there, a double-box semi blasted by at seventy-five miles an hour. The wind blew their hair back, rippled their clothes, and almost knocked Blakie over.

"Rachie, I'm scared! We're not supposed to go in the road!"

Tell me something I don't know, Rachel thought.

At home they weren't supposed to go any farther than the end of the driveway, and there was hardly any traffic on Fresh Winds Way in Falmouth. The traffic on the turnpike was far from constant, but the cars that *did* come along were going superfast. Besides, where was there to go? They might be able to walk in the breakdown lane, but it would be horribly risky. And there were no exits here, only woods. They could go back to the restaurant, but they would have to walk past the bad car.

A red sports car swept past, the guy behind the wheel blaring his horn in a constant *WAAAAAAAA* that made her want to cover her ears.

Blake was tugging her, and Rachel let herself be tugged. At one side of the ramp were guardrail posts. Blakie sat down on one of the thick cables running between them and covered his eyes with his chubby hands. Rachel sat next to him. She was out of ideas.

5. JIMMY GOLDING ('11 Crown Victoria)

A child's scream may be one of Mother Nature's more efficient survival mechanisms, but when it comes to turnpike travel, there's nothing like a parked state police cruiser. Especially if the black blank face of a radar detector is facing the oncoming traffic. Drivers doing seventy ease back to sixty-five; drivers doing eighty step on the brake and begin mentally figuring out how many points they'll lose off their licenses if the blue lights go on behind them. (It's a salutary effect that wears off quickly; ten or fifteen miles farther up or down the line, the stampeders are once again stampeding.)

The beauty of the parked cruiser, at least in Maine State Trooper Jimmy Golding's opinion, was that you didn't really need to *do* anything. You just pulled over and let nature (*human* nature, in this case) take its guilty course. On this overcast April afternoon, his Simmons SpeedCheck radar gun wasn't even on, and the traffic passing southbound on I-95 was just a background drone. All his attention was on the iPad propped against the lower arc of the steering wheel.

He was playing a Scrabble-like game called Words With Friends, his Internet connection provided by Verizon. His opponent was an old barracks-mate named Nick Avery, now with the Oklahoma State Patrol. Jimmy couldn't imagine why anyone would trade Maine for Oklahoma, seemed like a bad decision to him, but there could be no doubt that Nick was an *excellent* Words With Friends player. He beat Jimmy nine games out of every ten, and was leading in this one. But Nick's current lead was unusually small, and all the letters were out of the electronic draw-bag. If he, Jimmy, could play the four letters he had left, he would gain a hard-earned victory. Currently he was fixated on FIX. The four letters he had left were A, E, S, and another F. If he could somehow modify FIX, he would not only win, he would kick his old pal's ass. But it didn't look hopeful.

He was examining the rest of the board, where the prospects seemed even less fruitful, when his radio gave two high-pitched tones. It was an all-units alert from 911 in Westbrook. Jimmy tossed his iPad aside and turned up the gain.

"All units, attention. Who's close to the Mile 81 rest area? Anyone?"

Jimmy pulled his mike. "Nine-one-one dispatch, this is Seventeen. I'm currently at Mile 85, just south of the Lisbon-Sabattus exit."

The woman Rachel Lussier thought of as the 911 lady didn't bother to ask if anyone else was closer; in one of the new Crown Vic cruisers, Jimmy was just three minutes away, maybe less.

"Seventeen, I got a call three minutes ago from a little girl who says her parents are dead, and since then I've had multiple calls from people who say there are two unaccompanied little kids at the edge of that rest area."

He didn't bother to ask why none of those multiple callers had stopped. He had seen it before. Sometimes it was a fear of legal entanglements. More often it was just a severe case of don't-give-a-shit. There was a lot of that going around. Still . . . *kids*. Jesus, you'd think—

"Nine-one-one, I'm on this. Seventeen out."

Jimmy lit his blues, checked his rearview to make sure he had the road, and then peeled out of the gravel pass-through with its sign reading NO U-TURN, OFFICIAL VEHICLES ONLY. The Crown Vic's V-8 surged; the digital speedometer blurred up to 92, where it hung. Trees reeled giddily past on both sides of the road. He came up on a lumbering old Buick that stubbornly refused to pull over and swept around it. When he pulled back into the travel lane, Jimmy saw the rest area. And something else. Two little kids—a boy in shorts, a girl in pink pants—sitting on the guardrail cables beside the entrance ramp. They looked like the world's smallest vagrants, and Jimmy's heart squeezed hard enough to hurt. He had kids of his own.

They stood up when they saw the flashing lights, and for one terrible second Jimmy thought the little boy was going to step in front of his cruiser. God bless the little girl, who grabbed him by the arm and reeled him in.

Jimmy decelerated hard enough to send his citation book, logbook, and iPad cascading off the seat onto the floor. The Vic's front end drifted a little, but he brought it back and parked blocking the ramp, where several other cars were already parked. What was going on here?

The sun came out then, and a word completely unrelated to the current situation flashed through Trooper Jimmy Golding's mind: *AFFIXES. I can make AFFIXES, and go out clean.*

The little girl was running toward the driver's side

of the cruiser, dragging her weeping, stumbling kid brother with her. Her face, white and terrified, looked years older than it should have, and there was a big wet patch on the little boy's shorts.

Jimmy got out, being careful not to hit them with his door. He dropped on one knee to get on their level and they rushed into his arms, almost knocking him over. "Whoa, whoa, take it easy, you're all ri—"

"The bad car ate Mommy and Daddy," the little boy said, and pointed. "The bad car right there. It ate them all up like the big bad woof ate Riddle Red Riding Hoop. You have to get them back!"

It was impossible to tell which vehicle the chubby finger was pointing at. Jimmy saw four: a station wagon that looked like it had been rode hard along nine miles of woods road, a spandy-clean Prius, a Dodge Ram hauling a horse-trailer, and a Ford Expedition.

"Little girl, what's your name? I'm Trooper Jimmy."

"Rachel Ann Lussier," she said. "This is Blakie. He's my little brother. We live at Nineteen Fresh Winds Way, Falmouth, Maine, oh-four-one-oh-five. Don't go near it, Trooper Jimmy. It looks like a car, but it's not. It eats people."

"Which car are we talking about, Rachel?"

"That one in front, next to my daddy's. The muddy one."

"The muddy car ate Daddy and Mommy!" the little boy—Blakie—proclaimed. "You can get them back, you're a policeman, you got a gun!"

Still on one knee, Jimmy held the children in his arms and eyeballed the muddy station wagon. The sun went back in; their shadows disappeared. On the turnpike, traffic swished past, but slower now, mindful of those flashing blue lights.

No one in the Expedition, the Prius, or the truck. He was guessing there was no one in the horse-trailer, either, unless they were hunkered down, and in that case the horse would probably seem a lot more nervous than it did. The only vehicle he couldn't see into was the one these kids claimed had eaten their parents. Jimmy didn't like the way the mud was smeared on all its windows. It looked like *deliberate* mud, somehow. He didn't like the cracked cell phone lying by the driver's door, either. Or the ring beside it. The ring was downright creepy.

Like the rest of this isn't.

The driver's door suddenly creaked partway open, upping the Creepy Quotient by at least thirty percent. Jimmy tensed and put his hand on the butt of his Glock, but no one came out. The door just hung there, six inches ajar.

"That's how it tries to get you to come in," the little girl said in a voice that was little more than a whisper. "It's a *monster* car."

Jimmy Golding hadn't believed in monster cars since he saw that movie *Christine* as a kid, but he believed that sometimes monsters could lurk *in* cars. And someone was in this one. How else had the door opened? It could be one of the kids' parents, hurt and unable to cry out. It could also be a man lying down on the seat, so he wouldn't make a shape visible through the mud-smeared rear window. Maybe a man with a gun.

"Who's in the station wagon?" Jimmy called. "I'm a state trooper, and I need you to announce yourself."

No one announced himself.

"Come out. Hands first, and I want to see them empty."

The only thing that came out was the sun, printing the door's shadow on the pavement for a second or two before ducking back into the clouds. Then there was only the hanging door.

"Come with me, kids," Jimmy said, and shepherded them to his cruiser. He opened the back door. They looked at the backseat with its litter of paperwork, Jimmy's fleece-lined jacket (which he didn't need today), and the shotgun clipped and locked to the back of the bench seat. Especially that.

"Mommy n Daddy say never get into a stranger's car," the boy named Blakie said. "They say it at school, too. Stranger-danger."

"He's a policeman with a policeman's car," Rachel said. "It's okay. Get in. And if you touch that gun, I'll smack you."

"Good advice on the gun, but it's secured and the trigger lock's on," Jimmy said.

Blakie got in and peered over the seat. "Hey, you got a iPad!"

"Shut up," Rachel said. She started to get in, then looked at Jimmy Golding with tired, horrified eyes. "Don't touch it. It's *sticky*."

Jimmy almost smiled. He had a daughter only a year or so younger than this little girl, and she might have said the same thing. He guessed little girls divided naturally into two groups, tomboys and dirt-haters. Like his Ellen, this one was a dirt-hater.

It was with this soon-to-be fatal misconception of what Rachel Lussier meant by *sticky* that he closed them in the backseat of Unit 17. He leaned in the front window of the cruiser and snared his mike. He never took his eyes from the hanging front door of the station wagon, and so did not see the little boy standing next to the rest area restaurant, holding an imitation-leather saddlebag against his chest like a small blue baby. A moment later the sun peeked out again, and Pete Simmons was swallowed up by the restaurant's shadow.

Jimmy called in to the Gray barracks.

"Seventeen, come back."

"I'm at the old Mile 81 rest area. I have four abandoned vehicles, one abandoned horse, and two abandoned children. One of the vehicles is a station wagon. The kids say . . ." He paused, then thought *what the hell*. "The kids say it ate their parents."

"Come back?"

"I think they mean someone inside grabbed them. I want you to send all available units over here, copy?"

"Copy all available units, but it'll be ten minutes before the first one gets there. That's Unit Twelve. He's Code Seventy-three in Waterville."

Al Andrews, no doubt chowing down at Bob's Burgers and talking politics. "Copy that."

"Give me MML on the wagon, Seventeen, and I'll run it."

"Negative on all three. No plate. As far as make and model, the thing's so covered with mud I can't tell. It's American, though." *I think*. "Probably a Ford or a Chevy. The kids are in my cruiser. Names are Rachel and Blakie Lussier. Fresh Winds Way, Falmouth. I forget the street number."

"Nineteen!" Rachel and Blakie shouted together.

"They say—"

"I got it, Seventeen. And which car did they come in?"

"Daddy's Expundition!" Blakie cried, happy to be of help.

"Ford Expedition," Jimmy said. "Plate number three-seven-seven-two IY. I'm going to approach that station wagon."

"Copy. Be careful there, Jimmy."

"Copy that. Oh, and will you reach out to nine-one-one dispatch and tell her the kids are all right?"

"Is that you talking or Pete Townshend?"

Very funny. "Seventeen, I'm sixty-two."

He started to replace the mike, then handed it to Rachel. "If anything happens—anything *bad*—you push that button on the side and yell 'Thirty.' That means 'Officer needs help.' Have you got it?"

"Yes, but you shouldn't go near that car, Trooper Jimmy. It *bites* and it *eats* and it's *sticky*."

Blakie, who, in his wonder at being in an actual police car, had temporarily forgotten what had befallen his parents, now remembered and began to cry again. "I want Mommy n Daddy!"

In spite of the weirdness and potential danger of the situation, Rachel Lussier's eye-rolling *you see what I have to deal with* expression almost made Jimmy laugh. How many times had he seen that exact same expression on the face of five-year-old Ellen Golding?

"Listen, Rachel," Jimmy said, "I know you're scared, but you're safe in here, and I have to do my job. If your parents are in that car, we don't want them hurt, do we?"

"GO GET MOMMY N DADDY, TROOPER JIMMY!" Blakie trumpeted. *"WE DON'T WANT THEM HURRRT!"*

Jimmy saw hope spark in the girl's eyes, but not

as much as he might have expected. Like Agent Mulder on the old *X-Files* show, she wanted to believe . . . but, like Mulder's partner, Agent Scully, she couldn't quite do it. What had these kids seen?

"Be careful, Trooper Jimmy." She raised one finger. It was a schoolteacherly gesture made even more endearing by a slight tremble. *"Don't touch it."*

As Jimmy approached the station wagon, he drew his Glock service automatic but left the safety on. For the time being. Standing slightly south of the hanging door, he once again invited anyone inside to exit the vehicle, open and empty hands foremost. No one came out. He reached for the door, then remembered the little girl's parting admonition, and hesitated. He reached out with the barrel of his gun to swing the door open. Only the door didn't open, and the barrel of the pistol stuck fast. The thing was a glue-pot.

He was jerked forward, as if a powerful hand had gripped the Glock's barrel and yanked. There was a second when he could have let go, but such an idea never even surfaced in his mind. One of the first things they taught you at the Academy after weapons issue was that you never let go of your sidearm. *Never.*

So he held on, and the car that had already eaten his gun now ate his hand. And his arm. The sun came out again, casting his diminishing shadow on the pavement. Somewhere, children were screaming.

The station wagon AFFIXES itself to the trooper, he thought. *Now I know what she meant by stick—*

Then the pain bloomed large and all thought ceased. There was time for one scream. Only one.

6. THE KIDS ('10 Richforth)

From where he was standing, seventy yards away, Pete saw it all. He saw the state trooper reach out with the barrel of his gun to open the station wagon's door the rest of the way; he saw the barrel disappear *into* the door as if the whole car were nothing but an optical illusion; he saw the trooper jerk forward, his big gray hat tumbling from his head. Then the trooper was yanked through the door and only his hat was left, lying next to somebody's cell phone. There was a pause, and then the car pulled into itself, like fingers into a fist. Next came the tennis-racquet-on-ball sound—*pouck!*—and the muddy clenched fist became a car again.

The little boy began to wail; the little girl was for some reason screaming *thirty* over and over again, like she thought it was a magic word J. K. Rowling had somehow left out of her Harry Potter books.

The back door of the police car opened. The kids got out. Both of them were crying their asses off, and Pete didn't blame them. If he hadn't been so stunned by what he'd just seen, he'd probably be crying himself. A nutty thought came to him: another swig or two of that vodka might improve this situation. It would help him be less afraid, and if he was less afraid, he might be able to figure out what the fuck he should do.

Meanwhile, the kids were backing away again. Pete had an idea they might panic and take to their heels at any second. He couldn't let them do that; they'd run right into the road and get splatted by turnpike traffic.

"Hey!" he shouted. "Hey, you kids!"

When they turned to look at him—big, buggy eyes in pale faces—he waved and started walking toward them. As he did, the sun came out again, this time with authority.

The little boy started forward. The girl jerked him back. At first Pete thought she was afraid of him, then realized it was the car she was afraid of.

He made a circling gesture with his hand. "Walk around it! Walk around and come over here!"

They slipped through the guardrails on the left side of the ramp, giving the station wagon the widest berth possible, then cut across the parking lot. When they got to Pete, the little girl let go of her brother, sat down, and put her face in her hands. She had braids her mom had probably fixed for her. Looking at them and knowing the kid's mother would never fix them for her again made Pete feel horrible.

The little boy looked up solemnly. "It ate Mommy n Daddy. It ate the horse lady and Trooper Jimmy, too. It's going to eat everyone, I guess. It's going to eat the *world*."

If Pete Simmons had been twenty, he might have asked a lot of bullshit questions that didn't matter. Because he was only half that age, and able to accept what he had just seen, he asked something simpler and more pertinent. "Hey little girl. Are more police coming? Is that why you were yelling 'Thirty'?"

She dropped her hands and looked up at him. Her eyes were raw and red. "Yes, but Blakie's right. It will eat them, too. I told Trooper Jimmy, but he didn't believe me."

Pete believed her, because he had *seen*. But she was right. The police wouldn't believe. They would eventually, they'd have to, but maybe not before the monster car ate a bunch more of them.

"I think it's from space," he said. "Like on *Doctor Who*."

"Mommy n Daddy won't let us watch that," the little boy told him. "They say it's too scary. But this is scarier."

"It's alive." Pete spoke more to himself than to them.

"Duh," Rachel said, and gave a long, miserable sniffle.

The sun ducked briefly behind one of the unraveling clouds. When it came out again, an idea came with it. Pete had been hoping to show Normie Therriault and the rest of the Rip-Ass Raiders something that would amaze them enough to let him be part of their gang. Then George had given him a big-brother reality check: *They've all seen that baby trick a thousand times.*

Maybe so, but maybe that thing down there *hadn't* seen it a thousand times. Or even once. Maybe they didn't have magnifying glasses where it came from. Or sun, for that matter. He remembered a *Doctor Who* episode about a planet where it was dark all the time.

He could hear a siren in the distance. A cop was coming. A cop who wouldn't believe anything little kids said, because as far as grown-ups were concerned, little kids were all full of shit.

"You guys stay here. I'm going to try something."

"No!" The little girl grasped his wrist with fingers that felt like claws. "It'll eat you too!"

"I don't think it can move around," Pete told her, disengaging his hand. She had left a couple of bleeding scratches, but he wasn't mad and he didn't blame her. He probably would have done the same, if it had been his parents. "I think it's stuck in one place."

"It can *reach*," she said. "It can reach with its tires. They melt."

"I'll watch out," Pete said, "but I have to try this. Because you're right. Those cops will come, and it will eat them too. Stay put."

He walked toward the station wagon. When he was close (but not *too* close), he unzipped the saddlebag. *I have to try this,* he had told the kids, but the truth was a little balder: he *wanted* to try this. It would be like a science experiment. That would probably sound bizarre if he told someone, but he didn't have to tell. He just had to do it. Very . . . very . . . carefully.

He was sweating. With the sun out, the day had turned warm, but that wasn't the only reason, and he knew it. He looked up, squinting at the brightness. It made his HANGOVER ache, but so what. *Don't you go back behind a cloud. Don't you dare. I need you.*

He took his Richforth magnifying glass out of the saddlebag, and bent to put the saddlebag on the pavement. The joints of his knees cracked, and the station wagon's door swung open a few inches.

It knows I'm here. I don't know if it can see me, but it heard me just now. And maybe it smells me.

He took another step. Now he was close enough to touch the side of the station wagon. If he was fool enough to do so, that was.

"Watch out!" the little girl called. She and her brother were both standing now, their arms around each other. *"Watch out for it!"*

Carefully—like a kid reaching into a cage with a lion inside—Pete extended the magnifying glass. A circle of light appeared on the side of the station wagon, but it was too big. Too *soft.* He moved the glass closer.

"The tire!" the little boy screamed. *"Watch out for the TII-YIII-YII-RE!"*

Pete looked down and saw one of the tires melting. A gray tentacle was oozing across the pavement toward his sneaker. He couldn't back away without giving up his experiment, so he raised his foot and stood like a stork. The tentacle of gray goo immediately changed direction and headed for his other foot.

Not much time.

He moved the magnifying glass closer. The circle of light shrank to a brilliant white dot. For a moment nothing happened. Then tendrils of smoke began to drift up. The muddy white surface beneath the dot turned black.

From inside the station wagon there came an inhuman growling sound. Pete had to fight every instinct in his brain and body to keep from running. His lips parted, revealing teeth locked together in a desperate snarl. He held the Richforth steady, counting off seconds in his head. He'd reached seven when the growl rose to a glassy shriek that threatened to split his head. Behind him, Rachel and Blake had let go of each other so they could cover their ears.

At the foot of the rest area entrance ramp, Al Andrews brought Unit 12 to a sliding stop. He got out, wincing at that terrible shrieking sound. *It was like an air-raid siren broadcast through a heavy metal band's amplifiers,* he would say later. He saw a kid holding something out so it almost touched the surface of a muddy old Ford or Chevy station wagon. The boy was wincing in pain, determination, or both.

The smoking black spot on the flank of the station

wagon began to spread. The white smoke curling up from it began to thicken. It turned gray, then black. What happened next happened fast. Pete saw tiny blue flames pop into being around the black spot. They spread, seeming to dance *above* the surface of the car-thing. It was the way charcoal briquettes looked in their backyard barbecue after their father doused them with lighter fluid and then tossed in a match.

The gooey gray tentacle, which had almost reached the sneakered foot still on the pavement, snapped back. The car yanked in upon itself again, but this time the spreading blue flames stood out all around it in a corona. It pulled in tighter and still tighter, becoming a fiery ball. Then, as Pete and the Lussier kids and Trooper Andrews watched, it shot up into the blue spring sky. For a moment longer it was there, glowing like a cinder, and then it was gone. Pete found himself thinking of the cold darkness above the envelope of the earth's atmosphere—those endless leagues where anything might live and lurk.

I didn't kill it, I just drove it away. It had to go so it could put itself out, like a burning stick in a bucket of water.

Trooper Andrews was staring up into the sky, dumbfounded. One of his brain's few working circuits was wondering how he was supposed to write up a report on what he had just seen.

There were more approaching sirens in the distance.

Pete walked back to the two little kids with his saddlebag in one hand and his Richforth magnifying glass in the other. He sort of wished George and Normie were here, but so what if they weren't? He'd had quite an afternoon for himself without those guys, and he didn't care if he got grounded or not.

This made jumping bikes off the edge of a stupid sandpit look like *Sesame Street*.

You know what? I fuckin rock.

He might have laughed if the little kids hadn't been looking at him. They had just seen their parents eaten by some kind of alien—eaten *alive*—and showing happiness would be totally wrong.

The little boy held out his chubby arms, and Pete picked him up. He didn't laugh when the kid kissed his cheek, but he smiled. "Fanks," Blakie said. "You're a good kid."

Pete set him down. The little girl also kissed him, which was sort of nice, although it would have been nicer if she'd been a babe.

The trooper was running toward them now, and that made Pete think of something. He bent to the little girl and huffed into her face.

"Do you smell anything?"

Rachel Lussier looked at him for a moment, her expression far wiser than her years. "You'll be okay," she said, and actually smiled. Not a big one, but yes—a smile. "Just don't breathe on him. And maybe get some mints or something before you go home."

"I was thinking Teaberry gum," Pete said.

"Yeah," Rachel said. "That'll work."

For Nye Willden and Doug Allen,
who bought my first stories.

My mother had a saying for every occasion. ("And Steve remembers them all," I can hear my wife, Tabitha, say, with an accompanying roll of her eyes.)

One of her favorites was "Milk always takes the flavor of what it sits next to in the icebox." I don't know if that's true about milk, but it's certainly true when it comes to the stylistic development of young writers. When I was a young man, I wrote like H. P. Lovecraft when I was reading Lovecraft, and like Ross Macdonald when I was reading the adventures of PI Lew Archer.

Stylistic copying eventually wanes. Little by little, writers develop their own styles, each as unique as a fingerprint. Traces of the writers one reads in one's formative years remain, but the rhythm of each writer's thoughts—an expression of his or her very brainwaves, I think—eventually becomes dominant. In the end, no one sounds like Elmore Leonard but Leonard, and no one sounds like Mark Twain but Twain. Yet every now and then stylistic copying recurs, always when the writer encounters some new and wonderful mode of expression that shows him a new way of seeing and saying. 'Salem's Lot was written under the influence of James Dickey's poetry, and if *Rose Madder* sounds in places as if it were written by Cormac McCarthy, it's because while I was writing that book, I was reading everything by McCarthy I could get my hands on.

In 2009, an editor at *The New York Times Book Review* asked if I would do a double review of *Raymond Carver: A Writer's Life*, by Carol Sklenicka, and Carver's own collected stories, as published by Library of America. I agreed, mostly so I could explore some new territory. Although I am an omnivorous reader, I had somehow missed Carver. A large blind spot for a writer who came of literary age at roughly the same time Carver did, you might say, and you would be right. All I can say in my own defense is *quot libros, quam breve tempus*—so many books, so little time (and yes, I have the tee-shirt).

In any case, I was stunned by the clarity of Carver's style, and by the beautiful tension of his prose line. Everything is on the surface, but that surface is so clear that the reader can see a living universe just beneath. I loved those stories, and I loved the American losers Carver wrote about with such knowledge and tenderness. Yes, the man was a drunk, but he had a sure touch and a great heart.

I wrote "Premium Harmony" shortly after reading more than two dozen Carver stories, and it should come as no surprise that it has the feel of a Carver story. If I had written it at twenty, I think it would have been no more than a blurred copy of a much better writer. Because it was written at sixty-two, my own style bleeds through, for better or worse. Like many great American writers (Philip Roth and Jonathan Franzen come to mind), Carver seemed to have little sense of humor. I, on the other hand, see the humor in almost everything. The humor here is black, but in my opinion, that's often the best kind. Because—dig it—when it comes to death, what can you do but laugh?

Premium Harmony

They've been married for ten years and for a long time everything was okay—swell—but now they argue. Now they argue quite a lot. It's really all the same argument. It has circularity. It is, Ray sometimes thinks, like a dog track. When they argue they're like greyhounds chasing the mechanical rabbit. You go past the same scenery time after time, but you don't see the landscape. You see the rabbit.

He thinks it might be different if they'd had kids, but she couldn't have kids. They finally got tested, and that's what the doctor said. It was her problem. Something in her. A year or so after that, he bought her a dog, a Jack Russell she named Biznezz. Mary would spell it for people who asked. She wants everyone to get the joke. She loves that dog, but now they argue anyway.

They're going to Walmart for grass seed. They've decided to sell the house—they can't afford to keep it—but Mary says they won't get far until they do something about the plumbing and make the lawn nice. She says those bald patches make it look shanty Irish. It's been a hot summer with no rain to speak of. Ray tells her grass seed won't grow the lawn without rain no matter how good the grass seed is. He says they should wait.

"Then another year goes by and we're still there," she says. "We can't wait another year, Ray. We'll be bankrupts."

When she talks, Biz looks at her from his place in the backseat. Sometimes he looks at Ray when Ray talks, but not always. Mostly he looks at Mary.

"What do you think?" he says. "It's going to rain so you don't have to worry about going bankrupt?"

"We're in it together, unless you forgot," she says. They're driving through Castle Rock now. It's pretty dead. What Ray calls "the economy" has disappeared from this part of Maine. The Walmart is on the other side of town, near the high school where Ray is a janitor. The Walmart has its own stoplight. People joke about it.

"Penny wise and pound foolish," he says. "You ever hear that one?"

"A million times, from you."

He grunts. He can see the dog in the rearview mirror, watching her. Sometimes he hates the way Biz does that. It comes to him that neither of them knows what they are talking about. It is a depressing thought.

"And pull in at the Quik-Pik," she says. "I want to get a kickball for Tallie's birthday." Tallie is her brother's little girl. Ray supposes that makes her his niece, although he's not sure that's right, since all the blood is on Mary's side.

"They have balls at Walmart," Ray says, "and everything's cheaper at Wally World."

"The ones at Quik-Pik are purple. Purple is her favorite color. I can't be sure there'll be purple at Walmart."

"If there aren't, we'll stop at the Quik-Pik on the way back." He feels like a great weight is pressing down on his head. She'll get her way. She always does on things like this. Marriage is like a football game and he's quarterbacking the underdog team. He has to pick his spots. Make short passes.

"It'll be on the wrong side coming back," she says—as if they are caught in a torrent of city traffic instead of rolling through an almost deserted little town where most of the stores are for sale. "I'll just dash in and get the ball and dash right back out."

At two hundred pounds, Ray thinks, your dashing days are over, honey.

"They're only ninety-nine cents," she says. "Don't be such a pinchpenny."

Don't be so pound foolish, he thinks, but what he says is, "Buy me a pack of smokes while you're in there. I'm out."

"If you quit, we'd have an extra forty dollars a week."

He saves up and pays a friend in South Carolina to ship him a dozen cartons at a time. They're twenty dollars a carton cheaper in South Carolina. That's a lot of money, even in this day and age. It's not like he doesn't try to economize. He has told her this before and will again, but what's the point? In one ear, out the other. Nothing to slow down what he says in the middle.

"I used to smoke two packs a day," he says. "Now I smoke less than half a pack." Actually, most days he smokes more. She knows it, and Ray knows she knows it. That's marriage after awhile. That weight on his head gets a little heavier. Also, he can see Biz still looking at her. He feeds the damn thing, and he makes the money that *pays* for the food, but it's her he's looking at. And Jack Russells are supposed to be smart.

He turns in to the Quik-Pik.

"You ought to buy them on Indian Island if you've got to have them," she says.

"They haven't sold tax-free smokes on the rez for ten years," he says. "I've told you that, too. You don't listen." He pulls past the gas pumps and parks beside the store. There's no shade. The sun is directly overhead. The car's air conditioner only works a little. They are both sweating. In the backseat, Biz is panting. It makes him look like he's grinning.

"Well, you ought to quit," Mary says.

"And you ought to quit those Little Debbies," he says. He doesn't want to say this, he knows how sensitive she is about her weight, but out it comes. He can't hold it back. It's a mystery.

"I ain't had one in a year," she says.

"Mary, the box is on the top shelf. A twenty-four-pack. Behind the flour."

"Were you *snooping*?" she cries. A flush is rising in her cheeks, and he sees how she looked when she was still beautiful. Good-looking, anyway. Everybody said she was good-looking, even his mother, who didn't like her otherwise.

"I was looking for the bottle opener," he says. "I had a bottle of cream soda. The kind with the old-fashioned cap."

"Looking for a bottle opener on the top shelf of the goddam cupboard!"

"Go in and get the ball," he says. "And get me some smokes. Be a sport."

"Can't you wait until we get home? Can't you even wait that long?"

"You can get the cheap ones," he says. "That off-brand. Premium Harmony, they're called." They taste like old stale cowshit, but all right. If she'll only shut up about it. It's too hot to argue.

"Where are you going to smoke, anyway? In the car, I suppose, so I have to breathe it."

"I'll open the window, I always do."

"I'll get the ball. Then I'll come back. If you feel you *have* to spend four dollars and fifty cents to poison your lungs, *you* can go in. I'll sit with the baby."

Ray hates it when she calls Biz the baby. He's a dog, and he may be as bright as Mary likes to boast, but he still shits outside and licks where his balls used to be.

"Buy a few Twinkies while you're at it," he tells her. "Or maybe they're having a special on Ho Hos."

"You're so mean," she says. She gets out of the car and slams the door. He's parked too close to the concrete cube of a building and she has to sidle until she's past the trunk of the car, and he knows she knows he's looking at her, seeing how she's now so big she has to sidle. He knows she thinks he parked close to the building on purpose, to make her sidle, and maybe he did.

He wants a cigarette.

"Well, Biz, old buddy, it's just you and me."

Biz lies down on the backseat and closes his eyes. He may get up on his back paws and shuffle around for a few seconds when Mary puts on a record and tells him to dance, and if she tells him (in a jolly voice) that he's a *bad boy*, he may go into the corner and sit facing the wall, but he still shits outside.

The time goes by and she doesn't come out. Ray opens the glove compartment. He paws through the rat's nest of papers, looking for some cigarettes he might have forgotten, but there aren't any. He *does* find a Hostess Sno Ball still in its wrapper. He pokes it. It's as stiff as a corpse. It's got to be a thousand years old. Maybe older. Maybe it came over on the Ark.

"Everybody has his poison," he says. He unwraps the Sno Ball and tosses it into the backseat. "Want this, Biz? Go ahead, knock yourself out."

Biz snarks the Sno Ball in two bites. Then he sets to work licking up bits of coconut off the seat. Mary would have a shit fit, but Mary's not here.

Ray looks at the gas gauge and sees it's down to half. He could turn off the motor and unroll the windows, but then he'd really bake. Sitting here in the sun, waiting for her to buy a purple plastic kickball for ninety-nine cents when he knows they could get one for seventy-nine cents at Walmart. Only that one might be yellow or red. Not good enough for Tallie. Only purple for the princess.

He sits there and Mary doesn't come back. "Christ on a pony!" he says. Cool air traces over his face. He thinks again about turning off the engine, saving some gas, then thinks fuck it. She won't bring him the smokes, either. Not even the cheap off-brand. This he knows. He had to make that crack about those Little Debbies.

He sees a young woman in the rearview mirror. She's jogging toward the car. She's even heavier than Mary; great big tits shuffle back and forth under her blue smock. Biz sees her coming and starts to bark.

Ray unrolls the window.

"Is your wife a blond-haired woman?" She puffs the words. "A blond-haired woman wearing sneakers?" Her face shines with sweat.

"Yes. She wanted a ball for our niece."

"Well, something's wrong with her. She fell down. She's unconscious. Mr. Ghosh says he thinks she might have had a heart attack. He called nine-one-one. You better come."

Ray locks the car and follows her into the store. It's cold inside after the car. Mary is lying on the floor with her legs spread and her arms at her sides. She's next to a wire cylinder full of kickballs. The sign over the wire cylinder says HOT FUN IN THE SUMMER-TIME. Her eyes are closed. She might be sleeping there on the linoleum floor. Three people are standing over her. One is a dark-skinned man in khaki pants and a white shirt. A nametag on the pocket of his shirt says MR. GHOSH MANAGER. The other two are customers. One is a thin old man without much hair. He's in his seventies at least. The other is a fat woman. She's fatter than Mary. Fatter than the girl in the blue smock, too. Ray thinks by rights she's the one who should be lying out on the floor.

"Sir, are you this lady's husband?" Mr. Ghosh asks.

"Yes," Ray says. That doesn't seem to be enough. "I sure am."

"I am sorry to say but I think she might be dead," Mr. Ghosh says. "I gave the artificial respiration and the mouth-to-mouth, but . . ." He shrugs.

Ray thinks of the dark-skinned man putting his mouth on Mary's. Frenching her, sort of. Breathing down her throat right next to the wire cylinder full of plastic kickballs. Then he kneels down.

"Mary," he says. "Mary!" Like trying to wake her up after a hard night.

She doesn't appear to be breathing, but you can't always tell. He puts his ear by her mouth and hears nothing. He feels air moving on his skin, but that's probably just the air-conditioning.

"This gentleman called nine-one-one," the fat woman says. She's holding a bag of Bugles.

"Mary!" Ray says. Louder this time, but he can't quite bring himself to shout, not down on his knees with people standing around, one of them a dark-skinned man. He looks up and says, apologetically, "She never gets sick. She's healthy as a horse."

"You never know," the old man says. He shakes his head.

"She just fell down," says the young woman in the blue smock. "Didn't say a word."

"Did she grab her chest?" asks the fat woman with the Bugles.

"I don't know," the young woman says. "I guess not. Not that I saw. She just fell down."

There's a rack of souvenir tee-shirts near the kick-balls. They say things like MY PARENTS WERE TREATED LIKE ROYALTY IN CASTLE ROCK AND ALL I GOT WAS THIS LOUSY TEE-SHIRT. Mr. Ghosh takes one and says, "Would you like me to cover her face, sir?"

"God, no!" Ray says, startled. "She might only be unconscious. We're not doctors." Past Mr. Ghosh, he sees three kids, teenagers, looking in the window. One of them is taking pictures with his cell phone.

Mr. Ghosh looks where Ray's looking and rushes at the door, flapping his hands. "You kids get out of here! You kids get out!"

Laughing, the teenagers shuffle backwards, then turn and jog past the gas pumps to the sidewalk. Beyond them, the nearly deserted downtown shimmers. A car goes by pulsing rap. To Ray the bass sounds like Mary's stolen heartbeat.

"Where's the ambulance?" the old man says. "How come it's not here yet?"

Ray kneels by his wife while the time goes by. His back hurts and his knees hurt, but if he gets up, he'll look like a spectator.

The ambulance turns out to be a Chevy Suburban painted white with orange stripes. The red jackpot lights are flashing. CASTLE COUNTY RESCUE is printed across the front, only backwards. So you can read it in your rearview mirror. Ray thinks that's pretty clever.

The two men who come in are dressed in white. They look like waiters. One pushes an oxygen tank on a dolly. It's a green tank with an American flag decal on it.

"Sorry," this one says. "Just cleared a car accident over in Oxford."

The other one sees Mary lying on the floor, legs spread, hands to her sides. "Aw, gee," he says. Ray can't believe it.

"Is she still alive?" he asks. "Is she just unconscious? If she is, you better give her oxygen or she'll have brain damage."

Mr. Ghosh shakes his head. The young woman in the blue smock starts to cry. Ray wants to ask her what she's crying about, then knows. She has made up a whole story about him from what he just said. Why, if he came back in a week or so and played his cards right, she might toss him a mercy fuck. Not that he *would*, but he sees that maybe he could. If he wanted to.

Mary's eyes don't react to a penlight. One EMT listens to her nonexistent heartbeat, and the other takes her nonexistent blood pressure. It goes on like that for awhile. The teenagers come back with some of their friends. Other people too. Ray guesses they're drawn by the flashing red lights on top of the EMT Suburban the way bugs are drawn to a porch light. Mr. Ghosh runs at them again, flapping his arms. They back away again. Then, when Mr. Ghosh returns to the circle around Mary and Ray, they come back and start looking in again.

One of the EMTs says to Ray, "She was your wife?"

"Right."

"Well, sir, I'm sorry to say that she's dead."

"Oh." Ray stands up. His knees crack. "They told me she was, but I wasn't sure."

"Mary Mother of God bless her soul," says the fat lady with the Bugles. She crosses herself.

Mr. Ghosh offers one of the EMTs the souvenir tee-shirt to put over Mary's face, but the EMT shakes his head and goes outside. He tells the little crowd that there's nothing to see, as if anyone's going to believe a dead woman in the Quik-Pik isn't interesting.

The EMT pulls a gurney from the back of the rescue vehicle. He does it with a single quick flip of the wrist. The legs fold down all by themselves. The old man with the thinning hair holds the door open and the EMT pulls his rolling deathbed inside.

"Whoo, hot," the EMT says, wiping his forehead.

"You may want to turn away for this part, sir," the other one says, but Ray watches as they lift her onto the gurney. A sheet has been neatly folded down at the end of the gurney. They pull it all the way up until it's over her face. Now Mary looks like a corpse in a movie. They roll her out into the heat. This time it's the fat woman with the Bugles who holds the door for them. The crowd has retreated to the sidewalk. There must be three dozen, standing in the unrelieved August sunshine.

When Mary is stored, the EMTs come back. One is holding a clipboard. He asks Ray about twenty-five questions. Ray can answer all but the one about her age. Then he remembers she's three years younger than he is and tells them thirty-four.

"We're going to take her to St. Stevie's," the EMT with the clipboard says. "You can follow us if you don't know where that is."

"I know," Ray says. "What? Do you want to do an autopsy? Cut her up?"

The girl in the blue smock gives a gasp. Mr. Ghosh puts his arm around her, and she puts her face against his white shirt. Ray wonders if Mr. Ghosh is fucking her. He hopes not. Not because of Mr. Ghosh's brown skin, Ray doesn't care about that, but because he's got to be twice her age. An older man can take advantage, especially when he's the boss.

"Well, that's not our decision," the EMT says, "but probably not. She didn't die unattended—"

"*I'll* say," the woman with the Bugles interjects.

"—and it's pretty clearly a heart attack. You can probably have her released to the mortuary almost immediately."

Mortuary? An hour ago they were in the car, arguing.

"I don't have a mortuary," he says. "Not a mortuary, a burial plot, nothing. Why the hell would I? She's *thirty-four*."

The two EMTs exchange a look. "Mr. Burkett,

there'll be someone to help you with all that at St. Stevie's. Don't worry about it."

"Don't *worry*? What the hell!"

The EMT wagon pulls out with the lights still flashing but the siren off. The crowd on the sidewalk starts to break up. The counter girl, the old man, the fat woman, and Mr. Ghosh look at Ray as though he's someone special. A celebrity.

"She wanted a purple kickball for our niece," he says. "She's having a birthday. She'll be eight. Her name is Tallie. She was named for an actress."

Mr. Ghosh takes a purple kickball from the wire rack and holds it out to Ray in both hands. "On the house," he says.

"Thank you, sir," Ray says.

The woman with the Bugles bursts into tears. "Mary Mother of God," she says.

They stand around for awhile, talking. Mr. Ghosh gets sodas from the cooler. These are also on the house. They drink their sodas and Ray tells them a few things about Mary, steering clear of the arguments. He tells them how she made a quilt that took third prize at the Castle County fair. That was in '02. Or maybe '03.

"That's so sad," the woman with the Bugles says. She has opened them and shared them around. They eat and drink.

"My wife went in her sleep," the old man with the thinning hair says. "She just laid down on the sofa and never woke up. We were married thirty-seven years. I always expected I'd go first, but that's not the way God wanted it. I can still see her laying there on the sofa." He shakes his head. "I couldn't believe it."

Finally Ray runs out of things to tell them, and they run out of things to tell him. Customers are coming in again. Mr. Ghosh waits on some, and the woman in the blue smock waits on others. Then the fat woman says she really has to go. She gives Ray a kiss on the cheek before she does.

"You need to see to your business, Mr. Burkett," she tells him. Her tone is both reprimanding and flirtatious. Ray thinks she might be another mercy-fuck possibility.

He looks at the clock over the counter. It's the kind with a beer advertisement on it. Almost two hours have gone by since Mary went sidling between the car and the cinderblock side of the Quik-Pik. And for the first time he thinks of Biz.

When he opens the door, heat rushes out at him, and when he puts his hand on the steering wheel to lean in, he pulls it back with a cry. It's got to be a hundred and thirty in there. Biz is dead on his back. His eyes are milky. His tongue is protruding from the side of his mouth. Ray can see the wink of his teeth. There are little bits of coconut caught in his whiskers. That shouldn't be funny, but it is. Not funny enough to laugh, but funny in a way that's some fancy word he can't quite think of.

"Biz, old buddy," he says. "I'm sorry. I forgot all about you."

Great sadness and amusement sweep over him as he looks at the baked Jack Russell. That anything so sad should still be funny is just a crying shame.

"Well, you're with her now, ain't you?" he says, and this thought is so sad—yet so sweet—that he begins to cry. It's a hard storm. While he's crying it comes to him that now he can smoke all he wants, and anywhere in the house. He can smoke right there at her dining room table.

"You're with her now, Biz, old buddy," he says through his tears. His voice is clogged and thick. It's a relief to sound just right for the situation. "Poor old Mary, poor old Biz. Damn it all!"

Still crying, and with the purple kickball still tucked under his arm, he goes back into the Quik-Pik. He tells Mr. Ghosh he forgot to get cigarettes. He thinks maybe Mr. Ghosh will give him a pack of Premium Harmonys on the house as well, but Mr. Ghosh's generosity doesn't stretch that far. Ray smokes all the way to the hospital with the windows shut and Biz in the backseat and the air-conditioning on high.

Thinking of Raymond Carver

Sometimes a story arrives complete—a done thing. Usually, though, they come to me in two parts: first the cup, then the handle. Because the handle may not show up for weeks, months, or even years, I have a little box in the back of my mind full of unfinished cups, each protected in that unique mental packing we call memory. You can't go looking for a handle, no matter how beautiful the cup may be; you have to wait for it to appear. I realize that metaphor sort of sucks, but when you're talking about the process we call creative writing, most of them do. I have written fiction all my life, and still have very little understanding of how the process works. Of course, I don't understand how my liver works, either, but as long as it keeps doing its job, I'm good with that.

About six years ago, I saw a near-miss accident at a busy intersection in Sarasota. A cowboy driver tried to wedge his bigfoot truck—the kind with the huge tires—into a left-turn lane already occupied by another bigfoot truck. The guy whose space was being encroached upon hit his horn, there was a predictable screech of brakes, and the two gas-guzzling behemoths ended up inches apart. The guy in the turn lane unrolled his window and raised one finger to the blue Florida sky in a salute that is as American as baseball. The fellow who had almost hit him returned the greeting, along with a Tarzan chest-thump that presumably meant *Do you want a piece of me?* Then the light turned green, other drivers began to honk, and they went on their way with no physical confrontation.

The incident got me thinking about what might have happened if the two drivers had emerged from their vehicles and started duking it out right there on the Tamiami Trail. Not an unreasonable imagining; road rage happens all the time. Unfortunately, "it happens all the time" is not a recipe for a good story. Yet that near-accident stuck with me. It was a cup with no handle.

A year or so later, while eating lunch in an Applebee's with my wife, I saw a man in his fifties cutting up an elderly gent's chopped steak. He did it carefully, while the elderly gent stared vacantly over his head. At one point the old guy seemed to come around a little, and tried to grab the utensils, presumably so he could attend to his own meal. The younger man smiled and shook his head. The elderly gent let go and resumed his staring. I decided they were father and son, and there it was: the handle for my road rage cup.

Batman and Robin
Have an Altercation

Sanderson sees his father twice a week. On Wednesday evenings, after he closes the jewelry store his parents opened long ago, he drives the three miles to Crackerjack Manor and sees Pop there, usually in the common room. In his "suite," if Pop is having a bad day. On most Sundays, Sanderson takes him out to lunch. The facility where Pop is living out his final foggy years is actually called the Harvest Hills Special Care Unit, but to Sanderson, Crackerjack Manor seems more accurate.

Their time together isn't actually so bad, and not just because Sanderson no longer has to change the old man's bed when he pisses in it or get up in the middle of the night when Pop goes wandering around the house, calling for his wife to make him some scrambled eggs or telling Sanderson those damned Fredericks boys are out in the backyard, drinking and hollering at each other (Dory Sanderson has been dead for fifteen years and the three Fredericks boys, no longer boys, moved away long ago). There's an old joke about Alzheimer's: the good news is that you meet new people every day. Sanderson has discovered the real good news is that the script rarely changes. It means you almost never have to improvise.

Applebee's, for instance. Although they have been having Sunday lunch at the same one for over three years now, Pop almost always says the same thing: "This isn't so bad. We ought to come here again." He always has chopped steak, done medium rare, and when the bread pudding comes, he tells Sanderson that his wife's bread pudding is better. Last year, the pudding was off the menu of the Applebee's on Commerce Way, so Pop—after having Sanderson read the dessert choices to him four times and thinking it over for an endless two minutes—ordered the apple cobbler. When it came, Pop said that Dory served hers with heavy cream. Then he simply sat, staring out the window at the highway. The next time he made the same observation, but ate the cobbler right down to the china.

He can usually be counted on to remember Sanderson's name and the relationship, but he sometimes calls Sanderson Reggie, the name of his older brother. Reggie died forty years ago. When Sanderson prepares to leave the "suite" on Wednesdays—or, on Sundays, after he takes his father back to Crackerjack Manor—his father invariably thanks him, and promises that next time he will be feeling better.

In his young years—before meeting Dory Levin, who civilized him—Sanderson's pop-to-be was a roughneck in the Texas oilfields, and sometimes he reverts to that man, who never dreamed he would one day become a successful jewelry merchant in San Antonio. On these occasions he is confined to his "suite." Once he turned his bed over and paid for his efforts with a broken wrist. When the orderly on duty—José, Pop's favorite—asked why he did it, Pop said it was because that fucking Gunton wouldn't turn down his radio. There is no Gunton, of course. Not now. Somewhere in the past, maybe. Probably.

Lately, Pop has displayed a kleptomaniacal streak. The orderlies, nurses, and doctors have found all sorts of things in his room: vases, plastic utensils from the dining hall, the TV controller from the common room. Once José discovered an El Producto cigar box, filled with various jigsaw puzzle pieces and eighty or ninety assorted playing cards, under Pop's bed. Pop cannot tell anyone, including his son, why he takes these things, and usually denies that he has taken them at all. Once he told Sanderson that Gunderson was trying to get him in trouble.

"Do you mean Gunton, Pop?" Sanderson asked.

Pop waved a bony driftwood hand. "All that guy ever wanted was pussy. He was the original pussy hound from Pussyville."

But the klepto phase seems to be passing—that's what José says, anyway—and this Sunday his father is calm enough. It's not one of his clear days, but not one of the really bad ones, either. It's good enough for Applebee's, and if they get through it without his father pissing himself, all will be well. He's wearing continence pants, but of course there's a smell. For this reason, Sanderson always gets them a corner table. That's not a problem; they dine at two, and by then the after-church crowd is back home, watching baseball or football on TV.

"Who *are* you?" Pop asks in the car. It's a bright day, but chilly. In his oversize sunglasses and wool topcoat, he looks quite a lot like Uncle Junior, that old gangster from *The Sopranos*.

"I'm Dougie," Sanderson says. "Your son."

"I remember Dougie," Pop says, "but he died."

"No, Pop, hunh-uh. *Reggie* died. He . . ." Sanderson trails off, waiting to see if Pop will finish. Pop doesn't. "It was an accident."

"Drunk, was he?" Pop asks. This hurts, even after all the years. That's the bad news about what his father has—he is capable of random cruelties that, while unmeant, can sting like hell.

"No," Sanderson said, "that was the kid who hit him. And then walked away with nothing but a couple of scratches."

That kid will be in his fifties now, probably going silver at the temples. Sanderson hopes this grown version of the kid who killed his brother has scoliosis, he hopes the guy's wife died of ovarian cancer, hopes he got mumps and went both blind and sterile, but he's probably just fine. Managing a grocery store somewhere. Maybe even, God help them, managing an Applebee's. Why not? He was sixteen. All water over the dam. Youthful indiscretion. The records would be sealed. And Reggie? Also sealed. Bones inside a suit under a headstone on Mission Hill. Some days Sanderson can't even remember what he looked like.

"Dougie and I used to play Batman and Robin," Pop says. "It was his favorite game."

They stop for the light at the intersection of Commerce Way and Airline Road, where trouble will soon occur. Sanderson looks at his father and smiles. "Yeah, Pop, good! We even went out that way for Halloween one year, do you remember? I talked you into it. The Caped Crusader and the Boy Wonder."

His pop looks out through the windshield of Sanderson's Subaru, saying nothing. What is he thinking? Or has thought flattened to nothing but a carrier wave? Sanderson sometimes imagines the sound that flatline might make: *mmmmmmmm*. Like the old test-pattern hum on TV, back before cable and satellite.

Sanderson puts his hand on one thin topcoated arm and gives it a friendly squeeze. "You were drunk on your ass and Mom was mad, but I had fun. That was my best Halloween."

"I never drank around my wife," Pop says.

No, Sanderson thinks as the light turns green. Not once she trained you out of it.

"Want help with the menu, Pop?"

"I can read," his father says. He no longer can, but it's bright in their corner and he can look at the pictures even with his Uncle Junior gangsta sunglasses on. Besides, Sanderson knows what he will order.

When the waiter comes with their iced teas, Pop says he'll have the chopped steak, medium rare. "I want it pink but not red," he says. "If it's red, I'll send it back."

The waiter nods. "Your usual."

Pop looks at him suspiciously.

"Green beans or coleslaw?"

Pop snorts. "You kidding? All those beans were dead. You couldn't sell costume jewelry that year, let alone the real stuff."

"He'll have the slaw," Sanderson says. "And I'll have—"

"All those beans were dead!" Pop says emphatically, and gives the waiter an imperious look that says, Do you dare challenge me?

The waiter, who has served them many times before, merely nods and says, "They *were* dead," before turning to Sanderson. "For you, sir?"

They eat. Pop refuses to take off his topcoat, so Sanderson asks for one of the plastic bibs and ties it around his father's neck. Pop makes no objection to this, may not register it at all. Some of his slaw ends up on his pants, but the bib catches most of the mushroom gravy drips. As they are finishing, Pop informs the mostly empty room that he has to piss so bad he can taste it.

Sanderson accompanies him to the men's room, and his father allows him to unzip his fly, but when Sanderson attempts to pull down the elasticized front of the continence pants, Pop slaps his hand away. "Never handle another man's meat, Sunny Jim," he says, annoyed. "Don't you know that?"

This prompts an ancient memory: Dougie Sanderson standing in front of the toilet with his shorts puddled around his feet and his father kneeling beside him, giving instruction. How old was he then? Three? Only two? Yes, maybe only two, but he doesn't doubt the recollection; it's like a fleck of bright glass seen at the side of the road, one so perfectly positioned it leaves an afterimage. "Unlimber, assume the position, fire when ready," he says.

Pop gives him a suspicious look, then breaks Sanderson's heart with a grin. "I used to tell my boys that when I was getting them housebroke," he says. "Dory told me it was my job, and I did it, by God."

He unleashes a torrent, and most of it actually goes into the urinal. The smell is sour and sugary. Diabetes. But what does that matter? Sometimes Sanderson thinks the sooner the better.

• • •

Back at their table, still wearing the bib, Pop renders his verdict. "This place isn't so bad. We ought to come here again."

"How about some dessert, Pop?"

Pop considers the idea, gazing out the window, mouth hanging open. Or is it only the carrier wave? No, not this time. "Why not? I have room."

They both order the apple cobbler. Pop regards the scoop of vanilla on top with his eyebrows pulled together into a thicket. "My wife used to serve this with heavy cream. Her name was Dory. Short for Doreen. Like on *The Mickey Mouse Club.* Hi-there, ho-there, hey-there, you're as welcome as can be."

"I know, Pop. Eat up."

"Are you Dougie?"

"Yup."

"Really? Not pulling my leg?"

"No, Pop, I'm Dougie."

His father holds up a dripping spoonful of ice cream and apples. "We did, didn't we?"

"Did what?"

"Went out trick-and-treating as Batman and Robin."

Sanderson laughs, surprised. "We sure did! Ma said I was born foolish but you had no excuse. And Reggie wouldn't come near us. He was disgusted by the whole thing."

"I was drunk," Pop says, then begins eating his dessert. When he finishes, he belches, points out the window, and says, "Look at those birds. What are they again?"

Sanderson looks. The birds are clustered on a Dumpster in the parking lot. Several more are on the fence behind it. "Those're crows, Pop."

"Christ, I know that," Pop says. "Crows never bothered us back then. We had a pellet gun. Now listen." He leans forward, all business. "Have we been here before?"

Sanderson briefly considers the metaphysical possibilities inherent in this question, then says, "Yes. We come here most Sundays."

"Well, it's a good place. But I think we ought to go back. I'm tired. I want that other thing now."

"A nap."

"That other thing," Pop says, giving him that imperious look.

Sanderson motions for the check, and while he's paying it at the register, Pop sails on with his hands tucked deep in his coat pockets. Sanderson grabs his change in a hurry and has to run to catch the door before Pop can wander out into the parking lot, or even into the busy four lanes of Commerce Way.

"That was a good night," Pop says as Sanderson buckles his seatbelt.

"What night was that?"

"Halloween, you dummy. You were eight, so it was nineteen fifty-nine. You were born in 'fifty-one."

Sanderson looks at his father, amazed, but the old man is staring straight ahead at the traffic. Sanderson closes the passenger door, goes around the hood of his Subaru, gets in behind the wheel. They say nothing for two or three blocks, and Sanderson assumes his father has forgotten the whole thing, but he hasn't.

"When we got to the Foresters' house at the bottom of the hill—you remember the hill, don't you?"

"Church Street Hill, sure."

"Right! Norma Forester opened the door, and to

you she says—before you could—she says, 'Trick or treat?' Then she looks at me and says, 'Trick or drink?'" Pop makes a rusty-hinge sound that Sanderson hasn't heard in a year or more. He even slaps his thigh. "Trick or drink! What a card! You remember that, don't you?"

Sanderson tries, but comes up empty. All he remembers is how happy he was to have his dad with him, even though Dad's Batman costume—put together on the fly—was pretty lame. Gray pajamas, the bat emblem drawn on the front with Magic Marker. The cape cut out of an old bedsheet. The Batman utility belt was a leather belt in which his father had stuck an assortment of screwdrivers and chisels—even an adjustable wrench—from the toolbox in the garage. The mask was a moth-eaten balaclava that Pop rolled up to the nose so his mouth showed. Standing in front of the hallway mirror before going out, he pulled the top of the mask up on the sides, plucking at it to make ears, but they wouldn't stay.

"She offered me a bottle of Shiner's," Pop says. Now they're nine blocks up Commerce Way and approaching the intersection at Airline Road.

"Did you take it?" Pop is on a roll. Sanderson would love for it to continue all the way back to Crackerjack Manor.

"Sure did." He falls silent. As Commerce Way approaches the intersection, the two lanes become three. The one on the far left is a turn lane. The lights for straight-ahead traffic are red, but the one handling traffic in the left-turn lane is showing a green arrow. "That gal had tits like pillows. She was the best loving I ever had."

Yes, they hurt you. Sanderson knows this not

just from his own experience but from talking to others who have relatives in the Manor. Mostly they don't mean to, but they do. What memories remain to them are all in a jumble—like the pilfered puzzle pieces José found in the cigar box under Pop's bed—and there's no governor on them, no way of separating stuff that's okay to talk about from the stuff that isn't. Sanderson has never had a reason to think his father was anything but faithful to his wife for the entire forty-some years of their marriage, but isn't that an assumption all grown children make, if their parents' marriage was serene and collegial?

He takes his eyes off the road to look at his father, and that is why there is an accident instead of one of the near misses that happen all the time on busy roads like Commerce Way. Even so, it's not a terribly serious one, and though Sanderson knows his attention wandered from the road for a second or two, he also knows it still wasn't his fault.

One of those built-up pickup trucks with the oversize tires and the roof-lights on the cab swerves into his lane, wanting to get all the way left in time to turn before the green arrow goes out. There's no taillight blinker; this Sanderson notes just as the left front of his Subaru collides with the rear of the pickup truck. He and his father are both thrown forward into their locked seatbelts, and a ridge suddenly heaves up in the middle of his Subaru's previously smooth hood, but the airbags don't deploy. There's a brisk tinkle of glass.

"Asshole!" Sanderson cries. "Jesus!" Then he makes a mistake. He pushes the button that unrolls his window, sticks out his arm, and wags his middle finger at the truck. Later he will think he only did it because Pop was in the car with him, and Pop was on a roll.

Pop. Sanderson turns to him. "You okay?"

"What happened?" Pop says. "Why'd we quit?"

He's confused but otherwise fine. A good thing he was wearing his seatbelt, although God knows it's hard to forget them these days. The cars won't let you. Drive fifty feet without putting one on and they begin screaming with indignation. Sanderson leans over Pop's lap, thumbs open the glove compartment, gets out his registration and insurance card. When he straightens up again, the door of the pickup truck is standing open and the driver is walking toward him, taking absolutely no notice of the cars that honk and swerve to get around the latest fender-bender. There isn't as much traffic as there would be on a weekday, but Sanderson doesn't count this as a blessing, because he's looking at the approaching driver and thinking, I could be in trouble here.

He knows this guy. Not personally, but he's a south Texas staple. He's wearing jeans and a tee-shirt with the sleeves ripped off at the shoulders. Not cut, ripped, so that errant strings dangle against the tanned slabs of muscle on his upper arms. The jeans are hanging off his hipbones so the brand name of his underwear shows. A chain runs from one beltless loop of his jeans to his back pocket, where there will no doubt be a big leather wallet, possibly embossed with the logo of a heavy metal band. Lots of ink on his arms and hands, even crawling up his neck. This is the kind of guy, when Sanderson sees him on the sidewalk outside his jewelry shop via closed circuit TV, who causes him to push the button that locks the door. Right now he would like to push the button that locks his car door, but of course he can't do that. He should never have flipped the guy the bird, and he even had time to rethink his options, because he had to roll down the window in order to do it. But it's too late now.

Sanderson opens the door and gets out, ready to be placating, to apologize for what he shouldn't need to apologize for—it was the guy who cut across, for God's sake. But here is something else, something that makes little quills of dismay prickle the skin of his forearms and the back of his neck, which is sweating now that he's out of the AC. The guy's tattoos are crude, straggling things: chains around the biceps, thorns circling the forearms, a dagger on one wrist with a drop of blood hanging from the tip of the blade. No skin shop did those. That's jailhouse ink. Tat Man is at least six-two in his boots, and at least two hundred pounds. Maybe two twenty. Sanderson is five-nine and weighs a hundred and sixty.

"Look, I'm sorry I flipped you the bird," Sanderson says. "Heat of the moment. But you changed lanes without—"

"Look what you did to my truck!" Tat Man says. "I ain't had it but three months!"

"We need to exchange insurance information." They also need a cop. Sanderson looks around for one and sees only rubberneckers, slowing down to assess the damage and then speeding up again.

"You think I got insurance when I can barely make the payments on that bitch?"

You have to have insurance, Sanderson thinks, it's the law. Only a guy like this doesn't think he has to have anything. The rubber testicles hanging under his license plate are the final proof.

"Why the fuck didn't you let me in, asshole?"

"There was no time," Sanderson said. "You cut across, you never blinked——"

"I blinked!"

"Then how come it isn't on?" Sanderson points.

"Because you knocked out my fucking taillight, nummy! How am I supposed to tell my girlfriend about this? She fronted the fucking down payment! And get that fucking shit out of my face."

He strikes the insurance card and registration, which Sanderson is still holding out, from Sanderson's hand. Sanderson looks down at them, stunned. His papers are lying on the road.

"I'm going," Tat Man says. "I'll fix my damage, you fix yours. That's how it's going to work."

The damage to the Subaru is far worse than the damage to the absurdly oversize pickup, probably fifteen hundred or two thousand more, but that isn't what makes Sanderson speak up. It isn't being afraid the lug will get away clean, either—all Sanderson has to do is write down the number of the plate above those hanging rubber testes. It isn't even the heat, which is whopping. It's the thought of his gorked-out father sitting there in the passenger seat, not knowing what's happening, needing a nap. They should be halfway back to Crackerjack Manor by now, but no. No. Because this happy asshole had to cut across traffic. Just had to scoot under that green arrow before it went out, or the world would grow dark and the winds of judgment would blow.

"That's not how it's going to work," Sanderson says. "It was your fault. You cut in front of me without signaling. I didn't have time to stop. I want to see your registration, and I want to see your driver's license."

"Fuck your mother," the big man says, and punches Sanderson in the stomach. Sanderson bends over, expelling all the air in his lungs in a great whoosh. He should have known better than to provoke the driver of the pickup truck, he *did* know better, one look at those amateur tats and *anyone* would have known better, but he still went ahead because he didn't believe this would happen in broad daylight, at the intersection of Commerce Way and Airline Road. He belongs to the Jaycees. He hasn't been punched since the third grade, when the argument was over baseball cards.

"That there's my registration," Tat Man says. Big streams of sweat are running down the sides of his face. "I hope you like it. As for my driver's license, I don't have one, okay? Fuckin *don't*. I'm gonna be in a lot of trouble, and it's all your fuckin fault because you were jerkin off instead of looking where you were goin. Fuckin ringmeat!"

Then Tat Man loses it completely. Maybe it's the accident, maybe it's the heat, maybe it's Sanderson's insistence on looking at documents Tat Man doesn't have. It might even be the sound of his own voice. Sanderson has heard the phrase *he lost it* many times, but realizes he has never taken in its full meaning until now. Tat Man is his teacher, and he's a good teacher. He laces both of his hands together, making a double fist. Sanderson has just time enough to see there are blue eyes on Tat Man's knuckles before he's hit in the side of the face with a sledgehammer that drives him back against the newly distressed right side of his car. He slides along it, feeling a prong of metal tear his shirt and the skin beneath. Blood spills down his side, hot as fever. Then his knees buckle and he lands on the road. He stares down at his hands, not believing they are his hands. His right cheek is hot and seems to be rising like bread dough. His right eye is watering.

Next comes a kick to his wounded side, just above the beltline. Sanderson's head hits the right front hubcap of his Subaru and bounces off. He tries to crawl out from under Tat Man's shadow. Tat Man is yelling at him, but Sanderson can't make out any words; it's just *wah-wah-wah*, the sound adults make when they're talking to the kids in the animated *Peanuts* cartoons. He wants to tell Tat Man okay, okay, you say tomato and I say tomahto, let's call the whole thing off. He wants to say no harm and no foul (although he feels he has been fouled quite badly), you go your way and I'll go mine, happy trails to you, see you tomorrow, Mouseketeers. Only he can't catch his breath. He thinks he's going to have a heart attack, may be having one already. He wants to raise his head—if he's going to die he would like to do it looking at something more interesting than the surface of Commerce Way and the front of his own wounded car—but he can't seem to do it. His neck has become a noodle.

There's another kick, this time in the high meat of his left thigh. Then Tat Man gives a guttural cry, and red drops begin to splash the composition surface of the roadway. Sanderson at first thinks it's his nose—or maybe his lips, from the double-handed blow to his face—but then more warmth splashes the back of his neck. It's like a tropical rain shower. He crawls a little farther, past the hood of his car, then manages to turn over and sit. He looks up, squinting against the dazzle of the sky, and sees Pop standing beside Tat Man. Tat Man is bent over like a man suffering serious stomach cramps. He is also groping at the side of his neck, which has sprouted a piece of wood.

At first Sanderson can't understand what has happened, but then he gets it. The piece of wood is the handle of a knife, one he's seen before. He sees it almost every week. You don't need a steak knife to cut the kind of chopped meat Pop always has at their Sunday lunches, a fork does the trick very nicely, but they bring you a knife, anyway. It's all part of Applebee's service. Pop may no longer remember which son comes to visit him, or that his wife is dead, he probably no longer even remembers his middle name, but it seems he hasn't lost all the clever ruthlessness that enabled him to rise from a no-college oilfields roughneck to an upper-middle-class jewelry merchant in San Antonio.

He got me to look at the birds, Sanderson thinks. The crows on the Dumpster. That's when he took the knife.

Tat Man has lost interest in the man sitting in the road, and never casts a single glance at the older man standing beside him. Tat Man has begun coughing. A fine red spray comes from his mouth each time he does it. One hand is on the knife in his neck, trying to pull it out. Blood pours down the side of his tee-shirt and splatters his jeans. He begins walking toward the intersection of Commerce and Airline (where all traffic has stopped), still bent over and still coughing. With his free hand he gives a jaunty little wave: *Hi, Ma!*

Sanderson gets to his feet. His legs are trembling, but they hold him. He can hear sirens approaching. Sure, now the cops come. Now that it's all over.

Sanderson puts an arm around his father's shoulders. "You all right, Pop?"

"That man was beating on you," Pop says matter-of-factly. "Who is he?"

"I don't know." Tears are coursing down Sanderson's cheeks. He wipes them away.

Tat Man falls on his knees. He has stopped coughing. Now he's making a low growling sound. Most people hang back, but a couple of brave souls go to him, wanting to help. Sanderson thinks Tat Man is probably beyond it, but more power to them.

"Did we eat yet, Reggie?"

"Yeah, Pop, we did. And I'm Dougie."

"Reggie's dead. Didn't you tell me that?"

"Yeah, Pop."

"That man was beating on you." His father's face twists into the face of a child who is horribly tired and needs to go to bed. "I've got a headache. Let's blow this pop stand. I want to lie down."

"We have to wait for the cops."

"Why? What cops? Who *is* that guy?"

Sanderson smells shit. His father has just dropped a load.

"Let's get you in the car, Pop."

His father lets Sanderson lead him around the Subaru's crumpled snout. Pop says, "That was some Halloween, wasn't it?"

"Yeah, Pop, it was." He helps the eighty-three-year-old Caped Crusader into the car and closes the door to keep the cool in. The first city police car is pulling up, and they'll want to see some ID. The sixty-one-year-old Boy Wonder, hands pressed to his aching side, shuffles back to the driver's side to pick it up off the street.

For John Irving

As I said in the note to "Batman and Robin," sometimes—once in a great while—you get the cup with the handle already attached. God, how I love that. You're just going about your business, thinking of nothing in particular, and then, *ka-boom*, a story arrives Special Delivery, perfect and complete. The only thing you have to do is transcribe it.

I was in Florida, walking our dog on the beach. Because it was January, and cold, I was the only one out there. Up ahead I saw what looked like writing in the sand. When I got closer, I saw it was just a trick of sunlight and shadow, but writers' minds are junkheaps of odd information, and it made me think of an old quote from somewhere (it turned out to be Omar Khayyam): "The Moving Finger writes, and having writ, moves on." That in turn made me think of some magical place where an invisible Moving Finger would write terrible things in the sand, and I had this story. It has one of my very favorite endings. Maybe not up there with "August Heat," by W. F. Harvey—that one's a classic—but in the same neighborhood.

The Dune

As the Judge climbs into the kayak beneath a bright morning sky, a slow and clumsy process that takes him almost five minutes, he reflects that an old man's body is nothing but a sack in which he carries aches and indignities. Eighty years ago, when he was ten, he jumped into a wooden canoe and cast off, with no bulky life jacket, no worries, and certainly with no pee dribbling into his underwear. Every trip to the little unnamed island lying like a half-submerged submarine two hundred yards out in the Gulf began with a great and uneasy excitement. Now there is only unease. And pain that seems centered deep in his guts and radiates to everywhere. But he still makes the trip. Many things have lost their allure in these shadowy later years—most things—but not the dune on the far side of the island. Never the dune.

In the early days of his exploration, he expected it to be gone after every big storm, and following the 1944 hurricane that sank the USS *Warrington* off Vero Beach, he was sure it would be. But when the skies cleared, the island was still there. So was the dune, although the hundred-mile-an-hour winds should have blown all the sand away, leaving only the bare rocks and knobs of coral. Over the years he has debated back and forth about whether the magic is in him or in the island. Perhaps it's both, but surely most of it is in the dune.

Since 1932 he has crossed this short stretch of water thousands of times. Usually he finds nothing but rocks and bushes and sand, but every now and then there is something else.

Settled in the kayak at last, he paddles slowly from the beach to the island, his frizz of white hair blowing around his mostly bald skull. A few turkey buzzards wheel overhead, making their ugly conversation. Once he was the son of the richest man on the Florida Gulf coast, then he was a lawyer, then he was a judge on the Pinellas County Circuit, then he was appointed to the State Supreme Court. There was talk, during the Reagan years, of a nomination to the United States Supreme Court, but that never happened, and a week after the idiot Clinton became president, Judge Harvey Beecher—just the Judge to his many acquaintances (he has no real friends) in Sarasota, Osprey, Nokomis, and Venice—retired. Hell, he never liked Tallahassee, anyway. It's cold up there.

Also, it's too far from the island, and its peculiar dune. On these early-morning kayak trips, paddling the short distance on smooth water, he's willing to admit that he's addicted to it. But who wouldn't be addicted to a thing like this?

On the rocky east side, a gnarled bush juts from the split in a guano-splattered rock. This is where he ties up, and he's always careful to tie well. It wouldn't do to be stranded out here; his father's estate (that's how he still thinks of it, although the elder Beecher has been gone for forty years now) covers almost two miles of prime Gulf-front property, the main house is far inland, on the Sarasota Bay side, and there would be no one to hear him yelling. Tommy Curtis, the caretaker, might notice him gone and come looking; more likely, he would just assume the Judge was locked up in his study, where he often spends whole days, supposedly working on his memoirs.

Once upon a time Mrs. Riley might have gotten nervous when he didn't come out of the study for lunch, but now he hardly ever eats at noon (she calls him "nothing but a stuffed string," although not to his face). There's no other staff, and both Curtis and Mrs. Riley know he can be cross when he's interrupted. Not that there's really much to interrupt; he hasn't added so much as a line to the memoirs in two years, and in his heart he knows they will never be finished. The unfinished recollections of a Florida judge? No tragedy there. The one story he *could* write is the one he never will.

He's even slower getting out of the kayak than he was getting in, and turns turtle once, wetting his shirt and pants in the little waves that run up the gravelly shingle. Beecher is not discommoded. It isn't the first time he's fallen, and there's no one to see him. He supposes he's mad to continue these trips at his age, even though the island is so close to the mainland, but stopping them isn't an option. An addict is an addict is an addict.

Beecher struggles to his feet and clutches his belly until the last of the pain subsides. He brushes sand and small shells from his pants, double-checks his mooring rope, then spots one of the turkey buzzards perched on the island's largest rock, peering down at him.

"Yi!" he shouts in the voice he now hates—cracked and wavering, the voice of an old shrew in a black dress. "Yi-yi, you bugger! Get on about your business!"

After giving a brief rustle of its raggedy wings, the turkey buzzard sits right where it is. Its beady eyes seem to say, *But Judge—today* you're *my business.*

Beecher stoops, picks up a larger shell, and shies it at the bird. This time it does fly away, the sound of its wings like rippling cloth. It soars across the short stretch of water and lands on his dock. *Still,* the Judge thinks, *a bad omen.* He remembers Jimmy Caslow of the Florida State Patrol telling him once that turkey buzzards didn't just know where carrion was, but where carrion *would* be.

"I can't tell you," Caslow said, "how many times I've seen those ugly bastards circling a spot on the Tamiami where there's a fatal wreck a day or two later. Sounds crazy, I know, but just about any Florida road cop will tell you the same."

There are almost always turkey buzzards out here on the little no-name island. Judge Beecher supposes it smells like death to them, and why not?

He sets off on the little path he has beaten over the years. He will check the dune on the other side, where the sand is beach-fine instead of stony and shelly, and then he will return to the kayak and drink his little jug of cold tea. He may doze awhile in the morning sun (he dozes often these days, supposes most nonagenarians do), and when he wakes (*if* he wakes), he'll make the return trip. He tells himself that the dune will be just a smooth blank upslope of sand, as it is most days, but he knows better.

Goddam buzzard knew better, too.

He spends a long time on the sandy side, with his age-warped fingers clasped in a knot behind him. His back aches, his shoulders ache, his hips ache, his knees ache; most of all, his gut aches. But he pays these things no mind. Perhaps later, but not now.

He looks at the dune, and at what is written there.

Anthony Wayland arrives at Beecher's Pelican Point estate bang on seven o'clock p.m., just as promised. One thing the Judge has always appreciated—both in the courtroom and out of it—is punctuality, and the boy is punctual. Judge Beecher reminds himself never to call Wayland *boy* to his face (although, this being the South, *son* is okay). Wayland wouldn't understand that, when you're ninety, any fellow under the age of sixty looks like a boy.

"Thanks for coming," the Judge says, ushering Wayland into his study. It's just the two of them; Curtis and Mrs. Riley have long since gone to their homes in Nokomis Village. "You brought the necessary document?"

"Yes indeed, Judge." Wayland opens his big square attorney's briefcase and removes a thick document bound by a heavy clip. The pages aren't vellum, as they would have been in the old days, but they are rich and heavy just the same. At the top of the first, in heavy and forbidding type (what the Judge has always thought of as graveyard type), are the words **Last Will and Testament of HARVEY L. BEECHER.**

"You know, I'm kind of surprised you didn't draft this document yourself. You've probably forgotten more Florida probate law than I've ever learned."

"That might be true," the Judge says in his driest tone. "At my age, folks tend to forget a great deal."

Wayland flushes to the roots of his hair. "I didn't mean—"

"I know what you mean, son," the Judge says. "No offense taken. But since you ask . . . you know that old saying about how a man who serves as his own lawyer has a fool for a client?"

Wayland grins. "Heard it and used it plenty of times when I'm wearing my public defender hat and some sad-sack wife abuser or hit-and-runner tells me he plans to go the DIY route in court."

"I'm sure you have, but here's the unabridged version: a lawyer who serves as his own lawyer has a *great* fool for a client. Goes for criminal, civil, and probate law. So shall we get down to business? Time is short." This is something he means in more ways than one.

They get down to business. Mrs. Riley has left decaf coffee, which Wayland rejects in favor of a Co'-Cola. He makes copious notes as the Judge dictates the changes in his dry courtroom voice, adjusting old bequests and adding new ones. The major new one— four million dollars—is to the Sarasota County Beach and Wildlife Preservation Society. In order to qualify, they must successfully petition the state legislature to have a certain island just off the coast of Pelican Point declared forever wild.

"They won't have a problem getting that done," the Judge says. "You can handle the legal for them yourself. I'd prefer *pro bono*, but of course that's up to you. One trip to Tallahassee should do it. It's a little spit of a thing, nothing growing there but a few bushes. Governor Scott and his Tea Party cronies will be delighted."

"Why's that, Judge?"

"Because the next time Beach and Preservation

comes to them, begging money, they can say, 'Didn't old Judge Beecher just give you four million? Get out of here, and don't let the door hit you in the ass on your way out.'"

Wayland agrees that this is probably just how it will go, and the two men move on to the smaller bequests.

"Once I get a clean draft, we'll need two witnesses, and a notary," Wayland says when they've finished.

"I'll get all that done with this draft here, just to be safe," the Judge says. "If anything happens to me in the interim, it should stand up. There's no one to contest it; I've outlived them all."

"A wise precaution, Judge. It would be good to take care of it tonight. I don't suppose your caretaker and housekeeper—"

"Won't be back until eight tomorrow," Beecher says, "but I'll make it the first order of business. Harry Staines on Vamo Road's a notary, and he'll be glad to come over before he goes in to his office. He owes me a favor or six. You give that document to me, son. I'll lock it in my safe."

"I ought to at least make a . . ." Wayland looks at the gnarled, outstretched hand and trails off. When a state Supreme Court judge (even a retired one) holds out his hand, demurrals must cease. What the hell, it's only an annotated draft, anyway, soon to be replaced by a clean version. He passes the unsigned will over and watches as Beecher rises (painfully) and swings a picture of the Florida Everglades out on a hidden hinge. The Judge enters the correct combination, making no attempt to hide the touchpad from view, and deposits the will on top of what looks to Wayland like a large and untidy heap of cash. Yikes.

"There!" Beecher says. "All done and buttoned up! Except for the signing part, that is. How about a drink to celebrate? I have some fine single-malt Scotch."

"Well . . . I guess one wouldn't hurt."

"It never hurt me, although it does now, so you'll have to pardon me for not joining you. Decaf coffee and a little sweet tea are the strongest drinks I take these days. Stomach woes. Ice?"

Wayland holds up two fingers, and Beecher adds two cubes to the drink with the slow ceremony of old age. Wayland takes a sip, and color immediately dashes into his cheeks. It is the flush, Judge Beecher thinks, of a man who enjoys his tipple. As Wayland sets his glass down, he says, "Do you mind if I ask what the hurry is? You're all right, I take it? Stomach woes aside?"

The Judge doubts if young Wayland takes it that way at all. He's not blind.

"A-country fair," he says, seesawing one hand in the air and sitting down with a grunt and a wince. Then, after consideration, he says, "Do you really want to know what the hurry is?"

Wayland considers the question, and Beecher likes him for that. Then he nods.

"It has to do with that island we took care of just now. Probably never even noticed it, have you?"

"Can't say that I have."

"Most folks don't. It barely sticks up out of the water. The sea turtles don't even bother with that old island. Yet it's special. Did you know my grandfather fought in the Spanish-American War?"

"No, sir, I did not." Wayland speaks with exaggerated respect, and Beecher knows the boy believes his mind is wandering. The boy is wrong. Beecher's mind has never been clearer, and now that he's begun, he finds that he wants to tell this story at least once before . . .

Well, before.

"Yes. There's a photograph of him standing on top of San Juan Hill. It's around here someplace. Grampy claimed to have fought in the Civil War as well, but my research—for my memoirs, you understand— proved conclusively that he could not have done. He would have been a toddler, if born at all. But he was quite the fanciful gentleman, and he had a way of making me believe the wildest tales. Why would I not? I was only a child, not long from believing in Kris Kringle and the tooth fairy."

"Was he a lawyer like you and your father?"

"No, son, he was a thief. The original Light-Finger Harry. Anything that wasn't nailed down. Only, like most thieves who don't get caught—our current governor might be a case in point—he called himself a businessman. His chief business and chief thievery was land. He bought bug- and gator-infested Florida acreage cheap and sold it dear to folks who must have been as gullible as I was as a child. Balzac once said, 'Behind every great fortune there is a crime.' That's certainly true of the Beecher family, and please remember that you're my lawyer. Anything I say to you must be held in confidence."

"Yes, Judge." Wayland takes another sip of his drink. It is by far the finest Scotch he has ever drunk.

"Grampy Beecher was the one who pointed out that island to me. I was ten. He'd had the care of me for the day, and I suppose he wanted some peace and quiet. Or maybe what he wanted was a bit noisier. There was a pretty housemaid, and he may have been in hopes of investigating beneath her petticoats. So he told me that Edward Teach—better known as Blackbeard—had supposedly buried a great treasure out there. 'Nobody's ever found it, Havie,' he said—Havie's what he called me—'but you might be the one. A fortune in jewels and gold doubloons.' You know what I did next, I suppose."

"I suppose you went out there and left your grandfather to cheer up the maid."

The Judge nods, smiling. "I took the old wooden canoe we had tied up to the dock. Went like my hair was on fire and my tailfeathers were catching. Didn't take but five minutes to paddle out there. Takes me three times as long these days, and that's if the water's smooth. The island's all rock and brush on the landward side, but there's a dune of fine beach sand on the Gulf side. It never goes away. In the eighty years I've been going out there, it never seems to change."

"Didn't find any treasure, I suppose?"

"I did, in a way, but it wasn't jewels and gold. It was a name, written in the sand of that dune. As if with a stick, you know, only I didn't see any stick. The letters were drawn deep, and the sun struck shadows into them, making them stand out. Almost as if they were floating."

"What was the name, Judge?"

"I think you have to see it written to understand."

The Judge takes a sheet of paper from the top drawer of his desk, prints carefully, then turns the paper around so Wayland can read it: ROBIE LADOOSH.

"All right . . ." Wayland says cautiously.

"On any other day, I would have gone treasure-hunting with this very boy, because he was my best friend, and you know how boys are when they're best friends."

"Joined at the hip," Wayland says, smiling. Perhaps he's recalling his own best friend in bygone days.

"Tight as a new key in a new lock," Wayland agrees. "But it was summer and he'd gone off with his parents to visit his mama's people in Virginia or Maryland or some such northern clime. So I was on my own. But attend me closely, Counselor. The boy's *actual* name was Robert LaDoucette."

Again Wayland says, "All right . . ." The Judge thinks that sort of leading drawl could become annoying over time, but it isn't a thing he'll ever have to actually find out, so he lets it go.

"He was my best friend and I was his, but there was a whole gang of boys we ran around with, and everyone called him Robbie LaDoosh. You follow?"

"I guess," Wayland says, but the Judge can see he doesn't. That's understandable; Beecher has had a lot more time to think about these things. Often on sleepless nights.

"Remember that I was ten. If I had been asked to spell my friend's nickname, I would have done it just this way." He taps ROBIE LADOOSH. Speaking almost to himself, he adds: "So some of the magic comes from me. It *must* come from me. The question is, how much?"

"You're saying you didn't write that name in the sand?"

"No. I thought I made that clear."

"One of your other friends, then?"

"They were all from Nokomis Village, and didn't even know about that island. We never would have paddled out to such an uninteresting little rock on our own. Robbie knew it was there, he was also from the Point, but he was hundreds of miles north."

"All right . . ."

"My chum Robbie never came back from that vacation. We got word a week or so later that he'd taken a fall while out horseback riding. He broke his neck. Killed instantly. His parents were heartbroken. So was I."

There is silence while Wayland considers this. While they both consider it. Somewhere far off, a helicopter beats at the sky over the Gulf. The DEA looking for drug runners, the Judge supposes. He hears them every night. It's the modern age, and in some ways—in many—he'll be glad to be shed of it.

At last Wayland says, "Are you saying what I think you're saying?"

"Well, I don't know," the Judge says. "What do you think I'm saying?"

But Anthony Wayland is a lawyer, and refusing to be drawn is an ingrained habit with him. "Did you tell your grandfather?"

"On the day the telegram about Robbie came, he wasn't there to tell. He never stayed in one place for long. We didn't see him again for six months or more. No, I kept it to myself. And like Mary after she gave birth to God's only son, I considered these things in my heart."

"And what conclusion did you draw?"

"I kept canoeing out to that island to look at the dune. That should answer your question. There was nothing . . . and nothing . . . and nothing. I guess I was on the verge of forgetting all about it, but then I went out one afternoon after school and there was another name written in the sand. *Printed* in the sand, to be courtroom-exact. No sign of a stick that time, either, although I suppose a stick could have been thrown into the water. This time the name was Peter Alderson. It meant nothing to me until a few days later. It was my chore to go out to the end of the road and get the paper, and it was my habit to scan the front page while I walked back up the drive—which, as you know from driving it yourself, is a good quarter mile long. In the summer I'd also check on how the Washington Senators had done, because back then they were as close to a southern team as we had.

"This particular day, a headline on the bottom of the front page caught my eye: WINDOW WASHER KILLED IN FREAK FALL. The poor guy was doing the third-floor windows of the Sarasota Public Library when the scaffolding he was standing on gave way. His name was Peter Alderson."

The Judge can see from Wayland's face that he believes this is either a prank or some sort of elaborate fantasy the Judge is spinning out. He can also see that Wayland is enjoying his drink, and when the Judge moves to top it up, Wayland doesn't say no. And really, the young man's belief or disbelief is beside the point. It's just such a luxury to tell it.

"Maybe you see why I go back and forth in my mind about where the magic lies," Beecher says. "I *knew* Robbie, and the misspelling of his name was my misspelling. But I didn't know this window washer from Adam. In any case, that's when the dune really started to get a hold on me. I began going out almost every day, a habit that's continued into my very old age. I respect the place, I fear the place, and most of all, I'm addicted to the place.

"Over the years, many names have appeared on that

dune, and the people the names belong to always die. Sometimes it's within the week, sometimes it's two, but it's never more than a month. Some have been people I knew, and if it's by a nickname I knew them, it's the nickname I see. One day in nineteen forty I paddled out there and saw GRAMPY BEECHER drawn into the sand. He died in Key West three days later. It was a heart attack."

With the air of someone humoring a man who is mentally unbalanced but not actually dangerous, Wayland asks, "Did you never try to interfere with this . . . this process? Call your grandfather, for instance, and tell him to see a doctor?"

Beecher shakes his head. "I didn't *know* it was a heart attack until we got word from the Monroe County medical examiner, did I? It could have been an accident, or even a murder. Certainly there were people who had reasons to hate my grandfather; his dealings were not of the purest sort."

"Still . . ."

"Also, I was afraid. I felt, I *still* feel, as if there on that island, there's a hatch that's come ajar. On this side is what we're pleased to call 'the real world.' On the other is all the machinery of the universe, running at top speed. Only a fool would stick his hand into such machinery in an attempt to stop it."

"Judge Beecher, if you want your paperwork to sail through probate, I'd keep quiet about all this. You might think there's no one to contest your will, but when large amounts of money are at stake, third and fourth cousins have a way of appearing like rabbits from a magician's hat. And you know the time-honored criterion: 'being of sound mind.'"

"I've kept it to myself for eighty years," Beecher

says, and in his voice Wayland can hear *objection over-ruled*. "Never a word until now. And—perhaps I need to point it out again, although I shouldn't—whatever I say to you falls under the umbrella of privilege."

"All right," Wayland says. "Fine."

"I was always excited on days when names appeared in the sand—unhealthily excited, I'm sure—but terrified of the phenomenon only once. That single time I was *deeply* terrified, and fled back to the Point in my canoe as if devils were after me. Shall I tell you?"

"Please." Wayland lifts his drink and sips. Why not? Billable hours are, after all, billable hours.

"It was nineteen fifty-nine. I was still on the Point. I've always lived here except for the years in Tallahassee, and it's better not to speak of them . . . although I now think part of the hate I felt for that provincial backwater of a town, perhaps even most of it, was simply a masked longing for the island, and the dune. I kept wondering what I was missing, you see. *Who* I was missing. Being able to read obituaries in advance gives a man an extraordinary sense of power. Perhaps you find that unlovely, but there it is.

"So. Nineteen fifty-nine. Harvey Beecher lawyering in Sarasota and living at Pelican Point. If it wasn't pouring down rain when I got home, I'd always change into old clothes and paddle out to the island for a look-see before supper. On this particular day I'd been kept at the office late, and by the time I'd gotten out to the island, tied up, and walked over to the dune side, the sun was going down big and red, as it so often does over the Gulf. What I saw stunned me. I literally could not move.

"There wasn't just one name written in the sand that evening but many, and in that red sunset light they looked as if they had been written in blood. They were crammed together, they wove in and out, they were written over and above and up and down. The whole length and breadth of the dune was covered with a tapestry of names. The ones down by the water had been half erased.

"I think I screamed. I can't remember for sure, but yes, I think so. What I *do* remember is breaking the paralysis and running away as fast as I could, down the path to where my canoe was tied up. It seemed to take me forever to unpluck the knot, and when I did, I pushed the canoe out into the water before I climbed in. I was soaked from head to toe, and it's a wonder I didn't tump it over. Although in those days I could have easily swum to shore, and pushing the canoe ahead of me. Not these days; if I tipped my kayak over now, that would be all she wrote." He grins. "Speaking of writing, as we are."

"Then I suggest you stay onshore, at least until your will is signed, witnessed, and notarized."

Judge Beecher gives the young man a wintry smile. "You needn't worry about that, son," he says. He looks toward the window, and the Gulf beyond. His face is long and thoughtful. "Those names . . . I can see them yet, jostling each other for place on that bloodred dune. Two days later, a TWA plane on its way to Miami crashed in the 'Glades. All one hundred and nineteen souls on board were killed. The passenger list was in the paper. I recognized some of the names. I recognized *many* of them."

"You *saw* this. You saw those names."

"Yes. For several months after that I stayed away from the island, and I promised myself I would stay away for good. I suppose drug addicts make the same promises to themselves about their dope, don't they? And, like them, I eventually weakened and resumed my old habit. Now, Counselor: do you understand why I called you out here to finish the work on my will, and why it had to be tonight?"

Wayland doesn't believe a word of it, but like many fantasies, this one has its own internal logic. It's easy enough to follow. The Judge is ninety, his once ruddy complexion has gone the color of clay, his formerly firm step has become shuffling and tentative. He's clearly in pain, and he's lost weight he can't afford to lose.

"I suppose that today you saw your name in the sand," Wayland says.

Judge Beecher looks momentarily startled, and then he smiles. It is a terrible smile, transforming his narrow, pallid face into a death's-head grin.

"Oh no," he says. "Not *mine*."

Thinking of W. F. Harvey

Life is full of Big Questions, isn't it? Fate or destiny? Heaven or hell? Love or attraction? Reason or impulse?

Beatles or Stones?

For me it was always the Stones—the Beatles were just too soft once they became Jupiter in the solar system of pop music. (My wife used to refer to Sir Paul McCartney as "old dog eyes," and that kind of summed up how I felt.) But the early Beatles . . . ah, they played honest rock, and I still listen to those old tracks—mostly covers—with love. Sometimes I'm even moved to get up and dance a little.

One of my favorites was their version of the Larry Williams classic "Bad Boy," with John Lennon singing lead in a hoarse, urgent voice. I particularly liked the exhorted punchline: "Now Junior, *behave* yourself!" At some point, I decided I wanted to write a story about a bad little kid who moved into the neighborhood. Not a kid who was the devil's spawn, not a kid who was possessed by some ancient demon à la *The Exorcist*, but just bad for bad's sake, bad to the bone, the apotheosis of all the bad little kids who ever were. I saw him in shorts, and with a propeller beanie on his head. I saw him always causing trouble and absolutely *never* behaving himself.

This is the story that grew around that little kid: an evil version of Sluggo, Nancy's friend from the funny pages. An electronic version has appeared in France and also in Germany, where "Bad Boy" was no doubt a part of the Beatles' Star Club repertoire. This is its first publication in English.

Bad Little Kid

1

The prison was twenty miles from the nearest small city, on an otherwise empty expanse of prairie where the wind blew almost all the time. The main building was a looming stone horror perpetrated on the landscape at the beginning of the twentieth century. Growing from either side were concrete cellblocks built one by one over the previous forty-five years, mostly with federal money that began flowing during the Nixon years and just never stopped.

At some distance from the main body of the prison was a smaller building. The prisoners called this adjunct Needle Manor. Jutting from one side of it was an outdoor corridor forty yards long, twenty feet wide, and enclosed in heavy chainlink fencing: the Chicken Run. Each Needle Manor inmate—currently there were seven—was allowed two hours in the Chicken Run each day. Some walked. Some jogged. Most simply sat with their backs against the chainlink, either staring up at the sky or looking at the low grassy ridge that broke the landscape a quarter of a mile to the east. Sometimes there was something to look at. More often there was nothing. Almost always there was the wind. For three months of the year, the Chicken Run was hot. The rest of the time it was cold. In the winter, it was frigid. The inmates usually chose to go out even then. There was the sky to look at, after all. Birds. Sometimes deer feeding along the crest of that low ridge, free to go where they pleased.

At the center of Needle Manor was a tiled room containing a Y-shaped table and a few rudimentary pieces of medical equipment. Set in one wall was a window with drawn curtains. When pulled back, they disclosed an observation chamber no bigger than the living room of a suburban tract house with a dozen hard plastic chairs where guests could view the Y-shaped table. On the wall was a sign reading KEEP SILENT AND MAKE NO GESTURES DURING THE PROCEDURE.

There were an even dozen cells in Needle Manor. Beyond them was a guardroom. Beyond the guard-room was a monitoring station which was manned 24/7. Beyond the monitoring station was a consul-tation room, where a table on the inmate side was separated from the table on the visitor side by thick Plexiglas. There were no phones; inmates conversed with their loved ones or legal representatives through a circle of small punched holes, like those in the mouthpiece of an old-fashioned telephone.

Leonard Bradley sat down on his side of this com-munication port and opened his briefcase. He put a yellow legal pad and a Uniball pen on the table. Then he waited. The second hand on his watch made three revolutions and started a fourth before the door lead-ing to the inner regions of Needle Manor opened with a loud clack of withdrawing bolts. Bradley knew all the guards by now. This one was McGregor. Not a bad guy. He was holding George Hallas by the arm. Hallas's hands were free, but a steel snake of chain rattled along the floor between his ankles. There was a wide leather belt around the waist of his orange prison jumper, and when he sat down on his side of the glass, McGregor clipped another chain from a steel loop on the belt to a steel loop on the back of the chair. He locked it, gave it a tug, then tipped Bradley a two-finger salute.

"Afternoon, Counselor."

"Afternoon, Mr. McGregor."

Hallas said nothing.

"You know the deal," McGregor said. "As long as you want today. Or as long as you can take him, at least."

"I know."

Ordinarily, lawyer-client consultations were limited to an hour. Beginning a month before the client's scheduled trip into the room with the Y-shaped table, consultation time was upped to ninety minutes, during which the lawyer and his increasingly squirrelly partner in this state-mandated death waltz would discuss a diminishing number of shitty options. During the last week, there was no set time limit. This was true for close relatives as well as legal counsel, but Hallas's wife had divorced him only weeks after his conviction, and there were no children. He was alone in the world except for Len Bradley, but seemed to want little to do with any of the appeals—and consequent delays—Bradley had suggested.

Until today, that was.

He'll talk to you, McGregor had told him after a brief ten-minute consultation the month before, one where Hallas's end of the conversation had mostly been *no* and *no* and *no*.

When it gets close, he'll talk to you plenty. They get scared, see? They forget all about how they wanted to walk into the injection room with their heads up and their shoulders squared. They start figuring out it's not a movie, they're really going to die, and then they want to try every appeal in the book.

Hallas didn't look scared, though. He looked the same as ever: a small man with bad posture, a sallow complexion, thinning hair, and eyes that looked painted on. He looked like an accountant—which he had been in his previous life—who had lost all interest in the numbers that had previously seemed so important to him.

"Enjoy your visit, boys," McGregor said, and went over to the chair in the corner. There he sat, turned on his iPod, and stuffed his ears with music. His eyes never left them, however. The circle of speaking holes was too small to admit the passage of a pencil, but a needle was not out of the question.

"What can I do for you, George?"

For several moments Hallas didn't answer. He studied his hands, which were small and weak-looking—not the hands of a murderer at all, you would have said. Then he looked up.

"You're a pretty good guy, Mr. Bradley."

Bradley was surprised by this, and didn't know how to reply.

Hallas nodded, as if his lawyer had tried to deny it. "Yes. You are. You kept on even after I made it clear I wanted you to stop and let the process run its course. Not many court-appointeds would do that. They'd just say *yeah, whatever,* and go on to the next loser some judge hands them. You didn't do that. You told me what moves you wanted to make, and when I told you not to make them, you went ahead anyway. If not for you, I would've been in the ground a year ago."

"We don't always get what we want, George."

Hallas smiled briefly. "Nobody knows that better than me. But it hasn't been all bad; I can admit that now. Mostly because of the Chicken Run. I like going out there. I like the wind on my face, even when it's a cold wind. I like the smell of the prairie grass, or seeing the day-moon in the sky when it's full. Or deer. Sometimes they jump around up there on the ridge and chase each other. I like that. Makes me laugh out loud, sometimes."

"Life can be good. It can be worth fighting for."

"Some lives, I'm sure. Not mine. But I admire the way you've fought for it, just the same. I appreciate your dedication. So I'm going to tell you what I wouldn't say in court. And why I've refused to make any of the usual appeals . . . although I couldn't stop you from making them for me."

"Appeals made without the appellant's participation don't swing much weight in this state's courts. Or the higher ones."

"You've also been very good about visiting me, and I appreciate that too. Few people would show kindness to a convicted child murderer, but you have to me."

Once again, Bradley could think of no reply. Hallas had already said more in the last ten minutes than in all their visits over the last thirty-four months.

"I can't pay you anything, but I *can* tell you why I killed that child. You won't believe me, but I'll tell you, anyway. If you want to hear."

Hallas peered through the holes in the scratched Plexiglas and smiled.

"You do, don't you? Because you're troubled by certain things. The prosecution wasn't, but you are."

"Well . . . certain questions have occurred, yes."

"But I did it. I had a forty-five revolver and I emptied it into that boy. There were plenty of witnesses, and surely you know that the appeals process would simply have dragged out the inevitable for another three years—or four, or six—even if I had participated fully. The questions you have pale before the bald fact of premeditated murder. Isn't that so?"

"We could have argued diminished mental capacity." Bradley leaned forward. "And that's still possible. It's not too late, even now. Not quite."

"The insanity defense is rarely successful after the fact, Mr. Bradley."

He won't call me Len, Bradley thought. *Not even after all this time. He'll go to his death calling me Mr. Bradley.*

"Rarely isn't the same as never, George."

"No, but I'm not crazy now and I wasn't crazy then. I was never more sane. Are you sure you want to hear the testimony I wouldn't give in court? If you don't, that's fine, but it's all I have to give."

"Of course I want to hear," Bradley said. He picked up his pen, but ended up not making a single note. He only listened, hypnotized, as George Hallas spoke in his soft mid-South accent.

2

My mother, who was healthy all her short life, died of a pulmonary embolism six hours after I was born.

This was in 1969. It must have been a genetic defect, because she was only twenty-two. My father was eight years older. He was a good man and a good dad. He was a mining engineer, and worked mostly in the Southwest until I was eight.

A housekeeper traveled around with us. Her name was Nona McCarthy, and I called her Mama Nonie. She was black. I suppose he slept with her, although when I slipped into her bed—which I did on many mornings—she was always alone. It didn't matter to me, one way or the other. I didn't know what black had to do with anything. She was good to me, she made my lunches and read me the usual bedtime stories when my father wasn't home to do it, and that was all that mattered to me. It wasn't the usual setup, I suppose I knew that much, but I was happy enough.

In 1977 we moved east to Talbot, Alabama, not far from Birmingham. That's an army town, Fort John Huie, but also coal country. My father was hired to reopen the Good Luck mines—One, Two, and Three— and bring them up to environmental specifications, which meant breaking ground on new holes and designing a disposal system that would keep the waste from polluting the local streams.

We lived in a nice little suburban neighborhood, in a house the Good Luck Company provided. Mama Nonie liked it because my father turned the garage into a two-room apartment for her. It kept the gossip down to a dull roar, I suppose. I helped him with the renovations on weekends, handing him boards and such. That was a good time for us. I was able to go to the same school for two years, which was long enough to make friends and get some stability.

One of my friends was the girl next door. In a TV show or a magazine, we would have ended up sharing our first kiss in a treehouse, falling in love, and then going to the junior prom together when we finally made it to high school. But that was never going to happen to me and Marlee Jacobs.

Daddy never led me to believe we'd be staying in Talbot. He said there was nothing meaner than encouraging false hopes in a child. Oh, I might go to Mary Day Grammar School through the fifth grade, might even through the sixth, but eventually his Good Luck would run out and we'd be moving on. Maybe back to Texas or New Mexico; maybe up to West Virginia or Kentucky. I accepted this, and so did Mama Nonie. My dad was the boss, he was a good boss, and he loved us. Just my opinion, but I don't think you can do much better than that.

The second thing had to do with Marlee herself. She was . . . well, these days people would call her "mentally challenged," but back then the folks in our neighborhood just said she was soft in the head. You could call that mean, Mr. Bradley, but looking back on it, I think it's just right. Poetic, even. She saw the world that way, all soft and out of focus. Sometimes—often, even—that can be better. Again, just my opinion.

We were both in third grade when I met her, but Marlee was already eleven. We were both promoted to the fourth grade the next year, but in her case it was just so they could keep moving her along through the system. That's how things worked in places like Talbot back then. And it wasn't like she was the village idiot. She could read a little, and do some simple addition, but subtraction was beyond her. I tried to explain it every way I knew how, but she was just never going to get it.

We never kissed in a treehouse—never kissed at all—but we always held hands when we walked to school in the morning and back in the afternoon. I imagine we looked damn funny, because I was a shrimp and she was a big girl, at least four inches taller than me and already getting her breasts. It was her who wanted to hold hands, not me, but I didn't mind. I didn't mind that she was soft-headed, either. I would have in time, I suppose, but I was only nine when she died, still at an age when kids accept pretty much everything that's put before them. I think that's a blessed way to be. If everyone was soft in the head, do you think we'd still have wars? Balls we would.

If we'd lived another half a mile out, Marlee and I would have taken the bus. But since we were close to the Mary Day—six or eight blocks—we walked. Mama Nonie would hand me my bag lunch, and smooth down my cowlick, and tell me You be a good boy now, Georgie, and send me out the door. Marlee would be waiting outside *her* door, wearing one of her dresses or jumpers, with her hair done up in pigtails and ribbons and her lunchbox in her hand. I can still see that lunchbox. It had Steve Austin on it, the Six Million Dollar Man. Her mama would be standing in the doorway and she'd say Hey now, Georgie, and I'd say Hey now, Mrs. Jacobs, and she'd say You children be good, and Marlee would say We'll be good, Mama, and then Marlee would take hold of my hand and off we'd go down the sidewalk. We had the first couple of blocks to ourselves, but then the other kids would start streaming in from Rudolph Acres. That was where a lot of army families lived, because it was cheap and Fort Huie was only five miles north on Highway 78.

We must have looked funny—the pipsqueak with his sack lunch holding hands with the beanpole banging her Steve Austin lunchbox against one scabby knee—but I don't remember anyone making fun or teasing. I suppose they must have from time to time, kids being kids and all, but if so it was the light kind that doesn't mean much. Mostly once the sidewalk filled up it was boys saying stuff like Hey now, George, you want to play pickup after school or girls saying Hey now, Marlee, ain't those hairribbons some pretty. I don't remember anyone treating us bad. Not until the bad little kid.

One day after school Marlee didn't come out and didn't come out. This must have been not long after my ninth birthday, because I had my Bolo Bouncer. Mama Nonie gave it to me and it didn't last long— I hit it too hard and the rubber snapped—but I had it that day, and was going frontsies-backsies with it while I waited for her. Nobody ever told me I *had* to wait for her, I just did.

Finally she came out, and she was crying. Her face was all red and there was snot coming out of her nose. I asked her what was wrong and she said she couldn't find her lunchbox. She ate her lunch out of it same as always, she said, and put it back on the shelf in the cloakroom next to Cathy Morse's pink Barbie lunchbox, just like she always did, but when the going-home bell rang, it was gone. Somebody *stoled* it, she said.

No, no, somebody just moved it and it'll be there tomorrow, I said. You stop your fussing and stand still, now. You got a mess.

Mama Nonie always made sure I had a hankie when I left the house, but I wiped my nose on my sleeve like the other boys because a hankie seemed kind of sissy. So it was still clean and still folded when I took it out of my back pocket and wiped the snot off her face with it. She stopped crying and smiled and said it tickled. Then she took my hand and we walked on toward home, just like always, her talking six licks to the dozen. I didn't mind, because at least she'd forgotten her lunchbox.

Pretty soon all the other kids were gone, although we could hear them laughing and skylarking their way back to Rudolph Acres. Marlee was chitter-chattering along like always, anything that came into her head. I let it wash over me, saying Yeah and Uh-huh and Hey, mostly thinking about how I'd change into my old corduroys as soon as I got back, and if Mama Nonie didn't have any chores for me, I'd get my glove and run down to the Oak Street playground and get in on the pickup game that went on there every day until moms started yelling it was suppertime.

That is when we heard someone hollering at us from the other side of School Street. Only it was less like a voice and more like a donkey bray.

GEORGE AND MARLEE UP IN A TREE! K-I-S-S-I-N-G!

We stopped. There was a kid over there, standing by a hackberry bush. I'd never seen him before, not at Mary Day or anywhere else. He wasn't but four and a half feet tall, and stocky. He had on gray shorts that went down all the way to his knees, and a green sweater with orange stripes. It was rounded out up top with little boy-tits and a poochy belly underneath. He had a beanie on his head, the stupid kind with a plastic propeller.

His face was pudgy and hard at the same time. His hair was orange like the stripes on his sweater, that shade nobody loves. It was all sprayed out on the sides over his jug ears. His nose was a little blot underneath the brightest, greenest eyes I've ever seen. He had a sulky Cupid's bow of a mouth, the lips so red it looked like he was wearing his ma's lipstick. I've seen plenty of carrottops with those red lips since then, but none as red as that bad little kid's were.

We stood and stared at him. Marlee's chatter came to a halt. She had cat's-eye glasses with pink rims, and behind them her eyes were wide and magnified.

The kid—he couldn't have been more than six or seven—pooched up those red lips of his and made kissy-face noises. Then he put his hands on his butt and began to bump his hips at us.

GEORGE AND MARLEE UP IN A TREE! F-U-C-K-I-N-G!

Braying just like a donkey. We stared, amazed.

You better wear a scumbag when you fuck her, he called over, smirking those red lips. Less you want to have a bunch of retards just like her.

You shut up your face, I said.

Or what? he said.

Or I'll shut it up for you, I said.

I meant it, too. My father would have been mad if he knew I was threatening to beat up a kid who was younger and smaller, but he wasn't right to be saying those things. He looked like a little kid, but those weren't little-kid things he was saying.

Suck my dink, assface, he said, and then stepped behind the hackberry bush.

I thought about going over there, but Marlee was holding my hand so tight it almost hurt.

I don't like that boy, she said.

I said I didn't like him either, but to never mind. Let's go home, I said.

But before we could start walking again, the kid came back out from behind the hackberry bush, and he had Marlee's Steve Austin lunchbox in his hands. He held it up.

Lose something, fuckwit? he said, and laughed. Laughing wrinkled his face up and made it like a pig's face. He sniffed at the box and said, I guess it must be yours, cause it smells like cunt. Like *retarded* cunt.

Give me that, it's mine, Marlee yelled. She let go of my hand. I tried to hold it, but it greased out on the sweat of our palms.

Come and get it, he said, and held it out to her.

Before I tell you what happened next, I have to tell you about Mrs. Peckham. She was the first-grade teacher at Mary Day. I didn't have her, because I went to the first grade in New Mexico, but most of the kids in Talbot did—Marlee too—and they all loved her. *I* loved her, and I only had her for playground, when it was her turn to be monitor. If there was kickball, boys against the girls, she was always the pitcher for the girls' team. Sometimes she'd whip one in from behind her back, and that made everyone laugh. She was the kind of teacher you remember forty years later, because she could be kind and jolly but still make even the antsy-pantsy kids mind.

She had a big old Buick Roadmaster, sky-blue, and we used to call her Pokey Peckham because she never drove it more than thirty miles an hour, always sitting bolt straight behind the wheel with her eyes squinted. Of course, we only saw her drive in the neighborhood, which was a school zone, but I bet she drove pretty much the same way when she was on 78. Even on the interstate. She was careful and cautious. She would never hurt a child. Not on purpose, she wouldn't.

Marlee ran into the street to get her lunchbox. The bad little kid laughed and threw it at her. It hit the street and broke open. Her thermos bottle fell out and rolled. I saw that sky-blue Roadmaster coming and yelled for Marlee to look out, but I wasn't really worried because it was only Pokey Peckham, and she was still a block down, going slow as ever.

You let go of her hand, so now it's your fault, the kid said. He was looking at me and grinning, his lips drawn back so I could see all his little teeth. He said, You can't hold onto *nothing*, dink-sucker. He stuck out his tongue and blew a raspberry at me. Then he stepped back behind the bush.

Mrs. Peckham said her accelerator stuck. I don't know if the police believed her or not. All I know is she never taught first grade at Mary Day again.

Marlee bent over, picked up her thermos, and shook it. I could hear the rattle it made. She said, It's all broke inside, and started crying. She bent down again, to get her lunchbox, and that was when Mrs. Peckham's gas pedal must have stuck because the engine roared and her Buick just *leaped* down the road. Like a wolf on a rabbit. Marlee stood up with the lunchbox clutched to her chest in one hand and the broken thermos bottle in the other, and she saw the car coming, and she never moved.

Maybe I could have pushed her out of the way and saved her. Or maybe if I'd run out into the street, I would have gotten hit too. I don't know, because I was as frozen as she was. I just stood there. I didn't even move when the car hit her. Not even my head moved. I just followed her with my eyes when Marlee flew and then crashed down on her poor soft head. Pretty soon I heard screaming. That was Mrs. Peckham. She got out of her car and fell down and got up with her knees bleeding and ran for where Marlee was lying in the street with blood coming out of her head. So I ran too. When I got a little ways, I turned my head. By then I was far enough so I could see behind the hackberry bush. There was no one there.

3

Hallas stopped and put his face in his hands. At last he lowered them.

"Are you all right, George?" Bradley asked.

"Thirsty is all. I'm not used to talking so much. There's very little call for conversation on Death Row."

I waved my hand at McGregor. He took out his earbuds and stood up. "All finished, George?"

Hallas shook his head. "There's a lot more."

Bradley said, "My client would like a drink of water, Mr. McGregor. Is that possible?"

McGregor went to the intercom by the door to the monitoring station and spoke into it briefly. Bradley took the opportunity to ask Hallas just how big Mary Day Grammar School had been.

He shrugged. "Small town, small school. There couldn't have been more than a hundred and fifty kids, grades one to six."

The door of the monitoring room opened. A hand appeared, holding a paper cup. McGregor took it and brought it over to Hallas. He drank greedily and said thank you.

"Very welcome," McGregor said. He went back to his chair, replaced the earbuds, and once more lost himself in whatever he was listening to.

"And this kid—the bad little kid—was a carrottop? A *real* carrottop?"

"Hair like a neon sign."

"So if he'd gone to your school, you would have recognized him."

"Yes."

"But you didn't, and *he* didn't."

"No. I never saw him there before, and never afterward."

"So how did he get the Jacobs girl's lunchbox?"

"I don't know. But there's a better question."

"What would that be, George?"

"How did he get away from that hackberry bush? There was nothing but lawn on either side. He was just gone."

"George?"

"Yes?"

"Are you sure there really *was* a kid?"

"Her lunchbox, Mr. Bradley. It was in the street."

I don't doubt that, Bradley thought, tapping his Uniball on his legal pad. It would have been if she'd had it all along.

Or (here was a nasty thought, but nasty thoughts were par for the course when you were listening to the bullshit story of a child-killer) maybe *you* had her lunchbox, George. Maybe you took it from her and threw it into the street to tease her.

Bradley looked up from his pad and saw from his client's expression that what he was thinking might as well have been on a Teletype strip going across his forehead. He felt his face warming up.

"Do you want to hear the rest? Or have you already made up your mind?"

"Not at all," Bradley said. "Continue. Please."

Hallas drank the rest of his water, and took up his tale.

4

For five years or more I dreamed about that bad little kid with the carroty hair and the beanie cap, but eventually the dreams went away. Eventually I got to a place where I believed what you must believe, Mr. Bradley: that it was just an accident, that Mrs. Peckham's accelerator really did stick, as they sometimes will, and if there was a kid over there, teasing her . . . well, kids *do* tease sometimes, don't they?

My dad finished his job for the Good Luck Company and we moved up to eastern Kentucky, where he went to work doing much the same thing as he had in Alabama, only on a grander scale. Plenty of mines in that part of the world, you know. We lived in the town of Ironville long enough for me to finish high school. In my sophomore year, just for a lark, I joined the Drama Club. People would laugh if they knew, I suppose. A little mousy fellow like me, who made a living doing tax returns for small businesses and widows, acting in things like *No Exit*? Talk about Walter Mitty! But I did, and I was good. Everyone said so. I thought I might even have a career in acting. I knew I was never going to be a leading man, but someone has to play the president's economic adviser, or the bad guy's second-in-command, or the mechanic who gets killed in the first reel of a movie. I knew I could play parts like that, and I thought people might actually hire me. I told my dad I wanted to major in drama when I got to college. He said okay, great, go for it, just make sure you have something to fall back on. I went to Pitt, where I majored in theater arts and minored in business administration.

The first play I was cast in was *She Stoops to Conquer*, and that's where I met Vicky Abington. I was Tony Lumpkin and she was Constance Neville. She was a beautiful girl with masses of curly blond hair, very thin and high-strung. Far too beautiful for me, I thought, but eventually I got up enough nerve to ask her out for coffee. That was how it began. We'd sit for hours in Nordy's—that's the hamburger joint in Pitt Union—and she'd pour out all her troubles, which mostly had to do with her dominating mother, and tell me about her ambitions, which were all about the theater, especially serious theater in New York. Twenty-five years ago there still was such a thing.

I knew she got pills at the Nordenberg Wellness Center—maybe for anxiety, maybe for depression, maybe for both—but I thought, That's just because she's ambitious and creative, probably most really great actors and actresses take those pills. Probably Meryl Streep takes those pills, or did before she got famous in *The Deer Hunter*. And you know what? Vicky had a great sense of humor, which is something many beautiful women seem to lack, especially if they suffer from the nervous complaint. She could laugh at herself, and often did. She said being able to do that was the only thing that kept her sane.

We were cast as Nick and Honey in *Who's Afraid of Virginia Woolf?*, and got better reviews than the kids who played George and Martha. After that we weren't just coffee buddies, we were a couple. Sometimes we made out in a dark corner of the Union, although those sessions often ended with her crying and saying she knew she wasn't good enough, she'd fail at acting just like her mother said she would. One night— this was after the cast party for *Deathtrap*, our junior year—we had sex. It was the only time. She said she loved it, it was wonderful, but I guess it wasn't. Not for her, anyway, because she'd never do it again.

In the summer of 1990, we stayed on campus because there was going to be a summer production of *The Music Man* in Frick Park. It was a huge deal because Mandy Patinkin was going to direct it. Vicky and I both tried out. I wasn't a bit nervous, because I didn't expect to get anything, but that show had become the biggest thing in Vicky's life. She called it her first step to stardom, saying it the way people do when they're joking but not really. We were called in by sixes, each of us holding a card saying the part we were most interested in, and Vicky was shaking like a leaf while we waited outside the rehearsal hall. I put my arm around her and she quieted, but just a little. She was so white her makeup looked like a mask.

I went in and handed over my wish-card with *Mayor Shinn* written on it, because that's a smallish part in the show, and damned if I didn't end up getting the lead role—Harold Hill, the charming con man. Vicky tried out for Marian Paroo, the librarian who gives piano lessons. She's the female lead. She read all right, I thought—not great, not her best, but all right. Then came the singing.

It was Marian's big number. If you don't know it, it's this very sweet and simple song called "Goodnight, My Someone." She'd sung it for me—a capella—half a dozen times, and she was perfect. Sweet and sad and hopeful. But that day in the rehearsal hall, Vicky screwed the pooch. That girl was just clench-your-fists-and-close-your-eyes awful. She couldn't find her note and had to start again not once but twice. I could see Patinkin getting impatient, because he had half a dozen other girls waiting to read and sing. The accompanist was rolling her eyes. I wanted to punch her right in her stupid, horsey face.

By the time Vicky finished, she was trembling all over. Mr. Patinkin thanked her, and she thanked him, all very polite, and then ran. I caught up with her before she could get out of the building and told her she had been great. She smiled and thanked me and said we both knew better. I said that if Mr. Patinkin was as good as everyone said, he'd look past her nerves and see what a great actress she was. She hugged me and said I was her best friend. Besides, she said, there will be other shows. Next time I'll take a Valium before I try out. I was just afraid it would change my voice, because I've heard that some pills can do that. Then she laughed and said, But how much worse could it be than it was today? I said I'd buy her an ice cream at Nordy's, she said that sounded good, and off we went.

We were walking down the sidewalk, hand in hand, which made me remember all the times I walked back and forth to Mary Day Grammar holding hands with Marlee Jacobs. I won't say those thoughts summoned him, but I won't say they didn't, either. I don't know. I only know that some nights I lie awake in my cell, wondering.

I guess she was feeling a little better, because as we walked along she was talking about what a great Professor Hill I'd make, when someone yelled at us from the other side of the street. Only it wasn't a yell; it was a donkey bray.

GEORGE AND VICKY UP IN A TREE! F-U-C-K-I-N-G!

It was him. The bad little kid. Same shorts, same sweater, same orange hair sticking out from under that beanie with the plastic propeller on top. Over ten years had passed and he hadn't aged a day. It was like being thrown back in time, only now it was Vicky Abington, not Marlee Jacobs, and we were on Reynolds Street in Pittsburgh instead of School Street in Talbot, Alabama.

What in the *world*, Vicky said. Do you know that boy, George?

Well, what was I going to say to that? I didn't say anything. I was so far beyond surprise I couldn't even open my mouth.

You act like shit and you sing worse! he shouted. *CROWS* sing better than you do! And you're *UGLEEE! UGLEE VICKEE* is what you are!

She put her hands over her mouth, and I remember how big her eyes were, and how they were filling up with tears all over again.

Suck his dink, why don't you? he shouted. That's the only way an ugly no-talent cunt like you will ever get a part!

I started for him, only it didn't feel real. It felt like it was all happening in a dream. It was late afternoon and Reynolds Street was full of traffic, but I never thought of that. Vicky did, though. She caught me by the arm and pulled me back. I think I owe her my life, because a big bus went past only a second or two later, blaring its horn.

Don't, she said. He's not worth it, whoever he is.

There was a truck right behind the bus, and once they were both by us, we saw the kid running up the other side of the street with his big ass jouncing. He got to the corner and turned it, but before he did, he shoved down the back of his shorts, bent over, and mooned us.

Vicky sat down on a bench and I sat down beside her. She asked me again who he was, and I said I didn't know.

Then how did he know our names? she asked.

I don't know, I repeated.

Well, he was right about one thing, she said. If I want a part in *The Music Man*, I should go back and suck Mandy Patinkin's cock. Then she laughed, and this time it was real laughing, the kind that comes all the way up from the belly. She threw back her head and just let fly. Did you see that little ugly butt? she said. Like two muffins ready for the oven!

That got *me* going. We put our arms around each other, and put our heads together cheek to cheek, and really howled. I thought we were okay, but the truth of it—you never see these things at the time, do you?—is that we were both hysterical. Me because it was *the same kid* from all those years ago, Vicky because she believed what he said: she was no good, and even if she was, she'd never be able to get on top of her nerves enough to show it.

I walked her back to Fudgy Acres, this big old

apartment house that rented exclusively to young women—whom we still called coeds then—and she hugged me and told me again that I would make a great Harold Hill. Something about the way she said that worried me, and I asked if she was all right. She said, Of course I am, silly, and went running up the walk. That was the last time I saw her alive.

After the funeral, I took Carla Winston out for coffee, because she was the only girl in Fudgy Acres Vicky had been close to. I ended up pouring her cup into a glass, because her hands were shaking so badly I was afraid she'd burn herself. Carla wasn't just brokenhearted; she blamed herself for what happened. The same way I'm sure Mrs. Peckham blamed herself for what happened to Marlee.

She came across Vicky in the downstairs lounge that afternoon, staring at the TV. Only the TV was turned off. She said Vicky seemed distant and disconnected. She'd seen Vicky that way before, when she lost count of her pills and took one too many, or took them in the wrong order. She asked if Vicky wanted to go to the Wellness Center and get looked at. Vicky said no, she was fine, it had been a hard day but she'd be feeling better very soon.

There was a nasty little kid, Vicky told Carla. I fucked up my tryout, and then this kid started ragging on me.

That's too bad, Carla said.

George knew him, Vicky said. He told me he didn't, but I could tell he did. Do you want to know what I think?

Carla said sure. By then she was positive Vicky had screwed up her meds, smoked some dope, or both.

I think George put him up to it, she said. For a tease. But when he saw how upset I was, he was sorry and tried to make the kid stop. Only the kid wouldn't.

Carla said, That doesn't make sense, Vic. George would never tease you about a part. He likes you.

Vicky said, That kid was right, though. I might as well give up.

At this point in Carla's story, I told her the kid had nothing to do with me. Carla said I didn't even have to tell her that, she knew I was a good guy and how much I cared for Vicky. Then she started to cry.

It's *my* fault, not yours, she said. I could see she was screwed up, but I didn't do anything. And you know what happened. That's on me, too, because she didn't really mean to. I'm sure she didn't.

Carla left Vicky and went upstairs to study. A couple of hours later, she went down to Vicky's room.

I thought she might like to go out and get something to eat, she said. Or if the pills had worn off, maybe have a glass of wine. Only she wasn't there. So I checked the lounge, but she wasn't there, either. A couple of girls were watching TV, and one said she thought she saw Vicky going downstairs a little while ago, probably to do a wash.

Because she had some sheets, the girl said.

That worried Carla, although she wouldn't let herself think why. She went downstairs, but there was no one in the laundry room and none of the washers were going. The next room along was the box room, where the girls stored their luggage. She heard sounds from there, and when she went in, she saw Vicky with her back to her. She was standing on a little stack of suitcases. She'd tied two sheets together to make a hanging rope. One end was noosed around her neck. The other was tied to an overhead pipe.

But the thing was, Carla told me, there were only three suitcases, and plenty of slack in the sheets. If she'd meant business, she would have used one sheet and stood some girl's trunk on end. It was only what theater people call a dress rehearsal.

You don't know that for sure, I said. You don't know how many of her pills she might have taken, or how confused she was.

I know what I saw, Carla said. She could have stepped right off those suitcases and onto the floor without pulling the noose tight. But I didn't think of that then. I was too shocked. I just yelled her name.

That loud shout from behind startled her, and instead of stepping off the suitcases, Vicky jerked and toppled forward, the suitcases sliding along the floor behind. She would have hit the concrete floor smack on her belly, Carla said, but there wasn't *that* much slack in her rope. She still might have lived if the knot holding the two sheets together had given way, but it didn't. Her falling weight pulled the noose tight and yanked her head up hard.

I heard the snap when her neck broke, Carla said. It was loud. And it was my fault.

Then she cried and cried and cried.

I got her out of the coffee shop and into a bus shelter on the corner. I told her over and over again that it hadn't been her fault, and eventually she stopped crying. She even smiled a little.

She said, You're very persuasive, George.

What I didn't tell her—because she wouldn't have believed it—was that my persuasiveness came from absolute certainty.

5

"The bad little kid came after the people I cared about," Hallas said.

Bradley nodded. It was obvious that Hallas believed it, and if this story had come out at the trial, it might have earned the man a life sentence instead of a billet in Needle Manor. The jury very likely wouldn't have been completely sold, but it would have given them an excuse to take the death penalty off the table. Now it was probably too late. A written motion requesting a stay based on Hallas's story of the bad little kid would look like grasping at straws. You had to be in his presence, and see the absolute certainty on his face. To hear it in his voice.

The condemned man, meanwhile, was looking at him through the slightly clouded Plexiglas with a trace of a smile. "That kid wasn't just bad; he was also greedy. For him, it always had to be a twofer. One dead; one left to baste in a nice warm gravy of guilt."

"You must have convinced Carla," Bradley said. "She married you, after all."

"I never convinced her completely, and she never believed in the bad little kid at all. If she had, she would have been at the trial, and we'd still be married." He stared through the barrier at Bradley, his eyes dead level. "If she had, she would have been glad that I killed him."

The guard in the corner—McGregor—looked at his watch, removed his earbuds, and stood up. "I don't want to hurry you along, Counselor, but it's eleven thirty, and pretty soon your client has to be back in his cell for the midday count."

"I don't see why you can't count him right here," Bradley said . . . but mildly. It didn't do to get on the mean side of any guard, and although McGregor was one of the better ones, Bradley was sure he had a mean side. It was a requirement for men charged with overseeing hard cons. "You're looking at him, after all."

"Rules are rules," McGregor said, then raised his hand, as if to stifle a protest Bradley hadn't made. "I know you're entitled to as much time as you want this close to his date, so if you want to wait around, I'll bring him back after count. He'll miss his lunch, though, and probably you will too."

They watched McGregor return to his seat and once more replace his earbuds. When Hallas turned back to the Plexi barrier, there was more than a trace of a smile on his lips. "Hell, you could probably *guess* the rest."

Although Bradley was sure he could, he folded his hands on his blank legal pad and said, "Why don't you tell me anyway?"

6

I declined the part of Harold Hill and dropped out of Drama Club. I had lost my taste for acting. During my final year at Pitt, I concentrated on my business classes, especially accounting, and Carla Winston. The year I graduated, we were married. My father was my best man. He died three years later.

One of the mines he was responsible for was in the town of Louisa. That's a little south of Ironville, where he still lived with Nona McCarthy—Mama Nonie— as his "housekeeper." The mine was called Fair Deep.

One day there was a rockfall in its second parlor, which was about two hundred feet down. Not serious, everyone got out fine, but my father went down with a couple of company guys from the front office to look at the damage and try to figure out how long it would take to get things up and running again. He never came out. None of them did.

That boy keeps calling, Nonie said later. She had always been a pretty woman, but in the year after my father died, she bloomed out in wrinkles and dewlaps. Her walk turned into a shuffle, and she hunched her shoulders whenever anyone came into the room, as if she expected to be struck. It wasn't my father's death that did it to her; it was the bad little kid.

He keeps calling. He calls me a nigger bitch, but I don't mind that. I been called worse. That kind of thing rolls right off my back. What doesn't is him saying it happened because of the present I gave your father. Those boots. That can't be true, can it, Georgie? It had to've been something else. He had to've been wearing his felts. He *never* would have forgotten his felts after a mine accident, even one that didn't seem serious.

I agreed, but I could see the doubt eating into her like acid.

The boots were Trailman Specials. She gave them to him for his birthday not two months before the explosion in Fair Deep. They must have set her back at least three hundred dollars, but they were worth every penny. Knee high, leather as supple as silk, but tough. They were the kind of boots a man could wear all his life and then pass on to his son. *Hobnail* boots, you understand, and nails like that can strike sparks on the right surface, just like flint on steel.

My dad never would have worn nailboots into a mine where there might be methane or firedamp, and don't tell me he could have just forgot, not when he and those other two were toting respirators on their hips and wearing oxygen bottles on their backs. Even if he *had* been wearing the Specials, Mama Nonie was right—he would also have been wearing felts over them. She didn't need me to tell her; she knew how careful he was. But even the craziest idea can work its way into your mind if you're lonely and grief-stricken and someone keeps harping on it. It can wriggle in there like a bloodworm, and lay its eggs, and pretty soon your whole brain is squirming with maggots.

I told her to change her phone number, and she did, but the kid got the new one and kept calling, telling her my father had forgotten what he had on his feet and one of those hobnails struck a spark, and there went the old ballgame.

Never would have happened if you hadn't given him those boots, you stupid black bitch. That's the kind of thing he said, and probably worse that she wouldn't tell me.

Finally she had the phone taken out altogether. I told her she *had* to have a phone, living by herself like she did, but she wouldn't hear of it. She said, Sometimes he calls in the middle of the night, Georgie. You don't know how it is, lying awake and listening to the telephone ring and knowing it's that child. What kind of parents he has to let him do such things I can't imagine.

Unplug it at night, I said.

She said, I did. But sometimes it rings anyway.

I told her that was just her imagination. And I tried to believe it, but I never did, Mr. Bradley. If

that bad kid could get hold of Marlee's Steve Austin
lunchbox, and know how badly Vicky messed up her
tryout, and about the Trailman Specials—*if he could
stay young, year after year*—then sure, he could make
a phone ring even if it was unplugged. Bible says the
devil was set free to roam the earth, that God's hand
would not stay him. I don't know if that bad little kid
was *the* devil, but I know he was *a* devil.

Nor do I know if an ambulance call could have
saved Mama Nonie. All I know is that when she had
her heart attack, she couldn't call for one because the
phone was gone. She died alone, in her kitchen. A
neighbor lady found her the next day.

Carla and I went to the funeral, and after Nonie
was laid to rest, we spent the night in the house she
and my father had shared. I woke up from a bad
dream just before daybreak and couldn't get back to
sleep. When I heard the newspaper flop on the porch,
I went to get it and saw the flag was up on the mailbox. I walked down to the street in my robe and slippers and opened it. Inside there was a beanie with
a plastic propeller on top. I fished it out and it was
hot, like the person who'd just taken it off was burning up with fever. Touching it made me feel contami-
nated, but I turned it over and looked inside. It was
greasy with some sort of hair oil, the old-fashioned
stuff hardly anyone uses anymore. There were a few
orangey hairs sticking in it. There was also a note,
printed the way a kid might do it—the letters all
crooked and slanting downhill. The note said, KEEP
IT, I HAVE ANOTHER ONE.

I took the goddam thing inside—tweezed between
my thumb and index finger, that was as much as I
wanted to touch it—and stuck it in the kitchen

woodstove. I put a match to it and it went up all at once: *ka-floomp*. The flames were greenish. When Carla came down half an hour later, she sniffed and said, What's that awful smell? It's like low tide!

I told her it was most likely the septic tank out back, full up and needing to be pumped, but I knew better. That was the stink of methane, probably the last thing my father smelled before something sparked and blew him and those two others to kingdom come.

By then I had a job with an accounting firm—one of the biggest independents in the Midwest—and I worked my way up the ladder pretty quickly. I find that if you come in early, leave late, and keep your eye on the ball in between, that just about has to happen. Carla and I wanted kids, and we could afford them, but it didn't happen; she got her visit from the cardinal every month, just as regular as clockwork. We went to see an OB in Topeka, and he did all the usual tests. He said we were fine, and it was too early to talk about fertility treatments. He told us to go home, relax, and enjoy our sex life.

So that's what we did, and eleven months later, my wife's visits from the cardinal stopped. She had been raised Catholic, and stopped going to church when she was in college, but when she knew for sure she was pregnant, she started going again and dragged me with her. We went to St. Andrew's. I didn't mind. If she wanted to give God the credit for the bun in her oven, that was okay with me.

She was in her sixth month when the miscarriage happened. Because of the accident that wasn't really an accident. The baby lived for a few hours, then died. It was a girl. Because she needed a name, we named her Helen, after Carla's grandmother.

The accident happened after church. When mass was over, we were going to have a nice lunch downtown, then go home, where I'd watch the football game. Carla would put her feet up and rest and enjoy being pregnant. She *did* enjoy it, Mr. Bradley. Every day of it, even early on when she was sick in the mornings.

I saw the bad little kid as soon as we came out. Same baggy shorts, same sweater, same little round boy-tits and poochy belly. The beanie I found in the mailbox was blue, and the one he was wearing when we came out of the church was green, but it had the same kind of plastic propeller. I'd grown from a little boy to a man with the first threads of gray in his hair, but that bad little kid was still six years old. Seven at most.

He was standing back a little way. There was another kid in front of him. An *ordinary* kid, the kind who would grow up. He looked stunned and afraid. He had something in his hand. It looked like the ball on the end of the Bolo Bouncer Mama Nonie gave me all those years ago.

Go on, the bad little kid said. Unless you want me to take back that five bucks I gave you.

I don't want to, the ordinary kid said. I done changed my mind.

Carla didn't see any of this. She was standing at the top of the steps and talking to Father Patrick, telling him she'd enjoyed his homily, it had given her so much to think about. Those steps were granite, and they were steep.

I went to take her arm, I think, but maybe not. Maybe I was just frozen, the way I was when Vicky and I saw that kid after her lousy tryout for *The Music*

Man. Before I could unfreeze, or say anything, the bad little kid stepped forward. He reached into the pocket of his shorts and whipped out a cigarette lighter. As soon as he flicked it and I saw the spark, I knew what had happened that day in the Fair Deep mine, and it had nothing to do with the hobnails on my father's boots. Something started to fizz and spark on top of the red ball the ordinary kid was holding. He threw it just to get rid of it, and the bad little kid laughed. Except it was really a deep, snotty chuckle—*hgurr-hgurr-hgurr*, like that.

It struck the side of the steps, below the iron railing, and bounced back just before it went off with an ear-splitting bang and a flash of yellow light. That wasn't a firecracker or even a cherry bomb. That was an M-80. It startled Carla the way Carla herself must have startled Vicky that day in the box room at Fudgy Acres. I grabbed for her, but she was holding one of Father Patrick's hands in both of hers, and all I did was brush her elbow. They fell down the steps together. He broke his right arm and left leg. Carla broke an ankle and got a concussion. And she lost the baby. She lost Helen.

The kid who actually threw the M-80 walked into the police station the next day with his mother and owned up. He was devastated, of course, and said what kids always say and mostly mean after something goes wrong: it was an accident, he hadn't meant to hurt anyone. He said he wouldn't have thrown it at all, except the other boy lit the fuse and he was scared he'd lose his fingers. No, he said, he'd never seen the other kid before. No, he didn't know his name. Then he gave the policeman the five dollars the bad little kid had given him.

Carla didn't want to have much to do with me in the bedroom after that, and she stopped going to church. I kept on, though, and got involved with Conquest. You know what that is, Mr. Bradley, not because you're a Catholic, but because this is where you came in. I didn't bother with the religion part, they had Father Patrick for that, but I was happy to coach the baseball and touch football teams. I was always there for the cookouts and the campouts; I got a D code on my driver's license so I could take the boys to swim meets, amusement park fun days, and teen retreats in the church bus. And I always carried a gun. The .45 I bought at Wise Pawn and Loan—you know, the prosecution's Exhibit A. I carried that gun for five years, either in the glove compartment of my car, or in the toolbox of the Conquest bus. When I was coaching, I carried it in my gym bag.

Carla came to dislike my work with Conquest, because it took up so much of my free time. When Father Patrick asked for volunteers, I was always the first one to raise my hand. I'd have to say she was jealous. You're almost never home on weekends anymore, she said. I'm starting to wonder if you might be a little queer for those boys.

Probably I did seem a little queer, because I made a habit of picking out special boys and giving them extra attention. Making friends with them, helping them out. It wasn't hard. A lot of them came from low-income homes. Usually the single parent in those homes was a mom who had to work one minimum-wage job or even two or three to keep food on the table. If there was a car, she'd need it, so I'd be happy to pick my current special boy up for the Thursday-night Conquest meetings and bring him home again after. If I couldn't do that, I'd give the boys bus tokens. Never money, though—I found out early that giving those kids money was a bad idea.

I had some successes along the way. One kid—I think he had maybe two pairs of pants and three shirts to his name when I met him—was a math prodigy. I got him a scholarship at a private school and now he's a freshman at Kansas State, riding a full boat. A couple of others were dabbling in drugs, and I got at least one of them out of that. I think. You can never tell for sure. Another ran away after an argument with his mom and called me from Omaha a month later, right around the time his mother was deciding he was either dead or gone for good. I went and got him.

Working with those Conquest boys gave me a chance to do more good than I ever did filing tax returns and setting up tax-dodge corporations in Delaware. But that wasn't why I was doing it, only a side effect. Sometimes, Mr. Bradley, I'd take one of my special boys fishing out to Dixon Creek, or to the big river, on the lower city bridge. I was fishing, too, but not for trout or carp. For a long time I didn't feel a single nibble on my line. Then along came Ronald Gibson.

Ronnie was fifteen but looked younger. He was blind in one eye, so he couldn't play baseball or football, but he was a whiz at chess and all the other board games the boys played on rainy days. No one bullied him; he was sort of the group mascot. His father walked out on the family when he was nine or so, and he was starved for male attention. Pretty soon he was coming to me with all his problems. The main one, of course, was that bad eye. It was a congenital defect called a keratoconus—a misshapen cornea. A doctor told his mother it could be fixed with a corneal transplant, but it would be expensive, and his moms couldn't afford anything like that.

I went to Father Patrick, and between us we ran half a dozen fundraisers called Fresh Sight for Ronnie. We even got on TV—the local news on Channel 4. There was one shot of Ronnie and me walking in Barnum Park with my arm around his thin shoulders. Carla sniffed when she saw it. If you aren't queer for them, she said, people will say you are when they see that.

I didn't care what people said, because not long after that news report, I got the first tug on my line. Right in the middle of my head. It was the bad little kid. I'd finally caught his attention. I could *feel* him.

Ronnie had the surgery. He didn't get all the sight back in his bad eye, but he got most of it. For the first year afterward, he was supposed to wear special glasses that got dark in bright sunshine, but he didn't mind that; he said they made him look sort of cool.

Not too long after the operation, he and his mother came to see me one afternoon after school in the little Conquest office in the basement of St. Andrew's. She said, If there's ever anything we can do to pay you back, Mr. Hallas, all you have to do is ask.

I told them that wasn't necessary, it had been my pleasure. Then I pretended to get an idea.

There might be something, I said. Just a little thing.

What is it, Mr. H? Ronnie asked.

I said, One day last month I parked behind the church, and was halfway down the stairs when I remembered I hadn't locked up my car. I went back and saw a kid inside it, rummaging around. I shouted at him and he was out like a shot with my little change box, the one I keep in the glove compartment for tolls. I chased him, but he was too fast for me.

All I want, I told Ronnie and his moms, is to find him and talk to him. Tell him what I tell all you boys—stealing's the wrong start in life.

Ronnie asked me what he looked like.

Short and kind of pudgy, I said. Bright orange hair, a real carrottop. When I saw him, he was wearing gray shorts and a green sweater with stripes the same color as his hair.

Mrs. Gibson said, Oh my goodness. Was he wearing a little hat with a propeller on top?

Why, yes, I said, keeping my voice nice and steady. Now that you mention it, I believe he was.

I've seen him across the street, she said. I thought he moved into one of the projects over there.

What about you, Ronnie? I asked.

Nope, he said. Never seen him.

Well, if you do, don't say anything to him. Just come and get me. Will you do that?

He said he would, and I was satisfied. Because I knew the bad kid was back, and I knew I'd be around when he made his move. He'd *want* me to be around, because that was the whole point. I was the one he wanted to hurt. All the others—Marlee, Vicky, my father, Mama Nonie—were just collateral damage.

A week went past, then two. I was beginning to think the kid had sensed what I was planning. Then one day—*the* day, Mr. Bradley—one of the boys ran into the playground behind the church, where I was helping a bunch of them set up the volleyball net.

A kid knocked Ronnie down and stoled his glasses! this boy shouted. Then he ran off into the park! Ronnie's chasing him!

I didn't wait, just grabbed up my gym bag—I took it everywhere with me during the years when I had special boys—and ran through the gate into Barnum Park. I knew it wasn't the bad little kid who stole Ronnie's glasses; that wasn't his style. The glasses stealer would be as ordinary as the M-80 thrower, and just as sorry after whatever the bad little kid was planning played out. If I *let* it play out.

Ronnie wasn't an athletic boy, and he couldn't run fast. The glasses-stealing boy must have seen that, because he pulled up short on the far side of the park, waving them over his head and shouting, Come and get em, Ray Charles! Come and get em, Stevie Wonder!

I could hear the traffic on Barnum Boulevard, and knew exactly what that bad boy was planning. He thought what worked once would work again. It was a pair of special glare-reducing glasses instead of a Steve Austin lunchbox, but the basic idea was the same. Later the kid who took Ronnie's glasses would cry and say *he* didn't know what was going to happen, he thought it was just a joke, or a tease, or maybe payback for Ronnie pushing the pudgy little carrottop down on the sidewalk.

I could easily have caught up with Ronnie, but at first I didn't. He was my lure, you see, and the last thing I wanted was to reel him in too soon. When Ronnie got close, the boy doing the bad little kid's dirty work darted through the stone arch between the park and Barnum Boulevard, still waving Ronnie's glasses over his head. Ronnie ran after him and I came third. I jogged as I unzipped my gym bag, but once I had the revolver in my hand, I dropped the bag and went into overdrive.

Stay back! I shouted at Ronnie as I ran past him. Don't you go one step further!

He did what I said, and thank God for that. If anything had happened to him, I wouldn't be here waiting for the needle, Mr. Bradley; I would have killed myself.

When I got through the arch, I saw the bad little kid waiting on the sidewalk. He was the same as always. The big kid was handing him Ronnie's glasses, and the bad little kid was handing him a bill. When he saw me coming, he lost the nasty little smirk on those weird red lips of his for the first time. Because that wasn't the plan. The plan was Ronnie first, *then* me. Ronnie was supposed to chase the bad little kid into the street and be hit by a truck or a bus. I was supposed to come last. And see it.

Carrottop ran into Barnum Boulevard. You know what it looks like outside the park—at least you ought to, after the prosecution showed their video three times at the trial. Three lanes in each direction, two for travel and one for turning, with a concrete divider in the middle. The bad little kid looked back when he got to the divider, and by then he was a lot more than startled. That look was pure fear. Seeing it made me happy for the first time since Carla went upsy-turvy down those church steps.

One quick glimpse was all I got, then he charged into the southbound lanes without a single look to see what might be coming at him. I ran into the northbound lanes the same way. I knew I might get hit, but I didn't care. At least it would be a genuine accident, no mysterious stuck accelerator. You can call that suicidal, but it wasn't. I just couldn't let him slip away.

I might not have seen him for another twenty years, and by then I would have been an old man.

I don't know how close I came to getting creamed, but I heard plenty of screeching brakes and squalling tires. A car swerved to avoid the kid and sideswiped a panel truck. Someone called me a crazy asshole. Someone else shouted, What the fuck is he doing? That was just background noise. I had all my attention fixed on the bad little kid—eyes on the prize, right?

He was running as fast as he could, but no matter what kind of monster he was on the inside, on the outside he was stuck with short legs and a fat ass, and he never had a chance. All he could hope for was that a car would hit me, but none of them did.

He got to the far side and stumbled on the curb. I heard some woman—a stout lady with dyed blond hair—scream, That man has a gun! Mrs. Jane Hurley. She testified at the trial.

The kid tried to get up. I said, This is for Marlee, you little sonofabitch, and shot him in the back. That was number one.

He started crawling on his hands and knees. Blood was dripping onto the sidewalk. I said, This is for Vicky, and put another one in his back. That was number two. Then I said, This is for my dad and Mama Nonie, and put a bullet into the back of each knee, just where those baggy gray shorts ended. That was three and four.

Lots of people were screaming by then. Some man was yelling, Get it away from him, just tackle him! But no one did.

The bad little kid rolled over and looked at me. When I saw his face, I almost stopped. He didn't look six or seven anymore. Bewildered and in pain, he looked no more than five. His beanie had fallen off and lay next to him on its side. One of the two plastic propeller blades was all crooked. My God, I thought. I have shot a blameless child, and he's lying here at my feet, mortally wounded.

Yes, he almost got me. It was a good act, Mr. Bradley, real Academy Award stuff, but then the mask slipped. He could make most of his face all wounded and hurt, but not his eyes. That *thing* was still in his eyes. You can't stop me, his eyes were saying. You *won't* stop me until I'm done with you, and I'm not done with you yet.

Get the gun away from him, somebody! a woman yelled. Before he murders that child!

A big fellow ran toward me—he testified too, I believe—but I pointed my gun at him and he stepped away fast with his hands raised.

I turned back to the bad little kid and shot him in the chest and said, For Baby Helen. That was number five. By then blood was pouring out of his mouth and down his chin. My .45 was an old-fashioned six-shooter, so there was only one bullet left. I dropped to one knee in a puddle of his blood. It was red, but it should have been black. Like the goo that comes out of a poisonous insect when you step on it. I put the muzzle of the gun right between his eyes.

This is for me, I said. Now go back to whatever hell you came from. I pulled the trigger and that was number six. But just before I did, those green eyes of his met mine.

I'm not done with you, his eyes said. I'm not and I won't be until you stop drawing breath. Maybe not even then. Maybe I'll be waiting for you on the other side.

His head flopped over. One of his feet twitched and then went still. I put the gun down beside his body, raised my hands, and started to stand up. A couple of men grabbed me before I could. One of them kneed me in the groin. The other punched me in the face. A few more joined in. One was Mrs. Hurley. She got me at least two good ones. She didn't testify about *that* at the trial, did she?

Not that I blame her, Counselor. I don't blame any of them. What they saw lying on the sidewalk that day was a little boy so disfigured by bullets that his own mother wouldn't have recognized him.

Supposing he ever had one.

7

McGregor took Bradley's client back into the bowels of Needle Manor for the midday count, promising to bring him back afterward.

"I'll bring you some soup and a sandwich, if you want it," McGregor told Bradley. "You must be hungry."

Bradley wasn't. Not after all that. He sat waiting on his side of the Plexiglas partition, hands folded on his blank legal pad. He was meditating on the ruination of lives. Of the two under current consideration, the demolition of Hallas's was easier to accept, because the man was clearly mad. If he had taken the stand at his trial and told this story—and in the same reasonable, how-can-you-possibly-doubt-me tone of voice—Bradley felt sure Hallas would now be in one of the state's two maximum security mental institutions instead of awaiting sequential injections of sodium thiopental, pancuronium bromide, and potassium chloride: the lethal cocktail Needle Manor inmates called Goodnight, Mother.

But Hallas, most likely pushed over the edge of sanity by the loss of his own child, had gotten at least half a life. It had clearly been an unhappy one, beset by paranoid fantasies and delusions of persecution, but—to bend an old aphorism—half a life was better than none. The little boy was a far sadder case. According to the state medical examiner, the child who had just happened to be on Barnum Boulevard at the wrong time had been no more than eight and probably closer to six or seven. That wasn't a life, it was a prologue.

McGregor led Hallas back, chained him to his chair, and asked how much longer they'd be. "Because he didn't want any lunch, but I wouldn't mind having some."

"Not long," Bradley said. In truth he only had one question, and when Hallas was seated once more, he asked it.

"Why you?"

Hallas raised his eyebrows. "Beg pardon?"

"This demon—I presume that's what you think he was—why did he pick you?"

Hallas smiled, but it was a mere stretching of the lips. "That's rather naïve, Counselor. You might as well ask why one baby is born with a misshapen cornea, as Ronnie Gibson was, and the next fifty delivered in the same hospital are just fine. Or why a good man leading a decent life is struck down by a brain tumor at thirty and a monster who helped oversee the gas chambers of Dachau can live to be a hundred. If you're asking why bad things happen to good people, you've come to the wrong place."

You shot a fleeing child six times, Bradley thought, the last three or four at point-blank range. How in God's name does that make you a good person?

"Before you go," Hallas said, "let me ask *you* something."

Bradley waited.

"Have the police identified him yet?"

Hallas asked in the idle tone of a prisoner who is just making conversation in order to stay out of his cell a little longer, but for the first time since this lengthy visit began, his eyes shone with real life and interest.

"I don't believe so," Bradley replied carefully.

In fact, he knew they hadn't. He had a source in the prosecutor's office who would have given him the child's name and background well before the newspapers got hold of it and published it, as they were of course eager to do; Unknown Boy Victim was a human interest story that had gone nationwide. It had died down in the last four months or so, but following Hallas's execution, it would certainly flare up again.

"I'd tell you to think about that," Hallas said, "but I don't need to, do I? You've *been* thinking about it. It probably hasn't been keeping you up nights, but yes, you've been thinking about it."

Bradley didn't reply.

This time Hallas's smile was wide and genuine. "I know you don't believe a word of what I've told you, and hey, who could blame you? But just for a minute engage those brains of yours and think about it. This was a white male child—the sort of kid most apt to be missed and eagerly sought after in a society that still values white male children above all others. The kiddies are fingerprinted these days as a matter of course when they start school, to help ID them if they're lost, murdered, or abducted. I believe in this state it's even a law. Or am I wrong?"

"You're not." Bradley said this reluctantly. "But it would be wrong to make too much of it, George. This kid happened to fall through the cracks, that's all. It happens. The system is fallible."

Hallas's smile became a full-fledged grin. "Keep telling yourself that, Mr. Bradley. You just keep telling yourself that." He turned and waved to McGregor, who removed his earbuds and got to his feet.

"All done?"

"Yes," Hallas said. He turned back to Bradley as McGregor bent to unchain him. His grin—the only one Bradley had ever seen on his face—was gone as if it had never been. "Will you come? When it's time?"

"I'll be here," Bradley said.

8

And so he was, six days later, when the curtains in the observation room drew back at 11:52 a.m. to reveal the death chamber with its white tiles and Y-shaped table. Only two other witnesses were present. One was Father Patrick of St. Andrew's. Bradley sat with him in the back row. The district attorney was all the way down front with his arms folded across his chest and his eyes never leaving the room on the other side of the window.

The execution party (a grotesque term if ever there

was one, Bradley thought) was in place. There were five in all: Warden Toomey; McGregor and two other guards; a pair of medical personages in white coats. The star of the show lay on the table, his outstretched arms secured by Velcro straps, but when the curtains opened, Bradley's eye was first taken by the warden, who was weirdly sporty in an open-necked blue shirt that would have been more appropriate on the golf course.

Wearing a seatbelt around his waist and a three-point harness over his shoulders, George Hallas looked more ready to zoom off in a space capsule than to die by lethal injection. As per his request, there was no chaplain, but when he saw Bradley and Father Patrick, he raised one hand as far as the wrist straps would allow in a gesture of recognition.

Patrick raised a hand in return, then turned toward Bradley. His face was paper pale. "Have you ever attended one of these?"

Bradley shook his head. His mouth was dry, and he didn't trust himself to speak in a normal tone of voice.

"Me, either. I hope I'll be all right. He . . ." Father Patrick swallowed. "He was very good to all the children. They loved him. I just can't believe . . . even now I just can't believe . . . ."

Bradley couldn't, either. Yet he did. Had to.

The DA turned to them, frowning like Moses above his crossed arms. "Zip your lips, gentlemen."

Hallas looked around the last room he would ever inhabit. He seemed bewildered, as if he wasn't quite sure where he was or what was happening. McGregor laid a hand on his chest in a comforting gesture. It was now 11:58.

One of the whitecoats—an IV tech, Bradley

assumed—cinched a length of rubber tubing around Hallas's right forearm, then slipped in a needle and taped it down. The needle was attached to an IV line. The line went to a wall console, where three red lamps burned above three switches. The second whitecoat moved to the console and clasped his hands before him. Now the only movement in the death chamber came from George Hallas, who was blinking his eyes rapidly.

"Are they doing it?" Father Patrick whispered. "I can't tell."

"I can't either," Bradley whispered back. "Maybe, but—"

There was an amplified click that made them both jump (the state's legal representative remained as still as a statue). The warden said, "Can you folks hear me okay in there?"

The DA gave a thumbs-up, then crossed his arms again.

The warden turned to Hallas. "George Peter Hallas, you have been condemned to death by a jury of your peers, a sentence affirmed by this state's supreme court and the Supreme Court of the United States of America."

Like they ever said balls about it one way or the other, Bradley thought.

"Do you have any last words before sentence is carried out?"

Hallas began to shake his head, then appeared to change his mind. He peered through the glass and into the observation room.

"Hello, Mr. Bradley. I'm glad you came. Listen, okay? I'd watch out, if I were you. Remember, *it comes as a child*."

"Is that it?" the warden asked, almost jovially.

Hallas regarded the warden. "One more thing, I guess. Where in the *Christ* did you get that shirt?"

Warden Toomey blinked as if someone had suddenly flicked cold water in his face, then turned to the doctor. "Are you prepared?"

The whitecoat standing beside the panel nodded. The warden recited a mouthful of legal rigamarole, checked the clock, and frowned. It was 12:01 p.m., which made them a minute late. He pointed to the whitecoat like a stage director cueing an actor. The whitecoat flicked the switches and the three red lights turned green.

The intercom was still open and Bradley heard Hallas paraphrase Father Patrick. "Is it happening?"

No one answered. It didn't matter. His eyes closed. He made a snoring sound. A minute passed. Another long, ragged snore. Then two minutes. Then four. No snores and no movement. Bradley looked around. Father Patrick was gone.

9

A cold prairie wind was blowing when Bradley left Needle Manor. He zipped his coat and stood taking long breaths, trying to get as much outside as possible into his insides, and as fast as he could. It wasn't the execution per se; except for the warden's bizarre blue shirt, it had seemed as prosaic as getting a tetanus shot or a shingles vaccination. That was actually the horror of it.

Something moved at the corner of his eye in the Chicken Run, where the condemned prisoners took their exercise. Except there wasn't supposed to be anyone there. Exercise periods were canceled on days when an execution was scheduled. McGregor had told him this. And sure enough, when he turned his head, he saw the Chicken Run was empty.

Bradley thought, It comes as a child.

He laughed. He made himself laugh. It was just a well-deserved case of the whim-whams, no more than that. As if to prove it to himself, he shivered.

Father Patrick's elderly Volvo had departed. There was no car but his own in the small visitors' parking lot adjacent to Needle Manor. Bradley walked a few steps in that direction, then whirled suddenly toward the Chicken Run, the hem of his overcoat flapping around his knees. No one there. Of course not, Jesus Christ. George Hallas had been mad, and even if his bad little kid *had* been real, he was dead now. Six shots from a .45 pretty much guaranteed dead.

Bradley resumed walking, but when he got around the hood of his car, he once more came to a halt. An ugly scratch ran all the way from his Ford's front bumper to the rear left taillight. Someone had keyed his car. In a maximum security prison where you had to pass three walls and a like number of checkpoints, someone had keyed his car.

Bradley's first thought was of the DA, who had sat there with his arms crossed over his chest, a portrait of Talmudic self-righteousness. But the idea had no logic to support it. The DA had gotten what he wanted, after all; he had watched George Hallas die.

Bradley opened the car door, which he had not bothered to lock—he was in a *prison*, after all—and stood stock-still for several seconds. Then, as if controlled by a force outside himself, his hand rose slowly to his mouth and covered it. Lying on the driver's seat was a beanie with a propeller on top. One of the two plastic blades was crooked.

At last he bent and plucked it up, tweezing it between two fingers just as Hallas had done. Bradley turned it over. A note had been tucked inside, the letters crooked and bunched together and downslanted. A kid's printing.

KEEP IT, I HAVE ANOTHER ONE.

He heard a child's laughter, high and bright. He looked toward the Chicken Run, but it was still empty.

He turned the note over and saw another, even briefer communiqué:

SEE YOU SOON.

For Russ Dorr

In *The Hair of Harold Roux*, probably the best novel about writing ever published, Thomas Williams offers a striking metaphor, maybe even a parable, for how a story is born. He envisions a dark plain with a small fire burning on it. One by one, people come out of the dark to warm themselves. Each one brings a little fuel, and eventually the small fire becomes a blaze with the characters standing around it, their faces brightly lit and each beautiful in its own way.

One night as I lay drifting toward sleep, I saw a very small fire—a kerosene lantern, in fact—with a man trying to read a newspaper by its light. Other men came with their own lanterns, casting more light on a dreary landscape that turned out to be the Dakota Territory.

I have visions like this frequently, although it makes me uneasy to admit it. I don't always tell the stories that go with them; sometimes the fire goes out. This one had to be told, because I knew exactly what kind of language I wanted to use: dry and laconic, not like my usual style at all. I had no idea where the story was going, but I felt perfectly confident that the language would take me there. And it did.

A Death

Jim Trusdale had a shack on the west side of his father's gone-to-seed ranch, and that's where he was when Sheriff Barclay and half a dozen deputized townsmen found him, sitting in the one chair by the cold stove, wearing a dirty barn coat and reading an old issue of the *Black Hills Pioneer* by lantern light. Looking at it, anyway.

Sheriff Barclay stood in the doorway, mostly filling it up. He was holding his own lantern. "Come out of there, Jim, and do it with your hands up. I ain't drawn my pistol and don't want to."

Trusdale came out. He still had the newspaper in one of his raised hands. He stood there looking at the sheriff out of his flat gray eyes. The sheriff looked back. So did the others, four on horseback and two on the seat of an old buckboard with HINES MORTUARY printed on the side in faded yellow letters.

"I notice you ain't asked why we're here," Sheriff Barclay said.

"Why are you here, Sheriff?"

"Where is your hat, Jim?"

Trusdale put the hand not holding the newspaper

to his head as if to feel for his hat, which was a flat brown plainsman and not there.

"In your place, is it?" the sheriff asked. A cold breeze kicked up, blowing the horses' manes and flattening the grass in a wave that ran south.

"No," Trusdale said, "I don't believe it is."

"Then where?"

"I might have lost it."

"You need to get in the back of the wagon," the sheriff said.

"I don't want to ride in no funeral hack," Trusdale said. "That's bad luck."

"You got bad luck all over," one of the men said. "You're painted in it. Get in."

Trusdale went to the back of the buckboard and climbed up. The breeze kicked again, harder, and he turned up the collar of his barn coat.

The two men on the seat of the buckboard got down and stood either side of it. One drew his gun, the other did not. Trusdale knew their faces but not their names. They were town men. The sheriff and the other four went into his shack. One of them was Hines, the undertaker. They were in there for some time. They even opened the stove, which was unlit in spite of the cold evening, and dug through the ashes. At last they came out.

"No hat," Sheriff Barclay said, "and we would have seen it. That's a damn big hat. Got anything to say about that?"

"It's too bad I lost it. My father gave it to me back when he was still right in the head."

"Where is it, then?"

"Told you, I might have lost it. Or had it stoled. That might have happened, too. Say, I was going to bed right soon."

"Never mind going to bed. You were in town this afternoon, weren't you?"

"Sure he was," one of the men said, mounting up again. "I seen him myself. Wearing that hat, too."

"Shut up, Dave," Sheriff Barclay said. "Were you in town, Jim?"

"Yes, sir, I was," Trusdale said.

"In the Chuck-a-Luck?"

"Yes, sir, I was. I walked from here, and had two drinks, and then I walked home. I guess the Chuck-a-Luck's where I lost my hat."

"That's your story?"

Trusdale looked up at the black November sky. "It's the only story I got."

"Look at me, son."

Trusdale looked at him.

"That's your story?"

"Told you, the only one I got," Trusdale said, looking at him.

Sheriff Barclay sighed. "All right, let's go to town."

"Why?"

"Because you're arrested."

"Ain't got a brain in his fuckin head," one of the men remarked. "Makes his daddy look smart."

They went back to town. It was four miles. Trusdale rode in the back of the mortuary wagon with the collar of his coat turned up. Without turning around, the man holding the reins said, "Did you rape her as well as steal her dollar, you hound?"

"I don't know what you're talking about," Trusdale said.

The rest of the trip went in silence except for the wind. In town, people lined the street. At first they were silent. Then an old woman in a brown shawl

ran at the funeral hack in a sort of limping run and
spit at Trusdale. She missed, but there was a spatter
of applause.

At the jail, Sheriff Barclay helped Trusdale down
from the wagon. The wind was brisk now, and
smelled of snow. Tumbleweeds blew straight down
the main street and toward the town water tower,
where they piled up against a shakepole fence and
rattled there.

"Hang that baby-killer!" a man shouted, and
someone threw a rock. It went between Trusdale's
head and right shoulder and clattered on the board
sidewalk.

Sheriff Barclay turned and held up his lantern and
surveyed the crowd that had gathered in front of the
mercantile. "Don't do that," he said. "Don't act foolish. This is in hand."

The sheriff took Trusdale through his office, holding him by his upper arm, and into the jail. There
were two cells. Barclay led Trusdale into the one on
the left. There was a bunk and a stool and a waste
bucket. Trusdale made to sit down on the stool and
Barclay said, "No. Just stand there."

The sheriff looked around and saw the possemen
crowding into the doorway. "You all get out of here,"
he said.

"Otis," said the one named Dave, "what if he
attacks you?"

"Then I will subdue him. I thank you for doing
your duty, but now you need to scat."

When they were gone, he said, "Take off that coat
and give it to me."

Trusdale took off his barn coat and began shivering. Underneath he was wearing nothing but an

undershirt and corduroy pants so worn the wale was almost gone and one knee was out. Sheriff Barclay went through the pockets of the coat and found a twist of tobacco in a page of the J. W. Sears catalogue, and an old lottery ticket promising a payoff in pesos. There was also a black marble.

"That's my lucky marble," Trusdale said. "I had it since I was a boy."

"Turn out your pants pockets."

Trusdale turned them out. He had a penny and three nickels and a folded-up news clipping about the Nevada silver rush that looked as old as the Mexican lottery ticket.

"Take off your boots."

Trusdale took them off. Barclay took them and felt inside them. There was a hole in one sole the size of a dime.

"Now your stockings."

Barclay turned them inside out, and tossed them aside.

"Drop your pants."

"I don't want to."

"No more than I want to see what's in there, but drop them anyway."

Trusdale dropped his pants. He wasn't wearing underdrawers.

"Turn around and spread your cheeks."

Trusdale turned, grabbed his buttocks, and pulled them apart. Sheriff Barclay winced, sighed, and poked a finger into Trusdale's anus. Trusdale groaned. Barclay removed his finger, wincing again at the soft pop, and wiped his finger on Trusdale's undershirt.

"Where is it, Jim?"

"My hat?"

"You think I went up your ass looking for your hat? Or through the ashes in your stove? Are you being smart?"

Trusdale pulled up his trousers and buttoned them. Then he stood shivering and barefoot. Not long ago he had been at home, reading his newspaper and thinking about starting a fire in the stove, but that seemed long ago.

"I've got your hat in my office."

"Then why did you ask about it?"

"To see what you'd say. That hat is all settled. What I really want to know is where you put the girl's silver dollar. It's not in your house, or your pockets, or up your poop-chute. Did you get feeling guilty and throw it away?"

"I don't know about no silver dollar. Can I have my hat back?"

"No. It's evidence. Jim Trusdale, I'm arresting you for the murder of Rebecca Cline. Do you have anything you want to say to that?"

"Yes, sir. That I don't know no Rebecca Cline."

The sheriff left the cell, closed the door, took a key from the wall, and locked it. The tumblers screeched as they turned. The cell mostly housed drunks and was rarely locked. He looked in at Trusdale and said, "I feel sorry for you, Jim. Hell ain't too hot for a man who'd do such a thing."

"What thing?"

The sheriff clumped away without any reply.

Trusdale stayed in the cell for a week, eating grub from Mother's Best, sleeping on the bunk, shitting and pissing in the bucket, which was emptied every two days. His father didn't come to see him, because his father had gone foolish in his eighties and in his nineties was being cared for by a couple of squaws, one Sioux and the other Lakota. Sometimes they stood on the porch of the deserted bunkhouse and sang hymns in harmony. His brother was in Nevada, hunting for silver.

Sometimes children came and stood in the alley outside his cell, chanting *Hangman, hangman, come on down*. Sometimes men stood out there and threatened to cut off his privates. Once Rebecca Cline's mother came and said she would hang him herself, were she allowed. "How could you kill my baby?" she asked through the barred window. "She was only ten years old, and twas her birthday."

"Ma'am," Trusdale said, standing on the bunk so he could look down at her white upturned face, "I didn't kill your baby nor no one."

"Black liar," she said, and went away.

Almost everyone in town attended the child's funeral. The squaws went. Even the two whores who plied their trade in the Chuck-a-Luck went. Trusdale heard the singing from his cell, as he squatted over the bucket in the corner.

Sheriff Barclay telegraphed Fort Pierre, and eventually the circuit-riding judge came. He was newly appointed and young for the job, a dandy with long blond hair down his back like Wild Bill Hickok. His name was Roger Mizell. He wore small round spectacles, and in both the Chuck-a-Luck and Mother's Best proved himself a man with an eye for the ladies, although he wore a wedding band.

There was no lawyer in town to serve as Trusdale's defense, so Mizell called on George Andrews, owner of the mercantile, the hostelry, and the Good Rest Hotel. Andrews had gotten two years of higher education at a business school in Omaha. He said he would serve as Trusdale's attorney only if Mr. and Mrs. Cline agreed.

"Then go see them," Mizell said. He was in the barber shop, tilted back in the chair and taking a shave. "Don't let the grass grow under your feet."

"Well," Mr. Cline said, after Andrews had stated his business, "I got a question. If he doesn't have someone to stand for him, can they still hang him?"

"That would not be American justice," George Andrews said. "And although we are not one of the United States just yet, we will be soon."

"Can he wriggle out of it?" Mrs. Cline asked.

"No, ma'am," Andrews said. "I don't see how."

"Then do your duty and God bless you," Mrs. Cline said.

The trial lasted through one November morning and halfway into the afternoon. It was held in the municipal hall, and on that day there were snow flurries as fine as wedding lace. Slate-gray clouds rolling toward town threatened a bigger storm. Roger Mizell, who had familiarized himself with the case, served as prosecuting attorney as well as judge.

"Like a banker taking out a loan from himself and then paying himself interest," one of the jurors was overheard to say during the lunch break at Mother's Best, and although no one disagreed with this, no one suggested it was a bad idea. It had a certain economy, after all.

Prosecutor Mizell called half a dozen witnesses, and Judge Mizell never objected once to his line of questioning. Mr. Cline testified first and Sheriff Barclay came last. The story that emerged was a simple one. At noon on the day of Rebecca Cline's murder, there had been a birthday party with cake and ice cream. Several of Rebecca's friends attended. Around two o'clock, while the little girls were playing Pin the Tail on the Donkey and Musical Chairs, Jim Trusdale entered the Chuck-a-Luck and ordered a knock of whiskey. He was wearing his plainsman's hat. He made the drink last, and when it was gone, he ordered another.

Did he at any point take off the hat? Perhaps hang it on one of the hooks by the door? No one could remember.

"Only I never seen him without it," said Dale Gerard, the barman. "He was partial to that hat. If he did take it off, he probably laid it on the bar beside him. He had his second drink, and then he left."

"Was his hat on the bar when he left?" Mizell asked.

"No, sir."

"Was it on one of the hooks when you closed up shop for the night?"

"No, sir."

Around three o'clock that day, Rebecca Cline left her house at the south end of town to visit the apothecary on Main Street. Her mother told her she could buy some candy with her birthday dollar, but not eat it, because she had had sweets enough for one day. When five o'clock came and she hadn't returned home, Mr. Cline and some other men searched for her. They found her in Barker's Alley, between the stage depot and the Good Rest. She had been strangled. Her silver dollar was gone. It was only when the grieving father took her in his arms that the men saw Trusdale's broad-brimmed leather hat. It had been hidden beneath the skirt of the girl's party dress.

During the jury's lunch hour, hammering was heard from behind the stage depot and not ninety paces from the scene of the crime. This was the gallows going up. The work was supervised by the town's best carpenter, whose name, appropriately enough, was Mr. John House. Big snow was coming, and the road to Fort Pierre would be impassable, perhaps for a week, perhaps for the entire winter. There were no plans to jug Trusdale in the local calaboose until spring. There was no economy in that.

"Nothing to building a gallows," House told folks who came to watch. "A child could build one of these."

He told how a lever-operated beam would run beneath the trapdoor, and how it would be axle-greased to make sure there wouldn't be any last-minute hold-ups. "If you have to do a thing like this, you want to do it right the first time," House said.

In the afternoon, George Andrews put Trusdale on the stand. This occasioned some hissing from the spectators, which Judge Mizell gaveled down, promising to clear the courtroom if folks couldn't behave themselves.

"Did you enter the Chuck-a-Luck Saloon on the day in question?" Andrews asked when order had been restored.

"I guess so," Trusdale said. "Otherwise I wouldn't be here."

There was some laughter at that, which Mizell also gaveled down, although he was smiling himself and did not issue a second admonition.

"Did you order two drinks?"

"Yes, sir, I did. Two was all I had money for."

"But you got another dollar right quick, didn't you, you hound?" Abel Hines shouted.

Mizell pointed his gavel first at Hines, then at Sheriff Barclay, sitting in the front row. "Sheriff, escort that man out and charge him with disorderly conduct, if you please."

Barclay escorted Hines out, but did not charge him with disorderly conduct. He asked what had gotten into him instead.

"I'm sorry, Otis," Hines said. "It was seeing him sitting there with his bare face hanging out."

"You go on downstreet and see if John House needs some help with his work," Barclay said. "Don't come back in here until this mess is over."

"He's got all the help he needs, and it's snowing hard now."

"You won't blow away. Go on."

Meanwhile, Trusdale continued to testify. No, he hadn't left the Chuck-a-Luck wearing his hat, but hadn't realized it until he got to his place. By then, he said, he was too tired to walk all the way back to town in search of it. Besides, it was dark.

Mizell broke in. "Are you asking this court to believe you walked four miles without realizing you weren't wearing your damn hat?"

"I guess since I wear it all the time, I just figured it must be there," Trusdale said. This elicited another gust of laughter.

Barclay came back in and took his place next to Dave Fisher. "What are they laughing at?"

"Dummy don't need a hangman," Fisher said. "He's tying the knot all by himself. I guess it shouldn't be funny, but it's pretty comical, just the same."

"Did you encounter Rebecca Cline in that alley?"

George Andrews asked in a loud voice. With every eye on him, he had discovered a heretofore hidden flair for the dramatic. "Did you encounter her and steal her birthday dollar?"

"No, sir," Trusdale said.

"Did you kill her?"

"No, sir. I didn't even know who she was."

Mr. Cline rose from his seat and shouted, "You lying sonofabitch!"

"I ain't lying," Trusdale said, and that was when Sheriff Barclay believed him.

"I have no further questions," George Andrews said, and walked back to his seat.

Trusdale started to get up, but Mizell told him to sit still and answer a few more questions.

"Do you continue to contend, Mr. Trusdale, that someone stole your hat while you were drinking in the Chuck-a-Luck, and that someone put it on, and went into the alley, and killed Rebecca Cline, and left it there to implicate you?"

Trusdale was silent.

"Answer the question, Mr. Trusdale."

"Sir, I don't know what implicate means."

"Do you expect us to believe someone framed you for this heinous murder?"

Trusdale considered, twisting his hands together. At last he said, "Maybe somebody took it by mistake and throwed it away."

Mizell looked out at the rapt gallery. "Did anyone here take Mr. Trusdale's hat by mistake?"

There was silence, except for the wind. It was picking up. The snow was no longer flurries. The first big storm of winter had arrived. That was the one townsfolk called the Wolf Winter, because the wolves came

down from the Black Hills in packs to hunt for garbage.

"I have no more questions," Mizell said, "and due
to the weather, we are going to dispense with any
closing statements. The jury will retire to consider
a verdict. You have three choices, gentlemen—
innocent, manslaughter, or murder in the first
degree."

"Girlslaughter, more like it," someone remarked.

Sheriff Barclay and Dave Fisher retired to the
Chuck-a-Luck. Abel Hines joined them, brushing
snow from the shoulders of his coat. Dale Gerard
served them schooners of beer on the house.

"Mizell might not have had no more questions,"
Barclay said, "but I got one. Never mind the hat, if
Trusdale killed her, how come we never found that
silver dollar?"

"Because he got scared and threw it away," Hines
said.

"I don't think so. He's too bone-stupid. If he'd had
that dollar, he'd have gone back to the Chuck-a-Luck
and drunk it up."

"What are you saying?" Dave asked. "That you
think he's innocent?"

"I'm saying I wish we'd found that cartwheel."

"Maybe he lost it out a hole in his pocket."

"He didn't have any holes in his pockets," Barclay
said. "Only one in his boot, and it wasn't big enough
for a dollar to get through." He drank some of his
beer. The wind gusted, and tumbleweeds blew up
Main Street, looking like ghostly brains in the snow.

The jury took an hour and a half. "We voted to
hang him on the first ballot," Kelton Fisher said later,
"but we wanted it to look decent."

Mizell asked Trusdale if he had anything to say before sentence was passed.

"I can't think of nothing," Trusdale said. "Just I never killed that girl."

The storm blew for three days. John House asked Barclay how much he reckoned Trusdale weighed, and Barclay said he guessed the man went around one forty. House made a dummy out of burlap sacks and filled it with stones, weighing it on the hostelry scales until the needle stood pat on one forty. Then he hung the dummy while half the town stood around in the snowdrifts and watched. The trial run went all right.

On the night before the execution, the weather cleared. Sheriff Barclay told Trusdale he could have anything he wanted for dinner. Trusdale asked for steak and eggs, with homefries on the side soaked in gravy. Barclay bought it out of his own pocket, and sat at his desk cleaning his fingernails and listening to the steady clink of Trusdale's knife and fork on the china plate. When it stopped, he went in. Trusdale was sitting on his bunk. His plate was so clean Barclay figured he must have lapped up the last of the gravy like a dog. He was crying.

"Something just come to me," Trusdale said.

"What's that, Jim?"

"If they hang me tomorrow morning, I'll go into my grave with steak and eggs still in my belly. It won't have no chance to work through."

For a moment Barclay said nothing. He was horrified not by the image but because Trusdale had thought of it. Then he said, "Wipe your nose."

Trusdale wiped it.

"Now listen to me, Jim, because this is your last chance. You were in that bar in the middle of the afternoon. Not many people in there then. Isn't that right?"

"I guess it is."

"Then who took your hat? Close your eyes. Think back. See it."

Trusdale closed his eyes. Barclay waited. At last Trusdale opened his eyes, which were red from crying. "I can't even remember was I wearing it."

Barclay sighed. "Give me your plate, and mind that knife."

Trusdale handed the plate through the bars with the knife and fork laid on it, and said he wished he could have some beer. Barclay thought it over, then put on his heavy coat and Stetson and walked down to the Chuck-a-Luck, where he got a small pail of beer from Dale Gerard. Undertaker Hines was just finishing a glass of wine. He followed Barclay out into the wind and cold.

"Big day tomorrow," Barclay said. "There hasn't been a hanging here in ten years, and with luck there won't be another for ten more. I'll be gone out of the job by then. I wish I was now."

Hines looked at him. "You really don't think he killed her."

"If he didn't," Barclay said, "whoever did is still walking around."

The hanging was at nine o'clock the next morning. The day was windy and bitterly cold, but most of the town turned out to watch. Pastor Ray Rowles stood on the scaffold next to John House. Both of them were shivering in spite of their coats and scarves. The pages of Pastor Rowles's Bible fluttered. Tucked into House's belt, also fluttering, was a hood of homespun cloth dyed black.

Barclay led Trusdale, his hands cuffed behind his back, to the gallows. Trusdale was all right until he got to the steps, then he began to buck and cry.

"Don't do this," he said. "Please don't do this to me. Please don't hurt me. Please don't kill me."

He was strong for a little man, and Barclay motioned Dave Fisher to come and lend a hand. Together they muscled Trusdale, twisting and ducking and pushing, up the twelve wooden steps. Once he bucked so hard all three of them almost fell off, and arms reached up to catch them if they did.

"Quit that and die like a man!" someone shouted.

When they reached the platform, Trusdale was momentarily quiet, but when Pastor Rowles commenced Psalm 51, he began to scream. "Like a woman with her tit caught in the wringer," someone said later in the Chuck-a-Luck.

"Have mercy on me, o God, after Thy great goodness," Rowles read, raising his voice to be heard over the condemned man's shrieks to be let off. "According to the multitude of Thy mercies, do away with mine offenses."

When Trusdale saw House take the black hood out of his belt, he began to pant like a dog. He shook his head from side to side, trying to dodge the hood. His hair flew. House followed each jerk patiently, like a man who means to bridle a skittish horse.

"Let me look at the mountains!" Trusdale bellowed. Runners of snot hung from his nostrils. "I'll be good if you let me look at the mountains one more time!"

But House only jammed the hood over Trusdale's head and pulled it down to his shaking shoulders. Pastor Rowles was droning on, and Trusdale tried to run off the trapdoor. Barclay and Dave Fisher pushed him back onto it. Down below, someone cried, "Ride em, cowboy!"

"Say amen," Barclay told Pastor Rowles. "For Christ's sake, say amen."

"Amen," Pastor Rowles said, and stepped back, closing his Bible with a clap.

Barclay nodded to House. House pulled the lever. The greased beam retracted and the trap dropped. So did Trusdale. There was a crack when his neck broke. His legs drew up almost to his chin, then fell back limp. Yellow drops stained the snow under his feet.

"There, you bastard," Rebecca Cline's father shouted. "Died pissing like a dog on a fireplug. Welcome to hell." A few people clapped.

The spectators stayed until Trusdale's corpse, still wearing the black hood, was laid in the same hurry-up wagon he'd ridden to town in. Then they dispersed.

Barclay went back to the jail and sat in the cell Trusdale had occupied. He sat there for ten minutes. It was cold enough to see his breath. He knew what he was waiting for, and eventually it came. He picked up the small bucket that had held Trusdale's last drink of beer and vomited. Then he went into his office and stoked up the stove.

He was still there eight hours later, trying to read a book, when Abel Hines came in. He said, "You need to come down to the funeral parlor, Otis. There's something I want to show you."

"What?"

"No. You'll want to see it for yourself."

They walked down to the Hines Funeral Parlor & Mortuary. In the back room, Trusdale lay naked on a cooling board. There was a smell of chemicals and shit.

"They load their pants when they die that way," Hines said. "Even men who go to it with their heads up. They can't help it. The sphincter lets go."

"And?"

"Step over here. I figure a man in your job has seen worse than a pair of shitty drawers."

They lay on the floor, mostly turned inside out. Something gleamed in the mess. Barclay leaned closer and saw it was a silver dollar. He reached down and plucked it out of the crap.

"I don't understand it," Hines said. "Sonofabitch was locked up almost a month."

There was a chair in the corner. Barclay sat down in it so heavily he made a little woof sound. "He must have swallowed it the first time when he saw our lanterns coming. And every time it came out, he cleaned it off and swallowed it again."

The two men stared at each other.

"You believed him," Hines said at last.

"Fool that I am, I did."

"Maybe that says more about you than it does about him."

"He went on saying he was innocent right to the end. He'll most likely stand at the throne of God saying the same thing."

"Yes," Hines said.

"I don't understand. He was going to hang. Either way, he was going to hang. Do you understand it?"

"I don't even understand why the sun comes up. What are you going to do with that cartwheel? Give it back to the girl's mother and father? It might be better if you didn't, because . . ." Hines shrugged.

Because the Clines knew all along. Everyone in town knew all along. He was the only one that hadn't known. Fool that he was.

"I don't know what I'm going to do with it," he said.

The wind gusted, bringing the sound of singing. It was coming from the church. It was the Doxology.

Thinking of Elmore Leonard

I have written poetry since I was twelve and fell in love for the first time (seventh grade). Since then I've written hundreds of poems, usually scribbled on scraps of paper or in half-used notebooks, and have published less than half a dozen of them. Most are stowed in various drawers, God knows where—I don't. There's a reason for this; I'm not much of a poet. That's not lowballing, just the truth. When I *do* manage something I like, it's mostly by accident.

The rationale for including this piece of work is that it (like the other poem in this collection) is narrative rather than lyric. The first draft—long lost, like my original take on the story that became "Mile 81"—was written in college, and very much under the influence of Robert Browning's dramatic monologues, most notably "My Last Duchess." (Another Browning poem, "Childe Roland to the Dark Tower Came," became the basis of a series of books many of my Constant Readers know quite well.) If you've read Browning, you may hear his voice rather than mine. If not, that's fine; it's basically a story, like any other, which means it's to be enjoyed rather than deconstructed.

A friend of mine named Jimmy Smith read that lost first draft at a University of Maine Poetry Hour one Tuesday afternoon in 1968 or '69, and it was well received. Why not? He gave it his all, really belting it out. And people are captivated by a good story, whether it's in verses or paragraphs. This was a pretty good one, especially given the format, which allowed me to strip away all the prosy exposition. In the fall of 2008, I got to thinking about Jimmy's reading, and since I was between projects, I decided to try re-creating the poem. This is the result. How much resemblance it bears to the original I really can't say.

Jimmy, I hope you're out there someplace, and come across this. You rocked the house that day.

The Bone Church

If you want to hear, buy me another drink.
(Ah, this is slop, but never mind; what isn't?)
There were thirty-two of us went into that
    greensore,
Thirty days in the green and only three who rose
    above it.
Three rose above the green, three made it to the top,
Manning and Revois and me. And what does that
    book say?
The famous one? "Only I am left to tell you."
I'll die of the drink in bed, as many obsessed
    whoresons do.

And do I mourn Manning? Balls! It was his money
put us there, his will that drove us on, death by
    death.
But did *he* die in bed? Not that one! I saw to it!
Now he worships in that bone church forever. Life is
    grand!
(What slop is this? Still—buy me another, do. Buy
    me two!
I'll talk for whiskey; if you want me
to shut up, switch me to champagne.

Talk is cheap, silence is dear, my dear.
What was I saying?)

Twenty-nine dead on the march, and one a woman.
Fine tits she had, and an ass like an English saddle!
We found her facedown one morning,
as dead as the fire she lay in,
an ash-baby smoked at the cheeks and throat.
Never burnt; that fire must have been cold when she
     went in.
She talked the whole voyage and died without a
     sound;
what's better than being human? Do you say so?
No? Then balls to you, and your mother, too;
if she'd had a pair she'd have been a fucking king.

Anthropologist, arr, so she said. Didn't look like
no anthropologist when we pulled her out of the
ashes with char on her cheeks and the whites of her
     eyes
dusted gray with soot. Not a mark on her otherwise.
Dorrance said it might've been a stroke
and he was as close to a doctor as we had,
that poxy bastard. For the love of God bring
     whiskey,
for life's a trudge without it!

The green did em down day by day. Carson died of
     a stick
in his boot. His foot swole up and when we cut
     away
the boot leather, his toesies were as black
as the squid's ink that drove Manning's heart.
Reston and Polgoy, they were stung by spiders

big as your fist; Ackerman bit by a snake what
   dropped
out of a tree where it hung like a lady's fur stole
draped on a branch. Bit its poison into Ackerman's
   nose.
How strong a throe, you ask? Try this:
He ripped his own snoot clean off! Yes! Tore it away
like a rotten peach off a branch and died
spitin his own dyin face! Goddam life, I say,
if you can't laugh you might as well laugh anyway.
That's my goddam attitude, and I stick by it;
this ain't a sad world unless you're sane.
Now where was I?

Javier fell off a plank bridge and when we
hauled him out he couldn't breathe so
Dorrance tried to kiss him back to life
and sucked from his throat a leech as big as
a hothouse tomato. It popped free like a cork from
a bottle and split between em; sprayed both with the
   claret
we live on (for we're all alcoholics that way, if you
   see my figure)
and when the Spaniard died raving, Manning said
the leeches'd gone to his brain. As for me, I hold no
   opinion on that.
All I know is that Javy's eyes wouldn't stay shut but
   went on
bulging in and out even after he were an hour cold.
Something hungry there, all right, arr, yes there was!
And all the while the macaws screamed at the
   monkeys
and the monkeys screamed at the macaws and both
screamed for the blue sky they couldn't see,

for it was buried in the goddam green.
Is this whiskey or diarrhea in a glass?
There was one of those suckers in the Frenchie's
    pants—
did I tell you? You know what that one ate, don't
    you?

It was Dorrance himself went next; we were
climbing by then, but still in the green. He fell
in a gorge and we could hear the snap. Broke his
    neck,
twenty-six years of age, engaged to be married, case
    closed.
Arr, ain't life grand? Life's a sucker in the throat,
life's the gorge we all fall in, it's a soup
and we all end up vegetables. Ain't I philosophical?
Never mind. It's too late to count the dead,
and I'm too drunk. In the end we got there.
Just say that.

Climbed the high path out of all that
sizzling green after we buried Rostoy, Timmons,
the Texan—I forget his name—and Dorrance
and a couple of other ones. In the end most went
    down
of some fever that boiled their skin and turned it
    green.
At the end it was only Manning, Revois, and me.
We caught the fever too, but killed it before it killed
    us.
Only I ain't never really got better. Now whiskey's
my quinine, what I take for the shakes, so buy
me another before I forget my manners
and cut your fucking throat. I might even

drink what comes out, so be wise, sonny,
and trot it over, goddam you.

There was a road we came to, even Manning agreed
it was, and wide enough for elephants if the ivory
     hunters
hadn't picked clean the jungles and the plains
     beyond em
back when gas was still a nickel.
It bore up, that road, and we bore up with it on
     tilted slabs
of stone a million years jounced free of Mother
     Earth,
leaping one to another like frogs in the sun, Revois
still burning with the fever and me—oh, I was
     light!
Like milkweed gauze on a breeze, you know.
I saw it all. My mind was as clear then as clean
     water,
for I was as young then as horrid now—yes, I see
how you look at me, but you needn't frown so, for
it's your own future you see on this side o' table.
We climbed above the birds and there was the end,
a stone tongue poked straight into the sky.

Manning broke into a run and we ran after, Revois
trotting a right smart, sick as he was.
(But he wasn't sick long—hee!)
We looked down and saw what we saw.
Manning flushed red at the sight, and why not?
For greed's a fever, too.
He grabbed me by the rag that was once my shirt
and asked were it just a dream. When I said I saw
what he saw, he turned to Revois.

But before Revois could say Aye or Nay, we heard
    thunder
coming up from the greenroof we'd left behind,
like a storm turned upside down. Or say
like all of earth had caught the fever that stalked us
and was sick in its bowels. I asked Manning what he
    heard
and Manning said nothing. He was hypnotized by
that cleft, looking down a thousand feet of ancient
    air
into the church below: a million years' worth of bone
    and tusk,
a whited sepulcher of eternity, a thrashpit of prongs
such as you'd see if hell burned dry to the slag of its
    cauldron.

You expected to see bodies impaled on the
ancient thorns of that sunny tomb. There were none,
but the thunder was coming, rolling up from the
    ground
instead of down from the sky. The stones shook
beneath our heels as *they* burst free of the green
that took so many of us—Rostoy with his mouth
    harp,
Dorrance who sang along, the anthropologist
with the ass like an English saddle, twenty-six
    others.
They arrived, those gaunt ghosts, and shook the
    greenroof
from their feet, and came in a shuddering wave:
    elephants
stampeding from the green cradle of time.
Towering among em (believe what you want)
were mammoths from the dead age when man

was not, their tusks in corkscrews and their eyes
as red as the whips of sorrow;
wrapped around their wrinkled legs were jungle
    vines.
One come—yes!—with a flower stuck
in a fold of his chest hide like a boutonniere!

Revois screamed and put his hand over his eyes.
Manning said "I don't see that." (He sounded
like a man explaining to a fucking traffic cop.)
I pulled em aside and we three stumbled
into a stony cunt near the edge. From there
we watched em roll: a tide in the face of reality
that made you wish for blindness and glad for
    sight.
They went past us, never slowing,
the ones behind driving the ones before,
and over they went, trumpeting their way to
    suicide,
crashing into the bones of their oblivion a dusty
    mile below.
Hours it went on, that endless convention of
    tumbling death;
trumpets all the way down, a brass orchestra,
diminishing. The dust and the smell of their shit
near choked us, and in the end Revois ran mad.
Stood up, whether to pelt away or to join em
I don't never knew which, but join em he did,
headfirst and down with his bootheels in the sky and
all the nailheads winking.
One arm waved. The other . . . one of those giant flat
    feet
tore it off his body and the arm followed after,
    fingers

waving: "Bye-bye!" and "Bye-bye!" and "So long,
     boys!"
Har!

I leaned out to see him go and it was a sight to
     remember,
how he sprayed in pinwheels that hung in the air
after he was gone, then turned pink and floated away
on a breeze that smelled of rotten carnations.
His bones are with the others now, and where's my
     drink?
But—hear this, you idiot!—the only new bones
     were his.
Do you mark what I say? Then listen again, damn
     you:
His, but no others.
Nothing down there after the last of the giants had
     passed us
but for the bone church, which was as it was,
with one blot of red, and that was Revois.
For that was a stampede of ghosts or memories,
and who's to say they're not the same? Manning got
     up
trembling, said our fortunes were made (as if he
didn't already have one).
"And what about what you just saw?" I asked.
"Would you bring others to see such a holy place?
Why, next thing you know the pope himself will be
pissing his holy water over the side!" But Manning
only shook his head, and grinned, and held up hands
without a speck of dust on them—although not a
     minute
past we'd been choking on it by the bale,
and coated with it from top to toe.

He said it was hallucination
we'd seen, brought on by fever and stinkwater.
Said again that our fortunes were made, and
    laughed.
The bastard, that laugh was his undoing.
I saw that he was mad—or I was—and one of us
would have to die. You know which one it was,
since here I sit before you, drunk with hair that once
was black hanging in my eyes.

He said, "Don't you see, you fool—"
And said no more, for the rest was just a scream.
Balls to him!
And balls to your grinning face!

I don't remember how I got back; it's a
dream of green with brown faces in it,
then a dream of blue with white faces in it,
and now I wake at night in this city
where not one man in ten dreams of what
lies beyond his life—for the eyes they
use to dream with are shut, as Manning's
were, until the end, when not all the bank accounts
    in hell
or Switzerland (they may be the same) could save
    him.
I wake with my liver bellowing, and in the dark
I hear the lumbering thunder of those great ghosts
    rising
out of the greenroof like a storm set loose to harrow
    the earth,
and I smell the dust and the shit, and when the
    horde
breaks free into the sky of their undoing, I see

the ancient fans of their ears and the hooks of their
tusks; I see their eyes and their eyes and their eyes.
There's more to life than this; there are maps inside
    your maps.

It's still there, the bone church, and I'd like to
go back and find it again, so I could throw myself
over and be done this wretched comedy. Now turn
    away
your sheep's face before I turn it away for you.
Arr, reality's a dirty place with no religion in it.
So buy me a drink, goddam you!
We'll toast elephants that never were.

                    For Jimmy Smith

Morality is a slippery subject. If I didn't know that as a boy, I found out when I went to college. I attended the University of Maine on a slapped-together financial scaffolding of small scholarships, government loans, and summer jobs. During the school year, I worked the dish line in West Commons. The money never stretched far enough. My single mother, who was working as head housekeeper in a mental institution called Pineland Training Center, sent me $12 a week, which helped a little. After Mom died, I found out from one of her sisters that she had managed it by giving up her monthly beauty parlor visit and economizing on groceries. She also skipped lunch every Tuesday and Thursday.

Once I moved off-campus and away from West Commons, I sometimes supplemented my own diet by shoplifting steaks or packages of hamburger from the local supermarket. You had to do it on Fridays, when the store was really busy. I once tried for a chicken, but it was too fucking big to go under my coat.

Word got around that I would write papers for students who found themselves in a bind. I had a sliding scale for this service. If the student got an A, my fee was $20. I got $10 for a B. A grade of C was a wash, and no money changed hands. For a D or an F, I promised my client that I would pay him or her $20. I made sure I would never have to pay, because I couldn't afford it. And I was sly. (It embarrasses me to say that, but it's the truth.) I wouldn't take on a project unless the student in need could provide at least one paper he or she *had* written, so I could copy the style. I didn't need to do this a lot, thank God, but when I had to—when I was broke and simply couldn't live without a burger and fries at the Bear's Den in Memorial Union—I did.

Then, when I was a junior, I discovered that I had a fairly rare blood type, A-negative, roughly six percent of the population. There was a clinic in Bangor that would pay $25 per pint for A-neg. I thought that an excellent deal. Every two months or so, I drove my battered old station wagon up Route 2 from Orono (or hitchhiked when it was broke down, a frequent occurrence) and rolled up my sleeve. There was far less paperwork in those pre-AIDS years, and when your pint was in the bag, you had your choice of a small glass of orange juice or a small knock of whiskey. Being an alcoholic-in-training even then, I always opted for the whiskey.

Headed back to school after one of these donations, it occurred to me that if whoring is selling yourself for money, then I was a whore. Writing English essays and sociology term papers was also whoring. I had been raised mainstream Methodist, I had a clear fix on right and wrong, but there it was: I had become a whore, only peddling my blood and writing skills instead of my ass.

That realization raised questions of morality that still engage me to this day. It's a rubbery concept, isn't it? Uniquely stretchable. But if you stretch anything too far, it will tear. Nowadays I give my blood instead of selling it, but it occurred to me then and still seems true to me now: under the right circumstances, anyone might sell anything.

And live to regret it.

Morality

Chad knew something was up as soon as he walked in. Nora was home already. Her hours were from eleven to five, six days a week. The way it usually worked, he got home from school at four and had dinner on when she came in around six.

She was sitting on the fire escape, where he went to smoke, and she had some paperwork in her hands. He looked at the refrigerator and saw that the email printout was gone from beneath the magnet that had been holding it in place for almost four months.

"Hey, you," she said. "Come on out here." She paused. "Bring your butts, if you want."

Chad was down to just a pack a week, but that didn't make her like his habit any better. The health issue was part of it, but the expense was an even bigger part. Every cigarette meant forty cents up in smoke.

He didn't like smoking around her, even outside, but he got the current pack out of the drawer under the dish drainer and put it in his pocket. There was something about her solemn face that suggested he might want them.

He climbed out the window and sat down beside her. She had changed into jeans and one of her old blouses, so she had been home for awhile. Stranger and stranger.

They looked out over their little bit of the city for awhile without speaking. He kissed her and she smiled in an absent way. She had the agent's email; she also had the file folder with THE RED AND THE BLACK written on it in big capitals. His little joke, but not so funny. The file contained their financial stuff—bank and credit card statements, utility bills, insurance premiums—and the bottom line was red, not black. It was an American story these days, he supposed. There just wasn't enough. Two years ago they'd talked about having a kid. They didn't now. What they talked about now was getting out from under and maybe enough ahead to leave the city without a bunch of creditors snapping at their heels. Move north to New England. But not yet. At least here they were working.

"How was school?" she asked.

"Fine."

Actually, the job was a plum. But after Anita Biderman got back from maternity leave, who knew? Probably not another job at PS 321. He was high on the list of subs, but that didn't mean anything if the regular teaching roster was all present and accounted for.

"You're home early," he said. "Don't tell me Winnie died."

She looked startled, then smiled again. But they had been together for ten years, married for the last six, and Chad had seen that smile before. It meant trouble.

"Nora?"

"He sent me home early. To think. I've got a lot to think about. I'm . . ." She shook her head.

He took her by the shoulder and turned her to him. "You're what? Is everything okay with Winnie?"

"That's a good question. Go on, light up. Smoking lamp's lit."

"Tell me what's going on."

She had been cut from the staff of Congress Memorial Hospital two years ago during a "reorganization." Luckily for the Chad-and-Nora Corporation, she had landed on her feet. Getting the home nursing job had been something of a coup: one patient, a retired minister recovering from a stroke, thirty-six hours a week, very decent wages. She made more than he did, and by a good bit. The two incomes were almost enough to live on. At least until Anita Biderman came back.

"First, let's talk about this." She held up the agent's email. "How sure are you?"

"What, that I can do the work? Pretty sure. Almost positive. I mean, if I had the time. About the rest . . ." He shrugged. "It's right there in black and white. No guarantees."

With the hiring freeze currently in effect in the city's schools, subbing was the best Chad could do. He was on every list in the system, but there was no full-time position teaching fourth or fifth grade in his immediate future. Nor would the money be much better even if such a position opened up—just more reliable. As a sub, he sometimes spent weeks on the bench.

For awhile two years ago, the lay-off had been three months, and they almost lost the apartment. That was when the trouble with the credit cards had started.

Out of desperation and a need to fill up the empty hours when Nora was tending to the Reverend Winston, Chad had started a book he called *Living with the Animals: The Life of a Substitute Teacher in Four City Schools*. Words did not come easily to him, and on some days they did not come at all, but by the time he was called in to St. Saviour to teach second grade (Mr. Cardelli had broken a leg in a car accident), he had finished three chapters. Nora received the pages with a troubled smile. No woman wants the job of telling the man in her life that he's been wasting his time.

He hadn't been. The stories he told of the substitute teaching life were sweet, funny, and often moving— much more interesting than anything she'd heard over dinner or while they were lying in bed together.

Most of his query letters to agents weren't answered. A few were courteous enough to drop him a "sorry, but my plate's full" note. He finally found one who would at least look at the eighty pages he had managed to wring out of his old and limping Dell laptop.

The agent's name had a circus-y feel: Edward Ringling. His response to Chad's pages was long on praise and short on promise. "I might be able to get you a book contract based on this and an outline of the rest," Ringling had written, "but it would be a very small contract, likely a good deal less than you currently make as a teacher, and you might find yourself financially worse off than you are now— insane, I know, but today's market is pretty sick.

"What I suggest is that you finish another seven or eight chapters, possibly even the whole book. Then I might be able to take it to auction and get you a much better deal."

It made sense, Chad supposed, if you were oversee-ing the literary world from a comfy office in Manhat-tan. Not so much if you were hopscotching all over the boroughs, teaching a week here and three days there, trying to keep ahead of the bills. Ringling's letter had come in May. Now it was September, and although Chad had had a relatively good summer teaching (*God bless the dummies,* he sometimes thought), he hadn't added a single page to the manuscript. It wasn't lazi-ness; teaching, even when it was just subbing, was like having a pair of jumper cables attached to some critical part of your brain. It was good that the kids could draw power from that part, but there was pre-cious little left over. Many nights the most creative thing of which he found himself capable was reading a few chapters of the latest Linwood Barclay.

That might change if he spent another two or three months without work . . . except a few months of liv-ing on just his wife's salary would tip them over. Nor was anxiety helpful when it came to literary endeav-ors.

"How long would it take to finish it?" Nora asked. "If you were writing full-time?"

He drew out his cigarettes and lit one. He felt a strong urge to give an over-optimistic answer, but overcame it. He had no idea what was going on with her, but she deserved the truth.

"Eight months at least. Probably more like a year."

"And how much money do you think it would mean if Mr. Ringling held an auction and people actually came?"

Ringling hadn't mentioned numbers, but Chad had done his homework. "I'd guess the advance could be in the neighborhood of a hundred thousand."

A fresh start in Vermont, that was the plan. That was what they talked about in bed. A small town, maybe up in the Northeast Kingdom. She could catch on at the local hospital or get another private; he could land a full-time teaching position. Or maybe write another book.

"Nora, what's this about?"

"I'm afraid to tell you," she said, "but I will. Crazy or not, I will, because the number Winnie mentioned was bigger than a hundred thousand. Only one thing: I'm not quitting my job. He said I could keep it no matter what we decided, and we *need* that job."

He reached for the aluminum ashtray he kept tucked under the windowsill and butted his cigarette in it. Then he took her hand. "Tell me."

He listened with amazement, but not disbelief. He sort of wished he could disbelieve it, but he did not.

If asked before that day, Nora would have said she knew little about the Reverend George Winston and he knew next to nothing about her. In light of his proposal, she realized she had actually told him quite a bit. About the financial treadmill they were on, for one thing. The chance Chad's book offered to get them off it, for another.

And what had she actually known about Winnie? That he was a lifelong bachelor, that three years into his retirement from the Second Presbyterian Church of Park Slope (where he was still listed on the Church Slate as pastor emeritus), he had suffered a stroke that left him partially paralyzed on the right side. That was when she had entered his life.

He could now walk to the bathroom (and, on good days, to his rocker on the front porch) with the help of a plastic brace that kept his bad knee from buckling. And he could talk understandably again, although he still sometimes suffered from what Nora called "sleepy tongue." Nora had previous experience with stroke victims (it was what had clinched the job), and she had a large appreciation for how far he had come in a short time.

Until the day of his outrageous proposal, it had never occurred to her that he must be wealthy . . . although the house he lived in should have offered a clue. If she had assumed anything, it was that the house was a gift from the parish, and that her paid presence in his life was more of the same.

Her job had been called "practical care" in the last century. In addition to such nursely duties as giving him his pills and monitoring his blood pressure, she worked as a physical therapist. She was also a speech therapist, a masseuse, and occasionally—when he had letters to write—a secretary. She ran errands and sometimes read to him. Nor was she above light housekeeping on days when Mrs. Granger did not come in. On those days she made sandwiches or omelets for lunch, and she supposed it was over those lunches that he had drawn out the details of her own life—and done it so carefully and casually that Nora never realized what was going on.

"The one thing I remember saying," she told Chad, "and probably only because he mentioned it today, was that we weren't living in abject poverty or even in discomfort . . . that it was the *fear* of those things that got me down."

Chad smiled at that. "You and me both."

That morning Winnie had refused both the sponge bath and the massage. Instead he had asked her to put on his brace and help him into his study, which was a relatively long walk for him, certainly farther than the porch rocker. He got there, but by the time he fell into the chair behind his desk, he was red-faced and panting. She had gotten him a glass of orange juice, taking her time so he could get his breath back. When she returned he drained half the glass at a single go.

"Thank you, Nora. I want to talk to you now. Very seriously."

He must have seen her apprehension, because he smiled and made a waving-off gesture. "It's not about your job. You'll have that no matter what. If you want it. If not, I'll see that you have a reference that can't be beat."

Nice of him, but there weren't many jobs like this around.

"You're making me nervous, Winnie," she said.

"Nora, how would you like to make two hundred thousand dollars?"

She gawked at him. On either side, high shelves of smart books frowned down. The noises from the street were muffled. They might have been in another country. A quieter country than Brooklyn.

"If you think this is about sex, I assure you it is not. At least I don't think so; if one looks below the surface, and if one has read Freud, I suppose any aberrant act may be said to have a sexual basis. I don't know, myself. I haven't studied Freud since seminary, and even there my reading was cursory. Freud offended me. He seemed to feel that any suggestion of depth in human nature was an illusion. He seemed to be saying, *What you think of as an artesian well is actually a puddle*. I beg to differ. Human nature has no bottom. It is as deep and mysterious as the mind of God."

Nora stood up. "With all respect, I'm not sure I believe in God. And I'm not sure this is a proposal I want to hear."

"But if you don't listen, you won't know. And you'll always wonder."

She stood looking at him, unsure what to do or say. What she thought was, *That desk he's sitting behind must have cost thousands.* It was the first time she had really thought of him in connection with money.

"Two hundred thousand in cash is what I'm offering. Enough to pay off all the outstanding bills, enough to enable your husband to finish his book— enough, perhaps, to start a new life in . . . was it Vermont?"

"Yes." Thinking, *If you knew that, you've been listening a lot more carefully than I was.*

"No need to get the IRS involved, either." He had long features and white woolly hair. A sheeplike face she had always thought it before today. "Cash can be nice that way, and causes no problems if it's fed slowly into the stream of one's accounts. Also, once your husband's book is sold and you're established in New England, we need never see each other again." He paused. "Although if you decide not to stay on, I doubt if my next nurse will be half as competent as you have proved to be. Please. Sit down. You'll give me a stiff neck."

She did as he asked. It was the thought of two hundred thousand dollars in cash that kept her in the room. She found she could actually see it: bills stuffed into a padded brown envelope. Or perhaps it would take two envelopes to hold that much.

I suppose it would depend on the denomination of the bills, she thought.

"Let me talk for a bit," he said. "I haven't really done much of that, have I? Mostly I've been listening. It's your turn to listen now, Nora. Will you do that?"

"I suppose." She was curious. She supposed anybody would be. "Who do you want me to kill?"

It was a joke, but as soon as it was out of her mouth, she was afraid it might be true. Because it didn't *sound* like a joke. No more than the eyes in his long sheep's face looked like sheep's eyes.

To her relief, Winnie laughed. Then he said, "Not murder, my dear. We won't need to go that far."

He talked then, as he never had before. To anyone, probably.

"I grew up in a wealthy home on Long Island— my father was successful in the stock market. It was a religious home, and when I told my parents I felt called to the ministry, there was no puffing and blowing about the family business. On the contrary, they were delighted. Mother, especially. Most mothers are happy, I think, when their sons discover a vocation-with-a-capital-V.

"I went to seminary in upstate New York, after which I was assigned—as associate pastor—to a church in Idaho. I wanted for nothing. Presbyterians take no vow of poverty, and my parents made sure I never had to live as though I had. My father survived my mother by only five years, and when he passed on, I inherited a great deal of money, mostly in bonds and solid stocks. Over the years since, I have converted a small percentage of that to cash, a bit at a time. Not a nest egg, because I've never needed one, but what I'd call a *wish* egg. It's in a Manhattan safe deposit box, and it's that cash that I'm offering you, Nora. It may actually be closer to two hundred and forty thousand, but we'll agree, shall we, not to quibble over a dollar here and a dollar there?

"I wandered a few years in the hinterlands before coming back to Brooklyn and Second Presbo. After five years as an associate, I became the senior pastor. I served as such, without blemish, until two thousand six. My life has been one—I say it with neither pride nor shame—of unremarkable service. I have led my church in helping the poor, both in countries far from here and in this community. The local AA drop-in center was my idea, and it's helped hundreds of suffering addicts and alcoholics. I've comforted the sick and buried the dead. More cheerfully, I've presided over more than a thousand weddings, and inaugurated a scholarship fund that has sent many boys and girls to colleges they could not otherwise have afforded. One of our scholarship girls won a National Book Award in nineteen ninety-nine.

"And my only regret is this: in all my years, I have never committed one of the sins about which I have spent a lifetime warning my various flocks. I am not a lustful man, and since I've never been married, I never had so much as the opportunity to commit adultery. I'm not gluttonous by nature, and although I like nice things, I've never been greedy or covetous. Why would I be, when my father left me fifteen million dollars? I've worked hard, kept my temper, envy no one—except perhaps Mother Teresa—and have little pride of possessions or position.

"I'm not claiming I'm *without* sin. Not at all. Those who can say (and I suppose there are a few) that they have never sinned in deed or word can hardly say they've never sinned in thought, can they? The church covers every loophole. We hold out heaven, then make people understand they have no hope of achieving it without our help . . . because no one is without sin, and the wages of sin are death.

"I suppose this makes me sound like an unbeliever, but raised as I was, unbelief is as impossible for me as levitation. Yet I understand the cozening nature of the bargain, and the psychological tricks believers use to ensure the prosperity of those beliefs. The pope's fancy hat was not conferred on him by God, but by men and women paying theological blackmail money.

"I can see you fidgeting, so I'll come to the point. I want to commit a major sin before I die. A sin not of thought or word but of deed. This was on my mind—increasingly on my mind—before my stroke, but I thought it a frenzy that would pass. Now I see that it will not, because the idea has been with me more than ever during the last three years. But how great a sin can an old man stuck in a wheelchair commit, I asked myself? Surely not one very great, at least without being caught, and I would prefer not to be caught. Such grave matters as sin and forgiveness should remain between man and God.

"Listening to you talk about your husband's book and your financial situation, it occurred to me that I could sin by proxy. In fact, I could double my sin quotient, as it were, by making you my accessory."

She spoke from a dry mouth. "I believe in wrongdoing, Winnie, but I don't believe in sin."

He smiled. It was a benevolent smile. Also unpleasant: sheep lips, wolf teeth. "That's fine. But sin believes in you."

"I understand you think so . . . so why? It's *perverse!*"

His smile widened. "Yes! That's why! I want to know what it's like to do something entirely against my nature. To need forgiveness for the act and *more* than the act. Do you know what doubles sin, Nora?"

"No. I don't go to church."

"What doubles sin is saying to yourself, *I will do this because I know I can pray for forgiveness once it's done.* To say to yourself that you can have your cake and eat it, too. I want to know what being that deep in sin is like. I don't want to wallow; I want to dive in over my head."

"And take me with you!" She said it with real indignation.

"Ah, but you don't believe in sin, Nora. You just said so. From your standpoint, all I want is for you to get a little dirty. And risk arrest, I suppose, although the risk should be minor. For these things I will pay you two hundred thousand dollars. *Over* two hundred thousand."

Her face and hands felt numb, as if she had just come in from a long walk in the cold. She would not do it, of course. What she would do was walk out of this house and get some fresh air. She wouldn't quit, or at least not immediately, because she needed the job, but she *would* walk out. And if he fired her for deserting her post, let him. But first, she wanted to hear the rest. She wouldn't admit to herself that she was tempted, but curious? Yes, that much she would own.

"What is it you want me to do?"

Chad had lit another cigarette. She motioned with her fingers. "Give me a drag on that."

"Norrie, you haven't smoked a cigarette in five—"

"Give me a drag, I said."

He passed the cigarette to her. She dragged deep, coughed the smoke out. Then she told him.

That night she lay awake late, into the small hours, quite sure he was sleeping, and why not? The decision had been made. She would tell Winnie no and never mention the idea again. Decision made; sleep follows.

Still, she wasn't entirely surprised when he turned to her and said, "I can't stop thinking about it."

Nor could Nora. "I'd do it, you know. For us. If . . ."

Now they were face-to-face, inches apart. Close enough to taste each other's breath. It was two o'clock in the morning.

The hour of conspiracy if there ever was one, she thought.

"If?"

"If I didn't think it would taint our lives. Some stains don't come out."

"It's a moot question, Nor. We've decided. You play Sarah Palin and tell him thanks but no thanks for that bridge to nowhere. I'll find a way to finish the book without his weird idea of a grant-in-aid."

"When? On your next unpaid leave? I don't think so."

"It's decided. He's a crazy old man. The end." He rolled away from her.

Silence descended. Upstairs, Mrs. Reston—whose picture belonged in the dictionary next to *insomnia*—walked back and forth. Somewhere, maybe in deepest darkest Gowanus, a siren wailed.

Fifteen minutes went by before Chad spoke to the end table and the digital clock, which now read

2:17A. "Also, we'd have to trust him for the money, and you can't trust a man whose one remaining ambition in life is to commit a sin."

"But I *do* trust him," she said. "It's myself I don't trust. Go to sleep, Chad. This subject is closed."

"Right," he said. "Gotcha."

The clock read **2:26A** when she said, "It *could* be done. I'm sure of that much. I could change my hair color. Wear a hat. Dark glasses, of course. Which would mean it would have to be a sunny day. And there would have to be an escape route."

"Are you seriously—"

"I don't *know*! Two hundred thousand *dollars*! I'd have to work almost three years to make that much money, and after the government and the banks wet their beaks, there'd be next to nothing left. We know how that works."

She was quiet for awhile, looking at the ceiling above which Mrs. Reston trod her slow miles.

"And the *insurance*!" she burst out. "Do you know what we have for insurance? Nothing!"

"We have insurance."

"Okay, *next* to nothing. What if you got hit by a car? What if I turned up with an ovarian cyst?"

"Our coverage is okay."

"That's what everyone says, but what everyone knows is they fuck you at the drive-through! With this, we could be sure. That's what I keep thinking about. *We . . . could . . . be . . . sure!*"

"Two hundred thousand dollars makes my financial hopes for the book seem kind of small, though, don't you think? Why even bother?"

"Because this would be a onetime thing. And the book would be *clean*."

"*Clean?* You think this would make the book *clean?*" He rolled over and faced her. Part of him had grown hard, so perhaps part of this *was* about sex. On their end of the bargain, at least.

"Do you think I'll ever get another job like the one with Winnie?" She was angry, although with him or herself she couldn't tell. Nor did she care. "I'll be thirty-six in December. You'll take me to dinner for my birthday and a week later I'll get my real present: a past due notice for the last car loan payment."

"Are you blaming me for—?"

"*No.* I'm not even blaming the system that keeps us and everyone like us treading water. Blame is counterproductive. And I told Winnie the truth: I don't believe in sin. But I also don't want to go to jail." She felt tears growing in her eyes. "I don't want to hurt anyone, either. Especially not—"

"You're not going to."

He started to turn over, but she grabbed his shoulder.

"If we did it—if *I* did it—we could never talk about it afterward. Not one single time."

"No."

She reached for him. In marriages, deals were sealed with more than a handshake. This they both knew.

The clock said **2:58A** and he was drifting to sleep when she said, "Do you know anyone with a video camera? Because he wants—"

"Yes," he said. "Charlie Green."

After that, silence. Except for Mrs. Reston, walking slowly back and forth above them. Nora had an image—half a dream—of Mrs. Reston with a pedometer attached to the waistband of her pajama pants.

Mrs. Reston patiently walking off all those miles between her and dawn.

Nora fell asleep.

The next day, in Winnie's study.

"Well?" he said.

Her mother had never been a churchgoer, but Nora had attended Vacation Bible School every summer, and had enjoyed it. There were games and songs and flannelboard stories. She found herself remembering one of the stories now. She hadn't thought of it in years.

"I wouldn't have to really hurt the . . . you know, the person . . . to get the money?" she said. "I want to be very clear about that."

"No, but I expect to see blood flow. Let *me* be clear about *that*. I want you to use your fist, but a cut lip or bloody nose will be quite sufficient."

In one VBS story, the teacher put a mountain on the flannelboard. Then Jesus and a guy with horns. The teacher said the devil had taken Jesus up on top of a mountain and showed him all the cities of the earth. *You can have everything in those cities,* the devil had said. *Every treasure. All you have to do is fall down and worship me.* But Jesus was a stand-up guy. He'd said *Get thee behind me, Satan.*

"Well?" he asked again.

"Sin," she mused. "That's what's on your mind."

"Sin for its own sake. Deliberately planned and executed. Do you find the idea exciting?"

"No," she said, looking up at the frowning book-shelves.

Winnie let some time pass, then said for the third time: "Well?"

"If I got caught, would I still get the money?"

"If you lived up to your part of the agreement—and didn't implicate me, of course—you certainly would. And even if you were caught, the very worst to come of it would be probation."

"Plus court-ordered psychiatric evaluation," she said. "Which I probably need for even considering this."

Winnie said: "If you continue the way you are, dear, you'll need a marriage counselor, at the very least. In my time in the ministry, I counseled many partners, and while money worries weren't always the root cause of their problems, that's what it was in most cases. And that's *all* it was."

"Thank you for the benefit of your experience, Winnie."

He said nothing to this.

"You're crazy, you know."

He still said nothing.

She looked at the books some more. Most of them were on religion. Finally she turned her eyes back to his. "If I do this and you fuck me, I'll make you sorry."

He showed no discomfiture at her choice of language. "I'll honor my commitment. You may be sure of that."

"You speak almost perfectly now. Not even a lisp, unless you're tired."

He shrugged. "Being with me has trained your ear. It's like learning to understand a new language, I suppose."

She returned her eyes to the books. One of them was called *The Problem of Good and Evil*. Another was titled *The Basis of Morality*. That was a thick one. In the hall, an old Regulator clock was ticking steadily. Finally he said it again: "Well?"

"Isn't just putting this in front of me sin enough to satisfy you? You're tempting us both, and we're both considering the temptation. Isn't that enough?"

"It's sin in thought and word only. That will not satisfy my curiosity."

The Regulator ticked. Without looking at him, she said: "If you say *well* again, I'll walk out of here."

He didn't say *well* or anything else. She looked down at her hands, twisting in her lap. The most appalling thing: part of her was still curious. Not about what he wanted, that cat was out of the bag, but about what she wanted.

At last she looked up and gave her answer.

"Excellent," he said.

With the decision made, neither of them wanted the actual act hanging over their heads; it cast too big a shadow. They chose Forest Park in Queens. Chad borrowed Charlie Green's video camera and learned how to use it. They went to the park twice beforehand (on rainy days when it was mostly empty), and Chad video'd the area they decided on. They had a lot of sex during that period—nervous sex, fumbling sex, the kind teenagers have in the backseat of a car, but usually good sex. Hot, at least. Nora found her other major appetites dwindling. In the ten days between her agreement and the morning when she executed her part of the bargain, she lost nine pounds. Chad said she was starting to look like a college kid again.

On a sunny day in early October, Chad parked their old Ford on Jewel Avenue. Nora sat beside him, her hair dyed red and hanging to her shoulders, looking very un-Nora-like in a long skirt and an ugly brown smock top. She was wearing sunglasses and a Mets cap. She seemed calm enough, but when he reached out to touch her, she shied away.

"Nor, c'mon—"

"Have you got cab fare?"

"Yes."

"And a bag to put the videocam in?"

"Yes, of course."

"Then give me the car keys. I'll see you back at the apartment."

"Are you sure you'll be able to drive? Because the reaction to something like this—"

"I'll be fine. Give me the keys. Wait here fifteen minutes. If there's something wrong . . . if anything even *feels* wrong . . . I'll come back. If I don't, you go to the spot we picked out. Do you remember it?"

"Of course I remember it!"

She smiled—showed her teeth and dimples, at least. "That's the spirit," she said, and was gone.

It was an excruciatingly long fifteen minutes, but Chad waited through every one of them. Kids, all of them wearing clamshell helmets, pooted past on bikes. Women strolled in pairs, many with shopping bags. He saw an old lady laboriously crossing the avenue, and for one surreal moment he thought it was Mrs. Reston, but when she passed by, he saw that it wasn't. This woman was much older than Mrs. Reston.

When the fifteen minutes were almost up, it occurred to him—in a sane and rational way—that he could put a stop to this by driving away. In the park, Nora would look around and not see him. She would be the one to take the cab back to Brooklyn. And when she got there, she would thank him. She would say, *You saved me from myself.*

After that? Take a month off. No substitute teaching. He would turn all his resources to finishing the book. Throw his cap over the windmill.

Instead, he got out and walked to the park with Charlie Green's video camera in his hand. The paper bag that would hold it afterward was stuffed in the pocket of his windbreaker. He checked three times to make sure the camera's green power lamp was glowing. How terrible it would be to go through all this and discover he'd never turned on the camera. Or that he'd left the lens cap on.

He checked that again too.

Nora was sitting on a park bench. When she saw him, she brushed her hair back from the left side of her face. That was the signal. It was on.

Behind her was a playground—swings, a push merry-go-round, teeter-totters, bouncy horses on springs, that sort of thing. At this hour, there were only a few kids playing. The moms were in a group on the far side, talking and laughing, not really paying much attention to the kids.

Nora got up from the bench.

Two hundred thousand dollars, he thought, and raised the camera to his eye. Now that it was on, he felt calm.

He shot it like a pro.

II

Back at their building, Chad raced up the stairs. He felt sure that she wouldn't be there. He had seen her go skimming away at a full-out run, and the mothers had barely given her a look—they were converging on the child she had chosen, a boy of perhaps four—but he was still sure she wouldn't be there and that he would get a call telling him that his wife was at the police station, where she had collapsed and told everything, including his part in it. Worse, Winnie's part in it, thus ensuring it had all been for nothing.

His hand was shaking so badly that he couldn't get the key in the slot; it went chattering madly around the keyplate without even coming close. He was in the act of putting down the paper bag (now badly crumpled) with the videocam inside it, so he could use his left hand to steady his right, when the door opened.

Nora was now wearing cutoff jeans and a shell top, the clothes she'd had on beneath the long skirt and smock. The plan had been for her to change in the car, before driving away. She said she could do it like lightning, and it seemed she'd been right.

He threw his arms around her and hugged her so tightly he heard the thump as she came against him—not exactly a romantic embrace.

Nora bore this for a moment, then said, "Come inside. Get out of the hall." And as soon as the door to the outside world was closed, she said, "Did you get it? Tell me you did. I've been here for almost half an hour, pacing around like Mrs. Reston in the middle of the night . . . Mrs. Reston if she was on speed, that is . . . wondering—"

"I was worried too." He shoved his hair off his forehead, where the skin felt hot and feverish. "Norrie, I was scared to *death*."

She snatched the bag from his hands, peered inside, then glared at him. She had ditched the sunglasses. Her blue eyes burned. *"Tell me you got it."*

"Yeah. That is, I think so. I *must* have. I haven't looked yet."

The glare got hotter. He thought, *Watch out, Nor, your eyeballs will catch fire if you keep doing that.*

"You better have. You better have. The time I haven't been pacing around, I've been on the toilet. I keep having *cramps*—" She went to the window and looked out. He joined her, afraid she knew something he didn't. But there were only the usual pedestrians going back and forth.

She turned to him again, and this time grabbed his arms. Her palms were dead cold. "Is he all right? The kid? Did you see if he was okay?"

"He's fine," Chad said.

"Are you lying?" She was shouting into his face. "You better not be! *Was he all right?*"

"Fine. Standing up even before the mothers got to him. Bawling his head off, but I got worse at that kid's age when I was clopped in the back of the head by a swing. I had to go to the emergency room and have five sti—"

"I hit him much harder than I meant to. I was so afraid that if I pulled the punch . . . if Winnie *saw* I pulled it . . . he wouldn't pay. And the *adrenaline* . . . Christ! It's a wonder I didn't tear that poor kid's head right off! Why did I ever do it?" But she wasn't crying, and she didn't look remorseful. She looked furious. "Why did you *let* me?"

"I never—"

"Are you *sure* he's all right? You really saw him getting up? Because I hit him much harder than I . . ." She wheeled away from him, went to the wall, knocked her forehead against it, then turned back. "I walked into a playground and I punched a four-year-old child square in the mouth! For *money!*"

He had an inspiration. "I think it's on the tape. The kid getting up, I mean. You'll see for yourself."

She flew back across the room. "Put it on the TV! I want to see!"

Chad attached the VSS cable Charlie had given him. Then, after a little fumbling, he played the tape on the TV. He had indeed recorded the kid getting to his feet again, just before shutting the thing off and walking away. The kid looked bewildered, and of course he was crying, but otherwise he seemed fine. His lips were bleeding quite a lot, but his nose only a little. Chad thought he might have gotten the bloody nose when he fell down.

No worse than any minor playground accident, he thought. *Thousands of them happen every day.*

"See?" he asked her. "He's fi—"

"Run it again."

He did. And when she asked him to run it a third time, and a fourth, and a fifth, he did that too. At some point he became aware that she was no longer watching to see the kid get up. Neither was he. They were watching him go down. And the punch. The punch delivered by the crazy red-haired bitch in the sunglasses. The one who walked up and did her business and then took off with wings on her sneakers.

She said, "I think I knocked out one of his teeth."

He shrugged. "Good news for the Tooth Fairy."

After the fifth viewing, she said: "I want to get the red out of my hair. I hate it."

"Okay—"

"But first, take me in the bedroom. Don't talk about it either. Just do it."

• • •

She kept telling him to go harder, almost belting him with her upthrusting hips, as if she wanted to buck him off. But she wasn't getting there.

"Hit me," she said.

He did it. He was beyond rationality.

"You can do better than that. Fucking *hit* me!"

He hit her harder. Her lower lip split open. She dabbed her fingers in the blood. While she was doing it, she came.

"Show it to me," Winnie said. This was the next day. They were in his study.

"Show me the money." A famous line. She just couldn't remember from where.

"After I see the video."

The camera was still in the crumpled bag. She took it out, along with the cable. He had a little TV in the study, and she connected the cable to it. She pushed Play, and they looked at the woman in the Mets cap sitting on the park bench. Behind her, a few children were playing. Behind *them*, mothers were talking mommyshit: body wraps, plays they had seen or were going to see, the new car, the next vacation. Blah-blah-blah.

The woman got up from the bench. The video zoomed jerkily in. The picture shivered a bit, then steadied.

That was where Nora hit the Pause button. This was Chad's idea, and she had agreed to it. She trusted Winnie, but only so far.

"I want to see the money."

Winnie took a key from the pocket of the cardigan sweater he was wearing. He used it to open the center drawer of his desk, switching it to his left hand when the partially paralyzed right one wouldn't do his bidding.

It wasn't an envelope after all. It was a medium-sized Federal Express box. She looked inside and saw bundled hundreds, each bundle secured with a rubber band.

He said, "It's all there, plus some extra."

"All right. Look at what you bought. All you have to do is push Play. I'll be in the kitchen."

"Don't you want to watch it with me?"

"No."

"Nora? You appear to have had a small accident yourself." He tapped the corner of his mouth, the side that still turned down slightly.

Had she thought he had a sheep's face? How stupid of her. How *unseeing* of her. Nor was it a wolf's face, not really. It was somewhere in between. A dog's face, maybe. The kind of dog that would bite and then run.

"I ran into a door," she said.

"I see."

"All right, I'll watch it with you," she said, and sat down. She pushed Play herself.

They watched the video twice, in complete silence. The running time was about thirty seconds. That amounted to about sixty-six hundred dollars per second. Nora had done the math while she and Chad were watching it.

After the second time, he pushed Stop. She showed him how to eject the small cassette. "This is yours. The camera has to go back to the guy my husband borrowed it from."

"I understand." His eyes were bright. It seemed he'd actually gotten what he'd paid for. What he wanted. Incredible. "I shall have Mrs. Granger buy me another camera for future viewings. Or perhaps that's an errand you'd care to run."

"Not me. We're done."

"Ah." He didn't look surprised. "All right. But . . . if I may make a suggestion . . . you may want to get another job. So no one thinks it odd when those bills begin getting paid off at a faster clip. It's only your welfare I'm thinking of, my dear."

"I'm sure." She unplugged the cable and put it back in the bag with the camera.

"And I wouldn't leave for Vermont too soon."

"I don't need your advice. I feel dirty and you're the reason why."

"I suppose I am. But you won't get caught and no one will ever know." The right side of his mouth was drawn down, the left side lifted in what could have been a smile. The result was a serpentine **S** below his beak of a nose. His speech was very clear that day. She would remember that, and ponder it. As if what he called sin had turned out to be therapy. "And Nora . . . is feeling dirty always a bad thing?"

She had no idea how to answer this. Which, she supposed, was an answer in itself.

"I only ask," he said, "because the second time you ran the tape, I watched you instead of it."

She snatched up the bag with Charlie Green's vid-eocam inside and walked to the door. "Have a nice life, Winnie. Make sure you get an actual therapist as well as a nurse next time. Your father left you enough to afford both. And take care of that tape. For both our sakes."

"You're unidentifiable on it, dear. And even if

you weren't, would anyone care?" He shrugged. "It doesn't depict a rape or murder, after all."

She stood in the doorway, wanting to be gone but curious. Still curious.

"Winnie, how will you square this with your God? How long will it take to pray it off?"

He chuckled. "If an outrageous sinner like Simon Peter could go on to found the Catholic Church, I expect I'll be fine."

"Yes, but did Simon Peter keep the videotape to watch on cold winter evenings?"

This finally silenced him, and Nora left before he could find his voice again. It was a small victory, but one she grasped eagerly.

A week later he called the apartment and told her she was welcome to come back, at least until she and Chad left for Vermont. He hadn't hired anyone else, and if there was any possibility she might change her mind, he wouldn't.

"I miss you, Nora."

She said nothing.

His voice dropped. "We could watch the tape again. Wouldn't you like to do that? Wouldn't you like to see it again, at least once?"

"No," she said, and hung up. She started toward the kitchen to make tea, but then a wave of faintness came over her. She sat down in the corner of the living room and bent her head to her upraised knees. She waited for the faintness to pass. Eventually it did.

She got a job taking care of Mrs. Reston. It was only twenty hours a week, and the pay was nothing like what she had been making as Reverend Winston's employee, but money was no longer the issue, and the commute was easy—one flight of stairs. Best of all, Mrs. Reston, who suffered from diabetes and mild cardiac problems, was a featherbrained sweetie. Sometimes, however—especially during her endless monologues concerning her late husband—Nora's hand itched to reach out and slap her.

Chad kept his name on the sub list, but cut back on his hours. He set aside six of those newfound hours each weekend to work on *Living with the Animals,* and the pages began to mount up.

Once or twice he asked himself if the weekend pages were as good—as lively—as the work he had done before that day with the video camera, and told himself that the question had only occurred to him because some old and false notion of retribution was lodged in his mind. Like a kernel of popcorn between two back teeth.

Twelve days after the day in the park, there was a knock at the apartment door. When Nora opened it, a policeman was standing there.

"Yes, Officer?" she asked.

"Are you Nora Callahan?"

She thought calmly: *I will confess everything. And after the authorities have done to me whatever they do, I'll go to that boy's mother and stick out my face and say "Hit me with your best shot, Mama. You'll be doing both of us a favor."*

"Yes, I'm Mrs. Callahan."

"Ma'am, I'm here at the request of the Walt Whitman branch of the Brooklyn Public Library? You have four library books that are almost two months overdue, and one of them is quite valuable. An art book, I believe? Limited circulation."

She gawked at him, then burst out laughing. "You're a *library* policeman?"

He tried to keep a straight face, but then he laughed too. "Today I guess I am. Do you have those books?"

"Yes. I forgot all about them. Would you care to walk a lady to the library, Officer—" She looked at his nametag. "Abromowitz?"

"Happy to. Just bring your checkbook."

"Maybe they'll take my Visa," she said.

He smiled. "Probably will," he said.

That night, in bed.

"Hit me!" As though it wasn't lovemaking she had in mind but some nightmare blackjack game.

"No."

She was on top of him, which made it easy to reach down and smack him. The sound of her palm hitting the side of his face was like the report of an air gun.

"Hit me, I said! Hit m—"

Chad slapped her back without thinking. She began to cry, but he was stiffening under her. Good.

"Now do me."

He did her. Outside, someone's car alarm went off.

They went to Vermont in January. They went on the train. It was lovely, like a picture postcard. They saw a house they both liked about twenty miles outside of Montpelier. It was only the third one they looked at.

The real estate agent's name was Jody Enders. She was very pleasant, but she kept looking at Nora's right eye. Finally Nora said, with an embarrassed little laugh, "I slipped on a patch of ice while I was getting into a taxi. You should have seen me last week. I looked like a spouse-abuse ad."

"I can hardly see it," Jody Enders said. Then, shyly: "You're very pretty."

Chad put his arm around Nora's shoulders. "I think so too."

"What do you do for a living, Mr. Callahan?"

"I'm a writer," he said.

They made a down payment on the house. On the loan agreement, Nora checked OWNER FINANCED. In the DETAILS box, she wrote simply: *Savings*.

One day in February, while they were packing for the move, Chad went into Manhattan to see a movie at the Angelika and have dinner with his agent. Officer Abromowitz had given Nora his card. She called him. He came over and they fucked in the mostly empty bedroom. It was good, but it would have been better if she could have persuaded him to hit her. She asked, but he wouldn't.

"What kind of crazy lady are you?" he asked in that voice that people use when they mean *I'm joking but not really.*

"I don't know," Nora said. "I'm still finding out."

They were scheduled to make the move to Vermont on February 29. The day before—what would have been the last day of the month in an ordinary year—the telephone rang. It was Mrs. Granger, Pastor Emeritus Winston's housekeeper. As soon as Nora registered the woman's hushed tone, she knew why she had called, and her first thought was *What did you do with the tape, you bastard?*

"The obituary will say kidney failure," Mrs. Granger said in her hushed someone's-dead voice, "but I was in his bathroom. The medicine bottles were all out, and too many of the pills were gone. I think he committed suicide."

"Probably not," Nora said. She spoke in her calmest, surest, most nursely manner. "What's more likely is that he became confused about how many he'd taken. He may have even had another stroke. A small one."

"Do you really think so?"

"Oh yes," Nora said, and had to restrain herself from asking if Mrs. Granger had seen a new video camera around anywhere. Hooked up to Winnie's TV, most likely. It would be insane to ask such a question. She almost did, anyway.

"That's such a relief," Mrs. Granger said.

"Good," Nora said.

That night, in bed. Their last Brooklyn night.

"You need to stop worrying," Chad said. "If someone finds that tape, they probably won't look at it. And if they do, the chance they'd connect it with you is so small as to be infinitesimal. Besides, the kid's probably forgotten it by now. The mother too."

"The mother was there when a crazy lady assaulted her son and then ran away," Nora said. "Believe me, she hasn't forgotten it."

"All right," he said in an equable tone that made her want to hike her knee into his balls.

"Maybe I ought to go over and help Mrs. Granger neaten the place up."

He looked at her as if she were mad.

"Maybe I want to be suspected," she said, and gave

him a thin smile. What she thought of as her *inciting* smile.

He looked at her, then rolled away.

"Don't do that," she said. "C'mon, Chad."

"No," he said.

"What do you mean, no? Why?"

"Because I know what you think of when we do it."

She hit him. It was a pretty good thump on the back of the neck. "You don't know shit."

He turned over and raised a fist. "Don't do that, Nora."

"Go on," she said, offering her face. "You know you want to."

He almost did. She saw the twitch. Then he lowered his hand and unrolled the fingers. "No more."

She said nothing but thought: *That's what you think*.

Nora lay awake, looking at the digital clock. Until **1:41A** she thought, *This marriage is in trouble*. Then, as **1:41** became **1:42**, she thought: *No, that's wrong. This marriage is over*.

But it had another seven months to run.

Nora never expected any real closure in her association with the Right Reverend George Winston, but as she went to work rounding the new house into shape (she was going to put in not one but two gardens, one for flowers and one for vegetables), she had days when she never thought of Winnie at all. The hitting in bed had stopped. Or almost.

Then, one day in April, she got a postcard from him. It was a shock. It came in a US Postal Service envelope, because there was no more space on the card itself to scribble forwarding information. It had been everywhere, including Brooklyn, Maine, and Montpeliers in Idaho and Indiana. She had no idea why it hadn't reached her before she and Chad had left New York, and, considering its travels, it was a wonder it had reached her at all. It was dated the day before his death. She googled his obituary online just to be sure of that.

Maybe there's something to the Freud stuff, after all, it said. *How are you?*

Good, Nora thought. *I'm good.*

There was a woodstove in the kitchen of their house. She crumpled up the postcard, tossed it in, and set a match to it. *That's that.*

Chad finished *Living with the Animals* in July, writing the last fifty pages in a nine-day burst. He sent it to the agent. Emails and phone calls followed. Chad said Ringling seemed enthusiastic. If so, Nora thought he must have saved most of that enthusiasm for the phone calls. What she saw in the two emails was cautious optimism at best.

In August, at Ringling's request, Chad did some rewriting. He was quiet about this part of the work, a sign that it wasn't going particularly well. But he stuck to it. Nora hardly noticed. She was absorbed with her garden.

In September, Chad insisted on going to New York and pacing Ringling's office while the man made phone calls to the seven publishers to whom the manuscript had gone, hoping some of them would express an interest in meeting with the author. Nora thought about visiting a bar in Montpelier and picking someone up—they could go to a Motel 6—and didn't. It seemed like too much work for too little gain. She worked in her garden instead.

It was just as well. Chad flew back that evening instead of spending the night in New York as he had planned. He was drunk. He also professed to be happy. They had a handshake deal on the book with a good publisher. He named the publisher. She had never heard of it.

"How much?" she asked.

"That doesn't really matter, babe." *Doesn't* came out *dushn't*, and he only called her *babe* when he was drunk. "They really love the book, and that's what matters." *Mattersh*. She realized that when Chad was drunk, he sounded quite a bit like Winnie in the first months after Winnie's stroke.

"How much?"

"Forty thousand dollars." *Dollarsh*.

She laughed. "I probably made that much before I got from the bench to the playground. I figured it out the first time we watched—"

She didn't see the blow coming and didn't really feel it hit. There was a kind of big click in her head, that was all. Then she was lying on the kitchen floor, breathing through her mouth. She had to breathe through her mouth. He had broken her nose.

"You bitch!" he said, starting to cry.

Nora sat up. The kitchen seemed to make a large drunken circle around her before steadying. Blood pattered down on the linoleum. She was amazed, in pain, exhilarated, full of shame and hilarity.

I sure didn't see that one coming, she thought.

"That's right, blame me," she said. Her voice was foggy, hooting. "Blame me and then cry your stupid little eyes out."

He cocked his head as if he hadn't heard her—or couldn't believe what he'd heard—then made a fist and drew it back.

She raised her face, her now crooked nose leading the way. There was a beard of blood on her chin. "Go on," she said. "It's the only thing you're halfway good at."

"How many men have you slept with since that day? Tell me!"

"Slept with none. Fucked a dozen." A lie, actually. There had only been the cop and an electrician who'd come one day while Chad was in town. "Lay on, Macduff."

Instead of laying on, he opened his fist and let his hand drop to his side. "The book would have been fine if not for you." He shook his head as if to clear it. "That's not exactly right, but you know what I mean."

"You're drunk."

"I'm going to leave you and write another one. A better one."

"Pigs will whistle."

"You wait," he said, as tearfully childish as a little boy who has just lost in a schoolyard scuffle. "You just wait and see."

"You're drunk. Go to bed."

"You poison bitch."

Having delivered himself of this, he shuffled off to bed, walking with his head down. He even *walked* like Winnie after his stroke.

Nora thought about going to Urgent Care for her nose, but was too tired to think of a story that would have just the right touch of veracity. In her heart—her *nursely* heart—she knew there was no such story.

They would see through her no matter how good her story was. When it came to things like this, ER personnel always did.

She stuffed cotton up her nose and took two Tylenol with codeine. Then she went outside and weeded her garden until it was too dark to see. When she went inside, Chad was snoring on the bed. He had taken his shirt off, but his pants were still on. She thought he looked like a fool. This made her feel like crying, but she didn't.

He left her and went back to New York. Sometimes he emailed, and sometimes she emailed back. He didn't ask for his half of the remaining money, which was good. She wouldn't have given it to him. She had worked for that money and was still working *with* it, feeding it into the bank little by little, paying off the house. He said in his emails that he was subbing again and writing on the weekends. She believed him about the subbing but not about the writing. His emails had a strengthless, washed-out feeling that suggested he might not have much left when it came to writing. She'd always thought he was pretty much a one-book man, anyway.

She took care of the divorce herself. She found everything she needed on the Internet. There were papers she needed him to sign, and he signed them. They came back with no note attached.

The following summer—a good one; she was working full-time at the local hospital and her garden was an absolute riot—she was browsing in a used bookstore one day and came across a volume she had seen in Winnie's study: *The Basis of Morality*. It was a pretty beat-up copy, and she was able to take it home for two dollars, plus tax.

It took her the rest of the summer and most of the fall to read it cover-to-cover. In the end she was disappointed. There was little or nothing in it she did not already know.

For Jim Sprouse

I think that most people tend to meditate more on What Comes Next as they get older, and since I'm now in my late sixties, I qualify in that regard. Several of my short stories and at least one novel (*Revival*) have approached this question. I can't say "have *dealt* with it," because that implies some conclusion, and none of us can really draw one, can we? Nobody has sent back any cell phone video from the land of death. There's faith, of course (and a veritable deluge of "heaven is real" books), but faith is, by its very definition, belief without proof.

When you boil it down, there are only two choices. Either there's Something, or there's Nothing. If it's the latter, case closed. If it's the former, there are myriad possibilities, with heaven, hell, purgatory, and reincarnation being the most popular on the Afterlife Hit Parade. Or maybe you get what you always believed you would get. Maybe the brain is equipped with a deeply embedded exit program that starts running just as everything else is running down, and we're getting ready to catch that final train. To me, the reports of near-death experiences tend to support this idea.

What I'd like—I think—is a chance to go through it all again, as a kind of immersive movie, so I could relish the good times and good calls, like marrying my wife and our decision to have that third child. Of course I'd also have to rue the bad calls (I've made my share), but who wouldn't like to reexperience that first good kiss, or have a chance to relax and really enjoy the wedding ceremony that went by in such a nervous blur?

This story isn't about such a rerun—not exactly—but musing about the possibility led me to write about one man's afterlife. The reason fantasy fiction remains such a vital and necessary genre is that it lets us talk about such things in a way realistic fiction cannot.

Afterlife

William Andrews, an investment banker with Goldman Sachs, dies on the afternoon of September 23, 2012. It is an expected death; his wife and adult children are at his bedside. That evening, when she finally allows herself some time alone, away from the steady stream of family and condolence visitors, Lynn Andrews calls her oldest friend, who still lives in Milwaukee. It was Sally Freeman who introduced her to Bill, and if anyone deserves to know about the last sixty seconds of her thirty-year marriage, it's Sally.

"He was out of it for most of the last week—the drugs—but conscious at the end. His eyes were open, and he saw me. He smiled. I took his hand and he squeezed it a little. I bent over and kissed his cheek. When I straightened up again, he was gone." She has been waiting for hours to say this, and with it said, she bursts into tears.

Her assumption that the smile was for her is natural enough, but mistaken. As he is looking up at his wife and three grown children—they seem impossibly tall, creatures of angelic good health inhabiting a world he is now departing—Bill feels the pain he has lived with for the past eighteen months leave his body. It pours out like slop from a bucket. So he smiles.

With the pain gone, there's little left. His body feels as light as a fluff of milkweed. His wife takes his hand, reaching down from her tall and healthy world. He has reserved a little bit of strength, which he now expends by squeezing her fingers. She bends down. She is going to kiss him.

Before her lips can touch his skin, a hole appears in the center of his vision. It's not a black hole but a white one. It spreads, obliterating the only world he's known since 1956, when he was born in the small Hemingford County Hospital in Nebraska. During the last year, Bill has read a great deal about the passage from life to death (on his computer, always careful to obliterate the history so as not to upset Lynn, who is constantly and unrealistically upbeat), and while most of it struck him as bullshit, the so-called white light phenomenon seemed quite plausible. For one thing, it has been reported in all cultures. For another, it has a smidgen of scientific credibility. One theory he's read suggests the white light comes as a result of the sudden cessation of blood flow to the brain. Another, more elegant, posits that the brain is performing a final global scan in an effort to find an experience comparable to dying.

Or it may just be a final firework.

Whatever the cause, Bill Andrews is now experiencing it. The white light obliterates his family and the airy room from which the mortuary assistants will soon remove his sheeted breathless body. In his researches, he became familiar with the acronym NDE, standing for near-death experience. In many of these experiences, the white light becomes a tunnel, at the end of which stand beckoning family members who have already died, or friends, or angels, or Jesus, or some other beneficent deity.

Bill expects no welcoming committee. What he expects is for the final firework to fade to the blackness of oblivion, but that doesn't happen. When the brilliance dims, he's not in heaven or hell. He's in a hallway. He supposes it could be purgatory, a hallway painted industrial green and floored in scuffed and dirty tile could very well be purgatory, but only if it went on forever. This one ends twenty feet down at a door with a sign on it reading **ISAAC HARRIS MANAGER**.

Bill stands where he is for a few moments, inventorying himself. He's wearing the pajamas he died in (at least he assumes he died), and he's barefoot, but there's no sign of the cancer that first tasted his body, then gobbled it down to nothing but skin and skeleton. He looks to be back at about one ninety, which was his fighting weight (slightly soft-bellied, granted) before the cancer struck. He feels his buttocks and the small of his back. The bedsores are gone. Nice. He takes a deep breath and exhales without coughing. Even nicer.

He walks a little way down the hall. On his left is a fire extinguisher with a peculiar graffito above it: *Better late than never!* On his right is a bulletin board. On this a number of photographs have been pinned, the old-fashioned kind with deckle edges. Above them is a hand-printed banner reading COMPANY PICNIC 1956! WHAT FUN WE HAD!

Bill examines the photographs, which show executives, secretaries, office personnel, and a gaggle of romping kids smeared with ice cream. There are guys tending a barbecue (one wearing the obligatory joke toque), guys and gals tossing horseshoes, guys and gals playing volleyball, guys and gals swimming in a lake. The guys are wearing bathing suits that look almost obscenely short and tight to his twenty-first century eye, but very few of them are carrying big guts. *They have fifties' physiques,* Bill thinks. The gals are wearing those old-fashioned Esther Williams tank suits, the kind that make women look as if they have not buttocks but only a smooth and cleftless swoop above the backs of their thighs. Hot dogs are being consumed. Beer is being drunk. Everybody appears to be having a whale of a good time.

In one of the pictures he sees Richie Blankmore's father handing Annmarie Winkler a toasted marshmallow. This is ridiculous, because Richie's dad was a truck driver and never went to a company picnic in his life. Annmarie was a girl he dated in college. In another photo he sees Bobby Tisdale, a college classmate back in the early seventies. Bobby, who referred to himself as Tiz the Whiz, died of a heart attack while still in his thirties. He was probably on earth in 1956, but would have been in kindergarten or the first grade, not drinking beer on the shore of Lake Whatever. In this picture the Whiz looks about twenty, which would have been his age when Bill knew him. In a third picture, Eddie Scarponi's mom is baffing a volleyball. Eddie was Bill's best friend when the family moved from Nebraska to Paramus, New Jersey, and Gina Scarponi—once glimpsed sunning herself on the patio in filmy white panties and nothing else—was one of Bill's favorite fantasies when he was still on his masturbation learner's permit.

The guy in the joke toque is Ronald Reagan.

Bill looks closely, his nose almost pressing against the black-and-white photo, and there can be no doubt. The fortieth president of the United States is flipping burgers at a company picnic.

What company, though?

And where, exactly, is Bill now?

His euphoria at being whole again and pain free is fading. What replaces it is a growing sense of dislocation and unease. Seeing these familiar people in the photographs doesn't make sense, and the fact that he doesn't know the majority of them offers marginal comfort at best. He looks behind him, and sees stairs leading up to another door. Printed on this one in large red block letters is LOCKED. That leaves only Mr. Isaac Harris's office. Bill walks down there, hesitates, and then knocks.

"It's open."

Bill walks in. Beside a cluttered desk stands a fellow in baggy, high-waisted suit pants held up by suspenders. His brown hair is plastered to his skull and parted in the middle. He wears rimless glasses. The walls are covered with invoices and corny leg-art cheesecake pix that make Bill think of the trucking company Richie Blankmore's dad worked for. He went there a few times with Richie, and the dispatch office looked like this.

According to the calendar on one wall, it is March of 1911, which makes no more sense than 1956. To Bill's right as he enters, there's a door. To his left is another. There are no windows, but a glass tube comes out of the ceiling and dangles over a Dandux laundry basket. The basket is filled with a heap of yellow sheets that look like more invoices. Or maybe they're memos. Files are piled two feet high on the chair in front of the desk.

"Bill Anderson, isn't it?" The man goes behind the desk and sits down. There is no offer to shake hands.

"Andrews."

"Right. And I'm Harris. Here you are again, Andrews."

Given all Bill's research on dying, this comment actually makes sense. And it's a relief. As long as he doesn't have to come back as a dung beetle, or something. "So it's reincarnation? Is that the deal?"

Isaac Harris sighs. "You always ask the same thing, and I always give the same answer: not really."

"I'm dead, aren't I?"

"Do you feel dead?"

"No, but I saw the white light."

"Oh yes, the famous white light. There you were and here you are. Wait a minute, just hold the phone."

Harris breezes through the papers on his desk, doesn't find what he wants, and starts opening drawers. From one of them he takes a few more folders and selects one. He opens it, flips a page or two, and nods. "Just refreshing myself a bit. Investment banker, aren't you?"

"Yes."

"Wife and three kids? Two sons, one daughter?"

"Correct."

"Apologies. I have a couple of hundred pilgrims, and it's hard to keep them straight. I keep meaning to put these folders in some sort of order, but that's really a secretarial job, and since they've never provided me with one . . ."

"Who's *they*?"

"No idea. All communications come via the tube."

He taps it. The tube sways, then stills. "Runs on compressed air. Latest thing."

Bill picks up the folders on the client's chair and looks at the man behind the desk, eyebrows raised.

"Just put them on the floor," Harris says. "That'll do for now. One of these days I really am going to get organized. If there *are* days. Probably are—nights, too—but who can say for sure? No windows in here, as you will have noticed. Also no clocks."

Bill sits down. "Why call me a pilgrim, if it's not reincarnation?"

Harris leans back and laces his hands behind his neck. He looks up at the pneumatic tube, which probably *was* the latest thing at some time or other. Say around 1911, although Bill supposes such things might still have been around in 1956.

Harris shakes his head and chuckles, although not in an amused way. "If you only knew how *wearisome* you guys become. According to the file, this is our fifteenth visit."

"I've never been here in my life," Bill says. He considers this. "Except it's *not* my life. Is it? It's my afterlife."

"Actually, it's mine. You're the pilgrim, not me. You and the other bozos who parade in and out of here. You'll use one of the doors and go. I stay. There's no bathroom here, because I no longer have to perform toilet functions. There's no bedroom, because I no longer have to sleep. All I do is sit around and visit with you traveling bozos. You come in, you ask the same questions, and I give the same answers. That's *my* afterlife. Sound exciting?"

Bill, who has encountered all the theological ins and outs during his final research project, decides he had the right idea while he was still in the hall. "You're talking about purgatory."

"Oh, no doubt. The only question I have is how long I'll be staying. I'd like to tell you I'll eventually go mad if I can't move on, but I don't think I can do that any more than I can take a shit or a nap. I know my name means nothing to you, but we've discussed this before—not every time you show up, but on several occasions." He waves an arm with enough force to cause some of the invoices tacked on the wall to flutter. "This is—or *was*, I'm not sure which is actually correct—my earthly office."

"In nineteen eleven?"

"Just so. I'd ask if you know what a shirtwaist is, Bill, but since I know you don't, I'll tell you: a woman's blouse. At the turn of the century, I and my partner, Max Blanck, owned a business called the Triangle Shirtwaist Factory. Profitable business, but the women who worked there were a large pain in the keister. Always sneaking out to smoke, and—this was worse—stealing stuff, which they would put in their purses or tuck up under their skirts. So we locked the doors to keep them in during their shifts, and searched them on their way out. Long story short, the damned place caught fire one day. Max and I escaped by going up to the roof and down the fire escape. Many of the women were not so lucky. Although, let's be honest and admit there's lots of blame to go around. Smoking in the factory was strictly *verboten*, but plenty of them did it anyway, and it was a cigarette that started the blaze. Fire marshal said so. Max and I were tried for manslaughter and acquitted."

Bill recalls the fire extinguisher in the hall, with *Better late than never* printed above it. He thinks:

You were found guilty in the retrial, Mr. Harris, or you wouldn't be here. "How many women died?"

"A hundred and forty-six," Harris says, "and I regret every one, Mr. Anderson."

Bill doesn't bother correcting him on the name. Twenty minutes ago he was dying in his bed; now he is fascinated by this old story, which he has never heard before. That he remembers, anyway.

"Not long after Max and I got down the fire escape, the women crammed onto it. The damn thing couldn't take the weight. It collapsed and spilled two dozen of em a hundred feet to the cobblestones. They all died. Forty more jumped from the ninth- and tenth-floor windows. Some were on fire. *They* all died too. The fire brigade got there with life nets, but the women tore right through them and exploded on the pavement like bags filled with blood. A terrible sight, Mr. Anderson, terrible. Others jumped down the elevator shafts, but most . . . just . . . burned."

"Like nine-eleven with fewer casualties."

"So you always say."

"And you're here."

"Yes indeed. I sometimes wonder how many men are sitting in offices just like this. Women too. I'm sure there *are* women, I've always been forward-looking and see no reason why women can't fill low-level executive positions, and admirably. All of us answering the same questions and sending on the same pilgrims. You'd think that the load would lighten a little each time one of you decides to use the right-hand door instead of that one"—he points to the left—"but no. *No.* A fresh canister comes down the tube—*zoop*—and I get a new bozo to replace the old one. Sometimes two." He leans forward and speaks with great emphasis. "This is a shitty job, Mr. Anderson!"

"It's Andrews," Bill says. "And look, I'm sorry you feel that way, but Jesus, take a little responsibility for your actions, man! A hundred and forty-six women! And you *did* lock the doors."

Harris hammers his desk. "They were stealing us blind!" He picks up the folder and shakes it at Bill. "You should talk! Ha! Pot calling the kettle black! Goldman Sachs! Securities fraud! Profits in the billions, taxes in the millions! The *low* millions! Does the phrase *housing bubble* ring a bell? How many clients' trust did you abuse? How many people lost their life savings thanks to your greed and shortsightedness?"

Bill knows what Harris is talking about, but all that chicanery (well . . . most of it) went on far above his pay grade. He was as surprised as anyone when the excrement hit the cooling device. He's tempted to say there's a big difference between being beggared and burned alive, but why rub salt in the wound? Besides, it would probably sound self-righteous.

"Let's drop it," he says. "If you have information I need, why not give it to me. Fill me in on the deal, and I'll get out of your hair."

"*I* wasn't the one smoking," Harris says in a low and brooding tone. "*I* wasn't the one dropped the match."

"Mr. Harris?" Bill can feel the walls closing in. *If I had to be here forever I'd shoot myself,* he thinks. Only if what Mr. Harris says is true, he wouldn't want to, any more than he'd want to go to the toilet.

"Okay, all right." Harris makes a lip-flapping sound, not quite a raspberry. "The *deal* is this. Leave through the left door and you get to live your life over again. A to Z. Start to finish. Take the right one and you wink out. Poof. Candle-in-the-wind type of thing."

At first Bill says nothing to this. He's incapable of speech and not sure he can trust his ears. It's too good to be true. His mind first turns to his brother Mike, and the accident that happened when Mike was eight. Next, to the stupid shoplifting thing when Bill was seventeen. Just a lark, but it could have put a hole in his college plans if his father hadn't stepped in and talked to the right person. The thing with Annmarie in the fraternity house . . . that still haunts him at odd moments, even after all these years. And of course, the big one—

Harris is smiling, and the smile isn't a bit pleasant. "I know what you're thinking, because I've heard it all from you before. About how you and your brother were playing flashlight tag when you were kids, and you slammed the bedroom door to keep him out, and accidentally cut off the tip of his pinky finger. The impulse shoplifting thing, the watch, and how your dad pulled strings to get you out of it—"

"That's right, no record. Except with him. He never let me forget it."

"And then there's the girl in the frat house." Harris lifts the file. "Her name's in here somewhere, I imagine, I do my best to keep the files current—when I can find them—but why don't you refresh me."

"Annmarie Winkler." Bill can feel his cheeks heating up. "It wasn't date rape, so don't get that idea. She put her legs around me when I got on top of her, and if that doesn't say consent, I don't know what does."

"Did she also put her legs around the two fellows who came next?"

No, Bill is tempted to say, *but at least we didn't light her on fire.*

And still.

He'd be squaring up a putt on the seventh green or working in his woodshop or talking to his daughter (now a college student herself) about her senior thesis, and he would wonder where Annmarie is now. What she's doing. What she remembers about that night.

Harris's smile widens to a locker-room smirk. It may be a shitty job, but it's clear there are a few parts of it he enjoys. "I can see that's a question you don't want to answer, so why don't we move along. You're thinking of all the things you'll change during your next ride on the cosmic carousel. This time you won't slam the door on your kid brother's finger, or try to shoplift a watch at the Paramus Mall—"

"It was the Mall of New Jersey. I'm sure it's in your file somewhere."

Harris gives Bill's folder a get-away-fly flap and continues. "Next time you'll decline to fuck your semicomatose date as she lies on the sofa in the basement of your fraternity house, and—big one!—you'll actually make that appointment for the colonoscopy instead of putting it off, having now decided—correct me if I'm wrong—that the indignity of having a camera shoved up your ass is marginally better than dying of colon cancer."

Bill says, "Several times I've come close to telling Lynn about that frat house thing. I've never had the courage."

"But given the chance, you'd fix it."

"Of course—given the chance, wouldn't you unlock those factory doors?"

"Indeed I would, but there are no second chances. Sorry to disappoint you."

He doesn't look sorry. Harris looks tired. Harris looks bored. Harris also looks meanly triumphant. He points to the door on Bill's left.

"Use that one—as you have on every other occasion—and you begin all over again, as a seven-pound baby boy sliding from your mother's womb into the doctor's hands. You'll be wrapped in bunting and taken home to a farm in central Nebraska. When your father sells the farm in nineteen sixty-four, you'll move to New Jersey. There you will cut off the tip of your brother's little finger while playing flashlight tag. You'll go to the same high school, take the same courses, and make the same grades. You'll go to Boston College, and you'll commit the same act of semirape in the same fraternity house basement. You'll watch as the same two fraternity brothers then have sex with Annmarie Winkler, and although you'll think you should call a halt to what's going on, you'll never quite muster up the moral fortitude to do so. Three years later you'll meet Lynn DeSalvo, and two years after that you'll be married. You'll follow the same career path, you'll have the same friends, you'll have the same deep disquiet about some of your firm's business practices . . . and you'll keep the same silence. The same doctor will urge you to get a colonoscopy when you turn fifty, and you will promise—as you always do—that you'll take care of that little matter. You won't, and as a result you will die of the same cancer."

Harris's smile as he drops the folder back on his cluttered desk is now so wide it almost touches the lobes of his ears.

"Then you'll come here, and we'll have the same discussion. My advice would be to use the other door and have done with it, but of course that is your decision."

Bill has listened to this sermonette with increasing dismay. "I'll remember nothing? *Nothing?*"

"Not quite nothing," Harris says. "You may have noticed some photos in the hall."

"The company picnic."

"Yes. Every client who visits me sees pictures from the year of his or her birth, and recognizes a few familiar faces amid all the strange ones. When you live your life again, Mr. Anders—presuming you decide to—you will have a sense of *déjà vu* when you first see those people, a sense that you have lived it all before. Which, of course, you have. You will have a fleeting sense, almost a surety, that there is more . . . shall we say *depth* to your life, and to existence in general, than you previously believed. But then it will pass."

"If it's all the same, with no possibility of improvement, why are we even here?"

Harris makes a fist and knocks on the end of the pneumatic tube hanging over the laundry basket, making it swing. *"CLIENT WANTS TO KNOW WHY WE'RE HERE! WANTS TO KNOW WHAT IT'S ALL ABOUT!"*

He waits. Nothing happens. He folds his hands on his desk.

"When Job wanted to know that, Mr. Anders, God asked if Job was there when he—God—made the universe. I guess you don't even rate that much of a reply. So let's consider the matter closed. What do you want to do? Pick a door."

Bill is thinking about the cancer. The pain of the

cancer. To go through all that again . . . except he wouldn't remember he'd gone through it already. There's that. Assuming Isaac Harris is telling the truth.

"No memories at all? No changes at all? Are you sure? How can you be?"

"Because it's always the same conversation, Mr. Anderson. Each time, and with all of you."

"It's Andrews!" He bellows it, surprising both of them. In a lower voice, he says, "If I try, really try, I'm sure I can hold onto something. Even if it's only what happened to Mike's finger. And one change might be enough to . . . I don't know . . ."

To take Annmarie to a movie instead of to that fucking kegger, how about that?

Harris says, "There is a folk tale that before birth, every human soul knows all the secrets of life and death and the universe. But then, just before birth, an angel leans down, puts his finger to the new baby's lips, and whispers *'Shhh.'"* Harris touches his phil-trum. "According to the story, this is the mark left by the angel's finger. Every human being has one."

"Have you ever seen an angel, Mr. Harris?"

"No, but I once saw a camel. It was in the Bronx Zoo. Choose a door."

As he considers, Bill remembers a story they had to read in junior high: "The Lady or the Tiger." This decision is nowhere near as difficult.

I must hold onto just one thing, he tells himself as he opens the door that leads back into life. *Just one thing.*

The white light of return envelops him.

The doctor, who will bolt the Republican party and vote for Adlai Stevenson in the fall (something his wife must never know), bends forward from the waist like a waiter presenting a tray and comes up holding a naked baby by the heels. He gives it a sharp smack and the squalling begins.

"You have a healthy baby boy, Mrs. Andrews," he says. "Looks to be about seven pounds. Congratulations."

Mrs. Andrews takes the baby. She kisses his damp cheeks and brow. They will name him William, after her paternal grandfather. When the twenty-first century comes, he'll still be in his forties. The idea is dizzying. In her arms she holds not just a new life but a universe of possibilities. Nothing, she thinks, could be more wonderful.

Thinking of Surendra Patel

Ralph Vicinanza, a close friend who also sold the rights to publish my books in lots of foreign countries, had a way of coming to me with interesting ideas at just the right time—which is to say while I was between projects. I never talk much to people about what I'm working on, so he must have had some kind of special radar. He was the one who suggested I might like to try my hand at a serial novel, à la Charles Dickens, and that seed eventually blossomed into *The Green Mile*.

Ralph called not long after I finished the first draft of *Lisey's Story* and while I was waiting for that book to settle a bit (translation: doing nothing). He said that Amazon was launching their second-generation Kindle, and the company was hoping that some hotshit bestselling writer would help them out in the PR department by writing a story that used the Kindle as a plot element. (Such longish works of fiction and nonfiction later became known as Kindle Singles.) I thanked Ralph but said I had no interest, for two reasons. The first is that I've never been able to write stories on demand. The second is that I hadn't lent my name to any commercial enterprise since doing an American Express ad back in the day. And Jesus Christ, how bizarre was that? Wearing a tuxedo, I posed in a drafty castle with a stuffed raven on my arm. A friend told me I looked like a blackjack dealer with a bird fetish.

"Ralph," I said, "I enjoy my Kindle, but I have absolutely no interest in shilling for Amazon."

Yet the idea lingered, mostly because I've always been fascinated by new technologies, especially those having to do with reading and writing. One day not long after Ralph's call, the idea for this story arrived while I was taking my morning walk. It was too cool to remain unwritten. I didn't tell Ralph, but when the story was done, I sent it to him and said Kindle was welcome to use it for their launch purposes, if they liked. I even showed up at the event and read some of it.

I took a certain amount of shit about that from portions of the literary community that saw it as selling out to the business side, but, in the words of John Lee Hooker, "That don't confront me none." As far as I was concerned, Amazon was just another market, and one of the few that would publish a story of this length. There was no advance, but there were—and still are—royalties on each sale (or download, if you prefer). I was happy to bank those checks; there's an old saying that the workman is worthy of his hire, and I think it's a true saying. I write for love, but love doesn't pay the bills.

There was one special perk, though: a one-of-a-kind pink Kindle. Ralph got a kick out of that, and I'm glad. It was our last really cool deal, because my friend died suddenly in his sleep five years ago. Boy, I miss him.

This version of the story has been considerably revised, but you'll notice it's firmly set in an era when such e-reading devices were still new. That seems like a long time ago, doesn't it? And bonus points for you Roland of Gilead fans who catch references to a certain Dark Tower.

Ur

I—Experimenting with New Technology

When Wesley Smith's colleagues asked him—some with an eyebrow hoicked satirically—what he was doing with that gadget (they all called it a gadget), he told them he was experimenting with new technology. That was not true. He bought the Kindle purely out of spite.

I wonder if the market analysts at Amazon even have that particular motivation on their product-survey radar, he thought. He guessed not. This gave him some satisfaction, but not as much as he hoped to derive from Ellen Silverman's surprise when she saw him with his new purchase. That hadn't happened yet, but it would. It was a small campus, after all, and he'd only been in possession of his new toy (he called it his new toy, at least to begin with) for a week.

Wesley was an instructor in the English Department at Moore College, in Moore, Kentucky. Like all instructors of English, he thought he had a novel in him somewhere and would write it someday. Moore College was the sort of institution that people call "a pretty good school." Don Allman, Wesley's only friend in the English Department, explained what that meant.

"A pretty good school," Don said, "is one nobody has ever heard of outside a thirty-mile radius. People call it a pretty good school because they have no evidence to the contrary, and most people are optimists, although they may claim they are not. People who call themselves realists are often the biggest optimists of all."

"Does that make you a realist?" Wesley once asked him.

"I think the world is mostly populated by shitheads," Don Allman responded. "You take it from there."

Moore wasn't a good school, but neither was it a bad one. On the great scale of academic excellence, its place resided just a little south of mediocre. Most of its three thousand students paid their bills and many of them got jobs after graduating, although few went on to obtain (or even try for) graduate degrees. There was a fair amount of drinking, and of course there were parties, but on the great scale of party schools, Moore's place resided a little to the north of mediocre. It had produced politicians, but all of the small-water variety, even when it came to graft and chicanery. In 1978, one Moore graduate was elected to the US House of Representatives, but he dropped dead of a heart attack after serving only four months. His replacement was a graduate of Baylor.

The school's only marks of exceptionalism had to do with its Division Three football team and its Division Three women's basketball team. The football team (the Moore Meerkats) was one of the worst in America, having won only seven games in the last ten years. There was constant talk of disbanding it. The current coach was a drug addict who liked to tell people that he had seen *The Wrestler* twelve times and never failed to cry when Mickey Rourke told his estranged daughter that he was just a broken-down piece of meat.

The women's basketball team, however, was exceptional in a *good* way, especially considering that most of the players were no more than five feet seven and were preparing for jobs as marketing managers, wholesale buyers, or (if they were lucky) personal assistants to Men of Power. The Lady Meerkats had won eight conference titles in the last ten years. The coach was Wesley's ex-girlfriend, *ex* as of one month previous. Ellen Silverman was the source of the spite that had moved Wesley to buy a Kindle. Well . . . Ellen and the Henderson kid in Wesley's Introduction to Modern American Fiction class.

Don Allman also claimed the Moore faculty was mediocre. Not terrible, like the football team—that, at least, would have been interesting—but definitely mediocre.

"What about you and me?" Wesley asked. They were in the office they shared. If a student came in for a conference, the instructor who had not been sought would leave. For most of the fall and spring semesters this was not an issue, as students never came in for conferences until just before finals. Even then, only the veteran grade-grubbers, the ones who'd had permanently brown noses since elementary school, turned up. Don Allman said he sometimes fantasized about a juicy coed wearing a tee-shirt that said I WILL SCREW YOU FOR AN A, but this never happened.

"What about us?" Don replied. "Jesus Christ, just *look* at us, bro."

"Speak for yourself," Wesley said. "I'm going to write a novel." Although even saying it depressed him. Almost everything depressed him since Ellen had walked out. When he wasn't depressed, he felt spiteful.

"Yes! And President Obama is going to tab me as the new Poet Laureate!" Don Allman exclaimed. Then he pointed at something on Wesley's cluttered desk. The Kindle was currently sitting on *American Dreams*, the textbook Wesley used in his Intro to American Lit class. "How's that little bastard working out for you?"

"Fine," Wesley said.

"Will it ever replace the book?"

"Never," Wesley said. But he had begun to wonder.

"I thought they only came in white," Don Allman said.

Wesley looked at Don as haughtily as he himself had been looked at in the department meeting where his Kindle had made its public debut. "Nothing only comes in white," he said. "This is America."

Don Allman considered this, then said: "I heard you and Ellen broke up."

Wesley sighed.

Ellen had been his *other* friend, and one with benefits, until four weeks ago. She wasn't in the English Department, of course, but the thought of going to bed with anyone in the English Department, even Suzanne Montanaro, who was vaguely presentable, made him shudder. Ellen was five-two (eyes of blue!), slim, with a mop of short, curly black hair that made her look distinctly elfin. She had a dynamite figure and kissed like a dervish. (Wesley had never kissed a dervish, but could imagine.) Nor did her energy flag when they were in bed.

Once, winded, he lay back and said, "I'll never equal you as a lover."

"If you keep lowballing yourself like that, you won't be my lover for long. You're okay, Wes."

But he guessed he wasn't. He guessed he was just sort of . . . mediocre.

It wasn't his less-than-athletic sexual ability that ended their relationship, however. It wasn't the fact that Ellen was a vegan who ate Tofurky for Thanksgiving. It wasn't the fact that she would sometimes lie in bed after lovemaking, talking about pick-and-rolls, give-and-gos, and the inability of Shawna Deeson to learn something Ellen called "the old garden gate."

In fact, these monologues sometimes put Wesley into his deepest, sweetest, and most refreshing sleeps. He thought it was the calmness of her voice, so different from the often profane shrieks of encouragement she let out while they were making love. Her love-shrieks were eerily similar to the ones she uttered during games, running up and down the sidelines like a hare, exhorting her girls to "Pass the ball!" and "Drive the paint!" Wesley had even heard one of her sideline screams, "Go for the hole," in the bedroom from time to time.

They were well matched, at least in the short term; she was fiery iron, straight from the forge, and he—in his apartment filled with books—was the water in which she cooled herself.

The books were the problem. That, and the fact

that he had freaked out and called her an illiterate bitch. He had never called a woman such a thing in his life before, but she had surprised an anger out of him that he had never suspected. He might be a mediocre instructor, as Don Allman had suggested, and the novel he had in him might remain in him (like a wisdom tooth that never comes up, at least avoiding the possibility of rot, infection, and an expensive— not to mention painful—dental process), but he loved books. Books were his Achilles heel.

She had come in fuming, which was normal, but also fundamentally upset—a state he failed to recognize because he had never seen her in it before. Also, he was rereading James Dickey's *Deliverance*, reveling again in how well Dickey had harnessed his poetic sensibility, at least that once, to narrative, and he had just gotten to the closing passages, where the unfortunate canoeists are trying to cover up both what they have done and what has been done to them. He had no idea that Ellen had just been forced to boot Shawna Deeson off the team, or that the two of them had had a screaming fight in the gym in front of the whole team—plus the boys' basketball team, which was waiting their turn to practice their mediocre moves—or that Shawna Deeson had then gone outside and heaved a large rock at the windshield of Ellen's Volvo, an act for which she would surely be suspended. He had no idea that Ellen was now blaming herself, and bitterly, because "she was supposed to be the adult."

He heard that part—"I'm supposed to be the adult"—and said *Uh-huh* for the fifth or sixth time, which was one time too many for Ellen Silverman. She plucked *Deliverance* from Wesley's hands, threw it across the room, and said the words that would haunt him for the next lonely month:

"Why can't you just read off the computer, like the rest of us?"

"She really said that?" Don Allman asked, a remark that woke Wesley from a trancelike state. He realized he had just told the whole story to his officemate. He hadn't meant to, but he had. There was no going back now.

"She did. And I said, 'That was a first edition I got from my father, you illiterate bitch.'"

Don Allman was speechless. He could only stare.

"She walked out," Wesley said miserably. "I haven't seen or spoken to her since."

"Haven't even called to say you're sorry?"

Wesley had tried to do this, and had gotten only her voicemail. He had considered going over to the house she rented from the college, but thought she might put a fork in his face . . . or some other part of his anatomy. Also, he didn't consider what had happened to be entirely his fault. She hadn't even given him a *chance*. Plus . . . she *was* illiterate, or close to it. Had told him once in bed that the only book she'd read for pleasure since coming to Moore was *Reach for the Summit: The Definite Dozen System for Succeeding at Whatever You Do*, by Tennessee Lady Vols coach Pat Summitt. She watched TV (mostly sports), and when she wanted to dig deeper into some news story, she went to the *Drudge Report*. She certainly wasn't computer illiterate. She praised the Moore College Wi-Fi network (which was superlative rather than mediocre), and never went anywhere without her laptop slung over her shoulder. On the front was a picture of Tamika Catchings with blood running down

her face from a split eyebrow and the legend I PLAY
LIKE A GIRL.

Don Allman sat in silence for a few moments, tapping his fingers on his narrow chest. Outside their
window, November leaves rattled across Moore
Quadrangle. Then he said: "Did Ellen walking out
have anything to do with that?" He nodded to Wesley's new electronic sidekick. "It did, didn't it? You
decided to read off the computer, just like the rest of
us. To . . . what? Woo her back?"

"No," Wesley said, because he didn't want to tell
the truth: in a way he still didn't completely understand, he had done it to get back *at* her. Or make fun
of her. Or something. "Not at all. I'm merely experimenting with new technology."

"Right," said Don Allman. "And I'm Robert Frost,
stopping by the woods on a snowy fucking evening."

His car was in Parking Lot A, but Wesley elected to
walk the two miles back to his apartment, a thing he
often did when he wanted to think. He trudged down
Moore Avenue, first past the fraternity houses, then
past apartment houses blasting rock and rap from
every window, then past the bars and take-out res-
taurants that serve as a life-support system for every
small college in America. There was also a bookstore
specializing in used texts and last year's bestsellers
offered at fifty percent off. It looked dusty and dispir-
ited and was often empty.

Because people were home reading off the com
puter, Wesley assumed.

Brown leaves blew around his feet. His briefcase
banged against one knee. Inside were his texts, the
current book he was reading for pleasure (*2666*, by

Roberto Bolaño), and a bound notebook with beautiful marbleized boards. This had been a gift from Ellen on the occasion of his birthday.

"For your book ideas," she had said.

In July, that was, when things between them had still been swell and they'd had the campus pretty much to themselves. The blank book had over two hundred pages, but only the first one had been marked by his large, flat scrawl.

At the top of the page (printed) was: IDEAS FOR THE NOVEL!

Below that was: *A young boy discovers that his father and mother are both having affairs*

And

A young boy, blind since birth, is kidnapped by his lunatic grandfather who

And

A teenager falls in love with his best friend's mother and

Below this one was the final idea, written shortly after Ellen had thrown *Deliverance* across the room and stalked out of his life.

A shy but dedicated small college instructor and his athletic but largely illiterate girlfriend have a falling-out after

It was probably the best idea—write what you know, all the experts agreed on that—but he simply couldn't go there. Talking to Don had been hard enough. And even then, complete honesty had escaped him. Like not having said how much he wanted her back.

As he approached the three-room flat he called home—what Don Allman sometimes called his "swinging bachelor pad"—Wesley's thoughts turned to the Henderson kid. Was his name Richard or Robert? Wesley had a block about that, not the same as the block he had about fleshing out any of the fragmentary mission-statements for his novel, but probably related. He had an idea all such blocks were basically hysterical in nature, as if the brain detected (or thought it detected) some nasty interior beast and had locked it in a cell with a steel door. You could hear it thumping and jumping in there like a rabid raccoon that would bite if approached, but you couldn't see it.

The Henderson kid was on the football team—a noseback or point guard or some such thing—and while he was as horrible on the gridiron as any of them, he was a nice kid and a fairly good student. Wesley liked him. But still, he had been ready to tear the boy's head off when he spotted him in class with what Wesley assumed was a PDA or a newfangled cell phone. This was shortly after Ellen had walked out. In those early days of the breakup, Wesley often found himself up at three in the morning, pulling some literary comfort food down from the shelf: usually his old friends Jack Aubrey and Stephen Maturin, their adventures recounted by Patrick O'Brian. And not even that had kept him from remembering the ringing slam of the door as Ellen left his life, probably for good.

So he was in a foul mood and more than ready for backtalk as he approached Henderson and said, "Put it away. This is a literature class, not an Internet chat room."

The Henderson kid had looked up and given him a sweet smile. It hadn't lifted Wesley's foul mood, but it did dissolve his anger on contact. Mostly because he wasn't an angry man by nature. He supposed he was *depressive* by nature, maybe even dysthymic. Hadn't he always suspected that Ellen Silverman was too good for him? Hadn't he known, in his heart of hearts, that the doorslam had been waiting for him from the very beginning, when he'd spent the evening talking to her at a boring faculty party? Ellen played like a girl; he played like a wimp. He couldn't even stay mad at a student who was goofing with his pocket computer (or Nintendo, or whatever it was) in class.

"It's the assignment, Mr. Smith," the Henderson kid had said (on his forehead was a large purple bruise from his latest outing in the Meerkat blue). "It's 'Paul's Case.' Look."

The kid turned the gadget so Wesley could see it. It was a flat white panel, rectangular, less than half an inch thick. At the top was **amazon**kindle and the smile logo Wesley knew well; he was not entirely computer illiterate himself, and had ordered books from Amazon plenty of times (although he usually tried the bookstore in town first, partly out of pity; even the cat who spent most of its life dozing in the window looked malnourished).

The interesting thing on the kid's gadget wasn't the logo on top or the teeny-tiny keyboard on the bottom. It was mostly screen, and on that screen was not a video game where young men and women with buffed-out bodies were killing zombies in the ruins of New York, but a page of Willa Cather's story about the poor boy with the destructive illusions.

Wesley had reached for it, then paused. "May I?"

"Go ahead," the Henderson kid—Richard or Robert—told him. "It's pretty neat. You can download books from thin air, and you can make the type as big as you want. Also, the books are cheaper because there's no paper or binding."

That sent a minor chill through Wesley. He became

aware that most of his Intro to American Lit class was watching him. Wesley supposed it was hard for them to decide if he, as a thirty-five-year-old, was Old School (like the ancient Dr. Wence, who looked like a crocodile in a three-piece suit) or New School (like Suzanne Montanaro, who liked to play Avril Lavigne's "Girlfriend" in her Introduction to Modern Drama class). Wesley supposed his reaction to Henderson's Kindle would help them with that.

"Mr. Henderson," he said, "there will always be books. Which means there will always be paper and binding. Books are *real objects*. Books are *friends*."

"Yeah, but!" Henderson had replied, his sweet smile now becoming slightly sly.

"But?"

"They're also ideas and emotions. You said so in our first class."

"Well," Wesley had said, "you've got me there. But books aren't *solely* ideas. Books have a smell, for instance. One that gets better—more nostalgic— as the years go by. Does this gadget of yours have a smell?"

"Nope," Henderson replied. "Not really. But when you turn the pages . . . here, with this button . . . they kind of flutter, like in a real book, and I can go to any page I want, and when it sleeps, it shows pictures of famous writers, and it holds a charge, and—"

"It's a computer," Wesley had said. "You're reading off the computer."

The Henderson kid had taken his Kindle back. "It's still 'Paul's Case.' "

"You've never heard of a Kindle, Mr. Smith?" Josie Quinn had asked. Her tone was that of a kindly anthropologist asking a member of Papua New

Guinea's Kombai tribe if he had ever heard of electric stoves and elevator shoes.

"No," he said, not because it was true—he *had* seen something called Shop the Kindle Store when he bought books from Amazon online—but because, on the whole, he thought he would prefer being perceived by them as Old School. New School was somehow . . . mediocre.

"You ought to get one," the Henderson kid said, and when Wesley had replied, without even thinking, "Perhaps I will," the class had broken into spontaneous applause. For the first time since Ellen's departure, Wesley had felt faintly cheered. Because they wanted him to get a book-reading gadget, and also because the applause suggested they did see him as Old School. *Teachable* Old School.

He did not seriously consider buying a Kindle (if he was Old School, then books were definitely the way to go) until a couple of weeks later. One day on his way home from school he imagined Ellen seeing him with his Kindle, just strolling across the quad and bopping his finger on the little NEXT PAGE button.

What in the world are you doing? she would ask. Speaking to him at last.

Reading off the computer, he would say. *Just like the rest of you.*

Spiteful!

But, as the Henderson kid might put it, was that a bad thing? It occurred to him that spite was a kind of methadone for lovers, and better than going cold turkey.

When he got home he turned on his desktop Dell (he owned no laptop and took pride in the fact) and went to the Amazon website. He had expected the gadget to go for four hundred dollars or so, maybe more if there was a Cadillac model, and was surprised to find it was considerably cheaper than that. Then he went to the Kindle Store (which he had been so successfully ignoring) and discovered that the Henderson kid was right: the book prices were ridiculously low. Hardcover novels (*what* cover, ha-ha) were priced below most of the trade paperbacks he'd bought recently. Considering what he spent on books, the Kindle might pay for itself. As for the reaction of his colleagues—all those hoicked eyebrows—Wesley discovered he relished the prospect. Which led to an interesting insight into human nature, or at least the human nature of the academic: one liked to be perceived by one's students as Old School, but by one's peers as New School.

I'm experimenting with new technology, he imagined himself saying.

He liked the sound of it. It was New School all the way.

And of course he liked thinking of Ellen's reaction. He had stopped leaving messages on her phone, and he had begun avoiding places—The Pit Stop, Harry's Pizza—where he might run into her, but that could change. Surely *I'm reading off the computer, just like the rest of you* was too good a line to waste.

Oh, that's small, he scolded himself as he sat in front of his computer, looking at the picture of the Kindle. *That is spite so small it probably wouldn't poison a newborn kitten.*

True! But if it was the only spite of which he was capable, why not indulge it?

So he had clicked on the Buy Kindle box, and the gadget had arrived a day later, in a box stamped with

the smile logo and the words *ONE-DAY DELIVERY*.
Wesley hadn't opted for one-day, and would protest
that charge if it showed up on his MasterCard bill, but
he unpacked his new acquisition with real pleasure—
similar to the pleasure he felt when unpacking a box
of books, but sharper. Because there was that sense of
heading into the unknown, he supposed. Not that he
expected the Kindle to replace books, or to be much
more than a novelty item, really; an attention-getter
for a few weeks or months that would afterward stand
forgotten and gathering dust beside the Rubik's Cube
on the knickknack shelf in his living room.

It didn't strike him as peculiar that, whereas the
Henderson kid's Kindle had been white, his was pink.

Not at first.

II—Ur Functions

When Wesley got back to his apartment after his confessional conversation with Don Allman, the message
light on his answering machine was blinking. Two
messages. He pushed the playback button, expecting
to hear his mother complaining about her arthritis and
making trenchant observations about how some sons
actually called home more often than twice a month.
After that would come a robo-call from the Moore
Echo, reminding him—for the dozenth time—that
his subscription had lapsed. But it wasn't his mother
and it wasn't the newspaper. When he heard Ellen's
voice, he paused in the act of reaching for a beer and
listened bent over, with one hand outstretched in the
fridge's frosty glow.

"Hi, Wes," she said, sounding uncharacteristically unsure of herself. There was a long pause, long enough for Wesley to wonder if that was all there was going to be. In the background he heard hollow shouts and bouncing balls. She was in the gym, or had been when she left the message. "I've been thinking about us. Thinking that maybe we should try again. I miss you." And then, as if she had seen him rushing for the door: "But not yet. I need to think a little more about . . . what you said." A pause. "I was wrong to throw your book like that, but I was upset." Another pause, almost as long as the one after she'd said hi. "There's a preseason tourney in Lexington this weekend. You know, the one they call the Bluegrass. It's a big deal. Maybe when I get back, we should talk. Please don't call me until then, because I've got to concentrate on the girls. Defense is terrible, and I've only got one girl who can actually shoot from the perimeter, and . . . I don't know, this is probably a big mistake."

"It's not," he told the answering machine. His heart was pumping. He was still leaning into the open refrigerator, feeling the cold wafting out and striking his face, which seemed too hot. "Believe me, it's not."

"I had lunch with Suzanne Montanaro the other day, and she says you're carrying around one of those electronic reading thingies. To me that seemed . . . I don't know, like a sign that we should try again." She laughed, then screamed so loud that Wesley jumped. *"Chase down that loose ball! You either run or you sit!"* Then: "Sorry. I've got to go. Don't call me. I'll call you. One way or the other. After the Bluegrass. I'm sorry I've been dodging your calls, but . . . you hurt my feelings, Wes. Coaches have feelings too, you know. I—"

A beep interrupted her. The allotted message time had run out. Wesley uttered the word Norman Mailer's publishers had refused to let him use in *The Naked and the Dead*.

Then the second message started and she was back. "I guess English teachers also have feelings. Suzanne says we're not right for each other, she says we're too far apart in our interests, but . . . maybe there's a middle ground. I . . . I need to think about this. Don't call me. I'm not quite ready. Goodbye."

Wesley got his beer. He was smiling. Then he thought of the spite that had been living in his heart for the last month and stopped. He went to the calendar on the wall, and wrote PRESEASON TOURNEY across Saturday and Sunday. He paused, then drew a line through the days of the workweek after, a line on which he wrote ELLEN???

With that done he sat down in his favorite chair, drank his beer, and tried to read *2666*. It was a crazy book, but sort of interesting.

He wondered if it was available from the Kindle Store.

That evening, after replaying Ellen's messages for the third time, Wesley turned on his Dell and went to the Athletic Department website to check for details concerning the Bluegrass Preseason Invitational Tournament. He knew it would be a mistake to turn up there, and he had no intention of doing so, but he did want to know who the Meerkats were playing, and when Ellen would be back.

It turned out there were eight teams, seven from Division Two and only one from Division Three: the Lady Meerkats of Moore. Wesley felt pride on Ellen's behalf when he saw that, and was once more ashamed of his spite . . . which she (lucky him!) knew nothing about. She actually seemed to think he had bought the Kindle as a way of sending her a message: *Maybe you're right, and maybe I can change. Maybe we both can.* He supposed that if things went well, he would in time come to convince himself that was indeed so.

On the website he saw that the team would leave for Lexington by bus at noon this coming Friday. They would practice at Rupp Arena that evening, and play their first game—against the Bulldogs of Truman State, Missouri—on Saturday morning. Because the tourney was double elimination, they wouldn't be starting back until Sunday evening no matter what. Which meant he wouldn't hear from her until the following Monday at the earliest.

It was going to be a long week.

"And," he told his computer (a good listener!), "she may decide against trying again, anyway. I have to be prepared for that."

Well, he could try. And he could also call that bitch Suzanne Montanaro and tell her in no uncertain terms to stop campaigning against him. Why would she do that in the first place? She was a *colleague*, for God's sake!

Only if he did that, Suzanne might carry tales straight back to her friend (*friend?* who knew? who even suspected?) Ellen. It might be best to leave that aspect of things alone. Although the spite wasn't entirely out of his heart after all, it seemed. Now it was directed at Ms. Montanaro.

"Never mind," he told his computer. "George Herbert was wrong. Living well isn't the best revenge; loving well is."

He started to turn off his computer, then remembered something Don Allman had said about Wesley's Kindle: *I thought they only came in white.* Certainly the Henderson kid's had been white, but—what was the saying?—one swallow didn't make a summer. After a few false starts, Google (full of information but essentially dumb as a post) led him to Kindle Fan Sites. He found one called Kindle Kandle. At the top was a bizarre photo of a woman in Quaker garb reading her Kindle by candlelight. (Or possibly kandlelight.) Here he read several posts—complaints, mostly—about how the Kindle came in only one color, which one blogger called "plain old smudge-friendly white." Below it was a reply suggesting that if the complainer persisted in reading with dirty fingers, he should buy a custom sleeve for his Kindle. "In any color you like," she added. "Grow up and show some creativity!"

Wesley turned off his computer, went into the kitchen, got another beer, and pulled his own Kindle from his briefcase. His pink Kindle. Except for the color, it looked exactly the same as the ones on the Kindle Kandle website.

"Kindle-Kandle, bibble-babble," he said. "It's just some flaw in the plastic." Perhaps, but why had it come one-day express delivery when he hadn't specified that? Because someone at the Kindle factory wanted to get rid of the pink mutant as soon as possible? That was ridiculous. They would have just thrown it away. Another victim of quality control.

Could you use a Kindle to go on the Internet? He didn't know, and he remembered there was something else odd about his: no instruction booklet. He thought of going back to the Kindle Kandlers to check out his Internet question, then dismissed the idea. He was just goofing around, after all, beginning to while away the hours between now and next Monday, when he might hear from Ellen again.

"I miss you, kiddo," he said, and was surprised to hear his voice waver. He did miss her. He hadn't realized how much until he'd heard her voice. He'd been too wrapped up in his own wounded ego. Not to mention his sweaty little spite.

The screen titled Wesley's Kindle booted up. Listed were the books he had so far purchased—*Revolutionary Road*, by Richard Yates, and *The Old Man and the Sea*, by Hemingway. The gadget had come with *The New Oxford American Dictionary* preloaded. You only had to begin typing your word and the Kindle found it for you. It was, he thought, TiVo for bookworms.

But could you access the Internet?

He pushed the Menu button and was presented with a number of choices. The top one (of course) invited him to SHOP THE KINDLE STORE. But near the bottom was something called EXPERI-MENTAL. That looked interesting. He moved the cursor to it, opened it, and read this at the top of the screen: *We are working on these experimental prototypes. Do you find them useful?*

"Well, I don't know," Wesley said. "What are they?"

The first prototype turned out to be BASIC WEB. So, yes to the Internet question. The Kindle was apparently a lot more computerized than it looked at first blush. He glanced at the other experimental choices: music downloads (big whoop) and text-to-speech (which might come in handy if he were blind). He pushed the Next Page button to see if there were other experimental prototypes. There was one: Ur Functions.

Now what in the hell was that? Ur, so far as he knew, had only two meanings: a city in the Old Testament, and a prefix meaning "primitive" or "simple." The screen didn't help; although there were explanations for the other experimental functions, there was none for this. Well, there was one way to find out. He highlighted Ur Functions and selected it.

A new menu appeared. There were three items: Ur Books, Ur News Archive, and Ur Local (under construction).

"Huh," Wesley said. "What in the *world*."

He highlighted Ur Books, dropped his finger onto the Select button, then hesitated. Suddenly his skin felt cold, as when he'd been stilled by the sound of Ellen's recorded voice while reaching into the fridge for a beer. He would later think, *It was my own ur. Something simple and primitive deep inside, telling me not to push that button.*

But was he not a modern man? One who now read off the computer?

He was. He was. So he pushed it.

The screen blanked, then WELCOME TO UR BOOKS! appeared at the top . . . and in red! The Kandlers were behind the technological curve, it seemed; there *was* Kolor on the Kindle. Beneath the welcome message was a picture—not of Charles Dickens or Eudora Welty, but of a large black tower. There was something ominous about it. Below, also in red, was an invitation to *Select Author (your choice may not be available)*. And below that, a blinking cursor.

"What the hell," Wesley told the empty room. He

licked his lips, which were suddenly dry, and typed
ERNEST HEMINGWAY.

The screen wiped itself clean. The function, whatever it was supposed to be, didn't seem to work. After
ten seconds or so, Wesley reached for the Kindle,
meaning to turn it off. Before he could push the slide-
switch, the screen finally produced a new message.

10,438,721 URS SEARCHED
17,894 ERNEST HEMINGWAY TITLES
DETECTED
IF YOU DO NOT KNOW TITLE, SELECT UR
OR RETURN TO UR FUNCTIONS MENU
SELECTIONS FROM YOUR CURRENT UR
WILL NOT BE DISPLAYED

"What in the name of God is *this*?" Wesley asked
the empty room. Below the message, the cursor
blinked. Above it, in small type (black, not red), was
one further instruction: NUMERIC ENTRY ONLY.
NO COMMAS OR DASHES. YOUR CURRENT
UR: **117586**.

Wesley felt a strong urge (an *ur* urge!) to turn
the pink Kindle off and drop it into the silverware
drawer. Or into the freezer along with the ice cream
and Stouffer's frozen dinners, that might be even better. Instead, he used the teeny-tiny keypad to enter
his birth date. 7191974 would do as well as any number, he reckoned. He hesitated again, then plunged
the tip of his index finger down on the Select button.
When the screen blanked this time, he had to fight
an impulse to get up from the kitchen chair he was
sitting in and back away from the table. A crazy certainty had arisen in his mind: a hand—or perhaps a

claw—was going to swim up from the grayness of the Kindle's screen, grab him by the throat, and yank him in. He would exist forever after in computerized grayness, floating around the microchips and between the many worlds of Ur.

Then the screen produced type, plain old prosaic type, and the superstitious dread departed. He scanned the Kindle's screen (the size of a small paperback) eagerly, although what he was eager for he had no idea.

At the top was the author's full name—Ernest Miller Hemingway—and his dates. Next came a long list of his published works . . . but it was wrong. *The Sun Also Rises* was there . . . *For Whom the Bell Tolls* . . . the short stories . . . *The Old Man and the Sea*, of course . . . but there were also three or four titles Wesley didn't recognize, and except for minor essays, he thought he had read all of Hemingway's considerable output. Also . . .

He examined the dates again and saw that the death date was wrong. Hemingway had died on July 2, 1961, of a self-inflicted gunshot wound. According to the screen, he had gone to that great library in the sky on August 19, 1964.

"Birth date's wrong, too," Wesley muttered. He was running his free hand through his hair, pulling it into exotic new shapes. "I'm almost sure it is. Should be eighteen ninety-nine, not eighteen ninety-seven."

He moved the cursor down to one of the titles he didn't know: *Cortland's Dogs*. This was some lunatic computer programmer's idea of a joke, pretty much had to be, but *Cortland's Dogs* at least *sounded* like a Hemingway title. Wesley selected it.

The screen blanked, then produced a book cover.

The jacket image—in black-and-white—showed barking dogs surrounding a scarecrow. In the background, shoulders slumped in a posture of weariness or defeat (or both), was a hunter with a gun. The eponymous Cortland, probably.

In the woods of upper Michigan, James Cortland deals with the infidelity of his wife and his own mortality. When three dangerous criminals appear at the old Cortland farm, "Papa's" most famous hero is faced with a terrible choice. Rich in event and symbolism, Ernest Hemingway's final novel was awarded the Pulitzer Prize shortly before his death. $7.50

Below the thumbnail, Kindle asked: BUY THIS BOOK? Y N.

"Total bullshit," Wesley whispered as he highlighted Y and pushed the Select button.

The screen blanked again, then flashed a new message: *Ur novels may not be disseminated as according to all applicable Paradox Laws. Do you agree? Y N.*

Smiling—as befitted someone who got the joke but was going along with it anyway—Wesley selected *Y.* The screen blanked, then presented new information:

THANK YOU, WESLEY!
YOUR UR NOVEL HAS BEEN ORDERED
YOUR ACCOUNT WILL BE DEBITED $7.50
REMEMBER UR NOVELS TAKE LONGER
TO DOWNLOAD
ALLOW 2–4 MINS

Wesley returned to the Wesley's Kindle screen. The same items were there—*Revolutionary Road, The Old Man and the Sea,* the *New Oxford American*— and he was sure that wouldn't change. There was no

Hemingway novel called *Cortland's Dogs*, not in this world or any other. Nonetheless, he got up and went to the phone. It was picked up on the first ring.

"Don Allman," his officemate said. "And yes, I was indeed born a ramblin' man." No hollow gym sounds in the background this time; just the barbaric yawps of Don's three sons, who sounded as though they might be dismantling the Allman residence board by board.

"Don, it's Wesley."

"Ah, Wesley! I haven't seen you in . . . gee, it must be three hours!" From deeper within the lunatic asylum where Wesley assumed Don lived with his family, there came what sounded like a death scream. Don Allman was not perturbed. "Jason, don't throw that at your brother. Be a good little troll and go watch *SpongeBob*." Then, to Wesley: "What can I do for you, Wes? Advice on your love life? Tips on improving your sexual performance and stamina? A title for your novel in progress?"

"I have no novel in progress and you know it," Wesley snapped. "But it's novels I want to talk about. You know Hemingway's *oeuvre*, don't you?"

"I love it when you talk dirty."

"Do you or don't you?"

"Of course. But not as well as you, I hope. You're the twentieth-century American lit man, after all; I stick to the days when writers wore wigs, took snuff, and said picturesque things like *ecod*. What's on your mind?"

"To your knowledge, did Hemingway ever write any fiction about dogs?"

Don considered while another young child commenced shrieking. "Wes, are you okay? You sound a little—"

"Just answer the question. Did he or didn't he?"

Highlight Y or N, Wesley thought.

"All right," Don said. "So far as I can say without consulting my trusty computer, he didn't. I remember him once claiming the Batista partisans clubbed his pet pooch to death, though—how's that for a factoid? You know, when he was in Cuba. He took it as a sign that he and Mary should beat feet to Florida, and they did—posthaste."

"You don't happen to remember that dog's name, do you?"

"I think I do. I'd want to double-check it on the Internet, but I think it was Negrita. Something like that. Sounds slightly racist to me, but what do I know?"

"Thanks, Don." His lips felt numb. "I'll see you tomorrow."

"Wes, are you sure you're—*FRANKIE, PUT THAT DOWN! DON'T*—" There was a crash. "Shit. I think that was Delft. I gotta go, Wes. See you tomorrow."

"Right."

Wesley went back to the kitchen table. He saw that a fresh selection had appeared on the contents page of his Kindle. A novel (or *something*) called *Cortland's Dogs* had been downloaded from . . .

Where, exactly? Some other plane of reality called Ur (or possibly UR) 7191974?

Wesley no longer had the strength to call this idea ridiculous and push it away. He did, however, have enough to go to the refrigerator and get a beer. Which he needed. He opened it, drank half in five long swallows, belched. He sat down, feeling a little better. He highlighted his new acquisition

($7.50 would be mighty cheap for an undiscovered Hemingway, he reckoned) and a title page came up. The next page was a dedication: *To Sy, and to Mary, with love.* Then:

Chapter 1

A man's life was five dogs long, Cortland believed. The first was the one that taught you. The second was the one you taught. The third and fourth were the ones you worked. The last was the one that outlived you. That was the winter dog. Cortland's winter dog was Negrita, but he thought of it only as the scarecrow dog . . .

Liquid rose up in Wesley's throat. He ran for the sink, bent over it, and struggled to keep the beer down. His gorge settled, and instead of turning on the water to rinse puke down the drain, he cupped his hands under the flow and splashed it on his sweaty skin. That was better.

Then he went back to the Kindle and stared down at it.

A man's life was five dogs long, Cortland believed.

Somewhere—at some college a lot more ambitious than Moore of Kentucky—there was a computer programmed to read books and identify the writers by their stylistic tics and tocks, which were supposed to be as unique as fingerprints or snowflakes. Wesley had a vague recollection that this computer program had been used to identify the author of a pseudonymous novel called *Primary Colors*; the program had whiffled through thousands of writers in a matter of hours or days and had come up with a newsmagazine columnist named Joe Klein, who later owned up to his literary paternity.

Wesley thought that if he submitted *Cortland's Dogs* to that computer, it would spit out Ernest Hemingway's name. In truth, he didn't think he needed a computer.

He picked up the Kindle with hands that were now shaking badly. "What *are* you?" he asked.

III—Wesley Refuses to Go Mad

In a real dark night of the soul, Scott Fitzgerald had said, *it is always three o'clock in the morning, day after day.*

At three o'clock on that Tuesday morning, Wesley lay awake, feeling feverish and wondering if he might be cracking up himself. He had forced himself to turn off the pink Kindle and put it back in his briefcase an hour ago, but its hold over him remained every bit as strong as it had been at midnight, when he had still been deep in the Ur Books menu.

He had searched for Ernest Hemingway in two dozen of the Kindle's almost ten and a half million Urs, and had come up with at least twenty novels he had never heard of. In one of the Urs (it happened to be 6201949—which, when broken down, was his mother's birth date), Hemingway appeared to be a crime writer. Wesley had downloaded a title called *It's Blood, My Darling!*, and discovered your basic dime novel . . . but written in staccato, punchy sentences he would have recognized anywhere.

Hemingway sentences.

And even as a crime writer, Hemingway had

departed from gang wars and cheating, gore-happy debs long enough to write *A Farewell to Arms*. He *always* wrote *A Farewell to Arms*, it seemed; other titles came and went, but *A Farewell to Arms* was always there and *The Old Man and the Sea* was *usually* there.

He tried Faulkner.

Faulkner was not there at all, in any of the Urs.

He checked the regular menu, and discovered plenty of Faulkner. But only in this reality, it seemed.

This reality?

The mind boggled.

He checked Roberto Bolaño, the author of *2666*, and although it wasn't available from the normal Kindle menu, it was listed in several Ur Books submenus. So were other Bolaño novels, including (in Ur 101) a book with the colorful title *Marilyn Blows Fidel*. He almost downloaded that one, then changed his mind. So many authors, so many Urs, so little time.

A part of his mind—distant yet authentically terrified—continued to insist it was all an elaborate joke that had arisen from some loony computer programmer's imagination. Yet the evidence, which he continued to compile as that long night progressed, suggested otherwise.

James Cain, for instance. In one Ur Wesley checked, he had died exceedingly young, producing only two books: *Nightfall* (a new one) and *Mildred Pierce* (an oldie). Wesley would have bet on *The Postman Always Rings Twice* to have been a Cain constant—his ur-novel, so to speak—but no. Although he checked a dozen Urs for Cain, he found *Postman* only once. *Mildred Pierce*, on the other hand—which he considered very minor Cain, indeed—was always there. Like *A Farewell to Arms*.

He had checked his own name, and discovered what he feared: although the Urs were lousy with Wesley Smiths (one appeared to be a writer of Westerns, another the author of porno novels such as *Pittsburgh Panty Party*), none seemed to be him. Of course it was hard to be a hundred percent sure, but it appeared that he had stumbled on 10.4 million alternate realities and he was an unpublished loser in all of them.

Wide awake in his bed, listening to one lonely dog bark in the distance, Wesley began to shiver. His own literary aspirations seemed very minor to him at this moment. What seemed major—what loomed over his life and very sanity—were the riches hidden within that slim pink panel of plastic. He thought of all the writers whose passing he had mourned, from Norman Mailer and Saul Bellow to Donald Westlake and Evan Hunter; one after another, Thanatos stilled their magic voices and they spoke no more.

But now they could.

They could speak to him.

He threw back the bedclothes. The Kindle was calling him, but not in a human voice. It sounded like a beating heart, Poe's telltale heart, coming from inside his briefcase instead of from under the floorboards, and—

Poe!

Good Christ, he never checked Poe!

He had left his briefcase in its accustomed spot beside his favorite chair. He hurried to it, opened it, grabbed the Kindle, and plugged it in (no way he was going to risk running down the battery). He hurried to UR BOOKS, typed in Poe's name, and on his first try found an Ur—2555676—where Poe had lived until 1875 instead of dying at the age of forty in

1849. And this version of Poe had written novels! Six of them! Greed filled Wesley's heart as his eyes raced over the titles.

One was called *The House of Shame, or Degradation's Price.* Wesley downloaded it—the charge for this one was only $4.95—and read until dawn. Then he turned off the pink Kindle, put his head in his arms, and slept for two hours at the kitchen table.

He also dreamed. No images; only words. Titles! Endless lines of titles, many of them of undiscovered masterpieces. As many titles as there were stars in the sky.

He got through Tuesday and Wednesday—somehow— but during his Intro to American Lit class on Thursday, lack of sleep and overexcitement caught up with him. Not to mention his increasingly tenuous hold on reality. Halfway through his Mississippi Lecture (which he usually gave with a high degree of cogency) about how Hemingway was downriver from Twain, and almost all of twentieth-century American fiction was downriver from Hemingway, he realized he was telling the class that Papa had never written a great story about dogs, but if he had lived, he surely would have.

"Something more nutritious than *Marley and Me*," he said, and laughed with unnerving good cheer.

He turned from the blackboard and saw twenty-two pairs of eyes looking at him with varying degrees of concern, perplexity, and amusement. He heard a whisper, low, but as clear as the beating of the old man's heart to the ears of Poe's mad narrator: "Smithy's losin' it."

Smithy wasn't, not yet, but there could be no doubt that he was in *danger* of losing it.

I refuse, he thought. *I refuse, I refuse.* And realized, to his horror, that he was actually muttering this under his breath.

The Henderson kid, who sat in the first row, had heard it. "Mr. Smith?" A hesitation. "Sir? Are you all right?"

"Yes," he said. "No. A touch of the bug, maybe." *Poe's gold-bug,* he thought, and barely restrained himself from bursting into cackles of nutty laughter. "Class dismissed. Go on, get out of here."

And, as they scrambled for the door, he had presence of mind enough to add: "Raymond Carver next week! Don't forget! *Where I'm Calling From!*"

And thought: *What else is there by Raymond Carver in the worlds of Ur? Is there one—or a dozen, or a thousand— where he quit smoking, lived to be seventy, and wrote another half a dozen books?*

He sat down at his desk, reached for his briefcase with the pink Kindle inside, then pulled his hand back. He reached again, stopped himself again, and moaned. It was like a drug. Or a sexual obsession. Thinking of that made him think of Ellen Silverman, something he hadn't done since discovering the Kindle's hidden menus. For the first time since she'd walked out, Ellen had completely slipped his mind.

Ironic, isn't it? Now I'm reading off the computer, Ellen, and I can't stop.

"I refuse to spend the rest of the day looking into that thing," he said, "and I refuse to go mad. I refuse to look, and I refuse to go mad. To look or go mad. I refuse both. I—"

But the pink Kindle was in his hand! He had taken it out even as he had been denying its power over him!

When had he done that? And did he really intend to sit here in this empty classroom, mooning over it?

"Mr. Smith?"

The voice startled him so badly that he dropped the Kindle on his desk. He snatched it up at once and examined it, terrified it might be broken, but it was all right. Thank God.

"I didn't mean to startle you." It was the Henderson kid, standing in the doorway and looking concerned. This didn't surprise Wesley much. *If I saw me right now, I'd probably be concerned, too.*

"Oh, you didn't startle me," Wesley said. This obvious lie struck him as funny, and he almost giggled. He clapped a hand over his mouth to hold it in.

"What's wrong?" The Henderson kid took a step inside. "I think it's more than a virus. Man, you look awful. Did you get some bad news, or something?"

Wesley almost told him to mind his business, peddle his papers, put an egg in his shoe and beat it, but then the terrified part of him that had been cowering in the farthest corner of his brain, insisting that the pink Kindle was a prank or the opening gambit of some elaborate con, decided to stop hiding and start acting.

If you really refuse to go mad, you better do something about this, it said. *So how about it?*

"What's your first name, Mr. Henderson? It's entirely slipped my mind."

The kid smiled. A pleasant smile, but the concern was still in his eyes. "Robert, sir. Robbie."

"Well, Robbie, I'm Wes. And I want to show you something. Either you will see nothing—which means I'm deluded, and very likely suffering a nervous breakdown—or you will see something that completely blows your mind. Come to my office, would you?"

Henderson tried to ask questions as they crossed Moore's mediocre quad. Wesley shook them off, but he was glad Robbie Henderson had come back, and relieved that the terrified part of his mind had taken the initiative and spoken up. He felt better about the Kindle—*safer*—than at any time since discovering the hidden menus. In a story, Robbie Henderson would see nothing and the protagonist would decide he was going insane. Or had already gone. Wesley almost hoped for that, because . . .

Because I want it to be a delusion. If it is, and if with this young man's help I can recognize it as such, I'm sure I can avoid going mad. And I refuse to go mad.

"You're muttering, Mr. Smith," Robbie said. "Wes, I mean."

"Sorry."

"You're scaring me a little."

"I'm also scaring *me* a little."

Don Allman was in the office, wearing headphones, correcting papers, and singing about Jeremiah the bullfrog in a voice that went beyond the borders of tuneless and into the unexplored country of the truly execrable. He shut off his iPod when he saw Wesley.

"I thought you had class."

"Canceled it. This is Robert Henderson, one of my American Lit students."

"Robbie," Henderson said, extending his hand.

"Hello, Robbie. I'm Don Allman. One of the lesser-known Allman brothers. I play a mean tuba."

Robbie laughed politely and shook Don Allman's hand. Until that moment, Wesley had planned on asking Don to leave, thinking one witness to his mental collapse would be enough. But maybe this was that rare case where more really was merrier.

"Need some privacy?" Don asked.

"No," Wesley said. "Stay. I want to show you guys something. And if you see nothing and I see something, I'll be delighted to check into Central State Psychiatric." He opened his briefcase.

"Whoa!" Robbie exclaimed. "A pink Kindle! Sweet! I've never seen one of those before!"

"Now I'm going to show you something else that you've never seen before," Wesley said. "At least, I think I am."

He plugged in the Kindle and turned it on.

What convinced Don Allman was the *Collected Works of William Shakespeare* from Ur 17000. After downloading it at Don's request—because in this particular Ur, Shakespeare had died in 1620 instead of 1616—the three men discovered two new plays. One was titled *Two Ladies of Hampshire*, a comedy that seemed to have been written soon after *Julius Caesar*. The other was a tragedy called *A Black Fellow in London*, written in 1619. Wesley opened this one and then (with some reluctance) handed Don the Kindle.

Don Allman was ordinarily a ruddy-cheeked guy who smiled a lot, but as he paged through Acts I and II of *A Black Fellow in London*, he lost both his smile and his color. After twenty minutes, during which Wesley and Robbie sat watching him silently, he pushed the Kindle back to Wesley. He did it with the tips of his fingers, as if he really didn't want to touch it at all.

"So?" Wesley asked. "What's the verdict?"

"It could be an imitation," Don said, "but of course

there have always been scholars who claimed that Shakespeare's plays weren't written by Shakespeare. There are supporters of Christopher Marlowe . . . Francis Bacon . . . even the Earl of Derby . . ."

"Yeah, and James Frey wrote *Macbeth*," Wesley said. "What do *you* think?"

"I think this could be authentic Willie," Don said. He sounded on the verge of tears. Or laughter. Maybe both. "I think it's far too elaborate to be a joke. And if it's a hoax, I have no idea how it works." He reached a finger to the Kindle, touched it lightly, then pulled it away. "I'd have to study both plays closely, with reference works at hand, to be more definite, but . . . it's got his *lilt*."

Robbie Henderson, it turned out, had read almost all of John D. MacDonald's mystery and suspense novels. In the Ur 2171753 listing of MacDonald's works, he found seventeen novels in what was called "the Dave Higgins series." All the titles had colors in them.

"That part's right," Robbie said, "but the titles are all wrong. And John D.'s series character was named Travis McGee, not Dave Higgins."

Wesley downloaded one called *The Blue Lament*, hitting his credit card with another $4.50 charge, and pushed the Kindle over to Robbie once the book had been downloaded to the ever-growing library that was Wesley's Kindle. While Robbie read, at first from the beginning and then skipping around, Don went down to the main office and brought back three coffees. Before settling in behind his desk, he hung the little-used CONFERENCE IN PROGRESS DO NOT DISTURB sign on the door.

Robbie looked up, nearly as pale as Don had been after dipping into the never-written Shakespeare play about the African prince who is brought to London in chains.

"This is a lot like a Travis McGee novel called *Pale Gray for Guilt*," he said. "Only Travis McGee lives in Fort Lauderdale, and this guy Higgins lives in Sarasota. McGee has a friend named Meyer—a guy—and Higgins has a friend named Sarah . . ." He bent over the Kindle for a moment. "Sarah Mayer." He looked at Wesley, his eyes showing too much white around the irises. "Jesus Christ, and there's *ten million* of these . . . these other worlds?"

"Ten million, four hundred thousand and some, according to the UR BOOKS menu," Wesley said. "I think exploring even one author fully would take more years than you have left in your life, Robbie."

"I might die today," Robbie Henderson said in a low voice. "That thing could give me a freaking heart attack." He abruptly seized his Styrofoam cup of coffee and swallowed most of the contents, although the coffee was still steaming.

Wesley, on the other hand, felt almost like himself again. But with the fear of madness removed, a host of questions flooded his mind. Only one seemed completely relevant. "What do I do now?"

"For one thing," Don said, "this has to stay a dead secret among the three of us." He turned to Robbie. "Can you keep a secret? Say no and I'll have to kill you."

"I can keep one. But how about the people who sent it to you, Wes? Can *they* keep a secret? *Will* they?"

"How do I know that when I don't know who they are?"

"What credit card did you use when you ordered Little Pink here?"

"MasterCard. It's the only one I use these days."

Robbie pointed to the English Department computer terminal Wesley and Don shared. "Go online, why don't you, and check your account. If those . . . those Ur-books . . . came from Amazon, I'll be very surprised."

"Where else *could* they have come from?" Wesley asked. "It's their gadget, they sell the books for it. Also, it came in an Amazon box. It had the smile on it."

"And do they sell their gadget in Glow-stick Pink?" Robbie asked.

"Well, no."

"Dude, check your credit card account."

Wesley drummed his fingers on Don's Mighty Mouse mousepad as their office's outdated PC cogitated. Then he sat up straight and began to read.

"Well?" Don asked. "Share."

"According to this," Wesley said, "my latest MasterCard purchase was a blazer from Men's Wearhouse. A week ago. No downloaded books."

"Not even the ones you ordered the normal way? *The Old Man and the Sea* and *Revolutionary Road*?"

"Nope."

Robbie asked, "What about the Kindle itself?"

Wesley scrolled back. "Nothing . . . nothing . . . noth— Wait, here it—" He leaned forward until his nose was almost touching the screen. "Huh. I'll be damned."

"What?" Don and Robbie said it together.

"According to this, my purchase was denied. It says, 'wrong credit card number.'" He considered. "That could be. I'm always reversing two of the digits, sometimes even when I have the damn card right beside the keyboard. I'm a little dyslexic."

"But the order went through, anyway," Don said thoughtfully. "Someone . . . to some*one*. Some*where*. What Ur does the Kindle say we're in? Refresh me on that."

Wesley went back to the relevant screen and read back the number, 117586. "Only to enter that as a choice, you omit the comma."

Don said, "I bet that's the Ur this Kindle came from. In *that* Ur, the MasterCard number you gave is the right one for a Wesley Smith that exists there."

"What are the odds of something like that happening?" Robbie asked.

"I don't know," Don said, "but probably even steeper than ten point four million to one."

Wesley opened his mouth to say something, and was interrupted by a fusillade of knocks on the door. They all jumped. Don Allman actually uttered a little scream.

"Who is it?" Wesley asked, grabbing the Kindle and holding it protectively to his chest.

"Janitor," the voice on the other side of the door said. "You folks ever going home? It's almost seven o'clock, and I need to lock up the building."

IV—News Archive

They weren't done, couldn't be done. Not yet. Wesley in particular was anxious to press on. Although he hadn't slept for more than three hours at a stretch in days, he felt wide awake, energized. He and Robbie walked back to his apartment while Don went home to help his wife put the boys to bed. When that was done, he'd join them at Wesley's place for an extended skull session. Wesley said he'd order some food.

"Good," Don said, "but be careful. Ur-Chinese just doesn't taste the same, and you know what they say about German Chinese—an hour later you're hungry for power."

For a wonder, Wesley found he could actually laugh.

"So this is what an English instructor's apartment looks like," Robbie said, gazing around. "Man, I dig all the books."

"Good," Wesley said. "I loan, but only to people who bring back. Keep it in mind."

"I will. My parents have never been, you know, great readers. A few magazines, some diet books, a self-help manual or two . . . that's it. I might have been the same way, if not for you. Just bangin' my brains out on the football field, you know, with nothing ahead except maybe teaching PE in Giles County. That's in Tennessee. Yeehaw."

Wesley was touched by this. Probably because he'd been hurled through so many emotional hoops just lately. "Thanks, but remember there's nothing wrong with a good loud yeehaw. That's part of who you are, too. Both parts are equally valid."

He thought of Ellen, ripping *Deliverance* out of his hands and hurling it across the room. And why? Because she hated books? No, because he hadn't been listening when she needed him to. Hadn't it been Fritz Leiber, the great fantasist and science fiction writer, who had called books "the scholar's mistress"? And when Ellen needed him, hadn't he been in the arms of his other lover, the one who made no demands (other than on his vocabulary) and always took him in?

"Wes? What were those other things on the UR FUNCTIONS menu?"

At first Wesley didn't know what the kid was talking about. Then he remembered that there *had* been a couple of other items. He'd been so fixated on the BOOKS submenu that he had forgotten the other two.

"Well, let's see," he said, and turned the Kindle on. Every time he did this, he expected either the EXPERIMENTAL menu or the UR FUNCTIONS menu to be gone—the sort of thing that would happen in a *Twilight Zone* episode—but they were still right there.

"Ur News Archive and Ur Local," Robbie said. "Huh. Ur Local's under construction. Better watch out, traffic fines double."

"What?"

"Never mind, just goofin. Try the news archive."

Wesley selected it. The screen blanked. After a few moments, a message appeared.

WELCOME TO THE NEWS ARCHIVE!
ONLY *THE NEW YORK TIMES* IS
AVAILABLE AT THIS TIME
YOUR PRICE IS $1.00/4 DOWNLOADS
$10/50 DOWNLOADS
$100/800 DOWNLOADS
SELECT WITH CURSOR YOUR ACCOUNT
WILL BE BILLED

Wesley looked at Robbie, who shrugged. "I can't tell you what to do, but if *my* credit card wasn't being billed—in this world, anyway—I'd spend the hundred."

Wesley thought he had a point, although he wondered what the other Wesley (if there was one) would think when he opened his next MasterCard bill. He highlighted the $100/800 line and banged the Select button. This time the Paradox Laws didn't come up. Instead, the new message invited him to CHOOSE DATE AND UR. USE APPROPRIATE FIELDS.

"You do it," he said, and pushed the Kindle across the kitchen table to Robbie. This was getting easier to do, and he was glad. An obsession about keeping the Kindle in his own hands was a complication he didn't need, understandable as it was.

Robbie thought for a moment, then typed in *January 21, 2009.* In the Ur field he selected 1000000. "Ur one million," he said. "Why not?" And pushed the button.

The screen went blank, then produced a message reading ENJOY YOUR SELECTION! A moment later the front page of *The New York Times* appeared. They bent over the screen, reading silently, until there was a knock at the door.

"That'll be Don," Wesley said. "I'll let him in."

Robbie Henderson didn't reply. He was still transfixed.

"Getting cold out there," Don said as he came in. "And there's a wind knocking all the leaves off the—" He studied Wesley's face. "What? Or should I say, what now?"

"Come and see," Wesley said.

Don went into Wesley's book-lined living room—study, where Robbie remained bent over the Kindle. The kid looked up and turned the screen so Don could see it. There were blank patches where the photos should have gone, each with the message *Image Unavailable*, but the headline was big and black: **NOW IT'S HER TURN**. And below it, the subhead: **Hillary Clinton Takes Oath, Assumes Role as 44th President**.

"Looks like she made it after all," Wesley said. "At least in Ur 1000000."

"And check out who she's replacing," Robbie said, and pointed to the name. It was Albert Arnold Gore.

An hour later, when the doorbell rang, they didn't jump but rather looked around like men startled from a dream. Wesley went downstairs and paid the delivery guy, who had arrived with a loaded pizza from Harry's and a six-pack of Pepsi. They ate at the kitchen table, bent over the Kindle. Wesley put away three slices himself, a personal best, with no awareness of what he was eating.

They didn't use up the eight hundred downloads they had ordered—nowhere near it—but in the next four hours they skimmed enough stories from various Urs to make their heads ache. Wesley felt as though his *mind* were aching. From the nearly identical looks he saw on the faces of the other two—pale cheeks, avid eyes in bruised sockets, crazed hair—he guessed he wasn't alone. Looking into one alternate reality would have been challenging enough; here were over ten million, and although most were similar, not one was exactly the same.

The inauguration of the forty-fourth President of the United States was only one example, but a powerful one. They checked it in two dozen different Urs before getting tired and moving on. Fully seventeen front pages on January 21st of 2009 announced Hillary Clinton as the new president. In fourteen of them, Bill Richardson of New Mexico was her vice president. In two, it was Joe Biden. In one it was a senator none of them had heard of: Linwood Speck of New Jersey.

"He always says no to the vice-presidency when someone else wins the top spot," Don said.

"Who always says no?" Robbie asked. "Obama?"

"Yeah. He always gets asked, and he always says no."

"It's in character," Wesley said. "And while events change, character never seems to."

"You can't say that for sure," Don said. "We have a minuscule sample compared to the . . . the . . ." He laughed feebly. "You know, the whole thing. All the worlds of Ur."

Barack Obama had been elected in six Urs. Mitt Romney had been elected in one, with John McCain as his running mate. In that Ur, Romney ran against Obama, who was tapped after Hillary was killed in a helicopter crash late in the campaign.

They saw not a single mention of Sarah Palin. Wesley wasn't surprised. He thought that if they stumbled on her, it would be more by luck than by probability, and not just because Mitt Romney showed up more often as the Republican nominee than John McCain did. Palin had always been an outsider, a longshot, the one nobody expected.

Robbie wanted to check the Red Sox. Wesley felt it was a waste of time, but Don came down on the kid's side, so Wesley agreed. The two of them checked the sports pages for October in ten different Urs, plugging in dates from 1918 to 2009.

"This is depressing," Robbie said after the tenth try. Don Allman agreed.

"Why?" Wesley asked. "They win the Series lots of times."

"Which means there's no Curse," Don said. "Which is sort of boring."

"What curse?" Wesley was mystified.

Don opened his mouth to explain, then sighed. "Never mind," he said. "It would take too long, and you wouldn't get it, anyway."

"Look on the bright side," Robbie said. "The Bombers are always there, so it isn't *all* luck."

"Yeah," Don said glumly. "Fuckin Yankees. The military-industrial complex of the sporting world."

"Soh-*ree*. Does anyone want that last slice?"

Don and Wes shook their heads. Robbie scarfed it and said, "Check one more. Check Ur 4121989. It's my birthday. Gotta be lucky."

Only it was quite the opposite. When Wesley selected the Ur and added a date—January 20, 1973—not quite at random, what came up instead of **ENJOY YOUR SELECTION** was this: **NO *TIMES* THIS UR AFTER NOVEMBER 19, 1962**.

Wesley clapped a hand to his mouth. "Oh my dear sweet God."

"What?" Robbie asked. "What is it?"

"I think I know," Don said. He tried to take the pink Kindle.

Wesley, who guessed he had gone pale (but probably not as pale as he felt inside), put a hand over Don's. "No. I don't think I can bear it."

"Bear *what?*" Robbie nearly shouted.

"Didn't you cover the Cuban Missile Crisis in Twentieth Century American History?" Don asked. "Or didn't you get that far yet?"

"*What* missile crisis? Was it something to do with Castro?"

Don was looking at Wesley. "I don't really want to see, either," he said, "but I won't sleep tonight unless I make sure."

"Okay," Wesley said, and thought—not for the first time—that curiosity rather than rage was the true bane of the human spirit. "You'll have to do it, though. My hands are trembling too much."

Don filled in the fields for NOVEMBER 19, 1962. The Kindle told him to enjoy his selection, but he didn't. None of them did. The headlines were stark and huge:

NYC TOLL SURPASSES 6 MILLION
MANHATTAN DECIMATED BY RADIATION
RUSSIA SAID TO BE OBLITERATED
LOSSES IN EUROPE AND ASIA
"INCALCULABLE"
CHINESE LAUNCH 40 ICBMS

"Turn it off," Robbie said in a small, sick voice. "It's like that song says—I don't wanna see no more."

Don said, "Look on the bright side, you two. It seems we dodged the bullet in most of the Urs, including this one." But his voice wasn't quite steady.

"Robbie's right," Wesley said. He had discovered that the final issue of *The New York Times* in Ur 4121989 was only three pages long, and every article

was death. "Turn it off. I wish I'd never seen the damn
Kindle in the first place."

"Too late now," Robbie said. And how right he
was.

They went downstairs together and stood on the sidewalk in front of Wesley's apartment building. Main
Street was almost deserted. The rising wind moaned
around the buildings and rattled late-November
leaves along the sidewalks. A trio of drunk students
stumbled back toward Fraternity Row, singing what
might have been "Paradise City."

"I can't tell you what to do—it's your gadget—but
if it was mine, I'd get rid of it," Don said. "It'll suck
you in."

Wesley thought of telling him he'd already been
sucked, but didn't. "We'll talk about it tomorrow."

"Nope," Don said. "I'm driving the wife and kids
to Frankfort for a wonderful three-day weekend at my
in-laws'. Suzy Montanaro's taking my classes. And
after this little seminar tonight, I'm delighted to be
getting away. Robbie? Drop you somewhere?"

"Thanks, but no need. I share an apartment with a
couple of other guys two blocks up the street. Above
Susan and Nan's Place."

"Isn't that a little noisy?" Wesley asked. Susan
and Nan's was the local café, and opened at 6:00 a.m.
seven days a week.

"Most days I sleep right through it." Robbie
flashed a grin. "Also, when it comes to the rent, the
price is right."

"Good deal. Night, you guys," Don started for his
Tercel, then turned back. "I intend to kiss my kids
before I turn in. Maybe it'll help me get to sleep.

That last story—" He shook his head. "I could have done without that. No offense, Robbie, but stick your birthday up your ass."

They watched his diminishing taillights and Robbie said thoughtfully, "Nobody ever told me to stick my birthday before. That's a first."

"I'm sure he wouldn't want you to take it personally. And he's probably right about the Kindle, you know. It's fascinating—*too* fascinating—but useless in any practical sense."

Robbie stared at him, wide-eyed. "You're calling access to thousands of undiscovered novels by the great masters of the craft *useless*? Sheezis, what kind of English teacher are you?"

Wesley had no comeback. Especially when he knew that, late or not, he'd probably be reading more of *Cortland's Dogs* before turning in.

"Besides," Robbie said. "It might not be *entirely* useless. You could type up one of those books and send it in to a publisher, ever think of that? You know, submit it under your own name. Become the next big thing. They'd call you the heir to Vonnegut or Roth or whoever."

It was an attractive idea, especially when Wesley thought of the useless scribbles in his briefcase. But he shook his head. "It'd probably violate the Paradox Laws . . . whatever *they* are. More importantly, it would eat me like acid. From the inside out." He hesitated, not wanting to sound prissy, but wanting to articulate what felt like the real reason for not doing such a thing. "I would feel ashamed."

The kid smiled. "You're a good dude, Wes." They were walking in the direction of Robbie's apartment now, the leaves rattling around their feet, a quarter moon flying through the wind-driven clouds overhead.

"You think so?"

"I do. And so does Coach Silverman."

Wesley stopped, caught by surprise. "What do you know about me and Coach Silverman?"

"Personally? Not a thing. But you must know Josie's on the team. Josie Quinn from class?"

"Of course I know Josie." The one who'd sounded like a kindly anthropologist when they'd been discussing the Kindle. And yes, he *had* known she was a Lady Meerkat, although one of the subs who usually got into the game only if it was a total blowout.

"Josie says Coach has been really sad since you and her broke up. Grouchy, too. She makes them run all the time, and kicked one girl right off the team."

"She booted the Deeson girl before we broke up." Thinking: *In a way that's why we broke up.* "Um . . . does the whole team know about us?"

Robbie Henderson looked at him as though he were mad. "If Josie knows, they all know."

"How?" Ellen wouldn't have told them; briefing the team on your love life was not a coachly thing to do.

"How do women know anything?" Robbie asked. "They just do."

"Are you and Josie Quinn an item, Robbie?"

"We're going in the right direction. G'night, Wes. I'm gonna sleep in tomorrow—no classes on Friday—but if you drop by Susan and Nan's for lunch, come on up and knock on my door."

"I might do that," Wesley said. "Good night, Robbie. Thanks for being one of the Three Stooges."

"I'd say the pleasure was all mine, but I have to think about that."

• • •

Instead of reading ur-Hemingway when he got back, Wesley stuffed the Kindle in his briefcase. Then he took out the mostly blank bound notebook and ran his hand over its pretty cover. *For your book ideas,* Ellen had said, and it had to've been an expensive present. Too bad it was going to waste.

I could still write a book, he thought. *Just because I haven't in any of the other Urs doesn't mean I couldn't here.*

It was true. He could be the Sarah Palin of American letters. Because sometimes longshots came in.

Both for good and for ill.

He undressed, brushed his teeth, then called the English Department and left a message for the secretary to cancel his one morning class. "Thanks, Marilyn. Sorry to put this on you, but I think I'm coming down with the flu." He added an unconvincing cough and hung up.

He thought he would lie sleepless for hours, thinking of all those other worlds, but in the dark they seemed as unreal as actors when you saw them on a movie screen. They were big up there—often beautiful too—but they were still only shadows thrown by light. Maybe the Ur-worlds were like that, too.

What seemed real in this post-midnight hour was the sound of the wind, the beautiful sound of the wind telling tales of Tennessee, where it had been earlier this evening. Lulled by it, Wesley fell asleep, and he slept deeply and long. There were no dreams, and when he woke up, sunshine was flooding his bedroom. For the first time since his own undergraduate days, he had slept until almost eleven in the morning.

V—Ur Local (Under Construction)

He took a long hot shower, shaved, dressed, and decided to go down to Susan and Nan's for either a late breakfast or an early lunch, whichever looked better on the menu. As for Robbie, Wesley decided he'd let the kid sleep. He'd be out practicing with the rest of the hapless football team this afternoon; surely he deserved to sleep late. It occurred to him that, if he took a table by the window, he might see the Athletic Department bus go by as the girls set off for the Bluegrass Invitational, eighty miles away. He'd wave. Ellen mightn't see him, but he'd do it anyway.

He took his briefcase without even thinking about it.

He ordered Susan's Sexy Scramble (onions, peppers, mozzarella cheese) with bacon on the side, along with coffee and juice. By the time the young waitress brought his food, he'd taken out the Kindle and was reading *Cortland's Dogs*. It was Hemingway, all right, and one terrific story.

"Kindle, isn't it?" the waitress asked. "I got one for Christmas, and I love it. I'm reading my way through all of Jodi Picoult's books."

"Oh, probably not all of them," Wesley said.

"Huh?"

"She's probably got another one done already. That's all I meant."

"And James Patterson's probably written one since he got up this morning!" she said, and went off chortling.

Wesley had pushed the Main Menu button while

they were talking, wanting to hide the Ur-Hemingway novel. Because he was feeling guilty about what he was reading? Because the waitress might get a look and start screaming *That's not real Hemingway?* Ridiculous. But just owning the pink Kindle made him feel a little bit like a crook. It wasn't his device, after all, and the stuff he had downloaded wasn't really his, either, because he wasn't the one paying for it.

Maybe no one is, he thought, but didn't believe it. He thought one of the universal truths of life was that, sooner or later, someone always paid.

There was nothing especially sexy about his scramble, but it was good. Instead of going back to Cortland and his winter dog, he accessed the UR menu. The one function he hadn't peeked into was Ur Local. Which was *under construction.* What had Robbie said about that last night? *Better watch out, traffic fines double.* The kid was sharp and might get even sharper, if he didn't batter his brains out playing senseless Division Three football. Smiling, Wesley highlighted UR LOCAL and pushed the Select button. This message came up:

ACCESS CURRENT UR LOCAL SOURCE? Y N

Wesley selected Y. The Kindle thought some more, then posted a new message:

THE CURRENT UR LOCAL SOURCE IS
MOORE *ECHO*
ACCESS? Y N

Wesley considered the question while eating a strip of bacon. *The Echo* was a rag specializing in yard sales, area sports, and town politics. The residents scanned those things, he supposed, but mostly bought the paper for the obituaries and Police Beat. Everybody liked to know which of their neighbors had died or been jailed. Searching 10.4 million Moore, Kentucky, Urs sounded pretty boring, but why not? Wasn't he basically marking time, drawing his breakfast out, so he could watch the players' bus go by?

"Sad but true," he said, and highlighted the Y button. What came up was similar to a message he had seen before: *Ur Local is protected by all applicable Paradox Laws. Do you agree? Y N.*

Now *that* was strange. The *New York Times* archive wasn't protected by these Paradox Laws, whatever they were, but their pokey local paper was? It made no sense, but seemed harmless. Wesley shrugged and selected Y.

WELCOME TO *THE ECHO* PRE-ARCHIVE!
YOUR PRICE IS $40.00/4 DOWNLOADS
$350.00/10 DOWNLOADS
$2500.00/100 DOWNLOADS

Wesley put his fork on his plate and sat frowning at the screen. Not only was the local paper Paradox Law–protected, it was a hell of a lot more expensive. Why? And what the hell was a pre-archive? To Wesley, that sounded like a paradox in itself. Or an oxymoron.

"Well, it's under construction," he said. "Traffic fines double and so do download expenses. That's the explanation. Plus, I'm not paying for it."

No, but because the idea persisted that he might someday be forced to (someday *soon*!), he compromised on the middle choice. The next screen was similar to the one for the *Times* archive, but not quite the same; it just asked him to select a date. To him this suggested nothing but an ordinary newspaper archive, the kind he could find on microfilm at the local library. If so, why the big expense?

He shrugged, typed in *July 5, 2008*, and pushed Select. The Kindle responded immediately, posting this message:

FUTURE DATES ONLY
THIS IS NOVEMBER 20, 2009

For a moment he didn't get it. Then he did, and the world suddenly turned itself up to superbright, as if some supernatural being had cranked the rheostat controlling the daylight. And all the noises in the café—the clash of forks, the rattle of plates, the steady babble of conversation—seemed too loud.

"My God," he whispered. "No wonder it's expensive."

This was too much. *Way* too much. He moved to turn the Kindle off, then heard cheering and yelling outside. He looked up and saw a yellow bus with MOORE COLLEGE ATHLETIC DEPARTMENT printed on the side. Cheerleaders and players leaned out the open windows, waving and laughing and yelling stuff like *"Go, Meerkats!"* and *"We're number one!"* One of the young women was wagging a big foam Number One finger. The pedestrians on Main Street grinned and waved back.

Wesley lifted his own hand and waved feebly. The bus driver honked his horn. Flapping from the rear of the bus was a piece of sheeting with MEER-

KATS WILL ROCK THE RUPP spray-painted
on it. Wesley became aware that people in the café
were applauding. All this seemed to be happening in
another world. Another Ur.

When the bus was gone, Wesley looked down at
the pink Kindle again. He decided he wanted to uti-
lize at least one of his ten downloads, after all. The
locals didn't have much use for the student body as
a whole—the standard town-versus-gown thing—
but they loved the Lady Meerkats because everybody
loves a winner. The tourney's results, pre-season or
not, would be front-page news in Monday's *Echo*. If
they won, he could buy Ellen a victory gift, and if
they lost, he could buy her a consolation present.

"I'm a winner either way," he said, and entered
Monday's date: November 23, 2009.

The Kindle thought for a long time, then produced a newspaper front page.

The date was Monday's date.

The headline was huge and black.

Wesley spilled his coffee and yanked the Kindle
out of danger even as the lukewarm liquid soaked his
crotch.

Fifteen minutes later he was pacing the living room
of Robbie Henderson's apartment while Robbie—
who'd been up when Wesley came hammering at
the door but was still wearing the tee-shirt and
basketball shorts he slept in—stared at the screen of
the Kindle.

"We have to call someone," Wesley said. He was
smacking a fist into an open palm, and hard enough
to turn the skin red. "We have to call the police. No,
wait! The arena! Call the Rupp and leave a message

for her to call me, ASAP! No, that's wrong! Too slow! I'll call her now. That's what—"

"Relax, Mr. Smith—Wes, I mean."

"How can I relax? Don't you *see* that thing? Are you *blind*?"

"No, but you still have to relax. Pardon the expression, but you're losing your shit, and people can't think productively when they're doing that."

"But—"

"Take a deep breath. And remind yourself that according to this, we've got almost sixty hours."

"Easy for you to say. *Your* girlfriend isn't going to be on that bus when it starts back to—" Then he stopped, because that wasn't so. Josie Quinn was a member of the team, and according to Robbie, he and Josie had a thing going on.

"I'm sorry," he said. "I saw the headline and freaked. I didn't even pay for my breakfast, just ran up here. I know I look like I wet my pants, and I damn near did. Thank God your roommates are gone."

"I'm pretty freaked, too," Robbie admitted, and for a moment they studied the screen in silence. According to Wesley's Kindle, Monday's edition of *The Echo* was going to have a black border around the front page as well as a black headline on top of it. That headline read:

COACH, 7 STUDENTS KILLED IN HORRIFIC BUS CRASH; 9 OTHERS CRITICAL

The story itself really wasn't a story at all, only an item. Even in his distress, Wesley knew why. The accident had happened—no, was *going* to happen—at just short of 9:00 p.m. on Sunday night. Too late to report any details, although probably if they heated up Robbie's computer and went to the Internet—

What was he thinking? The Internet did not predict the future; only the pink Kindle did that.

His hands were shaking too badly to enter November 24. He pushed the Kindle to Robbie. "You do it."

Robbie managed, though it took him two tries. *The Echo*'s Tuesday story was more complete, but the headline was even worse:

DEATH TOLL RISES TO 10
TOWN AND COLLEGE MOURN

"Is Josie—" Wesley began.

"Yeah," Robbie said. "Survives the crash, dies on Monday. Christ."

> According to Antonia "Toni" Burrell, one of the Meerkats cheerleaders, and one of the lucky ones to survive Sunday night's horrific bus crash with only cuts and bruises, the celebration was still going on, the Bluegrass Trophy still being passed hand-to-hand. "We were singing 'We Are the Champions' for the twentieth time or so," she said from the hospital in Bowling Green, where most of the survivors were taken. "Coach turned around and yelled for us to keep it down, and that's when it happened."
>
> According to State Police Captain Moses Arden, the bus was traveling on Route 139, the Princeton Road, and was about two miles west of Cadiz when an

SUV driven by Candy Rymer of Montgomery struck it. "Ms. Rymer was traveling at a high rate of speed west along Highway 80," Captain Arden said, "and struck the bus at the intersection."

The bus driver, Herbert Allison, 58, of Moore, apparently saw Ms. Rymer's vehicle at the last moment and tried to swerve. That swerve, coupled with the impact, drove the bus into the ditch, where it overturned and exploded.

There was more, but neither of them wanted to read it.

"Okay," Robbie said. "Let's think about this. First, can we be sure it's true?"

"Maybe not," Wesley said. "But Robbie . . . can we afford to take the chance?"

"No," Robbie said. "No, I guess we can't. Of *course* we can't. But Wes, if we call the police, they won't believe us. You know that."

"We'll show them the Kindle! We'll show them the story!" But even to himself, Wesley sounded deflated. "Okay, how about this. I'll tell Ellen. Even if she won't believe me, she might agree to hold the bus for fifteen minutes or so, or change the route this guy Allison's planning to take."

Robbie considered. "Yeah. Worth a try."

Wesley took his phone out of his briefcase. Robbie had gone back to the story, using the Next Page button to access the rest.

The phone rang twice . . . three times . . . four.

Wesley was preparing to deliver his message to

voicemail when Ellen answered. "Wesley, I can't talk to you now. I thought you understood that—"

"Ellen, listen—"

"—but if you got my message, you know we're *going* to talk." In the background he could hear raucous, excited girls—Josie would be among them—and lots of loud music.

"Yes, I did get the message, but we have to talk n—"

"No!" Ellen said. "We *don't*. I'm not going to take your calls this weekend, and I'm not going to listen to your messages." Her voice softened. "And hon—every one you leave is going to make it harder. For us, I mean."

"Ellen, you don't understa—"

"Goodbye, Wes. I'll talk to you next week. Do you wish us luck?"

"Ellen, *please*!"

"I'll take that as a yes," she said. "And you know what? I guess I still care about you, even though you are a lug."

With that she was gone.

He poised his finger over Redial, then made himself not push it. It wouldn't help. Ellen was wearing her my-way-or-the-highway hat. It was insane, but there it was.

"She won't talk to me except on her schedule. What she doesn't realize is that after Sunday night she may not *have* a schedule. You'll have to call Ms. Quinn." In his current state, the girl's first name escaped him.

"Josie'd think I was prankin' on her," Robbie said. "A story like that, *any* girl'd think I was prankin' on her." He was still studying the Kindle's screen. "Want to know something? The woman who caused the accident—who *will* cause it—hardly gets hurt at all. I'll bet you next semester's tuition she was just as drunk as a goddam skunk."

Wesley hardly heard this. "Tell Josie that Ellen *has* to take my call. Have her say it's not about us. Tell her to say it's an emer—"

"Dude," Robbie said. "Slow down and listen. Are you listening?"

Wesley nodded, but what he heard most clearly was his own pounding heart.

"Point one, Josie would *still* think I was prankin' on her. Point two, she might think we *both* were. Point three, I don't think she'd go to Coach Silverman anyway, given the mood Coach has been in lately . . . and she gets even worse on game trips, Josie says." Robbie sighed. "You have to understand about Josie. She's sweet, she's smart, she's sexy as hell, but she's also a timid little mousie. It's sort of what I like about her."

"That probably says heaps of good things about your character, Robbie, but you'll pardon me if right now I don't give a rat's ass. You've told me what won't work; do you have any idea what might?"

"That's point four. With a little luck, we won't have to tell anybody about this. Which is good, since they wouldn't believe it."

"Elucidate."

"Huh?"

"Tell me what you've got in mind."

"First, we need to use another one of your *Echo* downloads."

Robbie punched in November 25, 2009. Another girl, a cheerleader who had been horribly burned in the explosion, had died, raising the death toll to eleven. Although *The Echo* didn't come right out and say so, more were likely to die before the week was out.

Robbie only gave this story a quick scan. What he was looking for was a boxed story on the lower half of page 1:

CANDACE RYMER CHARGED WITH MULTIPLE COUNTS OF VEHICULAR HOMICIDE

There was a gray square in the middle of the story—her picture, Wesley assumed, only the pink Kindle didn't seem able to reprint news photographs. But it didn't matter, because now he got it. It wasn't the bus they had to stop; it was the woman who was going to hit the bus.

Candace Rymer was point four.

VI—Candy Rymer

At five o'clock on a gray Sunday afternoon—as the Lady Meerkats were cutting down basketball nets in a not-too-distant part of the state—Wesley Smith and Robbie Henderson were sitting in Wesley's modest Chevy Malibu, watching the door of a roadhouse in Eddyville, twenty miles north of Cadiz. The parking lot was oiled dirt and mostly empty. There was almost certainly a TV inside The Broken Windmill, but Wesley guessed discriminating tipplers would rather do their drinking and NFL-watching at home. You didn't have to go inside the joint to know it was a hole. Candy Rymer's first stop had been bad, but this second one was worse.

Parked slightly crooked (and blocking what appeared to be the fire exit) was a filthy, dinged-up Ford Explorer with two bumper stickers on the back. MY CHILD IS AN HONOR STUDENT AT THE STATE COR-RECTIONAL FACILITY, one read. The other was even more telling: I BRAKE FOR JACK DANIELS.

"Maybe we oughta do it right here," Robbie said. "While she's inside slopping it up and watching the Titans."

It was a tempting idea, but Wesley shook his head. "We'll wait. She's got one more stop to make. Hop-son, remember?"

"That's miles from here."

"Right," Wesley said. "But we've got time to kill, and we're going to kill it."

"Why?"

"Because what we're up to is changing the future. Or trying to, at least. We have no idea how tough that is. Waiting as long as possible improves our chances."

"Wesley, that is one drunk chick. She was drunk when she got out of that first juke joint in Central City, and she's going to be a lot drunker when she comes out of yonder shack. I can't see her getting her car repaired in time to rendezvous with the girls' bus forty miles from here. And what if *we* break down while we're trying to follow her to her last stop?"

Wesley hadn't considered this. Now he did. "My instincts say wait, but if you have a strong feeling that we should do it now, we will."

Robbie sat up. "Too late. Here comes Miss America."

Candy Rymer emerged from The Broken Windmill in a kind of slalom. She dropped her purse, bent down to get it, almost fell over, cursed, picked it up, laughed, and then continued to where her Explorer was parked, digging her keys out as she went. Her face was puffy, not quite hiding the remains of what must once have been very good looks. Her hair, blond on top and black at the roots, hung around her cheeks in lank curls. Her belly pooched out the front of elastic-waist jeans just below the hem of what had to be a Kmart smock top.

She got in her beat-to-shit SUV, kicked the engine into life (it sounded in desperate need of a tune-up), and drove forward into the roadhouse's fire door. There was a crunch. Then her backup lights came on and she reversed so fast that for one sickening moment Wesley thought she was going to hit his Malibu, crippling it and leaving them on foot as she drove off to her appointment in Samarra. But she stopped in time and peeled onto the highway without pausing to look for traffic. A moment later Wesley was following as she headed east toward Hopson. And the intersection where the Lady Meerkats' bus would arrive in four hours.

In spite of the terrible thing she was going to do, Wesley couldn't help feeling a little sorry for her, and he had an idea Robbie felt the same. The follow-up story they'd read about her in *The Echo* told a tale as familiar as it was sordid.

Candace "Candy" Rymer, age forty-one, divorced. Three children, now in the custody of their father. During the last dozen years of her life she'd been in and out of four spin-dry facilities, roughly one every three years. According to an acquaintance (she seemed to have no friends), she had tried AA and decided it wasn't for her. Too much holy-rolling. She had been arrested for DUI half a dozen times. She had lost her license after each of the last two, but in both cases it had been restored, the second time by special petition. She needed her license to get to her job at the fertilizer factory in Bainbridge, she told Judge Wallenby. What she didn't tell him was that she had lost the job six months previous . . . and nobody checked. Candy Rymer was a booze-bomb waiting to go off, and the explosion was now very close.

The story hadn't mentioned her home address in Montgomery, but it didn't need to. In what Wesley considered a rather brilliant piece of investigative journalism (especially for *The Echo*), the reporter had retraced Candy's final binge, from The Pot O' Gold in Central City to The Broken Windmill in Eddyville to Banty's Bar in Hopson. There the bartender was going to try to take her keys. Unsuccessfully. Candy was going to give him the finger and leave, shouting "I'm done giving my business to this dive!" back over her shoulder. That was at seven o'clock. The reporter theorized that Candy must have pulled over somewhere for a short nap, possibly on Route 124, before cutting across to Route 80. A little farther down 80, she would make her final stop. A fiery one.

Once Robbie put the thought in his head, Wesley kept expecting his always-trustworthy Chevrolet to die and coast to a stop at the side of the two-lane blacktop, a victim of either a bad battery or the Paradox Laws. Candy Rymer's taillights would disappear from view and they would spend the following hours making frantic but useless calls (always assuming their phones would even work out here in the mid-South williwags) and cursing themselves for not disabling her vehicle back in Eddyville, while they still had a chance.

But the Malibu cruised as effortlessly as always, without a single gurgle or glitch. He stayed about a quarter mile behind Candy's Explorer.

"Man, she's all over the road," Robbie said. "Maybe she'll ditch the damn thing before she gets to the next bar. Save us the trouble of slashing her tires."

"According to *The Echo*, that doesn't happen."

"Yeah, but we know the future's not cast in stone, don't we? Maybe this is another Ur, or something."

Wesley was sure it didn't work that way with Ur Local, but he kept his mouth shut. Either way, it was too late now.

Candy Rymer made it to Banty's without going in the ditch or hitting any oncoming traffic, although she could have done either; God knew she had enough close calls. When one of the cars swerved out of her way and then passed Wesley's Malibu, Robbie said: "That's a family. Mom, Pop, three little kids goofin' around in the back."

That was when Wesley stopped feeling sorry for Rymer and started feeling angry at her. It was a clean, hot emotion that made his pique at Ellen feel paltry by comparison.

"That bitch," he said. His knuckles were white on the steering wheel. "That drunken who-gives-a-shit *bitch*. I'll kill her if that's the only way I can stop her."

"I'll help," Robbie said, then clamped his mouth so tightly shut his lips nearly disappeared.

They didn't have to kill her, and the Paradox Laws stopped them no more than the laws against drinking and driving had stopped Candy Rymer on her tour of southern Kentucky's more desperate watering holes.

The parking lot of Banty's was paved, but the buckling concrete looked like something left over from an Israeli bombing raid in Gaza. Overhead, a fizzing neon rooster flashed on and off. Hooked in one set of its talons was a moonshine jug with XXX printed on the side.

The Rymer woman's Explorer was parked almost directly beneath this fabulous bird, and by its stuttering orange-red glow, Wesley slashed open the elderly SUV's front tires with the butcher knife they had brought for that express purpose. As the *whoosh* of escaping air hit him, he was struck by a wave of relief so great that at first he couldn't get up but only hunker on his knees like a man praying. He only wished they'd done it back at The Broken Windmill.

"My turn," Robbie said, and a moment later the Explorer settled further as the kid punctured the rear tires. Then came another hiss. He had put a hole in the spare for good measure. By then Wesley had gotten to his feet.

"Let's park around to the side," Robbie said. "I think we better keep an eye on her."

"I'm going to do a lot more than that," Wesley said.

"Easy, big fella. What are you planning on?"

"I'm not planning. I'm beyond that." But the rage shaking through his body suggested something different.

According to *The Echo*, she had called Banty's a dive in her parting shot, but apparently that had been cleaned up for family consumption. What she actually threw back over her shoulder was, "I'm done doing business with this shitpit!" Only by this point she was so drunk the vulgarity came out in a slippery slur: *shi'pih*.

Robbie was so fascinated at seeing the news story played out before his eyes that he made no effort to grab Wesley as he strode toward her. He *did* call "Wait!" but Wesley didn't. He seized the woman and commenced shaking her.

Candy Rymer's mouth dropped open; the keys she'd been holding dropped to the cracked concrete tarmac.

"Leggo me, you bassard!"

Wesley didn't. He slapped her face hard enough to split her lower lip, then went back on her the other way. *"Sober up!"* he screamed into her frightened face. *"Sober up, you useless bitch! Get a life and stop fucking up other people's! You're going to kill people! Do you understand that? You are going to fucking KILL people!"*

He slapped her a third time, the sound as loud as a pistol shot. She staggered back against the side of the building, weeping and holding her hands up to protect her face. Blood trickled down her chin. Their shadows, turned into elongated gantries by the neon rooster, winked off and on.

He raised his hand to slap a fourth time—better to slap than to choke, which was what he really wanted to do—but Robbie grabbed him from behind and wrestled him away. "Stop it! Fucking stop it, man! That's enough!"

The bartender and a couple of goofy-looking patrons were now standing in the doorway, gawking. Candy Rymer had slid down to a sitting position. She was weeping hysterically, her hands pressed to her swelling face. "Why does everyone hate me?" She sobbed. "Why is everyone so goddam mean?"

Wesley looked at her dully, the anger out of him. What replaced it was a kind of hopelessness. You would say that a drunk driver who caused the deaths of at least eleven people had to be evil, but there was no evil here. Only a sobbing alkie sitting on the cracked, weedy concrete of a country roadhouse parking lot. A woman who, if the off-and-on light of the stuttering neon did not lie, had wet her pants.

"You can get to the person, but you can't get to the evil," Wesley said. His voice seemed to be coming from somewhere else. "The evil always survives. It flies off like a bigass bird and lands on someone else. That's the hell of it, wouldn't you say? The total hell of it?"

"Yeah, I'm sure, very philosophical, but come on. Before they get a really good look at you or the license plate of your car."

Robbie was leading him back to the Malibu. Wesley went as docilely as a child. He was trembling. "The evil always survives, Robbie. In all the Urs. Remember that."

"You bet, absolutely. Give me the keys. I'll drive."

"Hey!" someone shouted from behind them. "Why in the hell did you beat up that woman? She wasn't doing nothing to you! Come back here!"

Robbie pushed Wesley into the car, ran around the hood, threw himself behind the wheel, and drove away fast. He kept the pedal down until the stuttering rooster disappeared, then eased up. "What now?"

Wesley ran a hand over his eyes. "I'm sorry I did that," he said. "And yet I'm not. Do you understand?"

"Yeah," Robbie said. "You bet. It was for Coach

Silverman. And Josie too." He smiled. "My little mousie."

Wesley smiled.

"So where do we go? Home?"

"Not yet," Wesley said.

They parked on the edge of a cornfield near the intersection of Route 139 and Highway 80, two miles west of Cadiz. They were early, and Wesley used the time to fire up the pink Kindle. When he tried to access Ur Local, he was greeted by a somehow unsurprising message: THIS SERVICE IS NO LONGER AVAILABLE.

"Probably for the best," he said.

Robbie turned toward him. "Say what?"

"Nothing. It doesn't matter." He put the Kindle back in his briefcase.

"Wes?"

"What, Robbie?"

"Did we break the Paradox Laws?"

"Undoubtedly," Wes said.

At five to nine, they heard honking and saw lights. They got out of the Malibu and stood in front of it, waiting. Wesley observed that Robbie's hands were clenched, and was glad he himself wasn't the only one still afraid that Candy Rymer might still somehow appear.

Headlights breasted the nearest hill. It was the bus, followed by a dozen cars filled with Lady Meerkats supporters, all honking deliriously and flashing their high beams off and on. As the bus passed, Wesley heard sweet female voices singing "We Are the Champions" and felt a chill race up his back and lift the hair on his neck.

He raised his hand and waved.

Beside him, Robbie did the same. Then he turned to Wesley, smiling. "What do you say, Prof? Want to join the parade?"

Wesley clapped him on the shoulder. "That sounds like a damn fine idea."

When the last of the cars had passed, Robbie got in line. Like the others, he honked and flashed the Malibu's lights all the way back to Moore.

Wesley didn't mind.

VII—The Paradox Police

When Robbie got out in front of Susan and Nan's (where LADY MEERKATS RULE had been soaped on the window), Wesley said, "Wait a sec."

He came around the front of the car and embraced the kid. "You did good."

Robbie grinned. "Does this mean I get a gift A for the semester?"

"Nope, just some advice. Get out of football. You'll never make it a career, and your head deserves better."

"Duly noted," Robbie said . . . which was not agreement, as they both knew. "See you in class?"

"On Tuesday," Wesley said. But fifteen minutes later he had reason to wonder if *anyone* would see him. Ever again.

There was a car in the spot where he usually left the Malibu when he didn't leave it in Parking Lot A at the college. Wesley could have parked behind it, but chose the other side of the street instead. Something about the car made him uneasy. It was a Cadillac, and in the glow of the arc sodium beneath which it was parked, it seemed too bright. The red paint almost seemed to yell *Here I am! Do you like me?*

Wesley didn't. Nor did he like the tinted windows or the oversize gangsta hubcabs with their gold Cadillac emblems. It looked like a drug dealer's car. If, that was, the dealer in question also happened to be a homicidal maniac.

Now why would I think that?

"Stress of the day, that's all," he said as he crossed the deserted street with his briefcase banging against his leg. He bent down. Nobody was inside the car. At least he didn't *think* so. With the darkened windows, it was hard to be entirely sure.

It's the Paradox Police. They've come for me.

This idea should have seemed ridiculous at best, a paranoid fantasy at worst, but felt like neither. And when you considered all that had happened, maybe it wasn't paranoid at all.

Wesley stretched out a hand, touched the door of the car, then snatched it back. The door felt like metal, but it was warm. And it seemed to be *pulsing*. As if, metal or not, the car were alive.

Run.

The thought was so powerful he felt his lips mouth it, but he knew running wasn't an option. If he tried, the man or men who belonged to the loathsome red car would find him. This was a fact so simple that it defied logic. It *bypassed* logic. So, instead of running, he used his key to open the street door and went upstairs to his apartment. He did it slowly, because his heart was racing and his legs kept threatening to give way.

The door of 2B stood open, light spilling onto the upstairs landing in a long rectangle.

"Ah, here you are," a not-quite-human voice said. "Come in, Wesley of Kentucky."

There were two of them. One was young and one was old. The old one sat on his sofa, where Wesley and Ellen Silverman had once seduced each other to their mutual enjoyment (nay, ecstasy). The young one sat in Wesley's favorite chair, the one he always ended up in when the night was late, the leftover cheesecake tasty, the book interesting, and the light from the standing lamp just right. They both wore long mustard-colored coats, the kind that are called dusters, and Wesley understood, without knowing how he understood, that the coats were alive. He also understood that the men wearing them were not men at all. Their faces kept *changing*, and what lay just beneath the skin was reptilian. Or birdlike. Or both.

On their lapels, where lawmen in a Western movie would have worn badges, both wore buttons bearing a red eye. Wesley thought these too were alive. The eyes were watching him.

"How did you know it was me?"

"Smelled you," the older of the two replied, and the terrible thing was this: it didn't sound like a joke.

"What do you want?"

"You know why we're here," the young one said. The older of the two never spoke again at all until the end of the visit. Listening to one of them was bad enough. It was like listening to a man whose voicebox was stuffed with crickets.

"I suppose I do," Wesley said. His voice was steady, at least so far. "I broke the Paradox Laws." He prayed they didn't know about Robbie, and thought they might not; the Kindle had been registered to Wesley Smith, after all.

"You have no idea what you did," the man in the yellow coat said in a meditative voice. "The Tower trembles; the worlds shudder in their courses. The rose feels a chill, as of winter."

Very poetic, but not very illuminating. "What Tower? What rose?" Wesley could feel sweat breaking on his forehead even though he liked to keep the apartment cool. *It's because of them,* he thought. *These boys run hot.*

"It doesn't matter," his younger visitor said. "Explain yourself, Wesley of Kentucky. And do it well, if you would ever see sunshine again."

For a moment Wesley couldn't. His mind was filled with a single thought: *I'm on trial here.* Then he swept it aside. The return of his anger—a pale imitation of what he had felt toward Candy Rymer, but real enough—helped in this regard.

"People were going to die. Almost a dozen. Maybe more. That might not mean much to fellows like you, but it does to me, especially since one of them happens to be a woman I'm in love with. All because of one self-indulgent drunk who won't address her problems. And . . ." He almost said *And we,* but made the necessary course correction just in time. "And I didn't even hurt her. Slapped her a little, but I couldn't help myself."

"You boys can *never* help yourselves," the buzzing voice of the thing in his favorite chair—which would never be his favorite chair again—replied. "Poor impulse control is ninety percent of your problem. Did it ever cross your mind, Wesley of Kentucky, that the Paradox Laws exist for a reason?"

"I didn't—"

The thing raised its voice. "Of course you *didn't*. We know you *didn't*. We're here because you *didn't*. It didn't cross your mind that one of the people on that bus could become a serial killer, someone who might kill dozens, including a child who would otherwise grow up to cure cancer or Alzheimer's Disease. It didn't occur to you that one of those young women might give birth to the next Hitler or Stalin, a human monster who could go on to kill *millions* of your fellow humans on this level of the Tower. It didn't occur to you that you were meddling in events far beyond your ability to understand!"

No, he had not considered those things at all. Ellen was what he had considered. As Josie Quinn was what Robbie had considered. And together they had considered the others. Kids screaming, their skin turning to tallow and dripping off their bones, maybe dying the worst deaths God visits on His suffering people.

"Does that happen?" he whispered.

"We don't *know* what happens," the thing in the yellow coat said. "That's precisely the point. The experimental program you foolishly accessed can see clearly six months into the future . . . within a single narrow geographical area, that is. Beyond six months, predictive sight grows dim. Beyond a year, all is darkness. So you see, we don't know *what* you and your young friend may have done. And since we don't, there's no chance to repair the damage, if there was damage."

Your young friend. They knew about Robbie Henderson after all. Wesley's heart sank.

"Is there some sort of power controlling all this? There is, isn't there? When I accessed Ur Books for the first time, I saw a tower."

"All things serve the Tower," the man-thing in the yellow duster said, and touched the hideous button on its coat with a kind of reverence.

"Then how do you know I'm not serving it too?"

They said nothing. Only stared at him with their black, predatory bird-eyes.

"I never ordered it, you know. I mean . . . I ordered a Kindle, that much is true, but I never ordered the one I got. It just came."

There was a long silence, and Wesley understood that his life was teetering inside it. Life as he knew it, at least. He might continue some sort of existence if these two creatures took him away in their loathsome red car, but it would be a dark existence, probably an imprisoned existence, and he guessed he would not retain his sanity for long.

"We think it was a mistake in shipping," the young one said finally.

"But you don't know for sure, do you? Because you don't know where it came from. Or who sent it."

More silence. Then the older of the two repeated, "All things serve the Tower." He stood, and held out his hand. It shimmered and became a claw. Shimmered again and became a hand. "Give it to me, Wesley of Kentucky."

Wesley of Kentucky didn't have to be asked twice, although his hands were trembling so badly that he fumbled with the buckles of his briefcase for what felt like hours. At last the top sprang open, and he held the pink Kindle out to the older of the two. The creature stared at it with a crazed hunger that made Wesley feel like screaming.

"I don't think it works anymore, anyw—"

The creature snatched it. For one second Wesley

felt its skin and understood the creature's flesh had its own thoughts. Howling thoughts that ran along their own unknowable circuits. This time he *did* scream . . . or tried to. What actually came out was a low, choked groan.

They moved to the door, the hems of their coats making loathsome liquid chuckling sounds. The older one went out, still holding the pink Kindle in its claw-hands. The other paused for a moment to look back at Wesley. "You're getting a pass. Do you understand how lucky you are?"

"Yes," Wesley whispered.

"Then say thank you."

"Thank you."

It was gone without another word.

He couldn't bring himself to sit on the sofa, or in the chair that had seemed—in the days before Ellen—to be his best friend in the world. He lay down on his bed and crossed his arms over his chest in an effort to stop the shudders that were whipping through him. He left the lights on because there was no sense turning them off. He felt sure he would not sleep again for weeks. Perhaps never. He'd begin to drift off, then see those greedy black eyes and hear that voice saying *Do you understand how lucky you are?*

No, sleep was definitely out.

And with that, consciousness ceased.

VIII—The Future Lies Ahead

Wesley slept until the music-box tinkle of Pachelbel's "Canon in D" woke him at nine o'clock the next morning. If there were dreams (of pink Kindles, drunk women in roadhouse parking lots, or low men in yellow coats), he did not remember them. All he knew was that someone was calling his cell, and it might be someone he wanted to talk to very badly.

He ran into the living room, but the ringing ceased before he could get the phone out of his briefcase. He flipped it open and saw YOU HAVE 1 NEW MESSAGE. He accessed it.

"Hey, pal," Don Allman's voice said. "You better check the morning paper."

That was all.

He no longer subscribed to *The Echo*, but old Mrs. Ridpath, his downstairs neighbor, did. He took the stairs two at a time, and there it was, sticking out of her mailbox. He reached for it, then hesitated. What if his deep sleep hadn't been natural? What if he had been anesthetized somehow, so he could be booted into a different Ur, one where the crash had happened after all? What if Don had called to prepare him? Suppose he unfolded the paper and saw the black border that was the newspaper world's version of funeral crepe?

"Please," he whispered, unsure if it was God or that mysterious dark tower he was praying to. "Please let it still be my Ur."

He took the paper in a numb hand and unfolded it. The border was there, all right, boxing in the entire front page, but it was blue rather than black.

Meerkat blue.

The photo was the biggest he'd ever seen in *The Echo*; it took up half of the front page, under a headline reading **LADY MEERKATS TAKE BLUE-GRASS, AND THE FUTURE LIES AHEAD!** The team was clustered on the hardwood of Rupp Arena. Three were hoisting a shiny silver trophy. Another— it was Josie—stood on a stepladder, twirling a net over her head.

Standing in front of her team, dressed in the prim blue slacks and blue blazer she invariably wore on game days, was Ellen Silverman. She was smiling and holding up a handmade sign that read **I LOVE YOU WESLEY**.

Wesley thrust his hands, one still holding the newspaper, over his head and let out a yell that caused a couple of kids on the other side of the street to look around.

"Wassup?" one of them called.

"Sports fan!" Wesley called back, then raced upstairs. He had a call to make.

Thinking of Ralph Vicinanza

On July 26, 2009, a woman named Diane Schuler left the Hunter Lake Campground in Parksville, New York, driving her 2003 Ford Windstar. She had five passengers: her five-year-old son, her two-year-old daughter, and three nieces. She seemed fine—the last person to see her at the campground swears she was alert and had no liquor on her breath—and equally fine an hour later, when she fed the kids at a Mickey D's. Not long after that, however, she was observed vomiting beside the road. She called her brother and said she did not feel well. Then she turned onto the Taconic Parkway and drove the wrong way for nearly two miles, ignoring the horns, waves, and flashing lights of those who dodged around her. She eventually hit an SUV head-on, killing herself, all but one of her passengers (her son survived), and the three men in the SUV.

According to the toxicology reports, Schuler was processing the equivalent of ten drinks at the time of the crash, plus a large amount of marijuana. Her husband stated that his wife wasn't a drinker, but toxicology reports don't lie. Like Candy Rymer in the previous story, Diane Schuler was loaded to the max.

Did Daniel Schuler really not know, after at least five years of marriage and a period of courtship, that his wife was a secret drinker? It's actually possible. Abusers can be incredibly sly, and hide their addictions for a long time. They do it out of need and desperation.

What exactly happened in that car? How did she get drunk so fast, and when did she smoke the dope? What was she thinking when she refused to heed the drivers warning her that she was going the wrong way? Was it a booze and drug-fueled accident, a murder-suicide, or some weird combination of both? Only fiction can approach answers to these questions. Only *through* fiction can we think about the unthinkable, and perhaps obtain some sort of closure. This story is my effort to do that.

And by the way, Herman Wouk *is* still alive. He read a version of this story after it appeared in *The Atlantic*, and wrote me a nice note. Invited me to visit him, even. As a longtime fan, I was thrilled. He's pushing a hundred now, and I'm sixty-seven. Should I live long enough, I might just take him up on the invitation.

Herman Wouk
Is Still Alive

From the Portland (Maine) *Press-Herald*, September 19, 2010:

9 DIE IN HORRIFIC I-95 CRASH
Spontaneous Mourning at Scene
By Ray Dugan

Less than six hours after a one-vehicle accident in the town of Fairfield took the lives of two adults and seven children, all under the age of ten, the mourning has already begun. Bouquets of wildflowers in tin cans and insulated coffee mugs ring the scorched earth; a line of nine crosses has been placed in the picnic area of the adjacent rest area at Mile 109. At the site where the bodies of the two youngest children were found, an anonymous sign, words spray-painted on a piece of bedsheet, has been erected. It reads, ANGELS GATHER HERE.

I. *BRENDA HITS PICK-3 FOR $2,700 AND RESISTS HER FIRST IMPULSE.*

Instead of going out for a bottle of Orange Driver to celebrate with, Brenda pays off the MasterCard, which has been maxed like forever. Then calls Hertz and asks a question. Then calls her friend Jasmine, who lives in North Berwick, and tells her about the Pick-3. Jasmine screams and says, "Girl, you're rich!"

If only. Brenda explains how she paid off the credit card so she can rent a Chevy Express if she wants to. It's a van that seats nine, that's what the Hertz girl told her. "We could get all the kids in there and drive up to Mars Hill. See your folks and mine. Show off the grandchildren. Squeeze the home folks for a little more dough. What do you think?"

Jasmine is dubious. The glorified shack in Mars Hill that her folks call home doesn't have room, and she wouldn't want to stay with them even if it did. She hates her parents. With good reason, Brenda knows; it was Jazzy's own father who broke her in, a week after her fifteenth birthday. Her mother knew what was going on and did nothing. When Jaz went to her in tears, her ma said, "You got nothing to worry about, he's had his nuts cut."

Jaz married Mitch Robicheau to get away from them, and now, three men, four kids, and eight years later, she's on her own. And on welfare, although she gets sixteen hours a week at the Roll Around, handing out skates and making change for the video arcade, where the machines take only special tokens. They let her bring her two youngest. Delight sleeps in the office and Truth, her three-year-old, wanders around in the arcade hitching at his diapers. He doesn't get into too much trouble, although last year he got head-lice and the two women had to shave all his hair off. How he howled.

"There's six hundred left over after I paid off the credit card balance," Brenda says. "Well, four hundred if you count the rental, only I don't, because I can put that on MasterCard. We could stay at the Red Roof, watch Home Box. It's free. We can get take-out from downstreet and the kids can swim in the pool. What do you say?"

From behind her comes yelling. Brenda raises her voice and screams, *"Freddy, you stop teasing your sister and give that back!"* Then, oh goody, their squabbling wakes up the baby. Either that or Freedom has messed in her diapers and awakened herself. Freedom *always* messes in her diapers. To Brenda it seems like man-ufacturing poop is Free's life's work. Takes after her father that way.

"I suppose . . ." Jasmine says, drawing *suppose* out to four syllables. Maybe five.

"Come on, girl! Road trip! Get with the program! We take the bus to the Jetport and rent the van. Three hundred miles, we can be there in four hours. The girl says the rugrats can watch DVDs. *The Little Mermaid* and all that good stuff."

"Maybe I could get some of that government money from my ma before it's all gone," Jasmine says thoughtfully.

Her brother Tommy died the year before, in Afghanistan. It was an IED that took him. Her ma and dad got eighty thousand out of it. Her ma has promised her some, although not when the old man was in hearing distance of the phone. Of course it may be gone already. Probably is. She knows Mr. Fuck-A-Fifteen-Year-Old bought a Yamaha rice-rocket with some of it, although what he wants with a thing like that at his age Jasmine has no idea. And she knows things like government money are mostly a mirage. This is something they both know. Every time you see bright stuff, somebody turns on the rain machine. The bright stuff is never colorfast.

"Come on," Brenda says. She has fallen in love with the idea of loading up the van with kids and her best (her only) friend from high school, who ended up living just one town over. Both of them on their own, seven kids between them, too many lousy men in the rearview, but sometimes they still have a little fun.

She hears a thunk sound. Freddy starts to scream. Glory has whopped him in the eye with an action figure.

"Glory you stop that or I'll tear you a new one!" Brenda screams.

"He won't give back my Powerpuff!" Glory shrieks, and *she* starts to cry. Now they're all crying—Freddy, Glory, and Freedom—and for a moment grayness creeps over Brenda's vision. She's seen a lot of that grayness lately. Here they are in a three-room third-floor apartment, no guy in the picture (Tim, the latest in her life, took off six months ago), living pretty much on noodles and Pepsi and that cheap ice cream they sell at Walmart, no air-conditioning, no cable TV, she had a job at the Quik-Flash store but the company went bust and now the store's an On the Run and the manager hired some Taco Paco to do her job because Taco Paco can work twelve or fourteen

hours a day. Taco Paco wears a doorag on his head and a nasty little mustache on his upper lip and he's never been pregnant. Taco Paco's job is to get *girls* pregnant. They fall for that little mustache and then boom, the line in the little drugstore testing gadget turns blue and here comes another one, just like the other one.

Brenda has personal here-comes-another-one experience. She tells people she knows who Freddy's father is, but she really doesn't, she had a few drunk nights there when they *all* looked good, and besides, come on, how is she supposed to look for a job anyway? She's got these *kids*. What's she supposed to do, leave Freddy to mind Glory and take Freedom to the goddam job interviews? Sure, *that'll* work. And what is there, besides drive-up window girl at Mickey D's or the Booger King? Portland has a couple of strip clubs, but wide loads like her don't get that kind of work.

She reminds herself she hit the lottery. She reminds herself they could be in a couple of air-conditioned rooms tonight at the Red Roof—three, even! Why not? Things are turning around!

"Brennie?" Jaz sounds more doubtful than ever. "Are you like serious about this?"

"Yeah," Brenda says. "Come *on*, girl, I'm *approved*. The Hertz chick says the van is red." She lowers her voice and adds: "Your lucky color."

"Did you pay off the credit card online? How'd you do that?" Freddy and Glory got fighting last month and knocked Brenda's laptop off the bed. It fell on the floor and broke.

"I used the one at the library." She says it the way she grew up in Mars Hill saying it: *liberry*. "I had to wait awhile to get on, but it's worth it. It's free. So what do you say?"

"Maybe we could get a bottle of Allen's," Jaz says. She loves that Allen's Coffee Brandy, when she can get it. In truth, Jasmine loves anything when she can get it.

"No doubt," Brenda says. "And a bottle of Orange Driver for me. But I won't drink while I'm behind the wheel, Jaz. I have to keep my license. It's about all I got left."

"Can you really get any money out of your folks, do you think?"

Brenda tells herself that once they see the kids—assuming the kids can be bribed (or intimidated) into good behavior—she can. "But not a word about the lottery," she says.

"No way," Jasmine says. "I was born at night but it wasn't last night."

They yuk at this one, an oldie but a goodie.

"So what do you think?"

"I'll have to take Eddie and Rose Ellen out of school . . ."

"BFD," Brenda says. "So what do you *think*, girl?"

After a long pause on the other end, Jasmine says, "Road trip!"

"Road trip!" Brenda hollers back.

Then they are chanting it while the three kids bawl in Brenda's Sanford apartment and at least one (maybe two) are bawling in Jasmine's North Berwick apartment. These are the fat women nobody wants to see when they're on the streets, the ones no guy wants to pick up in the bars unless the hour is late and the mood is drunk and there's nobody better in sight. What men think when they're drunk—Brenda and Jasmine both know this—is that thunder thighs are better than no thighs at all. Especially at closing time. They went to high school together in Mars Hill and now they're downstate and they help each other when they can. They are the fat women nobody wants to see, they have a litter of children between them, and they are chanting *road trip*, *road trip* like a couple of cheerleading fools.

On a September morning, already hot at eight thirty, this is the way things happen. It's never been any different.

II. *SO THESE TWO OLD POETS WHO WERE ONCE LOVERS IN PARIS HAVE A PICNIC NEAR THE BATHROOMS.*

Phil Henreid is seventy-eight now, and Pauline Enslin is seventy-five. They're both skinny. They both wear spectacles. Their hair, white and thin, blows in the breeze. They've paused at a rest area on I-95 near Fairfield, which is about twenty miles north of Augusta. The rest area building is barnboard, and the adjacent bathrooms are brick. They're good-looking bathrooms. *State-of-the-art* bathrooms, one could say. There's no odor. Phil, who lives in Maine and knows this rest area well, would never have proposed a picnic here two months earlier. In the summertime, the traffic on the interstate swells with out-of-state vacationers, and the Turnpike Authority brings in a line of plastic Port-O-Sans. They make this pleasant grassy area stink like hell on New Year's Eve. But now the Port-O-Sans are in storage somewhere and the rest area is nice.

Pauline puts a checked cloth on the initial-scarred picnic table standing in the shade of an old oak, and anchors it with a wicker picnic basket against a slight warm breeze. From the basket she takes sandwiches, potato salad, melon wedges, and two slices of coconut-custard pie. She also has a large glass bottle of red tea. Ice cubes clink cheerfully inside.

"If we were in Paris, we'd have wine," Phil says.

"In Paris we never had another eighty miles to drive on the turnpike," she replies. "That tea is cold and it's fresh. You'll have to make do."

"I wasn't carping," he says, and lays an arthritis-swollen hand over hers (which is also swollen, although marginally less so). "This is a feast, my dear."

They smile into each other's used faces. Although Phil has been married three times (and has scattered five children behind him) and Pauline has been married twice (no children, but lovers of both sexes in the dozens), they still have quite a lot between them. Much more than a spark. Phil is both surprised and not surprised. At his age— late, but not quite last call—you take what you can and are happy to get it. They are on their way to a poetry festival at the University of Maine's Orono branch, and while the compensation for their joint appearance isn't huge, it's adequate. Since he has an expense account, Phil has splurged and rented a Cadillac from Hertz at the Portland Jetport, where he met her plane. Pauline jeered at the Caddy, said she always knew he was a plastic hippie, but she did so gently. He wasn't a hippie, but he was a genuine iconoclast, a one-of-a-kinder, and she knows it. As he knows that her osteoporotic bones have enjoyed the ride.

Now, a picnic. Tonight they'll have a catered meal, but the food will be a lukewarm, sauce-covered mess o' mystery supplied by the cafeteria in one of the college commons. Possibly chicken, possibly fish, it's always hard to tell. Beige food is what Pauline calls it. Visiting poet—food is always beige, and in any case it won't be served until eight o'clock. With some cheap yellowish-white wine seemingly created to saw at the guts of semiretired alcohol abusers such as themselves. This meal is nicer, and iced tea is fine. Phil even indulges the fantasy of leading her by the hand to the high grass behind the bathrooms once they have finished eating, like in that old Van Morrison song, and—

Ah, but no. Elderly poets whose sex drives are now permanently stuck in first gear should not chance such a potentially ludicrous site of assignation. Especially poets of long, rich, and varied experience, who now know that each time is apt to be largely unsatisfactory, and each time may well be the last time. *Besides,* Phil thinks, *I have already had two heart attacks. Who knows what's up with her?*

Pauline thinks, *Not after sandwiches and potato salad, not to mention custard pie. But perhaps tonight. It is not out of the question.* She smiles at him and takes the last item from the hamper. It is a *New York Times*, bought at the same Augusta convenience store where she got the rest of the picnic things, checked cloth and iced-tea bottle included. As in the old days, they flip for the Arts & Leisure section. In the old days, Phil— who won the National Book Award for *Burning Elephants* in 1970—always called tails and won far more times than the odds said he should. Today he calls heads . . . and wins again.

"Why, you snot!" she cries, and hands it over.

They eat. They read the divided paper. At one point she looks at him over a forkful of potato salad and says, "I still love you, you old fraud."

Phil smiles. The wind blows the gone-to-seed dandelion puff of his hair. His scalp shines gauzily through. He's not the young man who once came roistering out of Brooklyn, broad-shouldered as a longshoreman (and just as foul-mouthed), but Pauline can still see the shadow of that man, who was so full of anger, despair, and hilarity.

"Why, I love you, too, Paulie," he says.

"We're a couple of old crocks," she says, and bursts into laughter. Once she had sex with a king and a movie star at pretty much the same time on a balcony while "Maggie May" played on the gramophone, Rod Stewart singing in French. Now the woman *The New York Times* once called America's greatest living female poet lives in a walk-up in Queens. "Doing poetry readings in tank towns for dishonorable honorariums and eating alfresco in rest areas."

"We're not old," he says, "we're young, *bébé.*"

"What in the world are you talking about?"

"Look at this," he says, and holds out the first page of the Arts section. She takes it and sees a photograph. It's a dried-up string of a man wearing a straw hat and a smile.

Nonagenarian Wouk to Publish New Book
By Motoko Rich

By the time they reach the age of ninety-five— if they do—most writers have retired long ago. Not Herman Wouk, author of such famous novels as *The Caine Mutiny* (1951) and *Marjorie Morningstar* (1955). Many of those who remember the TV miniseries presentations of his exhaustive World War II novels, *The Winds of War* (1971) and *War and Remembrance* (1978), are now drawing Social Security themselves. It's a retirement premium Wouk became eligible for in 1980.

Wouk, however, is not done. He published a well-reviewed surprise novel, *A Hole in Texas*, a year shy of his ninetieth birthday, and expects to publish a book-length essay called *The Language God Talks* later this year. Is it his final word?

"I'm not prepared to speak on that subject, one way or the other," Wouk said with a smile. "The ideas don't stop just because one is old. The body weakens, but the words never do." When asked about his Continued on page 19

As she looks at that old, seamed face beneath the rakishly tilted straw hat, Pauline feels the sudden sting of tears. "The body weakens, but the words never do," she says. "That's beautiful."

"Have you ever read him?" Phil asks.

"*Marjorie Morningstar*, in my youth. It's an annoying hymn to virginity, but I was swept away in spite of myself. Have you?"

"I tried *Youngblood Hawke*, but couldn't finish it. Still . . . he's in there pitching. And, unbelievable as it may seem, he's old enough to be our father." Phil folds the paper and puts it into the picnic basket. Below them, light traffic on the turnpike runs beneath a high September sky full of fair-weather clouds. "Before we get back on the road, do you want to do swapsies? Like in the old days?"

She thinks about it, then nods. Many years have passed since she listened to someone else read one of her poems, and the experience is always a little dismaying—like having an out-of-body experience—but why not? They have the rest area to themselves. "In honor of Herman Wouk, who's still in there pitching. My work folder's in the front pocket of my carry bag."

"You trust me to go through your things?"

She gives him her old slanted smile, then stretches into the sun with her eyes closed. Relishing the heat. Soon the days will turn cold, but now there is heat. "You can go through my things all you want, Philip." She opens one eye in a reverse wink that is amusingly seductive. "Explore me to your heart's content."

"I'll keep that in mind," he says, and goes back to the Cadillac he has rented for them.

Poets in a Cadillac, she thinks. *The very definition of absurdity.* For a moment she watches the cars rush by. Then she picks up the paper and looks again at the narrow, smiling face of the old scribbler. Still alive. Perhaps at this very moment looking up at the high blue September sky, with his notebook open on a patio table and a glass of Perrier (or wine, if his stomach will still stand it) near to hand.

If there is a God, Pauline Enslin thinks, *She can occasionally be very generous.*

She waits for Phil to come back with her work folder and one of the steno pads he favors for composition. They will play swapsies. Tonight they may play other games. Once again she tells herself that it is not out of the question.

III. *SITTING BEHIND THE WHEEL OF THE CHEVY EXPRESS VAN, BRENDA FEELS LIKE SHE'S IN THE COCKPIT OF A JET FIGHTER.*

Everything is digital. There's a satellite radio and a GPS screen. When she backs up, the GPS turns into a TV monitor, so you can see what's behind you. Everything on the dashboard shines, that new-car smell fills the interior, and why not, with only seven hundred and fifty miles on the odometer? She has never in her life been behind the wheel of a motor vehicle with such low mileage. You can push buttons on the control stalk to show your average speed, how many miles per gallon you're getting, and how many gallons you've got left. The engine makes hardly any noise at all. The seats up front are twin buckets, upholstered in bone white material that looks like leather. The shocks are like butter.

In back is a pop-down TV screen with a DVD player. *The Little Mermaid* won't work because Truth, Jasmine's three-year-old, spread peanut butter all over the disk at some point, but they are content with *Shrek*, even though all of them have seen it like a billion times. The thrill is watching it *while they're on the road*! *Driving!* Freedom is asleep in her car seat between Freddy and Glory; Delight, Jasmine's six-month-old, is asleep in Jaz's lap, but the other five cram together in the two backseats, watching, entranced. Their mouths are hanging open. Jasmine's

Eddie is picking his nose and Eddie's older sister, Rose Ellen, has got drool on her sharp little chin, but at least they are quiet and not beating away at each other for once. They are hypnotized.

Brenda should be happy. The kids are quiet, the road stretches ahead of her like an airport runway, she's behind the wheel of a brand-new van, and the traffic is light once they leave Portland. The digital speedometer reads 70, and this baby hasn't even broken a sweat. Nonetheless, that grayness has begun to creep over her again.

The van isn't hers, after all. She'll have to give it back. A foolish expense, really, because what's at the far end of this trip? Mars Hill. Mars . . . fucking . . . Hill. Food brought in from the Round-Up, where she used to waitress when she was in high school and still had a figure. Hamburgers and fries covered with plastic wrap. The kids splashing in the pool before and maybe after. At least one of them will get hurt and bawl. Maybe more. Glory will complain that the water is too cold, even if it isn't. Glory always complains. She will complain her whole life. Brenda hates that whining and likes to tell Glory it's her father coming out . . . but the truth is the kid gets it from both sides. Poor kid. All of them, really. And the years stretch ahead, a march beneath a sun that never goes down.

She looks to her right, hoping Jasmine will say something funny and cheer her up, and is dismayed to see that Jaz is crying. Silent tears well up in her eyes and shine on her cheeks. In her lap, baby Delight sleeps on, sucking one of her fingers. It's her comfort finger, and all blistered down the inside. Once Jaz slapped her good and hard when she saw Dee sticking it in her mouth, but what good is slapping a kid that's only six months old? Might as well slap a door. But sometimes you do it. Sometimes you can't help it. Sometimes you don't want to help it. Brenda has done it herself.

"What's wrong, girl?" Brenda asks.

"Nothing. Never mind me, just watch your driving."

Behind them, Donkey says something funny to Shrek and some of the kids laugh. Not Glory, though; she's nodding off.

"Come on, Jaz. Tell me. I'm your friend."

"*Nothing*, I said."

Jasmine leans over the sleeping infant. Delight's baby seat is on the floor. Resting in it on a pile of diapers is the bottle of Allen's they stopped for in South Portland, before hitting the turnpike. Jaz has only had a couple of sips, but this time she takes two good long swallows before putting the cap back on. The tears are still running down her cheeks.

"Nothing. Everything. Comes to the same either way you say it, that's what I think."

"Is it Tommy? Is it your bro?"

Jaz laughs angrily. "They'll never give me a cent of that money, who'm I kidding? Ma'll blame it on Dad because that's easier for her, but she feels the same. It'll mostly be gone, anyway. What about you? Will your folks really give you something?"

"Sure, I think so."

Well. Yeah. Probably. Like forty dollars. A bag and a half's worth of groceries. Two bags if she uses the coupons in *Uncle Henry's Swap Guide*. Just the thought of flipping through that raggy little free magazine— the poor people's Bible—and getting the ink on her fingers causes the grayness around her to thicken. The afternoon is beautiful, more like summer than September, but a world where you have to depend on *Uncle Henry's* is a gray world. Brenda thinks, *How did we end up with all these kids? Wasn't I letting Mike Higgins cop a feel on me out behind the metal shop just yesterday?*

"Bully for you," Jasmine says, and snorks back tears. "My folks, they'll have three new gasoline toys in the dooryard and then plead poverty. And do you know what my dad'll say about the kids? 'Don't let em touch anything,' that's what he'll say."

"Maybe he'll be different," Brenda says. "Better."

"He's never different and he's never better," Jasmine says.

Rose Ellen is drifting off. She tries to put her head on her brother Eddie's shoulder and he punches her in the arm. She rubs it and begins to snivel, but pretty soon she's watching *Shrek* again. The drool is still on her chin. Brenda thinks it makes her look like an idiot, which she pretty close to is.

"I don't know what to say," Brenda says. "We'll have some fun, anyway. Red Roof, girl! Swimming pool!"

"Yeah, and some guy knocking on the wall at one in the morning, telling me to shut my kid up. Like, you know, I *want* Dee awake in the middle of the night because all those stinkin teeth are coming in at once."

She takes another slug from the coffee brandy bottle, then holds it out. Brenda knows better than to take it and risk her license, but no cops are in sight, and if she did lose her ticket, how much would she really be out? The car was Tim's, he took it when he left, and it was half dead anyway, a Bondo-and-chickenwire special. No great loss there. Besides, there's that grayness. She takes the bottle and tips it. Just a little sip, but the brandy's warm and nice, a shaft of dark sunlight, so she takes another one.

"They're closing the Roll Around at the end of the month," Jasmine says, taking the bottle back.

"Jazzy, *no!*"

"Jazzy yes." She stares straight ahead at the unrolling road. "Jack finally went broke. The writing's been on the wall since last year. So there goes *that* ninety a week." She drinks. In her lap, Delight stirs, then goes back to sleep with her comfort finger plugged in her gob. Where, Brenda thinks, some boy like Mike Higgins will want to put his dick not all that many years from now. *And she'll probably let him. I did. Jaz did too. It's just how things go.*

Behind them Princess Fiona is now saying something funny, but none of the kids laugh. They're getting glassy, even Eddie and Freddy, names like a TV sitcom joke.

"The world is gray," Brenda says. She didn't know she was going to say those words until she hears them come out of her mouth.

Jasmine looks at her, surprised. "Sure," she says. "Now you're getting with the program."

Brenda says, "Pass me that bottle."

Jasmine does. Brenda drinks some more, then hands it back. "Okay, enough of that."

Jasmine gives her her old sideways grin, the one Brenda remembers from study hall on Friday afternoons. It looks strange below her wet cheeks and bloodshot eyes. "You sure?"

Brenda doesn't reply, but she pushes the accelerator a little deeper with her foot. Now the digital speedometer reads 80.

IV. *"YOU FIRST," PAULINE SAYS.*

All at once she feels shy, afraid to hear her words coming out of Phil's mouth, sure they will sound booming yet false, like dry thunder. But she has forgotten the difference between his public voice—declamatory and a little corny, like the voice of a movie attorney in a summing-up-to-the-jury scene—and the one he uses when he's with just a friend or two (and hasn't had anything to drink). It is a softer, kinder voice, and she is pleased to hear her poem coming out of his mouth. No, more than pleased. She is grateful. He makes it sound far better than it is.

> "Shadow-print the road
> with black lipstick kisses.
> Decaying snow in farmhouse fields
> like cast-off bridal dresses.
> The rising mist turns to gold dust.
> The clouds boil apart in ragged tresses.
> It bursts through!
> For five seconds it could be summer
> and I seventeen with flowers
> folded in the apron of my dress."

He puts the sheet down. She looks at him, smiling a little, but anxious. He nods his head. "It's fine, dear," he says. "Fine enough. Now you."

She opens his steno pad, finds what appears to be the last poem, and pages through four or five scribbled drafts. She knows how he works and goes on until she comes to a version not in mostly illegible cursive but in small neat printing. She shows it to him. Phil nods, then turns to look at the turnpike. All of this is very nice, but they will have to go soon. They don't want to be late.

He sees a bright red van coming. It's going fast.

She begins.

V. *BRENDA SEES A HORN OF PLENTY SPILLING ROTTEN FRUIT.*

Yes, she thinks, *that's just about right. Thanksgiving for fools.*

Freddy will go for a soldier and fight in foreign lands, the way Jasmine's brother Tommy did. Jazzy's boys, Eddie and Truth, will do the same. They'll own muscle cars when and if they come home, always supposing gas is still available twenty years from now. And the girls? They'll go with boys. They'll give up their virginity while game shows play on TV. They'll believe the boys who tell them they'll pull out in time. They'll have babies and fry meat in skillets and put on weight, same as she and Jaz did. They'll smoke a little dope and eat a lot of ice cream—the cheap stuff from Walmart. Maybe not Rose Ellen, though. Something is wrong with Rose. She'll still have drool on her sharp little chin when she's in the eighth grade, same as now. The seven kids will beget seventeen, and the seventeen will beget seventy, and the seventy will beget two hundred. She can see a ragged fool's parade marching into the future, some wearing jeans that show the ass of their underwear, some wearing heavy-metal tee-shirts, some wearing gravy-spotted waitress uniforms, some wearing stretch pants from Kmart that have little MADE IN PARAGUAY tags sewn into the seams of the roomy seats. She can see the mountain of Fisher-Price toys they will own and which will later be sold at yard sales (which was where they were bought in the first place). They will buy the products they see on TV and go in debt to the credit card companies, as she did . . . and will again, because the Pick-3 was a fluke and she knows it. Worse than a fluke, really: a tease. Life is a rusty hubcap lying in a ditch at the side of the road, and life goes on. She will never again feel like she's sitting in the cockpit of a jet fighter. This is as good as it gets. There are no boats for nobody, and no camera is filming her life. This is reality, not a reality show.

Shrek is over and all the kids are asleep, even Eddie. Rose Ellen's head is once more on Eddie's shoulder. She's snoring like an old woman. She has red marks on her arms, because sometimes she can't stop scratching herself.

Jasmine screws the cap on the bottle of Allen's and drops it back into the baby seat in the footwell. In a low voice she says, "When I was five, I believed in unicorns."

"So did I," Brenda says. "I wonder how fast this fucker goes."

Jasmine looks at the road ahead. They flash past a blue sign that says REST AREA 1 MI. She sees no traffic northbound; both lanes are entirely theirs. "Let's find out," Jaz says.

The numbers on the speedometer dial rise from 80 to 85. Then 87. There's still some room left between the accelerator pedal and the floor. All the kids are sleeping.

Here is the rest area, coming up fast. Brenda sees only one car in the parking lot. It looks like a fancy one, a Lincoln or maybe a Cadillac. *I could have rented one of those,* she thinks. *I had enough money but too many kids. Couldn't fit them all in.* Story of her life, really.

She looks away from the road. She looks at her old friend from high school, who ended up living just one town away. Jaz is looking back at her. The van, now doing almost a hundred miles an hour, begins to drift.

Jasmine gives a small nod and then lifts Dee, cradling the baby against her big breasts. Dee's still got her comfort finger in her mouth.

Brenda nods back. Then she pushes down harder with her foot, trying to find the van's carpeted floor. It's there, and she lays the accelerator pedal softly against it.

VI. *"STOP, PAULIE, STOP."*

He reaches out and grabs her shoulder with his bony hand, startling her. She looks up from his poem (it is quite a bit longer than hers, but she's reached the last dozen lines or so) and sees him staring at the turnpike. His mouth is open and behind his glasses his eyes appear to be bulging out almost far enough to touch the lenses. She follows his gaze in time to see a red van slide smoothly from the travel lane into the breakdown lane and from the breakdown lane across the rest area entrance ramp. It doesn't turn in. It's going far too fast to turn in. It crosses the ramp, doing at least ninety, and plows onto the slope just below them, where it hits a tree. He hears a loud, toneless bang and the sound of breaking glass. The windshield disintegrates; glass pebbles sparkle for a moment in the sun and she thinks—blasphemously—*beautiful*.

The tree shears the van into two ragged pieces. Something—Phil Henreid can't bear to believe it's a child—is flung high into the air and comes down in the grass. Then the van's gas tank begins to burn, and Pauline screams.

He gets to his feet and runs down the slope, vaulting over the shakepole fence like the young man he once was. These days his failing heart is usually never far from his mind, but as he runs down to the burning pieces of the van, he never even thinks of it.

Cloud-shadows roll across the field, printing shadow-kisses on the hay and timothy. Wildflowers nod their heads.

Phil stops twenty yards from the burning remains, the heat baking his face. He sees what he knew he would see—no survivors—but he never imagined so many *non*-survivors. He sees blood on timothy and clover. He sees a shatter of taillight glass like a patch of strawberries. He sees a severed arm caught in a bush. In the flames he sees a melting baby seat. He sees shoes.

Pauline comes up beside him. She's gasping for breath. The only thing wilder than her eyes is her hair.

"Don't look," he says.

"What's that smell? Phil, what's that *smell*?"

"Burning gas and rubber," he says, although that's probably not the smell she's talking about. "Don't look. Go back to the car and . . . do you have a cell phone?"

"Yes, of course I have a—"

"Go back and call 911. Don't look at this. You don't want to see this."

He doesn't want to see it either, but cannot look away. How many? He can see the bodies of at least three children and one adult—probably a woman, but he can't be sure. Yet so many shoes . . . and he can see a DVD package with cartoon characters on it . . .

"What if I can't get through?" she asks.

He points to the smoke. Then to the three or four cars that are already pulling over. "Getting through won't matter," he says, "but try."

She starts to go, then turns back. She's crying. "Phil . . . how many?"

"I don't know. A lot. Maybe half a dozen. Go on, Paulie. Some of them might still be alive."

"You know better," she says through her sobs. "Damn thing was going six licks to the minute."

She begins trudging back up the hill. Halfway to the rest area parking lot (more cars are pulling in now), a terrible idea crosses her mind and she looks back, sure she will see her old friend and lover lying in the grass himself. Perhaps unconscious, perhaps dead of a final thunderclap heart attack. But he's on his feet, cautiously circling the blazing left half of the van. As she watches, he takes off his natty sport jacket with the patches on the elbows. He kneels and covers something with it. Either a small person or a part of a big person. Then he continues his circle.

Climbing the hill, she thinks that their lifelong efforts to make beauty out of words are an illusion. Either that or a joke played on children who have self-ishly refused to grow up. Yes, probably that. *Stupid selfish children like that,* she thinks, *deserve to be pranked*.

As she reaches the parking lot, now gasping for breath, she sees the *Times* Arts & Leisure section flip-ping lazily through the grass on the breath of a light breeze and thinks, *Never mind. Herman Wouk is still alive and writing a book about God's language. Herman Wouk believes that the body weakens, but the words never do. So* that's *all right, isn't it?*

A man and a woman rush up. The woman raises her own cell phone and takes a picture with it. Pauline Enslin observes this without much surprise. She supposes the woman will show it to friends later. Then they will have drinks and a meal and talk about the grace of God and how everything happens for a reason. God's grace is a pretty cool concept. It stays intact every time it's not you.

"What happened?" the man shouts into her face. "What in hell happened?"

Down below them a skinny old poet is happening. He has taken off his shirt to cover one of the other bodies. His ribs are a stack outlined against white skin. He kneels and spreads the shirt. He raises his arms into the sky, then lowers them and wraps them around his head.

Pauline is also a poet, and as such feels capable of answering the man in the language God speaks.

"What the fuck does it look like?" she says.

For Owen King and Herman Wouk

Where do you get your ideas and *Where did this idea come from* are different questions. The first is unanswerable, so I make a joke of it and say I get them from a little Used Idea Shop in Utica. The second is *sometimes* answerable, but in a surprising number of cases, it's not, because stories are like dreams. Everything is deliciously clear while the process is ongoing, but all that remains when the story's finished are a few fading traces. I sometimes think a book of short stories is actually a kind of oneiric diary, a way of catching subconscious images before they can fade away. Here is a case in point. I don't remember how I got the idea for "Under the Weather," or how long it took, or even where I wrote it.

What I *do* remember is that it's one of the very few stories I've written where the end was clear, which meant the story had to be built carefully to get there. I know that some writers prefer working with the end in sight (John Irving once told me he begins a novel by writing the last line), but I don't care for it. As a rule I like the ending to take care of itself, feeling that if I don't know how things come out, the reader won't either. Fortunately for me, this is one of those tales where it's okay for the reader to be one step ahead of the narrator.

Under the Weather

I've been having this bad dream for a week now, but it must be one of the lucid ones, because I'm always able to back out before it turns into a nightmare. Only this time it seems to have followed me, because Ellen and I aren't alone. There's something under the bed. I can hear it chewing.

You know how it is when you're really scared? Sure you do. I mean, it's pretty universal. Your heart seems to stop, your mouth dries up, your skin goes cold and goosebumps rise all over your body. Instead of meshing, the cogs in your head just spin. I almost scream, I really do. I think, *It's the thing I don't want to look at. It's the thing in the window seat.*

Then I see the fan overhead, the blades turning at their slowest speed. I see a crack of early-morning light running down the middle of the pulled drapes. I see the graying milkweed fluff of Ellen's hair on the other side of the bed. I'm here on the Upper East Side, fifth floor, and everything's okay. The dream was just a dream. As for what's under the bed—

I toss back the covers and slide down to my knees, like a man who means to pray. But instead of that, I lift the flounce and peer under the bed. I only see a dark shape at first. Then the shape's head turns and two eyes gleam at me. It's Lady. She's not supposed to be under there, and I guess she knows it (hard to tell what a dog knows and what it doesn't), but I must have left the door open when I came to bed. Or maybe it didn't quite latch and she pushed it open with her snout. She must have brought one of her toys with her from the basket in the hall. At least it wasn't the blue bone or the red rat. Those have squeakers in them, and would have wakened Ellen for sure. And Ellen needs her rest. She's been under the weather.

"Lady," I whisper. "Come out of there."

She only looks at me. She's getting on in years and not so steady on her pins as she used to be, but she's not stupid. She's under Ellen's side, where I can't reach her. If I raise my voice she'll have to come, but she knows (I'm pretty sure she knows) that I won't do that, because if I raise my voice, it will wake Ellen for sure.

As if to prove this, Lady turns away from me and the chewing recommences.

Well, I can handle that. I've been living with Lady for thirteen years, nearly half my married life. There are three things that get her on her feet. One is the rattle of her leash and a call of "Elevator!" Another is the thump of her food dish on the floor. The third—

I get up and walk down the short hall to the kitchen. From the cupboard I take the bag of Snackin' Slices, making sure to rattle it. I don't have to wait long for the muted clitter of cocker claws. Five seconds and she's right there. She doesn't even bother to bring her toy.

I offer her one of the little carrot-shapes, then toss it into the living room. A little mean, maybe, but the fat old thing can use the exercise. She chases her treat. I linger long enough to start the coffeemaker, then go back into the bedroom. I'm careful to pull the door all the way shut.

Ellen's still sleeping, and waking up before she does has one benefit: no need for the alarm. I turn it off. Let her sleep a little later. It's a bronchial infection. I was scared for awhile there, but now she's on the mend.

I go into the bathroom and officially christen the day by brushing my teeth (I've read that in the morning a person's mouth is as germicidally dead as it ever gets, but the habits we learn as children are hard to break). I turn on the shower, get it good and hot, and step in.

The shower's where I do my best thinking, and this morning I think about the dream. Five nights in a row I've had it. (But who's counting, right?) Nothing really awful happens in this dream, but in a way that's the worst part. Because I know—absolutely, positively—that something awful *will* happen. If I let it.

I'm in an airplane, in business class. I'm in an aisle seat, which is where I prefer to be, so I don't have to squeeze past anybody if I have to go to the toilet. My tray-table is down. On it are a bag of peanuts and an orange drink that looks like a Vodka Sunrise, a drink I've never ordered in real life. The ride is smooth. If there are clouds, we're above them. The cabin is filled with sunlight. Someone is sitting in the window seat, and I know if I look at him (or her, or possibly *it*), I'll see something that will turn my bad dream into a nightmare. If I look into the face of my seatmate, I may lose my mind. It could crack open like an egg and a tide of bloody darkness might pour out.

I give my soapy hair a quick rinse, step out, dry off. My clothes are folded on a chair in the bedroom. I take them and my shoes into the kitchen, which is now filling with the smell of coffee. Nice. Lady's curled up by the stove, looking at me reproachfully.

"Don't go giving me the stink-eye," I tell her, and nod toward the closed bedroom door. "You know the rules."

She puts her snout down between her paws and pretends to sleep, but I know she's still looking at me.

I choose cranberry juice while I wait for the coffee. There's OJ, which is my usual morning drink, but I don't want it. Too much like the drink in the dream, I suppose. I have my coffee in the living room with CNN on mute, just reading the crawl at the bottom, which is all a person really needs. Then I turn it off and have a bowl of All-Bran. Quarter to eight. I decide that if the day is nice when I take Lady out, I'll skip the cab and walk to work.

It's nice, all right, spring edging into summer and a shine on everything. Carlo, the doorman, is under the awning, talking on his cell phone. "Yuh," he says. "Yuh, I finally got hold of her. She says go ahead, no problem as long as I'm there. She don't trust nobody, for which I don't blame her. She got a lot of nice things up there. You come when? Three? You can't make it earlier?" He tips me a wave with one white-gloved hand as I walk Lady down to the corner.

We've got this down to a science, Lady and I. She does it at pretty much the same place every day, and I'm fast with the poop bag. When I come back, Carlo stoops to give her a pat. Lady waves her tail back and forth most fetchingly, but no treat is forthcoming from Carlo. He knows she's on a diet. Or supposed to be.

"I finally got hold of Mrs. Warshawski," Carlo tells me. Mrs. Warshawski is in 5-C, but only technically. She's been gone for a couple of months now. "She was in Vienna."

"Vienna, is that so," I say.

"She told me to go ahead with the exterminators. She was horrified when I told her. You're the only one on Four, Five, or Six who hasn't complained. The rest of them . . ." He shakes his head and makes a *whoo* sound.

"I grew up in a Connecticut mill town. It pretty well wrecked my sinuses. I can smell coffee, and Ellie's perfume if she puts it on thick, but that's about all."

"In this case, that's probably a blessing. How *is* Mrs. Franklin? Still under the weather?"

"It'll be a few more days before she's ready to go back to work, but she's a hell of a lot better. She gave me a scare for awhile."

"Me too. She was going out one day—in the rain, naturally—"

"That's El," I say. "Nothing stops her. If she feels like she has to go somewhere, she goes."

"—and I thought to myself, 'That's a real grave-yard cough.'" He raises one gloved hand in a *stop* gesture. "Not that I really thought—"

"I get it," I said. "It was on the way to being a stay-in-the-hospital cough, for sure. But I finally got her to see the doctor, and now . . . road to recovery."

"Good. Good." Then, returning to what's really on his mind: "Mrs. Warshawski was pretty grossed out when I told her. I said we'd probably just find some spoiled food in the fridge, but I know it's worse than that. So does anybody else on those floors with an intact smeller." He gives a grim little nod. "They're going to find a dead rat in there, you mark my words. Food stinks, but not like that. Only dead things stink like that. It's a rat, all right, maybe a couple of them. Mrs. W. probably put down poison and don't want to admit it." He bends down to give Lady another pat. "*You* smell it, don't you, girl? You bet you do."

There's a litter of purple notes around the coffee-maker. I take the purple pad they came from to the kitchen table and write another.

Ellen: Lady all walked. Coffee ready. If you feel well enough to go out to the park, go! Just not too far. Don't want you to overdo now that you're finally on the mend. Carlo told me again that he "smells a rat." I guess so does everyone else in the neighborhood of 5-C. Lucky for us that you're plugged up and I'm "nasally challenged." Haha! If you hear people down the hall, it's the exterminators. Carlo will be with them, so don't worry. I'm going to walk to work. Need to think some more about the latest male wonder drug. Wish they'd consulted us before they hung that name on it. Remember, DON'T OVERDO. Love you-love you.

I jot half a dozen *x*s just to underline the point, and sign it with a *B* in a heart. Then I add it to the other notes around the coffeemaker. I refill Lady's water dish before I leave.

It's twenty blocks or so, and I don't think about the latest male wonder drug. I think about the exterminators, who will be coming at three. Earlier, if they can make it.

The dreams have interrupted my sleep cycle, I guess, because I almost fall asleep during the morning meeting in the conference room. But I come around in a hurry when Pete Wendell shows a mock-up poster for the new Petrov Excellent campaign. I've seen it already, on his office computer while he was fooling with it last week, and looking at it again I know where at least one element of my dream came from.

"Petrov Excellent Vodka," Aura McLean says. Her wonderful breasts rise and fall in a theatrical sigh. "If that name's an example of the new Russian capitalism, it's dead on arrival." The heartiest laughter at this comes from the younger men, who'd like to see Aura's long blond hair spread on a pillow next to them. "No offense to you intended, Pete. Petrov Excellent aside, it's a great leader."

"None taken," Pete says with a game smile. "We do what we can."

The poster shows a couple toasting each other on a balcony while the sun sinks over a harbor filled with expensive pleasure boats. The cutline beneath reads SUNSET. THE PERFECT TIME FOR A VODKA SUNRISE.

There's some discussion about the placement of the Petrov bottle—right? left? center? below?—and Frank Bernstein suggests that actually adding the recipe might prolong the page-view, especially for webvertising and in mags like *Playboy* and *Esquire*. I tune out, thinking about the drink sitting on the tray in my airplane dream, until I realize George Slattery is calling on me. I'm able to replay the question, and that's a good thing. You don't ask George to chew his cabbage twice.

"I'm actually in the same boat as Pete," I say. "The client picked the name, I'm just doing what I can."

There's some good-natured laughter. There have

been many jokes about Vonnell Pharmaceutical's newest drug product.

"I may have something to show you by Monday," I tell them. I'm not exactly looking at George, but he knows where I'm aiming. "By the middle of next week for sure. I want to give Billy a chance to see what he can do." Billy Ederle is our newest hire, and doing his break-in time as my assistant. He doesn't get an invite to the morning meetings yet, but I like him. Everybody at Andrews-Slattery likes him. He's bright, he's eager, and I bet he'll start shaving in a year or two.

George considers this. "I was really hoping to see a treatment today. Even rough copy."

Silence. People study their nails. It's as close to a public rebuke as George ever gets, and maybe I deserve it. This hasn't been my best week, and laying it off on the kid doesn't look so good. It doesn't feel so good, either.

"Okay," George says at last, and you can feel the relief in the room. It's like a light cool breath of breeze, there and then gone. No one wants to witness a conference-room caning on a sunny Friday morning, and I sure don't want to get one. Too much other stuff on my mind.

George smells a rat, I think.

"How's Ellen doing?" he asks.

"Better," I tell him. "Thanks for asking."

There are a few more presentations. Then it's over. Thank God.

I'm almost dozing when Billy comes into my office twenty minutes later. Check that: I *am* dozing. I sit up fast, hoping the kid thinks he caught me deep in thought. He's probably too excited to have noticed either way. In one hand he's holding a piece of poster board. I think he'd look right at home in Podunk High School, putting up a big notice about the Friday-night dance.

"How was the meeting?" he asks.

"It was okay."

"Did they bring us up?"

"You know they did. What have you got for me, Billy?"

He takes a deep breath and turns his poster board around so I can see it. On the left is a prescription bottle of Viagra, either actual size or close enough not to matter. On the right—the power side of the ad, as anyone in advertising will tell you—is a prescription bottle of our stuff, but much bigger. Beneath is the cutline: PO-TENS, TEN TIMES MORE EFFECTIVE THAN VIAGRA!

As Billy looks at me looking at it, his hopeful smile starts to fade. "You don't like it."

"It's not a question of like or don't like. In this business it never is. It's a question of what works and what doesn't. This doesn't."

Now he's looking sulky. If George Slattery saw that look, he'd unload. I won't, although it might feel that way to him because it's my job to teach him. In spite of everything else on my mind, I'll try to do that. Because I love this business. It gets very little respect, but I love it anyway. Also, I can hear Ellen say, You don't let go, babe. Once you get your teeth in something, they stay there. Determination like that can be a little scary.

"Sit down, Billy."

He sits.

"And wipe that pout off your puss. You look like a kid who just dropped his binky in the toilet."

He does his best. Which I like about him. Kid's a trier, and if he's going to work in the Andrews-Slattery shop, he'd better be. Of course, he also has to be a doer.

"Good news is I'm not taking it away from you, mostly because it's not your fault Vonnell Pharmaceutical saddled us with a name that sounds like a multivitamin. But we're going to make a silk purse out of this sow's ear. In advertising, that's the main job seven times out of every ten. Maybe eight. So pay attention."

He gets a little grin. "Should I take notes?"

"Don't be a smartikins. First, when you're shouting a drug, you *never* show a prescription bottle. The logo, sure. The pill itself, sometimes. It depends. You know why Pfizer shows the Viagra pill? Because it's blue. Consumers like blue. The shape helps, too. Consumers have a very positive response to the shape of the Viagra tab. But people *never like to see the prescription bottle their stuff comes in*. Prescription bottles make them think of sickness. Got that?"

"So maybe a little Viagra pill and a big Po-TENS pill? Instead of the bottles?" He raises his hands, framing an invisible cutline. "'Po-TENS, ten times bigger, ten times better.' Get it?"

"Yes, Billy, I get it. The FDA will get it, too, and they won't like it. In fact, they could make us take ads with a cutline like that out of circulation, which would cost a bundle. Not to mention a very good client."

"*Why?*" It's almost a bleat.

"Because it *isn't* ten times bigger, and it isn't ten

times better. Viagra, Cialis, Levitra, Po-TENS, they all have about the same effectiveness when it comes to penis elevation. Do your research, kiddo. And a little refresher course in advertising law wouldn't hurt. Want to say Blowhard's Bran Muffins are ten times tastier than Bigmouth's Bran Muffins? Have at it, taste is a subjective judgment. What gets your prick hard, though, and for how long . . ."

"Okay," he says in a small voice.

"Here's the other half. 'Ten times more' anything is—speaking in erectile dysfunction terms—pretty limp. It went out of vogue around the same time as Two Cs in a K."

He looks blank.

"It's how advertising guys used to refer to their TV ads on the soaps back in the fifties. Stands for two cunts in a kitchen."

"You're joking!"

"Nope. Now here's something I've been playing with." I jot on a pad, and for a moment I think of all those notes scattered around the coffeemaker back in good old 5-B—why are they still there?

"Can't you just tell me?" the kid asks from a thousand miles away.

"No, because advertising isn't an oral medium. Never trust an ad that's spoken out loud. Write it down and show it to someone. Show it to your best friend. Or your . . . you know, your wife."

"Are you okay, Brad?"

"Fine. Why?"

"I don't know, you just looked funny for a minute."

"Just as long as I don't look funny when I present on Monday. Now—what does this say to you?" I turn the pad around and show him what I've printed there:

PO-TENS . . . FOR MEN WHO WANT TO DO IT
THE HARD WAY.

"It's like a dirty joke!" he objects.

"You've got a point, but I've printed it in block
caps. Imagine it in a soft italic type. Or maybe small,
in parentheses. Like a secret." I add the parens,
although they don't work with the caps. But they
will. It's a thing I just know, because I can see it.
"Now, playing off that, think of a photo showing a
big burly guy. In low-slung jeans that show the top
of his underwear. And a sweatshirt with the sleeves
cut off, let's say. See him with some grease and dirt
on his guns."

"Guns?"

"His biceps. And he's standing beside a muscle car
with the hood up. Now, is it still a dirty joke?"

"I . . . I don't know."

"Neither do I, not for sure, but my gut tells me it'll
pull the plow. But not yet. The cutline still doesn't
work, you're right about that, and it's got to, because
it'll be the basis of the TV and 'Net ads. So play with
it. Make it work. Just remember the key word . . ."

Suddenly, just like that, I know where the rest of
that damn dream came from. It snaps into place.

"Brad?"

"The key word is *hard*," I say. "Because a man . . .
when something's not working—his prick, his plan,
his *life*—he *takes* it hard. He doesn't want to give up.
He remembers how it was, and he wants it that way
again."

Yes, I think. He sure does.

Billy smirks. "I wouldn't know."

I manage a smile. It feels godawful heavy, as if
there are weights hanging from the corners of my

mouth. All at once it's like being in the bad dream again. Because there's something close to me I don't want to look at. Only this isn't a lucid dream I can back out of.

This is lucid reality.

After Billy leaves, I go to the can. It's ten o'clock, most of the guys in the shop have offloaded their morning coffee and are taking on more in our little break room, so I have the shithouse to myself. I drop my pants so if someone wanders in and happens to look under the door he won't think I'm weird, but the only business I've come in here to do is thinking.

Four years after coming on board at Andrews-Slattery, the Fasprin Pain Reliever account landed on my desk. I've had some special ones over the years, some breakouts, and that was the first. It happened fast. I opened the sample box, took out the bottle, and the basis of the campaign—what admen sometimes call the heartwood—came to me in an instant. I ditzed around a little, of course—you don't want to make it look *too* easy—then did some comps. Ellen helped. This was just after we found out she couldn't have babies. It was something to do with a drug she'd been given when she had rheumatic fever as a kid. She was pretty depressed. Helping with the Fasprin comps took her mind off it, and she really threw herself into the thing.

Al Peterson was still running things back then, and he was the one I took the comps to. I remember sitting in front of his desk in the sweat seat with my heart in my mouth as he shuffled slowly through the comps we'd worked up. When he finally put them down and raised his shaggy old head to look at me, the pause seemed to go on for at least an hour. Then he said, "These are good, Bradley. More than good, terrific. We'll meet with the client tomorrow afternoon. You do the prez."

I did the prez, and when the Dugan Drug VP saw the picture of the young working woman with the bottle of Fasprin poking out of her rolled-up sleeve, he flipped for it. The campaign brought Fasprin right up there with the big boys—Bayer, Anacin, Bufferin—and by the end of the year we were handling the whole Dugan account. Billing? Seven figures. Not a low seven, either.

I used the bonus to take Ellen to Nassau for ten days. We left from Kennedy, on a morning that was pelting down rain, and I still remember how she laughed and cried "Kiss me, beautiful" when the plane broke through the clouds and the cabin filled with sunlight. I did kiss her, and the couple on the other side of the aisle—we were flying in business class—applauded.

That was the best. The worst came half an hour later, when I turned to her and for a moment thought she was dead. It was the way she was sleeping, with her head cocked over on her shoulder and her mouth open and her hair kind of sticking to the window. She was young, we both were, but the idea of sudden death had a hideous possibility in Ellen's case.

"They used to call your condition 'barren,' Mrs. Franklin," the doctor said when he gave us the bad news, "but in this case, your inability to conceive could be a blessing. Pregnancy puts a strain on the heart, and thanks to a disease that was badly treated when you were a child, yours isn't strong. If you did happen to conceive, you'd be in bed for the last four months of the pregnancy, and even then the outcome would be dicey."

She wasn't pregnant when we left on that trip, and her last checkup had been fine, but the climb up to cruising altitude had been plenty rough . . . and she didn't look like she was breathing.

Then she opened her eyes. I settled back into my aisle seat, letting out a long and shaky breath.

She looked at me, puzzled. "What's wrong?"

"Nothing. The way you were sleeping, that's all."

She wiped at her chin. "Oh God, did I drool?"

"No." I laughed. "But for a minute there you looked . . . well, dead."

She laughed too. "And if I was, you'd ship the body back to New York, I suppose, and take up with some Bahama Mama."

"No," I said. "I'd take you, anyway."

"What?"

"Because I wouldn't accept it. No way would I."

"You'd have to after a few days. I'd get all smelly."

She was smiling. She thought it was still a game, because she hadn't really understood what the doctor was telling her that day. She hadn't—as the saying goes—taken it all the way to the heartwood. And she didn't know how she'd looked, with the sun shining on her winter-pale cheeks and smudged eyelids and slack mouth. But I'd seen, and I'd taken it to the heartwood. She *was* my heart, and I guard what's there. Nobody takes it away from me.

"You wouldn't," I said. "I'd keep you alive."

"Really? How? Necromancy?"

"By refusing to give up. And by using an adman's most valuable asset."

"Which is what, Mr. Fasprin?"

"Imagination. Now can we talk about something more pleasant?"

The call I've been expecting comes around three thirty. It's not Carlo. It's Berk Ostrow, the building super. He wants to know what time I'm going to be home, because the rat everybody's been smelling isn't in 5-C, it's in our apartment. Ostrow says the exterminators have to leave by four to get to another job, but that isn't the important thing. What's important is fixing what's wrong in there and by the way, Carlo says no one's seen your wife in over a week. Just you and the dog.

I explain about my deficient sense of smell, and Ellen's bronchitis. In her current condition, I say, she wouldn't know the drapes were on fire until the smoke detector went off. I'm sure Lady smells it, I tell him, but to a dog, the stench of a decaying rat probably smells like Chanel No. 5.

"I get all that, Mr. Franklin, but I still need to get in there to see what's what. And the exterminators will have to be called back. I think you're probably going to be on the hook for their bill, which is apt to be quite high. I could let myself in with the passkey, but I'd really be more comfortable if you were—"

"Yes, I'd be more comfortable, too. Not to mention my wife."

"I tried calling her, but she didn't answer the phone." I can hear suspicion in his voice now. I've explained everything, advertising men are good at that, but the convincing effect only lasts for sixty seconds or so. That's why you keep hearing the same ads and slogans over and over again: A little dab'll do ya. Save time, save money. Pepsi, for those who think young. I'm lovin' it. Breakfast of champions. It's like driving a nail. Driving it right into the heartwood.

"She's probably got the phone on mute. Plus, the medication the doctor gave her makes her sleep quite heavily."

"What time will you be home, Mr. Franklin? I can stay until seven; after that there's only Alfredo." The disparaging note in his voice suggests I'd be better off dealing with a street weirdo.

Never, I think. I'll never be home. In fact, I was never there in the first place. Ellen and I enjoyed the Bahamas so much we moved to Cable Beach, and I took a job with a little firm in Nassau. I shout Cruise Ship Specials ("The Ride Is the Destination!"), Stereo Blowout Sales ("Don't Just Hear It Better, Hear It Cheaper!"), and supermarket openings ("Save Under the Palms!"). All this New York stuff has just been a lucid dream, one I can escape at any time.

"Mr. Franklin? Are you there?"

"Sure. Just thinking. I've got one meeting I absolutely can't miss, but why don't you meet me in the apartment around six?"

"How about in the lobby, Mr. Franklin? We can go up together." In other words, *I'm not giving you a head start, Mr. Advertising Genius who maybe killed his wife.*

I think of asking him how he believes I'd beat him to the apartment and get rid of El's body—because that *is* what he's thinking. Maybe murder is not at the very front of his mind, but it's not all the way in back, either. Husband-murders-wife is very big on the Lifetime Channel. Maybe he thinks I'd use the service elevator, and stash her body in the box room. Or maybe dump it down the incinerator chute? DIY cremation.

"The lobby is absolutely okey-fine," I say. "Six. Quarter of, if I can possibly make it."

I hang up and head for the elevators. I have to pass the break room to get there. Billy Ederle's leaning in the doorway, drinking a Nozzy. It's a remarkably lousy soda, but it's all we vend. The company's a client.

"Where are you off to?"

"Home. Ellen called. She's not feeling well."

"Don't you want your briefcase?"

"No." I don't expect to be needing my briefcase for awhile. In fact, I may never need it again.

"I'm working on the new Po-TENS direction. I think it's going to be a winner."

"I'm sure," I say, and I am. Billy Ederle will soon be movin' on up, and good for him. "I've got to get a wiggle on."

"Sure, I understand." He's twenty-four and understands nothing. "Give her my best."

We take on half a dozen interns a year at Andrews-Slattery; it's how Billy Ederle got started. Most are terrific and at first Fred Willits seemed terrific too. I took him under my wing, and so it became my responsibility to fire him—I guess you'd say that, although interns are never actually "hired" in the first place—when it turned out he was a klepto who had decided our supply room was his private game preserve. God knows how much stuff he lifted before Maria Ellington caught him loading reams of paper into his briefcase one afternoon. Turned out he was also a bit of a psycho. He went nuclear when I told him he was through. Pete Wendell called security while the kid was yelling at me in the lobby and had him removed forcibly.

Apparently old Freddy had a lot more to say, because he started hanging around my building and haranguing me when I came home. He kept his distance, though, and the cops claimed he was just exercising his right to free speech. But it wasn't his mouth I was afraid of. I kept thinking he might have lifted a box-cutter or an X-Acto knife as well as printer cartridges and about fifty reams of copier paper. That was when I got Carlo to give me a key to the service entrance, and I started going in that way. All that was in the fall of the year, September or October. Young Mr. Willits gave up and took his issues elsewhere when the days turned cold, but Carlo never asked for the return of the key, and I never gave it back. I guess we both forgot.

That's why, instead of giving the taxi driver my address, I get him to let me out on the next block. I pay him, adding a generous tip—hey, it's only money—and then walk down the service alley. I have a bad moment when the key doesn't work, but when I jigger it a little, it turns. The service elevator has brown quilted movers' pads hanging from the walls. Previews of the padded cell they'll put me in, I think, but of course that's just melodrama. I'll probably have to take a leave of absence from the shop, and what I've done is a lease-breaker for sure, but—

What *have* I done, exactly?

For that matter, what have I been doing for the last week?

"Keeping her alive," I say as the elevator stops at the fifth floor. "Because I couldn't bear for her to be dead."

She *isn't* dead, I tell myself, just under the weather. It sucks as a cutline, but for the last week it has served me very well, and in the advertising biz the short term is all that counts.

I let myself in. The air is still and warm, but I don't smell anything. So I tell myself, anyway, and in the advertising biz, imagination is *also* what counts.

"Honey, I'm home," I call. "Are you awake? Feeling any better?"

I guess I forgot to close the bedroom door before I left this morning, because Lady slinks out. She's licking her chops. She gives me a guilty glance, then waddles into the living room with her tail tucked way down low. She doesn't look back.

"Honey? El?"

I go into the bedroom. There's still nothing to be seen of her but the milkweed fluff of her hair and the shape of her body under the quilt. The quilt is slightly rumpled, so I know she's been up—if only to have some coffee—and then gone back to bed again. It was last Friday when I came home and she wasn't breathing and since then she's been sleeping a lot.

I go around to her side and see her hand hanging down. There's not much left of it but bones and strips of flesh. I gaze at this and think there's two ways of seeing it. Look at it one way, and I'll probably have to have my dog—Ellen's dog, really, Lady always loved Ellen best—euthanized. Look at it another and you could say Lady got worried and was trying to wake her up. Come on, Ellie, I want to go to the park. Come on, Ellie, let's play with my toys.

I tuck the reduced hand under the sheets. That way it won't get cold. Then I wave away some flies. I can't remember ever seeing flies in our apartment before. They probably smelled that dead rat Carlo was talking about.

"You know Billy Ederle?" I say. "I gave him a slant on that damn Po-TENS account, and I think he's going to run with it."

Nothing from Ellen.

"You can't be dead," I say. "That's unacceptable."

Nothing from Ellen.

"Do you want coffee?" I glance at my watch. "Something to eat? We've got chicken soup. Just the kind that comes in the pouches, but it's not bad when it's hot." Not bad when it's hot, what a lousy slogan *that* would be. "What do you say, El?"

She says nothing.

"All right," I say. "That's all right. Remember when we went to the Bahamas, hon? When we went snorkeling and you had to quit because you were crying? And when I asked why, you said 'Because it's all so beautiful.'"

Now *I'm* the one who's crying.

"Are you sure you don't want to get up and walk around a little? I'll open the windows and let in some fresh air."

Nothing from Ellen.

I sigh. I stroke that fluff of hair. "All right," I say, "why don't you just sleep for another couple of hours? I'll sit here beside you."

And that's exactly what I do.

For Joe Hill

Yeah, it's about baseball, but give it a chance, okay? You don't have to be a sailor to love the novels of Patrick O'Brian, and you don't have to be a jockey— or even a bettor—to love the Dick Francis mysteries. Those stories come alive in the characters and the events, and I hope you'll find a similar liveliness here. I got the idea for this tale after watching a postseason playoff game where a bad call resulted in a near riot at Atlanta's Turner Field. Fans showered the field with cups, hats, signs, pennants, and beer bottles. After an umpire was bonked on the head with a pint whiskey bottle (by then empty, of course), the teams were pulled from the field until order could be restored. The TV commentators moaned about poor sportsmanship, as though such ventings of disgust and outrage had not gone on at America's ballparks for a hundred years or more.

I've loved baseball all my life, and wanted to write about the game as it was in a time when such energetic demurrals, accompanied by declarations of "Kill the ump!" and "Buy him a Seeing Eye dog!" were considered a valid part of the game. A time when baseball was almost as smashmouth as football, when players slid into second base with their cleats up, and colli-sions at the plate were expected rather than outlawed. Those were days when the reversal of a call based on a TV replay would have been regarded with horror, for the umpire's word was law. I wanted to use the lan-guage of those earlier ballplayers to summon up the texture and color of mid-century sporting America. I wanted to see if I could create something that was both mythic and—in a horrible way—sort of funny.

I also had a chance to put myself in the story, and I loved that. (My first paying gig as a writer was as a sports reporter for the Lisbon *Enterprise*, after all.) My sons call that sort of thing "metafiction." I just think of it as fun, and I hope that's what this story is: good old-fashioned fun, with the last line cribbed from a great movie called *The Wild Bunch*.

And watch out for the blade, Constant Reader. It *is* a Stephen King story, after all.

Blockade Billy

William Blakely?

Oh my God, you mean Blockade Billy. Nobody's asked me about him in years. Of course, no one asks me much of anything in here, except if I'd like to sign up for Polka Night at the K of P Hall downtown or something called Virtual Bowling. That's right here in the common room. My advice to you, Mr. King— you didn't ask for it, but I'll give it to you—is, don't get old, and if you do, don't let your relatives put you in a zombie hotel like this one.

It's a funny thing, getting old. When you're young, people always want to listen to your stories, especially if you were in pro baseball. But when you're young, you don't have time to tell them. Now I've got all the time in the world, and it seems like nobody cares about those old days. But I still like to think about them. So, sure, I'll tell you about Billy Blakely. Awful story, of course, but those are the ones that last the longest.

Baseball was different in those days. You have to remember that Blockade Billy played for the Titans only ten years after Jackie Robinson broke the color barrier, and the Titans are long gone. I don't suppose New Jersey will ever have another Major League team, not with two powerhouse franchises just across the river in New York. But it was a big deal then—*we* were a big deal—and we played our games in a different world.

The rules were the same. Those don't change. And the little rituals were pretty similar, too. Oh, nobody would have been allowed to wear their cap cocked to the side, or curve the brim, and your hair had to be neat and short (the way these chuckleheads wear it now, my God), but some players still crossed themselves before they stepped into the box, or drew in the dirt with the heads of their bats before taking up the stance, or jumped over the baseline when they were running out to take their positions. Nobody wanted to step on the baseline, it was considered the worst luck to do that.

The game was *local*, okay? TV had started to come in, but only on the weekends. We had a good market, because the games were on WNJ, and everyone in New York could watch. Some of those broadcasts were pretty comical. Compared to the way they do today's games, it was all amateur night in Dixie. Radio was better, more professional, but of course that was local, too. No satellite broadcasts, because there were no satellites! The Russians sent the first one up during the Yanks-Braves World Series that year. As I remember, it happened on an off-day, but I could be wrong about that. What I remember is that the Titans were out of it early that year. We contended for awhile, partly thanks to Blockade Billy, but you know how *that* turned out. It's why you're here, right?

But here's what I'm getting at: because the game was smaller on the national stage, the players weren't such a big deal. I'm not saying there weren't stars—guys like Aaron, Burdette, Williams, Kaline, and of course the Mick—but most weren't as well known coast-to-coast as players like Alex Rodriguez and Barry Bonds (a couple of drug-swallowing bushers, if you ask me). And most of the other guys? I can tell you in two words: working stiffs. The average salary back then was fifteen grand, less than a first-year high school teacher makes today.

Working stiffs, get it? Just like George Will said in that book of his. Only he said it like it was a good thing. I'm not so sure it was, if you were a thirty-year-old shortstop with a wife and three kids and maybe another seven years to go before retirement. Ten, if you were lucky and didn't get hurt. Carl Furillo ended up installing elevators in the World Trade Center and moonlighting as a night watchman, did you know that? You did? Do you think that guy Will knew it, or just forgot to mention it?

The deal was this: if you had the skills and could do the job even with a hangover, you got to play. If you couldn't, you got tossed on the scrap heap. It was that simple. And as brutal. Which brings me to our catching situation that spring.

We were in good shape during camp, which for the Titans was in Sarasota. Our starting catcher was Johnny Goodkind. Maybe you don't remember him. If you do, it's probably because of the way he ended up. He had four good years, batted over .300, put the gear on almost every game. Knew how to handle the pitchers, didn't take any guff. The kids didn't dare shake him off. He hit damn near .350 that spring, with maybe a dozen ding-dongs, one as deep and far as any I ever saw at Ed Smith Stadium, where the ball didn't carry well. Put out the windshield in some reporter's Chevrolet—ha!

But he was also a big drinker, and two days before the team was supposed to head north and open at home, he ran over a woman on Pineapple Street and killed her just as dead as a dormouse. Or doornail. Whatever the saying is. Then the damn fool tried to run. But there was a county sheriff's cruiser parked on the corner of Orange, and the deputies inside saw the whole thing. Wasn't much doubt about Johnny's state, either. When they pulled him out of his car, he smelled like a distillery and could hardly stand. One of the deputies bent down to put the cuffs on him, and Johnny threw up on the back of the guy's head. Johnny Goodkind's career in baseball was over before the puke dried. Even the Babe couldn't have stayed in the game after running over a housewife out doing her morning shop-around. I guess he wound up calling signs for the Raiford prison team. If they had one.

His backup was Frank Faraday. Not bad behind the plate, but a banjo hitter at best. Went about one sixty. No bulk, which put him at risk. The game was played hard in those days, Mr. King, with plenty of fuck-you.

But Faraday was what we had. I remember DiPunno saying he wouldn't last long, but not even Jersey Joe had an idea how short a time it was going to be.

Faraday was behind the plate when we played our last exhibition game that year. Against the Reds, it was. There was a squeeze play put on. Don Hoak at the plate. Some big hulk—I think it was Ted Kluszewski—on third. Hoak punches the ball right at Jerry Rugg, who was pitching for us that day. Big

Klew breaks for the plate, all two hundred and seventy Polack pounds of him. And there's Faraday, just about as skinny as a Flav'r Straw, standing with one foot on the old dishola. Couldn't help but end bad. Rugg throws to Faraday. Faraday turns to put the tag on. I couldn't look.

The little fella got the out, I'll give him that, only it was a spring-training out, as important in the great scheme of things as a low fart in a high wind. And that was the end of Frank Faraday's baseball career. One broken arm, one broken leg, a concussion—that was the score. I don't know what became of him. Wound up washing windshields for tips at an Esso station in Tucumcari, for all I know.

So we lost both our catchers in the space of forty-eight hours and had to go north with nobody to put behind the plate except for Ganzie Burgess, who converted from catcher to pitcher not long after the Korean War ended. The Ganzer was thirty-nine years old that season and only good for middle relief, but he was a knuckleballer, and as crafty as Satan, so no way was Joe DiPunno going to risk those old bones behind the plate. He said he'd put *me* back there first. I knew he was joking—I was just an old third-base coach with so many groin pulls my balls were practically banging on my knees—but the idea still made me shiver.

What Joe did was call the front office in Newark and say, "I need a guy who can catch Hank Masters's fastball and Danny Doo's curve without falling on his keister. I don't care if he plays for Testicle Tire in Tremont, just make sure he's got a mitt and have him at the Swamp in time for the National Anthem. Then get to work finding me a real catcher. If you want to have any chance at all of contending this season, that is." Then he hung up and lit what was probably his eightieth cigarette of the day.

Oh for the life of a manager, huh? One catcher facing manslaughter charges; another in the hospital, wrapped in so many bandages he looked like Boris Karloff in *The Mummy*; a pitching staff either not old enough to shave or about ready for the Sociable Security; God-knows-who about to put on the gear and squat behind the plate on Opening Day.

We flew north that year instead of riding the rails, but it still felt like a train wreck. Meanwhile, Kerwin McCaslin, who was the Titans' GM, got on the phone and found us a catcher to start the season with: William Blakely, soon to be known as Blockade Billy. I can't remember now if he came from Double or Triple A, but you could look it up on your computer, I guess, because I *do* know the name of the team he came from: the Davenport Cornhuskers. A few players came up from there during my seven years with the Titans, and the regulars would always ask how things were down there playing for the Cornholers. Or sometimes they'd call them the Cocksuckers. Baseball humor is not what you'd call sophisticated.

We opened against the Red Sox that year. Middle of April. Baseball started later back then, and played a saner schedule. I got to the park early—before God got out of bed, actually—and there was a young man sitting on the bumper of an old Ford truck in the players' lot. Iowa license plate dangling on chickenwire from the back bumper. Nick the gate guard let him in when the kid showed him his letter from the front office and his driver's license.

"You must be Bill Blakely," I said, shaking his hand. "Good to know you."

"Good to know you too," he said. "I brought my gear, but it's pretty beat up."

"Oh, I think we got you covered there, partner," I said, letting go of his hand. He had a Band-Aid wrapped around his second finger, just below the middle knuckle. "Cut yourself shaving?" I asked, pointing to it.

"Yup, cut myself shaving," he says. I couldn't tell if that was his way of showing he got my little joke, or if he was so worried about fucking up he thought he ought to agree with everything anyone said, at least to begin with. Later on I realized it was neither of those things; he just had a habit of echoing back what you said to him. I got used to it, even sort of got to like it.

"Are you the manager?" he asked. "Mr. DiPunno?"

"No," I said, "I'm George Grantham. The kids call me Granny. I coach third base. I'm also the equipment manager." Which was the truth; I did both jobs. Told you the game was smaller then. "I'll get you fixed up, don't worry. All new gear."

"All new gear," says he. "Except for the glove. I have to have Billy's old glove, you know. Billy Junior and me's been the miles."

"Well, that's fine with me." And we went on into what the sportswriters used to call Old Swampy in those days.

I hesitated over giving him 19, because it was poor old Faraday's number, but the uniform fit him without looking like pajamas, so I did. While he was dressing, I said: "Ain't you tired? You must have driven almost nonstop. Didn't they send you some cash to take a plane?"

"I ain't tired," he said. "They might have sent me some cash to take a plane, but I didn't see it. Could we go look at the field?"

I said we could, and led him down the runway and up through the dugout. He walked down to home plate outside the foul line in Faraday's uniform, the blue 19 gleaming in the morning sun (it wasn't but eight o'clock, the groundskeepers just starting what would be a long day's work).

I wish I could tell you how it felt to see him taking that walk, Mr. King, but words are your thing, not mine. All I know is that back-to he looked more like Faraday than ever. He was ten years younger, of course . . . but age doesn't show much from the back, except sometimes in a man's walk. Plus he was slim like Faraday, and slim's the way you want your shortstop and second baseman to be, not your catcher. Catchers should be built like fireplugs, the way Johnny Goodkind was. This guy looked like broken ribs and a rupture just waiting to happen.

He had a firmer build than Frank Faraday, though; broad in the butt and thick in the thighs. He was skinny from the waist up, but looking at him ass-end-going-away, I remember thinking he looked like what he probably was: an Iowa plowboy on vacation in scenic Newark.

He went to the plate and turned around to look out to dead center. He had blond hair, just like a plowboy should, and a lock of it had fallen on his forehead. He brushed it away and just stood there taking it all in— the silent, empty stands where over fifty thousand people would be sitting that afternoon, the bunting already hung on the railings and fluttering in the morning breeze, the foul poles painted fresh Jersey Blue, the groundskeepers just starting to water. It was an awesome sight, I always thought, and I could imagine what was going through the kid's mind, him that had probably been home pulling cow teats just a week ago and waiting for the Cornholers to start playing in mid-May.

I thought, *Poor kid's finally getting the picture. When he looks over here, I'll see the panic in his eyes. I may have to tie him down in the locker room to keep him from jumping in that old truck of his and hightailing it back to God's country.*

But when he looked at me, there was no panic in his eyes. Not even nervousness, which I would have said every player feels on Opening Day. No, he looked perfectly cool standing there behind the plate in his Levi's and light poplin jacket.

"Yuh," he says, like a man confirming something he was pretty sure of in the first place. "Billy can hit here."

"Good," I tell him. It's all I can think of to say.

"Good," he says back. Then—I swear—he says, "Do you think those guys need help with them hoses?"

I laughed. There was something strange about him, something off, something that made folks nervous . . . but that something made people take to him too. Kinda sweet. Something that made you want to like him in spite of feeling he wasn't exactly all there. Joe DiPunno knew he was light in the head right away. Some of the players did too, but that didn't stop them from liking him. I don't know, it was like when you talked to him what came back was the sound of your own voice. Like an echo in a cave.

"Billy," I said, "groundskeeping ain't your job.

Your job is to put on the gear and catch Danny Dusen this afternoon."

"Danny Doo," he said.

"That's right. Twenty and six last year, should have won the Cy Young, didn't. Because the writers don't like him. He's still got a red ass over that. And remember this: if he shakes you off, don't you dare flash the same sign again. Not unless you want your pecker and asshole to change places after the game, that is. Danny Doo is four games from two hundred wins, and he's going to be mean as hell until he gets there."

"Until he gets there." Nodding his head.

"That's right."

"If he shakes me off, flash something different."

"Yes."

"Does he have a changeup?"

"Does a dog piss on a fire hydrant? The Doo's won a hundred and ninety-six games. You don't do that without a changeup."

"Not without a changeup," he says. "Okay."

"And don't get hurt out there. Until the front office can make a deal, you're what we got."

"I'm it," he says. "Gotcha."

"I hope so."

Other players were coming in by then, and I had about a thousand things to do. Later on I saw the kid in Jersey Joe's office, signing whatever needed to be signed. Kerwin McCaslin hung over him like a vulture over roadkill, pointing out all the right places. Poor kid, probably six hours' worth of sleep in the last sixty, and he was in there signing five years of his life away. Later I saw him with Dusen, going over the Boston lineup. The Doo was doing all the talking, and the kid was doing all the listening. Didn't even ask a question, so far as I saw, which was good. If the kid had opened his head, Danny probably would have bit it off.

About an hour before the game, I went in to Joe's office to look at the lineup card. He had the kid batting eighth, which was no shock. Over our heads the murmuring had started and you could hear the rumble of feet on the boards. Opening Day crowds always pile in early. Listening to it started the butterflies in my gut, like always, and I could see Jersey Joe felt the same. His ashtray was already overflowing.

"He's not big like I hoped he'd be," he said, tapping Blakely's name on the lineup card. "God help us if he gets cleaned out."

"McCaslin hasn't found anyone else?"

"Maybe. He talked to Hubie Rattner's wife, but Hubie's on a fishing trip somewhere in Rectal Thermometer, Wisconsin. Out of touch until next week."

"Hubie Rattner's forty-three if he's a day."

"Tell me somethin I don't know. But beggars can't be choosers. And be straight with me—how long do you think that kid's gonna last in the bigs?"

"Oh, he's probably just a cup of coffee," I says, "but he's got something Faraday didn't."

"And what might that be?"

"Dunno. But if you'd seen him standing behind the plate and looking out into center, you might feel better about him. It was like he was thinking 'This ain't the big deal I thought it would be.'"

"He'll find out how big a deal it is the first time Ike Delock throws one at his nose," Joe said, and lit a cigarette. He took a drag and started hacking. "I got to quit these Luckies. Not a cough in a carload, my

ass. I'll bet you twenty goddam bucks that kid lets
Danny Doo's first curve go right through his wickets.
Then Danny'll be all upset—you know how he gets
when someone fucks up his train ride—and Boston'll
be off to the races."

"Ain't you the cheeriest Cheerio," I says.

He stuck out his hand. "Twenty bucks. Bet."

And because I knew he was trying to take the
curse off it, I shook his hand. That was twenty I won,
because the legend of Blockade Billy started that very
day.

You couldn't say he called a good game, because he
didn't call it. The Doo did that. But the first pitch—
to Frank Malzone—*was* a curve, and the kid caught it
just fine. Not only that, though. It was a cunt's hair
outside and I never saw a catcher pull one back so
fast, not even Yogi. Ump called strike one and it was
us off to the races, at least until Williams hit a solo
shot in the fifth. We got that back in the sixth, when
Ben Vincent put one out. Then in the seventh, we've
got a runner on second—I think it was Barbarino—
with two outs and the new kid at the plate. It was his
third at bat. First time he struck out looking, the second time swinging. Delock fooled him bad that time,
made him look silly, and the kid heard the only boos
he ever got while he was wearing a Titans uniform.

He steps in, and I looked over at Joe. Seen him sitting way down by the water cooler, just looking at his
shoes and shaking his head. Even if the kid worked a
walk, The Doo was up next, and The Doo couldn't hit
a slowpitch softball with a tennis racket. As a hitter
that guy was fucking terrible.

I won't drag out the suspense; this ain't no kids'
sports comic. Although whoever said life sometimes

imitates art was right, and it did that day. Count went to three and two. Then Delock threw the sinker that fooled the kid so bad the first time and damn if the kid didn't suck for it again. Except Ike Delock turned out to be the sucker that time. Kid golfed it right off his shoetops the way Ellie Howard used to do and shot it into the gap. I waved the runner in and we had the lead back, two to one.

Everybody in the joint was on their feet, screaming their throats out, but the kid didn't even seem to hear it. Just stood there on second, dusting the seat of his pants. He didn't stay there long, because The Doo went down on three pitches, then threw his bat like he always did when he got struck out.

So maybe it's a sports comic after all, like the kind you probably read behind your history book in junior high school study hall. Top of the ninth and The Doo's looking at the top of the lineup. Strikes out Malzone, and a quarter of the crowd's on their feet. Strikes out Klaus, and half the crowd's on their feet. Then comes Williams—old Teddy Ballgame. The Doo gets him on the hip, oh and two, then weakens and walks him. The kid starts out to the mound and Doo waves him back—just squat and do your job, sonny. So sonny does. What else is he gonna do? The guy on the mound is one of the best pitchers in baseball and the guy behind the plate was maybe playing a little pickup ball behind the barn that spring to keep in shape after the day's bovine tits was all pulled.

First pitch, goddam! Williams takes off for second. The ball was in the dirt, hard to handle, but the kid still made one fuck of a good throw. Almost got Teddy, but as you know, almost only counts in horseshoes. Now everybody's on their feet, screaming. The

Doo does some shouting at the kid—like it was the kid's fault instead of just a bullshit pitch—and while Doo's telling the kid he's a lousy choker, Williams calls time. Hurt his knee a little sliding into the bag, which shouldn't have surprised anyone; he could hit like nobody's business, but he was a leadfoot on the bases. Why he stole a bag that day is anybody's guess. It sure wasn't no hit-and-run, not with two outs and the game on the line.

So Billy Anderson comes in to run for Teddy and Dick Gernert steps into the box, .425 slugging percentage or something like it. The crowd's going apeshit, the flag's blowing out, the frank wrappers are swirling around, women are goddam crying, men are yelling for Jersey Joe to yank The Doo and put in Stew Rankin—he was what people would call the closer today, although back then he was just known as a short-relief specialist.

But Joe crossed his fingers and stuck with Dusen.

The count goes three and two, right? Anderson off with the pitch, right? Because he can run like the wind and the guy behind the plate's a first-game rook. Gernert, that mighty man, gets just under a curve and beeps it—not bloops it but *beeps* it—behind the pitcher's mound, just out of The Doo's reach. He's on it like a cat, though. Anderson's around third and The Doo throws home from his knees. That thing was a fucking *bullet*.

I know what you're thinking, Mr. King, but you're dead wrong. It never crossed my mind that our new rookie catcher was going to get busted up like Faraday and have a nice one-game career in the bigs. For one thing, Billy Anderson was no moose like Big Klew; more of a ballet dancer. For another . . . well . . . the kid was *better* than Faraday. I think I sensed that as soon as I saw him sitting on the bumper of his beshitted old Hiram Hoehandle truck with his wore-out gear stored in the back.

Dusen's throw was low but on the money. The kid took it between his legs, then pivoted around, and I seen he was holding out *just the mitt*. I just had time to think of what a rookie mistake that was, how he forgot that old saying *two hands for beginners*, how Anderson was going to knock the ball loose and we'd have to try to win the game in the bottom of the ninth. But then the kid lowered his left shoulder like a football lineman. I never paid attention to his free hand, because I was staring at that outstretched catcher's mitt, just like everyone else in Old Swampy that day. So I didn't exactly see what happened, and neither did anybody else.

What I *saw* was this: the kid whapped the glove on Anderson's chest while he was still three full steps from the dish. Then Anderson hit the kid's lowered shoulder. Anderson went ass over teakettle and landed behind the left-hand batter's box. The umpire lifted his fist in the *out* sign. Then Anderson started to yell and grab his ankle. I could hear it from the third-base coach's box, so you know it must have been good yelling, because those Opening Day fans were roaring like a force-ten gale. I could see that Anderson's left pants cuff was turning red, and blood was oozing out between his fingers.

Can I have a drink of water? Just pour some out of that plastic pitcher, would you? Plastic pitchers is all they give us for our rooms, you know; no glass pitchers allowed in the zombie hotel.

Ah, that's good. Been a long time since I talked so much, and I got a lot more to say. You bored yet? No? Good. Me neither. Having the time of my life, awful story or not.

Billy Anderson didn't play again until '58, and '58 was his last year—Boston gave him his unconditional release halfway through the season, and he couldn't catch on with anyone else. Because his speed was gone, and speed was really all he had to sell. The docs said he'd be good as new, the Achilles tendon was only nicked, not cut all the way through, but it was also stretched, and I imagine that's what finished him. Baseball's a tender game, you know; people don't realize. And it isn't only catchers who get hurt in collisions at the plate.

After the game, Danny Doo grabs the kid in the shower and yells: "I'm gonna buy you a drink tonight, rook! In fact, I'm gonna buy you *ten*!" And then he gives his highest praise: *"You hung the fuck in there!"*

"Ten drinks, because I hung the fuck in there," the kid says, and The Doo laughs and claps him on the back like it's the funniest thing he ever heard.

But then Pinky Higgins comes storming in. He was managing the Red Sox that year, which was a thankless job; things only got worse for Pinky and for the Sox as the summer of '57 crawled along. He was mad as hell, chewing a wad of tobacco so hard and fast the juice squirted from both sides of his mouth and splattered his uniform. He said the kid had deliberately cut Anderson's ankle when they collided at the plate. Said Blakely must have done it with his fingernails, and the kid should be put out of the game for it. This was pretty rich, coming from a man whose motto was "Spikes high and let em die!"

I was sitting in Joe's office drinking a beer, so me and DiPunno listened to Pinky's rant together. I thought the guy was nuts, and I could see from Joe's face that I wasn't alone.

Joe waited until Pinky ran down, then said, "I wasn't watching Anderson's foot. I was watching to see if Blakely made the tag and held onto the ball. Which he did."

"Get him in here," Pinky fumes. "I want to say it to his face."

"Be reasonable, Pink," Joe says. "Would I be in your office doing a tantrum if it had been Blakely all cut up?"

"It wasn't spikes!" Pinky yells. "Spikes are a part of the game! Scratching someone up like a . . . *a girl in a kickball match* . . . that *ain't*! And Anderson's in the game seven years! He's got a family to support!"

"So you're saying what? My catcher ripped your pinch runner's ankle open while he was tagging him out—and tossing him over his goddam shoulder, don't forget—and he did it with his *nails*?"

"That's what Anderson says," Pinky tells him. "Anderson says he felt it."

"Maybe Blakely stretched Anderson's foot with his nails, too. Is that it?"

"No," Pinky admits. His face was all red by then, and not just from being mad. He knew how it sounded. "He says that happened when he came down."

"Begging the court's pardon," I says, "but *finger-nails*? This is a load of crap."

"I want to see the kid's hands," Pinky says. "You show me or I'll lodge a goddam protest."

I thought Joe would tell Pinky to shit in his hat,

but he didn't. He turned to me. "Tell the kid to come in here. Tell him he's gonna show Mr. Higgins his nails, just like he did to his first-grade teacher after the Pledge of Allegiance."

I got the kid. He came willingly enough, although he was just wearing a towel, and didn't hold back showing his nails. They were short, clean, not broken, not even bent. There were no blood blisters, either, like there might be if you really set them in someone and raked with them. One little thing I did happen to notice, although I didn't think anything of it at the time: the Band-Aid was gone from his second finger, and I didn't see any sign of a healing cut where it had been, just clean skin, pink from the shower.

"Satisfied?" Joe asked Pinky. "Or would you like to check his ears for potato-dirt?"

"Fuck you," Pinky says. He got up, stamped over to the door, spat his cud into the wastepaper basket there—*splut!*—and then he turns back. "My boy says *your* boy cut him. Says he felt it. And my boy don't lie."

"Your boy tried to be a hero with the game on the line instead of stopping at third and giving Piersall a chance. He'd tell you the shit-streak in his skivvies was chocolate sauce if it'd get him off the hook for that. You know what happened and so do I. Anderson got tangled in his own spikes and did it to himself when he went whoopsy-daisy. Now get out of here."

"There'll be a payback for this, DiPunno."

"Yeah? Well, it's the same game time tomorrow. Get here early while the popcorn's hot and the beer's still cold."

Pinky left, already tearing off a fresh piece of chew. Joe drummed his fingers beside his ashtray, then asked the kid: "Now that it's just us chickens, did you do anything to Anderson? Tell me the truth."

"No." Not a bit of hesitation. "I didn't do anything to Anderson. That's the truth."

"Okay," Joe said, and stood up. "Always nice to shoot the shit after a game, but I think I'll go on home and fuck my wife on the sofa. Winning on Opening Day always makes my pecker stand up." He clapped our new catcher on the shoulder. "Kid, you played the game the way it's supposed to be played. Good for you."

He left. The kid cinched his towel around his waist and started back to the locker room. I said, "I see that shaving cut's all better."

He stopped dead in the doorway, and although his back was to me, I knew he'd done something out there. The truth was in the way he was standing. I don't know how to explain it better, but . . . I knew.

"What?" Like he didn't get me, you know.

"The shaving cut on your finger."

"Oh, *that* shaving cut. Yuh, all better."

And out he sails . . . although, rube that he was, he probably didn't have a clue where he was going.

Okay, second game of the season. Dandy Dave Sisler on the mound for Boston, and our new catcher is hardly settled into the batter's box before Sisler chucks a fastball at his head. Would have knocked his fucking eyes out if it had connected, but he snaps his head back—didn't duck or nothing—and then just cocks his bat again, looking at Sisler as if to say, *Go on, Mac, do it again if you want.*

The crowd's screaming like mad and chanting *RUN IM! RUN IM! RUN IM!* The ump didn't run Sisler, but he got warned and a cheer went up.

I looked over and saw Pinky in the Boston dugout, walking back and forth with his arms folded so tight he looked like he was trying to keep from exploding.

Sisler walks twice around the mound, soaking up the fan-love—boy oh boy, they wanted him drawn and quartered—and then he went to the rosin bag, and then he shook off two or three signs. Taking his time, you know, letting it sink in. The kid all the time just standing there with his bat cocked, comfortable as your gramma squatting on the living room sofa. So Dandy Dave throws a get-me-over fastball right down Broadway and the kid loses it in the left-field bleachers. Tidings was on base and we're up two to nothing. I bet the people over in New York heard the noise from Swampy when the kid hit that home run.

I thought he'd be grinning when he came around third, but he looked just as serious as a judge. Under his breath he's muttering, "Got it done, Billy, showed that busher and got it done."

The Doo was the first one to grab him in the dugout and danced him right into the bat rack. Helped him pick up the spilled lumber, too, which was nothing like Danny Dusen, who usually thought he was above such things.

After beating Boston twice and pissing off Pinky Higgins, we went down to Washington and won three straight. The kid hit safe in all three, including his second home run, but Griffith Stadium was a depressing place to play, brother; you could have machine-gunned a running rat in the box seats behind home plate and not had to worry about hitting any fans. Goddam Senators finished over forty back that year. Jesus fucking wept.

The kid was behind the plate for The Doo's second start down there and damn near caught a no-hitter in his fifth game wearing a big-league uniform. Pete Runnels spoiled it in the ninth—hit a double with one out. After that, the kid went out to the mound, and that time Danny didn't wave him back. They discussed it a little bit, and then The Doo gave an intentional pass to the next batter, Lou Berberet (see how it all comes back?). That brought up Bob Usher, and he hit into a double play just as sweet as you could ever want: ball game.

That night The Doo and the kid went out to celebrate Dusen's one hundred and ninety-eighth win. When I saw our newest chick the next day, he was very badly hungover, but he bore that as calmly as he bore having Dave Sisler chuck at his head. I was starting to think we had a real big leaguer on our hands, and wouldn't be needing Hubie Rattner after all. Or anybody else.

"You and Danny are getting pretty tight, I guess," I says.

"Tight," he agrees, rubbing his temples. "Me and The Doo are tight. He says Billy's his good luck charm."

"Does he, now?"

"Yuh. He says if we stick together, he'll win twenty-five and they'll have to give him the Cy Young even if the writers do hate his guts."

"That right?"

"Yessir, that's right. Granny?"

"What?"

He was giving me that wide blue stare of his: twenty-twenty vision that saw everything and understood almost nothing. By then I knew he could hardly read, and the only movie he'd ever seen was *Bambi*. He said he went with the other kids from Ottershow or Outershow—whatever—and I assumed it was his school. I was both right and wrong about that, but it ain't really the point. The point is that he knew how to play baseball—instinctively, I'd say—but otherwise he was a blackboard with nothing written on it.

"Tell me again what's a Cy Young?"

That's how he was, you see.

We went over to Baltimore for three before going back home. Typical spring baseball in that town, which isn't quite south or north; cold enough to freeze the balls off a brass monkey the first day, hotter than hell the second, a fine drizzle like liquid ice the third. Didn't matter to the kid; he hit in all three games, making it eight straight. Also, he stopped another runner at the plate. We lost the game, but it was a hell of a stop. Gus Triandos was the victim, I think. He ran headfirst into the kid's knees and just lay there as stunned, three feet from home. The kid put the tag on the back of his neck just as gentle as Mommy patting oil on Baby Dear's sunburn.

There was a picture of that putout in the Newark *Evening News*, with a caption reading *Blockade Billy Blakely Saves Another Run*. It was a good nickname, and caught on with the fans. They weren't as demonstrative in those days—nobody would have come to Yankee Stadium in '57 wearing a chef's hat to support Gary Sheffield, I don't think—but when we played our first game back at Old Swampy, some of the fans came in carrying orange road-signs reading DETOUR and ROAD CLOSED.

The signs might have been a one-day thing if two Indians hadn't got thrown out at the plate in our first game back. That was a game Danny Dusen pitched, incidentally. Both of those putouts were the result of great throws rather than great blocks, but the rook got the credit, anyway, and in a way he deserved it. The guys were starting to trust him, see? Also, they wanted to watch him slap the tag. Baseball players are fans too, and when someone's on a roll, even the most hard-hearted try to help.

Dusen got his hundred and ninety-ninth that day. Oh, and the kid went three-for-four, including a home run, so it shouldn't surprise you that even more people showed up with those signs for our second game against Cleveland.

By the third one, some enterprising fellow was selling them out on Titan Esplanade, big orange cardboard diamonds with black letters: ROAD CLOSED BY ORDER OF BLOCKADE BILLY. Some of the fans'd hold em up when Billy was at bat, and they'd all hold them up when the other team had a runner on third. By the time the Yankees came to town—this was going on to the end of April—the whole stadium would flush orange when the Bombers had a runner on third, which they did often in that series.

Because the Yankees kicked the living shit out of us and took over first place. It was no fault of the kid's; he hit in every game and tagged out Bill Skowron between home and third when the lug got caught in a rundown. Skowron was a moose the size of Big Klew, and he tried to flatten the kid, but it was Skowron who went on his ass, the kid straddling him with a knee on either side. The photo of that one in the paper made it look like the end of a Big Time Wrestling match with Pretty Tony Baba for once finishing off Gorgeous George instead of the other way around.

The crowd outdid themselves waving those ROAD CLOSED signs around. It didn't seem to matter that the Titans had lost; the fans went home happy because they'd seen our skinny catcher knock Mighty Moose Skowron on his ass.

I seen the kid afterward, sitting naked on the bench outside the showers. He had a big bruise coming on the side of his chest, but he didn't seem to mind it at all. He was no crybaby. He was too dumb to feel pain, some people said later; too dumb and crazy. But I've known plenty of dumb players in my time, and being dumb never stopped them from bitching over their ouchies.

"How about all those signs, kid?" I asked, thinking I would cheer him up if he needed cheering.

"What signs?" he says, and I could see by the puzzled look on his face that he wasn't joking a bit. That was Blockade Billy for you. He would have stood in front of a semi if the guy behind the wheel was driving it down the third base line and trying to score on him, but otherwise he didn't have a fucking clue.

We played a two-game series with Detroit before hitting the road again, and lost both. Danny Doo was on the mound for the second one, and he couldn't blame the kid for the way it went; he was gone before the third inning was over. Sat in the dugout whining about the cold weather (it wasn't cold), the way Harrington dropped a fly ball out in right (Harrington would have needed stilts to get to that one), and the bad calls he got from that sonofabitch Wenders behind the plate. On that last one he might have had a point. Hi Wenders didn't like The Doo any more than the sportswriters did, never had, ran him in two ball games the year before. But I didn't see any bad calls that day, and I was standing less than ninety feet away.

The kid hit safe in both games, including a home run and a triple. Nor did Dusen hold the hot bat against him, which would have been his ordinary behavior; he was one of those guys who wanted fellows to understand there was one big star on the Titans, and it wasn't them. But he liked the kid; really seemed to think the kid was his lucky charm. And the kid liked him. They went barhopping after the game, had about a thousand drinks and visited a whorehouse to celebrate The Doo's first loss of the season, and showed up the next day for the trip to KC pale and shaky.

"The kid got laid last night," Doo confided in me as we rode out to the airport in the team bus. "I think it was his first time. That's the good news. The bad news is that I don't think he remembers it."

We had a bumpy plane ride; most of them were back then. Lousy prop-driven buckets, it's a wonder we didn't all get killed like Buddy Holly and the Big Fucking Bopper. The kid spent most of the trip throwing up in the can at the back of the plane, while right outside the door a bunch of guys sat playing acey-deucey and tossing him the usual funny stuff: *Get any onya? Want a fork and knife to cut that up a little?* Then the next day the kid goes five-for-five at Municipal Stadium, including a pair of jacks.

There was also another Blockade Billy play; by then he could have taken out a patent. The latest victim was Cletis Boyer. Again it was Blockade Billy down with the left shoulder, and up and over Mr. Boyer went, landing flat on his back in the left batter's box. There were some differences, though. The rook used both hands on the tag, and there was no bloody foot or strained Achilles tendon. Boyer just got up and walked back to the dugout, dusting his ass and shaking his head like he didn't quite know where he was. Oh, and we lost the game in spite of the kid's five hits. Eleven to ten was the final score, or something like that. Ganzie Burgess's knuckleball wasn't dancing that day; the Athletics feasted on it.

We won the next game, and lost a squeaker on getaway day. The kid hit in both games, which made it sixteen straight. Plus nine putouts at the plate. Nine in sixteen games! That might be a record. If it was in the books, that is.

We went to Chicago for three, and the kid hit in those games, too, making it nineteen straight. But damn if we didn't lose all three. Jersey Joe looked at me after the last of those games and said, "I don't buy that lucky charm stuff. I think Blakely *sucks* luck."

"That ain't fair and you know it," I said. "We were going good at the start, and now we're in a bad patch. It'll even out."

"Maybe," he says. "Is Dusen still trying to teach the kid how to drink?"

"Yeah. They headed off to The Loop with some other guys."

"But they'll come back together," Joe says. "I don't get it. By now Dusen should hate that kid. Doo's been here five years and I know his MO."

I did, too. When The Doo lost, he had to lay the blame on somebody else, like that bum Johnny Harrington or that busher bluesuit Hi Wenders. The kid's turn in the barrel was overdue, but Danny was still clapping him on the back and promising him he'd be Rookie of the Goddam Year. Not that The Doo could blame the kid for that day's loss. In the fifth inning of his latest masterpiece, Danny had hucked one to the backstop in the fifth: high, wide, and handsome. That scored one. So then he gets mad, loses his control, and walks the next two. Then Nellie Fox doubled down the line. After that The Doo got it back together, but by then it was too late; he was on the hook and stayed there.

We got a little well in Detroit, took two out of three. The kid hit in all three games and made another one of those amazing home-plate stands. Then we flew home. By then the kid from the Davenport Cornholers was the hottest goddam thing in the American League. There was talk of him doing a Gillette ad.

"That's an ad I'd like to see," Si Barbarino said. "I'm a fan of comedy."

"Then you must love looking at yourself in the mirror," Critter Hayward said.

"You're a card," Si says. "What I mean is the kid ain't got no whiskers."

There never was an ad, of course. Blockade Billy's career as a baseball player was almost over.

We had three scheduled with the White Sox, but the first one was a washout. The Doo's old pal Hi Wenders was the umpire crew chief, and he gave me the news himself. I'd got to The Swamp early because the trunks with our road uniforms in them got sent to Idlewild by mistake and I wanted to make sure they'd been trucked over. We wouldn't need them for a week, but I was never easy in my mind until such things were taken care of.

Wenders was sitting on a little stool outside the umpire's room, reading a paperback with a blond in fancy lingerie on the cover.

"That your wife, Hi?" I asks.

"My girlfriend," he says. "Go on home, Granny. Weather forecast says that by three it's gonna be coming down in buckets. I'm just waiting for DiPunno and Lopez to call the game."

"Okay," I says. "Thanks." I started away and he called after me.

"Granny, is that wonder-kid of yours all right in the head? Because he talks to himself behind the plate. Whispers. Never fucking shuts up."

"He's no Quiz Kid, but he's not crazy, if that's what you mean," I said. I was wrong about that, but who knew? "What kind of stuff does he say?"

"I couldn't hear much the one time I was behind him—the second game against Boston—but I know he talks about himself. In that whatdoyoucallit, third person. He says stuff like 'I can do it, Billy.' And one time, when he dropped a foul tip that woulda been strike three, he goes, 'I'm sorry, Billy.' "

"Well, so what? Til I was five, I had an invisible friend named Sheriff Pete. Me and Sheriff Pete shot up a lot of mining towns together."

"Yeah, but Blakely ain't five anymore. Unless he's five up here." Wenders taps the side of his thick skull.

"He's apt to have a five as the first number in his batting average before long," I says. "That's all I care about. Plus he's a hell of a stopper. You have to admit that."

"I do," Wenders says. "That cockhound has no fear. Another sign that he's not all there in the head."

I wasn't going to listen to an umpire run down one of my players any more than that, so I changed the subject and asked him—joking but not joking—if he was going to call the game tomorrow fair and square, even though his favorite Doo-Bug was throwing.

"I always call it fair and square," he says. "Dusen's a conceited glory-hog who's got his spot all picked out in Cooperstown, he'll do a hundred things wrong and never take the blame once, and he's an argumentative sonofabitch who knows better than to start in with me, because I won't stand for it. That said, I'll call it straight up, just like I always do. I can't believe you'd ask."

And I can't believe you'd sit there scratching your ass and calling our catcher next door to a congenital idiot, I thought, *but you did.*

I took my wife out to dinner that night, and we had a very nice time. Danced to Lester Lanin's band, as I recall. Got a little romantic in the taxi afterward. Slept well. I didn't sleep well for quite some time afterward; lots of bad dreams.

Danny Dusen took the ball in what was supposed to be the afternoon half of a twi-nighter, but the world as it applied to the Titans had already gone to hell; we just didn't know it. No one did except for Joe DiPunno. By the time night fell, we knew we were royally fucked for the season, because our first twenty-two games were almost surely going to be erased from the record books, along with any official acknowledgment of Blockade Billy Blakely.

I got in late because of traffic, but figured it didn't matter because the uniform snafu was sorted out. Most of the guys were already there, dressing or playing poker or just sitting around shooting the shit and smoking. Dusen and the kid were over in the corner by the cigarette machine, sitting in a couple of folding chairs, the kid with his uniform pants on, Dusen still wearing nothing but his jock—not a pretty sight. I went over to get a pack of Winstons and listened in. Danny was doing most of the talking.

"That fucking Wenders hates my ass," he says.

"He hates your ass," the kid says, then adds: "That fucker."

"You bet he is. You think he wants to be the one behind the plate when I get my two hundredth?"

"No?" the kid says.

"You bet he don't! But I'm going to win today just to spite him. And you're gonna help me, Bill. Right?"

"Right. Sure. Bill's gonna help."

"He'll squeeze the plate like a motherfucker."

"Will he? Will he squeeze it like a motherf—"

"I just said he will. So you pull everything back real fast."

"Fast as Jack Lightning."

"You're my good luck charm, Billy-boy."

And the kid, serious as the preacher at a bigshot funeral: "I'm your good luck charm."

"Yeah. Now listen . . ."

It was funny and creepy at the same time. The Doo was *intense*—leaning forward, eyes flashing while he talked. The Doo was a competitor, see? He wanted to win the way Bob Gibson did. Like Gibby, he'd do anything he could get away with to make that happen. And the kid was eating it up with a spoon.

I almost said something, because I wanted to break up that connection. Talking about it to you, I think maybe my subconscious mind had already put a lot of it together. Maybe that's bullshit, but I don't think so.

But I left them alone, just got my ciggies and walked away. Hell, if I'd opened my bazoo, Dusen would have told me to put a sock in it, anyway. He didn't like to be interrupted when he was holding court, and while I might not have given much of a shit about that on any other day, you tend to leave a guy alone when it's his turn to toe the rubber in front of the forty thousand people who are paying his salary.

I went over to Joe's office to get the lineup card, but the office door was shut and the blinds were down, an almost unheard-of thing on a game day. The slats weren't closed, though, so I peeked in. Joe had the phone to his ear and one hand over his eyes. I knocked on the glass. He started so hard he almost fell out of his chair, and looked around. They say there's no crying in baseball, but he was crying, all right. First and only time I ever saw it. His face was pale and his hair was wild—what little hair he had.

He waved me away, then went back to talking on the phone. I started across the locker room to the coaches' office, which was really the equipment room. Halfway there I stopped. The big pitcher-catcher conference had broken up, and the kid was pulling on his uniform shirt, the one with the big blue 19. And I saw the Band-Aid was back on the second finger of his right hand.

I walked over and put a hand on his shoulder. He smiled at me. The kid had a real sweet smile when he used it. "Hi, Granny," he says. But his smile began to fade when he saw I wasn't smiling back.

"You all ready to play?" I asked.

"Sure."

"Good. But I want to tell you something before you hit the dirt. The Doo's a hell of a pitcher, but as a human being he ain't ever going to get past Double A. He'd walk on his grandmother's broken back to get a win, and you matter a hell of a lot less to him than his grandmother."

"I'm his good luck charm!" he says indignantly.

"Maybe so," I say back, "but that's not what I'm talking about. There's such a thing as getting *too* pumped up for a game. A little is good, but too much and a fellow's apt to bust wide open."

"I don't get you."

"If you popped and went flat like a bad tire, The Doo would just find himself a brand-new lucky charm."

"You shouldn't talk like that! Him and me's friends!"

"I'm your friend, too. More important, I'm one of the coaches on this team. I'm responsible for your welfare, and I'll talk any goddam way I want, especially to a rook. And you'll listen. Are you listening?"

"I'm listening."

I'm sure he was, but he wasn't looking; he'd cast his eyes down and sullen red roses were blooming on those smooth boy-cheeks of his.

"I don't know what kind of a rig you've got under that Band-Aid, and I don't want to know. All I know is I saw it in the first game you played for us, and somebody got hurt. I haven't seen it since, and I don't want to see it today. Because if you got caught, it'd be *you* caught, even if The Doo put you up to it."

"I just cut myself," he says, all sullen.

"Right. Cut yourself shaving your knuckles. But I don't want to see that Band-Aid on your finger when you go out there. I'm looking after your own best interests."

Would I have said that if I hadn't seen Joe so upset he was crying? I like to think so. I like to think I was also looking after the best interests of the game, which I loved then and now. Virtual Bowling can't hold a candle, believe me.

I walked away before he could say anything else. And I didn't look back. Partly because I didn't want to see what was under the Band-Aid, mostly because Joe was standing in his office door, beckoning to me. I won't swear there was more gray in his hair, but I won't swear there wasn't.

I came into the office and closed the door. An awful idea occurred to me. It made a kind of sense, given the look on his face. "Jesus, Joe, is it your wife? Or the kids? Did something happen to one of the kids?"

He started and blinked, like I'd popped a paper bag beside his ear. "Jessie and the kids are fine. But George . . . oh *God*. I can't believe it. This is such a mess." And he put the heels of his palms against his eyes. A sound came out of him, but it wasn't a sob. It was a laugh. The most terrible fucking laugh I ever heard.

"What is it? Who called you?"

"I have to think," he says—but not to me. It was himself he was talking to. "I have to decide how I'm going to . . ." He took his hands off his eyes, and he seemed a little more like himself. "You're managing today, Granny."

"*Me?* I can't manage! The Doo'd blow his stack! He's going for his two hundredth again, and—"

"None of that matters, don't you see? Not now."

"What—"

"Just shut up and make out a lineup card. As for that kid . . ." He thought, then shook his head. "Hell, let him play, why not? Shit, bat him fifth. I was gonna move him up, anyway."

"Of course he's gonna play," I said. "Who else'd catch Danny?"

"Oh, fuck Danny Dusen!" he says.

"Cap—Joey—tell me what happened."

"No," he says. "I got to think it over first. What I'm gonna say to the guys. And the reporters!" He slapped his brow as if this part of it had just occurred to him. "*Those* overbred, overpaid assholes! Shit!" Then, talking to himself again: "But let the guys have this game. They deserve that much. Maybe the kid, too. Hell, maybe he'll bat for the cycle!" He laughed some more, then went upside his own head to make himself stop.

"I don't understand."

"You will. Go on, get out of here. Make any old lineup you want. Pull the names out of a hat, why don't you? It doesn't matter. Only make sure you tell the umpire crew chief you're running the show. I guess that'd be Wenders."

I walked down the hall to the umpire's room like a man in a dream and told Wenders that I'd be making out the lineup and managing the game from the third base box. He asked me what was wrong with Joe, and I said he was sick. Which he sure was.

That was the first game I managed until I got the Athletics in '63, and it was a short one, because as you probably know if you've done your research, Hi Wenders ran me in the sixth. I don't remember much about it, anyway. I had so much on my mind that I felt like a man in a dream. But I did have sense enough to do one thing, and that was to check the kid's right hand before he ran out on the field. There was no Band-Aid on the second finger, and no cut, either. I didn't even feel relieved. I just kept seeing Joe DiPunno's red eyes and haggard mouth.

That was Danny Doo's last good game, and he never did get his two hundred. He tried to come back in '58, but no go. He claimed the double vision was gone and maybe it was true, but he couldn't hardly get the pill over the plate anymore. No spot in Cooperstown for Danny. Joe was right all along: that kid did suck luck. Like some kind of fucking voodoo prince.

But that afternoon Doo was the best I ever saw him, his fastball hopping, his curve snapping like a whip. For the first four innings they couldn't touch him at all. Just wave the stick and take a seat, fellows, thank you for playing. He struck out six and the rest were infield ground-outs. Only trouble was, Kinder was almost as good. We'd gotten one lousy hit, a two-out double by Harrington in the bottom of the third.

Comes the top of the fifth, okay? The first batter goes down easy. Then Walt Dropo comes up, hits one deep into the left field corner, and takes off like a bat out of hell. The crowd saw Harry Keene still chasing the ball while Dropo's legging for second, and they understood it could be an inside-the-park job. The chanting started. Only a few voices at first, then more and more. Getting deeper and louder. It put a chill up me from the crack of my ass to the nape of my neck.

"Bloh-KADE! Bloh-KADE! Bloh-KADE!"

The orange signs started going up. People were on their feet and holding them over their heads. Not waving them like usual, just holding them up. I have never seen anything like it.

"Bloh-KADE! Bloh-KADE! Bloh-KADE!"

At first I thought there wasn't a snowball's chance in hell; by then Dropo's steaming for third with all the stops pulled out. But Keene pounced on the ball and made a perfect throw to Barbarino at short. The rook, meanwhile, is standing on the third base side of home with his glove held out, making a target, and Si hit the goddam pocket.

The crowd's chanting. Dropo's sliding, with his spikes up. The kid don't mind; he goes on his knees and dives over em. Hi Wenders was where he was supposed to be—that time, at least—leaning over the play. A cloud of dust goes up . . . and out of it comes Wenders's upraised thumb. *"Yerrrr . . . OUT!"*

Mr. King, the fans went nuts. Walt Dropo did too. He was up and dancing around like a kid having an epileptic fit and trying to do the fucking Hully Gully at the same time. He couldn't believe it.

The kid was scraped halfway up his left forearm, not bad, just bloodsweat, but enough for old Bony Dadier—he was our trainer—to come out and slap a Band-Aid on it. So the kid got his Band-Aid after all, only this one was legit. The fans stayed on their feet during the whole medical consultation, waving their ROAD CLOSED signs and chanting *"Bloh-KADE! Bloh-KADE!"* like they wouldn't never get enough of it.

The kid didn't seem to notice. He was on another planet. He was that way the whole time he was with the Titans. He just hauled on his mask, went back behind the plate, and squatted down. Business as usual. Bubba Phillips came up, lined out to Lathrop at first, and that was the fifth.

When the kid came up in the bottom of the inning and struck out on three pitches, the crowd still gave him a standing O. That time he noticed, and tipped his cap when he went back to the dugout. Only time he ever did it. Not because he was snotty but because . . . well, I already said it. That other-planet thing.

Okay, top of the sixth. Over fifty years later and I still get a red ass when I think of it. Kinder's up first and loops out to third, just like a pitcher should. Then comes Luis Aparicio, Little Louie. The Doo winds and fires. Aparicio fouls it off high and lazy behind home plate, on the third base side of the screen. That was my side, and I saw it all. The kid throws away his mask and sprints after it, head back and glove out. Wenders trailed him, but not close like he should have done. He didn't think the kid had a chance. It was lousy goddam umping.

The kid's off the grass and on the track, by the low wall between the field and the box seats. Neck craned. Looking up. Two dozen people in those first- and second-row box seats also looking up, most of them waving their hands in the air. This is one thing I don't understand about fans and never will. It's a fucking *baseball*, for the love of God! An item that sold for seventy-five cents back then. But when fans see one in reach at the ballpark, they turn into fuck-ing greed-monsters. Never mind standing back and letting the man trying to catch it—*their* man, and in a tight ball game—do his job.

I saw it all, I tell you. Saw it clear. That mile-high pop-up came down on our side of the wall. The kid was going to catch it. Then some long-armed bozo in one of those Titans jerseys they sold on the Esplanade reached over and ticked it so the ball bounced off the edge of the kid's glove and fell to the ground.

I was so sure Wenders would call Aparicio out—it was clear interference—that at first I couldn't believe what I was seeing when he gestured for the kid to go back behind the plate and for Aparicio to resume the box. When I got it, I ran down the line, waving my arms. The crowd started cheering me and booing Wenders, which is no way to win friends and influence people when you're arguing a call, but I was too goddam mad to care. I wouldn't have stopped if Mahatma Gandhi had walked out on the field buttnaked and urging us to make peace.

"*Interference!*" I yelled. "*Clear as day, clear as the nose on your face!*"

"It was in the stands, and that makes it anyone's ball," Wenders says. "Go on back to your little nest and let's get this show on the road."

The kid didn't care; he was talking to his pal The Doo. That was all right. I didn't care that he didn't care. All I wanted at that moment was to tear Hi Wenders a fresh new asshole. I'm not ordinarily an argumentative man—all the years I managed the A's, I only got thrown out of games twice—but that day I would have made Billy Martin look like a peacenik.

"*You didn't see it, Hi! You were trailing too far back! You didn't see shit!*"

"I wasn't trailing and I saw it all. Now get back, Granny. I ain't kidding."

"*If you didn't see that long-armed sonofabitch—*" (here a lady in the second row put her hands over her little boy's ears and pursed up her mouth at me in an oh-you-nasty-man look) "*—that long-armed sonofabitch reach out and tick that ball, you were goddam trailing! Jesus Christ!*"

The man in the jersey starts shaking his head—who, me? not me!—but he's also wearing a big embarrassed suckass grin. Wenders saw it, knew what it meant, then looked away. "That's all you get," he says to me. And in the reasonable voice that means you're one smart crack from drinking a Rheingold in the locker room. "You've had your say. You can either shut the hell up or listen to the rest of the game on the radio. Take your pick."

I went back to the box. Aparicio stood back in with a big shit-eating grin on his face. He knew, sure he did. And made the most of it. The guy never hit many home runs, but when The Doo sent in a changeup that didn't change, Little Louie cranked it high, wide, and handsome to the deepest part of the park. Nosy Norton was playing center, and he never even turned around.

Aparicio circled the bases, serene as the *Queen Mary* coming into dock, while the crowd screamed at him, denigrated his relatives, and hurled hate down on Hi Wenders's head. Wenders heard none of it, which is the chief umpirely skill. He just got a fresh ball out of his coat pocket and inspected it for dings and doinks. Watching him do that, I lost it entirely. I rushed down to home plate and started shaking both fists in his face.

"That's your run, you fucking busher!" I screamed. *"Too fucking lazy to chase after a foul ball, and now you've got an RBI for yourself! Jam it up your ass! Maybe you'll find your glasses!"*

The crowd loved it. Hi Wenders, not so much. He pointed at me, threw his thumb back over his shoulder, and walked away. The crowd started booing and shaking their ROAD CLOSED signs; some threw bottles, cups, and half-eaten franks onto the field. It was a circus.

"Don't you walk away from me, you fatass blind lazy sonofabitching bastard!" I screamed, and chased after

him. Someone from our dugout grabbed me before I could grab Wenders, which I meant to do. I had lost it entirely.

The crowd was chanting *"KILL THE UMP! KILL THE UMP! KILL THE UMP!"* I'll never forget that, because it was the same way they'd been chanting *"Bloh-KADE! Bloh-KADE!"*

"If your mother was here, she'd yank down those blue pants and spank your ass, you bat-blind busher!" I screamed, and then they hauled me into the dugout. Ganzie Burgess, our knuckleballer, managed the last three innings of that horror show. He also pitched the last two. You might find that in the record books too. If there were any records of that lost spring.

The last thing I saw on the field was Danny Dusen and Blockade Billy standing on the grass between the plate and the mound. The kid had his mask tucked under his arm. The Doo was whispering in his ear. The kid was listening—he always listened when The Doo talked—but he was looking at the crowd, forty thousand fans on their feet, men, women, and children, yelling *KILL THE UMP! KILL THE UMP! KILL THE UMP!*

There was a bucket of balls halfway down the hall between the dugout and the locker room. I kicked it and sent balls rolling every whichway. If I'd stepped on one of them and fallen on my ass, it would have been the perfect end to a perfect fucking afternoon at the ballpark.

Joe was in the locker room, sitting on a bench outside the showers. By then he looked seventy instead of just fifty. There were three other guys in there with him. Two were uniformed cops. The third one was in a suit, but you only had to take one look at his hard roast beef of a face to know he was a cop, too.

"Game over early?" this one asked me. He was sitting on a folding chair with his big old cop thighs spread and straining his seersucker pants. The blue-suits were on one of the benches in front of the lockers.

"It is for me," I said. I was still so mad I didn't even care about the cops. To Joe I said, "Fucking Wenders ran me. I'm sorry, Cap, but it was a clear case of interference and that lazy sonofabitch—"

"It doesn't matter," Joe said. "The game isn't going to count. I don't think any of our games are going to count. Kerwin'll appeal to the Commissioner, of course, but—"

"What are you talking about?" I asked.

Joe sighed. Then he looked at the guy in the suit. "You tell him, Detective Lombardazzi," he said. "I can't bear to."

"Does he need to know?" Lombardazzi asked. He's looking at me like I'm some kind of bug he's never seen before. It was a look I didn't need on top of everything else, but I kept my mouth shut. Because I knew three cops, one of them a detective, don't show up in the locker room of a Major League baseball team if it isn't goddam serious.

"If you want him to hold the other guys long enough for you to get the Blakely kid out of here, I think you better put him in the picture," Joe says.

From above us there came a cry from the fans, followed by a groan, followed by a cheer. None of us paid any attention to what turned out to be the end of Danny Dusen's baseball career. The cry was when he got hit in the forehead by a Larry Doby line drive. The groan was when he fell on the pitcher's mound like a tagged prizefighter. And the cheer was when he picked himself up and gestured that he was okay. Which he was not, but he pitched the rest of the sixth, and the seventh, too. Didn't give up a run, either. Ganzie made him come out before the eighth when he saw The Doo wasn't walking straight. Danny all the time claiming he was perfectly okay, that the big purple goose egg raising up over his left eyebrow was nothing, he'd had lots worse, and the kid saying the same: it ain't nothing, it ain't nothing. Little Sir Echo. Us down in the clubhouse didn't know any of that, no more than Dusen knew he might've been tagged worse in his career, but it was the first time part of his brain had sprung a leak.

"His name isn't Blakely," Lombardazzi says. "It's Eugene Katsanis."

"Katz-*whatsis*? Where's Blakely, then?"

"William Blakely's dead. Has been for a month. His parents too."

I gaped at him. "What are you talking about?"

So he told me the stuff I'm sure you already know, Mr. King, but maybe I can fill in a few blanks. The Blakelys lived in Clarence, Iowa, a wide patch of not much an hour's drive from Davenport. Made it convenient for Ma and Pa, because they could go to most of their son's Minor League games. Blakely had a successful farm; an eight-hundred-acre job. One of their hired men wasn't much more than a boy. His name was Gene Katsanis, an orphan who'd grown up in The Ottershaw Christian Home for Boys. He was no farmer, and not quite right in the head, but he was a hell of a baseball player.

Katsanis and Blakely played against each other on

a couple of church teams, and together on the local Babe Ruth team, which won the state tournament all three years the two of them played together, and once went as far as the national semis. Blakely went to high school and starred on that team also, but Katsanis wasn't school material. Slopping-the-hogs material and ball-playing material is what he was, although he was never supposed to be as good as Billy Blakely. Nobody so much as considered such a thing. Until it happened, that is.

Blakely's father hired him because the kid worked cheap, sure, but mostly because he had enough natural talent to keep Billy sharp. For twenty-five dollars a week, the Blakely kid got a fielder and a batting-practice pitcher. The old man got a cow-milker and a shit-shoveler. Not a bad deal, at least for them.

Whatever you've found in your research probably favors the Blakely family, am I right? Because they had been around those parts for four generations, because they were rich farmers, and because Katsanis wasn't nothing but a state kid who started life in a liquor carton on a church step and had several screws loose upstairs. And why was that? Because he was born dumb or because he got the crap beaten out of him three and four times a week in that home before he got old enough and big enough to defend himself? I know a lot of the beatings came because he had a habit of talking to himself—that came out in the newspapers later on.

Katsanis and Billy practiced just as hard once Billy got into the Titans' farm system—during the off-season, you know, probably throwing and hitting in the barn once the snow got too deep outside—but Katsanis got kicked off the local town team, and wasn't allowed to go to the Cornholers' workouts during Billy's second season with them. During his first one, Katsanis had been allowed to participate in some of the workouts, even in some intersquad games, if they were a man shy. It was all pretty informal and loosey-goosey back then, not like now when the insurance companies shit a brick if a major leaguer so much as grabs a bat without wearing a helmet.

What I think happened—feel free to correct me if you know better—is that Katsanis, whatever other problems he might have had, continued to grow and mature as a ballplayer. Blakely didn't. You see that all the time. Two kids who both look like Babe Fuckin' Ruth in high school. Same height, same weight, same speed, same twenty-twenty peepers. But one of them is able to play at the next level . . . and the next . . . and the next . . . while the other one starts to fall behind. This much I did hear later: Billy Blakely didn't start out as a catcher. He got switched from center field when the kid who *was* catching broke his arm. And that kind of switch isn't a real good sign. It's like the coach is sending a message: "You'll do . . . but only until someone better shows up."

I think Blakely got jealous, I think his old man got jealous, and I think maybe Mom did, too. Maybe especially Mom, because sports moms can be wolverines. I think maybe they pulled a few strings to keep Katsanis from playing locally, and from showing up for the Davenport Cocksuckers' workouts. They could have done it, because they were a wealthy, long-established Iowa family and Gene Katsanis was a nobody who grew up in an orphan home that was probably hell on earth.

I think maybe Billy got ragging on the kid once too often and once too hard. Or it could've been the dad or the mom. Maybe it was over the way he milked the cows, or maybe he didn't shovel the shit just right that one time, but I'll bet the bottom line was baseball and plain old jealousy. The green-eyed monster. For all I know, the Cornholers' manager told Blakely he might be sent down to Single A in Clearwater, and getting sent down a rung when you're only twenty— when you're supposed to be going *up* the ladder—is a damned good sign that your career in organized baseball is going to be a short one.

But however it was—and *whoever*—it was a bad mistake. The kid could be sweet when he was treated right, we all knew that, but he wasn't right in the head. And he could be dangerous. I knew that even before the cops showed up, because of what happened in the very first game of the season: Billy Anderson's ankle.

"The county sheriff found all three Blakelys in the barn," Lombardazzi said. "Katsanis slashed their throats. Sheriff said it looked like a razor blade."

I just gaped at him.

"What must have happened is this," Joe said in a heavy voice. "Kerwin McCaslin called around for a backup catcher when our guys got hurt down in Florida, and the manager of the Cornhuskers said he had a boy who might fill the bill for three or four weeks, assuming we didn't need him to hit for average. Because, he said, this kid wouldn't do that."

"But he did," I says.

"Because he wasn't Blakely," Lombardazzi says. "By then Blakely and his parents must already have been dead a couple of days, at least. The Katsanis kid was keeping house all by himself. And not *all* his screws were loose. He was smart enough to answer the phone when it rang. He took the call from the manager and said sure, Billy'd be glad to go to New Jersey. And before he left—as Billy—he called around to the neighbors and the feed store downtown. Told em the Blakelys had been called away on a family emergency and he was taking care of things. Pretty smart for a loony, wouldn't you say?"

"He's not a loony," I told him.

"Well, he cut the throats of the people who took him in and gave him a job, and he killed all the cows so the neighbors wouldn't hear them bawling to be milked at night, but have it your way. I know the DA's going to agree with you, because he wants to see Katsanis get the rope. That's how they do it in Iowa, you know."

I turned to Joe. "How could a thing like this happen?"

"Because he was good," Joe said. "And because he wanted to play ball."

The kid had Billy Blakely's ID, and this was back in the days when picture IDs were pretty much unheard of. The two kids matched up pretty well, anyway: blue eyes, dark hair, six feet tall. But mostly, yeah—it happened because the kid was good. And wanted to play ball.

"Good enough to get almost a month in the pros," Lombardazzi said, and over our heads a cheer went up. Blockade Billy had just gotten his last big-league hit: a roundtripper. "Then, day before yesterday, the LP gas man went out to the Blakely farm. Other folks had been there before, but they read the note Katsanis left on the door and went away. Not the gas man. He filled the tanks behind the barn, and the barn was where the bodies were—cows and Blakelys both. The weather had finally turned warm, and he smelled em. Which is pretty much the way our story ends. Now, your manager here wants him arrested with as little fuss as possible, and with as little danger to the other players on your team as possible. That's fine with me. So your job—"

"Your job is to hold the rest of the guys in the dugout," Jersey Joe says. "Send Blakely . . . Katsanis . . . down here on his own. He'll be gone when the rest of the guys get to the locker room. Then we'll try to sort this clusterfuck out."

"What the hell do I tell them?"

"Team meeting. Free ice cream. I don't care. You just hold them for five minutes."

I says to Lombardazzi, "No one tipped? *No one?* You mean no one heard the radio broadcasts and tried calling Pop Blakely to say how great it was that his kid was tearing up the bigs?"

"I imagine one or two might have tried," Lombardazzi said. "Folks from Iowa *do* come to the big city from time to time, I'm told, and I imagine a few people visiting New York listen to the Titans or read about em in the paper—"

"I prefer the Yankees," one of the bluesuits chimes in.

"If I want your opinion, I'll rattle your cage," Lombardazzi said. "Until then, shut up and die right."

I looked at Joe, feeling sick. Getting a bad call and getting run off the field during my first managerial stint now seemed like the very least of my problems.

"Get him in here alone," Joe said. "I don't care how. The guys shouldn't have to see this." He thought it over and added: "And the kid shouldn't have to *see* them seeing it. No matter what he did."

If it matters—and I know it don't—we lost that game two to one. All three runs were solo shots. Minnie Minoso hit the game winner off of Ganzie in the top of the ninth. The kid made the final out. He whiffed in his first at bat as a Titan; he whiffed in his last one. Baseball is a game of inches, but it's also a game of balance.

Not that any of our guys cared about the game. When I got up there, they were gathered around The Doo, who was sitting on the bench and telling them he was fine, goddammit, just a little dizzy. But he didn't look fine, and our old excuse for a doc looked pretty grave. He wanted Danny down at Newark General for X-rays.

"Fuck that," Doo says, "I just need a couple of minutes. I'm all right, I tell you. Jesus, Bones, cut me a break."

"Blakely," I said. "Go on down to the locker room. Mr. DiPunno wants to see you."

"Coach DiPunno wants to see me? In the locker room? Why?"

"Something about the Rookie of the Month award," I said. It just popped into my head from nowhere. There was no such thing back then, but the kid didn't know that.

The kid looks at Danny Doo, and The Doo flaps his hand at him. "Go on, get out of here, kid. You played a good game. Not your fault. You're still lucky, and fuck anyone who says different." Then he says, "All of you get out of here. Gimme some breathing room."

"Hold off on that," I says. "Joe wants to see him alone. Give him a little one-to-one congratulations,

I guess. Kid, don't wait around. Just—" *Just scat* was how I meant to finish, but I didn't have to. Blakely or Katsanis, he was already gone.

You know what happened after that.

If the kid had gone straight down the hall to the umpire's room, he would have gotten collared, because the locker room was on the way. Instead, he cut through our box room, where luggage was stored and where we also had a couple of massage tables and a whirlpool bath. We'll never know for sure why he did that, but I think the kid knew something was wrong. Hell, he must have known the roof was going to fall in on him eventually; if he was crazy, it was like a fox. In any case, he came out on the far side of the locker room, walked down to the ump's room, and knocked on the door. By then the rig he probably learned how to make in The Ottershaw Christian Home was back on his second finger. One of the older boys probably showed him how, that's what I think. *Kid, if you want to stop getting beaten up all the time, make yourself one of these.*

He never put it back in his locker after all, just tucked it into his pocket. And he didn't bother with the Band-Aid after the game, which tells me he knew he didn't have anything to hide anymore.

He raps on the umpire's door and says, "Urgent telegram for Mr. Hi Wenders." Crazy like a fox, see? I don't know what would have happened if one of the other umps on the crew had opened up, but it was Wenders himself, and I'm betting his life was over even before he realized it wasn't a Western Union delivery boy standing there.

It *was* a razor blade, see? Or a piece of one. When it wasn't needed, it stayed inside a little tin band like a kid's pretend finger-ring. Only when he balled his right fist and pushed on the band with the ball of his thumb, that little sliver of blade slid out. Wenders opened the door and Katsanis swept it across his neck and cut his throat with it. When I saw the puddle of blood after he was taken away in handcuffs—oh my God, such a pool of it there was—all I could think of was those forty thousand people screaming *KILL THE UMP* the same way they'd been screaming *Bloh-KADE*. No one really means it, but the kid didn't know that, either. Especially not after The Doo poured a lot of poison in his ears about how Wenders was out to get *both* of them.

When the cops ran out of the locker room, Billy Blockade was just standing there with blood all down the front of his white home uniform and Wenders lying at his feet. Nor did he try to fight or slash when the bluesuits grabbed him. No, he just stood there whispering to himself. "I got him, Doo. Billy got him. He won't make no more bad calls now."

That's where the story ends, Mr. King—the part of it I know, at least. As far as the Titans go, you could look it up, as ol' Casey used to say: all those games canceled out, and all the doubleheaders we played to make them up. How we ended up with old Hubie Rattner squatting behind the plate after all, and how he batted .185—well below what they now call the Mendoza Line. How Danny Dusen was diagnosed with something called "an intercranial bleed" and had to sit out the rest of the season. How he tried to come back in 1958—that was sad. Five outings. In three of them he couldn't get the ball over the plate. In the other two . . . do you remember the last Red Sox–

Yankees playoff game in 2004? How Kevin Brown started for the Yankees, and the Sox scored six goddam runs off him in the first two innings? That's how Danny Doo pitched in '58 when he actually managed to get the ball over the dish. He had *nothing*. And still, after all that, we managed to finish ahead of the Senators and the Athletics. Only Jersey Joe DiPunno had a heart attack during the World Series that year. Might have been the same day the Russians put the Sputnik up. They took him out of County Stadium on a stretcher. He lived another five years, but he was a shadow of his former self and of course he never managed again.

He said the kid sucked luck, and he was more right than he knew. Mr. King, that kid was a *black hole* for luck.

For himself, as well. I'm sure you know how his story ended—how he was taken to Essex County Jail and held there for extradition. How he swallowed a bar of soap and choked to death on it. I can't think of a worse way to go. That was a nightmare season, no doubt, and still, telling you about it brought back some good memories. Mostly, I think, of how Old Swampy would flush orange when all those fans raised their signs: ROAD CLOSED BY ORDER OF BLOCKADE BILLY. Yep, I bet the fellow who thought those up made a goddam mint. But you know, the people who bought them got fair value. When they stood up with them held over their heads, they were part of something bigger than themselves. That can be a bad thing—just think of all the people who turned out to see Hitler at his rallies—but this was a good thing. *Baseball* is a good thing. Always was, always will be.

Bloh-KADE, bloh-KADE, bloh-KADE.

Still gives me a chill to think of it. Still echoes in my head. That kid was the real thing, crazy or not, luck-sucker or not.

Mr. King, I think I'm all talked out. Do you have enough? Good. I'm glad. You come back anytime you want, but not on Wednesday afternoon; that's when they have their goddam Virtual Bowling, and you can't hear yourself think. Come on Saturday, why don't you? There's a bunch of us always watches the Game of the Week. We're allowed a couple of beers, and we root like mad bastards. It ain't like the old days, but it ain't bad.

For Flip Thompson,
friend and high school catcher

Some stand-in for me in one of the early novels—I think it was Ben Mears in *'Salem's Lot*—says it's a bad idea to talk about a story you're planning to write. "It's like pissing it out on the ground" is how he puts it. Sometimes, though, especially if I'm feeling enthusiastic, I find it hard to take my own advice. That was the case with "Mister Yummy."

When I sketched out the rough idea of it to a friend, he listened carefully and then shook his head. "I don't think you've got anything new to say about AIDS, Steve." He paused and added, "Especially as a straight man."

No. And no. And especially: *no*.

I hate the assumption that you can't write about something because you haven't experienced it, and not just because it assumes a limit on the human imagination, which is basically limitless. It also suggests that some leaps of identification are impossible. I refuse to accept that, because it leads to the conclusion that real change is beyond us, and so is empathy. The idea is false on the evidence. Like shit, change happens. If the British and Irish can make peace, you gotta believe there's a chance that someday the Jews and Palestinians will work things out. Change only occurs as a result of hard work, I think we'd all agree on that, but hard work isn't enough. It also requires a strenuous leap of the imagination: what is it really like to be in the other guy or gal's shoes?

And hey, I never wanted to write a story about AIDS or being gay, anyhow—those things were only the framing device. What I wanted to write about was the brute power of the human sex drive. That power, it seems to me, holds sway over those of every orientation, especially when young. At some point—on the right or wrong night, in a good place or a bad one—desire rises up and will not be denied. Caution is swept away. Cogent thought ceases. Risk no longer matters.

That's what I wanted to write about.

Mister Yummy

I

Dave Calhoun was helping Olga Glukhov construct the Eiffel Tower. They had been at it for six mornings now, six *early* mornings, in the common room of the Lakeview Assisted Living Center. They were hardly alone in there; old people rise early. The giant flatscreen on the far side started blatting the usual rabble-rousing junk from Fox News at five thirty, and a number of residents were watching it with their mouths agape.

"Ah," Olga said. "Here's one I've been looking for." She tapped a piece of girder into place halfway down Gustave Eiffel's masterpiece, created—according to the back of the box—from junk metal.

Dave heard the tap of a cane approaching from behind him, and greeted the newcomer without turning his head. "Good morning, Ollie. You're up early." As a young man, Dave wouldn't have believed you could ID someone simply by the sound of his cane, but as a young man he had never dreamed he would finish his time on earth in a place where so many people used them.

"Good morning right back at you," Ollie Franklin said. "And to you, Olga."

She looked up briefly, then back down at the puzzle —a thousand pieces, according to the box, and most now where they belonged. "These girders are a *bugger*. I see them floating in front of me every time I close my eyes. I believe I'll go for a smoke and wake up my lungs."

Smoking was supposedly *verboten* in Lakeview, but Olga and a few other diehards were allowed to slip through the kitchen to the loading dock, where there was a butt can. She rose, tottered, cursed in either Russian or Polish, caught her balance, and shuffled away. Then she stopped and looked back at Dave, eyebrows drawn together. "Leave some for me, Bob. Do you promise?"

He raised his hand, palm out. "So help me God."

Satisfied, she shuffled on, digging in the pocket of her shapeless day dress for her butts and her Bic.

Ollie raised his own eyebrows. "Since when are you Bob?"

"He was her husband. You remember. Came here with her, died two years ago."

"Ah. Right. And now she's losing it. That's too bad."

Dave shrugged. "She'll be ninety in the fall, if she makes it. She's entitled to a few slipped cogs. And look at this." He gestured at the puzzle, which filled an entire card table. "She did most of it herself. I'm just her assistant."

Ollie, who had been a graphic designer in what he called his real life, looked at the nearly completed puzzle gloomily. "La Tour Eiffel. Did you know there was an artists' protest when it was under construction?"

"No, but I'm not surprised. The French."

"The novelist Léon Bloy called it a truly tragic streetlamp."

Calhoun looked at the puzzle, saw what Bloy had meant, and laughed. It did look like a streetlamp. Sort of.

"Some other artist or writer—I can't remember who—claimed that the best view of Paris was from the Eiffel Tower, because it was the only view of Paris without the Eiffel Tower in it." Ollie bent closer, one hand gripping his cane, the other pressed against the small of his back, as if to hold it together. His eyes moved from the puzzle to the scatter of remaining pieces, perhaps a hundred in all, then back to the puzzle. "Houston, you may have a problem here."

Dave had already begun to suspect this. "If you're right, it's going to ruin Olga's day."

"She should have expected it. How many times do you think this version of the Eiffel has been assembled, and then taken apart again? Old people are as careless as teenagers." He straightened up. "Would you walk outside in the garden with me? I have something to give you. Also something to tell you."

Dave studied Ollie. "You okay?"

The other chose not to answer this. "Come outside. It's a beautiful morning. Warming up nicely."

Ollie led the way toward the patio, his cane tapping out that familiar one-two-three rhythm, tossing a good-morning wave to someone as he passed the coffee-drinking coterie of TV watchers. Dave followed willingly enough, but slightly mystified.

II

Lakeview was built in a **U** shape, with the common room between two extending arms that comprised the "assisted living suites," each suite consisting of a sitting room, a bedroom, and the sort of bathroom that came equipped with handrails and a shower chair. These suites were not cheap. Although many of the residents were no longer strictly continent (Dave had begun suffering his own nighttime accidents not long after turning eighty-three, and now kept boxes of PM Pull-Ups on a high shelf in his closet), it was not the sort of place that smelled of piss and Lysol. The rooms also came with satellite TV, there was a snack buffet in each wing, and twice a month there were wine-tasting parties. All things considered, Dave thought, it was a pretty good place to run out the string.

The garden between the residence wings was lush—almost orgasmic—with early summer. Paths wandered and a central fountain splashed. The flowers rioted, but in a genteel, well-barbered way. Here and there were house telephones where a walker suddenly afflicted with shortness of breath or spreading numbness in the legs could call for assistance. There would be plenty of walkers later on, when those not yet arisen (or when those in the common room got their fill of Fox News) came out to enjoy the day before it heated up, but for the time being, Dave and Ollie had it to themselves.

Once they were through the double doors and down the steps from the wide flagstoned patio (both of them descending with care), Ollie stopped and began fumbling in the pocket of the baggy houndstooth check sportcoat he was wearing. He brought out a silver pocket watch on a heavy silver chain. He held it out to Dave.

"I want you to have this. It was my great-grandfather's. Judging by the engraving inside the cover, he either bought it or had it given to him in eighteen ninety."

Dave gazed at the watch, swinging on its chain from Ollie Franklin's slightly palsied hand like a hypnotist's amulet, with amusement and horror. "I can't take that."

Patiently, as if instructing a child, Ollie said, "You can if I give it to you. And I've seen you admire it many and many a time."

"It's a family heirloom!"

"Yes indeed, and my brother will take it if it's in my effects when I die. Which I'm going to do, and soon. Perhaps tonight. Certainly in the next few days."

Dave didn't know what to say.

Still in that same patient tone, Ollie said, "My brother, Tom, isn't worth the powder it would take to blow him to Des Moines. I have never said as much to him, it would be cruel, but I've said so many times to you. Haven't I?"

"Well . . . yes."

"I have supported him through three failed businesses and two failed marriages. I believe I've told you *that* many times, as well. Haven't I?"

"Yes, but—"

"I did well, and I invested well," Ollie said, beginning to walk and tapping his cane in his own personal code: *tap, tap-tap, tap, tap-tap-tap.* "I am one of the infamous One Percent so reviled by the liberal young. Not by a lot, mind you, but by enough to have lived comfortably here for the last three years while continuing to serve as my younger brother's safety net. I no longer have to perform that service for his daughter, thank God; Martha actually seems to be earning a living for herself. Which is a relief. I've made a will, all proper and correct, and in it I've done the proper thing. The *family* thing. Since I have no wife or children myself, that means leaving everything to Tom. Except this. This is for you. You've been a good friend to me, so please. Take it."

Dave considered, decided he could give it back when his friend's death premonition passed, and took the watch. He clicked it open and admired the crystal face. Twenty-two past six—right on time, as far as he could tell. The second hand moved briskly in its own little circle just above the scrolled 6.

"Cleaned several times, but repaired only once," Ollie said, resuming his slow ambulation. "In nineteen twenty-three, according to Grampy, after my father dropped it down the well on the old farm in Hemingford Home. Can you imagine that? Over a hundred and twenty years old, and only repaired once. How many human beings on earth can claim that? A dozen? Maybe only six? You have two sons and a daughter, am I right?"

"You are," Dave said. His friend had grown increasingly frail over the last year, and his hair was nothing but a few baby-fine wisps on his liver-spotted skull, but his mind was ticking along a little better than Olga's. Or my own, he admitted to himself.

"The watch isn't in my will, but it should go in yours. I'm sure you love all your children equally, you're that kind of guy, but liking is different, isn't it? Leave it to the one you like the best."

That would be Peter, Dave thought, and smiled.

Either returning the smile or catching the thought behind it, Ollie's lips parted over his remaining teeth and he nodded. "Let's sit down. I'm bushed. It doesn't take much, these days."

They sat on one of the benches, and Dave tried to hand the watch back. Ollie pushed his hands out in an exaggerated repelling gesture that was comical enough to make Dave laugh, although he recognized this as a serious matter. Certainly more serious than a few missing pieces in a jigsaw puzzle.

The smell of the flowers was strong, heavenly. When Dave Calhoun thought of death—not so far off now—the prospect he regretted most was the loss of the sensory world and all its ordinary luxuries. The sight of a woman's cleavage in a boatneck top. The sound of Cozy Cole going bullshit on the drums in "Topsy, Part Two." The taste of lemon pie with a cloud of meringue on top. The smell of flowers he could not name, although his wife would have known them all.

"Ollie, you may be going to die this week, God knows everyone in this place has one foot in the grave and the other on a banana peel, but there's no way you can know for sure. I don't know if you had a dream, or a black cat crossed your path, or something else, but premonitions are bullshit."

"I didn't just have a premonition," Ollie said, "I saw one. I saw Mister Yummy. I've seen him several times in the last two weeks. Always closer. Pretty soon I'll have a room visit, and that will be that. I don't mind. In fact, I'm looking forward to it. Life's a great thing, but if you live long enough, it wears out before it runs out."

"Mister Yummy," Calhoun said. "Who the hell is Mister Yummy?"

"It's not really him," Ollie said, as if he hadn't heard. "I know that. It's a *representation* of him. A summation of a time and place, if you like. Although there was a *real* Mister Yummy once. That's what my friends and I called him that night in Highpockets. I never knew his real name."

"I'm not following."

"Listen, you know I'm gay, right?"

Dave smiled. "Well, I think your dating days were over before I met you, but I had a pretty good idea, yes."

"Was it the ascot?"

It's the way you walk, Dave thought. Even with a cane. The way you run your fingers through what remains of your hair and then glance in the mirror. The way you roll your eyes at the women on that *Real Housewives* show. Even the still-life drawings in your room, which form a kind of timeline of your decline. Once you must have been so good, but now your hands shake. You're right—it wears out before it runs out.

"Among other things," Dave said.

"Have you ever heard someone say they were too old for one of America's military adventures? Vietnam? Iraq? Afghanistan?"

"Sure. Although what they usually say is they were too young."

"AIDS was a war." Ollie was looking down at his gnarled hands, from which the talent was departing. "And I wasn't too old for all of it, because no one is when the war's on one's native soil, wouldn't you say?"

"I guess that's true enough."

"I was born in nineteen thirty. When AIDS was first observed and clinically described in the United States, I was fifty-two. I was living in New York, and working freelance for several advertising firms. My friends and I still used to go around to the clubs in the Village once in awhile. Not the Stonewall—a hellhole run by the Mafia—but some of the others. One night I was standing outside Peter Pepper's on Christopher Street, sharing a jay with a friend, and a bunch of young men went in. Good-looking guys in tight bellbottom pants and the shirts they all seemed to wear back then, the kind with the wide shoulders and narrow waists. Suede boots with stacked heels."

"Yummy boys," Dave ventured.

"I guess, but not *the* yummy boy. And my best friend—his name was Noah Freemont, died just last year, I went to the funeral—turned to me and said, 'They don't even see us anymore, do they?' I agreed. They saw you if you had enough money, but we were too . . . dignified for that, you might say. Paying for it was demeaning, although some of us did, from time to time. Yet in the late fifties, when I first came to New York . . ."

He shrugged and looked off into the distance.

"When you first came to New York?" Dave prompted.

"I'm thinking about how to say this. In the late fifties, when women were still sighing over Rock Hudson and Liberace, when homosexuality was the love that dared not speak its name instead of the one that never shuts up, my sex drive was at its absolute peak. In that way—there are others, I'm sure, many others—gay men and straight men are the same. I read somewhere that when they are in the presence of an attractive other, men think about sex every twenty seconds or so. But when a man's in his teens and twenties, he thinks about sex *constantly*, whether he's in the presence of an attractive other or not."

"You get hard when the wind blows," Dave said.

He was thinking of his first job, as a pump jockey, and of a pretty redhead he'd happened to see sliding out of the passenger seat of her boyfriend's truck. Her skirt had rucked up, revealing her plain white cotton panties for a single second, two at most. Yet he had played that moment over and over in his mind while masturbating, and although he had only been sixteen at the time, the memory was still fresh and clear. He doubted if that would have been the case if he'd been fifty. By then he'd seen plenty of women's underwear.

"Some of the conservative columnists called AIDS the gay plague, and with ill-concealed satisfaction. It *was* a plague, but by nineteen eighty-six or so, the gay community had a pretty good fix on it. We understood the two most basic preventive measures—no unprotected sex and no sharing of needles. But young men think they're immortal, and as my grandma used to say when she was in her cups, a stiff dick has no conscience. It's especially true when the owner of that dick is drunk, high, and in the throes of sexual attraction."

Ollie sighed, shrugged.

"Chances were taken. Mistakes were made. Even after the transmission vectors were well understood, tens of thousands of gay men died. People are only beginning to grasp the magnitude of that tragedy now that most folks understand gays don't choose their sexual orientation. Great poets, great musicians, great mathematicians and scientists—God knows how many died before their talents could flower. They died in gutters, in cold-water flats, in hospitals, and the indigent wards, all because they took a risk on a night when the music was loud, the wine was flowing, and the poppers were popping. By choice? There are still plenty who say so, but that's nonsense. The drive is too strong. Too *primal*. If I'd been born twenty years later, I might have been one of the casualties. My friend Noah, as well. But he died of a heart attack in his bed, and I'll die of . . . whatever. Because by fifty, there are fewer sexual temptations to resist, and even when the temptation is strong, the brain is sometimes able to overrule the cock, at least long enough to grab a condom. I'm not saying that plenty of men my age didn't die of AIDS. They did—no fool like an old fool, right? Some were my friends. But they were fewer than the younger fellows who jammed the clubs every night.

"My own clique—Noah, Henry Reed, John Rubin, Frank Diamond—sometimes went out just to watch those young guys do their mating dances. We didn't drool, but we watched. We weren't so different from the middle-aged hetero golfing buddies who go to Hooters once a week just to watch the waitresses bend over. That sort of behavior may be slightly pitiful, but it's not unnatural. Or do you disagree?"

Dave shook his head.

"One night four or five of us dropped by a dance club called Highpockets. I think we had just about decided to call it a night when this kid walked in on his own. Looked a little like David Bowie. He was tall, wearing tight white bike shorts and a blue tee with cutoff sleeves. Long blond hair, combed up in a high pompadour that was funny and sexy at the same time. High color—natural, not rouge—in his cheeks, along with a spangle of silvery stuff. A Cupid's bow of a mouth. Every eye in the place turned to look at him. Noah grabbed my arm and said, 'That's him. *That's* Mister Yummy. I'd give a thousand dollars to take him home.'

"I laughed and said a thousand dollars wouldn't buy him. At that age, and with those looks, all he wanted was to be admired and desired. Also to have great sex as often as possible. And when you're twenty-two, that's often.

"Pretty soon he was part of a group of good-looking guys—although none as good-looking as he was—all of them laughing and drinking and dancing whatever dance was in back then. None of them sparing a glance for the quartet of middle-aged men sitting at a table far back from the dance floor and drinking wine. Middle-aged men still five or ten years from quitting their efforts to look younger than their age. Why would he look at us with all those lovely young men vying for his attention?

"And Frank Diamond said, 'He'll be dead in a year. See how pretty he is then.' Only he didn't just say it; he spit it out. Like that was some kind of weird . . . I don't know . . . *consolation* prize."

Ollie, who had survived the age of the deep closet to live in one where gay marriage was legal in most states, once more shrugged his thin shoulders. As if to say it was all water under the bridge.

"So that was our Mister Yummy, a summation of all that was beautiful and desirable and out of reach. I never saw him again until two weeks ago. Not at Highpockets, not at Peter Pepper's or the Tall Glass, not at any of the other clubs I went to . . . although

I went to those places less and less frequently as the so-called Reagan Era wore on. By the late eighties, going to the gay clubs was too weird. Like attending the masquerade ball in Poe's story about the Red Death. You know, 'Come on, everybody! Kick out the jams, have another glass of champagne, and ignore all those people dropping like flies.' There was no fun in that unless you were twenty-two and still under the impression that you were bulletproof."

"It must have been hard."

Ollie raised the hand not wedded to his cane and waggled it in a *comme ci, comme ça* gesture. "Was and wasn't. It was what the recovering alkies call life on life's terms."

Dave considered letting it go at that, and decided he couldn't. The gift of the watch was too dismaying. "Listen to your uncle Dave, Ollie. Words of one syllable: *you did not see that kid*. You might have seen someone who looked a little like him, but if your Mister Yummy was twenty-two back then, he'd be in his fifties himself by now. If he avoided AIDS, that is. It was just a trick your brain played on you."

"My *elderly* brain," Ollie said, smiling. "My going-on-*senile* brain."

"I never said senile. You're not that. But your brain *is* elderly."

"Undoubtedly, but it was him. It was. The first time I saw him, he was on Maryland Avenue, at the foot of the main drive. A few days later he was lounging on the porch steps below the main entrance, smoking a clove cigarette. Two days ago he was sitting on a bench outside the admission office. Still wearing that blue sleeveless tee and those blinding white shorts.

He should have stopped traffic, but nobody saw him.
Except for me, that is."

I refuse to humor him, Dave thought. *He deserves better.*

"You're hallucinating, pal."

Ollie was unfazed. "Just now he was in the common room, watching TV with the rest of the early birds. I waved to him, and he waved back." A grin, startlingly youthful, broke on Ollie's face. "He also tipped me a wink."

"White bike shorts? Sleeveless tee? Twenty-two and good-looking? I may be straight, but I think I would have noticed that."

"He's here for me, so I'm the only one who can see him. QED." He hoisted himself to his feet. "Shall we go back? I'm ready for coffee."

They walked toward the patio, where they would climb the steps as carefully as they had descended them. Once they had lived in the Reagan Era; now they lived in the Era of Glass Hips.

When they reached the flagstones outside the common room, they both paused for breath. When Dave had his, he said, "So what have we learned today, class? That death personified isn't a skeleton riding on a pale horse with a scythe over his shoulder, but a hot dancehall kid with glitter on his cheeks."

"I imagine different people see different avatars," Ollie said mildly. "According to what I've read, the majority see their mothers once they reach death's door."

"Ollie, the majority sees *no one*. And you're not in mortal—"

"My mother, however, died shortly after I was born, so I wouldn't even recognize her."

He started for the double doors, but Dave took his arm. "I'll keep the watch until the Halloween party, how's that? Four months. And I'll wind it religiously. But if you're still around then, you take it back. Deal?"

Ollie beamed. "Absolutely. Let's go see how Olga's doing with La Tour Eiffel, shall we?"

Olga was back at the card table, staring down at the puzzle. It was not a happy stare. "I left you the last three pieces, Dave." Unhappy or not, she was at least clear on who he was again. "But that will still leave four holes. After a week's work, this is very disappointing."

"Shit happens, Olga," Dave said, sitting down. He tapped the remaining pieces into place with a satisfaction that went all the way back to rainy days at summer camp. Where, he now realized, the common room had been quite a bit like this. Life was a short shelf that came with bookends.

"Yes it does," she said, contemplating the missing four pieces. "It certainly does. But so *much* shit, Bob. So *much*."

"Olga, I'm Dave."

She turned her frown on him. "That's what I said."

No sense arguing, and no sense trying to convince her that nine hundred and ninety-six out of a thousand was a fine score. *She's ten years from a hundred and still thinks she deserves perfection,* Dave thought. *Some people have remarkably sturdy illusions.*

He looked up and saw Ollie emerging from the closet-sized craft center adjacent to the common room. He was holding a sheet of tissue paper and a pen. He made his way to the table and floated the tissue onto the puzzle.

"Here, here, what are you doing?" Olga asked.

"Show some patience for once in your life, dear. You'll see."

She stuck out her lower lip like a pouty child. "No. I'm going to smoke. If you want to take that damn thing apart, be my guest. Put it back in the box or knock it on the floor. Your choice. It's no good the way it is."

She stalked off with as much hauteur as her arthritis would allow. Ollie dropped into her seat with a sigh of relief. "That's much better. Bending's a bitch these days." He traced two of the missing pieces, which happened to be close together, then moved the paper to trace the other two.

Dave watched with interest. "Will that work?"

"Oh yeah," Ollie said. "There are some cardboard FedEx boxes in the mail room. I'll filch one of them. Do some cutting and a little drawing. Just don't let Olga have a tantrum and disassemble the damn thing before I get back."

"If you want photos—you know, for matching purposes—I'll get my iPhone."

"Don't need it." Ollie tapped his forehead gravely. "Got my camera up here. It's an old Brownie box instead of a smartphone, but even these days it works pretty well."

III

Olga was still in a snit when she came back from the loading dock, and she did indeed want to disassemble the not-quite-complete jigsaw, but Dave was able to distract her by waving the cribbage board in her face.

They played three games. Dave lost all three, and was skunked in the last. Olga was not always sure who he was, and there were days when she believed she was back in Atlanta, living in an aunt's boardinghouse, but when it came to cribbage, she never missed a double run or a fifteen-for-two.

She's also really lucky, Dave thought, not without resentment. Who winds up with twenty points in the goddam crib?

Around quarter past eleven (Fox News had given way to Drew Carey flogging prizes on *The Price Is Right*), Ollie Franklin returned and made his way to the cribbage board. A shave and a neat short-sleeved shirt made him look almost dapper. "Hey, Olga. I have something for you, girlfriend."

"I'm not your girlfriend," Olga said. There was a small, meanly amused glint in her eye. "If you ever *had* a girlfriend, I'll be dipped in bearshit."

"Ingratitude, thy name is woman," Ollie said without rancor. "Hold out your hand." And when she did, he dropped four newly constructed jigsaw pieces into it.

She glared at them suspiciously. "What're these?"

"The missing pieces."

"Missing pieces to *what*?"

"The puzzle you and Dave were doing. Remember the puzzle?"

Dave could almost hear the clicking beneath her frizzy cloud of white hair as old relays and corroded memory banks came to life. "Of course I do. But these will never fit."

"Try them," Ollie invited.

Dave took them from her before she could. To him they looked perfect. One showed that lacework of girders; the two that had been close together showed part of a pink cloud at the horizon; the fourth showed the forehead and pertly cocked beret of a tiny *boulevardier* who could have been promenading on the Place Vendôme. It was pretty amazing, he thought. Ollie might be eighty-five, but he still had game. Dave returned the pieces to Olga, who tapped them in, one after the other. Each fit perfectly.

"*Voilà,*" Dave said, and shook Ollie's hand. "*Tout finit.* Wonderful."

Olga was bent so close to the puzzle that her nose was touching it. "This new girder piece doesn't quite match up with the ones around it."

Dave said, "That's a little thankless, even for you, Olga."

Olga made a *hmpf* sound. Over her head, Ollie waggled his eyebrows.

Dave waggled back. "Sit with us at lunch."

"I may skip lunch," Ollie said. "Our walk and my latest artistic triumph have tired me out." He bent to look at the puzzle and sighed. "No, they don't match. But close."

"Close only counts in horseshoes," Olga said. "*Boyfriend.*"

Ollie made his slow way toward the door opening on the Evergreen Wing, cane tapping its unmistakable one-two-three rhythm. He didn't appear at lunch, and when he didn't show up for dinner, that day's duty nurse checked on him and found him lying on the coverlet of his bed, with his talented hands laced together on his chest. He seemed to have died as he lived, peacefully and with no fuss.

That evening, Dave tried the door of his late friend's suite and found it open. He sat on the stripped bed with the silver pocket watch laid on his palm, the cover open so he could watch the second hand go around in the little circle above the 6. He looked at Ollie's possessions—the books on the shelf, the sketchpads on the desk, the various drawings taped to the walls—and wondered who would take them. The ne'er-do-well brother, he supposed. He fished for the name, and it came to him: Tom. And the niece was Martha.

Over the bed was a charcoal drawing of a handsome young man with his hair combed high and spangles on his cheeks. On his Cupid's-bow lips was a smile. It was small but inviting.

IV

The summer came full, then began to ebb. School-buses rolled down Maryland Avenue. Olga Glukhov's condition declined; she mistook Dave for her late husband more frequently. Her cribbage skills remained, but she began to lose her English. Although Dave's older son and daughter lived close by in the suburbs, it was Peter who came to visit most frequently, driving in from the farm in Hemingford County sixty miles away and often taking his father out to dinner.

Halloween rolled around. The staff decorated the common room with orange and black streamers. The residents of Lakeview Assisted Living Center celebrated All Hallows with cider, pumpkin pie, and popcorn balls for the few whose teeth were still up to the challenge. Many spent the evening in costume, which made Dave Calhoun think of something his old friend had said during their last conversation—

about how, in the late eighties, going to the gay clubs had been too much like attending the masquerade in Poe's story about the Red Death. He supposed Lakeview was also a kind of club, and sometimes it was gay, but there was a drawback: you couldn't leave, unless you had relatives willing to take you in. Peter and his wife would have done that for Dave if he had asked, would have given him the room where their son Jerome had once lived, but Peter and Alicia were getting on themselves now, and he would not inflict himself on them.

One warm day in early November, he went out onto the flagstone patio and sat on one of the benches there. The paths beyond were inviting in the sunshine, but he no longer dared the steps. He might fall going down, which would be bad. He might not be able to get back up again without help, which would be humiliating.

He spied a young woman standing by the fountain. She wore the kind of shin-length, frilly-collared dress you only saw nowadays in old black-and-white movies on TCM. Her hair was bright red. She smiled at him. And waved.

Why, look at you, Dave thought. *Didn't I see you not long after World War II ended, getting out of your boyfriend's pickup truck at the Humble Oil station in Omaha?*

As if hearing this thought, the pretty redhead tipped him a wink and then twitched up the hem of her dress slightly, showing her knees.

Hello, Miss Yummy, Dave thought, and then: *Once you did a lot better than that.* The memory made him laugh.

She laughed in return. This he saw but could not hear, although she was close and his ears were still sharp. Then she walked behind the fountain . . . and didn't come out. Yet Dave had reason to believe she would be back. He had glimpsed the life-force down there, no more and no less. The strong beating heart of beauty and desire. Next time she would be closer.

V

Peter came into town the following week, and they went out to dinner at a nice place close by. Dave ate well, and drank two glasses of wine. They perked him up considerably. When the meal was done, he took Ollie's silver watch from his inner coat pocket, coiled the heavy chain around it, and pushed it across the tablecloth to his son.

"What's this?" Peter asked.

"It was a gift from a friend," Dave said. "He gave it to me shortly before he passed on. I want you to have it."

Peter attempted to push it back. "I can't take this, Dad. It's too nice."

"Actually, you'd be doing me a favor. Because of the arthritis. It's very hard for me to wind it, and pretty soon I won't be able to at all. Darn thing's at least a hundred and twenty years old, and a watch that's made it that far deserves to run as long as it can. So please. Take it."

"Well, when you put it that way . . ." Peter took the watch and dropped it into his pocket. "Thanks, Dad. It's a beaut."

At the next table—so close Dave could have reached out and touched her—sat the redhead. There was no meal in front of her, but no one seemed to notice. At this distance, Dave saw that she was more than pretty; she was downright beautiful. Surely more beautiful than that long-ago girl had been, sliding out of her boyfriend's pickup with her skirt momentarily bunched in her lap, but what of that? Such revisions were, like birth and death, the ordinary course of things. Memory's job was not only to recall the past but to burnish it.

The redhead slid her skirt up farther this time, revealing one long white thigh for a second. Perhaps even two. And winked.

Dave winked back.

Peter turned to look and saw only an empty four-top table with a RESERVED sign on it. When he turned back to his father, his eyebrows were raised.

Dave smiled. "Just something in my eye. It's gone now. Why don't you get the check? I'm tired and ready to go back."

Thinking of Michael McDowell

There's a saying: "If you can remember the sixties, you weren't there." Total bullshit, and here's a case in point. Tommy wasn't his name, and he wasn't the one who died, but otherwise, this is how it went down, back when we all thought we were going to live forever and change the world.

Tommy

Tommy died in 1969.
He was a hippie with leukemia.
Bummer, man.

After the funeral came the reception at Newman
    Center.
That's what his folks called it: the reception.
My friend Phil said, "Isn't that what you have after a
    fucking *wedding*?"

The freaks all went to the reception.
Darryl wore his cape.
There were sandwiches to eat and grape drink in
    Dixie Cups.
My friend Phil said, "What is this grape shit?"
I said it was Za-Rex. I recognized it, I said, from MYF.
"What's *that* shit?" asked Phil.
"Methodist Youth Fellowship," I said.
"I went for ten years and once did
a flannelboard of Noah and the Ark."
"Fuck your Ark," said Phil.
"And fuck the animals who rode on it."
Phil: a young man with strong opinions.

After the reception, Tommy's parents went home.
I imagine they cried and cried.
The freaks went to 110 North Main.
We cranked up the stereo. I found some Grateful
    Dead records.
I hated the Dead. Of Jerry Garcia I used to say,
"I'll be grateful when he's dead!"
(Turned out I wasn't.)
Oh well, Tommy liked them.
(Also, dear God, Kenny Rogers.)
We smoked dope in Zig-Zag papers.
We smoked Winstons and Pall Malls.
We drank beer and ate scrambled eggs.

We rapped about Tommy.
It was pretty nice.
And when the Wilde-Stein Club showed up—all
    eight of them—we let them in
because Tommy was gay and sometimes wore
    Darryl's cape.

We all agreed his folks had done him righteous.
Tommy wrote down what he wanted and they gave
    him most of it.
He was dressed in his best as he lay in his new
    narrow apartment.
He wore his bellbottom blue jeans and his favorite
    tie-dye shirt.
(Melissa Big Girl Freek made that shirt.
I don't know what happened to her.
She was there one day, then gone down that lost
    highway.
I associate her with melting snow.

Main Street in Orono would gleam so wet and
    bright it hurt your eyes.
That was the winter The Lemon Pipers sang "Green
    Tambourine.")
His hair was shampooed. It went to his shoulders.
Man, it was clean!
I bet the mortician washed it.
He was wearing his headband
with the peace sign stitched in white silk.

"He looked like a dude," said Phil. He was getting
    drunk.
(Phil was always getting drunk.)
Jerry Garcia was singing "Truckin." It's a pretty
    stupid song.
"Fuckin Tommy!" said Phil. "Drink to the
    motherfucker!"
We drank to the motherfucker.

"He wasn't wearing his special button," said Indian
    Scontras.
Indian was in the Wilde-Stein Club.
Back then he knew every dance.
These days he sells insurance in Brewer.
"He told his mother he wanted to be buried wearing
    his button.
That is so bogus."
I said, "His mom just moved it under his vest. I
    looked."

It was a leather vest with silver buttons.
Tommy bought it at the Free Fair.
I was with him that day. There was a rainbow and

from a loudspeaker Canned Heat sang "Let's Work
    Together."
I'M HERE AND I'M QUEER said the button his
    mother moved beneath his vest.
"She should have left it alone," said Indian
    Scontras.
"Tommy was proud. He was a very proud queer."
Indian Scontras was crying.
Now he sells whole life policies and has 3
    daughters.
Turned out not to be so gay, after all, but
selling insurance is *very* queer, in my opinion.
"She was his mother," I said, "and kissed his scrapes
    when he was young."
"What does that have to do with it?" asked Indian
    Scontras.

"Fuckin Tommy!" said Phil, and raised his beer
    high.
"Let's toast the motherfucker!"
We toasted the motherfucker.

That was forty years ago.
Tonight I wonder how many hippies died in those
    few sunshine years.

Must have been quite a few. It's just statistics, man.
And I'm not just talking about
!!THE WAR!!
You had your car accidents.
Your drug overdoses.
    Plus booze
        bar fights

the occasional suicide
and let's not leave out leukemia.

All the usual suspects is all I'm saying.
How many were buried in their hippie duds?
This question occurs to me in the whispers of the
    night.
It must have been quite a few, although
it was fleeting, the time of the freaks.
Their Free Fair is now underground
where they still wear their bellbottoms and
    headbands
and there is mold on the full sleeves of their
    psychedelic shirts.

The hair in those narrow rooms is brittle, but still
    long.
"The Man's" barber has not touched it in forty
    years.
No gray has frosted it.
What about the ones who went down
clasping signs that said HELL NO WE WON'T
    GO?
What about the car accident boy buried with a
    McCarthy sticker
on the lid of his coffin?
What about the girl with the stars on her
    forehead?
(They have fallen now, I imagine, from her
    parchment skin.)

These are the soldiers of love who never sold
    insurance.

These are the fashion dudes who never went out of
fashion.

Sometimes, at night, I think of hippies asleep in the
earth.

Here's to Tommy.

Drink to the motherfucker.

For D. F.

In 1999, while taking a walk near my home, I was hit by a guy driving a van. He was doing about forty, and the collision should have killed me. I guess I must have taken some sort of half-assed evasive action at the last moment, although I don't remember doing that. What I do remember is the aftermath. An event that occurred in two or three seconds beside a rural Maine highway resulted in two or three years of physical therapy and slow rehabilitation. During those long months spent recovering some range of movement in my right leg and then learning to walk again, I had plenty of time to reflect on what some philosophers have called "the problem of pain."

This story is about that, and I wrote it years later, when the worst of my own pain had receded to a steady low mutter. Like several other stories in this book, "The Little Green God of Agony" is a search for closure. But, like *all* the stories in this book, its principal purpose is to entertain. Although life experiences are the basis of all stories, I'm not in the business of confessional fiction.

The Little Green God
of Agony

"I was in an accident," Newsome said.

Katherine MacDonald, sitting beside the bed and attaching one of four TENS units to Newsome's scrawny thigh just below the basketball shorts he now always wore, did not look up. Her face was carefully blank. She was a piece of human furniture in this big bedroom where she now spent most of her working life, and that was the way she liked it. Attracting Mr. Newsome's attention was usually a bad idea, as all of his employees knew. But her thoughts ran on, just the same.

Now you tell them that you actually caused the accident. Because you think taking responsibility makes you look like a hero.

"Actually," Newsome said, "I caused the accident. Not so tight, Kat, please."

She could have pointed out, as she had at the start, that TENS units lost their efficacy if they weren't drawn tight to the outraged nerves they were supposed to soothe, but she was a fast learner. She loosened the Velcro strap a little while her thoughts ran on.

The pilot told you there were thunderstorms in the Omaha area.

"The pilot told me there were thunderstorms in that part of the world," Newsome continued. The two men listened closely. Jensen had heard it all before, of course, but you always listened closely when the man doing the talking was the sixth-richest man not just in America but in the world. Three of the other five mega-rich guys were dark-complected fellows who wore robes and drove around desert countries in armored Mercedes-Benzes.

But I told him it was imperative that I make that meeting.

"But I told him it was imperative that I make that meeting."

The man sitting next to Newsome's personal assistant was the one who interested her—in an anthropological sort of way. His name was Rideout. He was tall and thin, maybe sixty, wearing plain gray pants and a white shirt buttoned all the way to his scrawny neck, which was red with overshaving. Kat supposed he'd wanted to get a close one before meeting the sixth-richest man in the world. Beneath his chair was the only item he'd carried in to this meeting, a long black lunchbox with a curved top meant to hold a thermos. A workingman's lunchbox, although what he claimed to be was a minister. So far Mr. Rideout hadn't said a word, but Kat didn't need her ears to know what he was. The whiff of charlatan about him was even stronger than the smell of his aftershave. In fifteen years as a nurse specializing in pain patients, she had met her share. At least this one wasn't wearing any crystals.

Now tell them about your revelation, she thought as

she carried her stool around to the other side of the bed. It was on casters, but Newsome didn't like the sound when she rolled on it. She might have told another patient that carrying the stool wasn't in her contract, but when you were being paid five grand a week for what were essentially human caretaking services, you kept your smart remarks to yourself. Nor did you tell the patient that emptying and washing out bedpans wasn't in your contract. Although lately her silent compliance was wearing a little thin. She felt it happening. Like the fabric of a shirt that had been washed and worn too many times.

Newsome was speaking primarily to the fellow in the farmer-goes-to-town getup. "As I lay on the runway in the rain among the burning pieces of a fourteen-million-dollar aircraft, most of the clothes torn off my body—that'll happen when you hit pavement and roll fifty or sixty feet—I had a revelation."

Actually, two of them, Kat thought as she strapped a second TENS unit around his other wasted, flabby, scarred leg.

"Actually, two revelations," Newsome said. "One was that it was very good to be alive, although I understood—even before the pain that's been my constant companion for the last two years started to eat through the shock—that I had been badly hurt. The second was that the word *imperative* is used very loosely by most people, including my former self. There are only two imperatives in human existence. One is life itself, the other is freedom from pain. Do you agree, Reverend Rideout?" And before Rideout could agree (for surely he would do nothing else), Newsome said in his waspy, hectoring, old man's voice: "Not so goddam *tight*, Kat! How many times do I have to tell you?"

"Sorry," she murmured, and loosened the strap.

Melissa, the housekeeper, looking trim in a white blouse and high-waisted white slacks, came in with a coffee tray. Jensen accepted a cup, along with two packets of artificial sweetener. The new guy, the bottom-of-the-barrel so-called reverend, only shook his head. Maybe he had some kind of holy coffee in his lunchbox thermos.

Kat didn't get an offer. When she took coffee, she took it in the kitchen with the rest of the help. Or in the summerhouse . . . only this wasn't summer. It was November, and wind-driven rain lashed the windows.

"Shall I turn you on, Mr. Newsome, or would you prefer that I leave now?"

She didn't want to leave. She'd heard the whole story many times before—the important meeting in Omaha, the crash, Andrew Newsome ejected from the burning plane, the broken bones, chipped spine, and dislocated hip, the twenty-four months of unrelieved suffering that had followed—and it bored her. But Rideout was kind of interesting. Other charlatans would undoubtedly follow, now that all reputable relief resources had been exhausted, but Rideout was the first, and Kat wanted to observe how the farmer-looking fellow would go about separating Andy Newsome from a large chunk of his cash. Or how he would try. Newsome hadn't amassed his fortune by being stupid, but of course he wasn't the same man he had been, no matter how real his pain might be. On that subject, Kat had her own opinions, but this was the best job she'd ever had. At least in terms of money. And if Newsome wanted to continue suffering, wasn't that his choice?

"Go ahead, honey, turn me on." He waggled his

eyebrows at her. Once the lechery might have been real (Kat thought Melissa might have information on that subject), but now it was just a pair of shaggy eyebrows working on muscle memory.

Kat plugged the cords into the control unit and flicked the switch. Properly attached, the TENS units would have sent a weak electrical current into Newsome's muscles, a therapy that seemed to have some ameliorative effects . . . although no one could say exactly why, or if they were entirely of the placebo variety. Be that as it might, they would do nothing for Newsome tonight. Hooked up as loosely as they were, they had been reduced to expensive joy-buzzers.

"Shall I—?"

"Stay!" he said. "Therapy!"

The lord wounded in battle commands, and I obey.

She bent over to pull her chest of goodies out from under the bed. It was filled with tools many of her past clients referred to as implements of torture. Jensen and Rideout paid no attention to her. They continued to look at Newsome, who might (or might not) have been granted revelations that had changed his priorities and outlook on life, but who still enjoyed holding court.

He told them about awakening in a cage of metal and mesh. There were steel gantries called external fixators on both legs and one arm to immobilize joints that had been repaired with "about a hundred" steel pins (actually seventeen; Kat had seen the X-rays). The fixators were anchored in the outraged and splintered femurs, tibiae, fibulae, humerus, radius, ulna. His back was encased in a kind of chain-mail girdle that went from his hips to the nape of his neck. He talked about sleepless nights that seemed to go on not for hours but for years. He talked about the crushing headaches. He told them about how even wiggling his toes caused pain all the way up to his jaw, and the shrieking agony that bit into his legs when the doctors insisted that he move them, fixators and all, so he wouldn't entirely lose their function. He told them about the bedsores and how he bit back howls of hurt and outrage when the nurses attempted to roll him on his side so the sores could be flushed out.

"There have been another dozen operations in the last two years," he said with a kind of dark pride.

Actually, Kat knew, there had been five, two of those to remove the external fixators when the bones were sufficiently healed. Unless you included the minor procedure to reset his broken fingers, that was. Then you could say there were six, but she didn't consider surgical stuff necessitating no more than local anesthetic to be "operations." If that were the case, she'd had a dozen herself, most of them while listening to Muzak in a dentist's chair.

Now we get to the false promises, she thought as she placed a gel pad in the crook of Newsome's right knee and laced her hands together on the hanging hot-water bottles of muscle beneath his right thigh. *That comes next.*

"The doctors promised me the pain would abate," Newsome said. His eyes were fixed on Rideout. "That in six weeks I'd only need the narcotics before and after my physical therapy sessions with the Queen of Pain here. That I'd be walking again by the summer of two thousand ten. *Last* summer." He paused for effect. "Reverend Rideout, those were false promises. I have almost no flexion in my knees at all, and the pain in my hips and back is beyond description. The doctors—*ah*! *Oh*! Stop, Kat, *stop*!"

She had raised his right leg to a ten-degree angle, perhaps a little more. Not even enough to hold the cushioning pad in place.

"Let it go down! Let it *down*, goddammit!"

Kat relaxed her hold on his knee, and the leg returned to the hospital bed. Ten degrees. Possibly twelve. Whoop-de-do. Sometimes she got it all the way to fifteen—and the left leg, which was a little better, to twenty degrees of flex—before he started hollering like a chickenshit kid who sees a hypodermic needle in the school nurse's hand. The doctors guilty of false promises had not been guilty of false advertising; they had told him the pain was coming. Kat had been there as a silent onlooker during several of those consultations. They had told him he would swim in pain before those crucial tendons, shortened by the accident and frozen in place by the fixators, stretched out and once again became limber. He would have plenty of pain before he was able to get the bend in his knees back to ninety degrees. Which meant before he would be able to sit in a chair or behind the wheel of a car. The same was true of his back and his neck. The road to recovery led through the Land of Pain, that was all.

These were true promises Andrew Newsome had chosen not to hear. It was his belief—never stated baldly, in words of one syllable, but undoubtedly one of the stars he steered by—that the sixth-richest man in the world should not have to visit the Land of Pain under any circumstances, only the Costa del Sol of Full Recovery. Blaming the doctors followed as day follows night. And of course he blamed fate. Things like this were not supposed to happen to guys like him.

Melissa came back with cookies on a tray. Newsome waved a hand—twisted and scarred in the accident—at her irritably. "No one's in the mood for baked goods, 'Lissa."

Here was another thing Kat MacDonald had discovered about those golden dollar-babies who had amassed assets beyond ordinary comprehension: they felt very confident about speaking for everyone in the room.

Melissa gave her little Mona Lisa smile, then turned (almost pirouetted) and left the room. *Glided* from the room. She had to be at least forty-five, but looked younger. She wasn't sexy; nothing so vulgar. Rather there was an ice-queen glamour about her that made Kat think of Ingrid Bergman. Icy or not, Kat supposed men would wonder how that chestnut hair would look freed from its clips and all mussed up. How her coral lipstick would look smeared on her teeth and up one cheek. Kat, who considered herself dumpy, told herself at least once a day that she wasn't jealous of that smooth, cool face. Or that tight, heart-shaped bottom.

Kat returned to the other side of the bed and prepared to lift Newsome's left leg until he yelled at her again to stop, goddammit, did she want to kill him? *If you were another patient, I'd tell you the facts of life,* she thought. *I'd tell you to stop looking for shortcuts, because there are none. Not even for the sixth-richest man in the world. I'd help you if you'd let me, but as long as you keep looking for a way to buy your way out of that bed, you're on your own.*

She placed the pad under his knee. Grasped the

hanging bags of flesh that should have been harden-
ing up again by now. Began to bend the leg. Waited
for him to scream at her to stop. And she would.
Because five thousand dollars a week added up to a
cool quarter mil a year. Did he know that part of what
he was buying was her complicity in his failure to
improve? How could he not?

*Now tell them about the doctors. Geneva, London,
Madrid, Mexico City.*

"I've been to doctors all over the world," he told
Rideout. The reverend still hadn't said a word, just
sat there with the red wattles of his overshaved neck
hanging over his buttoned-to-the-neck country
preacher shirt. He was wearing big yellow workboots.
The heel of one almost touched his black lunchbox.
"Teleconferencing would be the easier way to go, given
my condition, but of course that doesn't cut it in cases
like mine. So I've gone in person, in spite of the pain it
causes me. We've been everywhere, haven't we, Kat?"

"Indeed we have," she said, very slowly continuing
to bend the leg. On which he would have been walking
by now, if he weren't such a child about the pain. Such
a spoiled baby. On crutches, yes, but walking. And in
another year, he would have been able to throw the
crutches away. Only in another year he would still
be here, in this two-hundred-thousand-dollar state-
of-the-art hospital bed. And she would still be with
him. Still taking his hush money. How much would
be enough? Two million? She told herself that now,
but she'd told herself not so long ago half a million
would be enough, and had since moved the goalposts.
Money was wretched that way.

"We've seen specialists in Mexico, Geneva, London, Rome, Paris . . . where else, Kat?"

"Vienna," she said. "And San Francisco, of course."

Newsome snorted. "Doctor there told me I was manufacturing my own pain. Hysterical conversion, he said. To keep from doing the hard work of rehabilitation. But he was a Paki. And a queer. A queer Paki, how's that for a combo?" He gave a brief bark of laughter, then peered at Rideout. "I'm not offending you, am I, Reverend?"

Rideout moved his head side to side in a negative gesture. Twice. Very slowly.

"Good, good. Stop, Kat, that's enough."

"A little more," she coaxed.

"Stop, I said. That's all I can take."

She let the leg subside and began to manipulate his left arm. That he allowed. He often told people both of his arms had also been broken, but this wasn't true. The left one had only been sprained. He also told people he was lucky not to be in a wheelchair, but the all-the-bells-and-whistles hospital bed suggested strongly that this was luck on which he had no intention of capitalizing in the near future. The all-the-bells-and-whistles hospital bed *was* his wheelchair. He had ridden all over the world in it.

Neuropathic pain. It's a great mystery. Perhaps insoluble. The drugs no longer work.

"The consensus is that I'm suffering from neuropathic pain."

And cowardice.

"It's a great mystery."

Also a good excuse.

"Perhaps insoluble."

Especially when you don't try.

"The drugs no longer work and the doctors can't help me. That's why I've brought you here, Reverend

Rideout. Your references in the matter of . . . er . . . healing . . . are very strong."

Rideout stood up. Kat hadn't realized how tall he was. His shadow scared up behind him on the wall even higher. Almost to the ceiling. His eyes, sunken deep in their sockets, regarded Newsome solemnly. He had charisma, of that there could be no doubt. It didn't surprise her, the charlatans of the world couldn't get along without it, but she hadn't realized how much or how strong it was until he got to his feet and towered over them. Jensen was actually craning his neck to take him in. There was movement in the corner of Kat's eye. She looked and saw Melissa standing in the doorway. So now they were all here except for Tonya, the cook.

Outside, the wind rose to a shriek. The glass in the windows rattled.

"I don't heal," Rideout said. He was from Arkansas, Kat believed—that was where Newsome's latest Gulfstream IV had picked him up, at least—but his voice was accentless. And flat.

"No?" Newsome looked disappointed. Petulant. Maybe, Kat thought, a little scared. "I sent a team of investigators, and they assure me that in many cases—"

"I *expel*."

Up went the shaggy eyebrows. "I beg your pardon."

Rideout came to the bed and stood there with his long-fingered hands laced loosely together at the level of his crotch. His deep-set eyes looked somberly down at the man in the bed. "I exterminate the pest from the wounded body it's feeding on, just as a bug exterminator would exterminate termites feeding on a house."

Now, Kat thought, *I have heard absolutely everything.* But Newsome was fascinated. *Like a kid watching a three-card monte expert on a street corner,* she thought.

"You've been possessed, sir."

"Yes," Newsome said. "That's what it feels like. Especially at night. The nights are . . . very long."

"Every man or woman who suffers pain is possessed, of course, but in some unfortunate people—you are one—the problem goes deeper. The possession isn't a transient thing but a permanent condition. One that worsens. Doctors don't believe, because they are men of science. But *you* believe, don't you? Because you're the one who's suffering."

"You bet," Newsome breathed. Kat, sitting beside him on her stool, had to work very hard to keep from rolling her eyes.

"In these unfortunates, pain opens the way for a demon god. It's small, but dangerous. It feeds on a special kind of hurt produced only by certain special people."

Genius, Kat thought, *Newsome's going to love that.*

"Once the god finds its way in, pain becomes agony. It will feed until you are all used up. Then it will cast you aside, sir, and move on."

Kat surprised herself by saying, "What god would that be? Certainly not the one you preach about. That one is the God of love. Or so I grew up believing."

Jensen was frowning at her and shaking his head. He clearly expected an explosion from the boss . . . but a little smile had touched the corners of Newsome's lips. "What do you say to that, Rev?"

"I say that there are many gods. The fact that our Lord, the Lord God of Hosts, rules them all—and on the Day of Judgment will *destroy* them all—does not change that. These little gods have been worshipped by people both ancient and modern. They have their powers, and our God sometimes allows those powers to be exercised."

As a test, Kat thought.

"As a test of our strength and faith." Then Rideout turned to Newsome and said something that surprised her. "You are a man of much strength and little faith."

Newsome, although not used to hearing criticism, nevertheless smiled. "I don't have much in the way of Christian faith, that's true, but I have faith in myself. I also have faith in money. How much do you want?"

Rideout returned the smile, exposing teeth that were little more than tiny eroded gravestones. If he had ever seen a dentist, it had been many moons ago. Also, he was a tobacco chewer. Kat's father, who had died of mouth cancer, had had the same discolored teeth.

"How much would you pay to be free of your pain, sir?"

"Ten million dollars," Newsome replied promptly.

Kat heard Melissa gasp.

"But I didn't get to where I am by being a sucker. If you do whatever it is you do—expelling, exterminating, exorcising, call it what you want—you get the money. In cash, if you don't mind spending the night. Fail, and you get nothing. Except your first and only roundtrip on a private jet. For that there will be no charge. After all, *I* reached out to *you.*"

"No."

Rideout said it mildly, standing there beside the bed, close enough to Kat so she could smell the mothballs that had been recently keeping his dress pants (maybe his only pair, unless he had another to preach in) whole. She could also smell some strong soap.

"No?" Newsome looked frankly startled. "You tell me no?" Then he began to smile again. This time it was the secretive and rather unpleasant smile he wore when he made his phone calls and did his deals. "I get it. Now comes the curveball. I'm disappointed, Reverend Rideout. I really hoped you were on the level." He turned to Kat, causing her to draw back a bit. "You, of course, think I've lost my mind. But I haven't shared the investigators' reports with you. Have I?"

"No," she said.

"There's no curveball," Rideout said. "I haven't performed an expulsion in five years. Did your investigators tell you that?"

Newsome didn't reply. He was looking up at the thin, towering man with a certain unease.

Jensen said, "Is it because you've lost your powers? If that's the case, why did you come?"

"It's God's power, sir, not mine, and I haven't lost it. But an expulsion takes great energy and great strength. Five years ago I suffered a major heart attack shortly after performing one on a young girl who had been in a terrible car accident. We were successful, she and I, but the cardiologist I consulted in Jonesboro told me that if I ever exerted myself in such a way again, I might suffer another attack. This one fatal."

Newsome raised a gnarled hand—not without effort—to the side of his mouth and spoke to Kat and Melissa in a comic stage whisper. "I think he wants twenty million."

"What I want, sir, is seven hundred and fifty thousand."

Newsome just stared at him. It was Melissa who asked, "Why?"

"I am pastor of a church in Titusville. The Church of Holy Faith, it's called. Only there's no church anymore. We had a dry summer in my part of the world. There was a wildfire, started by drunken campers. My church is now just a concrete footprint and a few charred beams. I and my parishioners have been worshipping in an abandoned gas station–convenience store on the Jonesboro Pike. It is not satisfactory during the winter months, and there are no homes large enough to accommodate us. We are many but poor."

Kat listened with interest. As con-man stories went, this was an excellent one. It had all the right sympathy hooks.

Jensen, who still had the body of a college athlete to go with the mind of a Harvard MBA, asked the obvious question. "Insurance?"

Rideout once more shook his head in that deliberate way: left, right, left, right, back to center. He still stood towering over Newsome's state-of-the-art bed like some country-ass guardian angel. "We trust in God."

"You might have been better off with Allstate," Melissa said.

Newsome was smiling. Kat could tell from the stiff way he held his body that he was in serious discomfort—his pills were now half an hour over-due—but he was ignoring the pain because he was interested. That he *could* ignore it was something she'd known for quite awhile now. He could master the pain if he chose to. He had resources. She had thought she was merely irritated with this, but now, probably prompted by the appearance of the charlatan

from Arkansas, she discovered she was actually infuriated. It was so *wasteful*.

"I have consulted with a local builder—not a member of my flock, but a man of good repute who has
done repairs for me in the past and quotes a fair price.
He tells me that it will cost approximately seven hundred and fifty thousand dollars to rebuild."

Uh-huh, Kat thought.

"We don't have such monetary resources, of course.
But then, not even a week after speaking with Mr.
Kiernan, your letter came, along with the video disk.
Which I watched with great interest, by the way."

I'll bet you did, Kat thought. *Especially the part where
the doctor from San Francisco says the pain associated with
his injuries can be greatly alleviated by physical therapy.*
Stringent *physical therapy.*

It was true that nearly a dozen other doctors on
the DVD had claimed themselves at a loss, but Kat
believed Dr. Dilawar was the only one with the guts
to talk straight. She had been surprised that Newsome had allowed the disk to go out with that interview on it, but since his accident, the sixth-richest
man in the world had slipped a few cogs.

"Will you pay me enough to rebuild my church,
sir?"

Newsome studied him. Now there were small
beads of sweat just below his receding hairline. Kat
would give him his pills soon, whether he asked for
them or not. The pain was real enough, it wasn't as
though he were faking or anything, it was just . . .

"Would you agree not to ask for more? I'm talking
gentleman's agreement, we don't need to sign anything."

"Yes." Rideout said it with no hesitation.

"Although if you're able to remove the pain—*expel* the pain—I might well make a contribution of some size. Some *considerable* size. What I believe you people call a love offering."

"That would be your business, sir. Shall we begin?"

"No time like the present. Do you want everyone to leave?"

Rideout shook his head again: left to right, right to left, back to center. "I will need assistance."

Magicians always do, Kat thought. *It's part of the show.*

Outside, the wind shrieked, rested, then roused itself again. The lights flickered. Behind the house, the generator (also state-of-the-art) burped to life, then stilled.

Rideout sat on the edge of the bed. "Mr. Jensen there, I think. He looks strong and quick."

"He's both," Newsome said. "Played football in college. Running back. Hasn't lost a step since."

"Well . . . a few," Jensen said modestly.

Rideout leaned toward Newsome. His dark, deeply socketed eyes studied the billionaire's scarred face solemnly. "Answer a question for me, sir. What color is your pain?"

"Green," Newsome replied. He was looking back at the preacher with fascination. "My pain is green."

Rideout nodded: up, down, up, down, back to center. Eye contact never lost. Kat was sure he would have nodded with exactly the same look of grave confirmation if Newsome had said his pain was blue, or as purple as the fabled People-Eater. She thought, with a combination of dismay and real amusement: *I could lose my temper here. I really could. It would be the most expensive tantrum of my life, but still—I could.*

"And where is it?"

"Everywhere." It was almost a moan. Melissa took a step forward, giving Jensen a look of concern. Kat saw him shake his head a little and motion her back to the doorway.

"Yes, it likes to give that impression," Rideout said, "but it's a liar. Close your eyes, sir, and concentrate. Look for the pain. Look past the false shouts it gives—ignore the cheap ventriloquism—and locate it. You can do this. You *must* do it, if we're to have any success."

Newsome closed his eyes. For a space of ninety seconds there was no sound but the wind and the rain spattering against the windows like handfuls of fine gravel. Kat's watch was the old-fashioned wind-up kind, a nursing school graduation present from her father many years ago, and when the wind lulled, the room was quiet enough for her to hear its self-important ticking. And something else: at the far end of the big house: elderly Tonya Marsden singing softly as she neatened up the kitchen at the end of another day. *Froggy went a-courtin and he did ride, uh-huh.*

At last Newsome said, "It's in my chest. High in my chest. Or at the bottom of my throat, below the windpipe."

"Can you see it? Concentrate!"

Vertical lines appeared on Newsome's forehead. Scars from the skin that had been flayed open during the accident wavered through these grooves of concentration. "I see it. It's pulsing in time to my heartbeat." His lips pulled down in an expression of distaste. "It's nasty."

Rideout leaned closer. "Is it a ball? It is, isn't it? A green ball."

"Yes. Yes! A little green ball that *breathes*!"

Like the rigged-up tennis ball you undoubtedly have either up your sleeve or in that big black lunchbox of yours, Rev, she thought.

And, as if she were controlling him with her mind (instead of just deducing where this foolish little playlet would go next), Rideout said, "Mr. Jensen, sir. There's a lunchbox under the chair I was sitting in. Get it and open it and stand next to me. You need to do no more than that for the moment. Just—"

Kat MacDonald snapped. It was a snap she actually heard in her head. It sounded like Roger Miller snapping his fingers during the intro to "King of the Road."

She stepped up beside Rideout and shouldered him aside. It was easy. He was taller, but she had been turning and lifting patients for nearly half her life, and she was stronger. "Open your eyes, Andy. Open them right now. Look at me."

Startled, Newsome did as she said. Melissa and Jensen (now with the lunchbox in his hands) looked alarmed. One of the facts of their working lives—and Kat's own, at least until now—was that you didn't command the boss. The boss commanded you. You most certainly did not startle him.

But she'd had quite enough. In another twenty minutes she might be crawling after her headlights along stormy roads to the only motel in the vicinity, but it didn't matter. She simply couldn't do this any longer.

"This is bullshit, Andy," she said. "Are you hearing me? Bullshit."

"I think you better stop right there," Newsome said, beginning to smile—he had several smiles, and this wasn't one of the good ones. "If you want to keep your job, that is. There are plenty of other nurses in Vermont who specialize in pain therapy."

She might have stopped there, but Rideout said, "Let her speak, sir." It was the gentleness in his tone that drove her over the edge.

She leaned forward, into his space, and the words spilled out in a torrent.

"For the last sixteen months—ever since your respiratory system improved enough to allow meaningful physiotherapy—I've watched you lie in this goddam expensive bed and insult your own body. It makes me sick. Do you know how lucky you are to be alive, when everyone else on that airplane was killed? What a miracle it is that your spine wasn't severed, or your skull crushed into your brain, or your body burned—no, *baked*, baked like an apple—from head to toe? You would have lived four days, maybe even two weeks, in hellish agony. Instead you were thrown clear. You're not a vegetable. You're not a quadriplegic, although you choose to act like one. You won't do the work. You look for some easier way. You want to pay your way out of your situation. If you died and went to hell, the first thing you'd do is try to grease Satan's palm."

Jensen and Melissa were staring at her in horror. Newsome's mouth hung open. If he had ever been talked to in such a fashion, it had been long ago. Only Rideout looked at ease. *He* was the one smiling now. The way a father would smile at his wayward four-year-old. It drove her crazy.

"You could have been walking by now. God knows I've tried to make you understand that, and God knows I've told you—over and over—the kind of

work it would take to get you up out of that bed and
back on your feet. Dr. Dilawar in San Francisco had
the guts to tell you—he was the only one—and you
rewarded him by calling him a faggot."

"He *was* a faggot," Newsome said. His scarred
hands had balled themselves into fists.

"You're in pain, yes. Of course you are. It's man-
ageable, though. I've seen it managed, not once but
many times. But not by a rich man who tries to substitute his sense of entitlement for the plain old hard
work and tears it takes to get better. You refuse.
I've seen that, too, and I know what always happens
next. The quacks and confidence men come, the way
leeches come when a man with a cut leg wades into
a stagnant pond. Sometimes the quacks have magic
creams. Sometimes they have magic pills. The healers
come with trumped-up claims about God's power, the
way this one has. Usually the marks get partial relief.
Why wouldn't they, when half the pain is in their
heads, manufactured by lazy minds that only understand it will hurt to get better?"

She raised her voice to a wavering, childlike tre-
ble and bent close to him. "Daddy, it *hurrr-rrrts*! But
the relief never lasts long, because the muscles have
no tone, the tendons are still slack, the bones haven't
thickened enough to accommodate weight-bearing.
And when you get this guy on the phone to tell him
the pain's back—if you can—do you know what he'll
say? That you didn't have *faith* enough. If you used
your brains on this the way you did on your manufacturing plants and various investments, you'd know
there's no little living tennis ball sitting at the base of
your throat. You're too fucking old to believe in Santa
Claus, Andy."

Tonya had come into the doorway and now stood beside Melissa, staring with wide eyes and a dish-wiper hanging limp in one hand.

"You're fired," Newsome said, almost genially.

"Yes," Kat said. "Of course I am. Although I must say that this is the best I've felt in almost a year."

"If you fire her," Rideout said, "I'll have to take my leave."

Newsome's eyes rolled to the reverend. His brow was knitted in perplexity. His hands now began to knead his hips and thighs, as they always did when his pain medication was overdue.

"She needs educating, praise God's Holy Name." Rideout leaned toward Newsome, his own hands clasped behind his back. He reminded Kat of a pic-ture she'd seen once of Washington Irving's school-teacher, Ichabod Crane. "She's had her say. Shall I have mine?"

Newsome was sweating more heavily, but he was smiling again. "Have at her. Rip and roar. I believe I want to hear this."

Kat faced him. Those dark, socketed eyes were unsettling, but she met them. "Actually, so do I."

Hands still clasped behind his back, pink skull shining mutedly through his thin hair, long face sol-emn, Rideout examined her. Then he said, "You've never suffered yourself, have you?"

Kat felt an urge to flinch at that, or look away, or both. She suppressed it. "I fell out of a tree when I was eleven and broke my arm."

Rideout rounded his thin lips and whistled: one tuneless, almost toneless note. "Broke an *arm* while you were *eleven*. Yes, that must have been excruciat-ing."

She flushed. She felt it and hated it but couldn't stop the heat. "Belittle me all you want. I based what I said on years of experience dealing with pain patients. It is a *medical* opinion."

Now he'll tell me he's been expelling demons, or little green gods, or whatever they are, since I was in rompers.

But he didn't.

"I'm sure," he soothed. "And I'm sure you're good at what you do. I'm sure you've seen your share of fakers and posers. You know their kind. And I know yours, miss, because I've seen it many times before. They're usually not as pretty as you"—finally a trace of accent, *pretty* coming out as *purty*—"but their condescending attitude toward pain they have never felt themselves, pain they can't even conceive of, is always the same. They work in sickrooms, they work with patients who are in varying degrees of distress, from mild pain to deepest, searing agony. And after awhile, it all starts to look either overdone or outright fake to them, isn't that so?"

"That's not true at all," Kat said. What was happening to her voice? All at once it had grown small.

"No? When you bend their legs and they scream at fifteen degrees—or even at ten—don't you think, first in the back of your mind, then more and more toward the front, that they are lollygagging? Refusing to do the hard work? Perhaps even fishing for sympathy? When you enter the room and their faces go pale, don't you think, 'Oh, now I have to deal with *this* lazy slug of a thing again'? Haven't you—who once fell from a tree and broke your *arm*, for the Lord's sake—become more and more disgusted when they beg to be put back into bed and be given more morphine or whatever?"

"That's so unfair," Kat said . . . but now her voice was little more than a whisper.

"Once upon a time, when you were new at this, you knew agony when you saw it," Rideout said. "Once upon a time you would have believed in what you are going to see in just a few minutes, because you knew in your heart that a malignant outsider was there. I want you to stay so I can refresh your memory . . . and the sense of compassion that's gotten lost along the way."

"Some of my patients *are* whiners," Kat said, and looked defiantly at Newsome. "I suppose that sounds cruel, but sometimes the truth *is* cruel. Some *are* malingerers. If you don't know that, you're blind. Or stupid. I don't think you're either."

He bowed as if she had paid him a compliment—which, in a way, she supposed she had.

"Of course I know. But now, in your secret heart, you believe *all* of them are malingerers. Like a soldier who's spent too long in battle, you've become inured. Mr. Newsome is invaded, I tell you. *Infested*. There's a demon inside him so strong it has become a god, and I want you to see it when it comes out. It will improve matters for you considerably, I think. Certainly it will change your outlook on pain."

"And if I choose to leave?"

Rideout smiled. "No one will hold you here, Miss Nurse. Like all of God's creatures, you have free will. I would not ask others to constrain it, or constrain it myself. But I don't believe you're a coward, merely calloused. Case-hardened."

"You're a fraud," Kat said. She was furious, on the verge of tears.

"No," Rideout said, once more speaking gently.

"When we leave this room—with or without you—Mr. Newsome will be relieved of the agony that's been feeding on him. There will still be pain, but with the agony gone, he'll be able to deal with mere pain. Perhaps even with your help, miss, once you've had a necessary lesson in humility. Do you still intend to leave?"

"I'll stay," she said, then said: "Give me the lunch-box."

"But—" Jensen began.

"Give it over," Rideout said. "Let her inspect it, by all means. But no more talk. If I am meant to do this, it's time to begin."

Jensen gave her the long black lunchbox. Kat opened it. Where a workman's wife might have packed her husband's sandwiches and a little Tupperware container of fruit, she saw an empty glass bottle with a wide mouth. Inside the domed lid, held by a wire clamp meant to secure a thermos, was an aerosol can. There was nothing else. Kat turned to Rideout. He nodded. She took the aerosol out and looked at the label, nonplussed. "Pepper spray?"

"Pepper spray," Rideout agreed. "I don't know if it's legal in Vermont—probably not would be my guess—but where I come from, most hardware stores stock it." He turned to Tonya. "You are—?"

"Tonya Marsden. I cook for Mr. Newsome."

"Very nice to make your acquaintance, ma'am. I need one more thing before we begin. Do you have any sort of club? A baseball bat, perhaps?"

Tonya shook her head. The wind gusted again; once more the lights flickered and the generator burped in its shed behind the house.

"What about a broom?"

"Oh, yes, sir."

"Fetch it, please."

Tonya left. There was silence except for the wind. Kat tried to think of something to say and couldn't. Droplets of clear perspiration were trickling down Newsome's narrow cheeks, which had also been scarred in the accident. He had rolled and rolled, while the wreckage of the Gulfstream burned in the rain behind him.

I never said he wasn't in pain. Just that he could manage it, if he'd only muster half the will he showed during the years he spent building his empire.

But what if she was wrong?

Even if I am, that doesn't mean there's some sort of living tennis ball inside him, sucking his pain the way a vampire sucks blood.

There were no vampires, and no gods of agony . . . but when the wind blew hard enough to make the big house shiver in its bones, such ideas seemed almost plausible.

Tonya came back with a broom that looked like it had never swept so much as a single pile of floor-dirt into a dustpan. The bristles were bright blue nylon. The handle was painted wood, about four feet long. She held it up doubtfully. "This what you want?"

"I think it will serve," Rideout said, although to Kat he didn't sound entirely sure. It occurred to her that Newsome might not be the only one in this room who had slipped a few cogs lately. "I think you'd better give it to our skeptical nurse. No offense to you, Mrs. Marsden, but younger folks have quicker reflexes."

Looking not offended in the slightest—looking

relieved, in fact—Tonya held out the broom. Melissa took it and handed it to Kat.

"What am I supposed to do with it?" Kat asked. "Ride it?"

Rideout smiled, briefly showing the stained and eroded pegs of his teeth. "You'll know when the time comes, if you've ever had a bat or raccoon in the room with you. Just remember: first the bristles. Then the stick."

"To finish it off, I suppose. Then you put it in the specimen bottle."

"As you say."

"So you can put it on a shelf somewhere with the rest of your dead gods?"

He didn't respond to this. "Hand the spray can to Mr. Jensen, please."

Kat did so. Melissa asked, "What do I do?"

"Watch. And pray, if you know how. On my behalf, as well as Mr. Newsome's. For my heart to be strong."

Kat, who saw a fake heart attack coming, said nothing. She simply moved away from the bed, holding the handle of the broom in both hands. Rideout sat down beside Newsome with a grimace. His knees popped like pistol shots.

"Listen to me, Mr. Jensen."

"Yes?"

"You'll have time—it will be stunned—but be quick, just the same. As quick as you were on the football field, all right?"

"You want me to Mace it?"

Rideout once more flashed his brief smile, but Kat thought he really did look ill. "It's not Mace—that's illegal even where I come from—but you've got the idea, all right. Now I'd like silence, please."

"Wait a minute." Kat propped the broom against the bed and ran her hands first up Rideout's left arm, then his right. She felt only plain cotton cloth and the man's scrawny flesh beneath.

"Nothing up my sleeve, Miss Kat, I promise you."

"Hurry *up*," Newsome said. "This is bad. It always is, but the goddam stormy weather makes it worse."

"Hush," Rideout said. "All of you, hush."

They hushed. Rideout closed his eyes. His lips moved silently. Twenty seconds ticked past on Kat's watch, then thirty. Her hands were damp with perspiration. She wiped them one at a time on her sweater, then took hold of the broom again. *We look like people gathered at a deathbed,* she thought.

Outside, the wind snarled along the gutters.

Rideout opened his eyes and leaned close to Newsome.

"God, there is an evil outsider in this man. An outsider feeding on his flesh and bones. Help me cast it out, as Your Son cast out the demons from the possessed man of the Gadarenes. Help me speak to the little green god of agony inside Andrew Newsome in your own voice of command."

He leaned closer. He curled the long fingers of one arthritis-swollen hand around the base of Newsome's throat, as if he intended to strangle him. He leaned closer still, and inserted the first two fingers of his other hand into the billionaire's mouth. He curled them, and pulled down the jaw.

"Come out," he said. He had spoken of command, but his voice was soft. Silky. Almost cajoling. It made the skin on Kat's back and arms prickle. "Come out in the name of Jesus. Come out in the names of all the saints and martyrs. Come out in the name of God, who gave you leave to enter and now commands you to leave. Come out into the light. Leave off your gluttony and come out."

There was nothing.

"Come out in the name of Jesus. Come out in the names of the saints and martyrs." His hand flexed slightly, and Newsome's breath began to rasp. "No, don't go deeper. You can't hide, you small evil. Come out into the light. Jesus commands you. The saints and martyrs command you. God commands you to leave off dining on this man and come out."

A cold hand gripped Kat's upper arm and she almost screamed. It was Melissa. Her eyes were huge. Her mouth hung open. In Kat's ear, the housekeeper's whisper was as harsh as sandpaper. *"Look."*

A bulge like a goiter had appeared in Newsome's throat just above Rideout's loosely grasping hand. It began to move slowly mouthward. Kat had never seen anything like it in her life.

"That's right," Rideout almost crooned. His face was streaming with sweat; the collar of his shirt had gone limp and dark. "Come out. Come out into the light. You've done your feeding, you small thing of darkness."

The wind rose to a scream. Rain that was now half sleet blasted the windows like shrapnel. The lights flickered and the house creaked.

"The God that let you in commands you to leave. Jesus commands you to leave. All the saints and martyrs—"

He let go of Newsome's mouth, pulling his hand back the way a man does when he's touched something hot. But Newsome's mouth stayed open. More: it began to widen, first into a gape and then into a soundless howl. His eyes rolled back in his head and his feet began to jitter. His urine let go and the sheet over his crotch went as dark as Rideout's sweaty collar.

"Stop," Kat said, starting forward. "He's having a seizure. You have to st—"

Jensen yanked her back. She turned to him and saw his normally ruddy face had gone as pale as a linen napkin.

Newsome's jaw had dropped all the way to his breastbone. The lower half of his face disappeared into a mighty yawn. Kat heard temporomandibular tendons creak as knee tendons did during strenuous physical therapy: a sound like dirty hinges. The lights in the room stuttered off, on, off, then on again.

"Come out!" Rideout shouted. "Come out!"

In the darkness behind Newsome's teeth, a bladderlike thing rose. It was pulsing.

There was a rending, splintering crash and the window across the room shattered. Coffee cups fell to the floor and broke. Suddenly there was a branch in the room with them. The lights went out. The generator started up again. No burp this time but a steady roar. When the lights came back, Rideout was lying on the bed with Newsome, his arms flung out and his face planted on the wet patch in the sheet. Something was oozing from Newsome's gaping mouth, his teeth dragging grooves in its shapeless body, which was stippled with stubby green spikes.

Not a tennis ball, Kat thought. *More like one of those Kooshes the kids play with.*

Tonya saw it and fled back down the hall with her head hunched forward, her hands locked at the nape of her neck, and her forearms over her ears.

The green thing tumbled onto Newsome's chest.

"*Spray it!*" Kat screamed at Jensen. "*Spray it before it can get away!*" Yes. Then they would put it in the specimen bottle and screw the lid down tight. *Very* tight.

Jensen's eyes were huge and glassy. He looked like a sleepwalker. Wind blew through the room. It swirled his hair. A picture fell from the wall. Jensen pistoned out the hand holding the can of pepper spray and triggered the plastic nub. There was a hiss, then he leaped to his feet, screaming. He tried to turn, probably to flee after Tonya, but stumbled and fell to his knees. Although Kat felt too dumbfounded to move—to even stir a hand—part of her brain must still have been working, because she knew what had happened. He had gotten the can turned around, and instead of pepper-spraying the thing that was now oozing through the unconscious Reverend Rideout's hair, Jensen had sprayed himself.

"*Don't let it get me!*" Jensen shrieked. He began to crawl blindly away from the bed. "*I can't see, don't let it get me!*"

The wind gusted. Dead leaves tore free of the tree branch that had come through the window and swirled around the room. The green thing dropped from the nape of Rideout's creased and sunburned neck onto the floor. Feeling like a woman underwater, Kat swiped at it with the bristle end of the broom. She missed. The thing disappeared under the bed, not rolling but slithering.

Jensen crawled headfirst into the wall beside the doorway. "*Where am I? I can't see!*"

Newsome was sitting up, looking bewildered. "*What's going on? What happened?*" He pushed Ride-

out's head off him. The reverend slid bonelessly from
the bed to the floor.

Melissa bent over him.

"*Don't do that!*" Kat shouted, but it was too late.

She didn't know if the thing was truly a god or just
some weird kind of leech, but it was fast. It shot out
from under the bed, rolled along Rideout's shoulder,
onto Melissa's hand, and up her arm. Melissa tried to
shake it off and couldn't. *Some kind of sticky stuff on those
stubby little spikes,* the part of Kat's brain that would
still work told the part—the much larger part—that
still wouldn't. *Like the glue on a fly's feet.*

Melissa had seen where the thing came from and
even in her panic was wise enough to cover her own
mouth with both hands. The thing skittered up her
neck, over her cheek, and squatted on her left eye.
The wind screamed and Melissa screamed with it. It
was the cry of a woman drowning in a kind of pain
the one-to-ten charts in hospitals can never describe.
Melissa's agony was well over one hundred—that of
someone being boiled alive. She staggered backwards,
clawing at the thing on her eye. It was pulsing faster
now, and Kat could hear a low, liquid sound as the
thing resumed feeding. It was a *slushy* sound.

It doesn't care who it eats, Kat thought. She realized
she was walking toward the screaming, flailing
woman.

"Hold still! *Melissa, hold STILL!*"

Melissa paid no attention. She continued to back
up. She struck the thick branch now visiting the room
and went sprawling. Kat dropped to one knee beside
her and brought the broom handle smartly down on
Melissa's face. Down on the thing that was feeding on
Melissa's eye.

There was a splatting sound, and suddenly the thing was sliding limply down the housekeeper's cheek, leaving a wet trail of slime behind. It moved across the leaf-littered floor, intending to hide under the branch the way it had hidden under the bed. Kat sprang to her feet and stepped on it. She felt it splatter beneath her sturdy New Balance walking shoe. Green stuff shot out in both directions, as if she had stepped on a balloon filled with snot.

Kat went down again, this time on both knees, and took Melissa in her arms. At first Melissa struggled, and Kat felt a fist graze her ear. Then Melissa subsided, breathing harshly. "Is it gone? Kat, is it gone?"

"I feel better," Newsome said wonderingly from behind them, in some other world.

"Yes, it's gone," Kat said. She peered into Melissa's face. The eye the thing had landed on was bloodshot, but otherwise it looked all right. "Can you see?"

"Yes. It's blurry, but clearing. Kat . . . the pain . . . it was like the end of the world."

"Somebody needs to flush my eyes!" Jensen yelled. He sounded indignant.

"Flush your own eyes," Newsome said cheerily. "You've got two good legs, don't you? I think I might, too, once Kat throws them back into gear. Somebody check on Rideout. I think the poor sonofabitch might be dead."

Melissa was staring up at Kat, one eye blue, the other red and leaking tears. "The pain . . . Kat, you have no idea of the pain."

"Yes," Kat said. "Actually, I do. Now." She left Melissa sitting by the branch and went to Rideout. She checked for a pulse and found nothing, not even the wild waver of a heart that is still trying its best. Rideout's pain, it seemed, was over.

The generator went out.

"Fuck," Newsome said, still sounding cheery. "I paid seventy thousand dollars for that piece of Jap shit."

"I need someone to flush my eyes!" Jensen bellowed *"Kat!"*

Kat opened her mouth to reply, then didn't. In the new darkness, something had crawled onto the back of her hand.

For Russ Dorr

I've said before, and must reiterate, that stories are like dreams: vivid while in process, then quickly fading when the work is done. This is a clumsy (but truthful) prologue to a simple fact—I have no idea where this one came from, although I suppose I once did. It might have been a passing comment. It might have been a cookie jar with something written on it like NEVER LET THIS BE EMPTY. I just don't know.

I went to a movie recently, a matinee showing with very few people in attendance. Two of the concession guys were playing with a fuzzy duck one of them found after a showing of the latest animated kidtoon. I thought, *Maybe it's a magic duck, and when you squeak it, it grants wishes.* So I'm going to write a story called "Fuzzy Duck" just as soon as I get a chance. The point is simple. If someone asks me a year later about what inspired that particular yarn, I won't remember.

Unless, of course, I refer to this note.

Cookie Jar

1

There was a certain accord between them, right from the beginning. The boy thought the old man looked pretty good for ninety, and the old man thought the boy, whose name was Dale, looked pretty good for thirteen.

The kid started by calling him Great-Grandpa, but Barrett was having none of that. "It makes me feel even older than I am. Call me Rhett. That's what my father called me. I was a Rhett before there was a Rhett Butler—imagine that."

Dale asked him who Rhett Butler was.

"Never mind. It was a bad book and only a so-so movie. Tell me again about this project of yours."

"We're supposed to talk to our oldest relative, and ask what life was like when he was my age. Then I'm supposed to write a two-page report on how much things have changed. But Mr. Kendall hates generalities, so I'm supposed to concentrate on one or two specifics. That means—"

"I know what specifics are," Rhett said. "Which specifics have you got in mind?"

Dale considered the question. While he did so, Rhett considered the boy: healthy mop of hair, straight back, clear skin and eyes. There were seventy-seven years between them, and Dale Alderson probably considered that an ocean, but to Rhett it was only a lake. Maybe no more than a pond.

You'll get across it in no time, kiddo, he thought. *The brevity of the swim between your bank and mine will surprise you. It certainly surprised me.* He wasn't sure his great-grandson—the youngest of the lot—even thought of him as an actual human being. More like a talking fossil.

"Speak up, Dale. I've got all day, but you probably don't."

"Well . . . you remember before there was TV, right?"

Rhett smiled, even though he felt this was a question to which his great-grandson should already have known the answer. He restrained an urge to say, *Don't they teach you kids anything,* because it would have been curmudgeonly and impolite. Not to mention ungrateful. This boy had come to the Good Life Retirement Home for the sole purpose of hearing Barrett Alderson talk about the past, a subject that usually had kids running the other way as fast as they could go. It was only for a school assignment, true, but still. He had come all the way across town on the bus, which made Rhett think of trips he and his brother Jack had made on the interurban line to see their mother.

"Dale, I never even *saw* a television until I was twenty-one. Radar scopes, yes, but no TVs. I had my first confirmed sighting in an appliance-store window, after I got back from the war. I watched for twenty minutes, almost hypnotized."

"Which war was that?"

"Two," he said patiently. "Nazis? Hitler? Japanese in the Pacific? Ring any bells?"

"Sure, yeah, banzai charges and all that. I thought you might mean Korea."

"When Korea blew up, I was married with a couple of kids."

"Was my grandpa one of them?"

"Yup, he'd just made his appearance." *And when Vietnam rolled around, I was as old as your father is now. Maybe older.*

"So you were stuck with radio, huh?"

"Well, yes, but we didn't consider ourselves *stuck* with it."

Outside his room, from down the hall, came the electronically amplified voice of the retirement home's recreation director (or one of her minions) calling out bingo numbers. Rhett was happy not to be there, although he supposed he would be there tomorrow. He was measuring out the last years of his life—maybe down to months now, considering the blood that had started to show up in the bowl when he took a shit—not in coffee spoons but in coverall games.

"No?" Dale asked.

"Absolutely not. After supper, my dad and my brothers would—"

"Wait, wait, hold that thought." Dale dug into the pocket of his jeans and brought out an iPhone. He fiddled with it and the screen lit up. He fiddled with it some more and then set it on the bed.

"That thing records, too?" Rhett asked.

"Uh-huh."

"Is there anything it *doesn't* do?"

"Honey, it don't do windows," the boy said, and Rhett laughed. The kid might be a little foggy on twentieth-century history, but he was quick. And funny.

Dale smiled back at his great-grandfather, glad the old guy had gotten the joke, perhaps seeing him as a human being after all, or beginning to. Rhett could hope; even at ninety, he remained mostly optimistic, although optimism was a little harder to manage at three in the morning, lying awake and feeling the threads holding him to this life loosening.

"Are you sure it's hearing me?"

"Yeah, this baby's got great pickup. Also, I can see your voice on the screen." He held it up. "Say something."

"Our radio was a Philco table model," Rhett said, and watched sound waves roll across the iPhone's screen.

"See?"

"Yes. Great gadget. Don't know how we ever got along without them."

Dale checked the old man's face to be sure he was kidding. "Good one, Great-Grandpa."

"No, good one, *Rhett*."

"Good one, Rhett. So tell me about the radio."

Rhett talked for ten minutes or so, about how he and his two brothers would lie on the living-room rug after supper, them with their schoolbooks, his father in his easy chair with his feet up on the hassock, smoking his pipe, all of them listening to the Philco. He told Dale about *The Shadow* and *The Jack Benny Program*—how Jack was such a cheapskate—and his own favorite, *Major Bowes Amateur Hour,* where the host would hurry talky guests along by saying "All right, all right," and bang a gong if their performances were bad. But he began to slow down as more vivid memories slipped into the flow of his recollections. Those bus rides with Jack, for instance. And he thought, *Why not tell him? You have never told anyone, and you'll be dead soon enough. Blood in the toilet does not lie, not when you're ninety.*

"That amateur show was really sponsored by *cigarettes?*" Dale asked.

"Yup, Old Golds. 'If you want a treat instead of a treatment, smoke Old Golds. They're *good* for you!'"

"They could really say that?" The boy's eyes were shining with fascination.

"They did, but let's forget about the radio shows. I want to tell you something else I remember."

"Okay, but those old radio shows are pretty interesting."

"I can tell you something a lot more interesting, but turn off your gadget. I don't want you recording this."

"Really?"

"Really."

Dale turned off his iPhone and put it back in his pocket. He looked at his great-grandfather with some caution now, as if Rhett were about to tell him he'd robbed a few banks or enjoyed setting dogs on fire as a teenager.

"I had sort of a peculiar childhood, Dale, because my mother was peculiar. Not outright crazy, at least not crazy enough to be locked away in a sanitarium, but very, very peculiar. I was the youngest of three. In 1927, two years after I was born, she moved out of the house, bag and baggage, and into a little cottage on the other side of town—this side of town, in fact, and not far from here, although there's a shopping center there now. The place was hers by inheritance, from an old aunt, and not much bigger than a garage. She left my father to raise Pete, Jack, and me. Which he did, with the help of a woman who came in to do the housekeeping and watch us when we were too small to be trusted on our own."

"She never even gave a reason?" Dale asked.

"Said it was for our own protection. My father saw she had a good allowance for her necessaries, and he did it without complaint—those were tough times, but he had a shirt-and-tie job with the American Eagle Insurance Company, and her wants were small. They maintained a collegial relationship. Do you know what that means?"

"That they got along?"

"That's exactly right, and good for you. My brother Jack and I got along with her, too. Accepted the situation the way young kids usually do, without much complaining or too many questions. We went to visit her quite often. We'd play gin rummy and Crazy Eights and Monopoly. The place was cold in the winter and hotter than a stovepipe in the summer, even with a fan blowing the air around. We had a lot of laughs. She had a ukulele. Sometimes the three of us went out on the back stoop, and she'd play, and we'd sing. Stuff like 'Old Black Joe' and 'Massa's in the Cold, Cold Ground.'"

"Those were real songs?" Dale glanced at his iPhone. *Probably wishing it was still turned on,* Rhett thought. *Too bad, kid, but you're not playing this for anybody. Crazy is safer when it goes unrecorded.*

"Real songs. Not very politically correct by today's standards, but that was a different time. A different

world, really. We loved her like mad. She was energetic, as manic-depressives often are. Her laughter
was free and wild. It was different with Pete. He was
the oldest, almost seven when she moved out, and he
stayed angry at her until she died. Wouldn't visit her
unless my dad made him, which he eventually gave
up doing."

Then broke down at her funeral, Rhett thought. *Cried
so hard he fainted and had to be carried outside into the
fresh air to revive.*

"Probably his feelings were hurt," Dale said.
"Maybe he even thought he was to blame for her leaving."

Rhett smiled. "You're a wise child, son. I'm sure
it was all of that, and more. In any case, he rarely saw
her. Jack and I, though . . . we didn't just love her,
we were fascinated by her. Nineteen thirty-six was
her last good year. Jack was thirteen and I was eleven,
which made us old enough to ride across town on
the interurban, so we went to see her once or twice a
week. Usually on Saturdays, sometimes after school."

"My mom told me not to ask about yours," Dale
said.

"Because she committed suicide?"

"Yeah. Mom said she might just be a, like, historical figure to me, but she was a lot more to you. When
she asks me how it went—and she will—I'll have to
tell her you brought it up."

"That's fine," Rhett said. "And it did hurt. It hurt
plenty. I guess it most always does when your mother
dies, but suicide is in a class by itself. It hit Jack
harder than it did me, because he blamed himself.
He thought that because he was older, he should have
seen how much worse she was getting. Only it was

hard to see, because she was so full of life, and so . . . so interesting. She'd fly around that place, getting cards or board games or five-hundred-piece Tuco puzzles for the three of us to do. Sometimes she'd crank up her Victrola and try to teach us how to dance the Charleston, and when we wouldn't, she'd do it by herself, with her shadow on the wall. She'd tell jokes . . . play her uke . . . show us how to do magic tricks like the Disappearing Coin and the Floating Handkerchief. And—this is important—she had a big blue ceramic jar on a high shelf with cookies on the side in red. It was always full, and we'd eat them until we were stuffed. All different kinds, all good. That place of hers might not have been much bigger than a garage, but we had plenty of fun there. She saw to it, and I'm not sure even an adult could have seen the truth under all that camouflage."

"What truth?" Dale asked.

"That she was getting worse. She'd chat away about other worlds, right next to ours, and the alien races that lived there, and how something was out to get her. It talked to her through the electrical sockets, she said, so she unscrewed all the lightbulbs at night and put playing cards over the plug-in plates on the floor. She said the celluloid backs on the cards were very effective at stopping that voice. Only then she'd laugh, like it was all a big joke."

"Whoo," Dale said. "Far out."

"She drew a map on one of the walls, and she was always adding to it. She said it was a country in one of those other worlds. She called it Lalanka, and said it was full of *entities*. Do you know what that means?"

Dale shook his head.

"Creatures that wanted to come through into our

world, but couldn't. At least not yet. They were bottled up by some restraining force, which was a good thing, because they were hungry. She said that if they ever got into our world, they'd eat everything—not just the people and the animals, but lawns and cars and buildings and even the sky. About other things, though, she was completely rational. She did her little bit of grocery shopping, she kept herself clean and neat, she was very affectionate with me and Jack, and she never failed to ask about Pete. Before we left, she always told us to tell him that he was welcome anytime. 'I only moved out because it wouldn't have been safe for you boys and your father if I stayed,' she said."

"That's amazing."

Rhett shrugged and spread his liver-spotted hands. "Not to us, it wasn't. We just accepted it. That's what children do, Dale. But her map—that *was* amazing. In the last year of her life, there were new things on it every time we visited: mountain ranges, lakes, villages, castles, forests, roads."

"Did your dad ever see it?"

"Oh yes, many times. He thought it was a genuine work of art, and said it should have been in a gallery someplace. I think he believed that map was one of the few things keeping her on the rails. Along with our visits, of course. These days I suppose some people, smart people, would call it a coping mechanism. Sometimes we'd just sit in her little kitchen, eating sandwiches with the crusts cut off, and she'd ask us about school, and our friends, and quiz us if we had a test coming up. Jack was taking algebra and didn't get it, but she explained it to him by using cookies from the cookie jar. She'd draw an equals sign on a sheet of paper and put three cookies from the jar on one side and seven on the other. Next to the three cookies, she'd put an *x*, and tell Jack to stack more cookies on top of it until both sides of the equals sign were the same."

"Huh. Cool."

"But in between those rational, normal things, she'd tell us about what was going on in Lalanka, where the gobbits—those were creatures who lived in the deep woods—were producing a terrible white mist that killed small animals and gave larger ones convulsions, or the war between Red Henry and his renegade twin brother, Black John. One day when we came, she'd colored the woods around the biggest castle—Red Henry's castle—black. Because, she said, Black John had 'put the torch to the Long Forest.' And there was the stuff about how time had come to a stop in the West Kingdoms, and it was tearing holes in the fabric of existence. 'If the time-stop spreads to our world, boys, we're doomed,' she said. I had nightmares about it."

"I'm not surprised," Dale said. "I probably would, too."

"She called the white mist *forza,* and said it could travel in electric wires and telephone lines if it ever got over here. I had nightmares about that, too, and I got in the habit of checking our telephone to make sure forza wasn't coming out of the holes in the receiver. Only . . . " He trailed off.

"Only what?"

"I don't know how much of that she actually believed," Rhett said finally. "Back then I believed that *she* believed . . . do you get that?"

Dale said he did.

"And because *she* believed, *we* believed, but Jack

changed his mind after she was dead, and he convinced me. He said Lalanka was just a story she made up to distract her from one specific thing. Something that was real but not a part of this world. Something that couldn't be, but was. He said he didn't think a person could live with something like that. He called it a hole in reality. Lalanka and the gobbits, Red Henry and Black John, the forza mist, they were just . . . distractions. A way to cover that hole in reality the way you might cover a well with boards so no one would fall in." He thought about it and added, "What I mean is those stories were her way of staying sane. At least that's what Jack thought. I came to believe different."

"Are you serious?" Dale's eyes were shining.

"As a heart attack, kiddo. Anyway, all her distractions finally stopped working. Her uke, dancing with her shadow, the map on the wall, the playing cards over the wall sockets. Her stories stopped working for her, too. Because the thing she was afraid of was in the house with her all along."

"What? What was she afraid of?"

"She was afraid of the cookie jar."

2

After his wife's funeral, George Alderson told his three sons that he was going to empty the little house to the walls—sell what could be sold, and throw away the rest. But before he did it, he took them there and invited each of them to take one thing to remember her by. Jack chose the ukulele, and eventually learned to play it. Peter—a much quieter and less argumentative boy in the wake of his mother's untimely death—took the watch George had given her when she left for the little cottage. It was a man's watch, and she had worn it around her neck, like a ticking locket. Rhett took the blue ceramic cookie jar.

He kept it under his bed, and each night he and Jack ate a couple of the cookies—to remember her by, Rhett said. Pete was not invited in to share this ritual, and did not even know about it, because by then he had his own room. Although neither of the younger boys said so aloud, they felt Pete had no right to share in their cookie communion. He had mourned their mother after she was dead—strenuously—but had mostly turned his back on her while she was alive, sneering at the playing cards propped over the baseboard outlets and calling the map of Lalanka "goofy shit."

"He loved her," Rhett told his great-grandson, "but we felt he didn't love her enough. We were just kids, remember, and kids can be awfully judgmental." He paused, thinking. "Although in some ways, I still think we were right."

3

There came a night—it might have been a week after Moira Alderson's suicide, it might have been two—when Rhett and Jack Alderson shared a realization that should have come earlier, and would have, if their powers of observation hadn't been numbed by grief. They were sitting on Rhett's bed, the cookie jar between them.

"Whoa, Nellie," Jack said. "It's still full. How can that be?"

Rhett had no idea, but it was true. They had taken a lot of cookie communion since their mother's death, but the jar was still packed to the rim. On this particular night, the ones on top were macaroons. When Rhett stirred them aside, he saw chocolate chippers beneath. He started to burrow deeper to see if he could find the oatmeal-raisin cookies that were his personal favorites, but Jack grabbed his wrist and pulled his hand out.

"Don't do that."

"Why not?"

"Because it might be dangerous. Put the cover back on and stick it under your bed."

Rhett did so without argument, and Jack put out the light. They lay there in silence for awhile, neither sleepy. Rhett could feel the cookie jar underneath him, a small, dense planet with its own gravitational pull.

"It's like her ghost is in there," Rhett said finally, and his eyes filled with the tears that were always waiting since their mother had died.

"It's not her ghost, that's stupid," Jack said. Rhett could tell from the thickness of his voice that his brother was crying, too.

"What, then? Is it something to do with Lalanka? The forza? The. . ." It was hard to finish, because they were what he feared the most. "The gobbits?"

"Santa Claus isn't real, and neither are the gobbits or the forza mist, Rhett. None of that jazz is real. The map was just made up out of her head." Jack was trying to sound tough, but his voice was still thick. "She knew it, too. It was all just stuff she made up to keep her mind off the cookie jar."

"Then what's in there?"

"Cookies. And I don't want any more. I never want to eat another cookie in my life, not from that jar and not even from the bakery."

4

A week passed. The cookie jar stayed under Rhett's bed with the lid on. Then one night—it was a Saturday—Rhett was jerked back from the edge of sleep by the sound of his brother crying.

"Jack?" Rhett sat up. "What's wrong?"

"We would have gone over there today," Jack said. "We would have had bacon sandwiches, and played board games. I miss her. I miss Mom."

"I miss her, too."

Jack got out of bed, ghostly in his white pajamas, and sat down next to Rhett. "I was thinking of how her place smelled. How good it smelled."

"Like cookies," Rhett said. "That's how it always smelled. It was like a fairy-tale house that way, wasn't it?"

"Yes," Jack said, "only she was a good witch instead of a bad one."

They sat there for a little while, not talking, remembering the smell and her shadow dancing on the wall. How gone she was had finally gotten through to them. Even the map was gone, with the Long Forest and Lookout Hill and Castle Black and Castle Red. Their father might have said it belonged in a gallery when she was alive, but when she was gone, he scrubbed it away like a shopkeeper scrubbing a dirty word off the front of his store so his customers wouldn't be offended. He certainly couldn't sell the house with that crazy thing on the wall, he told the boys. It had to go. He took pictures of it first, but Kodak snaps weren't the same. Couldn't be.

"Get the jar," Jack said.

Rhett pulled it out from under the bed with relief, and cradled it in his lap. Jack lifted the cover. It was still full to the brim, but it was no longer macaroons on top. That Saturday night it was ginger snaps.

"She's been gone almost a month," Jack said. "They'll be stale."

But they weren't stale; they were as fresh as if they had been baked that very day.

Moira had cut her wrists and died in the bathtub on a hot August afternoon. Rhett and Jack discovered the cookie jar was always full right around the time school let in again. Halloween came, and Rhett went trick-or-treating by himself for the first time. He dressed as a pirate and came home with a bag of candy, but it wasn't very much fun without Jack, who had declared himself too old to put on a costume and go traipsing around the neighborhood begging for sweets. Thanksgiving came, and their father—now showing strands of gray at his temples—carved the turkey. Pete's girlfriend ate with them, and Pete ate with her family at Christmas. They became engaged on Valentine's Day of 1939, shortly after Pete turned eighteen. Summer came again, and Rhett spent most of it at the vacant lot down the street, playing baseball. Sometimes he pitched, even when there were bigger kids on the team. He had a great fastball.

Jack occasionally watched him, but rarely played. Mostly he went places by himself, usually with a sketchpad under his arm—he had inherited his mother's artistic ability, and then some.

"He might have been one of the great ones," Rhett told Dale. "Probably not, most kids never fulfill their potential, but we'll never know."

The lives of the two younger boys began to draw apart, slowly and subtly, but surely. Yet they still shared the same room, at night they took cookie communion, and the blue ceramic jar was always full, the cookies inside always fresh. Sometimes they were chocolate-covered grahams, sometimes they were sugar cookies, sometimes they were macaroons or chocolate chippers. They ate one or two apiece, sitting on Rhett's bed, more than a thousand cookies in the course of that long year before Pete got married and Jack moved into Pete's room.

By then Hitler had begun to dominate the news, and it seemed that in each day's paper more of the map on the front page was stamped with Nazi swastikas. Europe was pretty much gone, and England would be next.

"It can't hold out," George Alderson said, puffing his pipe. There were only two boys listening to the Philco table model with him now; Pete was living nine blocks away with his new wife, and on the road most of the time, selling beer and cigarettes and stocking jukeboxes with new records. "Thank God there's a long stretch of ocean between us and the maniac with the mustache."

As the swastikas on the front-page map continued to spread (Britain still holding out but Russia tottering), Rhett thought often of his mother's map. *Hitler is really Black John*, he thought, *and he's turning Europe into Lalanka*. And one day, while Rhett was downtown shopping for Christmas presents, a shopkeeper told him that the Japs had bombed Pearl Harbor.

"How old were you then?" Dale asked him.

"Sixteen. I still hadn't kissed a girl."

"Could you sign up to fight if you were sixteen?"

"No. I just hoped the war would last long enough for me to get in. And, unfortunately, it did."

5

Moira Alderson had sometimes called her oldest the plodder of the family—slow and steady wins the race—but Pete was Speedy Alka-Seltzer after Pearl Harbor. He was at the Navy recruiting office the very next day, with a fresh haircut and wearing his best suit. His new wife encouraged him, feeling he would be safer on board a big battleship than fighting the Japs hand-to-hand in the Pacific. On the day he left for Newport News, Pete gave Jack the Bulova watch their mother had worn around her neck, with instructions to keep it safe. "Because I'll want it back when I come home," he said.

Jack, the artistic one, joined the USAAF in early 1942, as soon as he turned eighteen. On the day before he left for Florida, where he would learn to fly the P-47 Thunderbolt at Hillsborough Army Airfield, he gave the wristwatch to Rhett.

"What about the uke?" Rhett asked him.

"Never mind the uke, greedyguts, I'm taking that with me. You just wear the watch, and keep it wound. It won't keep good time if you don't."

Rhett promised he would. They were sitting on his bed, and ate two cookies apiece from the blue jar. It was still full, and the cookies—gingerbread that night—were as tasty as ever.

Rhett enlisted in the army a year and a half later, one step ahead of the draft. There was no excitement in the thought of going to war, no thrill, only pessimism so strong it amounted to a premonition. He felt sure that he would be sent overseas, and that when the inevitable invasion happened—perhaps in 1944, perhaps not until 1945 or '46—he would be in the first wave, and killed by enemy machine-gun fire before he could even wade out of the water. He could actually see his body rocking back and forth in the waves, facedown, arms splayed.

It was in this fatalistic frame of mind that, on his last night home, he opened the cookie jar for the last time in almost three years. He didn't dare upend it—he had a vision of being buried in a never-ending avalanche of macaroons and shortbreads—but he began to reach in and take them out by the double handful, dropping them on his bed: sugar cookies, chocolate chippers, oatmeal raisin, ladyfingers, date-filled. When he had a hill of cookies on either side of him, he stopped and peered into the fat-bellied jar.

He had emptied it to a point more than halfway down, but the level was already rising. The cookies pushed up in the middle, then tumbled down the sides. It made him think of a high-school science lesson they'd had on volcano formation. Soon it would be full again, and what was he going to do with all of those he'd taken out of the jar? There were hundreds. He began to toss them back in, then saw something that froze him in place. He was wearing the Bulova, and as soon as his left wrist went past the rim of the jar, the second hand stopped. He snatched it back, then put it back in, just to be sure. Yes. When it was outside the jar, the second hand moved. Inside, it stood still.

Because Lalanka is real, he thought, *and the cookie jar is a kind of portal. One that opens on the West Kingdoms, where time has stopped.*

By then the jar was full to the brim again (pecan sandies on top that night). Rhett clapped the cover on it and stowed it under his bed. He put the left-overs in a paper sack marked for the trash the follow-ing morning—a final chore before leaving for what he assumed would be his own premature disposal. He told himself there *were* no West Kingdoms; he was too old to believe in such things. The cookie jar was a miracle, that much was undeniable. But miracles are scary things, and this one had been powerful enough to drive his mother out of her mind. It would do the same to him, if he let it, especially with the war about to swallow him up.

"I told myself it was some kind of magnetic field that stopped the second hand," he told Dale, "and I told myself I just wouldn't think about it anymore. Then I lay there wide awake until after midnight, thinking about nothing else. So I got up and took the damn thing up to the attic. Which is where it stayed until I came back from overseas."

6

Pete Alderson fought his version of Big Two from a desk in Hampton Roads, Virginia, and finished as a lieutenant commander. He sent many men into com-bat, but never heard a shot fired in anger. Jack learned to fly, and took his mother's ukulele to Guadalcanal with him. From there he flew dozens of sorties before his fighter was blown out from under him during the battle of Iwo Jima. A friend wrote to George Alderson, telling him that his son's canopy had jammed so he couldn't parachute to the water below. What he did not say (and perhaps did not have to) was that Jack, the artistic one, had burned like a torch in his cockpit before the shark-infested waters could put him out.

Rhett was indeed part of the invading force that landed at Normandy, but although men were shot to death all around him (their bodies rocked back and forth in the waves just as he had imagined), he survived that day and the booming, earth-shaking night that followed. He fought across France and into Germany, the vagabond watch that had made its way through the entire Alderson family ticking away on his wrist. He suffered from blisters and trench foot, he was gashed by blackberry brambles one afternoon when his squad happened upon a pocket of Kraut resistance holding a bridge near the German border, but he was never once wounded by enemy fire and he always kept the watch wound.

Sometimes there were cookies in their mess rations, usually hard as rocks and always stale. He ate them in bivouacs and foxholes and slit trenches, thinking of his mother's blue cookie jar.

In April of 1945, after facing only minimal resistance, Rhett was part of the Allied force that liberated a concentration camp named for the beech forests that surrounded it. The day was damp and overcast, with a heavy ground mist that sometimes hid the heaped bodies and sometimes revealed them. Living skeletons stood at the fences and outside the crematoriums, staring at the Americans. Some were horribly burned by white phosphorous.

"What the fuck have we gotten ourselves into?" asked a soldier standing at Rhett's elbow.

Rhett didn't reply, because what was in his mind— what he *knew*—would have sounded insane: They had gotten themselves into Lalanka, of course. The trailing mist was the forza, the heaped bodies in this dank charnel house were victims of the gobbits, and somewhere— probably in Berlin—Black Adolf, now barking mad, was determined to continue the slaughter.

Two weeks after Buchenwald came Dachau. Thirty-two thousand dead, many still lying in the trenches they had been forced to dig, their emaciated bodies rotting in the rain, their hair fallen out to lie beside their heads. These were the memories Rhett Alderson brought back from Europe, only they weren't exactly memories, because they weren't exactly over. He had seen too much for them ever to be over, and consequently brought the West Kingdoms of Lalanka home with him. The West Kingdoms, where time had stopped just as the second hand of the Bulova watch had stopped when he dipped it below the rim of the cookie jar.

7

All this was nothing to tell a boy of thirteen, so he merely said, "I was with the Americans who liberated two of the German death camps, near the end. It was pretty awful."

He was relieved when Dale didn't pursue this. His great-grandson had something else in mind. "Did you get the cookie jar out of the attic when you came home?"

"Eventually." Rhett smiled. "But the *first* thing I did was to give that watch back to my brother Pete, because it was the first thing he asked for."

"He sounds like kind of a dickhead," Dale said, then added hastily, "if you don't mind me saying."

"I don't, and he was, but he mellowed over time. He was a good husband and a good father."

Also, he never knew about the cookie jar, Rhett thought but didn't say. *And he never saw what I saw, from Omaha Beach in Normandy to Dachau, where the dead had lain in the open long enough to lose their hair.*

8

Rhett stayed with his father at first, his father who had grown prematurely old and moved slowly, his back humped into a shape like a turtle's shell. Pete had begun talking about putting him in a home, and Rhett supposed that would be the best thing, although it seemed cruel—like putting him out with the garbage. In the meantime, father and son rubbed along well enough, with Rhett doing the shopping and most of the housecleaning after putting in a day at the auto-repair shop where he had caught on as a mechanic (and which he later owned).

He worked hard, but slept badly.

One night in March of 1946, after his father had gone to bed and while a sleet-thickened wind slapped at the house, Rhett went up to the attic. The cookie jar was where he had left it, behind a carton of boxed-up glassware from when a sane mother had lived in this house. Rhett hefted it, half expecting it to be light, its magic gone, but it was still full.

He took it down the narrow flight of stairs cradled against his belly and sat with it on the bed, where Jack had sat beside him so many times. He lifted the lid and breathed deep, smelling chocolate and vanilla and cinnamon and butter. Good smells. Fresh smells. Ones he had remembered and longed for in the heat of a French summer and the cold of a German winter. The smell of newly baked cookies that had always pervaded his mother's little house, where she had danced to the Victrola and given them custard in little green cups.

My mother, the good witch, Rhett thought, *and this fucking thing drove her mad. The way my memories of the war will drive me mad, if I let them. Is there always a Red Henry, a Black Adolf? Does there have to be?* Why *does there have to be?*

The anger that had floated in him ever since Buchenwald—his own forza—coalesced into a dark cloud, and he upended the jar, spilling out a flood of cookies that overflowed the bed and made a mountain on the floor. At last, just when he began to think they would continue pouring out until he was drowning in ginger snaps and peanut-butter smoothies, they stopped. He raised the jar, tilting it up to the ceiling like a telescope, and peered in.

"What did you see?" Dale asked. "Was it just the bottom?"

"No," Rhett said. "Not the bottom."

Once, in late 1944, during a lull in the fighting between Thanksgiving and Christmas, the USO had arrived with a projector and a stack of film cans. There were popcorn and bottles of soda pop, and the soldiers watched, mesmerized, as a double-feature movie show was projected onto a bedsheet. There was a color cartoon ("Ehhh . . . what's up, Doc?"), a travelogue about Bali or Mali or one of those places, and then a double feature of *The Maltese Falcon* and *Yankee Doodle Dandy*. But what Rhett remembered when he peered into the uptilted cookie jar was the Movietone newsreel that came between the cartoon and the travelogue. There had been a feature about a scientific wonder of the Army Air Force called the Norden bombsight. What he saw through the bottom of the cookie jar was exactly like that, only without the crosshairs.

It was disorienting, because he was looking *down,* even though the jar grasped in his hands was tilted *up.* What he saw was distorted at the edges, but the central image was achingly clear. He could pick out each blackened, twisted tree in the Long Forest, burned by Black John's raiders. He could only see the top of Lookout Hill, because the rest had been obscured by drifting white clouds of forza, and he knew that everything beneath that mist—every animal, every human being—was dead. When he moved the cookie jar a bit ("Less than two inches to the left," he told Dale), leagues of land blurred past below, making him feel nauseous. When he held the jar still again, he saw Regency Road, curving like a snake on its way between Castle Black and Castle Red, just as it had on his mother's wall map all those years ago, before the world had gone insane for the second time in a single century.

"I saw a horse pulling a covered wagon," he told Dale. "A peddler's wagon. It was just as clear as could be. The front of it had been festooned with charms to ward off evil, but they didn't help, because two great white things came bursting out of the burnt husks of those trees and attacked it."

"Gobbits," Dale breathed.

"Yes. Gobbits. They were as big as timber wolves, but hairless and headless. Their shapes kept changing, as if they were made of jelly instead of flesh. I saw the man on the seat drop the reins and put his hands over his face. As if he wanted to die without seeing the horrors that were going to kill him. The strength ran out of my arms and I dropped the jar."

"Did it break? It did, didn't it?"

"No. I think it would have if it had landed on the floor, but instead it landed on cookies. That mountain of cookies. The bedroom stank of them."

The bingo game was over, and the inhabitants of the Good Life Retirement Home were making their slow way past Rhett's open door toward the next station of the cross, which would be lunch—noodles in some sort of sauce seemed likely. It was time to wrap this up, but he was not sorry he'd told the boy about his mother's cookie jar. Best-case scenario, Dale would see it as a kind of fable. Worst case, he'd think old Great-Gramps had gone gaga. And was that so wrong? Buchenwald and Dachau had knocked him crooked, and he'd never been really straight afterward. Yet he had done his best in small ways—volunteering in the city's soup kitchen, working with kids from homes that were poor, broken, or both—to straighten some things. He still thought things like that mattered; even two bits in a bum's upturned hat mattered. The world might be as awful as ever, but at least he had never joined the endlessly warring armies of Black John and Red Henry. Uncle Sam's army had been enough for him.

When he mustered out of that one, he mustered out for good.

"By the end of the war, my dad—your *great*-great-grandfather—was suffering from arthritis in his hips, knees, and ankles. Climbing the stairs every evening to go to bed was slow and painful. It hurt just to watch him. It was dangerous, too, because his balance was untrustworthy. Eventually I called my big brother on the phone, and the two of us converted Dad's study on the first floor into a bedroom. So I had the second floor entirely to myself, and considering the sea of cookies in my room after I dumped the jar, that was good. It was three nights before I could get rid of them. On the second night, he asked me what that vanilla smell was, coming from upstairs."

"What did you say?"

Rhett smiled. "That I didn't smell anything, of course. He said it reminded him of my mother. 'She baked so much that vanilla was her perfume,' he said."

Dale wasn't much interested in this, either. "How'd you get rid of them, Rhett? How'd you get rid of all those cookies?"

"Scooped them into galvanized trash cans I bought at the hardware store. Did it while Dad was asleep. I felt like a damn burglar. I put them out back, and on the third night I borrowed a pickup truck from where I worked and hauled them down to the river. I meant to throw them in, but in the end I couldn't do that."

"What stopped you?"

The memory of those walking skeletons, Rhett thought. *The ones that stared at us through the barbed wire with the mist drifting around them.* How could I remember those starving creatures, and then just dump four steel cans loaded with food into the water?

"I knew there were poor folks who came down to the river to fish. Back then the water was still clean enough to eat what you caught. And there were homeless people, too. They lived in the kind of camp we called a Hooverville, although I'm glad to say that it was gone by 1950 or so."

Just in time for the next war, he thought. *North Korea and South Korea, Black John and Red Henry.*

"I'm sure those folks had . . ." He trailed off.

"Rhett? You okay?"

"Yup. Just had a senior moment. I was going to say that I'm sure those homeless people had a cookie feast."

"At ninety, I guess you're entitled to all the senior moments you want," Dale said, and that made Rhett laugh. A good kid, fast on his feet. Would he ask the most obvious question? Rhett was betting he would. And Dale did.

9

Yes, he thought about throwing the blue ceramic jar away, but in the end could not bring himself to do it. Hauling cookies to the riverside in galvanized trash cans was one thing; throwing out a miracle, one that had belonged to his mother, was another.

Sometimes—often—he wondered how she had come by it in the first place. When he asked his father, George Alderson only shook his head. "That old blue cookie jar? No idea. But she used to haunt the church sales and rumble sales, called 'em the best entertainment in the world, and sometimes she brought things home. Cookie jar was probably one of them." He lit his pipe and blew out a fragrant cloud of Cherry Blend. "That was back when her mind was still right. Before all that map nonsense."

A week or so after he disposed of Cookie Mountain, Rhett returned the blue ceramic jar to the attic. Before he left, he took the cover off one last time. It was full to the brim, those enticing smells of vanilla and chocolate wafting up. Cookies that were as fresh as ever, sweetness masking a window into a blackened, blistered world that was always at war. He thought, *If I were wearing the Bulova watch and put it inside the rim, the second hand would stop. It might stop even if I laid it against the blue glaze of the jar's surface.* But the watch had gone back to Pete.

He thought about taking one more cookie—one more act of communion—and resisted the temptation. He put the cover back on and left the attic.

Too many sweets weren't good for you.

10

"We finally did put Dad in a home," Rhett said. "It was all right, but not as nice as this place. He didn't mind, because by then he'd started to get foggy upstairs, although he was only in his fifties. He aged all at once, it seemed. It wasn't fair, but—we sold the house—Pete and I did—and split the profits. I moved across town, and bought my own place. I brought along a few pieces of furniture I was attached to . . . and the cookie jar. I brought that, too, although I never opened it again."

"Never?" It was as if the kid couldn't get this straight in his mind.

"Never. I met a girl, I got married, I had kids—including your gramps—and I bought the business I was working in. Now there are Alderson Auto Shops all over the Midwest, and a few in the South, too."

"Wow, and you live here?"

"It's as good a place as any," Rhett said, and meant it. He was measuring out the end of his life in coverall games, but so what? He had a few friends, and you had to measure out the end of your life in something. "I lived with Pete's grandson for a little while—this would be your uncle, or maybe your great-uncle, I get all confused about such things—but when I sensed I was becoming a burden, I came here. Someone or other said that fish and guests both stink after three days, and I was at your uncle Bill's a lot longer than that. This is a roundabout way of getting back to your question, Dale, but first let me ask *you* a question. How much of this do you believe?"

The boy was quiet for a long time. Rhett respected his silence. At last he said, "I don't really know."

"A fair answer, but I think you can do better. If you want to. The last of my things are still stored in Bill Alderson's attic." Was he doing this wide-eyed, clear-skinned kid a favor by telling him that? Or cursing him? Well, either way, it was out now. "There are a few suits so old they might be back in fashion, some medals I won in the war—one of them's a Silver Star, believe it or not—and the cookie jar."

"Really?" Dale's voice was soft with awe, his eyes so wide he looked closer to six than thirteen.

"Unless it's been broken, yes. You could go see. In fact, I give it to you—think of it as a pre-death inheritance, and I'll be gone soon enough. Have a few cookies. I'm sure they're still fresh. Only . . . be careful."

"I will! I will!"

You won't, Rhett thought. *You won't be able to, any more than my mother was. Or I was. Any more than Jack would have been, if Jack had lived. In the end we all prefer the bitter to the sweet. It's our curse. So you'll turn the cookie jar upside down, and dump out all that's inside, and peer into that other world. After that . . .*

"Thanks, Rhett! Thanks!"

Rhett patted his great-grandson on the shoulder with one gnarled hand, and smiled, and thought, *After that, you're on your own.*

For Chuck Verrill

Public appearances aren't my favorite thing. When I stand before an audience, I always feel like an imposter. It isn't that I'm a solitary person, although I am, at least to a degree; I can drive from Maine to Florida by myself and feel perfectly content. It isn't stage fright, either, although I still feel it when I step in front of two or three thousand people. That is an unnatural situation for most writers. We're more accustomed to appearing before dedicated library groups of three dozen. That feeling of being the wrong person in the wrong place derives chiefly from knowing that whoever—or *whatever*—the audience came to see won't be there. The part of me that creates the stories exists only in solitude. The one who shows up to share anecdotes and answer questions is a poor substitute for the story-maker.

In November of 2013, I was being driven to my final appearance in Paris at Le Grand Rex, seating capacity 2,800. I felt nervous and out of place. I was in the backseat of a big black SUV. The streets were narrow and the traffic was heavy. I had my little sheaf of papers—a few remarks, a short reading—in a folder on my lap. At a stoplight we pulled up beside a bus, the two large vehicles snugged together so tightly they were almost touching. I looked in one of the bus windows and saw a woman in business dress, possibly headed home from work. I wished momentarily that I was sitting beside her, headed home myself, ready for a spot of dinner followed by a couple of hours reading a book in a comfy chair with good light, instead of being driven to a sold-out theater full of fans whose language I did not speak.

Perhaps *la femme* felt my gaze. More likely she was just bored with her newspaper. In any case, she raised her head and looked over at me, only feet away. Our eyes met. What I imagined I saw in hers was a wistful wish to be in the fancy SUV, going someplace where there would be lights and laughter and entertainment instead of back to her apartment, where there would be nothing but a small meal, perhaps taken from the freezer and heated up, followed by the evening news and the same old TV sitcoms. If we could have changed places, both of us might have been happier.

Then she looked back down at her newspaper and I looked back down at my folder. The bus went one way, the SUV another. But for a moment we were close enough to peer into each other's worlds. I thought of this story, and when I got back from my overseas tour, I sat down and wrote it in a burst.

That Bus
Is Another World

Wilson's mother, not one of the world's shiny happy people, had a saying: "When things go wrong, they keep going wrong until there's tears."

Mindful of this, as he was of all the folk wisdom he'd learned at his mother's knee ("An orange is gold in the morning and lead at night" was another gem), Wilson was careful to take out travel insurance—which he thought of as bumpers—ahead of occasions that were particularly important, and no occasion in his adult life was more important than his trip to New York, where he would present his portfolio and his pitch to the top brass at Market Forward.

MF was one of the most important advertising firms of the Internet age. Wilson's company, Southland Concepts, was just a one-man outfit based in Birmingham. Such chances as this didn't come around twice, which made a bumper vital. That was why he arrived at Birmingham-Shuttlesworth Airport at 4:00 a.m. for a 6:00 a.m. nonstop. The flight would put him into LaGuardia at nine twenty. His meeting—

actually an audition—was scheduled for two thirty. A five-hour bumper seemed travel insurance enough.

At first, all went well. The gate attendant checked and got approval for Wilson to store his portfolio in the first-class closet, although Wilson himself was of course flying coach. In such matters the trick was to ask early, before people started getting hassled. Hassled folks didn't want to hear about how important your portfolio was; how it might be the ticket to your future.

He did have to check one suitcase, because if he turned out to be a finalist for the Green Century account (and that could happen, he was actually very well positioned), he might be in New York for ten days. He had no idea how long the winnowing process would take, and he didn't want to send his clothes out to the hotel laundry any more than he intended to order meals from room service. Hotel extras were expensive in all big cities, and gruesomely expensive in the Big Apple.

Things didn't start going wrong until the plane, which took off on time, reached New York. There it took its place in an overhead traffic jam, circling and pogoing in gray air over that point of arrival the pilots so rightly called LaGarbage. There were not-so-funny jokes and outright complaints, but Wilson remained serene. His travel insurance was in place; his bumper was thick.

The plane landed at ten thirty, slightly over an hour late. Wilson proceeded to the luggage carousel, where his bag did not appear. And did not appear. And did not appear. Finally he and a bearded old man in a black beret were the only ones left, and the last unclaimed items remaining on the carousel were a pair of snowshoes and a large travel-stained plant with drooping leaves.

"This is impossible," Wilson told the old man. "The flight was nonstop."

The old man shrugged. "Must have mistagged them in Birmingham. Our shit could be on its way to Honolulu by now, for all we know. I'm toddling over to Lost Luggage. Want to accompany me?"

Wilson did, thinking of his mother's saying. And thanking God he still had his portfolio.

He was halfway through the Lost Luggage form when a baggage handler spoke up from behind him. "Does this belong to either of you gentlemen?"

Wilson turned and saw his tartan suitcase, looking damp.

"Fell off the back of the baggage-train," the handler said, comparing the claim check stapled to Wilson's ticket folder to the one on the suitcase. "Happens once in awhile. You should take a claim form in case something's broken."

"Where's mine?" asked the old man in the beret.

"Can't help you there," the handler said. "But we almost always find them in the end."

"Yeah," the old man said, "but the end is not yet."

By the time Wilson left the terminal with his suitcase, portfolio, and carry-on bag, it was closing in on eleven thirty. Several more flights had arrived in the meantime, and the taxi queue was long.

I have a bumper, he soothed himself. Three hours is plenty. Also, I'm under the overhang and out of the rain. Count your blessings and relax.

He rehearsed his pitch as he inched forward, visualizing each oversize showcard in his portfolio and reminding himself to be cool. To mount his very best charm offensive and put the potentially enormous change in his fortunes out of his mind the minute he walked into 245 Park Avenue.

Green Century was a multinational oil company, and its ecologically optimistic name had become a liability when one of its undersea wells had popped its top not far from Gulf Shores, Alabama. The gush had not been quite as catastrophic as the one following the *Deepwater Horizon* disaster, but bad enough. And oh dear, that name. The late-night comedians had been having a ball with it. (Letterman: "What's green and black and crap all over?") The Green Century CEO's first public whiny response—"We have to go after the oil where it is, you'd think people would understand that"—had not helped; an Internet cartoon showing an oil well poking out of the CEO's ass with his words captioned below had gone viral.

Green Century's PR team went to Market Forward, their longtime agency, with what they believed was a brilliant idea. They wanted to sub out the damage control campaign to a small southern ad agency, making hay from the fact that they weren't using the same old New York sharpies to soothe the American people. They were especially concerned with the opinions of those Americans living below what the New York sharpies no doubt referred to at their fancy cocktail parties as the Mason-Dumbass Line.

The taxi queue inched forward. Wilson looked at his watch. Five to twelve.

Not to worry, he told himself, but he was starting to.

He finally climbed into a Jolly Dingle cab at twenty past noon. He hated the idea of dragging his runway-dampened suitcase into a high-priced office suite in a Manhattan business building—how country that would look—but he was starting to think he might have to forgo a stop at the hotel to drop it off.

The cab was a bright yellow minivan. The driver was a melancholy Sikh living beneath an enormous orange turban. Lucite-encased pictures of his wife and children dangled and swung from the rearview mirror. The radio was tuned to 1010 WINS, its tooth-rattling xylophone ID playing every four minutes or so.

"Treffik very bad today," the Sikh said as they inched toward the airport exit. This seemed to be the extent of his conversation. "Treffik very, very bad."

The rain grew heavier as they crawled toward Manhattan. Wilson felt his bumper growing thinner with each pause and lurch of peristaltic forward motion. He had half an hour to make his pitch, half an hour only. Would they hold the slot for him if he were late? Would they say, "Fellows, of the fourteen small southern agencies we're auditioning today for the big stage—a star is born, and all that—only one has a proven record of working with firms that have suffered environmental mishaps, and that one is Southland Concepts. Therefore, let us not leave Mr. James Wilson out just because he's a bit late."

They *might* say that, but on the whole, Wilson thought . . . not. What they wanted most was to stop all those late-night jokes ASAP. That made the pitch all-important, but of course every asshole has a pitch. (That was one of his father's pearls of wisdom.) He had to be on time.

Quarter past one. When things go wrong they keep going wrong, he thought. He didn't want to think it, but he did. Until there are tears.

As they approached the Midtown Tunnel, he leaned

forward and asked the Sikh for an ETA. The orange turban wagged dolefully from side to side. "Cannot say, sir. Treffik very, very bad."

"Half an hour?"

There was a long pause, and then the Sikh said, "Perhaps." That carefully chosen placatory word was enough to make Wilson understand that his situation was critical going on dire.

I can leave my goddam suitcase at the Market Forward reception desk, he thought. Then at least I won't have to drag it into the conference room.

He leaned forward and said, "Never mind the hotel. Take me to Two forty-five Park."

The tunnel was a claustrophobe's nightmare: start and stop, start and stop. Traffic on the other side, moving crosstown on Thirty-Fourth Street, was no better. The minivan cab was just high enough for Wilson to see every dispiriting obstacle ahead. Yet when they reached Madison, he began to relax a little. It would be close, much closer than he liked, but there would be no need to make a humiliating call saying he was going to be a trifle late. Skipping the hotel had been the right move.

Only then came the broken water main, and the sawhorses, and the Sikh had to go around. "Worse than when Obama comes," he said, while 1010 WINS promised that if Wilson gave them twenty-two minutes, they'd give him the world. The xylophone chattered like loose teeth.

I don't want the world, he thought. I just want to get to 245 Park by quarter past two. Twenty past at the latest.

The Jolly Dingle eventually returned to Madison. It sprinted almost to Thirty-Sixth Street, then stopped short. Wilson imagined a football announcer telling the audience that while the run had been flashy, any gain on the play had been negligible. The windshield wipers thumped. A reporter talked about electronic cigarettes. Then there was an ad for Sleepy's.

Wilson thought, Take a chill pill. I can walk from here, if I have to. Eleven blocks, that's all. Only it was raining, and he'd be dragging his goddam suitcase.

A Peter Pan bus rolled up next to the cab and stopped with a chuff of airbrakes. Wilson was high enough to be able to look through his window and into the bus. Five or six feet away from him, no more than that, a good-looking woman was reading a magazine. Next to her, in the aisle seat, a man in a black raincoat was hunting through the briefcase balanced on his knees.

The Sikh honked his horn, then raised his hands, palms out, as if to say, *Look what the world has done to me.*

Wilson watched the good-looking woman touch the corners of her mouth, perhaps checking her lipstick's staying power. The man next to her was now rummaging through the pocket inside the lid of his briefcase. He took out a black scarf, put it to his nose, sniffed it.

Now why would he do that? Wilson wondered. Is it his wife's perfume or the scent of her powder?

For the first time since boarding the plane in Birmingham, he forgot about Green Century and Market Forward and the radical improvement of his circumstances that might result if the meeting, now less than half an hour away, went well. For the moment he was fascinated—more than fascinated, enthralled—by the woman's delicately probing fingers and the man with the scarf to his nose. It came to him that he was looking into another world. Yes. That bus was another world. That man and that woman had their own appointments, undoubtedly with balloons of hope attached. They had bills to pay. They had sisters and brothers and certain childhood toys that remained unforgotten. The woman might have had an abortion while in college. The man might have a penis ring. They might have pets, and if so, the pets would have names.

Wilson had a momentary image—vague and unformed but tremendous—of a clockwork galaxy where the separate wheels and cogs went through mysterious motions, perhaps to some karmic end, perhaps for no reason at all. Here was the world of the Jolly Dingle cab, and five feet away was the world of the Peter Pan bus. Between them were only five feet and two layers of glass. Wilson was amazed by this self-evident fact.

"Such treffik," the Sikh said. "Worse than Obama, I tell you."

The man dropped the black scarf from his nose. He held it in one hand and reached into the pocket of his raincoat with the other. The woman in the window seat of the bus flicked through her magazine. The man turned to her. Wilson saw his lips move. The woman lifted her head, eyes widening in apparent surprise. The man bent closer, as if to confide a secret. Wilson didn't realize the thing the man had taken from his raincoat pocket was a knife until he cut the woman's throat with it.

Her eyes widened. Her lips parted. She raised a hand toward her neck. The man in the raincoat used the hand holding the knife to push her hand gently but firmly down. At the same time he pressed the black scarf to the woman's throat and held it there. Then he kissed the hollow of her temple, looking through her hair as he did it. He saw Wilson, and his lips parted in a smile wide enough to show two rows of small, even teeth. He nodded to Wilson, as if to say either *have a nice day* or *now we have a secret*. There was a drop of blood on the woman's window. It fattened and ran down the glass. Still holding the scarf to the woman's throat, Raincoat Man slipped a finger into her slackening mouth. He was still smiling at Wilson as he did it.

"Finally!" the Sikh said, and the Jolly Dingle cab began to move.

"Did you see that?" Wilson asked. His voice sounded flat and unsurprised. "That man. That man on the bus. The one with the woman."

"What is it, sir?" the Sikh asked. The light on the corner turned yellow and the Sikh scooted through, ignoring a flourish of horns as he switched lanes. The Peter Pan bus was left behind. Ahead, Grand Central loomed in the rain, looking like a penitentiary.

It was only with the cab moving again that Wilson thought of his cell. He took it out of his coat pocket and looked at it. If he'd been a quick thinker (always his brother's department, according to their mother), he could have snapped Raincoat Man's picture. It was too late for that, but not too late to call 911. Of course he couldn't make such a call anonymously; his name and number would flash on some official screen as soon as the call went through. They would call him back to make sure he wasn't a prankster whiling away a rainy afternoon in New York City. Then they would want information, which he would have to give—no choice—at the nearest police station. They would want his story several times. What they would not want was his pitch.

The pitch was titled "Give us three years and we'll prove it." Wilson thought of how it was supposed to go. He would begin by telling the gathered PR flaks and executives that the spill had to be faced directly. It was there; volunteers were still washing oil-coated birds in Dawn detergent; it couldn't be swept under the rug. But, he would say, atonement doesn't have to be ugly and sometimes the truth can be beautiful. People want to believe in you guys, he would say. They need you, after all. They need you to get from Point A to Point B, and that makes them unwilling to see themselves as accessories in the rape of the environment. At this point he would open his portfolio and display the first card: a photo of a boy and girl standing on a pristine beach, backs to the camera, looking out at water so blue it almost hurt. ENERGY AND BEAUTY **CAN** GO TOGETHER, the copy read. GIVE US THREE YEARS AND WE'LL PROVE IT.

Calling 911 was so simple a child could do it. In fact, children did. When someone broke in. When Little Sister fell downstairs. Or if Daddy was tuning up on Mommy.

Next came his storyboard for a proposed TV commercial that would run in all the states on the Gulf, emphasis on local news and the cable twenty-fours like FOX and MSNBC. In time-lapse photography, a dirty, oil-smeared beach would become clean again. "We have a responsibility to fix our mistakes," the narrator would say (with the slightest southern twang). "It's how we do business and how we treat our neighbors. Give us three years and we'll prove it."

Next, the print ads. The radio ads. And in Phase Two—

"Sir? You said what?"

I could call, Wilson thought, but the guy will probably be off the bus and long gone before the police can get there. Probably? Almost certainly.

He turned to look behind him. The bus was way back there now. Maybe, he thought, the woman cried out. Maybe the other passengers are already piling onto the guy, the way passengers piled onto the Shoe Bomber when they figured out what he was up to.

Then he thought of the way the man in the raincoat had smiled at him. Also of how he'd put his finger in the woman's loose mouth.

Wilson thought, Speaking of pranks, it might not have been what I thought it was. It could have been a gag. One they played all the time. A flash-mob kind of thing.

The more he considered this, the more possible it seemed. Men cut women's throats in alleys and on TV shows, not on Peter Pan buses in the middle of the afternoon. As for himself, he had put together a fine campaign. He was the right man in the right place at the right time, and you rarely got more than one chance in this world. That had never been one of his mother's sayings, but it was a fact.

"Sir?"

"Let me out at the next light," Wilson said. "I can walk from there."

For Hesh Kestin

I saw lots of horror films when I was a kid (you probably guessed that). I was an easy target, and most of them scared me to death. It was dark, the images were so much bigger than you were, and the sound was so loud that the scares continued even when you shut your eyes. On TV, the scare quotient tended to be lower. There were commercials to break the rhythm of the thing, and the worst parts were sometimes snipped out to avoid giving complexes to any little shavers who might be watching (alas, already too late for me; I'd seen the dead woman rising out of the tub in *Diabolique*). As a last resort, you could always go into the kitchen and grab a Hires out of the fridge, lingering until the scary music was replaced by some local huckster screaming, *"Cars, cars, cars! No credit check! We'll sell to ANYONE!"*

One film I saw on TV did the job, however. At least the first hour or so of its seventy-seven-minute run did; the denouement wrecked the whole thing, and to this day I wish somebody would remake it and carry its hair-raising premise right through to the end. That film has perhaps the best horror-movie title of all time: *I Bury the Living*.

I was thinking of that movie when I wrote this story.

Obits

Keep it clear, and keep it in a straight line.

That was the gospel according to Vern Higgins, who headed up the journalism department at the University of Rhode Island, where I got my degree. A lot of what I heard at school went in one ear and out the other, but not that, because Professor Higgins hammered on it. He said that people need clarity and concision in order to start the process of understanding.

Your real job as journalists, he told his classes, is to give people the facts that allow them to make decisions and go forward. So don't be fancy. Don't go all twee and hifalutin. Start at the start, lay the middle out neatly, so the facts of each event lead logically to the next, and end at the end. Which, in reporting, he emphasized, is always the end for *now*. And don't you ever sink to that lazy crap about how *some people believe* or *the general consensus of opinion is*. A source for each fact, that's the rule. Then write it all in plain English, unadorned and unvarnished. Flights of rhetoric belong on the op-ed page.

I doubt if anyone will believe what follows, and my career at *Neon Circus* had very little to do with good writing, but I intend to do my best here: the facts of each event leading to the next. Beginning, middle, and end.

The end for now, at least.

Good reporting always begins with the five Ws: who, what, when, where, and why if you can find out. In my case, the why's a tough one.

The who is easy enough, though; your less-than-fearless narrator is Michael Anderson. I was twenty-seven at the time these things happened. I graduated from URI with a Bachelor of Arts in Journalism. For two years after college I lived with my parents in Brooklyn and worked for one of those Daily Shopper freebies, rewriting newswire items to break up the ads and coupons. I kept my résumé (such as it was) in constant rotation, but none of the papers in New York, Connecticut, or New Jersey wanted me. This didn't completely surprise my parents or me, not because my grades were lousy (they weren't), and not because my clip folder—mostly stories from the URI student newspaper, *The Good 5 Cent Cigar*—were badly written (a couple of them won awards), but because newspapers weren't hiring. Quite the opposite.

(If Professor Higgins saw all these parentheses, he'd kill me.)

My parents began urging me—gently, gently—to start looking for some other kind of job. "In a related field," my father said in his most diplomatic voice. "Maybe advertising."

"Advertising isn't news," I said. "Advertising is *anti*-news." But I caught his drift: he had visions of me still grabbing midnight snacks out of their fridge when I was forty. Slacker Deluxe.

Reluctantly, I began making a list of possible advertising firms that might like to hire a young copywriter with good chops but no experience. Then, on the night before I planned to begin sending out copies of my résumé to the firms on that list, I had a goofy idea. Sometimes—often—I lie awake nights wondering how different my life might have been if that idea had never crossed my mind.

Neon Circus was one of my favorite websites in those days. If you're a connoisseur of snark and schaden-freude, you know it: TMZ with better writers. They mostly cover the local "celeb scene," with occasional prospecting trips into the stinkier crevasses of New York and New Jersey politics. If I had to sum up its take on the world, I'd show you a photo we ran about six months into my employment there. It showed Rod Peterson (always referred to in the *Circus* as "the Barry Manilow of his generation") outside Pacha. His date is bent over, puking in the gutter. He's got a happy-ass grin on his face and his hand up the back of her dress. Caption: ROD PETERSON, THE BARRY MANILOW OF HIS GENERATION, EXPLORES NEW YORK'S LOWER EAST SIDE.

Circus is essentially a webazine, with lots of click-friendly departments: CELEB WALK OF SHAME, VILE CONSUMPTION, I WISH I HADN'T SEEN THAT, WORST TV OF THE WEEK, WHO WRITES THIS CRAP. There are more, but you get the idea. That night, with a stack of résumés ready to send out to firms I didn't really want to work for, I went to *Neon Circus* for a little revivifying junk food, and on the home page discovered that a hot young actor named Jack Briggs had OD'd. There was a photo of him staggering out of a downtown hotspot the week before, typical bad taste for *Neon Circus*, but the news item accompanying it was surprisingly straight, and not *Circus*-y at all. That was when inspiration struck. I did some research on the Internet, just screwing around, then wrote a quick and nasty obituary.

Jack Briggs, noted for his horrific performance in last year's Holy Rollers *as a talking bookshelf in love with Jennifer Lawrence, was found dead in his hotel room surrounded by some of his favorite powdered treats. He joins the 27 Club, which also contains such noted substance abusers as Robert Johnson, Jimi Hendrix, Janis Joplin, Kurt Cobain, and Amy Winehouse. Briggs shambled onto the acting scene in 2005, when . . .*

Well, you get it. Juvenile, disrespectful, downright nasty. If I'd been serious that night, I probably would have dragged the finished obit to the trash, because it seemed to go beyond even *Neon Circus*'s usual snark and into outright cruelty. But because I was just messing (it has since occurred to me to wonder how many careers have started while just messing), I sent it to them.

Two days later—the Internet speeds everything up—I got an email from someone named Jeroma Whitfield saying they not only wanted to run it, they wanted to discuss the possibility that I might perhaps write more in the same nasty-ass vein. Could I come into the city and discuss it at lunch?

My tie and sportcoat turned out to be a case of serious overdressing. The *Circus* offices on Third Avenue were filled with men and women who looked a lot more like boys and girls, all running around in rock-band tees. A couple of the women wore shorts, and I saw a guy in carpenter overalls with a Sharpie poked through his Mohawk. He was the head of the sports department, it turned out, responsible for one memorable story titled JINTS TAKE ANOTHER SHIT IN THE RED ZONE. I guess I shouldn't have been surprised. This was (and is) journalism in the Age of the Internet, and for every person in the offices that day, there were another five or six stringers working from home. For starvation wages, I hardly need add.

I have heard that once upon a gilded time, in New York's misty and mythic past, there were publishers' lunches at places like the Four Seasons, le Cirque, and the Russian Tea Room. Perhaps, but my lunch that day was in the cluttered office of Jeroma Whitfield. It consisted of deli sandwiches and Dr. Brown's Cream Soda. Jeroma was ancient by *Circus* standards (early forties), and I disliked her pushy abrasiveness from the start, but she wanted to hire me to write a weekly obituary column, and that made her a goddess. She even had a title for the new feature: Speaking Ill of the Dead.

Could I do it? I could.

Would I do it for shit money? I would. At least to start with.

After the column became the most-visited page on the *Neon Circus* site and my name had become associated with it, I dickered for more dough, partly because I wanted to move into my own apartment in the city and partly because I was tired of getting peon's wages for singlehandedly writing the page that was bringing in the most ad revenue.

That first dickering session was a modest success, probably because my demands were couched as tentative requests, and the requests were almost laughably humble. Four months later, when rumors began to circulate of a big corporation buying us for actual strutting money, I visited Jeroma's office and asked for a larger raise, this time with rather less humility.

"Sorry, Mike," she said. "In the memorable words of Hall and Oates, I can't go for that, no can do. Have a Yook."

Holding pride of place on Jeroma's cluttered desk was a large glass bowl filled with menthol-flavored eucalyptus drops. The wrappers were covered with gung-ho sayings. *Let's hear your battle cry,* read one. Another advised (it gives the grammarian in me chills to report this) *Turn can do into can did.*

"No thanks. Give me a chance to lay this out for you before you say no."

I marshaled my arguments; you might say I attempted to turn can do into can did. The bottom line was my belief that I was owed a wage more commensurate with the revenue Speaking Ill of the Dead was generating. Especially if *Neon Circus* was going to be bought out by a major corporate playa.

When I finally shut up, she unwrapped a Yook, popped it between her plum-colored lips, and said, "Okay! Great! If you've got that off your chest, you might want to get to work on Bump DeVoe. He's a tasty one."

He was indeed a tasty one. Bump, lead singer of the Raccoons, had been shot dead by his girlfriend while trying to sneak in through the bedroom window of her house in the Hamptons, probably as a joke. She had mistaken him for a burglar. What made the story such a deliciously fat pitch was the gun she used: a birthday present from the Bumpster himself, now the newest member of the 27 Club and perhaps comparing guitar chops with Brian Jones.

"So you're not even going to respond," I said. "That's how little respect you have for me."

She leaned forward, smiling just enough to show the tips of her little white teeth. I could smell menthol. Or eucalyptus. Or both. "Let me be frank, okay? For a guy who's still living with his parents in Brooklyn, you have an extremely inflated idea of your importance in the scheme of things. You think nobody else can piss on the graves of dimwit assholes who party themselves to death? Think again. I've got half a dozen stringers who can do it, and probably turn in copy funnier than yours."

"So why don't I walk, and you can find out if that's true?" I was pretty mad.

Jeroma grinned and clacked her eucalyptus drop against her teeth. "Be my guest. But if you go, Speaking Ill of the Dead doesn't go with you. It's my title, and it stays right here at *Circus*. Of course you *do* have some cred now, and I won't deny it. So here's your choice, kiddo. You can go back to your computer and get humping on Bump, or you can take a meeting at the *New York Post*. They'll probably hire you. You'll end up writing shit squibs on Page Six with no byline. If that floats your boat, go team."

"I'll write the obit. But we're going to revisit this, Jerri."

"Not on *my* watch, we're not. And don't call me Jerri. You know better than that."

I got up to go. My face was burning. I probably looked like a stop sign.

"And have a Yook," she said. "Hell, take two. They're very consoling."

I cast a disdainful look at the bowl and left, restraining (barely) a childish urge to slam the door.

• • •

If you're picturing a bustling newsroom like the one you see behind Wolf Blitzer on CNN, or in that old movie about Woodward and Bernstein nailing Nixon, reconsider. As I said, most of the *Circus* writers do their work from home. Our little news-nest (if you want to dignify what *Circus* does by calling it news) is roughly the size of a doublewide trailer. Twenty school desks are crammed in there, facing a row of muted TVs on one wall. The desks are equipped with battered laptops, each one bearing a hilarious sticker reading PLEASE RESPECT THESE MACHINES.

The place was almost empty that morning. I sat in the back row by the wall, in front of a poster showing a Thanksgiving dinner in a toilet bowl. Beneath this charming image was the motto PLEASE SHIT WHERE YOU EAT. I turned on the laptop, took my printouts concerning Bump DeVoe's short and undistinguished career from my briefcase, and shuffled through them while the cruncher booted. I opened Word, typed BUMP DeVOE OBIT in the proper box, then just sat there, staring at the blank document. I was paid to yuk it up in the face of death for twentysomethings who feel that death is always for the other guy, but it's hard to be funny when you're pissed off.

"Having trouble getting started?"

It was Katie Curran, a tall, svelte blond for whom I felt a strong lust that was almost certainly unrequited. She was always kind to me, and unfailingly sweet. She laughed at my jokes. Such characteristics rarely signal lust. Was I surprised? Not at all. She was hot; I am not. I am, if I may be frank, exactly that geek all the teenpix make fun of. Until my third month working at *Circus*, I even had the perfect geek accessory: spectacles mended with tape.

"A little," I said. I could smell her perfume. Some kind of fruit. Fresh pears, maybe. Fresh somethings, anyway.

She sat down at the next desk, a long-legged vision in faded jeans. "When that happens to me, I type *The quick brown fox jumped over the lazy dog* three times, real fast. It opens the creative floodgates." She spread her arms, showing me how floodgates open, and incidentally giving me a breathtaking view of breasts snugly encased in a black tank top.

"I don't think that will work in this case," I said.

Katie wrote her own feature, not as popular as Speaking Ill of the Dead, but still widely read; she had half a million followers on Twitter. (Modesty forbids me to say how many I had in those days, but go ahead and think seven figures; you won't be wrong.) Hers was called Getting Sloshed with Katie. The idea was to go out drinking with celebs we hadn't dissed yet— and even some we had went for the deal, go figure— and interview them as they got progressively more shitfaced. It was amazing what came out, and Katie got it all on her cute little pink iPhone.

She was supposed to get drunk right along with them, but she had a way of leaving a single drink but a quarter finished as they moved from one watering hole to another. The celebs rarely noticed. What they noticed was the perfect oval of her face, her masses of wheat-blond hair, and her wide gray eyes, which always projected the same message: Oh gosh, you're so interesting. They lined up for the chop even though Katie had effectively ended half a dozen careers since joining the *Circus* staff eighteen months or so before I came on board. Her most famous interview was with the family comedian who opined of Michael Jackson, "That candy-ass wanna-be-whitebread is better off dead."

"I guess she said no raise, huh?" Katie nodded toward Jeroma's office.

"How did you know I was going to ask for a raise? Did I tell you?" Mesmerized by those misty orbs, I might have told her anything.

"No, but everyone knew you were going to, and everyone knew she was going to say no. If she said yes, everyone would ask. By saying no to the most deserving, she shuts the rest of us down cold."

The most deserving. That gave me a little shiver of delight. Especially coming from Katie.

"So are you going to stick?"

"For now," I said. Talking out of the side of my mouth. It always works for Bogie in the old movies, but Katie got up, brushing nonexistent lint from the entrancingly flat midriff of her top.

"I've got a piece to write. Vic Albini. God, he could put it away."

"The gay action hero," I said.

"News flash: not gay." She gave me a mysterious smile and drifted off, leaving me to wonder. But not really wanting to know.

I sat in front of the blank Bump DeVoe document for ten minutes, made a false start, deleted it, and sat for another ten minutes. I could feel Jeroma's eyes on me and knew she was smirking, if only on the inside. I couldn't work with that stare on me, even if I was just imagining it. I decided to go home and write the DeVoe piece there. Maybe something would occur on the subway, which was always a good thinking place for me. I started to close the laptop, and that was when inspiration struck again, just as it had on the night when I saw the item about Jack Briggs departing for that great A-list buffet in the sky. I decided I *was* going to quit, and damn the consequences, but I would not go quietly.

I dumped the blank DeVoe document and created a new one, which I titled JEROMA WHITFIELD OBIT. I wrote with absolutely no pause. Two hundred poisonous words just poured out of my fingers and onto the screen.

Jeroma Whitfield, known as Jerri to her close friends (according to reports, she had a couple in pre-school), died today at—

I checked the clock.

—10:40 A.M. According to co-workers on the scene, she choked on her own bile. Although she graduated cum laude from Vassar, Jerri spent the last three years of her life whoring on Third Avenue, where she oversaw a crew of roughly two dozen galley slaves, all more talented than herself. She is survived by her husband, known to the staff of Neon Circus as Emasculated Toad, and one child, an ugly little fucker affectionately referred to by the staff as Pol Pot. Co-workers all agree that although she lacked even a vestige of talent, Jerri possessed a domineering and merciless personality that more than made up for it. Her braying voice was known to cause brain hemorrhages, and her lack of a sense of humor was legend. In lieu of flowers, Toad and Pot request that

*those who knew her express their joy at her demise by
sending eucalyptus drops to the starving children of
Africa. A memorial service will be held at the* Neon
Circus *offices, where joyful survivors can exchange
precious memories and join in singing "Ding Dong,
the Witch Is Dead."*

My idea as I started this diatribe was to print a
dozen copies, tape them up everywhere—including
the bathrooms and both elevators—then say see-
ya-wouldn't-want-to-be-ya to both the *Neon Circus*
offices and the Cough Drop Queen for good. I might
even have done it if I hadn't reread what I had written
and discovered it wasn't funny. It wasn't even close to
funny. It was the work of a child having a tantrum.
Which led me to wonder if *all* my obits had been
equally unfunny and stupid.

For the first time (you might not believe it, but I
swear it's true) it came to me that Bump DeVoe had
been a *real person*, and somewhere people might be
crying because he was gone. The same was probably
true of Jack Briggs . . . and Frank Ford (who I had
described as "noted *Tonight Show* crotch-grabber") . . .
and Trevor Wills, a reality-show star who committed suicide after being photographed in bed with
his brother-in-law. Those pix the *Circus* had cheerfully put online, just adding a black strip to cover the
brother-in-law's naughty bits (Wills's had been safely
out of sight, and you can probably guess where).

It also came to me that I was spending the most
creatively fecund years of my life doing bad work.
Shameful, in fact, a word that would never have
occurred to Jeroma Whitfield in any context.

Instead of printing the document, I closed it, dragged

it to the trash, and shut down the laptop. I thought about marching back into Jeroma's office and telling her I was done writing stuff that was the equivalent of a toddler throwing poo on the wall, but a cautious part of my mind—the traffic cop most of us have up there—told me to wait. To think it over and be absolutely sure.

Twenty-four hours, the traffic cop decreed. *Hit a movie this afternoon and sleep on it tonight. If you still feel the same way in the morning, go with God, my son.*

"Off so soon?" Katie asked from her own laptop, and for the first time since my first day here, I wasn't stopped cold in my tracks by those wide gray eyes. I just tipped her a wave and left.

I was attending a matinee of *Dr. Strangelove* at Film Forum when my mobile started vibrating. Because the living room–size theater was empty except for me, two snoozing drunks, and a couple of teenagers making vacuum cleaner noises in the back row, I risked looking at the screen and saw a text from Katie Curran: **Stop what you're doing and call me RIGHT NOW!**

I went out to the lobby without too much regret (although I always like to see Slim Pickens ride the bomb down) and called her back. It wouldn't be an exaggeration to say the first two words out of her mouth changed my life.

"Jeroma's dead."

"*What?*" I nearly screamed.

The popcorn girl glanced up at me over the top of her magazine, startled.

"Dead, Mike! *Dead!* She choked to death on one of those damn eucalyptus drops she's always sucking on."

Died at 10:40 A.M., I'd written. *Choked to death on her own bile.*

Only a coincidence, of course, but offhand I couldn't think of a more malefic one. God had turned Jeroma Whitfield from can do into can did.

"Mike? Are you there?"

"Yes."

"She had no second-in-command. You know that, right?"

"Uh-huh." Now I was thinking of her telling me to have a Yook, and clicking her own against her teeth.

"So I'm taking it on myself to call a staff meeting tomorrow at ten. Somebody's got to do it. Will you come?"

"I don't know. Maybe not." I was walking toward the door to Houston Street. Before I got there, I remembered that I'd left my briefcase by my movie seat and turned back to get it, yanking at my hair with my free hand. The popcorn girl was looking at me with outright suspicion now. "I'd pretty much made up my mind to quit this morning."

"I knew. I could see it on your face when you left."

The thought of Katie looking at my face might have tied up my tongue in other circumstances, but not then. "Did it happen at the office?"

"Yes. It was pushing on for two o'clock. There were four of us in the bullpen, not really working, just hanging out and swapping stories and rumors. You know how it goes."

I did. Those gossipy bull sessions were one of the reasons I went to the office instead of working at home in Brooklyn. Plus getting a chance to feast my eyes on Katie, of course.

"Her door was closed, but the blinds were open."

They usually were. Unless she was taking a meeting with someone she considered important, Jeroma liked to keep an eye on her vassals. "The first I knew was when Pinky said, 'What's wrong with the boss? She's all Gangnam Style.'

"So I looked, and she was jerking back and forth in her office chair, grabbing at her neck. Then she fell out of the chair and all I could see was her feet, drumming up and down. Roberta asked what we should do. I didn't even bother answering that."

They burst in. Roberta Hill and Chin Pak Soo lifted her up by the armpits. Katie got behind her and gave her the Heimlich. Pinky stood in the doorway and waved his hands. The first hard heave on her diaphragm did nothing. Katie shouted for Pinky to call 911 and went at her again. The second heave sent one of those eucalyptus drops flying all the way across the room. Jeroma took a single deep breath, opened her eyes, and spoke her last words (and very fitting they were, IMHO): "What the fuck?" Then she began to shudder all over again, and stopped breathing. Chin gave her artificial respiration until the paramedics arrived, but no joy.

"I checked the clock on her wall after she quit breathing," Katie said. "You know, that awful retro Huckleberry Hound thing? I thought . . . I don't know, I guess I thought someone might ask me for the time of death, like on *Law & Order*. Stupid what goes through your mind at a time like that. It was ten to three. Not even an hour ago, but it seems longer."

"So she could have choked on the cough drop at two forty," I said. Not *ten* forty, but *two* forty. I knew it was just another coincidence, like *Lincoln* and *Kennedy* having the same number of letters; forty past comes around twenty-four times a day. But I still didn't like it.

"I suppose, but I don't see what difference it makes." Katie sounded annoyed. "Will you come in tomorrow or not? Please come in, Mike. I need you."

To be needed by Katie Curran! Ai-yi-yi!

"Okay. But will you do something for me?"

"I guess so."

"I forgot to empty the trash on the computer I was using. The one back by the Thanksgiving dinner poster. Will you do it?" This request made no rational sense to me even then. I just wanted that bad joke of an obituary gone.

"You're crazy," she said, "but if you absolutely swear on your mother's name to come in tomorrow at ten, sure. Listen, Mike, this is a chance for us. We might end up owning a piece of the gold mine instead of just working in it."

"I'll be there."

Almost everyone was, except for stringers working among the primitives in darkest Connecticut and New Jersey. Even scabby little Irving Ramstein, who wrote a joke column called (I don't understand it, so don't ask me) Politically Incorrect Chickens, showed up. Katie ran the meeting with aplomb, telling us that the show would go on.

"It's what Jeroma would have wanted," Pinky said.

"Who gives a shit what Jeroma would have wanted," Georgina Bukowski said. "I just want to keep getting a paycheck. Also, if remotely possible, a piece of the action."

This cry was taken up by several others—*Action! Action! Piece-a-da-action!*—until our offices sounded like a messhall riot in an old prison movie. Katie let it run its course, then shushed them.

"How could she choke to death?" Chin asked. "The gumdrop came out."

"It wasn't a gumdrop," Roberta said. "It was one of those smelly cough drops she was always sucking on. Craptolyptus."

"Whatever, dude, it still came flying out when Kates gave her the Hug of Life. We all saw it."

"*I* didn't," Pinky said. "I was on the phone. And on fucking *hold*."

Katie said that she had interviewed one of the EMTs—no doubt using her large gray eyes to good effect—and had been told that the choking fit might have triggered a heart attack. And, in my effort to follow the dictum of Professor Higgins and keep all the relevant facts straight, I will jump ahead here and report the autopsy on our Dear Leader proved that to be the case. If Jeroma had gotten the *Neon Circus* headline she deserved, it probably would have been HEAD HONCHO POPS PUMP.

That meeting was long and loud. Already displaying talents that made her a natural to step into Jeroma's Jimmy Choos, Katie allowed them to fully vent their feelings (expressed mostly in bursts of wild, semihysterical laughter) before telling them to get back to work, because time, tide, and Internet waits for no man. Or woman, either. She said she would be talking with the *Circus*'s main investors before the week was out, and then invited me to step into Jeroma's office.

"Measuring the drapes?" I asked when the door was shut. "Or the blinds, in this case?"

She looked at me with what might have been hurt.

Or maybe just surprise. "Do you think I want this job? I'm a *columnist*, Mike, just like you."

"You'd be good at it, though. I know it and so do they." I jerked my head toward our excuse for a newsroom, where everyone was now either hunting and pecking or working the phones. "As for me, I'm just the funny-obit writer. Or was. I've decided to become an emeritus."

"I think I understand why you feel that way." She slipped a piece of paper from the back pocket of her jeans and unfolded it. I knew what it was before she handed it to me. "Curiosity comes with the job, so I peeped in your trash before dumping it. And found this."

I took the sheet, refolded it without looking (I didn't even want to see the print, let alone reread it), and put it in my own pocket. "Is it dumped now?"

"Yes, and that's the only hard copy." She brushed her hair away from her face and looked at me. It might not have been the face that launched a thousand ships, but it surely could have launched several dozen, including a destroyer or two. "I knew you'd ask. Having worked with you for a year and a half, I understand that paranoia is part of your character."

"Thanks."

"No offense intended. In New York, paranoia is a survival skill. But it's no reason to quit what could become a far more lucrative job in the immediate future. Even you must know that a freaky coincidence—and I admit this one's fairly freaky—is just a coincidence. Mike, I need you to stay on board."

Not *we* but *I*. She said she wasn't measuring the drapes; I thought she was.

"You don't understand. I don't think I could do

it anymore even if I wanted to. Not and be funny, at least. It would all come out . . ." I reached, and found a word from my childhood. "Goosh."

Katie frowned, thinking. "Maybe Penny could do it."

Penny Langston was one of those stringers from the darker environs, hired by Jeroma at Katie's suggestion. I had a vague idea that the two women had known each other in college. If so, they could not have been less alike. Penny rarely came in, and when she did, she wore an old baseball cap that never left her head and a macabre smile that rarely left her face. Frank Jessup, the sports guy with the Mohawk, liked to say that Penny always looked about two stress points from going postal.

"But she'd never be as funny as you are," Katie went on. "If you don't want to write obituaries, what *would* you want to do? Assuming you stay at *Circus*, which I pray you will."

"Reviews, maybe. I could write funny ones, I think."

"Hatchet jobs?" Sounding at least marginally hopeful.

"Well . . . yeah. Probably. Some of them." I was good at snark, after all, and I thought I could probably outsnark Joe Queenan on points, possibly by a knockout. And at least it would be dumping on live people who could fight back.

She put her hands on my shoulders, stood on tiptoe, and planted a soft kiss on the corner of my mouth. If I close my eyes, I can still feel that kiss today. She looked at me with those wide gray eyes—the sea on an overcast morning. I'm sure Professor Higgins would roll his eyes at that, but C-list guys like me rarely get kissed by A-list girls like her.

"Think about going on with the obits, would you?" Hands still on my shoulders. Her light scent in my nostrils. Her breasts less than an inch from my chest, and when she took a deep breath, they touched. I can still feel that today too. "This is not just about you or me. The next six weeks are going to be a critical time for the site and the staff. So *think*, okay? Even another month of obits would be helpful. It would give Penny—or someone else—a chance to work her way into the job, with guidance from you. And hey, maybe nobody interesting will die."

Except they always do, and we both knew it.

I probably told her I'd think about it. I can't remember. What I was actually thinking about was lip-locking her right there in Jeroma's office, and damn anyone in the bullpen who might see us. I didn't, though. Outside the rom-coms, guys like me rarely do. I said something or other and then I must have left, because pretty soon I found myself out on the street. I felt poleaxed.

One thing I do remember: when I came to a litter basket on the corner of Third and Fiftieth, I tore the joke obit that was no longer a joke into tiny shreds and threw them in.

That night I ate a pleasant enough dinner with my parents, then went into my room—the same one where I'd gone to sulk on days when my Little League team lost, how depressing is that—and sat down at my desk. The easiest way to get past my unease, it seemed to me, was to write another obit of a living person. Don't they tell you to get back on a horse right away if you've been thrown? Or climb right away to the top diving platform after your jackknife turns into a belly flop? All I needed to do was prove what I already knew: we live in a rational world. Sticking pins in voodoo dolls doesn't kill people. Writing your enemy's name on a scrap of paper and burning it while you recite the Lord's Prayer backwards doesn't kill people. Joke obituaries don't kill people, either.

Nevertheless, I was careful to make a list of possibles consisting solely of proven bad people, such as Faheem Darzi, who had claimed credit for the bus bombing in Miami, and Kenneth Wanderly, an electrician convicted on four counts of rape-murder in Oklahoma. Wanderly seemed like the best possibility on my short list of seven names, and I was about to whomp something up when I thought of Peter Stefano, a worthless fuck if there ever was one.

Stefano was a record producer who choked his girlfriend to death for refusing to record a song he had written. He was now doing time in a medium-security prison when he should have been at a black site in Saudi Arabia, dining on cockroaches, drinking his own pee, and listening to Anthrax played at top volume during the wee hours of the morning. (Just MHO, of course.) The woman he killed was Andi McCoy, who happened to be one of my all-time favorite female singers. If I had been writing joke obits at the time of her death, I never would have written hers; the idea that her soaring voice, easily the equal of the young Joan Baez's, could have been silenced by that domineering idiot still infuriated me five years later. God gives such golden vocal cords to only the chosen few, and Stefano had destroyed McCoy's in a fit of drugged-out pique.

I opened my laptop, typed PETER STEFANO OBIT in the proper field, and dropped the cursor onto the blank document. Once again the words poured out with no pause, like water from a broken pipe.

Slave-driving, no-talent record producer Peter Stefano was discovered dead in his jail cell at the Gowanda State Correctional Facility yesterday morning, and we all shout hooray. Although no official cause of death was announced, a prison source said, "It appears his anal hate-gland ruptured, thus spreading asshole poison through his body. In layman's terms, he had an allergic reaction to his own vile shit."

Although Stefano had his foot on the necks of a great many groups and solo artists, he is especially noted for ruining the careers of the Grenadiers, the Playful Mammals, Joe Dean (who committed suicide after Stefano refused to renegotiate his contract), and of course Andi McCoy. Not content with killing her career, Stefano choked her to death with a lamp cord while high on methamphetamines. He is survived by three grateful ex-wives, five ex-partners, and the two record companies he managed not to bankrupt.

It went on in that vein for another hundred words or so, and was not one of my better efforts (obviously). I didn't care, because it felt right. Not just because Peter Stefano was a bad man, either. It felt right as a *writer*, even though it was bad prose and part of me knew it was a bad thing. This might seem like a sidetrack, but I think (actually I know) it's at the heart of this story. Writing is hard, okay? At least it is for me. And yes, I know that most working stiffs talk about how hard their jobs are, it doesn't matter if they're butchers, bakers, candlestick makers, or obituary

writers. Only sometimes the work is *not* hard. Sometimes it's easy. When that happens you feel like you
do at the bowling alley, watching your ball as it rolls
over just the right diamond and you know you threw
a strike.

Killing Stefano in my computer felt like a strike.

I slept like a baby that night. Maybe some of it was
because I felt as if I'd done something to express my
own rage and dismay over that poor murdered girl—
the stupid waste of her talent. But I felt the same way
when I was writing the Jeroma Whitfield obit, and all
she did was refuse to give me a raise. Mostly it was the
writing itself. I felt the power, and feeling the power
was good.

My first compu-stop at breakfast the next day wasn't
Neon Circus but *Huffington Post*. It almost always was. I
never bothered scrolling down to the celebrity dish or
the side-boob items (frankly speaking, *Circus* did both
of those things much better), but the *Huffpo* headline
stories are always crisp, concise, and late-breaking.
The first item was about a Tea Party governor saying
something *Huffpo* found predictably outrageous. The
next one stopped my cup of coffee halfway to my lips.
It also stopped my breath. The headline read PETER
STEFANO MURDERED IN LIBRARY ALTERCA-
TION.

I put down my untasted coffee—carefully, carefully, not spilling a drop—and read the story. Stefano
and the trustee librarian had been arguing because
Andi McCoy's music was playing from the overhead
speakers in the library. Stefano told the librarian to
quit macking on him and "take that shit off." The
trustee refused, saying he wasn't macking on anybody,

just picked the CD at random. The argument escalated. That was when someone strolled up behind Stefano and put an end to him with some kind of prison shiv.

So far as I could tell, he had been murdered right around the time I finished writing his obit. I looked at my coffee. I raised the cup and sipped. It was cold. I rushed to the sink and vomited. Then I called Katie and told her I wouldn't be at the meeting, but would like to meet her later on.

"You said you'd come," she said. "You're breaking your promise!"

"With good reason. Meet me for coffee this afternoon and I'll tell you why."

After a pause, she said: "It happened again." Not a question.

I admitted it. Told her about making a "these guys deserve to die" list, and then thinking of Stefano. "So I wrote his obit, just to prove I had nothing to do with Jeroma's death. I finished around the same time he got stabbed in the library. I'll bring a printout with a time stamp, if you want to see it."

"I don't need to see a time stamp, I take your word. I'll meet you, but not for coffee. Come to my place. And bring the obituary."

"If you think you're going to put it online—"

"God, no, are you crazy? I just want to see it with my own eyes."

"All right." More than all right. *Her* place. "But Katie?"

"Yes?"

"You can't tell *anybody* about this."

"Of course not. What kind of person do you think I am?"

One with beautiful eyes, long legs, and perfect breasts, I thought as I hung up. I should have known I was in for trouble, but I wasn't thinking straight. I was thinking about that warm kiss on the corner of my mouth. I wanted another, and not on the corner. Plus whatever came next.

Her apartment was a tidy three-roomer on the West Side. She met me at the door, dressed in shorts and a filmy top, definitely NSFW. She put her arms around me and said, "Oh God, Mike, you look *awful*. I'm so sorry."

I hugged her. She hugged me. I sought her lips, as the romance novels say, and pressed them to mine. After five seconds or so—endless and not long enough—she pulled back and looked at me with those big gray eyes. "We've got *so* much to talk about." Then she smiled. "But we can talk about it later."

What followed was what geeks like me rarely get, and when they do get it, there's usually an ulterior motive. Not that geeks like me think about such things in the moment. In the moment, we're like any guy on earth: big head takes a walk, little head rules.

Sitting up in bed.

Drinking wine instead of coffee.

"Here's something I saw in the paper last year, or the year before," she said. "This guy in one of the flyover states—Iowa, Nebraska, someplace like that—buys a lottery ticket after work, one of those scratch-off thingies, and wins a hundred thousand dollars. A week later he buys a Powerball ticket and wins a hundred and forty million."

"Your point?" I saw her point, and didn't care. The

sheet had slipped down to reveal her breasts, every bit as firm and perfect as I'd expected they would be.

"Twice can *still* be a coincidence. I want you to do it again."

"I don't think that would be wise." It sounded weak even to my own ears. There was an armful of pretty girl within reaching distance, but all at once I wasn't thinking of the pretty girl. I was thinking of a bowling ball rolling over just the right diamond, and how it felt to stand watching it, knowing that in two seconds the pins were going to explode every whichway.

She turned on her side, looking at me earnestly. "If this is really happening, Mike, it's *big*. Biggest thing ever. The power of life and death!"

"If you're thinking about using this for the site—"

She shook her head vehemently. "No one would believe it. Even if they did, how would it benefit *Circus*? Would we run a poll? Ask people to send us names of bad guys who deserved the chop?"

She was wrong. People would be happy to participate in Death Vote 2016. It would be bigger than *American Idol*.

She linked her arms around my neck. "Who was on your hit list before you thought of Stefano?"

I winced. "Wish you wouldn't call it that."

"Never mind, just tell me."

I started listing the names, but when I got to Kenneth Wanderly, she stopped me. Now the gray eyes didn't just look overcast; they looked stormy. "Him! Write *his* obituary! I'll look up the background on Google so you can do a bang-up job, and—"

Reluctantly, I freed myself from her arms. "Why bother, Katie? He's on death row already. Let the state take care of him."

"But they won't!" She jumped out of bed and began to pace back and forth. It was a mesmerizing sight, as I'm sure I don't need to tell you. Those long legs, ai-yi-yi. "They *won't*! The Okies haven't done anyone since that botched execution two years ago! Kenneth Wanderly raped and killed four girls—*tortured* them to death—and he'll still be there eating government meatloaf when he's sixty-five! When he'll die in his sleep!"

She came back to the bed and threw herself on her knees. "Do this for me, Mike! *Please!*"

"What makes him so important to you?"

The animation ran out of her face. She sat back on her heels and lowered her head so that her hair screened her face. She stayed that way for maybe ten seconds, and when she looked at me again, her beauty was—not gone, but marred. *Scarred*. It wasn't just the tears streaming down her cheeks; it was the shamed droop of her mouth.

"Because I know what it's like. I was raped while I was in college. One night after a frat party. I'd tell you to write *his* obituary, but I never saw him." She drew a deep, shuddering breath. "He came up behind me. I was on my face the whole time. But Wanderly will do as a proxy. He'll do just fine."

I tossed back the sheet. "Turn on your computer."

Cowardly bald-headed rapist Kenneth Wanderly, who could only get it up when his prey was tied down, saved the taxpayers a bunch by committing suicide in his Oklahoma State Penitentiary cell on death row in the early hours of this morning. Guards found Wanderly (whose picture is next to "useless piece of shit" in the Urban Dictionary) hanging from a makeshift noose made of his own pants. Warden George Stockett immediately decreed a special celebratory dinner in the gen-pop dining hall tomorrow night, followed by a sock hop. When asked if the Suicide Trousers would be framed and placed with the penitentiary's other trophies, Warden Stockett refused to answer, but gave the hastily assembled press conference a wink.

Wanderly, a disease masquerading as a live birth, came into the world on October 27, 1972, in Danbury, Connecticut . . .

Another craptastic piece of work from Michael Anderson!

The worst of my Speaking Ill of the Dead obits were funnier and more trenchant (if you don't believe me, look them up for yourself), but that didn't matter. Once again the words came gushing out, and with that same sense of perfectly balanced power. At some point, far in the back of my mind, I realized it was more like throwing a spear than rolling a bowling ball. One with a sharply honed point. Katie felt it, too. She was sitting right next to me, crackling like static electricity flying from a hairbrush.

This next part is hard to write, because it makes me think there's a little Ken Wanderly in all of us, but since there's no way to tell the truth except to tell it, here it is: It made us horny. I grabbed her in a rough, ungeeky embrace as soon as it was done and carried her back to the bed. Katie locked her ankles at the small of my back and her hands at the nape of my neck. I think that second go-round might have lasted all of fifty seconds, but we both got off. And hard. People stink sometimes.

Ken Wanderly was a monster, okay? That's not

exclusively my judgment; he used the word to describe himself when he 'fessed up to everything in an unsuccessful effort to avoid the death sentence. I could use that to excuse what I did—what *we* did—except for one thing.

Writing his obituary was even better than the sex that followed it.

It made me want to do it again.

When I woke up the next morning, Katie was sitting on the couch with her laptop. She looked at me solemnly and patted the cushion beside her. I sat and read the *Neon Circus* headline on the screen: ANOTHER BAD BOY BITES THE DUST, "WICKED KEN" COMMITS SUICIDE IN HIS CELL. Only not by hanging. He had smuggled in a bar of soap—how was a mystery, because inmates are only supposed to have access to the liquid kind—and shoved it down his throat.

"Dear God," I said. "What a horrible way to die."

"Good!" She raised her hands, balled them into fists, and shook them beside her temples. *"Excellent!"*

There were things I didn't want to ask her. Number one on the list was if she had slept with me strictly so she could persuade me to kill a suitable stand-in for her rapist. But ask yourself this (I did): Would asking have done any good? She could give me a totally straight answer and I still might not have believed her. In a situation like that, the relationship may not be outright poisoned, but it's probably damn sick.

"I'm not going to do this again," I said.

"All right, I understand." (She didn't.)

"So don't ask me."

"I won't." (She did.)

"And you can never tell anybody."

"I already said I wouldn't." (She already had.)

I think part of me already knew this conversation was an exercise in futility, but I said okay and let it drop.

"Mike, I don't want to hurry you out of here, but I've got like a zillion things to do, and . . ."

"No worries, mate. I'm taillights."

In truth, I *wanted* to get out. I wanted to walk about sixteen aimless miles and think about what came next.

She grabbed me at the door and kissed me hard. "Don't go away mad."

"I'm not." I didn't know *how* I was going away.

"And don't you dare think about quitting. I need you. I've decided Penny would be all wrong for Speaking Ill of the Dead, but I totally understand you need a break from it. I was thinking maybe . . . Georgina?"

"Maybe," I said. I thought Georgina was the worst writer on the staff, but I didn't really care anymore. All I cared about right then was never seeing another obituary, let alone writing one.

"As for you, do all the nasty reviews you want. No Jeroma left to say no, am I right?"

"You're right."

She shook me. "Don't say it that way, you monkey. Show some enthusiasm. That old *Neon Circus* get-up-and-git. And say you'll stick around." She lowered her voice. "We can have our own conferences. *Private* ones." She saw my eyes drop to the front of her robe and laughed, pleased. Then she gave me a push. "Now go. Buzz on out of here."

A week passed, and when you're working for a site like *Neon Circus*, each week lasts three months. Celebs got drunk, celebs went into rehab, celebs came out of rehab and immediately got drunk, celebs got arrested, celebs got out of limos *sans* panties, celebs danced the night away, celebs got married, celebs got divorced, celebs "took a break from each other." One celeb fell into his pool and drowned. Georgina wrote a remarkably unfunny obituary, and a ton of *Where's Mike* tweets and emails arrived in its wake. Once that would have pleased me.

I did not visit Katie's apartment, because Katie was too busy for canoodling. In fact, Katie wasn't much in evidence. She was "taking meetings," a couple in New York and one in Chicago. In her absence, I somehow found myself in charge. I was not nominated, I did not campaign, I was not elected. It just happened. My consolation was that things would surely go back to normal when Katie returned.

I didn't want to spend time in Jeroma's office (it felt haunted), but other than our unisex bathroom, it was the only place where I could hold meetings with distraught staffers in relative privacy. And the staffers were *always* distraught. E-publishing is still publishing, and every publishing staff is a nest of old-fashioned complexes and neuroses. Jeroma would have told them to get the hell out (but hey, have a Yook). I couldn't do that. When I started feeling crazy, I reminded myself that soon I would be back in my accustomed seat by the wall, writing snarky reviews. Just another inmate in the madhouse.

The only real decision I can remember making that week had to do with Jeroma's chair. I absolutely could not put my ass where hers had been when she choked on the Cough Drop of Doom. I rolled it into the bullpen and brought in what I thought of as "my" chair, the one at the desk by the Thanksgiving poster reading PLEASE SHIT WHERE YOU EAT. It was a far less comfy perch, but at least it didn't feel haunted. Besides, I wasn't writing much anyway.

Late Friday afternoon, Katie swept into the office clad in a shimmery knee-length dress that was the antithesis of her usual jeans and tank tops. Her hair was in artfully tumbled beauty shop curls. To me she looked . . . well . . . sort of like a prettier version of Jeroma. I had a passing recollection of Orwell's *Animal Farm*, and how the chant of "Four legs good, two legs bad" had changed to "Four legs good, two legs better."

Katie gathered us and announced that we were being purchased by Pyramid Media out of Chicago, and there would be raises—small ones— for everybody. This occasioned wild applause. When it died down, she added that Georgina Bukowski would be taking over Speaking Ill of the Dead for good, and that Mike Anderson was our new kultcha kritic. "Which means," she said, "that he will spread his wings and fly slowly over the landscape, shitting where he will."

More wild applause. I stood up and took a bow, trying to look cheerful and devilish. On that score, I was batting .500. I hadn't been cheerful since Jeroma's sudden death, but I *did* feel like the devil.

"Now, everybody back to work! Write something eternal!" Glistening lips parted in a smile. "Mike, could I speak to you in private?"

Private meant Jeroma's office (we all still thought of it that way). Katie frowned when she saw the chair behind the desk. "What's *that* ugly thing doing in here?"

"I didn't like sitting in Jeroma's," I said. "I'll bring it back, if you want."

"I do. But *before* you do . . ." She moved close to me, but saw the blinds were up and we were being closely observed. She settled for putting a hand on my chest. "Can you come to my place tonight?"

"Absolutely." Although I wasn't as excited by the prospect as you might think. With the little head not in charge, doubts about Katie's motivations had continued to solidify. And, I have to admit, I found it a little upsetting that she was so eager to get Jeroma's chair back into the office.

Lowering her voice, even though we were alone, she said, "I don't suppose you've written any more . . ." Her glistening lips formed the word *obits*.

"I haven't even thought of it."

This was an extremely bodacious lie. Writing obits was the first thing I thought about in the morning, and the last thing I thought about at night. The way the words just flowed out. And the feeling that went with it: a bowling ball rolling over the right diamond, a twenty-foot putt heading straight for the hole, a spear thunking home in exactly the place you aimed at. Bullseye, dead center.

"What else *have* you been writing? Any reviews yet? I understand Paramount's releasing Jack Briggs's last movie, and I'm hearing it's even worse than *Holy Rollers*. That's *got* to be tempting."

"I haven't exactly been writing," I said. "I've been *ghost*writing. As in everyone else's work. But I was never cut out to be an editor. That's your job, Katie."

This time she didn't protest.

Later that day, I looked up from the back row, where I was trying (and failing) to write a CD review, and saw her in the office, bent over her laptop. Her mouth was moving, and at first I thought she must also be on her phone, but no phone was in evidence. I had an idea—almost certainly ridiculous, but weirdly hard to shake—that she had found a leftover stash of eucalyptus drops in the top drawer, and was sucking on one.

I arrived at her apartment shortly before seven, bearing bags of Chinese from Fun Joy. No shorts and filmy top that night; she was dressed in a pullover and baggy khakis. Also, she wasn't alone. Penny Langston was sitting on one end of the sofa (crouching there, actually). She wasn't wearing her baseball cap, but that strange smile, the one that said *touch me and I'll kill you*, was all present and accounted for.

Katie kissed my cheek. "I invited Penny to join us."

That was patently obvious, but I said, "Hi, Pens."

"Hi, Mike." Tiny mouse-voice and no eye contact, but she made a valiant effort to turn the smile into something a tad less creepy.

I looked back to Katie. I raised my eyebrows.

"I said I didn't tell anyone about what you can do," Katie said. "That . . . sort of wasn't the truth."

"And I sort of knew that." I put the grease-spotted white bags down on the coffee table. I didn't feel hungry anymore, and I didn't expect a whole lot of Fun Joy in the next few minutes. "Do you want to tell me what this is about before I accuse you of breaking your solemn promise and stalk out?"

"Don't do that. Please. Just listen. Penny works at

Neon Circus because I talked Jeroma into hiring her. I met her when she still lived here in the city. We were in a group together, weren't we, Pens?"

"Yes," Penny said in her tiny mouse-voice. She was looking at her hands, clasped so tightly in her lap that the knuckles were white. "The Holy Name of Mary Group."

"Which is what, exactly, when it's home with its hat off?" As if I had to ask. Sometimes when the pieces come together, you can actually hear the click.

"Rape support," Katie said. "I never saw my rapist, but Penny saw hers. Didn't you, Pens?"

"Yes. Lots of times." Now Penny was looking at me, and her voice grew stronger with each word. By the end, she was nearly shouting, and tears were rolling down her cheeks. "It was my uncle. I was nine years old. My sister was eleven. He raped her too. Katie says you can kill people with obituaries. I want you to write his."

I'm not going to tell the story she told me, sitting there on the couch with Katie next to her, holding one of her hands and putting Kleenex after Kleenex in the other. Unless you've lived in one of the seven places in this country not yet equipped for multimedia, you've heard it before. All you need to know is that Penny's parents died in a car accident, and she and her sister were shipped off to Uncle Amos and Aunt Claudia. Aunt Claudia refused to hear anything said against her husband. Figure the rest out for yourself.

I wanted to do it. Because the story was horrible, yes. Because guys like Uncle Amos need to take it in the head for preying on the weakest and most vulnerable, check. Because Katie wanted me to do it, absolutely. But in the end, it all came down to the sadly pretty dress Penny was wearing. And the shoes. And the bit of inexpertly applied makeup. For the first time in years, perhaps for the first time since Uncle Amos had begun making his nighttime visits to her bedroom, always telling her it was "our little secret," she had tried to make herself presentable for a male human being. It sort of broke my heart. Katie had been scarred by her rape, but had risen above it. Some girls and women can do that. Many can't.

When she finished, I asked, "Do you swear to God that your uncle really did this?"

"Yes. Again and again and again. When we got old enough to have babies, he made us turn over and used our . . ." She didn't finish this. "I bet it didn't stop with Jessie and me, either."

"And he's never been caught."

She shook her head vehemently, dank ringlets flying.

"Okay." I took my iPad out of my briefcase. "But you'll have to tell me about him."

"I can do better." She disengaged her hand from Katie's and grabbed the ugliest purse I've ever seen outside of a thrift-shop window. From it she took a crumpled sheet of paper, so sweat-stained it was limp and semitransparent. She had written in pencil. The looping scrawl looked like something a child might have done. It was headed AMOS CULLEN LANGFORD: HIS OBITUARY.

This miserable excuse for a man who raped little girls every chance he could get died slowly and painfully of many cancers in the soft parts of his body.

During the last week, pus came pouring out of his eyes. He was 63 years old and in his last extremity, his screams filled the house as he begged for extra morphine . . .

There was more. Much. Her handwriting was that of a child, but her vocabulary was terrific, and she had done a far better job on this piece than anything she'd ever written for *Neon Circus*.

"I don't know if this will work," I said, trying to hand it back. "I think I have to write it myself."

Katie said, "It won't hurt to try, will it?"

I supposed it wouldn't. Looking directly at Penny, I said, "I've never even seen this guy, and you want me to kill him."

"Yes," she said, and now she was meeting my eyes fair and square. "That's what I want."

"You're positive."

She nodded.

I sat down at Katie's little home desk, laid out Penny's handwritten death-diatribe beside my iPad, opened a blank document, and began transcribing. I knew immediately that it *was* going to work. The sense of power was stronger than ever. The sense of *aiming.* I quit looking at the sheet after the second sentence and just hammered the keyboard screen, hitting the main points and ended with this abjuration: *Funeral attendees—no one could call them mourners, given Mr. Langford's unspeakable predilections—are warned not to send flowers, but spitting on the coffin is encouraged.*

The two women were staring at me, big-eyed.

"Will it work?" Penny asked, then answered herself. "It will. I *felt* it."

"I think maybe it already has." I turned my attention to Katie. "Ask me to do this again, Kates, and I'll be tempted to write *your* obituary."

She tried to smile, but I could see she was scared. I hadn't meant to do that (at least I don't think I had), so I took her hand. She jumped, started to pull away, then let me hold it. The skin was cold and clammy.

"I'm joking. Bad joke, but I mean what I say. This needs to end."

"Yes," she said, and swallowed loudly, a cartoon *gulp* sound. "Absolutely."

"And no talking. Not to *anybody. Ever.*"

Once again they agreed. I started to get up and Penny leaped at me, knocking me back into the chair and almost spilling us both to the floor. The hug wasn't affectionate; it was more like the grip of a drowning woman muckling onto her would-be rescuer. She was greasy with sweat.

"Thank you," she whispered harshly. "Thank you, Mike."

I left without telling her she was welcome. I couldn't wait to get out of there. I don't know if they ate the food I brought, but I rather doubt it. Fun Joy, my rosy red ass.

I didn't sleep that night, and it wasn't thinking of Amos Langford that kept me awake. I had other things to worry about.

One was the eternal problem of addiction. I had left Katie's apartment determined that I would never wield that terrible power again, but it was a promise I'd made to myself before, and it wasn't one I was sure I could keep, because each time I wrote a "live obit," the urge to do it again grew stronger. It was like heroin. Use it once or twice, maybe you can stop. After awhile, though, you have to have it. I might not have reached that point yet, but I was on the edge of the pit and knew it. What I'd said to Katie was the absolute rock-bottom truth—this needed to end while I could still end it. Assuming it wasn't too late already.

The second thing wasn't quite as grim, but it was bad enough. On the subway back to Brooklyn, a particularly apropos Ben Franklin adage had come to mind: *Two can keep a secret, if one of them is dead*. There were already three people keeping this one, and since I had no intention of murdering Katie and Penny via obituary, that meant a really nasty secret was in their hands.

They'd keep it for awhile, I was sure. Penny would be especially keen to do so if she got a call in the morning informing her that dear old Uncle Amos had bitten the big one. But time would weaken the taboo. There was another factor, as well. Both of them were not just writers but *Neon Circus* writers, which meant spilling the beans was their business. Bean-spilling might not be as addictive as killing people with obits, but it had its own strong pull, as I well knew. Sooner or later there would be a bar, and too many drinks, and then . . .

Do you want to hear something really crazy? You have to promise not to tell anybody, though.

I pictured myself sitting in the newsroom by the Thanksgiving poster, occupied with my latest snarky review. Frank Jessup slides up, sits down, and asks if I've ever considered writing an obit for Bashar al-Assad, the Syrian dictator with the little tiny head, or—hey, even better!—that Korean butterball, Kim Jong-un. For all I knew, Jessup might want me to off the new head coach of the Knicks.

I tried to tell myself that one was ridiculous, and couldn't manage it. Mohawk Sports Boy was a crazed Knicks fan.

There was an even more horrific possibility (this I got to around three in the morning). Suppose word of my talent found its way to the wrong governmental ear? It seemed unlikely, but hadn't I read somewhere that the government had experimented with LSD and mind control on unsuspecting subjects back in the fifties? People capable of that might be capable of anything. What if some fellows from NSA appeared either at *Circus* or here at my folks' house in Brooklyn, and I wound up taking a one-way trip in a private jet to some government base where I would be installed in a private apartment (luxurious, but with guards on the door) and given a list of Al Qaeda and Isis militant leaders, complete with files that would allow me to write extremely detailed obituaries? I could make rocket-equipped drones obsolete.

Loony? Yuh. But at four in the morning, anything can seem possible.

Around five, just as the day's first light was creeping into my room, I found myself wondering yet again how I had come by this unwelcome talent in the first place. Not to mention how *long* I'd had it. There was no way of telling, because as a rule, folks do not write obituaries of live people. They don't even do that at *The New York Times*, they just stockpile the necessary info so it's at hand when a famous person dies. I could have had the ability all my life, and if I hadn't written that crappy bad joke about Jeroma, I never would have known. I thought of how I'd ended up writing for *Neon Circus* in the first place: by way of an unsolicited obituary. Of a person already dead, true, but an obit is an obit. And talent only wants one thing, don't you see? It wants to come out. It wants to put on a tuxedo and tap-dance all across the stage.

On that thought, I fell asleep.

My phone woke me at quarter to noon. It was Katie, and she was upset. "You need to come to the office," she said. "Right now."

I sat up in bed. "What's wrong?"

"I'll tell you when you get here, but I'll tell you one thing right now. You can't do it again."

"Duh," I said. "I think I told *you* that. And on more than one occasion."

If she heard me, she paid no attention, just steamed ahead. "*Not ever in your life*. If it was Hitler you couldn't do it. If your father had a knife to your mother's throat you couldn't do it."

She broke the connection before I could ask questions. I wondered why we weren't having this Code Red meeting in her apartment, which offered a lot more privacy than *Neon Circus*'s cramped digs, and only one answer came to mind: Katie didn't want to be alone with me. I was a dangerous dude. I had only done what she and her fellow rape survivor wanted me to do, but that didn't change the fact.

Now I was a dangerous dude.

She greeted me with a smile and a hug for the benefit of the few staffers on hand, quaffing their postlunch Red Bulls and plugging lackadaisically away at their laptops, but today the blinds in the office were down, and the smile disappeared as soon as we were behind them.

"I'm scared to death," she said. "I mean, I was last night, but when you're actually *doing* it—"

"It feels sort of good. Yeah, I know."

"But I'm a lot more scared now. I keep thinking of those spring-loaded gadgets you squeeze to make your hands and forearms stronger."

"What are you talking about?"

She didn't tell me. Not then. "I had to start in the middle, with Ken Wanderly's kid, and work both ways—"

"Wicked Ken had a *kid*?"

"A son, yes. Stop interrupting. I had to start in the middle because the item about the son was the first one I came across. There was a 'death reported' item in the *Times* this morning. For once they scooped the webs. Somebody at *Huffpo* or *Daily Beast* is apt to get taken to the woodshed for that, because it happened awhile ago. My guess is the family decided to wait until after the burial to release the news."

"Katie—"

"Shut up and listen." She leaned forward. *"There's collateral damage.* And it's getting worse."

"I don't—"

She put a palm over my mouth. "Shut. The fuck. Up."

I shut. She took her hand away.

"Jeroma Whitfield was where this started. So far as I can tell using Google, she's the only one in the world. *Was*, I mean. There are tons of *Jerome* Whitfields, though, so thank God she was your first, or it might have been attracted to some of them, anyway. The closest ones."

"It?"

She looked at me as if I were an idiot. "The power.

Your second . . ." She paused, I think because the word that came immediately to mind was *victim*. "Your second subject was Peter Stefano. Also not the world's most common name, but not completely weird, either. Now look at this."

From her desk she took a few sheets of paper. She eased the first from the paper clip holding them together and passed it to me. On it were three obituaries, all from small newspapers—one in Pennsylvania, one in Ohio, and one in upstate New York. The Pennsylvania Peter Stefano had died of a heart attack. The one in Ohio had fallen from a ladder. The one from New York—Woodstock—had suffered a stroke. All had died on the same day as the crazed record producer whose name they shared.

I sat down hard. "This can't be."

"It is. The good news is that I found two dozen *other* Peter Stefanos across the USA, and they're fine. I think because they all live farther away from Gowanda Correctional. That was ground zero. The shrapnel spread out from there."

I looked at her, dumbfounded.

"Wicked Ken came next. Another unusual name, thank God. There's a whole nest of Wanderlys in Wisconsin and Minnesota, but I guess that was too far. Only . . ."

She handed me the second sheet. First up was the news item from the *Times*: SERIAL KILLER'S SON DIES. His wife claimed Ken Wanderly Jr. had shot himself by accident while cleaning a pistol, but the item pointed out that the "accident" had happened less than twelve hours after his father's death. That it might actually have been suicide was left for the reader to infer.

"*I* don't think it was suicide," Katie said. Beneath her makeup, she looked very pale. "I don't think it was exactly an accident, either. *It homes in on the names*, Mike. You see that, right? And it can't spell, which makes it even worse."

The obit (I was coming to loathe that word) below the piece about Wicked Ken's son concerned one Kenneth Wanderlee, of Paramus, New Jersey. Like Peter Stefano of Pennsylvania (an innocent who had probably never killed anything but time), Wanderlee of Paramus had died of a heart attack.

Just like Jeroma.

I was breathing fast, and sweating all over. My balls had drawn up until they felt roughly the size of peach pits. I felt like fainting, also like vomiting, and managed to do neither. Although I did plenty of vomiting later. That went on for a week or more, and I lost ten pounds. (I told my worried mother it was the flu.)

"Here's the capper," she said, and handed me the last page. There were seventeen Amos Langfords on it. The biggest cluster was in the New York–New Jersey–Connecticut area, but one had died in Baltimore, one in Virginia, and two had kicked off in West Virginia. In Florida there were three.

"No," I whispered.

"Yes," she said. "This second one, in Amityville, is Penny's bad uncle. Just be grateful that Amos is also a fairly unusual name in this day and age. If it had been James or William, there could have been hundreds of dead Langfords. Probably not thousands, because it's still not reaching farther than the Midwest, but Florida's nine hundred miles away. Farther than any AM radio signal can reach, at least in the daytime."

The sheets of paper slipped from my hand and see-sawed to the floor.

"Now do you see what I meant about those squeezie things people use to make their hands and arms stronger? At first maybe you can only squeeze the handles together once or twice. But if you keep doing it, the muscles get stronger. That's what's happening to you, Mike. I'm sure of it. Every time you write an obit for a living person, the power gets stronger and reaches farther."

"It was your idea," I whispered. "Your goddam idea."

But she wasn't having that. "I didn't tell you to write Jeroma's obituary. That was *your* idea."

"It was a whim," I protested. "A *goof*, for God's sake. I didn't know what was going to happen!"

Only maybe that wasn't the truth. I flashed back to my first orgasm, in the bathtub, assisted by a bub-bly handful of Ivory Soap. I hadn't known what I was doing when I reached down and grabbed myself . . . only some part of me, some deep, instinctual part, *had* known. There's another old adage, this one not Ben Franklin's: *When the student is ready, the teacher will appear*. Sometimes the teacher is inside us.

"Wanderly was your idea," I pointed out. "So was Amos the Midnight Creeper. And by then you knew what was going to happen."

She sat on the edge of the desk—her desk, now—and looked at me straight on, which couldn't have been easy. "That much is true. But, Mike . . . I didn't know it was going to *spread*."

"Neither did I."

"And it really is addictive. I was sitting next to you when you did it, and it was like breathing sec-ondhand crack."

"I can stop," I said.

Hoping. Hoping.

"Are you sure?"

"Pretty. Now here's one for you. Can you keep your mouth shut about this? Like, for the rest of your life?"

She did me the courtesy of thinking it over. Then she nodded. "I have to. I could have a good thing here at *Circus*, and I don't want to bitch it up before I can get on my feet."

It was all about her, in other words, and what else could I have expected? Katie might not be sucking on Jeroma's eucalyptus drops, I could have been wrong about that, but she was sitting in Jeroma's chair, behind Jeroma's desk. Plus that new look-but-don't-touch tumbly hairdo. As Orwell's pigs might have said, blue jeans good, new dress better.

"What about Penny?"

Katie said nothing.

"Because my impression of Penny—*everybody's* impression of Penny, in fact—is that she doesn't have all four wheels on the road."

Katie's eyes flashed. "Are you surprised? She had an extremely traumatic childhood, in case you missed it. A *nightmare* childhood."

"I can relate, because I'm living my own nightmare right now. So save the support-group empathy. I just want to know if she'll keep her mouth shut. Like, forever. Will she?"

There was a long, long pause. At last Katie said, "Now that he's dead, maybe she'll stop going to the rape survivor meetings."

"And if she doesn't?"

"I guess she might . . . at some point . . . tell someone who's in especially bad shape that she knows a guy who could help that someone get closure. She wouldn't do it this month, and probably not this year, but . . ."

She didn't finish. We looked at each other. I was sure she could read what I was thinking in my eyes: there was one sure-shot, never-miss way to make sure Penny kept her mouth shut.

"No," Katie said. "Don't even think of it, and not only because she deserves her life and whatever good things there might be for her up ahead. It wouldn't be just her."

Based on her research, she was right about that. Penny Langston wasn't a super-common name, either, but there are more than three hundred million people in America, and some of the Penny or Penelope Langstons out there would win a very bad lottery if I decided to power up my laptop or iPad and write a new obit. Then there was the "in the neighborhood" effect. The power had taken a Wander*lee* as well as a Wander*ly*. What if it decided to take Petula Langstons? Patsy Langfords? Penny Langleys?

Then there was my own situation. It might take only one more obit for Michael Anderson to surrender completely to that high-voltage buzz. Just thinking about it made me want to do it, because it would take away, if only temporarily, these feelings of horror and dismay. I pictured myself writing an obituary for John Smith or Jill Jones to cheer myself up, and my balls shriveled even more at the thought of the mass carnage that could follow.

"What are you going to do?" Katie asked.

"I'll think of something," I said.

• • •

I did.

That night I opened a *Rand McNally Road Atlas* to the big map of the United States, closed my eyes, and dropped my finger. Which is why I now live in Laramie, Wyoming, where I'm a housepainter. *Primarily* a housepainter. I actually have a number of jobs, like many people in the small cities of the heartland— what I used to refer to, with a New Yorker's casual contempt, as "flyover country." I also work part-time for a landscaping company, mowing lawns, raking leaves, and planting bushes. In the winter, I plow out driveways and work at the Snowy Range ski resort, grooming trails. I'm not rich, but I keep my head above water. A little more above it than in New York, actually. Make fun of flyover country all you want to, but it's a lot cheaper to live out here, and whole days go by without anyone giving me the finger.

My parents don't understand why I chucked it all, and my father doesn't try to hide his disappointment; he sometimes talks about my "Peter Pan lifestyle," and says I'm going to regret it when I turn forty and start seeing gray in my hair. My mother is just as puzzled but less disapproving. She never liked *Neon Circus*, thought it was a sleazy waste of my "authorial abilities." She was probably right on both counts, but what I mostly use my authorial abilities for these days is jotting grocery lists. As for my hair, I saw the first strands of gray even before I left the city, and that was before I turned thirty.

I still dream about writing, though, and these are not pleasant dreams. In one of them I'm sitting at my laptop, even though I don't own a laptop anymore. I'm writing an obituary, and I can't stop. In this dream I don't want to, either, because that sense of power had never been stronger. I get as far as *Sad news, last night everyone in the world named John died* and then wake up, sometimes on the floor, sometimes rolled up in my blankets and screaming. On a couple of occasions it's a wonder I didn't wake the neighbors.

I never left my heart in San Francisco, but I did leave my laptop in dear old Brooklyn. Couldn't bear to give up my iPad, though (talk about addictions). I don't use it to send emails—when I want to get in touch with someone in a hurry, I call. If it's not urgent, I use that antique institution known as the United States Post Office. You'd be surprised how easy it is to get back into the habit of writing letters and postcards.

I like the iPad, though. There are plenty of games on it, plus the wind sounds that help me get to sleep at night and the alarm that wakes me up in the morning. I've got tons of stored music, a few audio books, lots of movies. When all else fails to entertain, I surf the Internet. Endless time-filling possibilities there, as you probably know yourself, and in Laramie the time can pass slowly when I'm not working. Especially in winter.

Sometimes I visit the *Neon Circus* site, just for old times' sake. Katie's doing a good job as editor—much better than Jeroma, who really didn't have much in the way of vision—and the site hovers around number five on the list of most visited Internet landing-spots. Sometimes it's a notch or two above the *Drudge Report*; mostly it lurks just below. Plenty of ads, so they're doing well in that regard.

Jeroma's successor is still writing her Getting Sloshed with Katie interviews. Frank Jessup is still covering sports; his not-quite-joking piece about wanting to see an All Steroids Football League got national attention and landed him a gig on ESPN, Mohawk and all. Georgina Bukowski wrote half a dozen unfunny Speaking Ill of the Dead obituaries, and then Katie shitcanned the column and replaced it with Celebrity Deathstakes, where readers win prizes for predicting which famous people will die in the next twelve months. Penny Langston is the master of ceremonies there, and each week a new smiling head-shot of her appears on top of a dancing skeleton. It's *Circus*'s most popular feature, and each week the comments section goes on for pages. People like to read about death, and they like to write about it.

I'm someone who knows.

Okay, that's the story. I don't expect you to believe it, and you don't have to; this is America, after all. I've done my best to lay it out neatly, just the same. The way I was taught to lay out a story in my journalism classes: not fancy, not twee or all hifalutin. I tried to keep it clear, in a straight line. Beginning leads to middle, middle leads to end. Old-school, you dig? Ducks in a row. And if you find the end a little flat, you might remember Professor Higgins's take on that. He used to say that in reporting, it's always the end for now, and in real life, the only full stop is on the obituary page.

For Stewart O'Nan

Here's an anecdote too good not to share, and I've been telling it at public appearances for years now. My wife does the major shopping for us—she says there'd never be a vegetable in the house otherwise—but she sometimes sends me on emergency errands. So I was in the local supermarket one afternoon, on a mission to find batteries and a nonstick frypan. As I meandered my way up the housewares aisle, having already stopped for a few other absolute necessities (cinnamon buns and potato chips), a woman came around the far end, riding one of those motorized carts. She was a Florida snowbird archetype, about eighty, permed to perfection, and as darkly tanned as a cordovan shoe. She looked at me, looked away, then did a double take.

"I know you," she said. "You're Stephen King. You write those scary stories. That's all right, some people like them, but not me. I like uplifting stories, like that *Shawshank Redemption*."

"I wrote that too," I said.

"No you didn't," she said, and went on her way.

The point is, you write some scary stories and you're like the girl who lives in the trailer park on the edge of town: you get a reputation. Fine by me; the bills are paid and I'm still having fun. You can call me anything, as the saying goes, just as long as you don't call me late for dinner. But the term *genre* holds very little interest for me. Yes, I like horror stories. I also love mysteries, tales of suspense, sea stories, straight literary novels, and poetry . . . just to mention a few. I also like to read and write stories that strike me funny, and that should surprise nobody, because humor and horror are Siamese twins.

Not long ago, I heard a guy talking about a fireworks arms race on a lake in Maine, and this story came to mind. And please don't think of it as "local color," okay? That's another genre I have no use for.

Drunken Fireworks

Statement given by Mr. Alden McCausland
Castle County Police Department
Statement taken by Police Chief Andrew Clutterbuck
Arresting Officer Ardelle Benoit also present
11:15 AM–1:20 PM
July 5, 2015

Yes, you could say Ma n me did a good deal of drinking and lounging around out to camp after Daddy died. No law against it, is there? If you don't get behind the wheel, that is, and we never did. We could afford it, too, because by then we were what you might call the idle rich. Never would have expected that, Dad being a carpenter all his life. Called himself a "skilled carpenter," and Ma always added, "Barely skilled n mostly distilled." That was her little joke.

Ma worked down to Royce Flowers over on Castle Street, but only full-time in November and December—a dab hand at those Christmas wreaths, she was, and not bad when it came to funeral arrangements, either. She did Dad's, you know. Had a nice yellow ribbon on it that said HOW WE LOVED THEE. Almost biblical, don't you think?

People cried when they saw it, even ones Dad owed money to.

When I got out of high school I went to work at Sonny's Garage, balancing wheels, doing oil changes, and fixing flats. Back in the old days I also used to pump gas, but accourse now that's all DIY. I also sold some pot, might as well admit it. Haven't done it for years, so I guess you can't charge me on that, but in the eighties that was a pretty good cash-and-carry business, especially in these parts. Always had enough jingle to go out steppin on Friday or Saturday night. I enjoy the company of women, but have stayed away from the altar, at least so far. I guess if I have any ambitions, one would be to see the Grand Canyon, and another would be to stay what they call a lifelong bachelor. Less problems that way. Besides, I got to keep an eye on Ma. You know what they say, a boy's best friend is his—

I will get to the point, Ardelle, but if you want it, you have to let me tell it my own way. If anyone should have a little sympathy for tellin the whole story, it's you. When we was in school together, you wouldn't shut up. Tongue hung in the middle and running at both ends, Mrs. Fitch used to say. Remember her? Fourth grade. What a card she was! Remember the time you put gum in the toe of her shoe? Ha!

Where was I? Camp, right? Out on Abenaki Lake.

Ain't nothing but a three-room cabin with a lick of beach and a old dock. Daddy bought it in ninety-one, I think it was, when he run into a little dividend from some job. That wasn't enough for the down payment, but when I added in the income from my herbal remedies, we was able to swing it. The place is pretty skeevy, though, I'm willing to admit that.

Ma called it the Mosquito Bowl, and we never fixed it up worth a tin shit, but Daddy kep to the payments pretty regular. When he missed, Ma n me chipped in. She bitched about giving away her flower money, but never too hard; she liked going out there from the first, bugs and leaky roof and all. We'd sit out on the deck and have a picnic lunch and watch the world go by. Even then she wouldn't say no to a six-pack or bottle of coffee brandy, although in those days she kep her drinking mostly to the weekends.

The place was all paid off around the turn of the century, and why not? It was on the town side of the lake—the west side—and you both know what it's like over there, all reedy and shallow, with plenty of puckerbrush. The east side is nicer, with them big houses the summer people have to have, and I imagine they looked acrost at the slums on our side, all shacks and cabins and trailer homes, and told themselves it was a shame how the locals had to live, without so much as a tennis court to their names. They could think whatever they wanted. Far as we were concerned, we were as good as anybody. Daddy'd fish a little off the end of our dock, and Ma would cook what he caught on the woodstove, and after oh-one (maybe it was oh-two), we had the runnin water and no longer had to trot to the outhouse in the middle of the night. Good as anybody.

We thought there'd be a little more money for fixin up once the place was paid off, but there never seemed to be; the way it disappeared was a mystery, because back then there was plenty of bank loans for people who wanted to build and Daddy was workin regular. When he died of a heart attack while on a job in Harlow, in oh-two that was, Ma n me thought we was pretty well skint. "We'll get by, though," she said, "and if it was whores he was spendin the extra on, I don't want to know." But she said we'd have to sell the place on Abenaki, if we could find someone crazy enough to buy it.

"We'll get showing it next spring," she said, "before the blackflies hatch out. That okay with you, Alden?"

I said it was, and even went to work sprucin it up. Got as far as new shingles and replacing the worst of the rotted boards on the dock, and that was when we had our first stroke of luck.

Ma got a call from an insurance company down in Portland, and found out why there never seemed to be any extra money even after the cabin and the two acres it stood on was paid off. It wasn't whores; Dad'd been putting the extra into life insurance. Maybe he had what you call a premonition. Stranger things happen in the world every day, like rains of frogs or the two-headed cat I seen at the Castle County Fair— gave me nightmares, it did—or that Loch Ness Monster. Whatever it was, we had seventy-five thousand dollars that we never expected just drop out of the sky and into our Key Bank account.

That was Stroke of Luck Number One. Two years after that call, two years almost to the day, here come Stroke of Luck Number Two. Ma was in the habit of buying a five-dollar scratch-off ticket once a week after she got her groceries at Normie's SuperShop. For years she'd been doin that and never won more than twenty dollars. Then one day in oh-four she matched 27 below to 27 above on a Big Maine Millions scratcher, and holy Christ on a bike, she seen that match was worth two hundred and fifty thousand dollars. "I thought I was going to pee my pants," she said. They put her pitcher in the window of the SuperShop. You might remember that, it was there for two months, at least.

A cool quarter million! More like a hundred and twenty thousand after all the taxes was paid, but still. We invested it in Sunny Oil, because Ma said oil was always gonna be a good investment, at least until it was gone, and we'd be gone by the time it was. I had to agree with that, and it turned out fine. Those were go-go years in the stock market, as you may remember, and that's when we commenced our life of leisure.

It's also when we got down to serious drinking. Some of it we done at the house in town, but not that much. You know how neighbors love to gossip. It wasn't until we were mostly shifted out to the Mosquito Bowl that we really went to work on it. Ma quit the flower shop for good in oh-nine, and I said toodleoo to patchin tires and replacin mufflers a year or so later. After that we didn't have much reason to live in town, at least until cold weather; no furnace out to the lake, you know. By twenty-twelve, when our trouble with those dagos across the lake started, we'd roll on out there a week or two before Memorial Day and stay until Thanksgiving or so.

Ma put on some weight—a hundred and fifty pounds, give or take—and I guess a lot of that was down to the coffee brandy, they don't call it fat ass in a glass for nothin. But she said she was never the Miss America type to begin with, or even Miss Maine. "I'm a *cuddly* kind of gal," she liked to say. What Doc Stone liked to say, at least until she stopped goin to him, was that she was going to be a dying-young kind of gal if she didn't quit drinkin the Allen's.

"You're a heart attack waiting to happen, Hallie," he said. "Or cirrhosis. You've already got Type Two diabetes, isn't that enough for you? I can give it to you in words of one syllable. You need to dry out, and then you need AA."

"Whew!" Ma said when she got back. "After a scoldin like that, I need a drink. What about you, Alden?"

I said I could use one, so we took our lawn chairs out to the end of the dock, as we most often did, and got royally schnockered while we watched the sun go down. Good as anyone, and better than many. And look here: somethin's gonna kill everyone, am I not right? Doctors have a way of forgettin that, but Ma knew.

"The macrobiotic sonofabitch is probably right," she said as we tottered back to the cabin—along about ten, this was, and both of us bit to shit in spite of the DEET we'd slathered ourselves with. "But at least when I go, I'll know I lived. And I don't smoke, everybody knows that's the worst. Not smoking should keep me going for awhile, but what about you, Alden? What are you going to do after I die and the money runs out?"

"I don't know," I said, "but I sure would like to see the Grand Canyon."

She laughed and tossed an elbow in my ribs and said, "That's my boy. You'll never get a stomach ulcer with that attitude. Now let's get some sleep." Which we did, waking up around ten the next day and starting to medicate our hangovers along about noon with Muddy Rudders. I didn't worry as much about Ma as the doc did; I figured she was havin too much fun to die. As it happened, she outlived Doc Stone, who got killed one night by a drunk driver on Pigeon Bridge. You could call that irony or tragedy or just the way life goes. Me, I ain't no philosopher. I was just glad the doc didn't have his family with him. And I hope his insurance was paid up.

All right, that's the background. Here's where we get down to business.

The Massimos. And that fuckin trumpet, pardon my francais.

I call it the Fourth of July Arms Race, and although it didn't really get up and runnin until twenty-thirteen, it really started the year before. The Massimos had the place directly across from us, a big white house with pillars and a lawn runnin down to their beach, which was pure white sand instead of gravel like ours. That place must have had a dozen rooms. Twenty or more if you count in the guest cottage. They called it Twelve Pines Camp, on account of the fir trees that was around the main house and kind of closed it in.

A camp! Sonny Jesus, that place was a mansion. And yes, they had a tennis court. Also badminton and a place on the side for throwin hoss-shoes. They'd come out near the end of June, and stay until Labor Day, and then close the sonofabitch up. A place that size, and they let it stand empty nine months out of every twelve. I couldn't believe it. Ma could, though. She said we were "accident rich," but the Massimos were real rich.

"Only those are ill-gotten gains, Alden," she said, "and I'm not talking about no quarter-acre pot patch, either. Everyone knows Paul Massimo is CON-NECTED." She always said it just like that, in big capital letters.

Supposedly the money came from Massimo Construction. I looked it up on the Internet, and it appeared as legal as could be, but they were Italian, and Massimo Construction was based in Providence, Rhode Island, and you're cops, you can connect the dots. As Ma always used to say, when you put two and two together, you never get five.

They used all of the rooms in the big white house when they were there, I'll say that much. And the ones in the "guest cottage," as well. Ma used to look across the water and toast them with her Sombrero or Muddy Rudder and say Massimos came cheaper by the dozen.

They knew how to have fun, I'll give em that. There were cookouts, and water tag, and teenage kids drivin those Jet Skis around—they must have had half a dozen of those babies, in colors so bright they'd burn your eyes if you looked at em too long. In the evenins they'd play touch football, usually enough Massimos to make two regulation teams of eleven each, and then, when it got too dark to see the ball, they'd sing. You could tell by the way they yelled out their songs, often in Italian, that they enjoyed a drink or three themselves.

One of em had a trumpet, and he'd blow it along with the songs, just wah-wah-wah, enough to make your eyes water. "Dizzy Gillespie he ain't," Ma said. "Someone ought to dip that trumpet in olive oil and stick it up his ass. He could fart out 'God Bless America.'"

Along about eleven, he'd blow "Taps," and that'd be it for the night. Not sure any of the neighbors would have complained even if the singing and that trumpet had gone on until three in the morning, not when most folks on our side of the lake believed he was the real-life Tony Soprano.

Come the Fourth of July that year—this is oh-twelve I'm talkin about—I had some sparklers, two or three packets of Black Cat firecrackers, and a couple of cherry bombs. I bought em from Pop Anderson at Anderson's Cheery Flea Mart on the road to Oxford. That ain't tattlin, neither. Not unless you're bone-stupid, and I know neither of you is. Hell, everyone knew you could get firecrackers at the Cheery Flea. But little stuff was all Pop'd sell, because back then fireworks was against the law.

Anyway, all those Massimos was runnin around across the lake, playin football and tennis and givin each other swimsuit wedgies, the little ones paddlin around the shore, the bigger ones divin off their float. Me n Ma was out at the end of the dock in our lawn chairs, feelin no pain, with our patriotic supplies laid out beside us. As dusk came down, I give her a sparkler, lit it, then lit mine off'n hers. We waved them around in the gloamin, and pretty soon the little ones over there on the other side seen em and started clamorin for their own. The two older Massimo boys handed em out, and they waved em back at us. Their sparklers was bigger n longer-lastin than ours, and the heads had been treated with some sort of chemical that made them go all different colors, while ours was only yellow-white.

The dago with the trumpet blew—wah-wah—as if to say, "This is what real sparklers look like."

"That's okay," Ma said. "Their sparklers may be bigger, but let's shoot some firecrackers and see how they like that."

We lit em one by one and then tossed em so they'd bang and flash before they hit the lake. The kids over there at Twelve Pines seen that, and started clamorin again. So some of the Massimo men went in the house and come back with a carton. It was full of firecrackers. Pretty soon the bigger kids was lightin em off a pack at a time. They must have had a couple hundred packs in all, and they went off like machine-gun fire, which made ours seem pretty tame.

Waah-waah, went the trumpet, as if to say, "Try again."

"Well, sugar-tit," Ma said. "Give me one of those cherry bumpers you been holdin back, Alden."

"All right," I said, "but you be careful, Ma. You've had a few, and you might still like to see all your fingers tomorrow morning."

"Just give one over and don't be smart," she said. "I didn't fall off a hayrick yesterday, and I don't like the sound of that trumpet. I bet they don't have any of these, because Pop don't sell to flatlanders. He sees their license plates and claims he's all out."

I gave her one and lit it with my Bic. The fuse sparked and she threw it high in the air. It went with a flash bright enough to hurt our eyes, and the bang echoed all the way down the lake. I lit the other one and flung it like Roger Clemens. Bang!

"There," Ma says. "Now they know who's boss."

But then Paul Massimo and his two oldest sons walked down to the end of their dock. One of em— big handsome young fella in a rugby shirt—had that goddam trumpet in a kind of holster thing on his belt. They waved to us, and then the old man handed each of the boys somethin. They held the somethins out so he could light the fuses. They flang em out over the lake, and . . . holy God! Not bang but boom! Two booms, loud as dynamite, and big white flashes.

"Those ain't cherry bombs," I said. "Them are M-80s."

"Where'd they get those?" Ma asked. "Pop don't sell those."

We looked at each other, and didn't even have to say it: Rhode Island. You could probably get anything in Rhode Island. At least if your name was Massimo, you could.

The old man handed each of them another, and lit them up. Then he lit one of his own. Three booms, loud enough to scare every fish in Abenaki up to the north end, I have no doubt. Then Paul waved to us, and the fella with the trumpet drew it out of its holster like a six-gun and blew three long blasts: Waaaah . . . waaaah . . . waaaah. As if to say, "Sorry about that, you poor-ass Yankees, better luck next year."

Wasn't nothin we could do about it, neither. We had another pack of Black Cats, but they would have sounded pretty lackluster after those M-80s. And over on the other side, that pack of dagos was applaudin and cheerin, the girls jumpin up n down in their bikini suits. Pretty soon they started singing "God Bless America."

Ma looked at me, and I looked at Ma. She shook her head and I shook mine. Then she said, "Next year."

"Yes," I said. "Next year."

She held up her glass—we were drinking Bucket Lucks that night, as I recall—and I raised mine. We drank to victory in oh-thirteen. And that was how the Fourth of July Arms Race began. Mostly I think it was that fucking trumpet.

Pardon my francais.

The followin June, I went to Pop Anderson and explained my situation; told him how I felt the honor of us on the west side of the lake had to be upheld.

"Well, Alden," he said, "I don't know what shootin off a bunch of gunpowder has to do with honor, but business is business, and if you come back in a week or so, I might have somethin for you."

I did just that. He took me into his office and put a box on his desk. Had a bunch of Chinese characters on it. "This is stuff I ordinarily don't sell," he said, "but me and your ma goes all the way back to grammar school together, where she spelled me by the wood-stove and helped me learn my times tables. I got you some big bangers they call M-120s, and there's not much bigger in the loud noise department unless you want to start tossin sticks of dynamite. And then there's a dozen of these." He brought out a cylinder sitting on top of a red stick.

"That looks like a bottle rocket," I said, "only bigger."

"Ayuh, you could call this the deluxe model," he said. "They're called Chinese Peonies. They shoot twice as high, then make a hell of a flash—some red, some purple, some yella. You stick em in a Coke or beer bottle, just like with ordinary bottle rockets, but you want to stand well back, because the fuses are going to fizz sparks all over the place when they lift off. Keep a towel handy so you don't start any brushfires."

"Well that's great," I said. "They won't be blowin no trumpet when they see those."

"I'll sell you the whole box for thirty bucks," Pop said. "I know that's dear, but I've also thrown in some Black Cats and a few Twizzlers. You can stick those in chunks of wood and send them off floatin. Awful pretty, they are."

"Say nummore," I told him. "It'd be cheap at twice the price."

"Alden," he said, "you never want to talk that way to a fella in my line of work."

I took em back to camp, and Ma was so excited she wanted to set off one of the M-120s and one of the Chinese Peonies right away. I didn't often put my foot down with Ma—she was apt to bite it right off your ankle—but I did that time. "Give those Massimos half a chance and they'll come up with something better," I said.

She thought it over, then kissed me on the cheek and said, "You know, for a boy who barely finished high school, you've got a head on your shoulders, Alden."

So here come the Glorious Fourth of oh-thirteen. The whole Massimo clan was gathered over at Twelve Pines like usual, must've been two dozen or more, and me n Ma was out on the end of our dock in our lawn chairs. We had our box of goodies set down between us, along with a good-size pitcher of Orange Driver.

Pretty soon Paul Massimo come out to the end of his dock with his own box of goodies, which was a bit bigger than ours, but that didn't concern me. It ain't the size of the dog in the fight, you know, but the size of the fight in the dog. His two grown boys was with him. They waved, and we waved back. Dusk commenced, and me n Ma started shooting off Black Cats, not one by one this time but by the pack. The little kids did the same over on their side, and when they got tired of that, they lit up their big sparklers and waved em around. The son with the trumpet blew a couple of times, kind of tunin up.

A bunch of the younger ones heard it and come out

on the Twelve Pines dock, and after some talk, Paul and his grown boys handed each of em a big gray ball that I recognized as M-80s. Sound carries across the lake real well, especially when there's no breeze, and I could hear Paul tellin the little ones to be careful and demonstratin how they was to chuck em out into the lake. Then Massimo lit em up.

Three of the kids threw high, wide, n handsome like they were s'posed to, but the youngest—couldn't have been more than seven—wound up like Nolan-friggin-Ryan and chucked his right onto the dock between his feet. It bounced and would've blown his nose off if Paul hadn't yanked him back. Some of the women screamed, but Massimo and his boys just about fell down laughin. I judge they might have had more than a few shots. Wine, most likely, because that's what those dagos like to drink.

"All right," Ma said, "enough friggin around. Let's show em up before that tall one starts honkin his god-dam horn."

So I took out a couple of the M-120s, which were black and looked like the bombs you sometimes see in those old-time cartoons, the ones the villain uses to blow up railroad tracks and gold mines and such.

"You be careful, Ma," I said. "Hold onto some-thing like this too long and you'd lose more than just your fingers."

"Don't you worry about me," she said. "Let's show those spaghetti-eaters."

So I lit em, and we threw em, and ka-pow! One after the other! Enough to rattle windows all the way to Waterford, I should judge. Mr. Hornblower froze with his trumpet halfway to his lips. Some of the lit-tle kids started to cry. All the women ran down to the beach to see what was goin on, if it was terrorists or what.

"That's got em!" Ma said, and she toasted to young Mr. Hornblower, standin over there with his trumpet in his hand and his thumb up his ass. Not really, you know, but in a manner of speakin.

Paul Massimo and his two sons walked back to the end of the dock, and there they huddled like a bunch of baseball players when the bases are loaded. Then they all walked up to the house together. I thought they was finished, and Ma was sure of it. So we lit up our Twizzlers, just to celebrate. I'd cut squares of Styrofoam from some packin material I found in the swill bucket out back of the cabin, and we stuck em in those and pushed em out into the water. By then it was that deep purple time that comes just before full dark, awful gorgeous, with the wishin star up there in the sky and all the others ready to peep out. Neither day nor night, and always the prettiest time there is, that's what I think. And them Twizzlers—they was a lot more than pretty. They was beautiful, floatin out there all red and green, waxin and wanin like candle flames, and reflectin on the water.

It was quiet again, too, so quiet you could hear the thumps of the fireworks show gettin started over Bridgeton way, plus frogs startin to croak again along the shoreline. The frogs thought all the noise n ruckus was over for the night. Little did they know, because just then Paul and his two grown boys come back down to their dock and looked across at us. Paul had somethin in his hand almost as big as a softball, and the grown boy without the trumpet—which made him the smarter of the two, in my opinion—lit him up. Massimo didn't waste time but slang it underhand, high above the water, and before I could tell Ma to cover her ears, it went off. Holy Jesus, the flash seemed to blot out the whole sky, and the blast was as loud as an artillery shell. This time it wasn't just the Massimo women and girls who came to see, but damn near everybody on the lake. And although half of em probably pissed their pants when that fucker went off, they were applaudin! Do you believe that?

Ma n me looked at each other because we knew what was comin next, and it surely did: Captain Hornblower raised his fuckin trumpet and blew it at us, one long blast: Waaaaah!

All the Massimos laughed and applauded some more, and so did everybody else on both sides of the water. It was humiliatin. You can understand that, can't you, Andy? Ardelle? We'd been outexploded by a bunch of Eye-Tie flatlanders from Rhode Island. Not that I don't like a plate of spaghetti myself from time to time, but every day? Get out!

"All right, fine," Ma said, squarin her shoulders. "Maybe they can outbang us, but we got those Chinese Peonies. Let's see how they like those." But I could see on her face that she felt they might best us there, too.

I set up a dozen beer n soda cans on the end of our dock, and slipped one of the Peonies into each one. The Massimo menfolk over on the other side stood watchin us, then the one who didn't think he could play the trumpet run back to the house for fresh ammunition.

Meanwhile I ran my lighter along the fuses, neat as you please, and the Chinese Peonies took off one after the other, with nary a malfunction. Awful pretty they were, even though they didn't last long. All the colors of the rainbow, just like Pop promised. There were oohs and ahhs—some from the Massimos, I'll give em that—and then the young man who ran away come back from his errand with another box.

Turned out it was full of fireworks that were like our Chinese Peonies, only bigger. Each one had its own little cardboard launchin pad. We could see, because by then there was lights on at the end of the Massimo dock, kind of shaped like torches, only electric. Paul lit those rockets and up they went, makin golden starbursts in the sky that was twice as big and bright as ours. They twinkled and made cracklin machine-gun noises when they came down. Everybody applauded even more, and accourse me n Ma had to do the same, or we'd be thought of as poor sports. And the trumpet blew: waaaaaaah-waaaaaaah-waaaaaaah.

Later on, after we'd shot off all our shit, Ma went stompin around the kitchen in her nightgown and tartan slippers, steam practically shootin out of her ears. "Where'd they get armaments like that?" she asked, but it was what you call a retropical question, and she didn't give me time to answer. "From his hoodlum friends back in Rhode Island, that's where. Because he's CONNECTED. And he's one of those people who's got to win at everything! You can tell just lookin at him!"

Sorta like you, Ma, I thought, but did not say. Sometimes silence really is golden, and never more than when your Ma's loaded on Allen's coffee brandy and madder than a wet hen.

"And I hate that friggin trumpet. Hate it with a purple passion."

I could agree with her there, and did.

She grabbed me by the arm, sloppin her last drink of the night all down the front of my shirt. "Next year!" she said. "We're going to show them who's boss next year! Promise me we'll shut up that trumpet in fourteen, Alden."

I promised to try—that was the best I could do. Paul Massimo had all his resources in Rhode Island, and what did I have? Pop Anderson, owner of a side o' the road flea market next to the discount sneaker store.

Still, I went to him the next day, and explained what had happened. He listened, and did me the courtesy of not laughin, although his mouth twitched a few times. I'm willin to sniculate that it did have its funny side—at least until last night it did—but not s'much when you had Hallie McCausland breathin down your neck.

"Yes, I can see how that would get your ma's goat," Pop said. "She was always a heller when someone tried to get the best of her. But for Christ's sake, Alden, it's only fireworks. When she sobers up she'll see that."

"I don't think so," I said, not wantin to add that Ma never really sobered up anymore, just went from tiddly to crocked to asleep to hungover and then back to tiddly again. Not that I was much better. "It ain't s'much the fireworks as it is that trumpet, you see. If she could shut up that fuckin trumpet on the Fourth of July, I think she'd be satisfied."

"Well, I can't help you," Pop said. "There's plenty of bigger fireworks out there for sale, but I won't truck in them. I don't want to lose my vendor's license, for one thing. And I don't want to see no one get hurt, that's another. Drunks shootin explosives is always a recipe for disaster. But if you're really determined, you ought to take a ride up to Indian Island and talk to a fella there. Great big Penobscot named Howard Gamache. Biggest goddam Indian in Maine, maybe in the whole world. Rides a Harley-Davidson and has feathers tattooed on his cheeks. He's what you might call connected."

Somebody connected! That's exactly what we needed! I thanked Pop, and wrote the name *Howard Gamache* in my notebook, and next April I took a ride up to Penobscot County with five hundred dollars cash in the glovebox of my truck.

I found Mr. Gamache sittin at the bar of the Harvest Hotel in Oldtown, and he was as big as advertised—six foot eight, I'd guess, and would weigh around three fifty. He listened to my tale of woe, and after I'd bought him a pitcher of Bud, which he drank down in less than ten minutes, he said, "Well, Mr. McCausland, let's you and me take a little jaunt up the road to my wigwam and discuss this in more detail."

He was ridin a Harley Softail, which is a mighty big sled, but when he was on it, that thing looked like one of the little bikes the clowns ride in the circus. Butt cheeks hung right down to the saddlebags, they did. His wigwam turned out to be a nice little two-story ranch with a pool out back for the kiddies, of which he had a passel.

No, Ardelle, the bike and the pool *ain't* particularly important to the story, but if you want it, you'll have to take it my way. And I find it interestin. There was even a home theater set up in the basement. Jeezly Crow, I felt like movin in.

The fireworks was in his garage under a tarp, all stacked up in wooden crates, and there was some pretty awesome stuff. "If you get caught with it," he said, "you never heard of Howard Gamache. Isn't that right?"

I said it was, and because he seemed like an honest enough fella who wouldn't screw me—at least not too bad—I asked him what five hundred dollars would buy. I ended up gettin mostly cakes, which are blocks of rockets with a single fuse. You light it, and up they go by the dozen. There was three cakes called Pyro Monkey, another two called Declaration of Independence, one called Psycho-Delick that shoots off big bursts of light that look like flowers, and one that was extra-special. I'll get to that.

"You think this stuff will shut down those dagos?" I asked him.

"You bet," Howard said. "Only as someone who prefers to be called a Native American rather than a redskin or a Tomahawk Tom, I don't care much for such pejorative terms as dagos, bog-trotters, camel jockeys, and beaners. They are Americans, even as you and I, and there's no need to denigrate them."

"I hear you," I said, "and I'll take it to heart, but those Massimos still piss me off, and if that offends you, it's a case of tough titty said the kitty."

"Understood, and I can fully identify with your emotional condition. But let me give you some advice, paleface: keep-um to speed limit going home. You don't want to get caught with that shit in your trunk."

When Ma saw what I'd bought, she shook her fists over her head and then poured us a couple of Dirty Hubcaps to celebrate. "When they experience these, they're gonna shit nickels!" she said. "Maybe even silver dollars! See if they don't!"

Only it didn't turn out that way. I guess you know that, don't you?

Come the Fourth of July last year, Abenaki Lake was loaded to the gunwales. Word had got around, you see, that it was the McCausland Yankees against the Massimo Dagos for the fireworks blue ribbon. Must have been six hundred people on our side of the lake. Not so many over on their side, but there was a bunch, all right, more than ever before. Every Massimo east of the Mississippi must have shown up for the oh-fourteen showdown. We didn't bother with piddling stuff like firecrackers and cherry bombs that time, just waited for deep dusk so we could shoot the big stuff. Ma n me had boxes with Chinese characters stacked on our dock, but so did they. The east shore-front was lined with little Massimos waving spar-klers; looked like stars that had fallen to earth, they did. I sometimes think sparklers are enough, and this morning I sure wish we'd stuck to em.

Paul Massimo waved to us and we waved back. The idiot with the trumpet blew a long blast: Waaaaaah! Paul pointed to me, as if to say you first, monsewer, so I shot off a Pyro Monkey. It lit up the sky and every-one went aahhhh. Then one of Massimo's sons lit off something similar, except it was brighter and lasted a little longer. The crowd went ooooh, and off went the fuckin trumpet.

"Never mind the Funky Monkeys, or whatever they are," Ma said. "Give em the Declaration of Inde-pendence. That'll show em."

I did, and it was some gorgeous, but those goddam Massimos topped that one too. They topped every-thing we shot off, and every time theirs went brighter n louder, that asshole blew his trumpet. It pissed off

Ma n me no end; hell, it was enough to piss off the pope. The crowd got one hell of a fireworks show that night, probably as good as the one they have in Portland, and I'm sure they went home happy, but there was no joy on the dock of the Mosquito Bowl, I can tell you that. Ma usually gets happy when she's in the bag, but she wasn't that night. It was full dark by then, all the stars out, and a haze of gunpowder driftin across the lake. We was down to our last and biggest item.

"Shoot it," Ma said, "and see if they can beat it. Might as well. But if he blows that friggin trumpet one more time, my head's gonna explode right off my shoulders."

Our last one—the extra-special—was called the Ghost of Fury, and Howard Gamache swore by it. "A beautiful thing," he told me, "and totally illegal. Stand back after you light it, Mr. McCausland, because it goes a gusher."

Goddam fuse was thick as your wrist. I lit it and stood back. For a few seconds after it burned down there was nothin, and I thought it was a dud.

"Well, don't that just impregnate the family dog," Ma said. "Now he'll blow that bastardly trumpet."

But before he could, the Ghost of Fury went off. First it was just a fountain of white sparks, but then it shot up higher and turned rose-pink. It started blowin off rockets that exploded in starbursts. By then the fountain of sparks on the end of our dock was at least twelve feet high and bright red. It shot off even more rockets, straight up into the sky, and they boomed as loud as a squadron of jets breakin the sound barrier. Ma covered her ears, but she was laughin fit to split. The fountain went down, then spurted up one last time—like an old man in a whorehouse, Ma said—and shot off this gorgeous red n yella flower into the sky.

There was a moment of silence—awed, don't you know—and then everybody on the lake started applaudin like crazy. Some people who was in their campers tooted their horns, which sounded mighty thin after all those bangs. The Massimos was applaudin too, which showed they was good sports, which impressed me, because you know folks who have to win at everything usually ain't. The one with the trumpet never took the damn thing out of its holster.

"We did it!" Ma shouted. "Alden, give your Ma a kiss!"

I did, and when I looked across the lake, I seen Paul Massimo standin at the end of his dock, in the light of those electric torches they had. He put up one finger, as if to say, "Wait and watch." It gave me a bad feelin in the pit of my stomach.

The son without the trumpet—the one I judged might have a lick of sense—put down a launcher cradle, slow and reverent, like an altar boy puttin out the Holy Communion. Settin in it was the biggest fuckin rocket I ever seen that wasn't on TV at Cape Canaveral. Paul dropped down on one knee and put his lighter to the fuse. As soon as it started to spark, he grabbed both his boys and ran em right off the dock.

There was no pause, like with our Ghost of Fury. Fucker took off like Apollo 19, trailin a streak of blue fire that turned purple, then red. A second later the stars was blotted out by a giant flamin bird that covered the lake almost from one side to the other. It blazed up there, then exploded. And I'll be damned if little birds didn't come out of the explosion, shootin off in every direction.

The crowd went nuts. Them grown boys was huggin their father and poundin him on the back and laughin.

"Let's go in, Alden," Ma said, and she never sounded so sad since Daddy died. "We're beat."

"We'll get em next year," I said, pattin her shoulder.

"No," she said, "them Massimos will always be a step ahead. That's the kind of people they are—people with CONNECTIONS. We're just a couple of poor folks livin on a lucky fortune, and I guess that'll have to be enough."

As we went up the steps of our shitty little cabin, there come one final trumpet blast from the fine big house across the lake: Waaaa-aaaah! Made my head ache, it did.

Howard Gamache told me that last firework was called the Rooster of Destiny. He said he'd seen videos of em on YouTube, but always with people talkin Chinese in the background.

"How this Massimo gentleman got it into this country is a mystery to me," Howard said. This was about a month later, toward the end of last summer, when I finally got up enough ambition to make the drive up to his two-story wigwam on Indian Island and tell him what happened—how we give em a good battle but still come off on the short end when all was said and told.

"It's no mystery to me," I said. "His friends in China prob'ly threw it in as an extra with his last load of opium. You know, a little gift to say thanks for doin business with us. Have you got anything that'll top it? Ma's awful depressed, Mr. Gamache. She don't want to compete next year, but I was thinkin if there was anything . . . you know, the topper to top all toppers . . . I'd pay as much as a thousand dollars. It'd be worth it just to see my ma smilin on Fourth of July night."

Howard sat on his back steps with his knees stickin up around his ears like a couple of boulders—God, what a mighty man he was—and thought about it. Cogitated on it. Judged his way around it. At last he said, "I have heard rumors."

"Rumors about what?"

"About a special something called Close Encounters of the Fourth Kind," he said. "From a fellow I correspond with on the subject of gunpowder amusements. His native name is Shining Path, but mostly he goes by Johnny Parker. He's a Cayuga Indian, and he lives near Albany, New York. I could give you his email address, but he won't reply unless I email him first and tell him you're safe."

"Will you do that?" I asked.

"Of course," he said, "but first you must pay heap big wampum, paleface. Fifty bucks should do it."

Money passed from my small hand to his big one, he emailed Johnny Shining Path Parker, and when I got back to the lake and sent him an email of my own, he answered right back. But he wouldn't talk about what he called CE4 except in person, claimed the government read all Native American emails as a matter of course. I didn't have no argument with that; I bet those suckers read everyone's email. So we agreed to meet, and along about the first of October last year, I went up.

Accourse Ma wanted to know what sort of errand

would take me all the way to upstate New York, and I didn't bother tellin her no made-up story, because she always sees through em and has since I was knee-high to a collie. She just shook her head. "Go on, if it'll make you happy," she said. "But you know they'll come back with somethin even bigger, and we'll be stuck listenin to that Eye-Tie cock-knocker blow his trumpet."

"Well, maybe," I said, "but Mr. Shining Path says this is the firework to end all fireworks."

As you now see, that turned out to be nothing but the truth.

I had a pretty drive, and Johnny Shining Path Parker turned out to be a nice fella. His wigwam was in Green Island, where the houses are almost as big as the Massimos' Twelve Pines, and his wife made one hell of an enchilada. I ate three with that hot green sauce and got the shits on the way home, but since that ain't part of the story and I can see Ardelle's gettin impatient again, I'll leave it out. All I can say is thank God for Handi-Wipes.

"CE4 would be a special order," Johnny said. "The Chinese make only three or four a year, in Outer Mongolia or someplace like that, where there's snow nine months of the year and the babies are purportedly raised with wolf cubs. Such explosive devices are usually shipped to Toronto. I guess I could order one and bring it in from Canada myself, although you'd have to pay for my gas and my time, and if I got caught, I'd probably end up in Leavenworth as a terrorist."

"Jesus, I don't want to get you in no trouble like that," I said.

"Well, I'm exaggerating a bit, maybe," he said, "but CE4's one hell of a firework. Never been one like it. I couldn't give you your money back if your pal across the lake happened to have something to beat it, but I'd give you back my profit on the deal. That's how sure I am."

"Besides," Cindy Shining Path Parker said, "Johnny loves an adventure. Would you like another enchilada, Mr. McCausland?"

I passed on that, which probably kep me from explodin somewhere in Vermont, and for awhile I almost forgot the whole thing. Then, just after New Year's—we're gettin close now, Ardelle, don't that make you happy?—I got a call from Johnny.

"If you want that item we were discussing last fall," he said, "I've got it, but it'll cost you two thousand."

I sucked in breath. "That's pretty steep."

"I can't argue with you there, but look at it this way—you white folks got Manhattan for twenty-four bucks, and we've been looking for payback ever since." He laughed, then said, "But speaking seriously now, and if you don't want it, that's fine. Maybe your buddy across the lake would be interested."

"Don't you ever," I said.

He laughed harder at that. "I have to tell you, this thing is pretty awesome. I've sold a lot of fireworks over the years, and I've never seen anything remotely like this."

"Like what?" I asked. "What is it?"

"You have to see for yourself," he said. "I have no intention of sending you a pitcher over the Internet. Besides, it doesn't look like much until it's . . . uh . . . in use. If you want to roll on up here, I can show you a video."

"I'll be there," I said, and two or three days later I was, sober and shaved and with my hair combed.

Now listen to me, you two. I ain't gonna make excuses for what I done—and you c'n leave Ma out of it, I was the one that got the damn thing, and I was the one who set it off—but I am gonna tell you that the CE4 I saw in that video Johnny showed me and the one I set off last night wasn't the same. The one in the video was a lot smaller. I even remarked on the size of the crate mine was in when Johnny and me put it in the back of the truck. "They sure must have put a lot of packing in there," I said.

"I guess they wanted to make sure nothing would happen to it in shipping," Johnny said.

He didn't know either, you see. Cindy Shining Path Parker asked if I didn't want to at least open the crate and have a look, make sure it was the right thing, but it was nailed up tight all over, and I wanted to get back before dark, on account of my eyes ain't as good as they used to be. But because I come here today determined to make a clean breast of it, I have to tell you that wasn't the truth. Evenin is my drinkin time, and I didn't want to miss any of it. That's the truth. I know that's kind of a sad way to be, and I know I have to do somethin about it. I guess if they put me in jail, I'll get a chance, won't I?

Me n Ma unnailed the crate the next day and took a look at what we'd bought. This was at the house in town, you understand, because we're talkin January, and colder than a witch's tit. There was some packin material, all right, Chinese newspapers of some kind, but not nearly so much as I expected. The CE4 was probably seven feet on the square, and looked like a package done up in brown paper, only the paper was kind of oily, and so heavy it felt more like canvas. The fuse was stickin out the bottom.

"Do you think it will really go up?" Ma asked.

"Well," I said, "if ours don't, what's the worst that can happen?"

"We'll be out two thousand bucks," Ma said, "but that ain't the worst. The worst'd be it rises up two or three feet and then fizzles into the lake. Followed by that young Eye-talian who looks like Ben Afflict blowin his trumpet."

We put it in the garage and there it stayed until Memorial Day, when we took it out to the lake. I didn't buy nothing else of a firework nature this year, not from Pop Anderson and not from Howard Gamache, either. We was all in on the one thing. It was CE4 or bust.

All right; here we are at last night. Fourth of July of oh-fifteen, never been nothin like it on Abenaki Lake and I hope there never will be again. We knew it had been a goddam dry summer, accourse we knew, but that never crossed our minds. Why would it? We were shootin over the water, weren't we? What could be safer?

All the Massimos was there and havin fun—playin their music and playin their games and cookin weenies on about five different grills and swimmin near the beach and divin off the float. Everyone else was there, too, on both sides of the lake. There was even some at the north and south ends, where it's all swampy. They were there to see this year's chapter of the Great Fourth of July Arms Race, Eye-Ties versus Yankees.

Dusk drew down and finally the wishin star come out, like she always does, and those electric torches at the end of the Massimo dock popped on like a couple of spotlights. Out onto it struts Paul Massimo, flanked by his two grown sons, and goddam if they weren't dressed like for a fancy country club dance! Father in a tuxedo, sons in white dinner jackets with red flowers in the lapels, the Ben Afflict–lookin one wearin his trumpet down low on his hip, like a gunslinger.

I looked around and seen the lake was lined with more folks than ever before. Must have been at least a thousand. They'd come expectin a show, and those Massimos was dressed to give em one, while Ma was in her usual housedress and I was in a pair of old jeans and a tee-shirt that said KISS ME WHERE IT STINKS, MEET ME IN MILLINOCKET.

"He ain't got no boxes, Alden," Ma said. "Why is that?"

I just shook my head, because I didn't know. Our single firework was already at the end of our dock, covered with an old quilt. Had been there all day.

Massimo held out his hand to us, polite as always, tellin us we should start. I shook my head and held out mine right back, as if to say nope, after you this time, monsewer. He shrugged and made a twirlin gesture in the air, sort of like when the ump is sayin it's a home run. About four seconds later, the night was filled with uprushin trails of sparks, and fireworks started to explode over the lake in starbursts and sprays and multiple canister blasts that shot out flowers and fountains and I don't know what-all.

Ma gasped. "Why, that dirty dog! He went and hired a whole fireworks crew! *Professionals!*"

And yes, that's just what he done. He must've spent ten or fifteen thousand dollars on that twenty-minute sky-show, what with the Double Excalibur and the Wolfpack that come near the end. The crowd on the lake was whoopin and hollerin to beat the band, bammin on their car horns and cheerin and screamin. The Ben Afflict–lookin one was blowin his trumpet hard enough to give him a brain hemorrhage, but you couldn't even hear him over the gunnery practice goin on in the sky, which was lit up bright as day, and in every color. Sheets of smoke rose from where the fireworks crew was settin off their goods down on the beach, but none of it blew across the lake. It blew toward the house instead. Toward Twelve Pines. You could say I should have noticed that, but I didn't. Ma didn't, either. Nobody did. We was too gobsmacked. Massimo was sendin us a message, you see: It's over. Don't even think about it next year, you poor-ass Yankees.

There was a pause, and I was just decidin he'd shot his load when up goes a double gusher of sparks, and the sky filled with a great big burnin boat, sails n all! I knew from Howard Gamache what that one was too: an Excellent Junk. That's a Chinese boat. When it finally went out and the crowd around the lake stopped goin bananas, Massimo signaled to his fireworks boys one last time and they sparked up an American flag on the beach. It burned red white n blue and threw off fireballs while someone played "America the Beautiful" through the sound system.

Finally, the flag burned out to nothin but orange cinders. Massimo was still at the end of his dock, and he held his hand out to us again, smiling. As if to say, Go on n shoot whatever paltry shit you got over there, McCausland, and we'll be done with it. Not just this year but for good.

I looked at Ma. She looked at me. Then she slatted whatever was left of her drink—we was drinkin

Moonquakes last night—into the water and said,
"Go on. It probably won't amount to a pisshole in the
snow, but we bought the damn thing, might as well
set her off."

I remember how quiet it was. The frogs hadn't
started up again yet, and the poor old loons had
packed it in for the night, maybe for the rest of the
summer. There was still plenty of people standin at
the water's edge to see what we had, but a lot more
was goin back to town, like fans will when their
team is gettin blown out and has no chance of comin
back. I could see a chain of lights all the way down
Lake Road, that hooks up with Highway 119, and
to Pretty Bitch, the one that eventually takes you to
TR-90 and Chester's Mill.

I decided if I was gonna do it, I ought to make a
fair show of it; if it misfired, the ones that were left
could laugh as much as they wanted. I could even
put up with the goddam trumpet, knowin I wouldn't
have to listen to it blowed at me next year, because I
was done, and I could see from her face that Ma felt
the same. Even her boobs seemed to be hangin their
heads, but maybe that was just because she left off her
bra last night. She says it pinches her terrible.

I whipped off that piece of quilt like a magician doin a trick, and there was the square thing I'd
bought for two thousand dollars—prob'ly half what
Massimo paid for just his Excellent Junk alone—all
wrapped in its heavy canvasy paper, with the short
thick fuse stickin out the end.

I pointed to it, then pointed to the sky. Them three
dressed-up Massimos standin at the end of their dock
laughed, and the trumpet blew: Waaaa-aaaaah!

I lit the fuse and it started to spark. I grabbed

Ma and pulled her back, in case the friggin thing should explode on the launchin pad. The fuse burned down to the box, then disappeared. Fuckin box just sat there. The Massimo with the trumpet raised it to his lips, but before he could blow it, fire kind of squashed out from under the box and up she rose, slow at first, then faster as more jets—I guess they was jets—caught fire.

Up n up. Ten feet, then twenty, then forty. I could just make out the square shape against the stars. It made fifty, everyone cranin their necks to look, and then it exploded, just like the one in the YouTube video Johnny Shining Path Parker showed me. Me n Ma cheered. Everyone cheered. The Massimos only looked perplexed, and maybe—hard to tell from our side of the lake—a little contemptuous. It was like they was thinkin, an exploding box, what the fuck is that?

Only the CE4 wasn't done. When people's eyes adjusted, they gasped in wonder, for the paper stuff was unfoldin and spreadin even as it began to burn every color you ever saw and some you never did. It was turnin into a goddam flyin saucer. It spread and spread, like God was openin his own holy umbrella, and as it opened it began shootin off fireballs every whichway. Each one exploded and shot off more, makin a kind of rainbow over that saucer. I know you two have seen cell phone video of it, probably everybody who had a phone was makin movies of it which I don't doubt will be evidence at my trial, but I'm tellin you you had to be there to fully appreciate the wonder of it.

Ma was clutchin my arm. "It's beautiful," she said, "but I thought it was only eight feet across. Isn't that what your Indian friend said?"

It was, but the thing I'd unleashed was *twenty* feet across and still growin when it popped a dozen or more little parachutes to keep it elevated while it shot off more colors and sparklers and fountains and flash bombs. It was maybe not so grand as Massimo's fireworks show in the altogether, but grander than his Excellent Junk. And, accourse, it came last. That's what people always remember, don't you think, what they see last?

Ma seen the Massimos starin up at the sky, their jaws hung down like doors on busted hinges, lookin like the purest goddam ijits that ever walked the earth, and she started to dance. The trumpet was danglin down Ben Afflict's hand, like he'd forgotten he had it.

"We beat em!" Ma screamed at me, shakin her fists. "We finally did it, Alden! Look at em! They're beat and it was worth *every fuckin penny*!"

She wanted me to dance with her, but I seen something I didn't much care for. The wind was pushin that flyin saucer east'rds across the lake, toward Twelve Pines.

Paul Massimo seen the same thing and pointed at me, as if to say, You put it up there, you bring it down while it's still over the water.

Only I couldn't, accourse, and meanwhile the goddam thing was still blowin its wad, shootin off rockets and cannonades and swirly fountains like it would never stop. Then—I had no idea it was gonna happen, because the video Johnny Shining Path showed me was silent—it started to play music. Just five notes over and over: doo-dee-doo-dum-dee. It was the music the spaceship makes in *Close Encounters of the Third Kind*. So it's toodlee-dooin and toodleedeein, and that's when the goddam saucer caught afire. I don't know if that was an accident or if it was s'posed to be the final effect. The parachutes holdin it up, they caught, too, and the whoremaster started to sink. At first I thought it'd go down before it ran out of lake to land in, maybe even on the Massimos' swimmin float, which would've been bad, but not the worst. Only just then a stronger gust of wind blew up, as if Mother Nature herself was tired of the Massimos. Or maybe it was just that fuckin trumpet the old girl was tired of.

Well, you know how their place got its name, and them dozen pines was plenty dry. There was two of em on either side of the long front porch, and those were what our CE4 crashed into. Them trees went up right away, lookin sort of like the electric torches at the end of Massimo's dock, only bigger. First the needles, then the branches, then the trunks. Massimos started runnin every whichway, like ants when someone kicks their hill. A burnin branch fell on the roof over the porch, and pretty soon that was burnin merry hell, too. And all the while that little tootlin tune went on, doo-dee-doo-dum-dee.

The spaceship tore in two pieces. Half of it fell on the lawn, which wasn't s'bad, but the other half floated down on the main roof, still shootin off a few final rockets, one of which crashed through an upstairs window, lightin the curtains afire as it went.

Ma turned to me and said, "Well, *that* ain't good."

"No," I said, "looks pretty poor, don't it?"

She said, "I guess you better call the fire department, Alden. In fact, I guess you better call two or three of em, or there's gonna be cooked woods from the lake to the Castle County line."

I turned to run back to the cabin and get my phone, but she caught my arm. There was this funny little smile on her face. "Before you go," she said, "take a glance at that."

She pointed across the lake. By then the whole house was afire, so there wasn't no trouble seein what she was pointin at. There was no one on their dock anymore, but one thing got left behind: the goddam trumpet.

"Tell em it was all my idea," Ma said. "I'll go to jail for it, but I don't give a shit. At least we shut that friggin thing up."

Say, Ardelle, can I have a drink of water? I'm dry as an old chip.

Officer Benoit brought Alden a glass of water. She and Andy Clutterbuck watched him drink it down— a lanky man in chinos and a strap-style tee-shirt, his hair thin and graying, his face haggard from lack of sleep and the previous night's ingestion of sixty-proof Moonquakes.

"At least no one got hurt," Alden said. "I'm glad of that. And we didn't burn the woods down. I'm glad of that, too."

"You're lucky the wind died," Andy said.

"You're also lucky the fire trucks from all three towns were standing by," Ardelle added. "Of course they have to be on Fourth of July nights, because there are always a few fools setting off drunken fireworks."

"This is all on me," Alden said. "I just want you to understand that. I bought the goddam thing, and I was the one who fired it up. Ma had nothing to do with it." He paused. "I just hope Massimo understands that, and leaves my ma alone. He's CONNECTED, you know."

Andy said, "That family has been summering on Abenaki Lake for twenty years or more, and according to everything I know, Paul Massimo is a legitimate businessman."

"Ayuh," Alden said. "Just like Al Capone."

Officer Ellis knocked on the glass of the interview room, pointed at Andy, cocked his thumb and little finger in a telephone gesture, and beckoned. Andy sighed and left the room.

Ardelle Benoit stared at Alden. "I've seen some tall orders of shit flapjacks in my time," she said, "and even more since I got on the cops, but this takes the prize."

"I know," Alden said, hanging his head. "I ain't makin any excuses." Then he brightened. "But it was one hell of a show while it lasted. People won't never forget it."

Ardelle made a rude noise. Somewhere in the distance, a siren howled.

Andy eventually came back and sat down. He said nothing at first, just looked off into space.

"Was that about Ma?" Alden asked.

"It *was* your ma," Andy said. "She wanted to talk to you, and when I told her you were otherwise occupied, she asked if I would pass on a message. She was calling from Lucky's Diner, where she just finished having a nice sit-down brunch with your neighbor from across the lake. She said to tell you he was still dressed in his tuxedo and it was his treat."

"Did he threaten her?" Alden cried. "Did that sonofabitch—"

"Sit down, Alden. Relax."

Alden settled slowly from a half-risen crouch, but his hands were clenched into fists. They were big hands, and looked capable of doing damage, if their owner felt provoked.

"Hallie also said to tell you that Mr. Massimo isn't going to press any charges. He said that two families got into a stupid competition, and consequently both families were at fault. Your mother says Mr. Massimo wants to let bygones be bygones."

Alden's Adam's apple bobbed up and down, reminding Ardelle of a monkey-on-a-stick toy she'd had as a child.

Andy leaned forward. He was smiling in the painful way folks do when they don't really want to smile but just can't help it. "She said Mr. Massimo also wants you to know he was sorry about what happened with the rest of your fireworks."

"The *rest* of em? I told you we didn't have nothing this year except for—"

"Hush while I'm talking. I don't want to forget any of the message."

Alden hushed. Outside they could hear a second siren, and then a third.

"The ones in the kitchen. *Those* fireworks. Your ma said you must have put the boxes too close to the woodstove. Do you remember doing that?"

"Uh . . ."

"I urge you to remember, Alden, because I have a deep desire to bring down the curtain on this particular shit-show."

"I guess . . . I sorta do," Alden said.

"I won't even ask why you had your stove going on a hot July night, because after thirty years in the policing business, I know drunks are apt to take any half-baked notion into their heads. Would you agree with that?"

"Well . . . ayuh," Alden admitted. "Drunks are unpredictable. And those Moonquakes are deadly."

"Which is why your cabin out there on Abenaki Lake is now burning to the ground."

"Jesus Christ on a crutch!"

"I don't think we can blame this fire on the Son of God, Alden, crutch or no crutch. Were you insured?"

"Gorry, yes," Alden said. "Insurance is a good idea. I learned that when Daddy passed away."

"Massimo was insured, as well. Your mother told me to tell you that too. She said the two of them agreed over bacon and eggs that it all evens out. Would you agree with that?"

"Well . . . his house was a hell of a lot bigger than our cabin."

"Presumably his policy will reflect the difference." Andy stood up. "I suppose there'll be some kind of hearing eventually, but right now you're free to go."

Alden said thank you. And left before they could change their minds.

Andy and Ardelle sat in the interview room, looking at each other. Eventually Ardelle said, "Where was Mrs. McCausland when the fire broke out?"

"Until Massimo came to treat her to lobster Benedict and homefries at Lucky's, right here at the station," Andy said. "Waiting to see if her boy was going to court or county jail. Hoping for court so she could bail him out. Ellis said that when she and Massimo left, he had his arm around her waist. Which must have been quite a reach, considering her current girth."

"And who do you think set the fire at the McCausland cabin?"

"We'll never know for sure, but were I forced to

guess, I'd say it was Massimo's boys, before sunrise. Put some of their own unused fireworks next to the stove—or right on top of it—and then stuffed that Pearl full of kindling so it would burn nice and hot. Not much different from putting a bomb on a timer, when you think about it."

"Damn," Ardelle said.

"What it comes down to is drunks with fireworks, which is bad, and one hand washing the other, which is good."

Ardelle thought about that, then puckered her lips and whistled the five-note melody from *Close Encounters of the Third Kind*. She tried to do it again, but began to laugh and lost her pucker.

"Not bad," Andy said. "But can you play it on the trumpet?"

Thinking of Marshall Dodge

What better place to end a collection than with a story about the end of the world? I've done at least one sprawling book on this subject, *The Stand*, but here the focus is narrowed to little more than a pinprick. I don't have much to say about the story itself, other than that I was thinking about my beloved 1986 Harley Softail, which I've now put away, and probably for good—my reflexes have slowed enough to make me a danger to myself and others when I'm on the road and doing 65. How I loved that bike. After I wrote *Insomnia*, I rode it from Maine to California and remember an evening somewhere in Kansas, watching the sun set in the west while the moon rose, huge and orange, in the east. I pulled over and just watched, thinking it was the finest sunset of my life. Maybe it was.

Oh, and "Summer Thunder" was written in a place much like the one where we find Robinson, his neighbor, and a certain stray dog named Gandalf.

Summer Thunder

Robinson was okay as long as Gandalf was. Not okay in the sense of everything is fine, but in the sense of getting along from one day to the next. He still woke up in the night, often with tears on his face from vivid dreams where Diana and Ellen were alive, but when he picked Gandalf up from the blanket in the corner where he slept and put him on the bed, he could more often than not go back to sleep again. As for Gandalf, he didn't care where he slept, and if Robinson pulled him close, that was okay, too. It was warm, dry, and safe. He had been rescued. That was all Gandalf cared about.

With another living being to take care of, things were better. Robinson drove to the country store five miles up Route 19 (Gandalf sitting in the pickup's passenger seat, ears cocked, eyes bright) and got dog food. The store was abandoned, and of course it had been looted, but no one had taken the Eukanuba. After June Sixth, pets had been the last thing on people's minds. So Robinson deduced.

Otherwise, the two of them stayed by the lake. There was plenty of food in the pantry, and boxes of stuff downstairs. He had often joked about how Diana expected the apocalypse, but the joke turned out to be on him. Both of them, actually, because Diana had surely never imagined that when the apocalypse finally arrived, she would be in Boston with their daughter, investigating the academic possibilities of Emerson College. Eating for one, the food would last longer than he did. Robinson had no doubt of that. Timlin said they were doomed.

He never would have expected doom to be so lovely. The weather was warm and cloudless. In the old days, Lake Pocomtuck would have buzzed with powerboats and Jet Skis (which were killing the fish, the old-timers grumbled), but this summer it was silent except for the loons . . . only there seemed to be fewer of them crying each night. At first Robinson thought this was just his imagination, which was as infected with grief as the rest of his thinking apparatus, but Timlin assured him it wasn't.

"Haven't you noticed that most of the woodland birds are already gone? No chickadee concerts in the morning, no crow music at noon. By September, the loons will be as gone as the loons who did this. The fish will live a little longer, but eventually they'll be gone, too. Like the deer, the rabbits, and the chipmunks."

About such wildlife there could be no argument. Robinson had seen almost a dozen dead deer beside the lake road and more beside Route 19, on that one trip he and Gandalf had made to the Carson Corners General Store, where the sign out front—BUY YOUR VERMONT CHEESE & SYRUP HERE!—now lay facedown next to the dry gas pumps. But the greatest part of the animal holocaust was in the woods. When the wind was from the east, toward the lake rather than off it, the reek was tremendous. The warm days didn't help, and Robinson wanted to know what had happened to nuclear winter.

"Oh, it'll come," said Timlin, sitting in his rocker and looking off into the dappled sunshine under the trees. "Earth is still absorbing the blow. Besides, we know from the last reports that the Southern Hemisphere—not to mention most of Asia—is socked in beneath what may turn out to be eternal cloud cover. Enjoy the sunshine while we've got it, Peter."

As if he could enjoy anything. He and Diana had been talking about a trip to England—their first extended vacation since the honeymoon—once Ellen was settled in school.

Ellen, he thought. Who had just been recovering from the breakup with her first real boyfriend and was beginning to smile again.

On each of these fine late-summer postapocalypse days, Robinson clipped a leash to Gandalf's collar (he had no idea what the dog's name had been before June Sixth; the mutt had come with a collar from which only a State of Massachusetts vaccination tag hung), and they walked the two miles to the pricey enclave of which Howard Timlin was now the only resident.

Diana had once called that walk snapshot heaven. Much of it overlooked sheer drops to the lake and forty-mile views into New York. At one point, where the road buttonhooked sharply, a sign that read MIND YOUR DRIVING! had been posted. The summer kids of course called this hairpin Dead Man's Curve.

Woodland Acres—private as well as pricey before the world ended—was a mile farther on. The centerpiece was a fieldstone lodge that had featured a restaurant with a marvelous view, a five-star chef, and a "beer pantry" stocked with a thousand brands. ("Many undrinkable," Timlin said. "Take it from me.") Scattered around the main lodge, in various bosky dells, were two dozen picturesque "cottages," some owned by major corporations before June Sixth put an end to corporations. Most of the cottages had still been empty on June Sixth, and in the crazy ten days that followed, the few people who were in residence fled for Canada, which was rumored to be radiation-free. That was when there was still enough gasoline to make flight possible.

The owners of Woodland Acres, George and Ellen Benson, had stayed. So had Timlin, who was divorced, had no children to mourn, and knew the Canada story was surely a fable. Then, in early July, the Bensons had swallowed pills and taken to their bed while listening to Beethoven on a battery-powered phonograph. Now it was just Timlin.

"All that you see is mine," he had told Robinson, waving his arm grandly. "And someday, son, it will be yours."

On these daily walks down to the Acres, Robinson's grief and sense of dislocation eased; sunshine was seductive. Gandalf sniffed at the bushes and tried to pee on every one. He barked bravely when he heard something in the woods, but always moved closer to Robinson. The leash was necessary only because of the dead squirrels and chipmunks. Gandalf didn't want to pee on those, he wanted to roll in what was left of them.

Woodland Acres Lane split off from the camp road where Robinson now lived the single life. Once the lane had been gated to keep lookie-loos and wage-slave rabble such as himself out, but now the gate stood permanently open. The lane meandered for half a mile through forest where the slanting, dusty light seemed almost as old as the towering spruces and pines that filtered it, passed four tennis courts, skirted a putting green, and looped behind a barn where the trail horses now lay dead in their stalls. Timlin's cottage was on the far side of the lodge—a modest dwelling with four bedrooms, four bathrooms, a hot tub, and its own sauna.

"Why did you need four bedrooms, if it's just you?" Robinson asked him once.

"I don't now and never did," Timlin said, "but they *all* have four bedrooms. Except for Foxglove, Yarrow, and Lavender. They have five. Lavender also has an attached bowling alley. All mod cons. But when I came here as a kid with my family, we peed in a privy. True thing."

Robinson and Gandalf usually found Timlin sitting in one of the rockers on the wide front porch of his cottage (Veronica), reading a book or listening to his battery-powered CD player. Robinson would unclip the leash from Gandalf's collar and the dog—just a mutt, no real recognizable brand except for the spaniel ears—raced up the steps to be made a fuss of. After a few strokes, Timlin would gently pull at the dog's gray-white fur in various places, and when it remained rooted, he would always say the same thing: "Remarkable."

On this fine day in mid-August, Gandalf only made a brief visit to Timlin's rocker, sniffing at the man's bare ankles before trotting back down the steps and into the woods. Timlin raised his hand to Robinson in the How gesture of an old-time movie Indian.

Robinson returned the compliment.

"Want a beer?" Timlin asked. "They're cool. I just dragged them out of the lake."

"Would today's tipple be Old Shitty or Green Mountain Dew?"

"Neither. There was a case of Budweiser in the storeroom. The King of Beers, as you may remember. I liberated it."

"In that case, I'll be happy to join you."

Timlin got up with a grunt and went inside, rocking slightly from side to side. Arthritis had mounted a sneak attack on his hips two years ago, he had told Robinson, and, not content with that, had decided to lay claim to his ankles. Robinson had never asked, but judged Timlin to be in his mid-seventies. His slim body suggested a life of fitness, but fitness was now beginning to fail. Robinson himself had never felt physically better in his life, which was ironic considering how little he now had to live for. Timlin certainly didn't need him, although the old guy was congenial enough. As this preternaturally beautiful summer wound down, only Gandalf actually needed him. Which was okay, because for now, Gandalf was enough.

Just a boy and his dog, he thought.

Said dog had emerged from the woods in mid-June, thin and bedraggled, his coat snarled with bur-dock stickers and with a deep scratch across his snout. Robinson had been lying in the guest bedroom (he could not bear to sleep in the bed he had shared with Diana), sleepless with grief and depression, aware that he was edging closer and closer to just giving up and pulling the pin. He would have called such an action cowardly only weeks before, but had since come to recognize several undeniable facts. The pain would not stop. The grief would not stop. And, of course, his life was not apt to be a long one in any case. You only had to smell the decaying animals in the woods to know what lay ahead.

He'd heard rattling sounds, and at first thought it might be a human being. Or a surviving bear that had smelled his food. But the gennie was still running then, and in the glare of the motion lights that illuminated the driveway he had seen a little gray dog, alternately scratching at the door and then huddling on the porch. When Robinson opened the door, the dog at first backed away, ears back and tail tucked.

"I guess you better come in," Robinson had said, and without much further hesitation, the dog did.

Robinson gave him a bowl of water, which he lapped furiously, and then a can of Prudence corned beef hash, which he ate in five or six snaffling bites. When the dog finished, Robinson stroked him, hoping he wouldn't be bitten. Instead of biting, the dog licked his hand.

"You're Gandalf," Robinson had said. "Gandalf the Grey." And then burst into tears. He tried to tell himself he was being ridiculous, but he wasn't. He was no longer alone in the house.

"What news about that motorhuckle of yours?" Timlin asked.

They had progressed to their second beers. When Robinson finished his, he and Gandalf would make the two-mile walk back to the house. He didn't want to wait too long; the mosquitoes got thicker when twilight came.

If Timlin's right, he thought, the bloodsuckers will inherit the earth instead of the meek. If they can find any blood to suck, that is.

"The battery's dead," he told Timlin. Then: "My wife made me promise to sell the bike when I was fifty. She said after fifty, a man's reflexes are too slow to be safe."

"And you're fifty when?"

"Next year," Robinson said. And laughed at the absurdity of it.

"I lost a tooth this morning," Timlin said. "Might mean nothing at my age, but . . ."

"Seeing any blood in the toilet bowl?"

Timlin had told him that was one of the first signs of advanced radiation poisoning, and he knew a lot more about it than Robinson did. What Robinson knew was that his wife and daughter had been in Boston when the frantic Geneva peace talks had gone up in a nuclear flash on the fifth of June, and they were still in Boston the next day, when the world killed itself. The eastern seaboard of America, from Hartford to Miami, was now mostly slag.

"I'm going to take the Fifth Amendment on that," Timlin said. "Here comes your dog. Better check his paws—he's limping a bit. Looks like the rear left."

But they could find no thorn in any of Gandalf's paws, and this time when Timlin pulled gently at his fur, a patch on his hindquarters came out. Gandalf seemed not to feel it. The two men looked at each other.

"Could be the mange," Robinson said at last. "Or stress. Dogs do lose fur when they're stressed, you know."

"Maybe." Timlin was looking west, across the

lake. "It's going to be a beautiful sunset. Of course, they're all beautiful now. Like when Krakatoa blew its stack in eighteen eighty-three. Only this was ten thousand Krakatoas." He bent and stroked Gandalf's head.

"India and Pakistan," Robinson said.

Timlin straightened up again. "Well, yes. But then everyone else just had to get into the act, didn't they? Even the Chechens had a few, which they delivered to Moscow in pickup trucks. It's as though the world willfully forgot how many countries—and groups, fucking *groups*!—had those things."

"Or what those things were capable of," Robinson said.

Timlin nodded. "That too. We were too worried about the debt ceiling, and our friends across the pond were concentrating on stopping child beauty pageants and propping up the euro."

"You're sure Canada's just as dirty as the lower forty-eight?"

"It's a matter of degree, I suppose. Vermont's not as dirty as New York, and Canada's probably not as dirty as Vermont. But it will be. Plus, most of the people headed up there are already sick. Sick unto death, if I may misquote Kierkegaard. Want another beer?"

"I'd better get back." Robinson stood. "Come on, Gandalf. Time to burn some calories."

"Will I see you tomorrow?"

"Maybe in the late afternoon. I've got an errand to run in the morning."

"May I ask where?"

"Bennington, while there's still enough gas in my truck to get there and back."

Timlin raised his eyebrows.

"Want to see if I can find a motorcycle battery."

Gandalf made it as far as Dead Man's Curve under his own power, although his limp grew steadily worse. When they got there, he simply sat down, as if to watch the boiling sunset reflected in the lake. It was a fuming orange shot through with arteries of deepest red. The dog whined and licked at his back left leg. Robinson sat beside him for a little while, but when the first mosquito scouts called for reinforcements, he picked Gandalf up and started walking again. By the time they got back to the house, Robinson's arms were trembling and his shoulders were aching. If Gandalf had weighed another ten pounds, maybe even another five, he would have had to leave the mutt and go get the truck. His head also ached, perhaps from the heat, or the second beer, or both.

The tree-lined driveway sloping down to the house was a pool of shadows, and the house itself was dark. The gennie had given up the ghost weeks ago. Sunset had subsided to a dull purple bruise. He plodded onto the porch and put Gandalf down to open the door. "Go on, boy," he said. Gandalf struggled to rise, then subsided.

Just as Robinson was bending to pick him up again, Gandalf made another effort. This time he lunged over the doorsill and collapsed on his side in the entryway, panting. On the wall above the dog were at least two dozen photographs featuring people Robinson loved, all now deceased. He could no longer even dial Diana's and Ellen's phones and listen to their recorded voices. His own phone had died shortly after the generator, but even before that, all cell service had ceased.

He got a bottle of Poland Spring water from the pantry, filled Gandalf's bowl, then put down a scoop of kibble. Gandalf drank some water but wouldn't eat. When Robinson squatted to scratch the dog's belly, fur came out in bundles.

It's happening so fast, he thought. This morning he was fine.

Robinson went out to the lean-to behind the house with a flashlight. On the lake, a loon cried—just one. The motorcycle was under a tarp. He pulled the canvas off and shone the beam along the bike's gleaming body. It was a 2014 Fat Bob, several years old now, but low mileage; his days of riding four and five thousand miles between May and October were behind him. Yet the Bob was still his dream ride, even though his dreams were mostly where he'd ridden it over the last couple of years. Air-cooled. Twin cam. Six-speed. Almost seventeen hundred ccs. And the sound it made! Only Harleys had that sound, like summer thunder. When you came up next to a Chevy at a stoplight, the cager inside was apt to lock his doors.

Robinson skidded a palm along the handlebars, then hoisted his leg over and sat in the saddle with his feet on the pegs. Diana had become increasingly insistent that he sell it, and when he did ride, she reminded him again and again that Vermont had a helmet law for a reason . . . unlike the idiots in New Hampshire and Maine. Now he could ride it without a helmet if he wanted to. There was no Diana to nag him, and no County Mounties to pull him over. He could ride it buckass naked, if he wanted to.

"Although I'd have to mind the tailpipes when I

got off," he said, and laughed. He went inside without putting the tarp back on the Harley. Gandalf was lying on the bed of blankets Robinson had made for him, nose on one of his front paws. His kibble was untouched.

"Better eat up," Robinson said, giving Gandalf's head a stroke. "You'll feel better."

The next morning there was a red stain on the blankets around Gandalf's hindquarters, and although he tried, he couldn't make it to his feet. After he gave up the second time, Robinson carried him outside, where Gandalf first lay on the grass, then managed to get up enough to squat. What came out of him was a gush of bloody stool. Gandalf crawled away from it as if ashamed, then lay down, looking at Robinson mournfully.

This time when Robinson picked him up, Gandalf cried out in pain. He bared his teeth but did not bite. Robinson carried him into the house and put him down on his blanket bed. He looked at his hands when he straightened up and saw they were coated with fur. When he dusted his palms together, the fur floated away like milkweed.

"You'll be okay," he told Gandalf. "Just a little upset stomach. Must have gotten one of those goddam chipmunks when I wasn't looking. Stay there and rest up. I'm sure you'll be feeling more like yourself by the time I get back."

There was still half a tank of gas in the Silverado, more than enough for a sixty-mile roundtrip to Bennington. Robinson decided to go down to Woodland Acres first and see if Timlin wanted anything.

His last neighbor was sitting on the porch of Veronica in his rocker. He was extremely pale, and there were purple pouches under his eyes. When Robinson told him about Gandalf, Timlin nodded. "I was up most of the night, running to the toilet. We must have caught the same bug." He smiled to show it was a joke, although not a very funny one.

No, he said, there was nothing he wanted in Bennington, but perhaps Robinson would stop by on his way back. "I've got something *you* might want," he said.

The drive to Bennington was slower than Robinson expected, because the highway was littered with abandoned cars. It was close to noon by the time he pulled into the front lot of Kingdom Harley-Davidson. The show windows had been broken and all the display models were gone, but there were plenty of bikes out back. These had been rendered theft-proof with steel cables sheathed in plastic and sturdy bike locks.

That was fine with Robinson; he only wanted to steal a battery. The Fat Bob he settled on was a year or two newer than his, but the battery looked the same. He fetched his toolbox from the bed of his pickup and checked the battery with his Impact (the tester had been a gift from his daughter two birthdays back), and got a green light. He removed the battery, went into the showroom, and found a selection of maps. Using the most detailed one to suss out the back roads, he made it back to the lake by three o'clock.

He saw a great many dead animals, including an extremely large moose lying beside the cement block steps of someone's trailer home. On the trailer's crab-grassy lawn, a hand-painted sign had been posted, only two words: HEAVEN SOON.

The porch of Veronica was deserted, but when Robinson knocked on the door, Timlin called for him to come in. He was sitting in the ostentatiously rustic living room, paler than ever. In one hand he held an oversize linen napkin. It was spotted with blood. On the coffee table in front of him were three items: a picture book titled *The Beauty of Vermont*, a hypodermic needle filled with yellow fluid, and a revolver.

"I'm glad you came," Timlin said. "I didn't want to leave without telling you goodbye."

Robinson recognized the absurdity of the first response that came to mind—*Let's not be hasty*—and stayed silent.

"I've lost half a dozen teeth," Timlin said, "but that's not the major problem. In the last twelve hours or so, I seem to have expelled most of my intestines. The eerie thing is how little it hurts. The hemorrhoids I was afflicted with in my fifties were worse. The pain will come—I've read enough to know that—but I don't intend to stick around long enough to experience it in full flower. Did you get the battery you wanted?"

"Yes," Robinson said, and sat down heavily. "Jesus, Howard, I'm so fucking sorry."

"Much appreciated. And you? How do you feel?"

"Physically? Fine." Although this was no longer completely true. Several red patches that didn't look like sunburn were blooming on his forearms, and there was another on his chest, above the right nipple. They itched. Also . . . his breakfast was staying down, but his stomach seemed far from happy with it.

Timlin leaned forward and tapped the hypo. "Demerol. I was going to inject myself, then look at pictures of Vermont until . . . until. But I've changed my mind. The gun will be fine, I think. You take the hypo."

"I'm not quite ready."

"Not for you, for the dog. He doesn't deserve to suffer. It wasn't dogs that built the bombs, after all."

"I think maybe he just ate a chipmunk," Robinson said feebly.

"We both know that's not it. Even if it was, the dead animals are so full of radiation it might as well have been a cobalt capsule. It's a wonder he's survived as long as he has. Be grateful for the time you've had with him. A little bit of grace. That's what a good dog is, you know. A little bit of grace."

Timlin studied him closely.

"Don't you cry on me. If you do, I will too, so man up. There's one more six-pack of Bud in the fridge. I don't know why I bothered to put it in there, but old habits die hard. Why don't you bring us each one? Warm beer is better than no beer; I believe Woodrow Wilson said that. We'll toast Gandalf. Also your new motorcycle battery. Meanwhile, I need to spend a penny. Or, who knows, this one might cost a little more."

Robinson got the beer. When he came back Timlin was gone, and remained gone for almost five minutes. He came back slowly, holding onto things. He had removed his pants and cinched a bath sheet around his midsection. He sat down with a little cry of pain, but took the can of beer Robinson held out to him. They toasted Gandalf and drank. The Bud was warm, all right, but not that bad. It was, after all, the King of Beers.

Timlin picked up the gun. "Mine will be the classic Victorian suicide," he said, sounding pleased at the prospect. "Gun to temple. Free hand over the eyes. Goodbye, cruel world."

"I'm off to join the circus," Robinson said without thinking.

Timlin laughed heartily, lips peeling back to reveal his few remaining teeth. "It would be nice, but I doubt it. Did I ever tell you that I was hit by a truck when I was a boy? The kind our British cousins call a milk float?"

Robinson shook his head.

"Nineteen fifty-seven, this was. I was fifteen, walking down a country road in Michigan, headed for Highway Twenty-two, where I hoped to hook a ride into Traverse City and attend a double-feature movie show. I was daydreaming about a girl in my homeroom—such long, lovely legs and such high breasts—and wandered away from the relative safety of the shoulder. The milk float came over the top of a hill—the driver was going much too fast—and hit me square on. If it had been fully loaded, I surely would have been killed, but because it was empty it was much lighter, thus allowing me to live to the age of seventy-five, and experience what it's like to shit one's bowels into a toilet that will no longer flush."

There seemed to be no adequate response to this.

"There was a flash of sun on the float's windshield as it came over the top of the hill, and then . . . nothing. I believe I will experience roughly the same thing when the bullet goes into my brain and lays waste to all I've ever thought or experienced." He raised a professorly finger. "Only this time, nothing will not give way to something. Just a flash, like sun on the windshield of a milk float, followed by nothing. I find the idea simultaneously awesome and terribly depressing."

"Maybe you ought to hold off for awhile," Robinson said. "You might . . ."

Timlin waited politely, eyebrows raised.

"Fuck, I don't know," Robinson said. And then, surprising himself, he shouted, *"What did they do? What did those motherfuckers do?"*

"You know perfectly well what they did," Timlin said. "And now we live with the consequences. I know you love that dog, Peter. It's displaced love—what the psychiatrists call hysterical conversion—but we take what we can get, and if we've got half a brain, we're grateful. So don't hesitate. Stick him in the neck, and stick him hard. Grab his collar in case he flinches."

Robinson put his beer down. He didn't want it anymore. "He was in pretty bad shape when I left. Maybe he's dead already."

But Gandalf wasn't.

He looked up when Robinson came into the bedroom and thumped his tail twice on his bloody pad of blankets. Robinson sat down next to him. He stroked Gandalf's head and thought about the dooms of love, which were really so simple when you peered directly into them. Gandalf put his head on Robinson's knee and looked up at him. Robinson took the hypo out of his shirt pocket and removed the protective cap from the needle.

"You're a good guy," he said, and took hold of Gandalf's collar, as Timlin had instructed.

While he was nerving himself to go through with it, he heard a gunshot. The sound was faint at this distance, but with the lake so still, there was no mistaking it for anything else. It rolled across the hot summer air, diminished, tried to echo, failed. Gandalf cocked his ears, and an idea came to Robinson, as comforting as it was absurd. Maybe Timlin was wrong about the nothing. It was possible. In a world where you could look up and see an eternal hallway of stars, he reckoned anything was. Maybe—

Maybe.

Gandalf was still looking at him as he slid the needle home. For a moment the dog's eyes remained bright and aware, and in the endless moment before the brightness left, Robinson would have taken it back if he could.

He sat there on the floor for a long time, hoping that last loon might sound off one more time, but it didn't. After awhile, he went out to the lean-to, found a spade, and dug a hole in his wife's flower garden. There was no need to go deep; no animal was going to come along and dig Gandalf up.

When he woke up the next morning, Robinson's mouth tasted coppery. When he lifted his head, his cheek peeled away from the pillow. Both his nose and his gums had bled in the night.

It was another beautiful day, and although it was still summer, the first color had begun to steal into the trees. Robinson wheeled his Fat Bob out of the lean-to and replaced the dead battery, working slowly and carefully in the deep silence.

When he finished, he turned the switch. The green neutral light came on, but stuttered a little. He shut the switch off, tightened the connections, then tried again. This time the light stayed steady. He hit the ignition and that sound—summer thunder—shattered the quiet. It seemed sacrilegious, but—this was strange—in a good way.

Robinson wasn't surprised to find himself thinking of his first and only trip to attend the annual Sturgis motorcycle rally in South Dakota, 1998 that had been, the year before he met Diana. He remembered rolling slowly down Junction Avenue on his Honda GB 500, one more sled in a parade of two thousand, the combined roar of all those bikes so loud it seemed a physical thing. Later that night there had been a bonfire, and an endless stream of Stones and AC/DC and Metallica roaring from Stonehenge stacks of Marshall amps. Tattooed girls danced topless in the firelight; bearded men drank beer from bizarre helmets; children decorated with decal tattoos of their own ran everywhere, waving sparklers. It had been terrifying and amazing and wonderful, everything that was right and wrong with the world in the same place and in perfect focus. Overhead, that hallway of stars.

Robinson gunned the Fat Boy, then let off the throttle. Gunned and let off. Gunned and let off. The rich smell of freshly burned gasoline filled the driveway. The world was a dying hulk but the silence had been banished, at least for the time being, and that was good. That was fine. Fuck you, silence, he thought. Fuck you and the horse you rode in on. This is *my* horse, my iron horse, and how do you like it?

He squeezed the clutch and toed the gearshift down into first. He rolled up the driveway, banked right, and toed up this time, into second and then third. The road was dirt, and rutted in places, but the bike took the ruts easily, floating Robinson up and down on the seat. His nose was spouting again; the blood streamed up his cheeks and flew off behind him in fat droplets. He took the first curve and then the second, banking harder now, hitting fourth gear as he came onto a brief straight stretch. The Fat Bob was eager to go. It had been in that goddam lean-to too long, gathering dust. On Robinson's right, he could see Lake Pocomtuck from the corner of his eye, still as a mirror, the sun beating a yellow-gold track across the blue. Robinson let out a yell and shook one fist at the sky—at the universe—before returning it to the handgrip. Ahead was the buttonhook, with the MIND YOUR DRIVING! sign that marked Dead Man's Curve.

Robinson aimed for the sign and twisted the throttle all the way. He just had time to hit fifth gear.

For Kurt Sutter and Richard Chizmar